Happy Reading!

Cleopatra Selene

Legacy of the Sun & Moon

Sharon M. Desruisseaux

PublishAmerica
Baltimore

First printing

All characters in this book are fictitious, and any resemblance to real persons, living or dead, is coincidental.

PublishAmerica has allowed this work to remain exactly as the author intended, verbatim, without editorial input.

Hardcover 978-1-4512-6164-6
Softcover 978-1-4512-6165-3
Pocketbook 978-1-61582-668-1
PUBLISHED BY PUBLISHAMERICA, LLLP
www.publishamerica.com
Baltimore

Printed in the United States of America

This book is dedicated to my three daughters Alexaundra, Jacqueline and Tiffany. May they be proud of where they came from and what they will be.

And to my parents with their undying faith and loyalty in my writing and my cherished friends.
Thank you!

Legacy of the Sun and Moon

By Sharon DesRuisseaux

"To have a legacy like mine would seem to most a joy, but in retrospect has been our silent destruction through the many generations from the most famous to bear my name, the infamous Cleopatra VII, the Last Pharaoh of Egypt. I am just known as Cleopatra and five generations down from her. The following is the chronicles of her legacy and how it intertwined zealously with that of the Rome she left us to. I am the family historian and have traveled the known world to compile all that she had left behind in her wake. I am also the narrator of this tale I leave for those we left behind to judge us and our actions, now that you are armed with the truth.

-Princess Cleopatra of the Iceni of Britannia"

Cleopatra Selene

Legacy of the Sun & Moon

Part one

From the chronicles of Cleopatra Selene…

I

65 B.C.E through 30 B.C.E.

"My name is Cleopatra Selene and I am the oldest daughter of the legendary Cleopatra VII and her consort Marcus Antonii of Rome. For I am also the keeper of the family chronicles and the truth despite the all too popular misconceptions brought forth to public light as distorted by Roman historians such as Cicero, who barely knew my parents, especially my mother and others. Their writings which have circulated the world have a curious historical bend to them and have been swayed politically by the favor of their patrons. Therefore the history popularly laid out for all, has been tragically biased and has shed nothing but an ill view of those people who gave me life and a powerful foundation.

Cleopatra VII was the daughter of Ptolemy XI, to the Romans he was known as Auletes for his flute playing and the Princess Cleopatra V, Tryphaena of Egypt. The father of Cleopatra VII was the King of Rome and a Friend and ally of the Roman people. Her father's first wife was his sister, Berenice IV, and she was the mother of her older brother's both named Ptolemy. Her mother was his second wife, the daughter of Ptolemy IX Soter, who was married into the Seleucid line of Syria, and his cousin. She was the last in the legitimate line of the Ptolemy, which secured Ptolemy XI legitimately into the Ptolemy house by the marriage to his cousin and later the mother of Cleopatra VII, my mother.

Cleopatra was known as the daughter of Isis, who like the Goddess was the mother of all. She, like Isis was the epitome of devotion. Isis was the sister and cherished wife of the God Osiris. She wept a river of tears when her husband and lover was torn apart by their brother Seth. For Seth was jealous of the love that Isis and Osiris shared, and he wanted Isis for himself and therefore, destroyed Osiris to reach his prize. He never counted on the devotion of Isis, for she and her sister Nepthys wandered for eons, to recover the severed body parts of Osiris. When the search was complete, Isis remolded the pieces of Osiris to make him whole once more. However, much to the dismay of the loyal Isis, he lacked the necessary part that made him a man. Being also the Goddess of creativity, she called upon the forces of nature to solve her dilemma. For she desperately needed this part to create the future and to fill her womb with life. Nepthys and she conspired and had arrived at the same solution, and created the missing part from the sands of the Nile. She then joined in union in the form of a hawk with her now complete husband, to create the first pharaoh in her womb named Horus. Horus was the first of their joined blood. It is legend, further, that Horus forever seeks his Uncle Seth in vengeance for the crime that he committed against his brother. It is the tradition in the land in which she was born, the mighty Egypt, that all of the pharaohs claimed that they are the child of the reanimated Osiris and his devoted wife and sister, Isis. Seth, will forever be known to physically and spiritually possess the enemies to the throne, while Isis till the end of eternity stands guardian over her descendants.

Cleopatra VII resembled her infamous ancestor Goddess in more ways than that. She was the third child of Ptolemy Auletes. In mention of his flute playing, Cleopatra had told her children of several instances in which he would annoy the inhabitants of the palace with the endless musical dissonance that echoed through the gilded halls of Bruchion and only seemed to echo even more in volume against the monotony of the waves in the harbor. No one had told this to the King of Egypt, it was just whispered by everyone in his wake. She loved her father, and to the day of her death, a tear would glisten, at the sound of a flute.

She had an aunt who shared the same name as she. She could not recall much of her, only that she later went in league with her older Aunt Berenice. The older Cleopatra was more of a follower, than anything. How odd for the first born in that generation of the Ptolemy family. For these were the sisters that her father had brought into power and placed on the throne in his absence.

To my knowledge, the very first Cleopatra of this family was the sister of Alexander the Great, and the wife of his general, Ptolemy. The Macedonian power that conquered the ancient land of Kemet, now referred to as Egypt, over four hundred years before my birth and three hundred years before the birth of Cleopatra VII; cast it's influence over Egypt and intermarried with the old line to further fortify their influence and rule over the conquered.

There was a daunting number of Cleopatra's, Ptolemy's, Berenice's, and Arsinoe's in the family line. It can be rather confusing trying to disentangle the particular ones noted in ancient scrolls that were the point of reference without confusing that person with a sibling or parent with the same name. There could have been as many as three others than the person referenced of the same name in the same generation. There was some respite however, when the name was followed by a Greek reference name, such as philopater or brotherly love.

The story's were told of Berenice, the sister of my grandfather . She was allegedly so beautiful that the court was dripping with admirers singing of her in adoration and of the rapture of emotions from one stolen glance from her legendary violet eyes. She was noted to have been as tall and as graceful as a gazelle. Frequent were the memories of my mother rolling her eyes in jealousy over the ludicrous descriptions of her young and ambitious aunt.

Several years subsequent to "the Berenice of the violet eyes", my mother first toppled into the arms of her royal parents. She was Macedonian Greek in ancestral origin, after three hundred years in Egypt of the Ptolemy lineage. The most famous Cleopatra of all was a very beautiful and charismatic woman to others and an adoring and protective force to be reckoned with in concern to her children. Her long dark chestnut tresses were very wavy and soft and often smelled of the beautiful white petals of jasmine that were planted all over the palace. Her soft hair often captured different hues of the rainbow in the glow of the golden oil lamps that hung throughout the palace. She would playfully toss them about in mock exaggeration and imitation of the "beloved Berenice". Her frame was small in comparison to others in her family, who were noted as tall to chroniclers of that time. Her eyes were hazel flecked with gold and rimmed in a deep forest green with long black lashes and were almond in shape. Her eyes were described as the most charismatic part of her distinction by so many others who had the luxury of her personal presence. Those famous eyes were known to cast many a spell to entice those in her presence into her causes. So, great was her casting the illusion of glamour, that it was said to have been based on her training as a priestess of Isis. Her gait was strong for such a petite woman, she emanated confidence and power to the unsteady precipice of the politics that surrounded her in those turbulent times. She always had the appearance of being late, though in her life, she never was. For punctuality was her nature and discipline, and if one were late, good luck if that inauspicious soul should desire another audience with her. Her clothing was immaculate and later in her life was noted to be primarily in the ancient Egyptian style, unlike those of her predecessor Ptolemy's who preferred the Macedonian attire of their far removed homeland. She was the first Ptolemy to adopt the Egyptian lifestyle and religion, which enfolded her with the people of the land so that she was made Pharaoh, unlike her father who was only the King of Egypt. As Pharaoh, she had absolute control and owned everything in that country, which was far more than being just the King of Egypt.

"The Ptolemy's before her were Macedonian Greek in worship, apparel, language, and everything else. For almost the entire length of their dynasty since the days of Alexander the Great, they had looked down upon the people of the land that they had conquered. Her family line had placed those of Macedonian influence in positions of power, leaving the Egyptians to labor over the land and them with the smallest positions possible and little to no influence in the rule of the land.

The ceremonial costumes donned by Cleopatra the Great were noted in many descriptions of her. She would immortalize the ancient pharonaic queens who ruled the land thousands of years before her footsteps graced the remains of the ancient temples in worship. She would don for the many festivals and religious ceremonies her glamorously braided wigs and heavy gold ornament, in such imitation of the old that some were bedazzled to imagine that one were in the presence of the mighty Nefertiti or Hapshepsut themselves incarnate in the form of the tiny Cleopatra VII. She had a passion for the study of the land in which she was born. She had attempted to emulate the power of those ancient women written about in dusty tombs and temples, and would have succeeded had she been granted just a little more time and had she not been ruled so completely by her heart. She was a woman of passion who stood strong in the face of adversity and those who stood in the way of her powerful vision of a mighty alliance of the greatest powers in the world at that time . Though what had been reaped, after good initial intentions began to feel the suction and slow corruption of waning attention as the beginning of the slow demise of the Roman power started it's final descent into the lands of Egypt.

She instilled in us a strong pride in our lineage, in which the stories of those before her were collected and written down and handed to those in each generation after her to protect and to eventually reveal when the world was ready for the truth.

II

Cleopatra VII had taken her children frequently to the tomb of Alexander the Great, and especially Cleopatra Selene. She would stand in awe of his decayed presence, hidden under the marble sarcophagus. Never did the cold, damp chamber cease to amaze Cleopatra Selene, for their mother had the power to captivate the enchantment of history in oratorical glory of those special visits with her daughter. The histories of the older Ptolemys would set an impression in her that was recorded vehemently in her own chronicles of her lifetime.

Cleopatra VII would describe her childhood in the palace of Bruchion to her children in so much detail that one would almost believe the reality of those halls in their full splendor as in her lifetime, not the decaying remnants of a grandeur long past it's prime. This palace overlooked the Great Harbor in Alexandria and was on an island. The streets of the city were wide and straight with tall columns and a dazzling whiteness that made the city glow in it's Greek beauty and magnificence. Many treks were made to that library, the most famous in the world, by Cleopatra and her daughter Selene.

The city of Alexandria was in Lower Egypt at the bottom of the backward flowing mighty Nile River. This river was in a harbor in the mighty Roman Sea and was an epicenter in trade and world commerce. This city was above Lake Mareotis which was between two harbors that held the nestled Greek city in the land of ancient Egypt. Both harbors were separated by a narrow strip that connected the mainland to the famous Island of Pharos. To the Northwest and above the whole of the city was the Roman Sea known as the Mediterranean. The sea was the success of the city and the dream of the Great Alexander which he never saw in full fruition. The city in the time of Cleopatra VII was metropolitan and a leader in trade and learning. Which was the reason that the Romans and Julius Caesar and later Octavian were so eager to gain power over this land and famous port. This opulent city was built three hundred years prior to her lifetime and sparked the blood of the Great Alexander's dream in their bloodline. He died without issue, so the Ptolemy family descent is not direct. But, it left enough of an impression to hold them dear to the keeping and preservation and later longing for that white sparkling city long after their footsteps were forbidden there.

The land of Kemet or Egypt had many older capitals before that one was built by an usurping Greek. There was Thebes in the middle of the land, and before that was Abydos, the legendary burial site of the God Osiris. These prior capitols are now dust under the hot sweltering sun of the relentless desert that eventually engulfed all memory of their greatness. Each time this land was conquered a new capitol was founded along the Great River Nile which was their main source of life.

A culture and religion worshipping such had sprung up along it's banks untouched for thousands of lifetimes and reigns of timeless pharaohs and dynasties. The first writing ever was on direct order of the original King of Egypt the legendary Scorpion King, whose tomb lies next to that of Osiris in Abydos near the top of this river.

The mighty and ferocious Nile is compliant in shape at it's origins. The source of which flowed from the hostile lands of the kingdom of Punt, just below, and reached far up to spread out like a blossoming lotus flower to spread its daring petals to kiss the Sea of the Mediterranean. The city was located in it's western branch and was connected by an extensive system of aqueducts. Which fed on the waters of the same Nile.

The palace of Bruchion was fashioned in the Greek style and emulated the artistry of the ancient Egyptians which supported hallways adorned with miniature Greek fashioned sphinxes carved in precious marble of various colors and hues. The size of the palace cast a shadow on the city from the island in which it stood. With snakelike tendrils, the rooms and corridors formed a labyrinth for those not born in the palace enclosure, thus many were often lost. The rooms were lavishly adorned with the spoils of their Greek ancestors who ruled this land far away from Macedonia from the many territories conquered and brought under wing. Cleopatra VII and her children grew up in a sealed off paradise far from the rest of the world, in a cocoon of luxury and love and constant pampering as befit their station in life. Cleopatra Selene was known to describe in such complete and absolute detail her childhood palace of Bruchion; she described in loving memory that in her later years she could still taste the salt breeze that wafted in from the harbor to the palace enclosure with the intense sea salt that would tangle in her hair, so powerful were the impressions of her youth stamped in her soul. She had painted a picture so perfect and immaculate to her children of the powerful tendrils of light that pierced her window from the legendary lighthouse on the banks of the Pharos that would lead ships safely into their harbor. Her daughter would recall every detail to writing as described to her in bedtime story.

This same lighthouse was the subject of many travelers journals, so powerful and modern was its light that it was known throughout the world. Cleopatra VII used it often in metaphor to her children. She had tried desperately to protect her family and to give them all of her soul and knowledge in the illusion of safety with a bond of family love that did not exist for herself in childhood, not even in illusion.

Growing up as a child for Cleopatra VII was anything but safe, even in her own family. It was treacherous and perilous to say the very least from her own aunts and older brothers Ptolemy as well as her other siblings. Something she fervidly erased in her own children. She established a bond between the siblings from her womb that has lasted through many other generations. She had to constantly look over her shoulder for any possible assassin, even in the guise of her own family or guards. Danger clawed at any illusion of safety from the murkiest and most dismal of corners, even in the most bright and sunny ones! The possibilities of her death throughout her childhood and until the time of her actual death was as plentiful as the locusts that would sometimes swarm the very banks of the Nile that she later ruled over.

She had two brothers who shared the name of her father, Ptolemy who were at the top of the list for the assassins that kissed her cheek and praised her in admiration. Her brothers were extremely pliable and easily influenced by their tutors and any other voices in the wind that praised them in favor. Their very nature precarious and transiliant as the change of the wind.

She also had a younger sister by the name of Arsinoe, who was as shifty and as dangerous as a cobra. She always had to be on guard from anything coming from the direction of her sister's sweet praises. Her younger sister was always plotting some advantageous scheme to bring her to the throne sooner than her fated birth allowed her. However Cleopatra knew that Arsinoe only followed the voices of those whispers that led her, not from any whim of her own. Though she knew that she would not spare anyone in her path, regardless of relation or even a past cradle mate like herself. It was more than feasible that Cleopatra was suspicious of her, though pity was primary in her feelings for the younger sister. To be so malleable to the vises and opinions of another was intolerable to Cleopatra VII. Little Arsinoe, with hair the color of the summer sands. She had tried to love this sister and care for her as their mother could not do since she had died when they were very young.

III

Often told and related down to her children were the delicious tales of the father's relentless flute playing. Cleopatra VII would roll in the throes of laughter in description of the times that he would play the flute for the Roman debt collectors as they dared to call upon his court. He would play that flute so loudly and so aimlessly without possibility of making sense that they would run from the palace screaming for an end to their torment. He would dance for them as if possessed by the God Dionysus himself in persecution of the boring and mundane that the tax collectors represented and threatened to wake the dead in that racket he called music.

IV

Then in the somberness of the respect for her father's death, Cleopatra would relate further on her upbringing to be chronicled properly by her daughter the noted Cleopatra Selene. She was raised in a Macedonian Greek court, almost in mockery over the land in which her family ruled for over three hundred years. She was taught Macedonian principles and values under a slowly encroaching Roman dominion. The Romans were effortlessly closing their all destroying grip on their fertile Nile River and its dominions. It still held the death grip over the family in the future generations.

In the time of her childhood they were under the rule by necessity of the Roman domination and slowly becoming a part of their empire. The powerful triumvirate of Gaius Julius Caesar, Pompey and Crassus held sway while Cleopatra VII was under the waning tutorship of her father.

The last legitimate Ptolemy XI Alexander II, was the puppet of the Dictator of Rome—Sulla, before he was torn to pieces by the angry

Alexandrian mob after the brutal murder of his ageing mother Cleopatra Berenice. Their kingdom, initially separate, had reluctantly become a vassal to that enormous power. Her father was the last of a weakening line of Ptolemys that had grown up under the spell of luxury in which their potential for power was diminished in their fight over each other for the throne. Their kingdom had been slowly dissipating over the centuries while they fought their own siblings and parents for the past legendary power that their family held while wasting vast resources in this single minded though genetic quest for power. Thus, they had to seek help from Rome financially in order to preserve their illusion of royalty and oasis of learning. Her tutors were Macedonian and imported from there in a prayer of preservation for the kingdom of the Ptolemy's. Her father preached oratory and rhetoric and mumbled the theories of Pythagoras. Her father worshipped the essence of a good education and shunned the uninformed. She learned her zest for learning from her beloved father, the flute player.

When Cleopatra was nine years old, Gaius Julius Caesar was elected to the counsul in Rome. He was the political heir with Pompey to the famous Sulla. He was almost thirty years older than Cleopatra VII and was born of a noble and ambitious family. Cleopatra Selene had noted that her mother had loved him mainly due to his fairness and resourceful education. Her mother recalled that many evenings were spent together in ruthless debate over some issue or matter. His mind was acute and forever expanding in constant absorption on many venues. For she wrote that he was a superb orator and would baffle any who would have the nerve to oppose his interest on the matter at issue. He even took over the governorship of the Cisalpine Gaul ten years before her birth. He had a late political start compared to most born even with the same august lineage, though he was well established many years before her own birth. Yet, he forever wanted more. He tasted the sweet ambrosia of success and wanted to seduce every last drop and wasted no time in this process. Cleopatra VII was so enamored in her youth of the powerful confidence of this personae, that she herself wasted no time and finding the appropriate moment to reveal herself to him in her full allure! She had set a challenge that she was inspired by.

V

Cleopatra VII was nervous of the disintegrating kingdom and power of her family, and abhorred the idea of it warming the hands of the Roman power. She had studied all she could on the past exploits of her challenge and waited for the opportune moment for their initial meeting. For she always knew that the initial impression could set a very powerful stage and would raise or destroy her kingdom. She chose when young, not to roll the dice that her father had, but to create her own stakes.

While she waited for that moment, she would while away the languorous days by absorbing herself into the history of the land that she wanted so desperately to rule. She had contained all too rational fears of her aunts Berenice and the silent follower, the older Cleopatra; holding the knowledge of their plans to capture the throne unjustly from her own father. She did not want the wiles of Berenice gaining any possible contact with power. For that dreaded contact would almost surely go to her head. She sadly witnessed her father's glory dissolve around him and eventually surround him in the cloak of insanity. His stature was not so powerful as she had envisioned in her childhood. Her father was like a God to the people and their land, as well as to her youthful self. Though his flute indifferently and recklessly played on and on. Forever echoing through the extensive labyrinth of their home. His once proud frame began to fade and sag under the burden of a falling kingdom and his incapacity to fight it in the glory of his ancestors. A sad victim to the Roman world around him, one in which he did not want to play a part. He lost himself in his music. He was afraid to let the old Gods of Greece, his never seen homeland, die inside of him. His once Godly eminence, slowly appeared all too human to her.

She had written in the first personal chronicles of the family which had been lost until the later generations; that the sweet memory of his God did not restore his youth and vigor. That must have been a deep disappointment to her shattered soul. She would bend her head in the telling of her father's all too eventual demise. She mournfully related of the day in which the Romans had snatched his victory and with it his pride, from his weakened grasp. She mournfully explained the day when the once mighty Auletes, ran from his court in the ceaseless demands of the debt collectors. He bent his head down in shame at his retreat and of the countless bribes to Rome to restore his power in Egypt, which they held on a string and dangled in front of him. This fact tore at her soul, for she held in her heart the image of his retreat with his head bent down in shame, a silent admission of his lost power. This time he did not play his flute, for it was thrown out after his diminishing form. To witness this shame of her father must have devastated and her must have sown the seeds of revenge. Her cocoon of childhood illusions was finally and irreparably shattered from that day forth. For the child she was until that very moment, was lost on that day and a ruler was born.

Those who knew her well could almost picture her revealing to the world her shield of indifference, while secretly plotting a pretense of vengeance in her all too able mind and inner sanctuary. Only her daughter Cleopatra Selene, could have read her mother's soul thoughts in her bright hazel eyes that she draped in mystery to all others, had she existed at that time.

Cleopatra VII had not assumed her rule at that time and was only fourteen years old. There were others before her and she fervently prayed for her father's return to rule. From my own research into the family, those years in my family were very turbulent. At that age, she was almost a woman. Falling into an ever expanding abyss before her while she treaded water carefully. She was a victor by nature, for she would ride out any wave in those days that the Romans would throw at her, with an uncanny sense of grace and style that would baffle those around her in admiration. It was almost as if she had always anticipated the problems and was in wait to utilize the impending chaos to point her way. She probably earned this talent in her own research and chronicles of her family. Her own writing was lost in a secret family artifact that was passed down, though related directly in memory by her daughter Cleopatra

Selene in the tattered papyrus I glance at in the telling of this compiled chronicle.

Plato and Cicero would in later years smear the memory of Cleopatra VII with the slurs and accusations of her alleged wanton-hood. The insufferable Roman called Plato never actually knew her and had heard tales from a man in the employ of his father. Cicero did meet her though and raved in patriarchal rage at the idea of a woman in power and ranted that the only way that a woman could hold any power was through sex and did not have the capabilities of thought to control anything, not even her husband! Some of the words mentioned on the reign of her mother's family I had found out not to be true, since Berenice was placed on the throne by her grandfather, it was not stolen as was mentioned in the memoirs of Cleopatra Selene.

VI

As written by Cleopatra Selene on the life of her mother in that turbulent time...

"Berenice slipped into the palace in the shadows of the night and set up her pathetic rule in my grandfather's stead. The older Cleopatra, followed her and sat beside her in their imagined rule. They proclaimed themselves as the legitimate rulers of Egypt. What a nerve she had, that Berenice! My mother must have fumed over her lessons and paced the floors wearing down the imported marble tile in her soft pink slippers. She would pace and mumble to herself, as I actually witnessed as a child, probably planning some scheme or another. She was always intense in her planning on matters to be dealt with, for she would always win the battles that she would wage, except of course in the end-the most important one of all.

One had to be devious to survive the cunning and intrigues of her daily palace life. One had to think on their feet, since the ground was always being dragged up from under their feet by their own family members. Well, she did think on her feet and hid herself in the refectory in contemplation, knowing her. She must have choked on her figs, ever so gracefully of course; when she received word of her aunts proclaimed rule. Berenice IV indeed!

My mother was the most convincing of actresses when the need suited her. I could almost see her now toying with the kingdom in the mock pretense and ignorance of the politics which enveloped the land. An act which had definitely saved her life. She would shroud herself in her beloved papyrus scrolls and velum books in half mock rapture, pretending that politics annoyed her and were not of her concern, since she was only a mere child at that time.

For this was the year in which she first met my father, Marcus Antonii. She told me of the very day which she held dear to her heart to the very end. She told me that she had been toiling over her lessons in hieroglyphs all morning, composing a hymn to Osiris. She had forgotten the time as she hid in fervent study, of when she was told that she must ready herself for the banquet for the Roman officials that had just arrived that evening. She laughed and recalled how she ran through her toiletries and grasped around frantically for a garment suitable enough for the Romans. At that time Egypt was still a client kingdom of Rome, and one must set an amiable impression and appear the able ruling family that they were. So she hurried in rapt pursuit of a garment in mock of that. She must have run her slaves rabid at the tone of her voice. Garment after garment was tried on until she finally made her choice. The first one that she would make her appearance in public in. Finally considered old enough to appear as a part of the family in functions of state, though not old enough to be a threat to her sisters. She earnestly thought that it would create quite the gabble around the kingdom, and indeed it did, though not in the way that she had planned.

She wore the finest of linen, almost transparent, though not quite. The finest linen from Thebes, that had the straightest of plaits. Her belt of gold probably cuddled her tiny waist just so. The softest of pink slippers adorned her miniature feet and she strode purposefully down the hall. She mentioned that even her wig was of Egyptian ebony silk plaits, that fell down her waist, her own hair pinned perfectly underneath to complete the illusion. She told me that she had placed on her dainty head, the crown that she wore in the play on the wedding of Isis and Osiris. The finest of chiseled gold had circled her head, with horns on each side tapered up to encompass the golden disc between them in the grasp of the golden arms.

What a spectacle she must have made on the palace occupants, striding down the hall as if she were the Goddess Isis walking on the Nile itself. Silently she must have praised the Goddess that gave her this ingenious idea in mock subservience to the Romans. She must have shone ever so brightly among all who observed her and bowed down in her path. She told me that she then approached the throne room where her aunt sat on the throne of Upper and Lower Egypt, with the ever silent older sibling by her side to her left. Berenice and everyone else in the chamber were in the flowing drapes of the popular Roman style, and she in her Egyptian splendor. Berenice sat on the throne in her Roman apparel and her Egyptian headdress of the Upper and Lower Egypt with the look of aggravation on her tiny brow. Oh, how royally disturbed she must have been so see my mother thus, and to create ridicule among her family. For my mother completed her approach to kiss the toe of her aunt and to sit meekly beside them.

She had told me that it was at that moment when she first settled to the side of her aunts, that she had observed the reaction of the room. She would mimic the open mouthed expressions of all who beheld her image. My mother had mentioned that the silence was stifling. She stated that the room was filled with the haughtiness of grandeur in their Roman magnificence and august presence. Not one plebian in sight from her description of that scene. She stated that she wished to back up the whole evening, to when she first arrived at the thought of her ridiculous plan. There was no where left to go and hide.

He older brothers stood meekly beside the thrones of their aunts. Silent as the hush that fell over the room at the approach of my mother.

She recalled scanning the room for any possible escape, when her eyes rested upon those of my father. He was the youngest of Romans in her line of vision for her eyes not only rested on his eyes but lingered. In his youth he was tall and slender with broad hips to take command. He had a powerful and demanding jaw line that met the perfect aquiline nose. His eyes were blue with sensitive lids. He always, in my own memory, looked at someone as if they were the most important person to him. His expression forever deserved loyalty from all who gazed upon him. That expression never left his face, even in his later years. For the rest, from that moment on, was history…

"After that day, Berenice grasped the throne for another eight months and then lost it upon the return to court of my grandfather. She had tried in his absence to vacate him completely from rule. There were whispers of the involvement of Berenice in the mysterious death of the older Cleopatra, who died in agony one sunny morning. Only one of my family members at that time and prior had actually died a natural death, especially if they were close in line to the throne. For the only person in my lineage to die of natural causes and old age was the first Ptolemy. So, naturally suspicion was always in the forefront upon the death of any family member, no matter how insignificant it seemed initially. It was believed that her Aunt Cleopatra had succumbed to the poison of a mushroom so potent that it gave her several miserable and tormented hours of agony prior to her death. Berenice probably had something to do with that tragedy, for my mother recalled that Berenice was annoyed at her sister's apparent weakness in joint leadership and probably wished to have the throne all to herself. Berenice then fled Egypt to the mountains of Persia in fear of the wrath of my grandfather. Who, though a weak man, was not known for a forgiving nature. He would shake the very foundations of Hades in his festering rages on some slight, real or imagined. Even the shadows would tremble in fear of his steam.

Shortly after that he must have run to the scribes in fear of such an episode to occur again and established that my mother, the remaining Cleopatra and her brother Ptolemy Achilles were to be married. In accordance with Egyptian dynastic and pharonaic custom, the lineage of the rule could then be kept pure with the intermarriage of close kin of brother to sister and even in some cases of father to daughter, and other such close blood connections.

VII

"How the years must have passed as centuries for her in dread anticipation of the event, even through it was her expected duty and nothing new. Apparently her father had learned something of the evening when she appareled herself in the splendor of the Nile. For it had taught him how they had neglected the customs of the very kingdom in which they precariously ruled over. Of how the ruling family had never taken up the garb of the land in which they ruled. He would not allow that any further. He allowed her to dress in the Egyptian mode and secretly encouraged her to do so, for he had grown accustomed to the Greek and Roman apparel and their volumous drapery for he stated that it suited their climate fine and even provided some comfort of air circulation under the toga in their fierce desert sun.

"Some years had passed by without incident and they then waited out the rest of their destiny, which would all too soon crash at their feet once again. The images of the execution of Berenice in the court square after her capture, had even began to dim in the eyes of my mother, though the lesson was all too real for her.

In those years that would follow, my grandfather would play the flute solemnly at the example he had set with the deaths of his sisters. He never forgave Berenice, yet I am sure he had wondered as to where he had gone wrong with her. It must have wasted him away at those thoughts and others, for he seemed to fall into a saving oblivion after those events.

At that point, the news of Gaius Julius Caesar had reached the confines of the palace harem, of his newly declared governorship of the Cisalpine Gaul. My mother's palace informants were always on the lookout for the latest news of this powerful man. She was simply intrigued by him.

Her father was weakening by the day, and she was constantly by his bedside reading to him from the piles of scrolls in the confines of the palace suit. Together they would work on improving the policy for the people as well as attempting to settle the debts incurred by Rome.

Anything to placate his tiring nerves on his eventual deathbed. Cleopatra must have reveled in the attention given to her by her father in those days. As a daughter to a Greek man, she was never paid much attention to prior to this time. Now, as Ptolemy Auletes was nearing the door to the underworld in which all souls go, according to the religion of the ancients of the land, he realized the value of his third child. He must have observed the spark of power on her concentrated brow as they waited away his last days together pondering the issues brought before him.

For she told me of how she devoted the last days to her father by his side, in learning all about the rule of the magical land of Kemet. For he had to depend on her and that of her younger brother, of whom she was married to. Her brother was just not ready to grasp the mature concept of the rule about to be placed on them upon their father's death. In his youth, her brother was headstrong and impulsive, qualities that were inherited from their father. Though upon the observation allowed him in this weakened physical state, he realized those as not the greatest of qualities that a ruler should have. Her brother gave no indication of quenching his irrational pride either, so her father resorted to a dependence on his daughter and her good sense and objective opinions.

"To back up a bit, Kemet, was the name given to the land by the ancients, it meant "the black land". This was in reference to the rich black soil deposited on the banks of the Nile, of which the people had for thousands of years depended on for the prosperity and their very lives. This soil would be deposited luminously on the banks of the mighty river with each inundation of the Nile, which occurred once a year.

Nilometers were set up at various intervals along the river and were used to determine the amount that the river would flood. The amount was essential in establishing whether or not they would have enough to support the people in the ensuing year and of how much to tax them. The Nilometer consisted of a marked area along the banks of the river, which consisted of many steps, on which the water of the Nile would rise during the inundation. Records were kept and the result of which would determine whether the crops would be bountiful that year or not, depending on which step the water would settle. There was even a mark named the "cubit of death" which would indicate famine for the people in that the crops would not receive the water and precious enriched soil for the survival of the crops. The rich black soil that was deposited contained the necessary minerals needed in the soil to attain profitable crops. From the time that she was a child she would attend the officials who maintained the records at the Nilometers and record the process. Her father told her that in doing this she would become a part of this vital land and understand the people. Something he realized too late in his reign was essential for their families' survival.

For in the last years of his reign the Nile had not risen to a profitable height and had maintained itself just below the "cubit of death". He was aware of this and of how important it was to the people who worked along the shores and provided sustenance for the land over which they ruled. For he hoped that it would rise again and the prosperity would return. He felt it very wise that his daughter had ingrained herself to their people to gain her popularity and hoped that it would help despite the level of the infamous Nilometer.

VIII

"Those final days of my grandfather must have been difficult for her and the rest of the palace. For the flute ceased it's music, the enchantment of the day was over, the curtain had finally fallen on a man who loved life so much. He was never that much of a pharaoh, though who could control that station that one was born in life to fulfill. What he did do which was essential for the maintenance of the land, was done in his last years and behind closed curtains. The people only saw and remembered his merry façade, and not the lines that creased his brow with worry. Thus, the people did not witness the actual deeds of Ptolemy Auletes. My mother always said that he should have been on the stage, since he was never one to enjoy the staunch protocol of the throne. He performed his duties in secret and joined publicly in revels and amusements with his people. He never had the head for foreign politics and could never fit well in the intrigues of the world's issues. He only had a heart for his homeland that touched the powerful Nile and had eventually granted the peace he so longed for in the end. He taught her a lot in those days of their country and it's power. He taught her the value of acting, for one must always appear strong before the subjects of their rule, no matter what they may feel inside, unlike his example. He taught her the value of knowledge. For he was an insidious bibliophile as well as she. He had meant well during his reign, and he did do a lot, though it was never enough to keep Rome away from his door and the people from reminding him of his illegitimacy. Most of those people were long gone, and his daughter did not have that burden. He probably, at one time, cherished dreams of his sons claiming the throne, when the futile reality of this had forced him to depend on my mother in those last moments of his life.

He was never officially meant for the throne for he was the illegitimate son of the last Ptolemy IX Alexander Soter II and under the care of Syria in his youth. He had paid a heavy bribe to Julius Caesar to secure the throne. For the last in the legitimate line was his son and half brother to my grandfather; Ptolemy XI Alexander Soter II. Ptolemy XI had been brutally torn apart by the angry Alexandrian mob for the murder of his mother Queen Cleopatra Berenice. That Ptolemy had been raised a Hellenistic prince and was the puppet of the Roman dictator Sulla who was placed by him on the throne of Alexandria to marry his ageing mother who had assumed the sole rule over Egypt for the twenty years prior. The Alexandrians did not like that the last legitimate Ptolemy had grown tired after only three weeks of marriage to his mother and had brutally arranged her execution. They avenged this and tore him to pieces in the gymnasium. Which left the throne vacant for my grandfather. He came to rule with the help of the Romans and his money and gained the title "Friend and Ally of the Roman People".

When the Romans annexed Cyprus they deposed my grandfather Ptolemy XII, and the Alexandrians again grew angry in his not helping his half brother who had the throne briefly before him, after the death of their father-so fickle was their favor. So Ptolemy brought his sisters Cleopatra VI and Berenice IV to the throne. After that Cleopatra's death, Ptolemy XII paid another bribe to Rome and paid and even greater bribe to Rome to secure his throne once again and upon his return had Berenice

IV executed. He held the throne until his death, which was remarkably the only other natural death of that great family and momentous time in our history.

Thus, in my mother's lifetime, she had witnessed most of this and had realized the power of the money of her family, as well as a woman's in rule over Egypt, Berenice IV. It is confusing for anyone to research my family line with the vast repetition of names and the marriages of siblings and family members with the same names. For despite my mother's jealousy over her aunt Berenice IV, research proved that she was a more able rule that Cleopatra VII's own father.

Her brothers were an interesting sort. After all of the intrigue in their family they turned their back on duty to the various gaming tables that the Romans brought over with them and to the theater that their father loved so much. They had no interest in the rule except when guided by their tutors.

To the great dismay of my grandfather, not one of his son's knocked on the doors of his Chambers for tutelage. They both had inherited his love of revelry and his poor business sense. Their ears were forever yearning for more gossip and seedy tales of the elite and inner circle, the unfortunates, who were the subject of the palace gossip and slander. The Nilometer was just another set of boring stairs to them, one they would not run the risk of slipping on while parading about in their silken slippers.

"Then came the day when the trumpets sounded the last breath of my grandfather, and my mother was to walk the steps of her destiny all alone. For she knew that the wedding feast would be set out for her and her older Ptolemy brother. She must have held her head up high and choked on the tears as she walked down the aisle as many have before her. Drowning in her misery over the loss of her father and of the beginning of her fate without his guidance. Though, how like her to do something about it. She must have begun her plot when the trumpet sounded.

According to his wishes and in hopes of the future adoration of the people of the land whom he precariously ruled over, he abandoned the customary Greek funeral that his family dynasty had adhered to for the prior three hundred years or so. In respect of his rather unusual request, she made sure that her father was laid to rest after the seventy customary days of waiting for the mummification process. She knew the process of the death ritual of the rulers of the land of Kemet. The Egyptians believed that the most important part of a person was the heart, where after death it was weighed on the scale against the feather of the Goddess Maat. If the heart proved strong enough and did not tip the scale, the person was ready to travel onwards to the underworld, where Osiris awaited them. There was a whole ceremony performed by the priests who attended the ceremony of their ruler . The priests had been anxiously awaiting summons from the ruling family for way too long. They eagerly obeyed this latest request and offered much instruction to the ruling family of their traditions and meanings so thankful that they had finally been called into service.

They had informed the curious Cleopatra of the secret ceremony that would be ritually adhered to. They had explained to her that in accordance of a four thousand year old tradition, the corpse of the ruler would be drawn upon by the scribe to await the knife of the cutter. The cutter would remove certain parts of the body to be placed in canopic jars with the figures of Gods adorning the lids in protection. It was perilous for the person deemed as the initial cutter, for after that first penetration with the knife on the skin, the cutter had to run for his life. For the others in the room would run in pursuit of the cutter pelting him with rocks. This was a strange custom, for it held to the belief that it was improper to cut the body in life and in death. However, it was a necessary part in the preparation for the dead in this land, and the ceremony of pelting the cutter with rocks was to ease this infraction of the immoral incision. The cutter, would then resume in the preparation after his flight throughout the room.

The brain matter was discarded in the generations before them, since it was considered of no use in the afterlife. Though in the most current of dynasties it was left intact following the wisdom of the Greeks. The heart was the most valued part and had it's own container. After this was done, the body was prepared in spices and wrapped. The body was then laid to rest for seventy days in nitron, which was a special preserving compound made of salt from the Nile and a soda-like powder. The exact ingredients were kept to the sacred priesthood only. After the seventy days were over, they would wash the body again and wrap it up artistically in the finest of linens. Certain charms were placed in the linen wrapping to guard the shell of the body left behind on the person's descent to the Afterlife. For it was believed that at the proper time Osiris would return to the shell of the person left behind and breathe life into him. That is why the bodies were preserved and great tombs were prepared with many games and food for the after life when the breath was restored to the body. The final sarcophagus would be made of the heaviest stone available to protect the resting shell of the person left behind. Each coffin from the body to the heaviest one would be more elaborate to the inner one that surrounded the body. At last the body was placed in a tomb for the final resting place after the necessary ritual ceremonies were held. The tomb for each pharaoh was commenced in the beginning of the reign and therefore, the longer the pharaoh lived the more elaborate the tomb would be. Each tomb was loaded with everything that the deceased person loved and needed in life. The sarcophagus would be surrounded with vivid paintings and carvings of statues of the things most enjoyed in life. Statues of those people and family members that the deceased person loved in life were placed in there for comfort, as well as statues of the servants to serve them in the afterlife. The Book of the Dead was inscribed along the walls of the tomb to guide my grandfather to the underworld and the arms of Osiris.

Knowing my grandfather, he probably had a devoted slave place a silver penny on his lips in secret payment to the ferryman of the River Styx, by the name of Charron. For my grandfather did not believe in the "rabble of the Egyptians". He though that it was nonsense. For his heart leaned towards Zeus and Olympus and the Greek Pantheon of his beliefs. However, it was protocol to adhere to the calling of the throne he sat upon and he fervently hoped that this would endear his daughter and son's reign to his people that he had left behind. For he was finally at home in the arms of his beloved Dionysus, his God, and could play his flute forever.

My Aunt Arsinoe must have whined as to why she was not placed on the throne, but what could she do, for she was still younger than my mother. I could imagine the plots filling her ears from her faithful advisors all the while.

IX

"My mother dove mercilessly among the books of the books of the library at her disposal, built by her ancestor, Ptolemy, the first of the name to rule over this land so long ago. A library that I have not seen since I was a small child, led by the sure hands of my mother. I will never forget the endless cubicles leading to eternity, overflowing with scrolls both numerous and ancient. The musty smell that permeated the halls was intoxicating and overwhelmed the senses. For the dust covered the words of the wisest men and women who ever lived. And all of this was at her disposal her whole life. This library contained every work from every civilization in our world. There was the science of the Greeks, of which the Romans only seem to copy or not even grasp at all, and the sacred holy texts of the Jews in a complete canon. Noted amongst those works were the texts compiled by one of their oldest patriarchs Abraham, a mystical work on the many phases of heaven and of armies of angels and of their fierce God Yadaboath of their first God/Goddess the Pistis Sophia which was the all and everything both male and female. A very interesting philosophy held sacred to their priests. The average Jew worships only one God and have died for this in the monotheistic colonies where they dwell since they long ago left their homeland. These sacred works were there for only a few to peruse, including my mother. The secret works of the known world rested here.

There were even works of an ancient civilization that disappeared beneath the sea six thousand years ago. This civilization was more advanced when compared to anything that she knew of the world that she lived in. It was written and yet to be discovered that they had built temples off an unknown island to the far east of Alexandria and lay deep in the ocean. This ancient language was still in the process of being translated. For they contained incredible secrets of the universe of which they believed that this world was only a small part of. To imagine what those texts would uncover! The Greeks had only glimpsed on that theory to believe that the world was round and spun on an invisible axis and then in turn rotated on a spherical path around the sun. The Greeks had uncovered so many of the hidden mysteries of that civilization over a thousand years before my time, in was truly incredible. The writings of every civilization, as well as the origins of the world lay at your fingertips in those marbled halls.

All one had to do was look. For this was all meticulously maintained by the master keeper of the texts, a Greek by the name of Demicretus. He was old and frail by the time that I walked the halls. His eyes would twinkle at the sight of my mother. For she loved the written word as well as he. They would talk for hours debating one writing in comparison with another. How she would playfully adore in stumping him with her inquiries, and I am sure that the feeling was reciprocated.

My mother perused the writings of the mystics as well as in statecraft. I supposed that this is how she developed a love for the land that she eventually gained rule over. She would ponder for hours and days over the sacred texts of the temples of the land. She later shared that knowledge with me as best as she could since I was only a child of ten the last time that I saw her. She never saw age as a barrier in her teaching. My mother would laboriously translate every word for me to hear for as long as I could remember. We even developed a game with the hieroglyphs that covered the walls of the sacred temples of the land. Her family never bothered to learn the meanings of this magical text. For she always loved a challenge. The knowledge of the ancient religion, instilled in her a strong desire to restore as many of the ancient buildings that during most of the reign of the Ptolemy's past, had fallen into decay from the ceaseless battering of millenniums of desert winds.

In her learning about her people's religion, she developed a love for the Goddess Isis. She even joined the temple to learn the arts of healing and dream reading. She would frequent the temple of Isis, and had even included me in some of those treks in pilgrimage. The closest temple was located at the base of the lighthouse on the small Island of Philo. In this temple she would tend to the ill, and even divine the dreams of her own subjects. She would not do this as a pharaoh or queen but as a priestess of

Isis and no more. The stoic in her buried deep inside and passed on during those last days of her father, saw people as equals and even debated over the issue of slavery. My mother and later I in turn would ponder this philosophy often and would lay awake late at night trying to find someway that she could live this philosophy more. That was one of the dreams she never realized in her short life.

The people of her land observed their Queen in reverence to their own Gods and Goddesses, and had wept in tears of joy at the return to the old ways. For so long, their religion, had been tossed aside for the worship of the Gods of their conquerors. The people would madly cheer the approach of my mother, whenever she made a public appearance.

Her brothers sat idly by on the sidelines and eagerly listened to the fruitless promises from their tutors and advisors of more treasures and the wars to wage for the acquisition of them. In contrast, my mother devoted most of her time in pleasing the people of Kemet and shining her charismatic eyes upon the Romans and other dignitaries who came to visit. She knew that her kingdom was only a client kingdom to the vast power of Rome. This mighty power, which crushed people as if they were ants. Lands and kingdoms fell away at their feet and eventually paid them honor. Rome would not only destroy the lands they conquered but send in their people to populate the lands they conquered by marrying into and living amongst them. The latter was the way in which most of the world was eventually conquered by the Romans. My mother hated even what she saw in her own time. She decided to play their own game by capturing the most powerful Roman of all. She must have learned that the only way to survive, was to gain the favor of her enemy, and only then would she have access to their weaknesses. She decided that Gaius Julius Caesar, would be a very important man for her to meet. Knowing her she concocted plans in which she would seduce him with her glamour that she had learned from the teachings of Isis.

"For soon after her claiming the throne she was ousted by her older brother Ptolemy, the older of the two Ptolemys who was her husband and her younger sister Arsinoe. Their advisors must have warned them of the increasing power that my mother had with the people and the disfavor they had incurred from the same. Both conspired and denounced her from the throne and palace, my mother was forced to flee in the dead of night under the cover of the screeching dessert winds.

Though she learned a valuable lesson from her father, and of her own actions while Berenice claimed rule. Life is always full of lessons, one only had to ponder long enough to learn from them. She had learned that there would be times when it would be a wise move to appear weak and ignorant, to bide the time that was needed for her to strike back. She just never assumed that it would occur during her own reign. Her own father did the same and appeared to others as if he was driven out of the country, when in reality, he was preparing the military strength and forces essential to his re-admittance to his seat of power and repairing his faults in this respite as well. When the time was auspicious for him, he struck with a vengeance. I often wondered if my grandfather had exaggerated his insanity before his flight to Rome, to hide any of the plans that he was creating and could not commit to at that time, since it was definitely not his time. My, mother in a flight similar, might have wondered those very same thoughts on the matter. She probably used her acting skills to conceal her smile as she hid her thoughts over dusty scrolls in her earlier youth.

"I do recall her telling me of the many plays she and her family attended in her youth. For her family vastly encouraged the arts as in turn did ours. Knowing my mother, she probably imagined herself one of the characters in a play in those times, such as the voracious Cassandra of Troy, the prophetess and priestess of Apollo sister of Paris of Troy. The Iliad, which as compiled by Horace just before the time of my mother was one of her favorite plays. A volume of tales handed down from the Greeks to be converted into plays for the Romans amusements and her own delight. Cassandra was one of the main characters of the play who had the least amount of lines. The listener knew that she had the most knowledge, though the other characters involved in the dramae had no such knowledge and mocked the dooming prophesies she uttered on the destruction of Troy. Did my mother see herself as the doomed Cassandra, a woman no one would believe until too late. A character misunderstood?

Cassandra also waited in silence, until she felt that the time was right, though what did it gain either of them in the end?

X

"My mother told me of the time that she had to wait silently in the desert for the proper opportunity to seize the chance to take back her throne. She had received word that her brother and Arsinoe sat side by side on the thrones in mockery of her retreat.

The truth of it all was that she was recouping her armies and deciding on her best vantage point. She realized that Caesar would be a mighty ally for her to have, for he might be the absolute power in Rome someday. The rate he was seizing power and gaining territory for Rome was remarkable in itself. She had to have an audience with this man.

She had gained the knowledge that he had set up residence in the palace where her brothers and sister were. Her younger Ptolemy brother was probably playing with his friends oblivious to the situation and probably even wondered where she was. For he was truly the only sibling who actually cared for her, though was useless as a political ally and power. The palace was probably crawling with guards, since their situation was so unstable, especially in the presence of Caesar. They must have shook in their delicate sandals in the fear that he might set up rule on their throne. She knew that Arsinoe had set up her new and loyal guards to prevent this, to treat that more as a threat than the thought of Cleopatra's return. Rome was just too powerful an enemy to provoke, even if they had to pay homage to them. The Roman's were still kind enough to let the Ptolemy's pretend they had the throne, were they not?

The mighty Cleopatra, my mother, my driving force and inspiration; told me of how incredible this advantage really was to her at that time. They were more concerned with guarding the inside of the palace from their powerful guest, than they were of a single girl of nineteen years. It did not matter to them that she was the legal heir and uprooted Queen. To them she was just a mere girl and far from a threat of the Roman army.

And wait did she for the perfect moment… In the meanwhile she had received reports of the pathetic image her brother made of the garishly decorated throne. Of how his stature was weak and unimposing, unlike what was expected of the pharaoh by the people. He almost appeared as if he was a little boy playacting that he was king. How foolish he must have looked to the people, for he was really twenty-three, though had the care for rule as an eight year old child. He cared only for the pageantry and power of the rule, not bothering to actually do anything to gain the respect of the people. The people of Alexandria were extremely weary by now of the rule of the Ptolemy's who had grown weaker in each successive generation with nothing substantial done by any of them for the past two hundred years.

"She had heard that upon the actual arrival to the city of Alexandria by Gaius Julius Caesar, he was greeted at the steps of the palace by her brother's and sister, the Lord High Chamberlain Potheinus and their vapid tutor Theodotus. They had presented Caesar with a gift which they thought would completely surprise the mighty Roman and bring them to their cause. For wrapped in a heavy embroidered cloth to cover the element of surprise it lay on the ground in front of the feet of Caesar. "If you will, Sir." Potheinus foppishly beckoned Caesar to receive his gift that was placed at his feet. Caesar bowed in thankfulness and proceeded to unwrap his gift in rapt curiosity. When he realized to his horror what it was he had to step back in appraisal of the situation and how best to deal with it. He had realized they truly meant only to win his side and not to bring about the vast reaction that stole freakishly through his veins. For in the bag was the severed head of his friend and fellow triumvirate Pompey the great. For he was in Alexandria to mend a disagreement that they recently had and to resume their friendship. Pompey was an old friend and was even married to his beloved only child Julia. Julia and his grandson had died only five years prior and he and Pompey had been on odds with each other. Pompey, the only man he found good enough for his only child, how they loved each other once. Caesar lamented the dreadful present and negated this day until the date of his death. He never forgave himself for not making amends sooner with his missed friend.

Though noted for his composure, he said little politically though they gained the idea on the impression it made with Caesar and he decided to cut off his campaign and settle for a time and Alexandria to clear the trouble with the leadership. For he had guessed correctly whose idea it was…Potheinus and none other. He would make sure that his rule over the Ptolemy children would end fast.

"My mother had secretly prepared an army that would rise against her brother and sister in their fantasy rule. For she deemed that it was time for it to cease. In the end, I know not what higher power made her act in the way that she eventually did, for it proved to be a much more favorable outcome indeed. Not since the execution of her aunt Berenice, had she been more frightened. Though that fright proved to be her greatest ally in her time of need, for it made her proceed in every venture from that moment on with caution. Stress proved to be her greatest strength. She vowed that she would not end up like her obstreperous aunt, still warm in her tomb.

She then proceeded to plant the first seeds of her plan to capture the heart of a man who should have been king. She did believe that he had the aura of an emperor, probably as powerful as Alexander the Great. Though Rome preached it's abhorrence to the thought of an autocracy, the people were presenting a populace that so desperately needed one.

XI

"One evening she was able to set her plan in motion…she had secretly donned herself in the silkiest and gauziest apparel known to man. She whispered of how this strange silk from Cathay, could tempt the most pious of men when worn by a woman who knew what she was doing. It was as if the material were handed down to women as a tantalizing weapon to strike the unaware men that it was donned for. Such was her weapon of choice for that darkest of evenings in the wake of a new moon that covered her scheme.

She must have laughed at the simplicity of her plan, as her eyes would twinkle in the tell of it and in remembrance of its fruition. She must have summoned the breath of Isis to aid her that eve, for the easel of the Gods rapidly filled with enchanted mists to cloud her approach to the palace. She summoned the power of Isis to enter her form as she ventured forth to seduce the descendant of a God. She also contained the sexual power of the Goddess in her breast, so silkily adorned.

Alone, she walked to the bank of the canal and laid down silently to submit to the next part of the plan. The only other person who had knowledge of her plans was the simple fisherman who she lured in with her plight and brilliant idea. Not even he, truly knew who she was, for she appeared to him in his simplicity—as the Goddess Isis. He eagerly obeyed the whims of his Goddess before him and proceeded to roll her in a Persian rug. He obeyed her command and rowed the carefully concealed Goddess to the gates of the palace enclosure. He even recalled his instructions as to what he had to say to the guard to gain him admittance to the palace main. He informed the guards that the rug was a gift for the Roman who was named Caesar, who was in residence at the palace at that time. Under the stars of Nut, the Goddess of the sky, she was carried faithfully by the fisherman, to the very feet of Gaius Julius Caesar that eve.

She knew that everything had to be perfect to aid her in this scheme. For she had selected the most exquisite rug she could attain. Surely this would escape the eyes of the guard and lead them to believe that it was truly a gift. She must have prayed fervently to Isis, and probably even Aphrodite as well!

Her prayers were surely answered that eve, for what an entrance she must have made! I would have given anything to see the look upon him face, when he bent down over the rug to unroll it, oblivious to the contents therein! Well, the rest is history known only to the two of them. Though to say the very least, she had won the very heart and soul of Gaius Julius Caesar. For from that day forward, their hearts were entwined in rapture, or so she told me, omitting all details for her daughter of course. With her Greek upbringing, she held her heart open for him for all the time that he lived.

In a way, I believed that her plans on attaining his heart, had failed in a way due to her strength of love for him. For it did get in the way. She could no longer be objective in order to gain any political achievements with their alliance. Her heart yearned to gain control and sometimes did. She did not plan on having any feelings for him, she had only meant to conquer his heart, not to entangle hers in the process. At that time she had truly felt that he was her destined soul mate, and she would have no other, to her dismay. She would not even honor her marital obligations to her brother as she should have. For she feared that she could not maintain the coldness towards him that she deemed as necessary for the goal that she had in mind. She did not want anyone to have power over her emotions; as only Julius Caesar regretfully did to hold the reigns which set her carefully placed kindling she lay before him into a raging inferno until his last breath.

XII

"They spent the whole evening talking, or so she had claimed to her daughter. Though I am not an innocent any longer to that tale and have become a woman of my own right at the writing of this. I knew that much more than words were required to seal any bargain and lure the fiery soul of this powerful Roman. I had heard much of his Roman wife that he left behind named Calpurnia, as well as of his many amorous affairs that were legendary. There were even jokes around Rome that had urged the men in Rome to hide their wives from the wiles of Julius Caesar! I had gained this knowledge in my pursuit of the real woman behind the love I have for my infamous mother. I wanted to hear all sides of the story. He had left a trail of broken hearts and cuckolded husbands. Had he really been entranced by my mother, or was she merely just another of his political pawns. For there was also the legend of his affair with King Juba of Numidia's wife, which was another of Cicero's sordid tales. For the noted Cicero was on campaign against Julius Caesar and my mother and later my father as well. There was constant source for the venom which he spread from his lips against any who trod his path. Though Romans were notorious for their jokes on each other, for Cicero was only a family nickname which meant Chickpea, due to his father's lack of height.

She must have done or said something to spark his next actions. Together they made a political alliance. They each had their motives. My mother had her designs, as well did Caesar. For he, at that time, was still steaming over the death of his fellow leader and triumvirate of Rome. For he told of this upon their initial meeting of the occurrence at his arrival in Rome. He had informed her that the Ptolemy that had sat on the throne gave his numb approval of that idea. He then, due to that mass blunder, had set up his residence in the palace and began to plan his pretext on being the guest at the palace of Bruchion. Her brother had looked so pitiful at the mention of that horrible deed. Was Arsinoe a part of this? She then set up an investigation into the matter, unofficial of course.

Anyways, Caesar had set into motion his own cleaning of the palace, at the approval of my mother. Many more lessons in statecrafts were taught to my mother from the greatest of them. For they had both agreed on the disposal of her older brother Ptolemy from the throne and of Arsinoe. Unfortunately, he escaped with his head, though not with any wits-which he never had in the first place. Arsinoe was captured and placed under guard to await her transport to Rome.

The rest of the events to the time of her death was known as the Alexandrian war. Though it was mainly drafted by the Romans, it did provide an accurate account of the military events that occurred. My mother approved of most of the account. Some histories were tailored to the writers cultural side and were known to have heavily embellished events in their countries favor. Alas, she had felt that the accounts that she had gained access to were fairly accurate as well as those written by her lover Caesar.

Eventually the older Ptolemy was found after the battles in the marshes by the canal. He was one of the many who had perished in the confusion of their evacuation of the city. What a gruesome fate indeed for anyone. He must have felt that he was so powerful, to finally surrender to a force such as water in the end.

XIII

Caesar married my mother in the Egyptian fashion in the full glory that it entailed. He must have quieted her with the promises of divorcing his Roman wife Calpurnia. For relented did she to the persuasions of his words and shared with him her kingdom of gold. They followed the wedding with a tour down the Nile to display to the people their rulers power in uniting Egypt to the greatest of Rome.

She soon bore him a son, too soon after the wedding. My mother must have chuckled at this, knowing that the Goddess must have been with her indeed to have conceived with her first meeting of Caesar, or so soon after. For she never did reveal any of the details of that evening to anyone. Though one could easily have done the math of her lunar cycle. Her son was named Ptolemy Caesar, to show the whole world the paternity he held. For even upon one glance, the truth of that was revealed. I had heard it said that he was the very image of Caesar in his youth. Too closely did he resemble his father in his appearance in fairness and golden curls. My mother called him Caesarion and delighted in his golden ringlets, just slightly darker in shade than those of his father. He would stomp around with his toddler legs wearing a miniature toga of white, bordered in purple and waiving his wooden sword. My mother always tolerated this Roman fancy well, though wished to enter her son into the teachings of the temple of Amun, though her Gaius would not hear of it. That must have distressed her so, to be led even in part by a man. She did soften a bit with his wishes on that latter matter though, for she had often dreams of her son ruling both Egypt and Rome which kept her busy enough in the planning to the reality of it. Though on that last matter, he did not intercede in her wishes. She probably bided her time to wait for the proper moment for her cherished wish of the divorce of Calpurnia. She must have silently seethed in the fact that she had once again to hold her tongue on an issue.

"She even recalled a time when her brothers had laid the foundation of vicious propaganda against her and her charming Gaius. As if any mob could deter a proud personae as she in her day! Even Gaius must have mocked the hubris of the very thought of it.

Despite all of that, she held her court, like the mighty Isis in attendance of her subjects. For she was trained as a high priestess of Isis, and reared me in her footsteps to the best of her ability and her short time as my mother.

I cannot even fathom the thoughts that ran rapid through my younger uncle's mind as she led her campaign. The deep chasm that separated any possible love from any of the members of her immediate household, was simply immense; and thus, never breached in all of her years. I know that they all plotted against each other, even in their sleep it seemed. By the time that she had married Caesar in the Egyptian fashion, Ptolemy Achilles had drowned in the river during the war that had destroyed too much of her beloved and metropolitan city. To this very day, I still hear the remnants of the poison spread initially by my older uncle. It is so pathetic, it is not even wasting any ink over. Much blood was lost to my Uncle Ptolemy Achilles and my Aunt Arsinoe when they joined forces against my mother. She even mentioned that Arsinoe had proclaimed herself the true Pharaoh of Egypt. Though, that of course did not last that long in duration. For she was captured by Caesar and brought to Rome in chains.

XIV

"Both Gaius and my mother had their own battles to wage, each in their own realms. Gaius had to struggle for ground in the civil wars in Rome, while my mother had to face the angry hordes on her own soil. They both had their hands full just in attempting to hold their own ground.

XV

From the information that I had gained on my mother's first husband, it was apparent that at that time, the Romans were initially concerned with the dissolution of the old city-state constitution that they were so proud to have in their history. Gradually, Gaius had managed to wrench, bit by bit, the power of the republic away from the people of Rome, to govern over while the old way was being questioned. The people needed to implement a new way of rule over the conquered and the already established peoples of Rome.

Sulla, who had the prior dictatorship and rule over the people, had attempted to reenact the old city-state constitution, though to no fruition. Pompey and Crassius ruled the senate until Gaius became counsul when my mother was a mere seven years old. He rose steadily in power like a mercurial comet from Olympus. The three of them concorded a political alliance as the triumvirate, when they agreed to heed each other in further advancements.

"Caesar was born of an august line of Romans and extremely educated in literary pursuits, his capability immense. He was the descendant of the Roman Goddess Venus. He was a phenomenal orator, relying on his affable wit and charisma. The people adored him.

Hispania saw the first of his noted military campaigns, which had sown the seeds of an even greater love from the people of Rome. He became governor of Cisalpine Gaul when my mother was ten years of age. His genius knew no common bounds. Though he had initiated his career rather late compared to the average Roman in his thirties. Alexander the Great had conquered most of the known world by the time that he was thirty-two and Caesar was just getting started. Caesar had the name though not the money in his youth.

He was raised in a humble insulae subdura in the depths of the city and had to rely on his Julii family name and associates to establish his political tie to Rome, which he did greatly.

When my mother was eleven, he had conquered all of Gaul, which had further ingrained him in the hearts of the Romans. The senators were so stunned by this victory and conservatively feared that if he were to return to Rome, he would have enough forces behind him to conquer the city as Sulla had. Their fears were to the naught, for he had only wanted to return to his home after eight years on campaign.

"His victory in Gaul was to a chieftain by the name of Vercingetorix. Vercingetorix was the thorn in the side of the mighty and until then, unconquerable Gaius Julius Caesar. For Vercingetorix led his undefeated army against Caesar on many a chase throughout the countryside of the vast wilderness of Gaul.

Before he met up with Vercingetorix, he had gained his fame through his defeat of pirates that had been ravaging the shoreline of Italia for many prior decades. Julius Caesar was captured by them and eventually defeated them, gaining the trust and admiration of Rome.

"Vercingetorix was of tall stature, I have heard from my own inquiries on the man. It almost seems as if all of the old heroes were of tall build, and probably ego as well. Almost as if he were one if the titans I hear so much about from the Romans in their history annals. Even his name fit perfectly for a hero for it meant "King of a hundred heads". This must have been utterly intended to inspire fear amongst the enemy combatants of the time on the battle field. This character was of noble deed and word for the Gauls worshipped him. For he was the first leader of their race to ban together the tribes of the fearsome Celts (or Keltoi peoples from the Greek records) in their whole known history. They were forever warring amongst themselves, when the right hero bade them to cease this and to realize the all too real threat of the Romans encroachment of their lands.

The Keltoi peoples of Vercingetorix were known to occupy the land named by the Romans as "Long-Haired Gaul" on their charts of the region. This was due to their vanity for long hair and how during battle, they fearsomely decorated it to inspire fear among their enemies. This land that they occupied was large in mass and was south of the Germanic territory and North of Greater Gaul located in the northern part of Italia. There were fierce mountain ranges that bordered most of the land in which they occupied, which had to be crossed by the Romans in invasion and probably contributed to their fiery ways that they had inherited which enabled them to survive in that harsh climate.

Vercingetorix was the son of a chieftain by the name of Cetlillos. He successfully banded the warring tribes together in common deed-which was a remarkable feat indeed! The Keltoi peoples were mainly a farming community at that time, and abhorred the threat of the urban development of the Romans. They banded together in their hate against the vast insurgence of Roman feet upon their soil.

A series of battles were fought to prevent any urbanization of the Romans. Vercingetorix gathered the forces of the following tribes; Leones, Parisii, Pictones, Cardurci, Suroni, Cenomai, Lemovicis, Alerci, Andes, Amorcan, and many others. The only opposition at that time within the Keltoi peoples of "Long Haired Gaul" in this common cause, was from the uncle of Vercingetorix who was named Gobannito; who had raised a band of ruffians and traitors to is cause.

The battle turned for the worse against the Romans, when the forces of Vercingetorix had entered the settlement of Avaricum-which had maintained the largest wheat supplies for the people. For by then the supplies of the Romans were low and had desperately required replenishment before marching on. This was one of Gauls richest dominions. Due to the season, there was no grass in the fields nor wheat in the barns, which added in favor to the Gauls. The brave Vercingetorix did all that was in his power to tarry the advancement of the large forces of Caesar. Therefore, all of the towns in the immediate vicinity were set on fire by the Gauls in order to deter the advancing pace of the Romans. Over twenty towns of the Biturges were put to the torch under the command of the Gauls.

This honorable character had changed the events of history against him due to his noble heart. There are a great many songs and poems written of this man and of his noble heart. Unfortunately history has no such place for noble deeds in reality, especially in the time of my mother and before. For in his generosity to the people in granting their wishes, he had turned the table of time against him, which had forever his valiant dreams.

For the people of the town of Avaricum had begged the valiant Vercingetorix for his mercy on their valued city and its contents. He must have paused and weighed the extreme situation and consequences in his mind. The Celtic heart had much room and need for such inspired epics. With his decision to grant the people their town, his fate was sealed. The

Gauls had done everything else that they could think of to delay the inevitable disaster. For skillful tacticians were employed in the building and navigation of ditches to surround the walls of the settlement. Traps and pits scattered the desolate landscape before the Romans, leading to the city gates. There followed a series of small battles and skirmishes on those very lands. The frantic leader probably paced the streets of the settlement, his mind wavering towards the original idea of torching the very settlement that he was in—the closest the Keltoi would get to a Roman city at that time. He probably stared in rapt horror at the dwindling size of his troops.

Finally, a vicious attack was launched and the town was seized in it's last effort. A Large massacre was the seedless result of this chaos and destruction. For the corpses lined the streets in mock hubris to the Gods that had failed them in ignorance of their fervent prayers. The glory of the Gauls was seized and destroyed by the vainglorious Romans, much to their horror.

Though I heard in Roman accounts that prior to the destruction of that city the Gauls in their desperation had made an attempt to save the woman and the children by handing them over to the Romans to feed. Vercingetorix had probably figured that their own woman and children would fare much better under the treatment of the Romans, even in slavery, than to die in the slow torture of starvation. However, the Romans were starving themselves in not being able to find any food before they had reached this city in its being destroyed by the Gauls before they arrived. When the woman were turned over to the camps of the Romans, they were ignored and left to wander in-between both camp and city to beg for food. Many of the woman and children belonged to the defenders of the city. For days they wandered until the last of them had succumbed to the clutches of hysteria and starvation.

Whatever the truth of the matter Avaricum was weakened by too many defeats and losses of those they loved and had witnessed the helpless deaths of the weak who had depended on them for survival in a cruel world.

The Romans were able to secure their provisions from that battle in the plunder that followed, and were thus able to greet the next day of battle that awaited them.

Such a pity that nobility was not the answer to that battle. Though I often wonder why the Gauls considered him noble when he watched the helpless women and children die before their very eyes. Though I suppose that Caesar was noble in his own rights, he was just able to foresee what was needed for a victory in that matter.

"Vercingetorix had retreated then to Georgovia, which happened to be on a plateau and a good vantage point against the Roman forces. One of the tribes had planted the seeds of turbulence for the mighty Caesar. The Gauls and Georgovia had helped out against the Romans in a new set of skirmishes. It was Caesar that was defeated during that span of battles. Vercingetorix was then voted by the Gauls, the supreme commander to the unification of the tribes, as a result of that victory. For then, he had in his command a larger number of Calvary than the Roman legions.

His choice in launching the premature assault had leaned against him. He had lost an irrefutable amount of horsemen in this battle, which turned the tables against him once again.

"Another serious error was to follow this, when he chose to lead his forces into refuge in the settlement of Mandibrian. For he should have cut his losses and held back his forces to lead order to small bands of harassment against the Romans. However, he chose once again in the wrong, which depressed any hope of victory.

When he took this refuge in the Mandibrian fortress of Alesia, Caesar had set siege upon the forces of Vercingetorix. At this point too many critical mistakes had led to the finite casualty of his forces by the numerous and replenished Romans.

The tribes had gone so far as to oust Vercingetorix as their leader and raised Comminos to the fore. This new man had so many of the needed qualities of the leader that they so desperately needed then, however, he came forward too late. Should he had come forward prior to then, the history may have been quite different from what we now read. Thus, the forces held a meeting on what course of action to take; in which Vercingetorix had elected that all of the noncombatants be led out of town, instead of sacrificing them as was suggested. Comminos refused this request of their prior leader. Such songs were sung to the honor of Vercingetorix from the hearts of the people, of this fateful meeting of the minds.

Alas, being that the request was denied, the battles of the determination of history were thus fought. Trenches were dug around the city in which stakes were placed and concealed therein. Much to the dismay of the forces of Caesar.

The courage and bravery that evening led to epics! My mother told me Caesar's version of that eve. The wasted remains of the city were silhouetted in the splendor of the barbarian sunset. The burgundy hues magnified the beauty of the destruction and set the stage for the entrance of a figure he had conquered, yet admired. Out of the rubble Vercingetorix, proudly marched with his bare arms extended towards the victors. He was arrayed in all of the magnificence of his cherished rank, in the splendor of the chief of chiefs. Comminos was nowhere to be seen. He walked forward, and time stood still to receive his eminence and fearful visage. His bronzed physique was heightened by the hues of the brilliance emanated by the Gods of the moment. The gold that covered his marvelous frame, shone with grandeur, to the marvel of all who beheld such a sight! His garments were embroidered with colorful symbols and designs, as was the paint on his skin. The colors wove the labyrinth they so believed was the doorway to all they held so sacred. A druid accompanied him in his short trek to the fore of the battlefield. The man was covered in a long black woolen robe, the voluminous robe concealed his expression, which led to the enchantment of the moment. Vercingetorix held his arms aloft, as if to grasp the very Gods in their heavens, and boldly granted his men and forces to the leadership of the victorious Caesar. Such a moment! Ah, to only have been there to witness this fierce bravery that even the mighty Caesar admired.

I was further told, that the defeated Gauls were led in captivity to the Urban environs of Rome to back their victory. In chains they were led to the gate of the city and displayed to the people of Rome. Such a worthy adversary and foe. Caesar had greatly admired the courage and bravery of this man, and told my mother, and in turn she told us, of the legend of the fall of Gaul.

I render unto you, the mixture of both the Roman version from the chronicles of events by Julius Caesar, as well as the Keltoi version as told later by various other witnesses whom I have met in my research on this great moment in history.

XVI

"All of this occurred away from the land of Kemet and my mother. Many events unfolded away from her and before they met, though eventually landed in the hands and chronicles of my mother for her to record. Those records are lost at the time of this writing, for they were hidden away in a last desperate moment.

For with the tale of the epic battle of Julius Caesar and Vercingetorix, I write of the foundation that was established already in the man that my mother had known. For this all occurred many years before they had met in Alexandria.

XVII

"She had even told me of a time when the relationship was young, when Caesar had set fire to the city of Alexandria in hopes of ousting the older Ptolemy from his leadership during the Alexandrian wars. My mother told me of the horror of awakening to find her harbor was on fire and had reached the very portal of her much cherished library! What a sight that had appeared to Gaius in the form of the wrath of my mother! She fortunately had to hold her temper even in that moment, and coolly requested his forces to withdraw. This must have scorched her so. The power and the voice to her future lay with Rome, and with Rome—Gaius Julius Caesar.

Due to her many powers of persuasion to the opposite sex, she held sway, and was jointly enlisted with Caesar as her consort, to the rule of the empire of Egypt. Her rhetoric held true to her, while her oratory skills gained the day. Soon after that time she had my brother Caesarion, several months later while Caesar was away on yet, another campaign.

Meanwhile, the triumvirate fell apart in Rome. Caesar still had his power beside Cleopatra and governed wisely.

"Subsequent to the wedding in the Egyptian rite, Caesar was accepted to the priesthood as the incarnation of Amun to appease my mother and the people. More, sting to my uncle, the older of the Ptolemy's, who must have turned violently in his tomb at the very whisper of this. My mother built a temple in Caesar's honor in the city of Thebes and had devoted it to the Goddess Hathor. Hathor is the Goddess of my people, of love and merriment. She obviously felt this appropriate in her situation with Caesar. Especially since he was the descendant of Venus, the Roman equivalent.

Her studies had noted the similarities of divinities of various cultures of her time and of the past. She told me that she believed that Venus and Hathor were one and the same in her eyes, which was her reasoning for the temple. On the walls she had a portrait painted in the style of the ancients of my half brother Caesarion.

XVIII

"Unfortunately for my mother and her dreams, the Roman law considered her son from Caesar as illegitimate; due to his marriage to Calpurnia as well as his not being born from a mother of Roman citizenship. There was a Roman law that would not, no matter what, accept the legitimacy of any child of a non-roman citizen, even if they were married in Rome. My mother was Greek and Ruled Egypt. Caesarion would never be considered for a rule in Rome with those laws. It must have shattered my mother's hopes even further that Calpurnia was barren. She contained silently the knowledge of the existence of a daughter of Caesar from a prior marriage, named Julia, whom he still adored though long dead.

XIX

"She recalled a time when she had moved her court to the very gates of Rome and had set up residence in his guest house. That must have assuredly burned any hopes that Calpurnia had of her husband! She must have secretly learned of the liaison with the visiting ruler of Egypt and of her husband. For during public appearances, Calpurnia maintained the semblance of grace and emanated the epitome of devotion to her husband, though in the privacy of their chambers she must have had her word. For my mother had hinted at the true Calpurnia, and of how she held her head up high, despite the turmoil in her marriage. She was determined not to let the public of Rome make a mockery of her.

"My mother had a special barge created in the magic of the ancient beauty of her country. I do not know if this vessel was seaworthy due to the barge's assumed weight in gold, however, it was able to stay afloat on the Tiber and anchored at the dock. That great palace boat is to this very day (if it was not eventually plundered by the Romans) docked in the Great Harbor of Alexandria, where I last held my eyes in it's grandeur. This boat was spectacular indeed for it was ostentatious enough for Isis herself!

She and my half-brother Caesarion would be carried through the streets of Rome in the magnificence of Egypt and her station. My mother at that time, was caring for her sickly remaining brother, the younger of the Ptolemy's. He would spend most of his time attended by her famed physician Olympos, in the chambers of the guest house provided for her by Caesar. He did not fare well with the harsh climate of Rome and of the changing weather. I knew she cared for her brother, for a tear would glimmer in her eyes in the telling of his tale. Their retinue was large in number, not including those she had placed in the care of her brother. Olympos, her trusted physician was in constant care of her brother and his failing health.

Her brother would escort her in the most important of state festivities, though would soon retire to the care of her physician in his chambers. Her son was cherished in the arms of the Greek nurse, she bade care for him in her absence in the required affairs of her station as the ruler of her country.

"To while away her time, she would entertain the most august of the inhabitants of the city. She was often entertained by the philosophers such as Ovid and Plato, and others less noteworthy. She learned of Cicero, and of his ravings and supposed vast area of knowledge. Often, with her quick wit, she would conspire to stump this charming figure when he came to visit. Though her only way was in Greek, since she had never learned to speak Latin. She had to rely on Greek, since any learned individual at that time had a knowledge of that language. Alas, to no avail, since Cicero had no desire for her company, after the initial formal visit that he made. He had no room in his life to listen to what he uttered as the worthless prattle of a woman, no matter what her status. As could be expected, she turned her attentions elsewhere to gain success with this visit.

Her visionage would delight the population of Rome, in the mysterious Eastern apparel she was known to have worn on her official visits. She would frequent the Temple of Isis, though old and ill-kept, to pay her respects to the Goddess. This was not a popular temple at the time for the people of Rome, though slowly a new interest was sparked in the women of Rome who were enamored at that strange and beautiful Queen. They slowly began to seek the temple in curiosity at the mysterious eloquence of the east.

"One day, after she had been in Rome for almost a year, she was presented with a gift from Caesar. She followed him one day at his summons to the vast area of the Roman Forum on the Palantine Hill. On that day they were dressed as commoners, for he wanted to share his secret with her alone, and did not want to share it with the public rabble. She followed him with intensely growing anticipation into a large area surrounded by columns and palisades. Temples devoted to various Roman Gods dotted the area in their opulence. It was in the middle of the evening and their presence went unnoticed by the few restless souls about.

They stood side by side and marveled in awe at the magnificence of this new temple, Caesar had told her that he had it created in honor of his families patron Goddess, Venus. His gift to the city. He felt it important in his growing fame, that he should replace the old and dilapidated structure that had existed prior to this on the same spot.

He had softly hinted to her that there was something more and bade her to follow him into the temple. He must have planned ahead on this surprise, since he did not have to search for illumination inside of the temple that was bathed in an uncommon darkness and hollow silence. He hushed her and swiftly lit the oil lamp almost produced from nowhere until suddenly the chamber danced with life. The warm glow of the lamp shed a comfortable amber glow that paraded upon the walls in its brilliance.

In the center of the chamber stood a statue that was three times the height of my mother. The figure of the Goddess enchanted them with her presence and had a demeanor of pride that almost seemed to throw itself into the eyes and souls of those who glimpsed upon her form. Slowly the eyes of my mother adjusted to the illumination's birth and threw the haze from her mind, until she realized that she shared an uncanny resemblance with the Goddess as depicted. The idea would not leave her mind that they were one and the same. She felt a little bit uncomfortable at the thoughts that raced through her inquisitive mind while Caesar just stood there studying her reaction. He often did that, when presenting a gift to someone. He would study the person in silence uncannily deciphering any emotion of the claimant upon the receipt of his gift. He must have chuckled at the expressions of wonder and confusion that she had tried to conceal in the softness of the lamps luminescence.

However, the warmth of the illumination and the smallness of it in the grand chamber, must have exaggerated any sliver that escaped her attempts to quash. For she knew him enough to know that he was appraising her every emotion and could not stand this game that he always played. He suddenly jumped up from his concentration and proceeded to her side to wrap her in his encompassing embrace and chuckled. He told her that she gave the reaction that he craved from her. It was difficult for anyone to put something past his scrutiny of everything, he had wanted to amaze and confuse her—but most of all he wanted to show her how much she meant to him, that she was his Venus, his own Goddess of love.

My mother's other thoughts rang true with the passing of time after the eventual unveiling of the temple to the city. With this sculpture, he had made a public announcement of their love in having it fashioned in her likeness and in the form that it represented.

When their embrace of the moment, and the glow of the lamp was extinguished, and their footsteps faded away and separated to their own separate abodes…her thoughts must have ran rampant. She must have turned about in sleepless slumber, haunted with her summations of the event. Her mind was much more the acute when away from his presence, which seemed to dull her otherwise normally acute perceptions on matters.

"When initially told of his reasoning of the statue, she was in ecstatic joy and easily melted into his arms to his welcoming and accepting embrace. Though as his footsteps faded away from hers, she realized the fate of the sculpture and of how it marbleized her reality. This certainty of the statue must have struck her with a vicious force when she had finally reached her lonely reality. The thoughts on this matter must have struck her equally so by the time that she reached the cold comforts of her sleeping chamber and empty bed. Did she hear the sleeping gurgles of her son in the next chamber, that only sealed her growing apprehension? Her son, who was not recognized as the legal hear of Gaius Julius Caesar—his own father.

She told me later of her appraisals of the situation from her own confines of that luxurious sleeping chamber. She felt at that moment as if she were the statue itself. Forever doomed to represent a love that would never receive the warmth of the real thing. She believed that he did love her in his own way, which was not her way. He loved her as one would a mistress, a conquest, to escape the dullness of the political marriage that he was forced into for state. He showered her with gifts and poems and praises of her glory and intelligence. Though she realized dismally, he would never give to her what he valued most of all—his name. His august name and lineage. Sure, he married her in her own tradition, though first and foremost—he was Roman. He often told her of how Rome would not accept a marriage to any woman of foreign birth. He gave her his kisses and caresses and the most tender passion she could ever dream of. For she had known no one else in that intimate way prior to their meeting, and swore that she would know no other. Yet, she read and daydreamed on the words and sonnets of the poets. She knew that hers was a love so rare, yet destined for disaster.

She gave her heart and soul to him and yet cared naught for mercy. When absent from her side, she prayed to all of the Gods she could, for his presence to light up her solitude. She had an innocent love for him and did not realize the complete depth of her emotions. She languored in a school girl passion, kindled mostly by her flame alone. For she knew from the first time that evening, that he would give himself to no one person in full. He would only give himself to Roma Dea and all that it entailed.

That cold statue of marble in the magnificent chamber reminded her of herself and her reality. Both were surrounded in opulence and luxury and both received the devotions of the multitudes. Yet, both were utterly and completely alone in the evening hours, lingering in the cherished yearnings for an embrace from their creator. For both were created by Caesar. One of marble to serve as a Goddess in the temple for the people, the other as a woman, to serve as a vessel for the Goddess for her people. Both stood tall and proud and both felt the chill of the echoing chambers around them.

She knew that Rome would be the only true and real love for Caesar, for everything that he did was for the betterment of Rome. At their first meeting that fateful evening long before that moment that wound their lives together; he must have looked upon her as another conquest for the glory of Rome. He must have played with her innocence in the beginning, as she in her naiveté basked in his charisma and warmth. Yet she knew that he did fall in love with her, as she had of him. For they had spent countless evenings together in the beginning taking on every matter of importance in the birth of their relationship together. Though she fruitlessly realized that she would never enter the center of his soul that was saved for the dirt of Rome. She pondered as to why he would value dirt over her warm embrace.

She did not know it then, but with all of those realities stark before her, she had grown from a child to a woman. She began to make mortal a man whom in her innocence she held as a God, prior to this. She had learned to accept him for his weakness and appreciated any love that he had to offer to her. Either that, or to do something about it. She chose to accept, due to the son that they shared. Mayhap, she would work on easing his thoughts towards the legitimacy of their son, sound asleep in the next chamber. She would devote her time to sway his rock solid stance on the matter. For she knew that he would not release his bond to his marriage with Calpurnia. He felt that it would not fare well in the eyes of Rome. She must have laughed at this, since she knew that all of Rome knew of their dalliance and had even heard whispers directed towards their son. The son that Calpurnia could not even give to him and yet she, Cleopatra VII the Pharaoh of Egypt—did, and of their own love!"

XX

"Days melted into months before them, and still no change in his thoughts on the matter. Calpurnia walked before all of Rome as his faithful and devoted wife, while he secretly stole into Queen Cleopatra's chambers in the dead of nights to share her embrace.

All of Rome was giddily recounting lurid tales of her seducing their devoted ruler with her charms and wiles. They talked of her as if she were a whore, using him for her own gain and power forgetting that she was young and that he had a vast history and reputation before he even met the Queen. No one defended her in her misery. For, to Rome he appeared in public as a faithful and devoted husband, while in her bed, he whispered to her of his dreams and his love for her. She must have quaked with the irony of the situation, though was held weak in his spell and enchantment. For it was truly she, who was bewitched. She had almost forgotten her own country, and left it to the hands of others to rule in her absence. She was in the heart of Roma Dea to chase her love and her hopes of having the man totally and completely.

She would visit the statue, in her image, the one the city called Venus Genetrix, and pray to the Goddess to shine the light for her to see through the blindness of her love.

"Cicero, an eminent ally and friend of her Gaius, detested the glorious Cleopatra! He set out more slander against her image to the Romans' all to eager ears. He placed in their minds, that she was enchanting their august countryman with mad ideas. Even Caesar's friend Brutus, scowled as she passed him on the street, or when they chanced to meet at some occasion or another. Even his nephew Octavian had almost growled at her on occasion! Yet, she bravely wove a dazzling facade of charm and grace, which led to the heightened fuel of her adversaries. While Cicero and his cronies lamented in public of they could not stand a woman in any charge, other than in their beds. The very thought of an ambitious woman, probably made their skin crawl! Their carefully draped togas had stifled their thoughts with ice and bitter venom.

It was common knowledge of what a bore that Octavian really was, and of the snores that escaped the rooms during one of his speeches. Yet, the people endured him, due to his great lineage. Caesar, even took a great liking to his nephew, and was followed everywhere by the boy, who was awed in the admiration of his esteemed uncle. Caesar displayed his nephew like a show horse and jabbered on and on of his achievements to all who would listen.

Sure the boy was handsome, he had the Caesar pedigree in his blood, as was obvious. It was if the Gods had carved this family out of gold, so bright were their curly locks and lashes. Their eyes were as blue as the Mediterranean on a sunny day. Octavian might have been boring, though the charisma of his family had wrapped the rays of illusion around him on several occasions.

She had observed the times when his soft and soothing voice would numb his listeners and seduce them to his opinion. She saw through this cunning and soft-spoken exterior, his joy in exhibiting to the populace at large. She truly believed that deep inside, he had the core of selfishness that was his true motive. He had no true love of country like his uncle, he had the most amazing love for his self that he appeared the perfect Roman. Though he was cunning enough to hide this from his unwary companions and those who were easily swayed in his soft charisma. She had noted this in his careful attention to his apparel and detail orientation with his surroundings. Not a fold was out of place in his garment, and not a hair out of place on his head. He cared too much of what the people had thought of him, and paid every attention in the illusion he allowed them.

He would eye her in scrutiny behind his uncle's back, and made sure that she was aware of this. He abhorred the very idea of her. He did not have a strong liking for a woman in any other role other than bed-companion and breeder, and despised her position and rule. For his amorous liaisons were numerous, for he was known to sleep anywhere else besides his own marital bed with Scribonia.

Octavian abhorred the thought that his uncle told Cleopatra his dreams as he told no one else, not even his own nephew. She had breached the circle that no one else had in the past.

She pretty much ignored the empty threats of Octavian, though she had respected his love and deep admiration for his uncle. She did not appreciate his selfishness of it, for she truly did not realize her true position to Caesar. For he was a man who never had let anyone into his world besides her. She did not gain that knowledge until after his death.

XXI

"Yet, she was the master of waiting for the opportune moment. For that she had relayed to me, was the key to any plan. Unfortunately for her dreams, that day that she had long waited for had never arrived. She had waited too long to approach him with her feelings in his marriage and of their son. For on the Ides of March, that doomed and ominous day, had dawned with the vilest of omens. She claimed that she felt uneasy at her awakening that morning. She knew that there was something about to occur, though she could not place her finger on it. The thought faded and she reluctantly went about her day, with the thoughts of her plans on her mind, and wondering when she would have the opportunity to give voice to her emotions and ideas. She had the fervent prayer of her son inheriting both Egypt and the life dictatorship after Caesar on her lips, ready for the chance to depart to his ears.

That thought never reached his hearing, though I am sure that he was waiting for it. I often wonder if that thought even crossed his mind on that eventful day. For he went about his business in the usual way and had approached the steps of the council house eager to attend a meeting with the senate.

Recently, he had disbanded the forever-present guards of the Roman lictors who would follow him wherever he went. He despised the idea of being protected by so loud a presence, and felt that it made him appear weak. Despite warnings from my father, Marcus Antonii and others who correctly feared for his safety while in Rome. Julius Caesar had ignored the many threats that had circulated throughout Rome and of the genuine threat of a covert rebel group called the "Liberators". This group felt that Julius Caesar was to closely assuming the power of a King and had voraciously hated the idea of Rome returning to the ancient monarchy that had been abolished hundreds of years prior. This group and preached throughout the populace that it wanted a return to the Republic, which they felt that Julius Caesar was taking away from them.

"My mother had told me that on the evening prior, he had relayed to her of what he had hopes of announcing to the senate that very next day. He told her that they wanted to grant him with the laurel of supreme leadership to place upon his head. He was secretly hesitant to tell them that he could not accept it. She told me that he had even worked out a plan with her on how he would not accept it without offending them. For this honor had not been bestowed on anyone in their republican history of hundreds of years. It would set them back to an old an vanquished millennia of the dreaded monarchy.

He passionately delved into all of his thoughts of the republic and dreams for time to return the grandeur of it's origin. He had sadly watched his land crawl back to it's barbarous past of monarchy. My mother must have squirmed at his summation of her position in life, though must have quieted to realize he was rendering to her his fear.

She was a different sort of ruler when compared with what Rome had in the past. And he had assuaged her of this. He was just afraid of the ability of the Romans to twist an idea such as monarchy into corruption. He felt threatened. Though, that evening my mother had eventually resolved on the idea to delay the inevitable; which is why there was more purpose in his stride as he approached the steps of his doom unknown to him then.

"When she received word of his fate, she screamed to her Goddess for this to only be a nightmare, which she prayed that she would awaken soon from. She crumpled on the cold mosaic marble floor in abandon. Frantically, she tried to gather all of the slivers of her reality, which was shattered all too cruelly before her. She did not feel the soft touch of my half-brother in her loss, until his tears had joined hers on the cold and polished floors of the domus. The Domus that was Caesar's guest house. Guest house. Upon the sudden realization of this, she ran to her room scooping Caesarion in her arms as she ran. She told me that as she lay on her empty bed, still ruffled from his presence the eve before, had made his absence all the more blatant and powerful. She told me of what felt to her in that moment that was his way of letting her know his true feelings for her, that he never had shown to her in life. She mentioned that this feeling, this presence surrounded first she and then their son, and almost appeared as if were to enter him and then faded therein. Mayhap, this was her message that he felt love for her and their son.

The tale had also reached her ears of the supposed prediction of the event by his Roman wife Calpurnia. She had allegedly dreamed the evening prior of some dire event that was to occur, if he went to the senate house the next day. It was mentioned that she brutally begged her husband not to go to the senate house that morning. This seemed all too wonderfully convenient for the famed matron of Rome!

"For she had also gained that knowledge of the reality of his death. He was brutally murdered by the hands of men with whom he gave his trust.

The very men in the group called throughout Rome as the Liberators, whom he a silently mocked. The final death blow of the dagger that had pierced his heart, was wielded by his closest friend and companion Brutus! Who knew what his thoughts were when he saw the face of his murderer and bent down to watch his dreams and visions pour out of him, as his blood poured from the numerous dagger wounds inflicted upon his body. There were twenty-three wounds counted upon his corpse, though legend had added more over the years! His plans died with him that day, and of any hopes that he had of restoring the grandeur of the republic… on the steps of the senate. My mother truly believed that had that event never occurred, he had the power to set his dreams into motion. Yet, the event had set into reality the true path of Rome, that was to be the first step in the destruction of the republic. With the death of Gaius Julius Caesar, the death of the Republic was initially and irreparably set into the motion.

"Thus, the way was paved for the entrance of my father into my mother's loving arms and of a real love, immortal.

"In the meantime, she had received word of the reading of the will of Caesar. Her heart was broken in the wake of his death. As she watched the city gather at the pyre of the most powerful man they had ever known, her former dreams she had with him, drifted as the smoke spiraled to the sky. Dissolved in the fire of the passion of the people. For she had recently learned that Caesar had left in his will, everything to his Roman wife. There was not even one mention of her nor Caesarion! He had formally adopted his nephew as his son, and bade him to use the name of Julius Caesar in public. He acknowledged and accepted this soft-spoken relative as his one and only son! In the flames of the lost passion of her soul, she silently screamed to the Goddess of her own people. She felt as cold as the statue in the temple deep inside her heart.

XXII

“Alas, my mother placed her foot on the path to her destiny together with Marcus Antonius of the family Antonii. She had met him during her stay in Rome as well as his wife Drusilla. She had grown to admire him in her stay and had often sought out his company in friendship, for she valued his honest counsel. She had observed his devotion and admiration for his distant relative, Caesar. He had recognized the true paternity of her son, one of which Rome denied. She knew that he was not swayed by the twisted tales told about her, and judged her from his own experience. She welcomed his compassion at the death of Caesar. For he knew that she mourned his loss and comforted her, as no one else did.

In the days after his death, she silently slipped into the background, hiding from the wake of his passing. She had decided then that it was time for her to return to her home and to be a queen to her people once again. She knew that she was not wanted here, and was afraid that the people would rise up against her. For the people of Rome had looked upon her with hatred scorn. They immortalized their Caesar into a God, and comforted the laments of his devoted wife Calpurnia. The woman was made a martyr by the people and looked at Cleopatra as the seductress and marriage destroyer.

XXIII

“So, she stood up strait and packed her things as well as her memories of her life and loaded them on the barge. Marcus Antonii assisted her in her return. He was the only light in her darkness at that time; besides the dimming light of her son by Julius Caesar, which had faded at the realization of his father’s death. He found it very difficult to believe that that wonderful man would never bring him sweets nor toss him about in the air. He had on his father’s helmet, too large for his tiny golden ringleted head, and carried his father’s sword which was wrapped up in a bundle that was almost as large as he was. His mother took the bundle from her son and added it to the luggage gathered on the deck of their ship. His tears followed the bundle as it was loaded on the deck.

XXIV

"Marcus Antonius of the Antonii, had large shoes to fill when compared with Gaius. For prior to his death, he had established more than twenty colonies throughout the Mediterranean, and most of them were located in the barbarous lands of Gaul. The colonies were important in establishing the power and influence of Roman and the Hellenistic civilization. The assignation set off a civil war among the citizens of Rome. His once so noble and proud stature, was burned in the forum, as the tears of thousands joined the clouds that evening. The Gods took their brilliant son into their midst.

His rise to fame and immortality was dizzying to those who stood witness to his accomplishments. He became Quaestor when he was fifty one, and then served in Hispanoli as an Assizer for the next eight years. He then was granted the title of Aedile, when he incurred large sums on the games he held in the circus. He then became the Pontifex Maximus a year later, and then went on to his numerous military exploits in Hispanoli, which paved the way to even further august titles. His title of triumvirate was one of his crowning achievements that soon followed, to only be topped when he became the Supreme Dictator of Rome and it's people. In the years before that last title, he spent nine years in Gaul for the famed Gallic Wars, which led to the defeat of Vercingetorix. Also, near the end of his life, he led two campaigns to Britannia, after he reinstituted his authority with his fellow triumvir, Pompey. He waved his hands at the threats of his being replaced as uttered in open threats by his ally, Lucius Domitius Ahenobarbus.

Success in his military ventures paved his way to the top. It also made imminent that he had such illustrious and august blood in his veins. He was born of one of the most noble families in Rome, and had a history that went as far back as the beginning of the republic.

He held his triumphs in Rome to show his military genius over Africa and Egypt, with how he successfully routed out Ptolemy XIII to stop the civil wars. In this march, his chariot was followed by his half-sister Arsinoe among the captors. I wonder to this day, how she explained such to her weak brother and her son, as to why Arsinoe was led in chains before them!

Why, just before his death, he was revered by his people as semi-divine! And of course, completely divine upon his death.

For the people truly loved him for the many things that he gave. For instance, when he returned from the civil wars, he gave the people ten processions of grandeur and feasts for all those who greeted him. Not only that, but he gave the people a year's rent for the tenants who paid 2,000 sesterces or less a year. He gave his legions 24,000 sesterces! Such generosity was received lovingly by the populace. This sum was enough to outright rent a cheap apartment house in an insula, or to purchase a smaller domus outside of Rome.

This astounding man also renovated the roman calendar, which was off by a month in the usual reckoning of the calendar. He created a year of 12 months to commence on January the 1st. It became known as the Julian calendar.

To further his generosity during his reign, he gave all of the practicing doctors in Rome full citizenship. This was a good idea from the sound of it, however, it paved the way for any charlatan with charismatic notions to enter the scene of the much desired rite of citizenship. Large fortunes were gained in this venture, I could not even imagine it, though I constantly see the results thereof.

So much has reached my ears on this illustrious predecessor of my father. I had even heard that during his election to the counsel, his supporter by the name of Clodius had promoted a law to the people in Caesar's name to give wheat to the people for free! Can one even imagine the commotion that must have caused? And all to gain the electoral support for the young Julius Caesar!

He even provided entertainment for free for the people at the circus! This probably was meant for a short time to appease the people until he thought out a more feasible plan.

With the free rations of grain, it unfortunately brought out in hordes the poor farmers from outside of Rome who gave up their futile struggles and fled to the gates of Rome for their rations! A large amount of people freed their slaves so that they no longer would have to feed them. For the grain rations were only for the freed peoples and citizens of Rome. What a ruckus that must have caused. I suppose that he must have meant well, though the population must have sat around on their lazy arses in eager anticipation.

After his campaign with the Civil War, he had to cope with the disaster that awaited his return. The people of Rome were receiving wheat for free for the whole time of his leave. He eventually reduced the list to a hundred and fifty thousand. Since he was the supreme dictator at the time for the people, he was able to do this act without starting a revolt of the people. He had the manpower to prevent the possibility of this unfortunate occurrence. A name could only added to the list, upon the death of a past recipient. His predecessor in Rome, Octavian/ Augustus, not only kept up the dole, he increased it as well, by the old amount prior to the list that he created.

There was even a story about him at the time that he was captured by pirates on his way to study under Apollonius Molo for his oratorical skills in Rhodes. This has been briefly mentioned early on in this history of true events. He was kidnapped and held for ransom for the sum of 12,000 gold pieces. He made a sacred vow to seek vengeance on them all, during his captivity. He eventually lived out those fateful words, to each and every one of them! He sought them out and crucified all of them, which he showed no mercy.

“It was found out later, that Cassius and Brutus had been the foremost conspirators in the party formed in opposition to his rule. They had named the faction the Liberators, in which they reiterated the ancient sources that proclaimed the evil omens that would precede his passing. He ignored their empty threats and fell to the daggers of his enemies.

I suppose of one of his worst traits was one that was admired among everyone else; he forgave his enemies too easily and openly. This was probably the reason why he walked so easily into the path of his enemies and met his death!

My mother must have seethed when she gained wind of his second marriage to a woman named Pompea, whom he divorced due to her alleged affair with Clodius. She was the granddaughter of the infamous Sulla. What an alliance. She never even knew of her existence. Only of his first wife by the name of Cornelia, who bore their daughter Julia, and of his wife at the time of his death, Calpurnia. She honestly held the notion that he was utterly against divorce! She probably misinterpreted him when he told her that he hated divorce, meaning the process and heartache he underwent. Which she mistook in her youthful ignorance as he did not believe in divorce at all!

Thus, a small list of the many accomplishments of such a great name. This man did indeed hold the key to the world in those days, and would have probably had so much more, were his life not cut so short. He served the people with a greater devotion than my father or my grandfather, and by the side of my mother he must have been magnificent indeed!

XXV

"Caesar's eighteen year old nephew was named as his heir, not my brother. No doubt Calpurnia had the winning hand in this deal.

Octavian had then joined forces with two of Caesar's lieutenants by the names of Marcus Antonius (Antonii) and Lepidus. They became known as the second triumvirate of Rome and it's dominions. Together, they banded, and tracked down those responsible for the death of their supreme dictator.

Octavian's worst adversary proved to be, no other than my father, in the eyes of Rome. He was soon branded a traitor to Rome and it's peoples. My mother had chosen wrong this time in whom to lend her support. But, alas, love had no reason in some matters. And this was one time that it was definitely not the right choice. Though, to those who loved him, and received his love in return, this was the wisest of choices.

XXVI

"My mother probably walked into this one unawares initially. For in the beginning they were the closest of friends. He assisted her with her final affairs in Rome, and she gave him wise counsel on matters of state, which had to be clarified in the absence of their supreme dictator. They formed a bond in their innocent confidences, which was soon to lay the foundation of their fate together in a love immortal.

XXVII

"My father, Marcus Antonius was over twenty years my mother's senior. He was a notable character as well. Though he tended to walk on the clouds and to even charm the birds out of their nests, than to walk on the stable ground as did Gaius Julius Caesar! That could have been his fortune as well as his folly.

His father was an unsuccessful admiral by the name of Antonius Creticus. While his mother was the much admired Julia of the Julian clan, thus, his relationship to Caesar in a distant way as his cousin. His father died when he was very young, and soon after his mother married Cornelius Lentulus. Before he began the romantic affair with my mother, his adoptive father was strangled on the orders of Cicero. Cicero raped Cornelius Lentulus of any dignity when he rallied the people against him, uttering slanderous words on his involvement in the famed Cataline Affair. This act was never forgotten by my father, who would spit venom at the mere utterance of the name Cicero. He adored his adoptive father who had lovingly taught him everything that he knew.

When he was in his thirties, he traveled to Syria and joined the army of Gabinius, where he served as a cavalry commander in Egypt. He even told me that he was in Gaul and had served as a staff member for Caesar for a year! This connection with Caesar, assisted him to further distinction when he became a quaestor and was noted as one of Julius Caesar's most dedicated and charismatic of his followers.

He supported Caesarion's father with loyalty and vetoed the Senate's decree to order Caesar stripped of his command. He stated that he was serving Caesar, at the time, as his tribune in Rome. He then joined his friend and cousin in Gaul to assist him in the stanching of the civil outbreaks there. He proved his devotion when he served over the interest of Caesar, while he was in Hispanoli. While there, my father had even commanded Caesar's left wing forces at the battle of Pharsulus. At that battle they both watched in horror, as Pompey met his defeat. Caesar recognized this honesty in his admirer and named him his co-counsul soon after.

"Whatever plans Julius Caesar had for my father, came to naught at the hands of the Liberators on the eve of his death. My father was the person who seized the papers of Caesar, and read them to the people, and gave the oration at his funeral. I heard later that there was even a rumor that he had occupied Caesar's land and told the people that he was the true heir, not Octavian.

I assumed that she sailed out the day of Caesar's funeral in silence and obscurity, her state of mourning blocking any such rabble of the people from reaching her ears. For she had too much in mind when it came the eventual return to her own people.

"Eventually my father gained control of the Cisalpine Gaul and faced his adversaries Brutus and Caesar's other assassins. The adversarial forces were soon joined, much to his dismay by the lecherous Cicero and Octavian, huddled at his side. How pathetic they must have looked in their mockery of a joined force. I'll bet that Caesar must have rolled his eyes from the heavens at this turnout. For he had failed or refused to see their true devious nature in his lifetime.

Unfortunately, the battles were not in favor of my father, for he was defeated from setbacks at the Forum Gallorum and Mutina. He had to retreat to join forces with the provincial governors of the west with whom he gained a new alliance. Lepidus was once again by his side.

He then became part of the second Triumvirate in November of that year with Octavian and Lepidus. Together the three of the men and their forces faced the Republicans at Phillipi the very next year. Antony gained control of the east, where the last of the snakes from the Liberators had fallen in battle. He still, at that time, had held the belief that Octavian had no ill will toward him. He must have inherited the same in naiveté in the faces of his foes as had Caesar.

My mother delayed him in Tarsus, while he was on his way to follow the wishes of Octavian in the Parthian expeditions. For Tarsus was a most memorable event to the heart of my mother.

I suppose one of the feasible daggers that edged Octavian, was when my father's Roman wife at the time named Fulvia, had joined forces with his brother Lucius, in opposition to Octavian. Fulvia took hold of the reign without Antony and rode the shining Octavian wave. I suppose my mother, had she not had her heart latched to my father, and met her in a different circumstance, would have actually admired the woman. For she had the strength of heart that was not common in women of their time, especially a Roman woman.

The death of Fulvia had ceased any dispute at the time between Octavian and my father. For a stalemate was reached. By this time the relationship between my parents was at it's zenith.

In the meanwhile, peace was made between Antony and Octavian at Brundisium and to seal the bargain, gave his sister Octavia in marriage to my father. My mother had found out one evening while presiding over the common pittances of her peoples. I had heard some rather interesting portrayals on her demeanor at the hearing of those fateful words. For she had been setting the notion in his head on how it would be a good idea for them to marry.

My father would later console her and tell her that he could not attain a divorce from his wife Fulvia, since it just would not be proper and at that time he needed the political alliance that it brought along with his stability in Rome. She must have truly come apart when she gained the news of the death of Fulvia and of his instant marriage to the sister of Octavian! For he had assailed her with the hopes that he would take care of the matter on his way to Brundisium, and that he did—though obviously not to her liking at all!

XXVIII

"Eventually, he soon realized the direness of his situation and the lies of Octavian. He admitted to my mother his brutal mistake in taking Octavia as his wife in return for Octavian taking his rule over the Cisalpine Gaul region. He truly believed that the deal was made in friendship.

XXIX

"Soon after, my parents sat side by side in rule over the land of Kemet, the dominion city of Rome. My mother regulated most of the rule over her land, while my father sat complacently and in respect for his patron God Bacchus. I suppose that was one of the things that attracted her to him, that he paid homage to a God the same as that of her father. The two Gods presided over the merry and the drunk. Most revered at banquets and festivals. However, not much of a God for the governing of a land and it's peoples.

XXX

"My father was at the peak of his power when Lepidus fell from the triumvirate at my father's victory at Armenia. This left the power of Rome to the rule of both Octavian and Antony. Both had blood that contained the genius of Caesar, and one carried his name, while the other dared to repeat history in the planning of his strategies. Both, just did not have that genius contained and laid out with a rare execution that was upheld immortal in a man that the word would probably never see the likes of again.

They probably both realized this, though they both laid an attempt to repeat and further the history laid clean before them. They had both worked under his command and learned from his talent that made Rome what it was. They each held the word in the palms of their hands, a gift from a god who was once a man as mortal as they. Those of the blood that were left behind had enormous shoes to fill to be even half of what he was.

I realized in my life at the side of my father, that he was only too mortal. He lacked the incredible discipline of emotion so characteristic of Julius Caesar. He trembled in the face of danger and mocked the Gods in his moments of glory. I suppose that that was what I loved most about him. That he was real. I do not know how I would have taken the hardness the impeccable accurateness of Caesarion's father.

For my father knew all too well that he was human and found it difficult to hide such from those that he loved. He made mistakes and laughed about the frailties of his humanity. My mother told me that Caesar made few mistakes, if anything his rock solid continence in the face of adversity—made whims appear to all others as divine and untouched by the marred blemishes of humanity as emanated by my father. Caesar held no such lofty opinions of himself as those around him did, nor did he tremble in fear, nor laugh at his mistakes. He voiced in the confidence of only my mother of his mistakes. To the world, he was solid as the pillars of Hercules. He was the voice of reason, judgment unhampered by any emotion.

With my ability to look back in retrospect, I have observed that he had let some of his decisions grow tainted by his fierce and dominant emotions. This was probably what led him to a defeat that was inevitable. How he let his emotions pave the road of his decisions. As a leader, one must be prepared for any sacrifice for the benefit of the land that one ruled over. My mother was Antony's match in this, for she let her love for two men get in the way of the greater good of Egypt.

Granted, she was an excellent ruler in keeping her land bountiful and the people's bellies full and satiated. Yet, she left her country to seek out Caesar with my brother. Had she been in her land and abandoned this quest, she would have led her country to it's climax with her incredible powers of ruler-ship when she applied herself. My parents, in their love for each other, had been blind to the objective side in some issues that led to their downfall.

"As a daughter, I greatly appreciated their love for each other, for they provided a most stable and comfortable home life. Our palace was made into a warm cocoon of love, to protect us from the harsh world outside. As a product of their love, I was shown what love should truly be. I grew up with the most unique of parents who actually loved each other and were the best of friends.

In this age, political marriages are the norm and the expected. My eyes were opened to what was impossible for a daughter born of my lineage. I was led to believe that all such people when they were married, had married for the love of one another. In my position, that should never have reached my eyes. For it taught me to dream and believe that I would as well find a love similar to that of my parents. It had seemed all too normal to me in the innocence of my youth.

"Of course, in that innocence I had failed to see the obvious, that my mother was queen, a queen who stood alone. It was miraculous how she actually reached that height and status, since she was the third born in succession to the line. It was something that should not have happened. In a time when the throne was passed down to the first male of each generation, it was a rarity indeed for one to attain the throne who was truly capable to carry the crook and the flail, especially from her family. So many destined to sit in the throne before her, had failed to hold the weight of their power adequately. Though my mother attained rule by a freak of nature, when she ruled, she ruled well.

My parents shared their dreams and their love for their countries. My father had a passion, equal to that of Caesar before him, for the domains of Rome. My mother had such a love for her land, that she willfully took on the culture of it's past rulers. This culture had been abandoned by the royalty of Kemet for three hundred years. Yet my mother had the patience and perseverance to learn the glyphs of the ancients and to understand the words faded in the temples and monuments of her own homeland. She had such a love for the past of her country, that she strove to preserve it's past and let it shine once again.

XXXI

"In the East, my father who was enamored with the fruit of power, fought to attain it's juices. For he had dreams of expanding the territories of Rome and of Egypt. He gathered his forces and sought out the power for his own and to pass down to those that he loved.

XXXII

"My mother, was constantly at his side about his divorcing his Roman wife. She did not make the fatal mistake in this one issue, as she had with Caesar. She did not wait until it was too late. Eventually he succumbed to the persuasion and ultimatum made all to strong by the will of my mother. He relented and eventually released his legal bounds to Octavian. At this time, my twin brother and I were already old enough to talk and run in play. She told him that he must relinquish Octavia as wife, and that he did, despite her having two daughters born from him. His two daughters born of he and Octavia were known as Antonia Major and Antonia Minor . For he had abandoned them as well as his Roman wife.

"My father had learned of our birth, only after that fact. My mother had too much pride to tell him when he was preparing for battle and on his way to Brundisium. She was led to believe that if he truly loved her, he would return to her arms on his own. She held her feelings at bay and waited for his return. Instead, she had attained the knowledge of their victory, and of his alliance with Octavian. She had also, in the learning of this, attained the knowledge of the death of Fulvia and of his political marriage with Octavia. And she held close to her the knowledge of her pregnancy, which she would not be able to hide for much longer. She had to live with the stigma of her pregnancy without a husband, for her second brother, who was made her husband at the death of the older Ptolemy in name only, had succumbed to the wasting disease and was embalmed and thus, with his Gods. She ruled alone at that point and had waited for Antony to join her side.

In his absence, we were born and the prophesy was told. My mother told me that she was brought into an early labor, as the destruction of her heart at that news. Our birth had given her a whole new strength. She then made a vow, that everything she would do would be for the benefit of her children for their eventual rule.

Soon after she had learned of the birth of his daughter Antonia Minor, the second of his children from Octavia.

When my father returned to her side he told her that he would not ever abandon her side again and professed his love for her. She told him that in order for him to prove this, he must sever his ties to his wife in Rome.

He was reluctant to do this due to the eventual repercussions that would in definite soon follow. He knew that if he divorced Octavia, he would sever the last precarious tie to Rome that remained. Though, for the love that he had for my mother, he agreed. He had hesitated due to the fruit of that particular union, for Octavia had born him two daughters and had even raised those from Fulvia. She was the doomed and martyred matriarch that Rome grew to love as much as Calpurnia. The Romans had admired her strength and will to raise the children that perhaps never knew the love of their father. She took on this task with a strong chin, and thrived in maintaining his abandoned household in Rome. She fought the demons of despair, that her husband had left her to be at the side of his Egyptian lover. She must have been a strong woman indeed, to face that, and at the same time to raise his children in the absence of his shadow. My mother was blind to the emotions of this other woman in her own pain.

Why must men weave such webs of disappear in those they love, and go forth in such blindness to their burdens that they must bear? Though, I suppose he must have weighted the burdens on each of these women that he had caused unknowing, since he did hesitate to cut the ties of one. He must have felt Octavia's pain, for he did have incredible empathy.

"The Romans had woven delirious tales of my father and my mother. My father was portrayed as a monster to abandon his faithful and devoted wife for the harlot of Egypt, who allegedly was seduced by her alluring magic. Cicero wrote of my father as an idiot and a weakling, powerless in the dominance of my mother. They said that my mother used her power of seduction for her selfish gains only. What an exaggerated and ugly picture they painted of a love so pure. They raised Octavia on a pedestal in her matriarchdom and devotion. My mother was painted as a whore and my father cuckolded in her selfish wrath. How disgusting were they in their blindness. Caricatures were passed out of my mother painted up gaudily as a temple prostitute and my father small and shriveling under her whip. Octavian was so venomous due to Antony's daring divorce of his sister. My parents probably took this as a childish demonstration of his temper. They probably laughed about it!

It was odd how Octavian looked so adversely upon the divorce of his sister, when he had sought divorce himself from such a political marriage. I had even received news that when he married that poor woman, the marriage was not even consummated, she was just tossed aside when he was through with the particular alliance that he needed at that time. How odd he looked upon what my father did, with such hatred. For at least Antony consummated the marriage and took it seriously in the beginning, much to the dismay of my mother. Yet, he treated it seriously, not in jest as what Octavian did in his mockery of a marriage. Even my mother knew the bonds of a marriage made of state, for she had married both of her brothers in the name of Egypt. Like Octavian, both of the marriages were in name only. For both of her brothers she pitied. Ptolemy Achilles, she pitied for his blindness and weakness to poor counsel. The younger Ptolemy, she pitied due to his youth and innocence to the intrigues of the world. He was weak in soul, treating her as the mother he never knew and adored the ground that she walked on. His weakness in body, led to his eventual death at such a tender age. In both of those marriages, she had made the most of it in her treatment of them and treated it as a political marriage. Loving the younger Ptolemy like he so desperately needed. Both, Octavian and my mother were caught in the political necessity of their marriages and had yielded to them each in their different ways. My father, had relented to his marriages and acted out of duty to do what he thought was right.

Three completely different people, bound together by common threads. What a shame that they never shared the similarities and became friends. Ha, the thought of it could rumble ceaseless laughter out of the mighty throats of the Gods above in their counsel.

XXXIII

"When my parents were eventually married, they soon after embarked on a wedding tour of the Nile to greet the people and introduce the land to my father. The people accepted him with wild applause, for he had an eloquence in speech that could have easily led the people of Egypt into believing that Dionysus himself spoke through his mouth. His voice demanded respect, admiration and love. His gaze would enrapture all caught in the midst of it.

"Upon their return to the palace of Bruchion, they eventually settled down into the routine that my mother had set for them. My mother had formulated in the palace, a strict code of regulation and schedule that maintained the immaculate upkeep of the palace.

She had also created a warm and cozy cocoon of shelter from the world outside. She needed that place of comfort as a ruler would and my father accepted it willingly. Easily adjusting to her structured and loving world that she had created for her own sanity and those that she loved.

I suppose she created this world out of need to escape from the daunting reality of the kingdom that she maintained. She felt that no matter what occurred outside of the gates, she would keep the fires burning safely in her domain for our protection. She told me that she wanted us to be strong rulers as was our destiny, though she had wanted to preserve our youth, as hers never was. She sheltered us from the coldness and cruelty of the world that she had to face so young.

XXXIV

"Upon her return to her rule she gloriously upheld the legendary crook and flail of her rule. She regulated the taxes for her subjects. She had also built up the banks of the canal and brought prosperity and produce to the glamorous and mysterious land of Kemet. She granted this to the people, despite the reading of the Nilometer barely reaching above the cubit of death. Her magic powers held sway over all in her wake. Her actions revealed the love that she had for the people of the land that she ruled over.

She gave the native Egyptians (unprecedented in the Ptolemy dynasty) positions of power in her illustrious court. Her family in the past had given those posts to only to those of Greek origin, which in turn were inherited by subsequent generations. This in turn had created a weak governing body that had grown more insipid and jaded with each passing generation. She not only wanted to oust them, but to hire in those positions a more qualified personnel, which consisted mainly of those born on the Egyptian soil as it had turned out.

She beautified her hearth city of Alexandria, the seat of power in the land of Kemet. She had added to the already magnificent library as well as to the Museon. She encouraged the patronage of the poets and philosophers to add to the mysticism of the city's knowledge. She encouraged the works and endeavors of the chemists of her time to find new cures and treatments for ailments. She even expanded the venue for the discovery of new poisons. People flocked to the gates of this cosmopolitan city, with their wisdom in their hands to be given to her and to the world.

XXXV

"My parents shared the grandest of love affairs in known history, their love knew no boundaries. She built for him an obelisk in front of the Grecian style temple that she had built. She had named this temple, the temple of the sun, which was located in Heliopolis. She set this up in honor of the love she had for my father. This was a great shaft of granite for which she had commissioned the finest artists of the time to make immortal her voice raised in love for him. This was originally located at the first cataract of the Nile.

XXXVI

"On the Roman front, my father and Octavian had become rivals in the rule of it's people. Egypt, knowing the whim of my mother, remained neutral in this matter.

XXXVII

"To back up a little bit and to recite a truth to a legend from the words of my mother about an event that occurred in the beginning of the relationship. One day, my father had summoned my mother to Tarsus in Asia Minor for her support in an issue that had arose. She, however, went on with her own terms remaining neutral in her position in matters, though needing to be at his side. She arrived in her usual pomp and splendiferous manner before him. She was hardly twenty-nine at that time and in the very apex of her beauty. I cannot even begin to fathom the reaction of my father at the very sight of her and her entourage. For the very time that she was summoned and his resonance to her presence, was the very beginning of their famous love for her. She sent a counter invitation, requesting his presence before her to dine lavishly on her barge that was docked at the bay. He arrived to the wonder of a fantasy land that she created with her vivid imagination. For on the deck of the barge one had to walk though a carpet of rose petals. Upon each step, from each person on board, the scents were released to the heavens after they would assail the noses of those privileged to be on board. The music was soft and magical, meant to allure and enchant him. He told me that that was the very moment that he had fallen hopelessly under her spell. He felt as if he had walked in the presence of the Goddess herself, so magnificent was her attire which fully emanated the glamour of the Goddess upon all who were in her presence. So ruthlessly had she loved to set forth her power on others, who would always surrender to her will. And since he worshipped a flamboyant God such as Bacchus, he could dine with the best. For lavishly and with much ceremony was the only way that she could dine. He so loved to entertain and to be entertained. The wine and food forever flowed as if by magic in those evenings, as it did always. Only this time their senses had the added stimulation of the rose petals to add to the magic of the evening. For he was not an abstainer like Caesar before him. He willfully embraced the power of the wines set before him. He gave up his future in Rome to be at her side in Kemet.

She had even played a little trick on him, which only wound the net to his soul ever tighter into her grasp. For that very evening, she had wanted to display to him her wealth and power. For that she had ordered a special glass of wine be prepared for her ruse. Into the glass she lavishly tossed in a large pearl that she had taken from one of her earrings. This particular pearl was large and enchanting and very rare and valuable due to it's rather large size. She then drank from that very same glass, appearing to consume the pearl as if she had many others like it and was of no real value to her! She never told me how this was managed in reality, though I know from her that it was somehow slipped into a secret pocket that was sewn into her silken garment! My father was lured in with her lackadaisical manner towards the illusion of her vast wealth. For she had during her reign attained great riches of her own, but not that much. Ah well, such was the humor of my mother.

XXXVIII

"She could never win in the eyes of the stingy Romans. For months subsequent to that union of their souls, my brother and I had entered the picture. From the very beginning, I had only loving memories of my mother.

She was often away working on this matter or that. However, the moments she was here at our side, were generous indeed. Her soft voice echoed through the halls in song to us and to Isis. From the start, we cherished to hear another of her cleverly made up melodies. We would accompany her with tiny cisterns or even a small wooden harp that my father had made for me. We would while away those few stolen moments of her precious time.

I vividly recall the long evenings that would linger at the absence of her whimsical smile. I would often wander into her suite when she was not around and crawl into her silken bed and roll myself in her robes that were smothered in her mysterious scent. For she so loved the scent of Jasmine, that she would pay dearly for it in vast amounts. Whenever I happen to catch the scent in the present, my mind cannot help but to linger on the memories of her love.

XXXIX

"My brother and I resembled each other so much from the early years, that it was difficult to tell us apart! As my mother thought fit, my brother had his head shorn at the appropriate time, with the lock of youth left to the side of his head, as befitting the style of the ancient Egyptians. I would wear my hair down in long curls. It was there that the resemblance fled. For our locks told us apart, or rather, his lack of hair except for the lock of youth.

The two of us were inseparable from conception. We were constantly creating miniature kingdoms over which to rule as our parents did in reality. There were many monsters and evil Gods which were constantly attacking our kingdoms. Then Caesarion would come crashing through the battle lines in full torrential speed, and knock down all of our carefully laid out armies. He would yell and roar like the mightiest and most powerful of the evil Gods and wreak havoc on our meticulously planned out sand cities, and crush the whole thing. Oh, it was countless how many times he had done that to us. However, we gathered our scattered forces and rebuilt every time.

Oh, Caesarion! He so resembled a cherub on the exterior, though on the inside—he contained the very steam that would rock the pillars of

Hercules from their foundations! He must have glorified in our screams of terror whenever he destroyed each and everything that we had worked so hard to create! Though I look back now and think, how like a typical older brother he was, and nothing more…However, one could easily see the solid and beautiful form of his father and know his emotions were that of my mother with her mischievousness and fiery resolve. This would only reveal itself when least expected from him, it would exhibit itself to ones bafflement at the calm posterior that he maintained so like his father.

XL

"My father on the other hand, was not like the teetotaler that Caesar was, oh how he loved the sweet liquid ambrosia, that seemed to flow from the very walls of the palace! Always a goblet materialized in his hand, and at the tilt of his head another would appear. The amphorae were especially imported from far away regions of the world for the consumption of my father and his vast entourage! My mother never denied him his wine. My mother had even told me of a gathering of people he had founded that would disguise themselves and wander the taverns of the city. She related that they favored to call themselves "the Incomparables"! I would definitely say that in the very least, for I was told that the group was always on one adventure or another under their guise of illusion to the general populace. How they would shudder at the thought of who was really under the robes!

I suppose that he meant well, he probably missed his homeland of Rome and all that it might have held for him had he stayed behind. I doubt that he missed his ex-wife Octavia though. Unfortunately she was the sister of Octavian himself! That probably had a lot to do with his unpleasant standing in the union. For the mighty Octavian so loved to besmear his once mighty name as well as that of my mother.

After my parents were married in the fashion of Kemet, my mother had built him a temple in his honor. She did not spare one expense in the creation of this temple to comfort the banks of the mighty Nile. Though my mother never did do anything without grandeur.

XLI

"Marcus Antonius, he so loved to spark one hubris after another, just to see the reaction of the populace. For he broke the unwritten rule of holding a triumph outside of the gates of Rome. For it was written somewhere, that a triumph could only be held in Rome. He held his in Alexandria. In celebration of his victory for Rome on his Asian campaigns, he marched through the gates of Rome on a golden chariot, pulled by six rare milk white horses! As was natural, the captives were to follow this grand entrance in chains behind their valiant and so noble conqueror. All of the vanquished kings were in chains with the rest of the captured, which must have been quite a site, had I only remembered this. Alas, This I was told on a very rare rainy evening to us all as we cuddled beside the skirts of my mother by the light of the oil lamp's glow. The shadows cast only manipulated our pliable minds to see the picture in greater definition. The voice of my father bellowing the speeches to our amazed ears. Oh, how they loved to tell us tales of the olden days!

XLII

"Rome could not tolerate the crass behavior of my father, nor could Octavian. Then again he did not tolerate much of what my parents did then. He had always found a way of tarnishing any of the good that my parents tried to do. Octavian did not like the fact that Alexandria had become the capitol of the Eastern empire, especially since it had everything to do with my parents. It almost seemed as if he was obsessed with the two of them and their eminent destruction. Was it really about what my father had done to his sister, or was it really about his pride. Then again all that I knew about that man was from the mouths of my parents, and their voices were a bit biased.

This man I would love to meet. For I had only seen him on the morbid occasion of my capture. That I will delve into another time. For I have heard so much about this man and the many different sides that he displayed for all to see.

XLIII

"Despite Octavian's lack of affection towards the two people who gave me life, they still managed to lead a normal semblance of a life. My father was always more than generous in the bestowing gifts to my mother. For after his campaign in Asia Minor, he gave my mother the lands he conquered as a wedding gift. Octavian and the senate felt that it should have gone to the Roman empire instead!

However, she was the type who always hungered for more than what she had. She was constantly coercing him that he give her Judea as well. This she assured him would return Egypt in domain to the land it once was under the rule of Alexander the great. Yet, my father was in alliance with King Herod of Judea and considered him a friend. She even mustered the audacity and took it upon herself to meet with King Herod herself to request that he lease the land to her. On the land that she desired, were produced her adored balsam trees, for this was the only place in which they were grown. She desired them so completely she sought out Herod to negotiate. She offered a request for her to rent the land at two hundred tablets of gold a year. Good thing that she made her departure when she did, since Herod was furious with her, and even went so far as attempting to have her killed. Lucky for her that the shadow of Rome fell heavily upon his gaunt shoulder. For he had to call off the attempt on her life made in haste at the expense of is anger. He then reluctantly agreed to her demand.

He soon had his revenge on behalf of her reputation, when even more slander on her had poured forth from his city gates to the ears of the military elsewhere. She, on the other hand, was not content with the proceeds from the rental of the gardens of her precious balsam trees, for she had some roots cut to be planted in Maurenia near Heliopolis, as well as some seeds for her gardens, under her direct supervision. She must have reveled in the fact that the gardens were no longer unique to Herod's land, that she had them at her fingertips as well, for her very own pleasure. Alas, one of the many eccentricities lashed forth from my mother.

XLIV

"At this point she added the name of King of Kings, to the name of her son Caesarion. For she was one to hold delusions of grandeur close to her breast. She had such great ambitions for her son. She never stopped her dreams with him, they went to herself and to her other children as well. For myself, she wanted the position of queen as well as High Priestess of Isis after a marriage with Caesarion. For my own twin brother Alexander Helios, she wanted to head the priesthood of the order of Isis as well as vizier to my brother Caesarion. She had trained us for these rolls from our cradles.

"Meanwhile, many battles were fought between my father and Octavian, and the ever encroaching control of the dominion of Rome. Cleopatra made it her life long struggle to attain her land from the grasp of the Romans. She made it her personal quest. My father, in turn, made it more personal between he and Octavian. Octavian was constantly smearing the good names of my parents, that he had almost made it an obsession to ply for their eventual destruction and demise.

The two pieces of the opposing armies met on the game board of Actium. Octavian had made his move and laid in wait for the fleet of my father in order to trap him. Marcus Antonius' forces were defeated, since my mother had mistakenly misinterpreted his instructions. For the man of the deck of the fleet belonging to her, had misread the flag, and had left with the reinforcements. My father's forces were defeated at this insipid turn of events. My father was rather perturbed by this and had refused to talk to my mother and to listen to her reason. He followed her off the battleground, and refused to converse with her in the process. This, I could imagine, must have brought her to her boiling point. As a result of this, for months they were estranged from each other.

XLV

"Gradually their love bounced back and re-strengthened it's immortal continuum. They had forged the way to an even deeper love after their difference's were resolved. Never would her armies confuse the signs in future battles, for they had worked together for weeks to devise a new system with colors and flags.

My mother had muttered one evening after music and revelry, for I was there at that time, "We will build our fleet to fight Octavian another day." For her voicing out thoughts on the matter, seemed to alleviate her fears for the time being. For at that time, never did he have the slightest comprehension on just how deadly the fields of Actium would prove to be for him at a later date.

XLVI

"In the months that followed that brief disaster, my father eventually recouped in strength, especially with the wine and spirits that went along with it. The parties increased in number and became so elaborate that an extra wing was added to the palace. The room was inlaid with exquisite carvings in ivory from Numidia. The deepest of Persian rugs had covered the expansive tiling, to create a warm retreat for ones bare feet, if so inclined to indulge without the sandals. Elaborate and colorful wall screens were hung to the wide windows in maintaining coolness of the room during the summer months. The screens were soaked almost hourly and re-stretched tight across the windows in hopes of catching all of the heat that slipped through the windows and transferred it to a cool breeze to soothe those throughout the room. This was one of her favorite tricks in maintaining the coolness of the room, for she had these contraptions all over the palace for her comfort.

"The voices of their many noble guests had constantly filled the rooms and kept us up at night, when we finally gave in to the throes of slumber and to the underworld dream journeys.

XLVII

"He ate and drank himself into oblivion in those days, and even had built himself a hermitage along the Harbor of Safe Return. He would often jest about residing in seclusion to our horror, like Timon of Athens. He would tease us about living out the rest of his days in rags and eating shellfish that he could catch in the multitudes. I do not know what brought out this sudden change in his usual people seeking mode. For he spent many a day in the solitude of his thoughts in his own created isolation. He drifted in and out of his dream world for awhile. When he was around, it was only his shell and half of the usual facade that he would normally project. This was a new side of him, one we had never met before. So, in those days, we just bided our time and waited impatiently for our father to return to the material world and the brighten the light of day, that he seemed to hide from in this new reverie of his.

He was not only the king or pharaoh of Egypt, he was the king of sarcasm as well. One could never tell with the tone of his voice whether he was serious or if he was in jest, since he maintained his composure so well. He was always talking of some adventure or another that he had intended on taking for the purpose of saving his soul or Ba. He would often tease my mother on how he was only paving his way in gold that would lead to Osiris and the underworld. For he knew all too well, that it was one journey that everyone someday had to partake of. He mentioned on how he would provide the Goddess Maat with a new scale of electrum to weight his heart, during the famous Opening of the Mouth ceremony. For this ceremony was one that was required of all Egyptians in their journey of the underworld. He would further tease that the Goddess would probably even more appreciate a new electrum scale, which would hopefully grant him the leverage of the scale weighing in his favor. I suppose that in his moments of jest with my mother on her newfound religion, it was his way of accepting her beliefs and was possibly even questioning them himself then. He would often jest with those he loved, it was his way of acceptance in their differences. He found acceptance of peoples idiosyncrasies, since he had so many of his own, and was not a hypocrite.

XLVIII

"The infamous Cleopatra had never forgotten her own ticket to the underworld, and made the necessary arrangements to insure the unavoidable venture that she would take regardless of her future. She had a mausoleum constructed to insure that unavoidable result of her life. The mausoleum was built for her, my father, and her children, on a rocky promontory on the outskirts of the city that she held so close to her heart. This as located near a small grotto by the shores of the Mediterranean Sea, and near in locale to the shrine of Isis. For I suppose that in the afterlife, she wanted to have easy access for her worship and for her literary pursuits that she enveloped herself in so ruthlessly in her life. She had a tunnel carved into the depths of the earth that led to a small room in the colossal library, that held copies of her favorite writings.

She employed her favorite architect, Anuses for this valuable endeavor. For he toiled away into the early morning hours in hopes of creating the perfect plans for her and Marcus Antony. His toil had proved true, for he utterly impressed them both. He and the workers in the surrounding villages set off immediately to materialize his dream and inspiration.

The workers that they hired were rewarded as was natural of my mother and her generosity. For she believed that the best of work was created when the workers were paid, for they were more inclined to work well since they were rewarded for their efforts.

A village was erected nearby for them and even a small area was laid aside for their own advancement to the underworld. For the majority of her workers maintained the traditions of the ancient religion of the land. The people loved her for embracing their faith and greeted her warmly when she graced them with her presence.

Most of the people had not the monetary means to insure their safe travel throughout the underworld to the final resting place and the eventual union of the five parts of their personality. The Ba and the Ka, being only two of them. For in order to do so a Book of the Dead must be obtained and certain trained individuals had to be hired to perform the rites and the proper incantations to the deceased individual. My mother had insured this for all of the people who participated in the building of her temple, who happened to lose their lives under her employ. There was also the immense cost of preserving the body and the wrapping of it as well. This, as one could imagine, was costly, when done properly. My parents had taken care of their funerary needs, since they were working for their own advancement in the underworld. Fortunately for her coffers there were relatively few deaths that had occurred, probably due to their high morale and good treatment.

I remember that as a child, my mother would take the three of us along to see how they were doing. She would explain how important it was for gaining a place in the underworld, and insuring her a place by the side of Isis and Osiris. For she was the daughter of Isis incarnate. She was very pregnant in those days, and eagerly looked forward to those walks with us, before she would be confined in the later stages of her pregnancy. It must have been odd for her to be contemplating plans for her death, when she felt the quickening of life inside of her.

XLIX

"Eventually those walks had reached an end, when she grew too awkward for those treks along the rocky shores. She was then confined to the elegance of the palace enclosure and the luxury of her rooms, where we all were in attendance to her. She was glorious in state of pregnancy, for she blossomed and appeared even younger, since her face had filled out. The love beamed from her very eyes and danced upon her cheeks. All of the lines of worry and the weight of her rule, were softened quite a bit in those days. She required no makeup in those days, for there was no stress to cover. She basked in her rare luxury of a break from the daily palace. Though naturally, she would ponder for hours over plans and maps and records, just to while away the endless time. For she was the type of person, who could never accept a true holiday from her duties. She had to keep a grip somehow, and did this in the solitude of the family suite in the palace. She performed no public functions and enjoyed the luxury of her time with her family.

My father was forever in attendance to her every desire, which I am truly sure was a rarity in that. For he was often away attending this matter or that. He filled her rooms with the most wonderful menagerie of birds. Birds from every country were sought in his inquisitous quest for her. Each one chosen for their plumage and the delight which sprang forth from their beaks. Their cages, another mission of his. He contacted the most famed of artists to craft and assemble this exotic collection of hers. Cages of every discretion enclosed their cries of joy. There were ivory cages and ones of cypress, and even those of silver and gold. Their cages did not often hold their charges for very long though. For my mother grasped an even greater joy in letting them fly free about the many chambers of her suite, to all of our amusement. They would fly about the rooms a myriad of colors and rainbows in delicious free flight. Every color in our dreams flew about in front of our eyes, their song filling our tiny ears at the enchantment of the sound. She would even have musicians perform to them for either their rest or inspiration, I know naught which, but play they did for her birds. She was always thinking of others, even her birds. She constantly strove to create a world of happiness and wonder about her, possibly as her escape from the world of pain outside of the walls of the palace. We never tired of this, which was eagerly anticipated after our lessons at court spent in colorless clay rooms toiling over our glyphs and histories. They were usually rushed in those days for we much awaited the visits to the colorful rooms of our mother at the end of each day.

L

"When the tomb was completed it made the eventual future death of my parents all the more eminent and real to our young and innocent minds. I would pray that the fantasy world that my mother had created in her boredom of her maternity confinement would never end. I prayed that they would never have to actually use those tombs, that they would forever be at my side. I would cry myself to sleep at night, hoping they would never die, for I did not think that I could handle that eventual future reality. But, naturally, being a child, those gloomy days were only fleeting, and were swept away by the joy of the reality of the embrace of my parents.

LI

"My mother soon ended her confinement and returned to the rest of the world with the birth of my sister Arsinoe.

"The first thing on her agenda upon her return was to see the family tomb in it's final stage of completion. For it was all of her feelings of life eternal in stone, her message to the world long after her last breath. It was absolutely magnificent to behold. It was airy and pristine. The opulence absolutely seeped out from the enclosure to captivate ones eyes and senses. It was a true work of art, I felt. One could almost forget the real reason for it's construction.

The paintings that covered the walls were splendidly bright. For the latest in chemicals were used to ensure the lasting effects of the colors. The style of the art was of a softer version of the ancient technique that one could find in temples along the Nile that were thousands of years old. The scenes that were portrayed, were captured from the Book of the Dead, and displayed for the eyes to behold in their magnificence. The hieroglyphs were finely rendered and delighted even those who could not read them, for each one was a work of art in it self.

When I finally rested my young eyes upon the area where their sarcophaguses would be placed, the reality of the construction loomed bold before my eyes. For this would be the residence of my parents for all eternity after they left the earthly realm. There was even an area for each of us to rest by their sides. Would we be forever young to them in the afterworld? Would my father truly become Osiris and my mother Isis?

The place for our own tombs, frightened me a little, I must have swayed slightly in my reverie, for my mother walked over to me and placed her hand upon my shoulder. She bent down and looked in my eyes, "Do not worry precious one, for in the afterlife, we will never be separated, even if we happen to be in our lives. For every living thing on this earth, soon will die. We just believe that our lives on this earthly realm is only one small step and the next will be taken in the afterlife. That is why we put into our tombs the things we most cherish while we still breathe-so that they may comfort us on that next step, which will last much longer than this life—for eternity. For eternity lasts much longer than either you nor I could possibly imagine!" She then paused, possibly looking for a better phrase to not frighten me, and then continued, "We must take it upon ourselves to fill our life with joy and happiness and love in all of our waking moments; for everything that we do, will be a thousand-fold in the life after we leave our body's shell. I hope you learn the significance of these words, for I believe that it is true. If you give forth love and justice, it will return to you not only in this life, but a thousand fold in the under-realm. If we part in life, we will be united with all we love in death. In this shrine we will be together and forever celebrate our happiest moments in life for eternity. So, do not fret about death, wipe it from your mind, yet never forget," She turned to us all, capturing us all to her gaze and said, "I hope we will never have to be laid inside of these tombs, yet it is silly to mock our fates. I vow I will do everything possible to give you joy and love while I breathe from these lips that so love to kiss each one of you. It might frighten you to think of something such as death, for here I strive to give you the comfort that we will never part our souls, no matter what life brings each one of us. These walls will call you all together to be at my side and your father's for all of eternity, when our last breaths have failed." She then turned away with baby Arsinoe in her arms to a corner of the room. I suppose she needed a few moments to compose herself, for her mind was probably filled with running thoughts of her words and the reality thereof. I cherish in my heart the multitudes of love she had for each and every one of us.

Even after that speech, so eloquently stated by my mother, the reality of death failed to penetrate my young and delicate mind. The thought of that eventual state, was as far away as the very shores of Atlantis. Their death was even shadowed by their all to vivid presence and perpetual aura in life. Never, in that time, did I actually believe that they would be entombed there. That could never happen. For the Gods needed them here to raise us! How could such vivid life be extinguished to the dust and shell that would lie in those tombs?

LII

"My little sister was a joy from the very start of her life. Her amber curls caught even the smallest ray of light to shine her bright facade. We all took pleasure in each little gurgle and bubbly smile that would fill the room. For we all begged to hold her and to listen to her tiny baby speech. For our mother had told us that when each baby was born, they spoke the ancient language of the Gods, and as they grew, they would lose that magical language that would be heard and understood directly by the Gods. The language, therefore, had to be relearned at one's death in order to pass on in the next journey. This language, insured my mother, made sure that a baby's every desire was met. Well, whatever Arsinoe had said to the Gods, I certainly did not understand one word of it. Perhaps I had forgotten that language that I once knew. I wonder, if it was the quest of each individual to try to find those words in our lifetime. Yet, mother assured us, that the only thing that we had to know of the language, was to give all of our love to baby Arsinoe, since that was the most important word in that ancient language, and one that we should never forget. For the Gods would take care of the rest, until they learned our language. I may not have understood the language at that time, I do recall for sure, that I sought to obey each gurgle and smile.

"Soon after, almost a year, came the gurgles of my baby brother Ptolemy Philedelphos, which translated as brotherly and sisterly love. I suppose the Gods must have chortled in that play of words for the little rebel that he turned out to be. From day one, he brought about a ruckus in the walls of the nursery and ripped apart our tiny little sibling alliance we created for ourselves. Demanding, he was from every possible source that would heed his ear piercing cries and wails. He needed to be the center of attention from the very beginning. His cries would not only outnumber those of Arsinoe, but the range far exceeded her in distance as well. For servants and slaves would race from the lengths of the palace in order to placate those aggravating squalls that bellowed from such a tiny orifice! My mother would practically tear her hair in mock reverence to him. The two were as opposite as could be. As fire was to water in a placid pond. For placid was Arsinoe, as she was almost forgotten in the scrambles towards my tiny brother.

Alas one more followed, though not for very long. For my mother soon gave birth to Berenice, who was sickly from birth. She did not grace us with her presence for very long. For her cries had ceased eight months after her entrance into this world that was too much for her frail presence.

LIII

"The walls of the palace were crowded with our voices and cries of attention. For it was indeed wonderful to be raised as the child to Gods incarnate! For our every wish was fulfilled, we never knew want. Our plates were filled to overflowing with every delicacy of the known world. Our food was transported great distances to tempt our tiny refined palates.

Our clothes, changed very often were in an array of the vastness of the rainbow in stark contrast to the bleak mud-brick walls of the palace enclosures. Our tiny feet rang through the halls in pursuit of some such imaginary foe or delight. Our imaginations reigned supreme in those brightest of days. Arsinoe would follow and obey our every command. She did not take to Philedelphos that well. For he was always setting her up in some trap or another. We always had to extricate her from those predicaments. Poor Arsinoe! She was dainty indeed and completely naive. Forever susceptible to the torments of our baby brother. For he soon grew to heights beyond all of us.

Caesarion, our oldest brother, was not always there in those days for he was being trained in the aptitude of the future rule that would eventually be placed upon his shoulders. No more would that monster chase us or storm out our castles. Oh well, he still doted on our every desire when he did have the time. For he found joy in our smiles, as did our loving parents.

Alexander Helios, whom I called Helios after the birth of my little brother, was always by my side. He and I would practice with Arsinoe and Philedelphos, some play or performance for my parents when they were in residence. We would work for days prior to their return on some work of art for their entertainment. I would spend hours with my handmaiden, Arial, in toil over the costumes. For I was still very young in those days, so my stitches were quite laborious. She would lose herself in the rapture of the creation. Her work was marvelous!

I know my parents delighted in our creations and amusements for them. They were so proud of us then. That is why I never would have suspected the eventual outcome of events that were soon to follow those sun-brightened days.

LIV

"Towards the end of our calendar, before the inundation of the Nile and at the end of one of our harvests; Octavian created a challenge for my father to meet. He awaited the presence of my father at the Canopic Gates of the city, in full battle attire. My father, despite the protests of my siblings, met that challenge.

To the dismay of all, my father, Marcus Antonius of the family Antonii, was defeated. He fell on his sword in appeal to the Gods at this moment of Hell on earth. Our wails must have been heard to the very gates of the underworld. For he was mortally wounded in this act. Why, oh why did he do this? Did he not love us? Did he not want to see the play we had worked so hard on? Did he not long for the embraces of my mother and his children? For those cries were not heard by any God. His dying body was carried to the palace and to the feet of my mother.

I did not understand why we were all sent away, for we were never to hear his last wishes. They only went to the ears of our mother. It must have almost killed her to see him in that state. A man she had thought to be invulnerable, the descendant of Hercules himself, had at last succumbed to the throes of death. It must have destroyed her. For her wails of morning rang through the palace. My body still quivers at the remembrance of those moments, that summed the inevitable death of my father. I know that he died in her arms. It took eight slaves to pry her lose from the stiff embrace of her lover, husband, and father of her children. For she had lost all sense of reality, and her dreams had perished at the moment of his death. For she probably thought that she had no one to share them with, who would understand. Were we forgotten in her pain? How could she forget about our future? This distressed me so that dreary day and still does. For she had unknowingly forgot about us in her mourning.

For never were we again to hear his silly jokes, or to be held in his mighty embrace! Or to rapture in the loving lock of his gaze and attention. Our father was dead!!! How was I ever to carry on, especially without the attention from mother. Our life had ended with the last breath of our father. For our magical world of happiness and wonder had ceased on that very day. For all we knew from that day forth… was want. We had want for the love of our mother that was taken away from us on that day, that shell that had once been filled with our fathers essence, to be taken away for his funeral and placement in the tomb that was so recently finished. I never actually believed that the tomb would contain even one of our bodies.

Our mother, under the trance of her grief, had torn most of her once beautiful locks of hair from her sorrow-drowned head. Her wails of desperation were heard throughout the environs of our expansive palace, in the privacy of the dark of the night. For during the day, she bore the continence of grace in her state matters. For she was a queen first and foremost, however deep her sorrow. She must hide it from the eyes of the public. My sister, and brothers, and I, were left alone in the pains and suffering of our own nightmare. We wanted to die and be there with them. For our mother was death walking to our eyes. We cried alone. For we begged of her to tell us that nothing would ever change, that everything would go back to normal and this was just a scary play. We never heard those words of comfort, never!

For our once tranquil world was torn even more asunder. In her grief-stricken state, she pitifully appealed to Octavian. I know not what means she may have used for that. For I had heard that he was disgusted in her pathetic attempt. His obsession was so unforgiving. I had heard that he actually laughed in her face. The horror of it still upsets me to this very day that I write. She was captured then and placed in the deepest of her own prisons to await his so "august" presence. That second audience never came. He informed her by messenger, that she and her children were to be taken to Rome for his triumphal parade and games. As was custom, we were to walk in chains behind his golden chariot. That thought must have repulsed any pride that she might have had left in those moments. For she spat at the messenger and at the words of the new Caesar. She could not handle the very thought of the idea, for she had lived to bear witness to the humiliation of her sister Arsinoe, who walked in the wake of Caesar's chariot throughout the streets of Rome bearing the heavy chains of her imprisonment.

LV

"In her imprisonment, we all shared the sorrow of confinement. We all were kept in the chambers of the palace under guard and she was let in to see us on occasion from her much more abysmally allotted cell. One evening, she was brought to us who were timeless in our loss of tears. As she entered the place of our confinement, we rushed into her arms. Our voices cried out all at once to cover her with a joyous cacophony of love. We hoped that she would never leave our side again, we fought to keep her in our embrace. Her head bent low to shower us with her tears of joy at the sight of us.

She covered us with kisses and promises of a return to a normal life. She mentioned that she was in the process of creating a plan for her return to the throne and to our normal life in the palace.

At that moment all of the wear of our last days in captivity, had disappeared with her hugs and kisses. All of our sorrow abandoned in view of her form in the room with us. For she was only our mother in that moment, and we missed her dreadfully. With her form, was brought to us our childish hopes of a life that would soon return to normal, and the thoughts that our nightmare would soon come to an end. Her words encouraged those visions, and made them strong in our hearts. Our mother was all powerful to us, we felt that she could do anything. For we knew all that she could give. She was a goddess to us then, we felt that she could do anything. The illusion held us together in her absence, made all the more real to us when she again was before us to hold.

"I have etched in my soul the memory of her last moments with us, not the words, for they were unimportant. For her words were the promises a mother made to her children in times dire. The words were those of comfort and love, words that we had heard in a time that seemed so far away to us then. Of a time of light and happiness without the constraints of captivity. For what I recall dearly was her face, which was wrapped in utter despair as she initially walked in the door—to be suddenly washed away at the sight of our faces. She showered us with words of love and kisses to our eager faces. For we had truly believed that she had returned to us, the mother we had lost with our father. She was adorned in a linen that was wrapped about her in the draped style of the Romans and trailed the dust of the un swept floor of our room. The dust which was swept up in her wake had surrounded her in a cloud making her appear even more goddess-like. Her touch when she bent down, gave us the reality of her comfort so long denied us.

I recall the last time that she walked out of that room, with promises on her lips of her eventual return. As she backed out of the room, she paused, as if to memorize that moment. She turned and proudly walked out of the room, leaving a swirl of dust in her wake. The door closed then as she was led away at the hands of her captors. The door was closed forever to us of her love, though we did not know it then. She had left us with the dreams of the end of our captivity and to run again in the halls of the palace in the freedom of before. Not even Arsinoe cried, for she too held the thoughts of what she had last told us.

For she had told us that we had the blood of the Ptolemys in our veins, and thus, we had to be brave in our captivity. For we were soldiers and we must be proud in the face of adversity. For our line will endure, she promised us, and we would all look back upon this time and remember our strength. Philedelphos, was the only one who dared to break the silence when she left the room. For he was oblivious to our predicament and our father's death. He thought that this was some sort of play that we all were in probably. He demanded for sweets. Would it have been that simple, I gladly would have retrieved them for him myself! Yet, the rest of us kept our promise and sat there pretending that we were strong and proud.

In those days of our captivity before we were brought to Rome we were left in the solitude of our selves, the children of a great queen. We were kept in an old abandoned suite of our palace and locked inside. Guards stood sentinel at the door and brought us simple meals. We, in our innocence, thought it was wondrous to have such bizarre food. For the only food that graced our palates before the confinement, was that which was strenuously prepared by the most talented of chefs. We pretended that our simple fare, was that of soldiers, and that we were in our barracks preparing for our final battle to return us to the throne. We made games in this solitude during the light of the day, mocking Octavian, this enemy that we never saw. Only Caesarion had laid eyes upon him, and we used his stores of memories of him in our plays.

The nights were filled with muffled tears, for we had all fought to be brave for our mother. We fought so desperately hard.

LVI

One day, there came a slight knock upon the door in the early hours of the morning. We thought, perhaps, that it was the food that was prepared to break our fast. In appeared one of our servants, a young woman covered from head to toe in the drapery of the Romans. She lowered her head to us, revealing a tear streaked face, that had been recently swept clean. The tears had made trails in the dust of her finely chiseled face that had smeared upon her wiping them away in our presence. I vividly recalled her face and her large ebony eyes. I even recall the freckles dotted across her nose. The drapery about her made her look older than her obvious years, when one looked closely upon her face.

She called us all to her presence then. Reluctantly we obeyed. Finding this foreign to us that a servant should command. Though in our situation, the normalities of our past were fading to us. We gathered by her skirts in anticipation. She bent down to us and held us deep in her gaze and told us words we did not want to hear…

She told us that our mother left her imprisonment in chains in the company of her valued attendants, Iras and Charmian. We nodded at this, because we knew and loved them both. She continued to tell us that our mother locked herself in our family mausoleum for some reason. These two followed, since they obeyed her every wish. They followed my mother to the grotto she had built by the sea, and to the arms of the rose quartz Isis, that protected the harbor. I cannot even begin to grasp what was on her mind at that time, or even how she managed to leave her prison under the guard of the Romans. Though, she did that, and found her way to the tomb. She had proceeded to lock herself and her attendants who served her too well into her newly built tomb.

We were then told that a slave had brought in to them a basket of figs for their refreshment and their desolate confinement. For all I knew and hoped, she was busy inside with plans and schemes. For that we dared to hope for.

Unfortunately that basket had concealed an asp. Did Octavian place the asp inside for her defiance, or was it the wish of my mother to end her grief. For the later, was what the Romans would have us believe. But they had not seen the love and the hope in her eyes that last time that we shared with her. They had not felt her warm embrace and overpowering love that she gave us. I will never know the truth, until the day I meet her in the underworld at the side of her Osiris, my father. For in that basket of figs was the very death of one so prominent a figure in life for all time. Her death she shared with her most beloved of attendants. Was this

Octavian's final 'favor' to Cleopatra, or was it truly her desire to be by the side of my father for eternity? I tend to tell myself over and over again that she did not know what was really inside of the basket other than the figs that she had requested in that last act of defiance. For she was not the kind of person to bow down to defeat. An asp was the only thing that could be claimed as her eventual demise, for the marks upon their forms when found. The lack of the actual asp, was a mystery to all. Though in it's stead, Octavian had won that final bloodless battle that very evening.

LVII

The rest of our last moments in Alexandria were spent in a daze of unreality. Brought forth from our confinement to bear witness to the funeral of my parents. We trembled by each other for comfort and struggled to stand tall and proud. For we were the heirs to the throne of Egypt on the outside, but deep inside…we were only children who desperately wanted their parents to return. To the people who observed Cleopatra's children, we appeared to them as hollow shells of children, draped in the formality that was grilled in us from the time of our cradles. We gave them the semblance of royalty. We revealed to them the proud line of the Ptolemys for them to bear witness in our strength. Through our silent tears, we saw the bodies of our parents wrapped together side by side, as was the wish of my mother.

Throughout the land of Kemet and beyond, the people praise the love and the devotion of the attendants of Cleopatra, who followed their mistress to her death, making sure that she would not go there alone. Altars and small shrines were erected throughout the land to bestow honor upon their memory of their devotion. Statues were made in their image and later placed by the doorways of homes as a sign of protection as well. Iras and Charmian had served their mistress to the very end.

LVIII

My sister and brothers and I were then walked, as was the wish of Octavian, behind his golden chariot upon his return to Rome. We arrived in the city in a daze after a forgotten journey. When normally we would have roamed on the decks of the ship at the rarity and newness of the voyage. For we had never left the borders of our homeland. Though this time, we remained below in the comfort of each others' arms. For we knew that we were all that we had, and we did not know how long even that would last.

We walked in chains behind his chariot of gold in the sweet oblivion and numbness in that face of despair. For very young we all were. The chains were lighter that the norm, for they were for the effect and the symbolism of the victory. Not caring our fate, only desperately yearning the arms of our mother who was taken away from us! Crying for her to sing us to sleep and for the sweet scent of Jasmine that was always in her presence.

I could still feel the weight of the chains that we carried through the streets of Rome. The silence of the crowd as we approached. The loud cheers that resounded the streets had ceased as we walked by. All the world was silent, only the sound of our tiny footsteps across the paved streets, softly thudding on and on. Oh, how that dreadfully gaudy chariot creaked the misery of our thoughts and crushed hopes! For the chains were not the only things that weighted upon our forms, for the deaths of our parents weighed even more heavily upon our souls in the added burden of our captivity!

We saw the last of each other then, for were separated a day after the end of the march. We were woken from our slumber, our bodies were all tangled together for comfort in a strange and cruel world. We had felt that we were on display as if the whole world had watched our tears. For by the end of the march our heads could no longer be held up high in our forced pride, they were bent low in sorrow and the tears that fell were witnessed by the whole populace of Rome who gathered to witness us in chains. We were pulled apart by several strange hands that we had never seen before.

For all that was familiar to us had vanished. We cried and screamed and kicked. Caesarion boldly told them to unhand us, for we were princes and princesses…"We are Ptolemys" he screamed out. And that he was the heir to the throne. They laughed at him as if he was a mere delusional child! He told him that they would pay for the way that they handled us when he attained the throne for his parents. They laughed even harder. Then he told them that if they were to see to our freedom, he would make sure that they would be rewarded richly, for we knew the location of the riches of the Ptolemys. Our cries had hushed upon his pleas. His promises were ignored in their cruel laughter. When they regained their composure, they began again to separate us. We screamed all the louder as we were forced apart. We yelled with all of our power for our parents to hear in the underworld, so they could return to save us. Our cries were ignored. A different adult was assigned to each one of us. We were carried out wailing and kicking with all of our might. For we had promised our mother that we would always be together. The day of broken promises fell upon us all when we saw the last of each other. The very last memory I have of each one of them in that most horrible moment of my life, were their cries as they grew farther apart from my own. Of how they seemed to mingle together as the sight vanished of them as we were led off in different directions, until they were finally muffled out by the echoes in the streets of my own tears, and they were met by no others…."

* * * * *

"Two small children wandered aimlessly along the beach beside the vast sea before them. The two little heads bobbed this way and that in attendance with the languorous strides they took along with the pounding of the waves. The voices of the waves drowned out their giggles as they picked up the pace in a race to nowhere. Long light brown hair of the same honeyed hue, trailed out after their lithe bodies. The boy's hair was shaved except for a long lock of dark blonde hair, as long as the girl's. They were twins, these two.

Playfully, they ran into each other and began to tangle into each one another's laughter. Arms and legs all over the place, and sand flying in their wake.

"Selene, lets build a castle and make an army in the sand"

"That sounds wonderful, let's hope Caesarion does not find out, that would be bad." She sat there in the reverie of her own grand plans for the building. Her eyes wandered over the beach to a large clam shell half exposed in the sand. She walked over to the shell and began to dig.

"Hopefully this hole does not get deep enough to reach the gates of the underworld."

"Aye, that would be bad indeed!" He giggled and joined in with his hands. Together they managed to build the walls of the battlements. Laboriously the walls wound around and around, forming a labyrinth. "Osiris himself could get lost in there, do you think, Selene?" Together their giggles reached new heights. She nodded and continued to dig.

Slowly the labyrinth twisted towards a pit, that they started to work on. "This will be the deepest pit in the world, this is where the bad people will go." Selene added with a mocking look of anger upon her tiny brow-line. "The bad people will fall in and not be able to get out. Then there will be only good people on this earth!" Her tone changed with a new vengeance. Helios dug on in oblivion to her last statement. He was wrapped up in the ease of inspiration.

"And this wall will make sure that no one will ever leave." He stooped over to ponder their creation. "We need an army to protect the good people who live in these walls over here." His gaze trailed over to a small sand village to the side.

"Wouldn't it be great if we could lead Octavian to this maze?" He looked up at her waiting for a response. She nodded and continued to dig, while the hole filled with even more sand.

"I wish that Octavian would get stuck in here and drown." Helios looked up at her and continued with his digging, "Yea, that would be great!"

The little girl stopped abruptly her digging and her plans while her thoughts begin to wander. Slowly she fell into the grip of a trance. Her thoughts raced inside hr head, while she tried to gain a hold onto where her thoughts were leading her. Her eyes locked onto a water pool, losing her self to it's depth. And she learned the prophesy of her family… she learned that death will await them by water. It was clear to her in that moment that it was only she and her own who could protect them all. She was given the stage for her mind to learn of the prophesy to be told to her when she was older… when her family truly needed it."

LIX

Cleopatra Selene had thought to herself as she paused to receive her memory in the course of her writing. She thought of the constant visions of her mind that would overturn any reality at that moment, making her oblivious of her surroundings. She recalled the one that she had while a child on the beach, as one of her earliest daytime dreams. She pondered as to why she even had those visions that would torment her. For some reason, she would store the visions to be recalled at a later date. She had in later years received the scroll written about the first twin prophetess in her family, Cleopatra III.

Slowly she stretched out her arms before her loosening the cramps that had begun to form from the endless writing. She bent her head in sorrow at all of the memory that returned at the writing of this. Though still she was determined to continue. Her very soul cried out for the truth about her mother to be told. She did not want to depend on the ravings of a madman to spill horrible lies about the virtue of her mother. She continued to write to take her away from that part of her memory in which she was not ready to dwell.

LX

"I feel this need deep in my soul, to tell people of my mother, from the point of view of someone who knew and loved her well. Let not the poisonous words taint the truth from the ears of the future. Not from the demented perspective of the obsessed Octavian or the pathetic mumblings of Virgil. They have not had chances enough to see the spark of genius that illuminated from her thoughtful gaze. Unfortunately the warped visions and pitiful mumblings of these men are heard by many people, and are thus believed.

My mother was not wanton in any way. She loved and adored her husbands, especially my father. She devoted her life to making her dreams a reality, and for passing them down to her children. She wove the web of life around all of those who touched her. Her magical words lit up many a dull moment in laughter to her witty epitaphs. She made all of those around her worship her wit and wisdom, though we were never made to feel inferior by her. She made all around her shine, though never dimming her light in the process.

I dread to think that she may have seen what her children have suffered subsequent to her last breath. Did she witness from the Underworld the blade of the Roman sword fall on the neck of my oldest brother—her first-born? Did she watch in dread our tears as they fell upon our innocent cheeks, as we walked in chains behind the golden chariot of our conqueror? Octavian stole the title of pharaoh for himself, as he stole the innocence at the deaths of our parents. Did he in fact take the life from my mother, does he wash her blood from his hands? He was so obsessed with their destruction, I tend to wonder at what fate had handed to them, or was it simply the wish of Octavian. The very same Octavian who gave himself the name of Caesar Augustus after his own victory over the blood of my parents.

When we were made to walk through the streets of Rome in chains we were all so very young. My brother and I had just turned eleven at the time. So untried and innocent to life. Arsinoe was of the tender age of five, while Philedelphos only three years of age. When my brother Caesarion was executed, he was sixteen years old and too close in age to inherit the formidable throne of Kemet. Caesarion had made his escape from our captivity in Rome and had eventually met up with his tutor Rhodon. In the depths of the evening, they made their escape. Unfortunately, they were easy prey to the clutches of the 'mighty' Augustus and his forces who all too soon caught up with them. He planned for their prompt execution, which was performed in silence in some dark dismal cellar deep in the Roman city.

We were children, forced in chains to walk a path which we did nothing to create. Our parents obviously had no foresight to the future when it was in the negative. For their dreams were for the gain only, there was no place for the all too evident defeat, that we alone as children had to face. We were the innocent victims of a battle which we never fought, though had only leaned of behind the skirts of our mother. Our tears, we felt, were enough to overflow the mighty banks of the Nile, which had disappeared from the horizon to us. Too young were we to hear of our fate until we actually had to walk the reality of it. The sheltered bubble in which were raised had burst in a fury, a fury we had never laid our eyes upon prior to that nightmare in which we found ourselves in.

Days passed into evenings in our separation in all we had grown to know. As our shadowed remnants of our living nightmare had grown into a reality, we gradually adapted to the situation in which we found ourselves, for we had no choice.

"Now it is ten years after the event, and the tears have not dried, nor has the agony escaped my soul. I know not, the fate of my brothers and sister, as I sit here and contemplate my reality all to vivid before me. They were brought back on to the house where I was kept captive by Octavia. She was the sister of Octavian and the Roman wife of my father. More of that time will be revealed later in this scroll. The past, seems a remnant dream that all too stubbornly wisps away at the rise of the sun.

I have heard rumors on the fates of my siblings with which I will share to the reader of this chronicle of the truth. For know you, that these fates of my siblings are only rumors. I bore witness to the dismal fate of my oldest brother Caesarion, that I reveal as fate. I last saw him in chains being led into the depths of one of the many similar facaded buildings in this city. A child to die for a station that he never requested. A station that he was still so unprepared to carry out. He was still, till that time, under the tutelage of my parents. Because of the fate of his line in birth, he died.

LXI

"For I have silent aspirations that someday, I will complete her dreams. I hope and send fervent prayer to Isis that my mother looks down upon me and is proud of how I handled this predicament. Though, she was not in captivity as long as we have been, I envision that she would have done the same were she in my shoes. I like to think of her spirit in conjunction with mine, aiding me in my plight. Rendering guidance in my life in the shadows and in my dreams. For I am her firstborn daughter, and therefore must carry on her wishes, learning from any mistakes that she had made.

LXII

"Octavian made himself first man in Rome and Imperator, thus the people call his personae Emperor. He has named himself Augustus, for he was officially adopted by Caesar as his only son upon his death. This man controls such a vast amount of land, and I have heard, that he does this wisely, that he is a just emperor. Just indeed. Does no one see the blood of my parents on his hands? He had such an obsession over their destruction that he never ceased his hold on them until they were both dead!

"Augustus had told the people that he found a city of mud, and left a city of marble. Seeing with eyes, I find this a bit exaggerated, though I have heard the city is constantly in remodeling and construction of new delights for the people. The new marble before me does soften my vision of him.

I have also heard of the wondrous things that he has done for his people. He had reorganized Rome into fourteen regions, and had even set up a more feasible government for them to add order to the prior chaos.

In Rome itself, he set a limit of seventy feet for the height of the new construction. He also set forth new rules and regulations for the safety of the new buildings that brighten the landscape. Slowly, the marble begins to take shape over the all too common and colorless buildings that had once dominated the landscape. In it's place lie the more prominent scaffolding erected all over in the avid preparation of the new city of the dreams of Augustus.

I have seen on rare excursions, the large sundial that he built on the field of Mars, their mighty war god. A large obelisk was erected to measure the movement of the sun. He tactfully contracted the aid of a famous mathematician to guarantee it's accuracy.

The news has reached my ears of Augustus' sleepless nights when in residence, working on his dream for his people of Rome. I suppose all of his physical weaknesses and lack of height, has balanced itself in his aptitude in ruler-ship. He intends to allow benefits for the growth of the city. This interests me, as does all politics.

I am like my mother in that respect, am constantly entangling myself in the web of intrigue. I have learned the art from my mother, and plan to learn from her mistakes. For I will not let anyone steal my heart and my plans to blind me from the true objectivity which I ultimately seek. Never will I let the rays of the sun blind me from my true vision. I must learn to look upon all who rule in the light of truth, and never will I let my feelings cloud my judgment and observations. There, for I must look upon the truth of my true enemy and not be clouded by the past.

LXII

"Octavian also supports the arts, I have heard. He also supports the young aspiring poet Virgil. Though he does not follow the works of Ovid, whom I love. For I believe that Ovid has an Egyptian heart and soul when he writes. Which is why, I suppose that Augustus cannot tolerate his works, for it probably strikes to close to him of the memory of my parents. His writings portray freedom unheard of by the stuffy Romans, on the subject of love. My parents hold to torch of soliloquy and reverence in living out his writing and in making them immortal.

It is difficult to surmise the fact that is all too planned of whom they chose to join me in marriage. For my mother had the freedom to chose of her own free will. Free will, I know not the ring of that in reality, though I had all too frequented in my childhood. Freedom was all around me then. I was free to walk the halls of the palace, and free to roam the endless sands of the beaches that stretched to the horizon. I was also free to read anything that I chose, that is what I could comprehend in language; that as my only boundary. My mother made such that there were no boundaries for her. For she believed that the key to greatness in leadership was in the learning of as many languages possible. She knew and could write fourteen of them, including ancient Egyptian and Hebrew. For she did not trust the words of an interpreter in her political dealings and preferred to deal in their own language. This had ultimately gained the respect of all the leaders in which she had met with. For she made sure that no doors were closed to her, as they normally would have been to a woman, no matter what her title. She made sure that by knowing the language of her allies they would have no excuse to omit her from any meeting and counsel.

She also had the talent in dealing with the accounts of her country as well. For her meticulous maintenance of her books, made sure of the profit of her land. Nothing passed her scrutinous eyes in her all too often perusal of her books.

She also had the advantage of learning military techniques from one of the greatest soldiers of all time, Julius Caesar. We all learned, as her children and future, how to read maps at a very young age. For she was always hiring out the most brilliant of cartographers to maintain the accuracy of the maps of her dominions. She must have learned quite a bit on her own to keep Egypt from the greedy claws of the Romans for so long. For she had well deserved pride in her navy that she had built. Which was renown as one of the largest of her time. Unfortunately, most of them were lost in the battle of Actium.

The most valuable lesson I have attained from my mother was in her learnings with the temple of Isis. She had impeccable retention skills and therefore memorized many prayers to our deity. She taught me to love and be loved by the mighty and all powerful Isis. She knew the skills of healing and was often by the side of Olympos her physician comparing experiments and notes on results.

She even dabbled in magic and of learning the secrets of the world. She believed that there was a mighty force in the universe that mankind had only begun to understand. She delved hungrily into the secrets and mystique of many cultures ancient and current.

For I knew that everything that she had learned, she had planned inevitably to share with us. And all that she gained was for us to carry on her future. I listened well when under her tutelage and plans, when I gain my freedom to increase my store of knowledge. For my mother, I will prove that her blood is all too strong in my veins."

Part two

I

29 B.C.E.

She felt the exhaustion of her writing binge as it caught up with her. She trembled in waves of consumption in the repletion of her soul that she forced out through her stylus filling up fields of the once empty papyrus. She hung her head and succumbed to throes of slumber which her body and soul cried all to vehemently for. She sank down into her bed in defeat, yet the smile of victory painted her lips as slumber gripped her soul. For she cherished the completion of her dreams of setting to paper the true memoirs of her mother. She would not let Rome mock the brilliance of her matriarch. She was further eased with the safekeeping of her document from the wrong eyes. She carefully placed the rolls of her papyrus into a secret compartment of her wardrobe. Alas, she settled into the throes of a sweet and all too deserved slumber in ease.

II

She awoke with the grandeur of Isis, shining her love upon her daughter. For she knew that she was loved. For she desperately longed for some acknowledgment on behalf of her mother on her plans and endeavors. Instead she prepared for her day of freedom when she could activate her plans for reinstitution of the throne to the Ptolemys.

Slowly she emerged from her slumber to greet the bright rays of hope that fell upon her form. She collected her energy to rise from her bed to set forth the day before her. One by one her long legs burst from their warm cocoon of blankets. Her arms reached out to catch the rays as they danced upon the walls of her bedchamber. She rose in full stature and walked pridefully to her altar that she had set up in her chamber.

Her altar was prepared with the greatest of care and devotion. It rose to half of her full height in it's entirety. There was a sapphire silk blanket that hid the simple wooden table. On it were the tools of her worship. There was the image of the Goddess herself inlayed in gold with wings that spread out sideways. The goddess held her arms out in front of her, her head held high. To crown her head of gold, was a crown in the image of a crescent moon reaching it's tendrils heavenward. On the table were objects collected for their symbolism. In a chipped bowl, there contained some pebbles worn to smoothness in their constant handling by her alone. She choose the stones for their properties and healing powers and knew that the Goddess added to their power on her altar. There was a platter of silver which contained her offerings to the goddess in whatever forms she could contrive. Most often they were the remnants of her own meals and even the smooth white feather that she had found one day. There was also a bowl of great antiquity from her homeland, of which hieroglyphs danced upon the surface and ancient prayer to her Goddess. For the pictures were displayed on the outside of the vessel, inside was inlayed in pure gold. In this vessel, she would fill with petals from a rose and clear running water, onto which she would divine the future. For water, she had learned was her vessel to seeing through the eyes of Isis. This was her doorway.

She glanced at the altar and placed bits of bread on the offering platter and dutifully lit the incense gathered in a pot of iron for her ritual. She kneeled before the altar and subjugated her will to the Goddess. This was her greeting to the day, her prayer of thanks to her Goddess. Her head tilted and her hair cascaded around her shoulders touching the mosaic floor of her bed chamber. She was shielded from the world behind her amber tresses. She focused on locking her inner eye to the form of the goddess and sang her praise…

"Great mother of sunshine and bringer of life
I pray to thee.
Wrap your wings of strength over me
and shield me with your love.
Help me to be the best that I can be
and let me love as you do.
Give me wings with which I can sour
and reach the fullness of your love.
Give me the wisdom of which I seek in truth.
And never let the taint of lies defeat me.

Great mother and bringer of life
I pray to thee.
For the knowledge you gave me the eyes to see,
and the wisdom you gave me the strength to divine
the truth I seek in all about me.
You have taught me your love and courage.

For this I thank you, Oh great Isis!
I thank you for the breath of life that falls from my lips,
and the earth which cushions my feet.
I thank you for what you make of me
and from where I am from.

With all you bestow upon your daughter,
she will use in sharing your love
with all who grace her life.

I welcome with love this new day before me
And thank you for giving me another chance."

After her devotion to her beloved goddess, she gracefully settled in for a day of reading. For her captor had indulged her whims in providing her with the manuscripts that she had modestly requested.

She would lose herself and the passing of hours as she enveloped her self in the writing of others and happily entwined herself in the knowledge she gleaned from others. The sun passed unknowing to her across the horizon, interrupted by the slaves as they brought forth her meals, respectful of her silence.

III

After a completely uneventful day, another day left to wonder at what road her future would take. Cleopatra Selene crossed the room to where her bed lay. Wearily she laid down for the night and to open her thoughts to any dreams that Isis might send to her in her journey of the underworld, where one roams in slumber. For the evening is the time of the Gods, when the mighty Goddess Nut spreads her body over all of the world. For during the day, the God Ra rides his golden chariot of the sun across the sky to return it to the underworld in preparation for the journey of the next day.

Her thoughts are whisked away into the world of slumber while she eagerly awaits word of whom she will marry. For she knows how valuable she is. She and her brother Helios, are the oldest heirs to the throne of the upper and lower kingdom of Kemet.

She does not know the fate of her country, or the fate of her siblings, she can only wonder about her own…

IV

A new day unfolds before her in anticipation of her fate, for today is the day when she will hopefully receive word of whom she will marry. Of course no one had consulted her in this decision, for it is only in the hands and power of the emperor Augustus.

She waited eagerly in her bed watching the glorious dawn approach her window in all it's majesty. The colors light up to comfort her form as she reclined in retrospect of all that she had accomplished prior to this new day.

She recalled the first day that she was brought to this house on the Palatine Hill, overlooking the grandeur of Rome. Her captor was the illustrious Octavia, sister of Augustus and the widow of her own father, Marc Antony. Only a few meetings over the weeks, enough to know that she worships the Roman Goddess Vesta, the most reverent Goddess in all of Rome. For this Goddess guards the hearth held sacred by the Romans. A shrine to the Goddess is set up in every home of the Romans.

For Octavia in her reverence constantly strove to live a life worthy of the Goddess, in keeping a well maintained home, and faithful worship to the Goddess. The wax masks of the ancestors were kept in a large wooden chest near the alter. For at the eve of a death close to the home, the masks were adorned by the head of the house in reverence to the worthy ancestors. Octavia maintained the masks, and kept incense lighted at all times on the altar nearby. Her strict maintenance and observance of these rites would please any Goddess.

She recalled the times when they would both sit about and describe the attributes of each of their Goddesses and the observations of them. There were many similarities. For both of the Goddess' are revered as mothers. They respected the worship of others.

Octavia would often come to Selene for the telling of her future, which she sees in her scrying bowl. In the waters of the golden bowl filled with rose petals, Selene would see many paths stretched out before her and sometimes of those whose paths crossed hers, as was in the case for Octavia. Together they would sit for a spell in hope for some valuable message from the Goddess Isis, who used the body of Selene in those moments, as a vessel for her voice. Octavia would sneak out on several occasions in the hope that Selene would talk with the voice of her Goddess. Selene smiled in remembrance of those moments.

Selene could not help but feel sorry for her Mistress Domina Octavia in the fate of her duty to not only care for her children from first marriage to Marcellus; the two Antonia's from her second marriage; as well as those children from Marc Antony's first wife Fulvia and from his mistress and my mother Cleopatra. For all of these children were now under the care of Octavia the devoted Roman matron.

V

Kateiran, a Gaulish slave in the household of Octavia, was placed over the care of the Ptolemy children. He would run errands for them and make sure their needs were met. He was four years older than she and Helios. She had spent many dreary summer days in conversation with this strange person who met their daily needs.

VI

She found their world similar and agreed often with his philosophic meanderings and contemplations. He taught her valuable lessons on his Gods and Goddesses. For she found amazing similarities to hers.

She knew that he was captured as a slave when he had reached the gates of manhood. Caught from his quest in the learning of the strange druidry. He had the knowledge of the ancients of his land stored in the confines of his memory. For they believed that all learning must be done verbally and inscribed in ones memory. They did not value the written word and felt it utter blasphemy to rely on words to record their sacred knowledge. They encouraged impeccable retention skills to store the vast knowledge of their path to druidry.

Perchance this is why he had so much knowledge. For she found that area of which she lacked. She recalled the various scrolls in reference, though not the exact wording therein. He could recite verbatim, various chants and healing potions. Such wonder stored in the recesses of his mind. She was utterly amazed at that skill. Would that her culture implied the same format of learning and did not have to rely on words. Perhaps the secrets of the world in her culture would be easier to acquire, and not left to the fortunate few of financial means. For the written record was extremely valuable and rather difficult to obtain for the average person.

She did not value the accessibility of a great library next door, until it was taken away from her.

She secretly found her heart aflutter at the sound of his voice, she could not find any meaning to this mystery. She found curious, her anticipation of each meeting with her slave. She did not treat him as such that often, she was more his companion.

She thanked Isis above, for granting to her the company of her Kateiran. For she knew that he was acquired for the purpose of easing her mind in her captivity. She reveled in gratitude for their gift.

For all to often in his absence, she would find herself lost to his image and the comfort he brought her. He had a tall stature to that of the Romans and was at least a head taller than most. His hair was full and hung unshorn down his back. Pulled together at the nape of his neck by a bronze clasp. She secretly found pleasure in how the rays of the sun would weave wondrous gold on his soft mane of hair. She felt that he had the eyes of the dreamer that he was. Heavily lidded, he looked always as if he had only just awoke. Inside of which, peered out the most intense gaze of azure. A color that was dulled to the ice color in the eyes of the rare Roman possessed with eyes of blue. His fingers were long and tapered, he had the hands of a scholar, yet he knew the feel of nature. For he believed that nature was his shrine. He believed that one could only worship in the outdoors under the sky.

He taught her of the runes and of how one could predict the future with them. They would spend hours dropping sticks to the ground and reading the sacred symbols they made when they landed on the ground. Just how many hours were spent in each others company? She eagerly anticipated each visit and the chance to gaze at his azure eyes in his unawares. He seemed oblivious in her secret longing for him. She prayed to Isis that she would not be separated from him when she was to be married. She begged the Goddess to give her a husband as beautiful to look at as he. His eyes were large with a dreamy look to them. His shoulders broad with a narrow waist. His skin so white, was bronzed in the summer months with the kiss of the Goddess. His frame seemed so powerful to her. She would often find herself wondering what it would be like wrapped up in his arms. Alas that reality would never reach her, for their stations in life forbade any thought. Ah well, in the land of dreams they meet, that is enough to comfort her in her youth.

In this state she lay in her bed, thoughts wandering from her in reverie, when the ominous footsteps to her door had reached her ears. Her thoughts ceased to the tremor of her heart, was it the word of her fate, of her future husband. With this she had many mixed emotions on the matter. Excitement as the release, yet dread that she would eventually be parted from her Kateiran and his company. This she feared. Would she have any hopes of bargaining for him, maybe…

The footsteps had reached her door and lifted the latch to enter upon her domain softly. Ah, relief, for twas only the foot steps belonging to the slave with her morning food.

The slave bowed to the floor in supplication to her majesty. "Thank you." Selene slowly sat up from her bed and walked over to the Roman couch in her quarters close to the window. She then gracefully sat down upon it and reclined in the Roman way in anticipation to break her fast of the evening behind her.

The slave was a young girl with long waist length hair flowing down to her shoulders. She guessed the slave was of Babylonian descent for the milky white skin of her face and beautiful long lashes topped with blue black silky hair. She knew this to be one of the house slaves raised here from her birth. She had known nothing else but servitude in her life.

Still bowing to Selene she left the tray on a small wooden table beside her and silently took leave from the room. Left alone to the constant silence of her confinement.

Before she partook the food that was given to her, she silently bowed her head in subservience to her Goddess in a silent whispered thank you. She whispered a greeting to the Goddess and to the new day before her and to the adventures that possibly awaited her outside the door.

When finished she deftly picked up the silver platter and nonchalantly glanced at it's contents. Figs, which she left to the side of her plate to be untouched, and slice of heavy wheatened bread adorned with some sort of nut that she was not familiar with. A chunk of orange cheese awaited her palate as well. A small carafe was provided for her to quench her thirst with water fresh from the Tiber, that flowed to the City where she resided.

This she ate thankfully, with a respectful prayer in morning for all those that she loved, in hopes that they knew no hunger or thirst in their captivity.

She knew that before the seventh hour of the day, she would hear news of her fate. The Romans counted their hours of their day from the first light of the sun. The seventh hour was in the middle of the day for them.

After she finished her meal she reclined again in wait for something to happen, anything to keep her thoughts from straying.

In her thoughts she noticed the travel of the sun as the hours whiled away from her. Knowing that she cannot trap the travel of time, she waited patiently for her summons or any such means of an answer to her fate.

VII

Taken to twirling her long silken hair in her delicate fingers, she was startled by a knock upon her door. She was so absorbed in her thoughts that she did not hear the impending footsteps.

Kateiran entered in his usual way, sauntering his long strides to where she lay reclined in her thoughts on the couch.

"Mistress, you answer is here, the mistress awaits her highness." He bowed and sent one of his winning smiles in her direction. She giggled as she untangled her hair from her fingers.

"I shall follow thee to the depths of the underworld, my devoted servant" She giggled in response to his game. She fervently tried to hide any trembling that had begun in her stomach at the reality of her predicament. She rose and with a wave of her hand, summoned him to lead the way to her impending fate.

Out of her chambers she glided with strides of purpose on the path ahead of her. She followed his graceful lead and long strides through the corridor of the domus that ringed the outside of the courtyard. She noticed the shadows cast by the Corinthian columns that bordered the corridor from the courtyard. They walked past the mosaic displays of classic Greek plays framed in between the numerous doorways and arches.

At last his steps ceased as they reached the portal of the room that contained the vast study of her captor, Octavia. Kateiran smiled at her outside of the room, encouraging her to venture forth inside. She knew he felt empathy with her plight. For he, as well as she, had really no right in the decisions of their own future. He knew all to well the reality of the invisible chains that bound them both.

She held her head up high with all of the pride that she could muster, and strongly rapped on the frame of the door in request for an entrance inside.

VIII

In a world of constant intrigue, Octavia was a formidable matron of Rome. She carried herself with the air of royalty she would have had had Rome chosen a monarchy instead of their intrepid republic that was dissolving around them anyways. Octavia was the sister of Octavian and born to the famous and ancient Octavii family. She was the spoiled daughter of Caesar Octavius and Atia. Her father being the sister of Julius Caesar's mother Julia. Though their alliance to the Julian family was more advantageous. Her brother even gave the funeral oration of his grandmother and Julius Caesar's mother Julia at the age of eleven. Her mother raised she and her brother when their father died over twenty years ago. She had to overcome rumors that their father was a money changer, though he had been born into wealth. Though the rumors persisted and she had a childhood of surviving under the constant stab of Rome and it's propensity to gossip about any patrician family. Her father had used his wealth to launch his avid political career, initially as praetor and then as the governor of Macedonia where he earned the praise of Cicero. Upon his return to Rome after his governorship was completed for further office he died one night in his sleep. She recalled the early days of her childhood of her father's absence and upon his eventual return to be taken away from her forever.

She was married young to the counsul Gaius Marcellus and had three children by him. Her eldest son of that union was Marcus Claudius Marcellus, who is currently betrothed to the daughter of Sextus Pompey, Pompeia. Octavia spent some of her time in persuasion of her son to cease the futile battles with Marcus Agrippa, her brother's most loyal supporter. For she was an ample judge of character in people and saw that Marcus Agrippa would eventually reach vast amounts of power and influence with her brother. She knew that her son was the heir to the power that her brother waged, though urged her son vehemently to use more caution with her brother's mercurial affections. Recently her brother was granted tribunician power with the aid of Marcus Agrippa, who was of common birth and was in such constant close company of her brother that one would have thought they were brother's themselves.

Her brother was battling with the people in that he had no wish to become the leader or the Dictator of Rome. He used the plunder of Egypt to pay for his troops with out pinching the treasury which added joy to the people of Rome and gained even further praise. Octavian realized the value of the republican institutions and in the sound judgment in keeping it to ensure the further prosperity of the Roman state.

In the past year alone he had begun his reforms in the army while Marcus Agrippa was creating a census of the population of Rome to better serve them. After paying off his troops from the Egyptian plunder, her gave his veterans land to farm and colonize and thus, reduced his legions, though the Roman influence in the provinces was assured by his good will.

Her brother's power was gaining at a rapid pace before her eyes. She was leery and cautious when she had any dealings with her brother and watched closely his rise in power. She saw wonderful things ahead for her family by the advancement of her older brother Octavian. She recalled that as a youth he was sickly and required the constant pampering of their mother and supervision of his studies to overcome any possible weakness that anyone outside of the family might have seen. Their mother made sure that they were introduced to their Uncle Julius Caesar and were in the vicinity of his presence quite often. This proved rather remarkable in that it resulted in her brother being made the only true heir to the revered

Julius Caesar, who was later deified after his death. Her brother became the son of a God, did that make her the sister of one? If it did, she watched her step to make sure that she would not do anything to tarnish her family name or to hinder in any way the advancement of her brother, who was fast assuming even more power than their illustrious Uncle Julius.

She wondered how her daughters, Marcella the elder and the younger were faring. They were from her first marriage with Marcellus. She recalled those days as the wife of Gaius Marcellus who she truly cared for, though he was much older than she. She was married very young and genuinely fell under the spell of his protection and doting on his young and precocious wife. Her second child, Marcella the Elder was married to her brother's valued ally and best of friend's Marcus Agrippa.

Tremendous pain and conflict was caused during her marriage to Marcellus, when her brother in one of his short whims of fancy wanted her to marry Pompey and abandon Marcellus. This caused the both of them tremendous grief especially after their third child had died at the tender and precious age of three, Marcella the Younger. It was especially difficult when both of the Marcella's resembled their father so strongly and was left with the remaining Marcella who held such close remnants of her baby sister. The ice blonde Marcellian ringlets adorned her tiny precious angel and was revived in her older sister. Her two children hung impatiently in wait under the further orders of her brother regarding their marriages since neither of her husbands were there to assist her in this and he held the paterfamilias in their stead in that he was their closest male relative.

When her husband had died she was soon married off to cement the alliance with her brother and Marcus Antonius. From that union she bore him two daughters, Antonia Major and Antonia Minor. She was halfway through her pregnancy with Antonia Minor when her husband had abandoned her and the marriage to live with Queen Cleopatra of Egypt. That woman bore her husband twins soon after her Antonia Minor was born and then two more children.

She recalled the days when she clung desperately to the hope that her husband would soon return from his sojourn with the Queen of Egypt. His actions caused further unrest of her brother's affections for him and eventually ended up in her husband's defeat and of his mistress in Actium. Though as a matron of Rome she endured her woes which were compounded when she had to take in the children of her husband and his mistress the so-called Queen of Egypt. She was already raising the remaining son of her second husband's first marriage with Fulvia, Antonius Iullus, or as the children called him Iully. The other son had perished with Cleopatra's first born son Caesarion for his assistance with his father in Actium.

It was certainly not a surprise to Octavia when she had heard of this in Antonius being so like his mother Fulvia in his strong will and perseverance no matter what the odds were. Iully was a lesser version of his brother and mother. She recalled the turbulence which always surrounded Fulvia and her whims in politics. She delved into the business as mercilessly as if she had been born a man. Fulvia was the daughter of Marcus Fulvius Bambalio and had been married before Marcus Antonius to Scribonius Curio, and then to Clodius Pulcher and then at last to Marcus Antonius. Her second husband, Publius Clodius Pulcher was murdered. There are still questions surrounding that incident to this very day.

Her second husband was a violent and ambitious man who profaned the house of Caesar during the rites of the Bona Dea when he allegedly dressed up as a woman and violated the festival which only allowed females to attend in it's mysteries. He even tried to use her beloved friend Cicero in his alibi, but Cicero would have nothing to do with it when Clodius was later brought to trial. Cicero mentioned that he had only been with Clodius for three hours which did not end up in condemning him since at that time he was a quaestor and was able to bribe the judges. Clodius never forgave Cicero for this. They became the most vicious of enemies which had bothered her brother Octavian to no end with their constant complaints of one another.

Fulvia's infamous husband Clodius had then been adopted into a patrician family which enabled him to add further trouble to Rome. He gained influence with the first triumvirate of Pompey, Crassius and Caesar and used that force to condemn Cicero and the notorious Cato Utensius who were exiled from Rome. Even though he gained the status of aedileship, he could not prevent the return of Cicero to Rome and went into decline himself politically. He thus, tried to intimidate Pompey, which only proved fatal and had sent gangs to roam the streets of Rome to bully Pompey. Pompey retaliated and sent after Clodius an Annius Milo in counterattack which ensued in a bloodbath. Legally and maliciously they battled in the environs of Rome until Clodius ran for praetorship and Milo ran for the consul. And then on the Apian Way one evening a fierce determined battle played out in which Clodius was killed. The supporters of Fulvia's Clodius ran amuck in Rome and created such chaos that the opposite occurred. The anarchy was subdued only after they had burned the house of the senate! The people were so devastated that Pompey was created in sole counsul as a result and of his assistance in quelling the rebellion which was originally caused by him.

Fulvia learned mostly from her second husband's strong will which caused much aggravation with her third husband with her constant meddling into his business. She gained her personal power after the death of Julius Caesar when the survivors of the revolution had struggled to gain some sort of control over the senate. Fulvia maintained her control and even went so much further as to pursue matter which she thought to be in the best interest of her husband while he was away in Phillipi.

At the creation of the second triumvirate, she proved all the more cunning and bold in her attack on Octavia's brother Octavian. Her brother had only received Italy in his share of the triumvirate to find himself in a lock of wills with the wife of his other triumvirate Marcus Antonius.

Fulvia had met her match though, especially when she united her forced with the brother of Marcus Antonius by the name of Lucius Antonius and by their actions started the Perusine War. She and Lucius fled to Athens.

Marcus had told Octavia during the course of their marriage in retrospect that he had been aware of the strife between Fulvia and

Octavian, but never in his wildest imaginings would he have seen that it would lead to the war that was eventually waged in his name. Learning of the struggle of Fulvia and Octavian, he rushed over to her to hear the accounting of the events and only met with her ceaseless condemnations of Octavian according to him in his explanation of the events.

Probably the bitter taste of her ambitions ate at her to cause her increasing illness, until she was finally forced to retire to Sicyon where she later died. Upon her death the strife between Marcus and Octavian had finally ended and lasted until their eventual conflict which led to the death of her husband and the events which have led her to this day. She even recalled a short period of time when her brother was married to Claudia, who was Fulvia's daughter from Clodius Pulcher. The dust only just started to settle recently from that period of constant battle of wills. And she was left to deal with the remains. It was always she who was left behind to pick up the pieces of battles that she never fought.

Her brother was currently married to his third wife Livia. His first wife was Scribonia who was divorced for his beloved Livia after Scribonia gave birth to their daughter Julia. Scribonia was the daughter of Lucius Scribonius Libo who was the father-in-law of Pompey creating a fortuitous political advantage at that time. When the political advantage soon waned after the power of Pompey had ceased with his death, he found a better political match and divorced Scribonia to marry his favored Livia, besides Scribonia was much older than her brother and had been married twice prior. Also their union had been riddled with constant disagreements and he accused her of being a constant nag and needed to get away from her.

Livia was a wonderful woman and a fierce protector of her own as was Octavia. The two women shared an overwhelming pride in their children and helped to create advantages for them as well as incredible power in Rome. Livia Drusilla was first married to Tiberius Claudius Nero and the daughter of the powerful and ambitious Marcus Livius Drusus Claudius who was a nobleman. Her immense wealth was the attraction of many men in Rome, though she had fallen drastically for the strong protective hands of Tiberius Claudius Nero. Her husband was an adversary of

Octavia's brother Octavian and had even fled to the protection of her late husband Marcus. Livia had then fled with her infant son Tiberius at the time to Campagnia to where her Marcus was at that time.

After Octavian divorced Scribonia after the birth of their Julia, Octavia's favorite niece; her own brother convinced Livia's husband to divorce her so that he could marry his Livia. Tiberius went into a rage, though had no option but to agree due to the power of her brother even at that time. Livia was six months pregnant at that time and her son Tiberius Claudius Nero had even attended the wedding of their mother and was present to the held back tears of his father. Octavia was mortified when the people of Rome had the audacity in the pain of the events of utter after the birth of Livia's son Drusus, "Only the privileged can have a child in three months", which added to the rightful horror of the eloquent Tiberius Claudius Nero who could do nothing but stand idly by at that drastic turn of events. She valued Livia and her advice since they shared similar turmoil's of fate and some brought about by her brother Octavian, the Imperator of Rome.

Her last husband Marcus had created many a mess as did her brother, though none so daunting and damaging as the dirt thrown oratorical by her one-time friend Cicero. He was a two-faced slimy viper who did not know when to stop wagging his tongue. He ruthlessly slandered the name of Marcus in which ended up in being one of his finest addresses to win over the heart of her brother after the death of Julius Caesar. It was called the *Philippics* and tore viciously even upsetting the general populace, who did not favor Marcus at that time.

When the new triumvirate was signed, Cicero's name had appeared on the list of those condemned to die. He fled as he had so many times in his life from the results of his words, though was eventually caught. Octavia recalled the time that she had actually gone to the Rostra to witness the nailing up of Cicero's head and hands. The stench was enough to make that visit a short one, though it never left her memory. She would forever after utilize extreme caution in her dealings with people in the future, for any person could just turn and use anything possible against her or her own.

Such was the life that she was born into. Sitting on the sidelines, a pawn in her brother's great scheme in life. She learned much from her older friend and mentor, Livia. She, like Livia would rule Rome through their children and all they taught to them. Since, women held no sway—as was commonly believed in the general male population of Rome. These two powerful women knew better. Let them think they are kings as they wage their battles in our lives and in the world around us, but let them not forget who raised them and who whispers to them at night in soft persuasion. The women are truly the rule over the supposed world of men. For if a woman played her part right, she was the true power behind all of the laws and battles waged. Octavia had learned her part to perfection and even remembered this in her role as guardian over the children of Marcus and his mistress and former wife. With all of those children in her household and in such a young and malleable age, she would have much work to do. She made sure that she was an almost constant presence to all of the children in her household and hid any emotions she had especially from the children of Cleopatra. For all in all, they were innocent of what their parents had done and they were without their own mother.

Octavia held her own counsel silently in a world ruled by men. It was common practice, though more in the time of her father—for the whole family of the man condemned by Rome to perish as well as the accused. Families would be massacred and some even went so far as to wipe out even associations of the condemned person as well as the blood ties. She, being first and foremost a mother—sat her own counsel on these tender young and adorable children of Marcus and Cleopatra. She had already grown attached to Fulvia's son Iully, whom the children all adorned and fought to gain attention from.

Octavia was truly an empath and reacted as if she were their mother (despite her feeling's toward her) and treated the children accordingly. Despite her growing fondness for all of the children, Octavia knew that her brother had set his attention on Cleopatra Selene and knew she had to detach herself from the child. Cleopatra Selene was of marriageable age and very important to her brother politically. She knew all too well the duty of a daughter to the Republic of Rome.

She knew that her brother was growing apprehensive of Juba II the son of the conquered Juba, who was growing in maturity and already twenty one. The son of Juba was raised in Rome under the constant supervision of allies of her brother and family and was extremely Romanized. The only fear was the dormant province of Numidia which needed Roman rule to cease the rebellions that have occurred after being leaderless for quite some time now.

She had become quite attached to Arsinoe and her curly summery locks of gold and her eruptions in giggling fits. She even delighted in the Stoic behavior of the displaced Helios and of his aggressive younger brother Philedelphos. She had witnessed the devotion that Helios had for his twin and envied their secret closeness that she never had with a sibling of her own. She even saw the growing friendship despite their beginnings of her daughter the younger Antonia and of Cleopatra Selene.

It was difficult to remain neutral in the development of the marriage contract of Juba with Selene in her youth. For Selene was of the same age that she was when she had married a much older Metellius, which had proved to be a strong and stable marriage until his eventual death. She also was aware of her brother's interest and her persuasions on the marriage of her Metillia and of her brother's confidant Marcus Agrippa. Hopefully her daughter would have a better marriage than she did with her own Marcus.

For she knew deep down in her heart that if her husband had not been on so many foreign campaigns away from their hearth in Rome, he would have grown fond of her as her Metellius had. Marcus had only sought the bed of Cleopatra in his loneliness for he constantly needed to have someone there for him.

IX

"Come in, Come in, my child" chimed a melodious voice from within the chamber.

Cleopatra Selene attempted to hide her obvious hesitation, and strode forth into the chamber that was once the study of her own father. It absolutely reeked of his essence in all that was displayed in the room. For the mosaics were almost loud and beckoning, painted in bright vivid colors and energetic scenes of his male Gods at the play of sports and hunting.

Octavia was sitting at a couch by a window that overlooked the courtyard of her domus. The light was utilized in her study as she sat at the chair, piles of scrolls lay at her feet cast aside in abandonment all too recent. Her father was once a busy man, which she gleaned from the crowdedness of the room and the many apertures for the containment of documents and scrolls. This was not a man who read for pleasure, of that she was sure. Her eyes swept this room, for she had never been inside prior to this. She had never known this side of her father's past before. She stood in complete amazement.

She then let her eyes trail to Octavia's form on the couch. The sister of Octavian and her father's former Roman wife was of small build like her own mother was. Seemingly fragile, yet she knew that there was much more to this woman who held her fate in her regal hands. Her hair was the color of a summer dawn like her younger sister Arsinoe and wavy under the confines of her matronly bun. Tendrils escaped in argument. This was a woman of power despite her predicament. She was the one who cared for the most important children of Rome.

Octavia's children of her first marriage to Marcellus; which produced a son named Marcellus and two daughter's to the best of her memory, were already married off being around the age of Caesarion. Her children from Marc Antony, the famous Antonia's; Antonia Major and Antonia Minor were still in the children's wing as was the remaining child of Marcus Antonius and Fulvia, who was Antonius Iullus—Antyllus was executed alongside Caesarion, he had acted as messenger during that battle with Octavian.

The Antonia's who were neglected soon after their birth when her father Marcus Antonii left their mother for hers—and had abandoned them and his marriage with Octavia.

Her memory of what she heard about Fulvia was that she was a powerful women in her own rights and locked wills with Octavian after Julius Caesar was murdered on the steps of the senate. She heard that

Fulvia had joined forces with her uncle Lucius staring the Perusine war. Octavian surprised them with an easy victory when she and Lucius fled to Athens. Marcus Antonius had crossed over to where she was and had demanded some meaning to her reckless actions. Whatever ills she had caused with the trouble that followed her it manifested physically and eventually killed her during her retirement in Sicyon. Her death brought about an immediate cessation of the hostilities in which Octavian and Marcus Antonius had created a peace at Brundisium that lasted until the battles with the parents of Selene and Helios. Octavian then married his sister with Marcus Antonius and he himself had married at that time Claudia, the daughter of Fulvia with her former husband Clodius.

So much had passed in the stamp of history by the parents of the unaware children in the nursery, for they were all young. Selene often wondered what the famous Fulvia was like since the historians were completely in favor of Octavian and had written a complete political tarnishment in the memory of both her own mother and Fulvia, the two women who opposed the power of the Caesar and Rome. For Fulvia had opposed her own husband the father of Cleopatra Selene. Selene wondered how he would have reacted if her mother had opposed his will, which would have eventually happened had their deaths not occurred when they did.

The blood of countess battles and betrayals had scarred the cries in the nursery wing of the domus of Octavia. The woman who serenely sat on the couch in the study that used to be her late husband's. She reigned this vast domus and answered to the will of her brother, the current power of Rome. Her long fingers gracefully clutched a scroll which Selene had guessed to be her future and the wishes of Octavian.

"Selene, you will be married in state tomorrow to Juba II of Numidia and hopefully soon Mauretania as well. The papers have been prepared and you are to ready for the journey to your new home." Selene stood there as still as marble at her fate and enveloped it gracefully as a princess should. She silently embraced the confines of the chamber in which they stood, that had once belonged to her father. She ran her eyes across the many scrolls and vellums piled about the room. The chaos apparently untouched since he was last there. Had this been planned that Selene was to see what her father had left behind for her mother. That she actually was present in the room was an act of the twisted wills of the Gods in itself, a graceful knife in her side for the sins of her parents by the abandoned wife.

"That will be all, Kateiran…" with that she was dismissed to her fate, one not chosen by her parents, but by the woman her own mother had despised. Dismissed by the sister of Octavian. Gracefully, she held back her tears and accepted her fate with a grace that would have made her mother proud. They left that chamber of reminders to walk back to the nursery and to the other children.

X

Inside the wing for the children there was silence due to the absence of them, for they had all gone earlier that morning on an outing to the market. She had the valued space to gather her belongings and then collapse on her pallet to shed all of her anger and sadness. She would not see her brothers and baby sister Arsinoe for probably a long time. And to the Antonia's and her mentor Iully, the son of her father and of Fulvia, she would miss his strong body holding back tears from the torments of her brothers. The Antonia's and their lessons to her on beauty would be sorely missed by Selene, but they would practice on Arsinoe when she left. She and her half sister Antonia Minor had just begun a friendship and all to be torn away by the hatred of Octavia and her brother.

How fast events were turning for her and upside down and backwards things were. She was a princess and must hold her head up high and win favor with her new husband and maybe bring her siblings and Antonia Minor back to Numidia with her.

Her weary eyes swayed listlessly around her chamber and tried to gather a memento from those that she would leave behind in her duty. A flower picked for her from Arsinoe that she removed from a vase and placed into her lesson book. A bracelet from her mother, a rock that was her brother Philedelphos' soldier abandoned by him in play the day before. A stylus used by her brother in his battle memoirs (he liked to fancy that he was like their father and Julius Caesar and would be a famous general someday and thus kept a journal). From Antonia Minor she held the key to their secret writing they established for themselves and made a silent vow to write to her as much as possible. For Antonia Minor was only a few months older than she and her half sister and promised best friends for life. Antonia Major was spoiled and all she did was complain and wait for her husband, she had no goals and aspirations as did Selene and Antonia Minor. Soon after her betrothal, she learned that Antonia Major was to married to Lucius Domitius Ahenobarbus. She wondered who would be chosen for her best friend Antonia Minor.

She gathered all of her mementos and slid softly into her bed which lead her to a troubled sleep. It was amazing for a child who had everything from birth to value the slightest of things and to be reduced to nothing with no say in her life.

XI

The day dawned with impeccable certainty and the beginning of her future apart from her family, broken though it was. She felt as if she were no longer a child, but an adult of twelve. She held her head up to meet the rays of the sun and her destiny with the grace that her mother had taught her.

Kateiran was there to help her with her belongings and her brothers and sisters were gathered to see her off. The unreality of the moment cut the air like a knife in that nursery. Their playful lives were shattered by the absence of someone they all loved and played with.

Arsinoe was held by Iully and cried and wriggled in his grasp, his own eyes glistened with tears that he refused to shed trying hard to be a man. Helios looked at her numbly and realized that his other half was to be taken from his side. He stood frozen deep in his own thoughts. Philedelphos just ran around the room and pretended that this was all some kind of joke and refused to grasp the reality of this moment as his big sister was leaving them as had his own parents.

Antonia Major ran to retrieve little Philedelphos into her arms to kiss Selene in her departure. While Antonia Minor broke from the side of her half brother Iully to the embrace of her sister. Crying they held each other knowing the destiny they both had before them. Bittersweet promises to write everyday escaped their tiny lips in fervent prayer of that harsh moment.

The moment ended all too soon when they heard the approaching footsteps of Octavia enter their wing. She opened the door and beckoned to Selene to make ready her departure to the study of her brother and the finality of the papers. A small spark of empathy escaped the confines of the rigid demeanor of Octavia in that split second, but disappeared just as rapidly. She held out her long regal finger to those of Selene and bowed solemnly to the others in the room and for the parting to end gracefully. Just then Arsinoe broke free from Iully and ran to her side, "don weave Seeny, don weave!" She screamed, "you weave jus wike momma and poppa, take me! Take me Seeny!" Octavia's eyes found those of Antonia Major and Iully to take hold of Arsinoe and with a wave of her hand she left the room.

Selene rushed in her wake of flowing robes with Kateiran gasping for air to keep up with all of Selene's belongings. Through the halls of the domus, to the portico and out to the entrance they followed her, the echoes of Arsinoe being hushed and muffled had mingled with the sounds of the baggage train.

She was placed into a curtained litter and hefted up into movement to the footsteps carrying her off to the unknown. Her mind wandering to all of the sounds that the curtains tried to muffle, those that she had left behind without any time to grasp hold of them or anything, just the regimented footsteps into the rest of her life. She held with all of her strength her small leather bag with the remnants of her past.

XII

When the litter stopped she was lifted out and made to follow Octavia, who was in their entourage along with many other strangers who played a role in her future. A red veil was placed upon her head by a servant as she was ushered into the building She stood in a large hall and was finally face to face with Octavian. She glimpsed at her fate through scarlet-rose tinted lace. Reddish hues marred the brother and sister who bowed slightly to each other in acknowledgement and then swiftly began the business at hand.

To the side of Octavian who sat so smugly on a marble bench sat another man. "Juba, do you take this Cleopatra Selene as you wife and Queen to our client kingdom of Numidia?" He almost choked on the Cleopatra in her name, which was barely perceptible. This was all happening too quickly for Selene to take the reality of it in. This grown man before her was to be her husband! This man who appeared ten years older than herself, handsome and very sure of himself.

Octavian beckoned to Juba who nodded his head in agreement and uttered "That I do, Caesar." For everyone called Octavian Caesar in that he was the legal heir of Julius Caesar and was willed to be called by that name upon his death.

With those words her new husband moved to the fore of her view and she was able to grasp in detail —her new husband. He stood tall and had sun darkened skin, though appeared scholarly by his stylus-molded fingers. His hair was worn long and hung down in chestnut waves to his waist, very handsome indeed. His robes were Roman in fashion and draped very nobly, though colorful hand embroidered bands bordered the toga as a sign of his station as a King and client to Rome. He bent his head in acceptance to his fate with out missing a heartbeat he bowed to Selene.

With that Caesar concluded the bargain and added his seal. Her veil was lifted off of her astonished face as she glanced at her new husband with out the color to mar any defects. None were further found as she was led like chattel to follow her new husband.

However, from her silent place amongst the proceedings, Octavia stepped out and into the hands of Selene she placed and small scroll and a dark violet cloth that held something inside.

When inside the curtained litter, curiosity raged within her soul as she looked at her new husband and he nodded his assent and encouragement to open the small package and scroll placed in her hands by the mysterious Octavia.

"***Cleopatra Selene,***

Congratulations my child in your new journey in life. I wanted to make sure that you knew where I stood in your life. I am concerned about you and your future, though note that no such paltry emotions are allowed to play a part in the grand scheme of life that we daughters of Roma Dea find ourselves valuable players in. Please know that you will always have a home here and caring words of comfort from myself in your time of need. I wish that we would have had more time together and am truly sorry for the circumstances for which we have been brought together in this life. Please write often to all of us here and tell us of your many adventures. I hear the children cry out for you as I write this in haste and want you to leave here with the knowledge that you are truly loved by all here. Maybe, if we had met under another fate, your mother and I would have been friends? I took the liberty to slip you a membrance of your late father, his ring that he had given his son Antyllus that had belonged to his step-father who had raised him. I had begged of this from my brother to give to you. Please accept this and try not to forget all of us here and understand why I was too afraid to grow attached to you. For child, I knew long before I met you, how valuable my brother would see you to the cause of Rome.

-Octavia"

Wrapped in the heavy dark purple cloth was a wide banded ring that she knew she would have to wear on a chain around her neck. The ring was silver and had a worn and barely discernable carving of the name Cornelius inside. Very odd in that her Uncle Julius' first wife was Cornelia who had been the mother of his only child Julia. It was probably the same family somehow, it seemed to her that all of Rome was connected though not as closely as her own family. She did cherish the thoughtfulness of Octavia in this last minute and unexpected gift. For she had recalled a few years back when her father had given this ring to Antyllus at the very beginning of those battles that later led to Actium and the loss of both of her parents. She recalled Antyllus and his pride in wearing the ring that we all knew meant so much to our father in that most of what he valued most in life and the progress in life were lessons learned from his much loved step-father. She found it extremely comforting much the same as her own mother would have done at this moment in Selene's life in peeking into the bag held close to her body in sleep. This touching gift had proved that Octavia was more like herself that she ever thought before, though lamented that had her mother been alive-due to her aggressive and possessive personality—she would not have had a friendship with Octavia. Though had they met in a completely different life under opposite circumstances, maybe—but then perchance their lives and personalities would have been completely altered too and would not have been the strong women she knew.

Juba sat back and let his young new wife slip away in her reverie, as he too often did upon his own youth.

XIII

Juba had reflected silently about how he arrived at this very moment. His child-wife next to him lost in her own thoughts in their litter that they shared lost in the rhythmic beat at the pace set by the slaves that carried them off to the rest of their destiny.

He recalled the first glimpse that he had of his equally royal wife, her small form hidden in the voluminous Roman robes with the purple border to further elevate her royal status and prize in this marriage of state. Thus, she held her hidden form regally and slowly trod to her place beside the Imperator and his benefactor, Octavian or Gaius Julius Caesar, the name that he had taken in accordance to the wishes of his Uncle who had adopted him upon his own death a few years before who was his original benefactor since his parents were conquered and Numidia became a client state to Rome.

Under the traditional Roman wedding veil of red he could faintly make out a promise of the woman that she was soon destined to be. Her eyes were guarded and dropped to the floor, perhaps in resignation to the moment. Her chin held high gave away any false hope that he would possibly have had of a resigned character. She was probably born with the fiery temper of her late mother. For she had only spent a short time in Rome, unlike himself who had been there since the age of six, when his own father, the first Juba was conquered on the fields of battle as her own parents were.

Yet, he had spent most of his known life in the beautiful city of Rome and was taken in eventually as a son, though not in name by Octavian and his wife Scribonia.

His own history and that of the country that he would bring this young and hopefully fruitful bride back to, Numidia had it's own tumultuous past like that of her own country of Egypt.

The fierce pride of his own countrymen were of only legend now that they were on the path to being subdued by Rome. He was descended from many great Kings and conquerors such as Masinissa and from a sister of Hannibal.

Masinissa led an exemplary and long life which had begun almost two hundred years before his time, though had started their line to greatness. He was born the son of Gaia who was a King of the eastern most tribe the Massyli, one of the two main tribes in that area now known as Africa Novae. The western tribe was ruled by his brother Syphax II. As a child he had spent most of his early life as a hostage due to his father's opposition to Carthage, though took advantage of that internment to obtain a vast and diverse education from the Carthaginian hosts and learning several neighboring languages as well.

His first major campaign was against the Massaesylians that occurred five years into the Second Punic War. Rome had survived a few military defeats at that point and the older Scipio brother's were gaining fame from their success in preventing Hadrubal from sending reinforcements to Hannibal in Italia. They were slowly sending the war to Africa to join with the forces of Syphax, when Hadrubal responded by crossing over from Hispanoli and joining forces with Gaia's Massylians. Syphax was defeated once again, though somehow eluded capture to make his peace with Carthage.

Juba's ancestor Masinissa joined the Carthaginian forces in Hispanoli and was known to have played a major role in the battles that had defeated the elder Scipios. He then returned to Africa for reinforcements and became engaged to his most notable wife Sophonisba who was the daughter of a general from Carthage named Hasdrubal Gisco.

When he returned to Hispanoli and was accompanied by his young nephew Massiva he was met by the younger Publius Cornelius Scipio, who later became the future Africanus. The younger brother Scipio was in Hispanoli to salvage his position there. In their first encounter, Massiva was captured by Scipio and Masinissa was very bitter about it.

In an absolute turn of fate, Massiva had returned to Masinissa loaded down with gifts from Scipio instead of the horrid fate that Masinissa had predicted. This was never forgotten by Masinissa and played and important part in the future with him and through the family in future generations.

There were other battles waged in his lifetime with Rome and upon learning of the death of his father-in-law after his defeat of Hispanoli, he and his men roamed in attempt to be recruited by the Carthaginians to try to settle matters with Scipio. Masinissa had joined forces with the men of Hasdrubal Gisco, Mago Barca, as well as his own to face Scipio's much small gathered forces near Ilipa in southern Hispanoli.

However, a series of smaller battles had occurred since then to make Masinissa determine the possibility in switching sides and joining Rome due the vast defeats Carthage suffered in the interim.

Suddenly, plans were curtailed by the death of Gaia and his son went into deep mourning. His father's throne had passed then to his ageing Uncle Oezacles in accordance to a pact that they had made as children, though he soon died and the throne was then passed over him to his uncle's elder son Capussa, who again was killed in a revolt soon after that and the throne was passed over him yet again to Lacumazes who was only eight years old and obviously the puppet king of a chieftan named Mazaetullus who was responsible for the death of the elder brother. With the tribes thrown into such instability, there were constant battles over the rightful leadership of the country.

Masinissa and Mazaetullus eventually faced each other in battle, and with the all too eminent defeat of Mazaetullus and his puppet Lacumazes, they were forced to flee to Carthage. Meanwhile the rest of the Massaesylians had joined to the side of Masinissa. After this breach of peace was restored, Masinissa then started to attach Syphax II who was busy occupying the rest of the lands not taken over by Masinissa.

The people of Carthage were angered by the constant battles on their land and had begged Syphax to send out an emissary to hunt down Masinissa, which ended up in scattering all of the troops that he had gathered from the defeat of Mazaetullus. The forces of Masinissa were finally cornered in near the town of Clupea.

Masinissa was wounded in this skirmish, though escaped with four men and plunged into the rain soaked wadi in a desperate escape. Two of the men he was with had drowned in full view of Bucar, the emissary sent by Syphax II to destroy him, and who was later convinced that Masinissa had followed them to the grave.

Masinissa had ominously escaped and hid in a cold damp cave to heal his wounds. When he was fully healed he had returned to show that he was still alive and had recruited a great force behind him due to his incredible survival skills. He continued to raid his enemies and had even occupied the capitol of Cirta and Hippo Regius on the coast.

Syphax again stood his ground to battle his almost undefeatable foe in hopes on conquering all of the area of the kingdoms as his own and had sent his son, Vermina in pursuit of Masinissa from behind while he attacked them in the front lines. The Massylians were again defeated and this time Masinissa escaped with only sixty of his valued cavalry and had made his way to Syrtis Minor since it was too dangerous for him to remain in Numidia or Carthage and hid out in the lands between the Carthaginian Emporia and the land of the Garamantes.

He had learned later that year that Scipio was in Sicily preparing to invade Africae. Due to this, Masinissa had sent his legate Gaius Laulius to raid the African coast. He raced across the coast to meet with his legate and complained bitterly to him about Scipio's lack of action, yet renewed in earnest his pledge to serve the Romans upon their arrival in Africa.

He began to recruit more followers in his cause and eventually met with Scipio to destroy the Carthaginian cavalry. Hasdrubal and Syphax fled inland and then followed Scipio in pursuit to crush their army. Masinissa fought valiantly in the plains as was his right. Hasdrubal escaped and Scipio sent after the remaining forces of Syphax, his ally Masinissa and his legate. Masinissa had defeated Syphax along the Amapsaga River which was east of Cirta and was captured after he was thrown from his horse. Masinissa led Syphax through Carthage in chains and with that view of their defeated leader, the rest of the city surrendered.

Sophonisba pleaded with Scipio and Masinissa not to let the Romans take her away in chains due to the damage done by her father in aid of Syphax, for she was the daughter of Hasdrubal. Masinissa had relented to her pleas since he was deeply in love with her and was afraid that she would take her own life rather than be a prisoner. He married her that very day in attempt to assuage her cries of grief and to save her from captivity.

The legate of Masinissa, Laelius was so enraged at the thoughtless actions of Masinissa that he had even tried to drag the pleading Sophonisba from the wedding bed, though failed when he had persuaded him to let Scipio decide the matter instead.

When Masinissa had finally met with Scipio on the matter, Scipio used flattery and politics to inform him that Rome would never accept a marriage that they had not chosen and especially to Sophonisba the daughter of their defeated foe. Masinissa reluctantly accepted the verdict and sent a slave after Sophonisba to offer her poison as the only honorable alternative to capture.

Scipio was truly distraught over this and had rebuked the young Masinissa over that thoughtless tragedy in that it had been taken so far.

Though in reality, Scipio had not truly known how much Masinissa's people had resented the idea of capture of any kind. In battles of his people, vast armies would dissipate with any hint of loss and the treat of capture—they would flee with the winds.

To calm his hot-blooded ally, he placed Masinissa to the fore of the troops and created feasts in his honor and gave him many gifts in appreciation of their friendship and even had him proclaimed king of all Numidia.

It was around this time that Hannibal had returned to Africa and began organizing his army for his final battle with Scipio. When Scipio received word of this gathering of forces he sent a request for Masinissa to join him. At Zama, Hannibal could not catch up with Scipio before the forces of Masinissa had joined his formidable enemy. With the defeat of Hannibal, his sister was taken by Masinissa as a trophy and a wife, where his blood had mingled with his to form such a noble line. Juba II's bloodline was mingled with the Greeks, Phoenicians and even with the Egyptians before the Ptolemy line was established, as well as the bloodlines of Mesopotamia and Sumer.

With that final War at its conclusion, Masinissa was able to reform his new country and to lead the people away from its scattered origins as nomads, to unify their strength with all that he had learned from the Romans. He had even greatly enhanced the cavalry and gave it order which had proved to be so valuable that his tactics were still maintained in their army at the present time. Juba knew that Masinissa greatly admired Rome, though he still looked to Carthage for inspiration and had unified the language to Punic and Greek and even adopted their religious practices. He recruited Greek and Italian settlers to create a much needed urban development to his new domain.

Masinissa had continued his support of Rome and sent them troops when needed. And even had the time through all of this to maintain a vast harem due to his status and was known for his forty-four son's not to mention his numerous daughters. He lived to be ninety years old.

In his long life-time, Masinissa even continued to torment Carthage and it's territories which Rome favored since it made them weak. His territory eventually stretched from Tacapae and all of Tripolitania from the River Muluchat in the west to Cyrene in the east.

After troubles in Rome during this time caused by Scipio's adversary Marcus Porcius Cato Censorinus which led Rome to send out a commission on behalf of the protests of Cato; for Masinissa to return some of the lands of Carthage to Rome.

In all of the turmoil caused by this in that Cato did not want either Masinissa nor Scipio to have so much power, two sons of Masinissa were attacked after their being refused entry into Carthage to plead for the exiles release. Masinissa was enraged and invaded Carthage's territory and laid siege to the town of Oroscopa. In the following battles of Carthage's retaliations, two of Masinissa's dissatisfied illegitimate son's of slaves in his harem had joined on the side of Carthage against their father. Carthage had tried to persuade the grandson of Scipio to intercede but to no avail. Masinissa and his troops swept down on Carthage and it's environs and forced their eventual surrender. After the Carthagians marched out of the camp, they were massacred by the Numidians.

The Roman state had already decided to destroy Carthage and were happy to learn of it's defeat. However, they were there to make sure that Masinissa would not gain control of it either. They sent a large retinue and began to destroy Carthage. After it's defeat, Masinissa was upset as to the verdict of the Romans in his not being able to complete his dreams and ambitions for the City at it's destruction. He was especially angered when the Romans placed the other Numidian general Hasdrubal in charge of the destroyed city of Carthage. Masinissa was reluctant to wage any battles against his own grandson.

Masinissa had refused help to the Romans after this especially when the Romans had suffered a number of setbacks and defeats and required the assistance of Masinissa. Masinissa had not aided the Romans again until his death at the age of ninety in remembrance of their betrayal. However, he did not let his anger deter him from his friendship with Scipio that was forged when he was very young. It was stipulated in his will that Scipio was to determine the division of his kingdom between his three surviving legitimate sons. Scipio, upon the death of his dear friend had given Micipsa the control of Cirta, the government and treasury. To Gulussa the control of the army and to Mastabal the control of the judicial matters setting up a wise system of checks and balances to prevent any from overthrowing the other upon the wishes of his dear friend and ally Masinissa.

Numidia joined Rome and Gulussa was by the side of Scipio at the fall of Carthage four years later.

That was the beginning of Rome's presence in Numidia. Any possible conflict between the brothers was ceased when Gulussa and Mastabal had succumbed to violent deaths from a plague that had struck the coastal cities a few years after that. The remaining son of Masinissa named Micipsa had gained control over the whole of the kingdom as well as the additional inherited lands near Carthage that the brothers had received after the death of their father.

The armies of Juba II's land became well known in their support during the reign of Micipsa in their aid of the Romans in battle. Better relations were established in the wisdom of the future kingdoms the growing power of Rome and had prospered as a result of this.

There were no conflicts until the time of Jugartha, when Rome had interceded unnecessarily in Numidia's own matters. Jugartha was the illegitimate grandson of Masinissa and originally chosen to be his heir when his remaining son Micispa had not produced his own heir to the throne. After the succession was well established in Numidia of Jugartha the son of Mastabal, suddenly the wife of Micispa had two sons one after the other and both had proved to be healthy. They were Hiempsal and Adherbal.

Jugartha had learned his military strength again from the Romans when a few years prior to that, he was sent by Micipsa, who had adopted him as heir before the birth of his two sons to support the Roman troops in their attack on Numantea. In that experience, it allowed Jugartha to learn war tactics which served him well in his later years and battles for the kingdom that he believed to be right-fully his.

Shortly after the death of Micipsa, he had Hiempsal assassinated to attain full control of Numidia. Adherbal had fled to Rome to report how Jugartha had broken the will of his father. Despite the opposition on that from Rome he aggressively acted on Rome and their complaints on his taking over the accession. He was defeated and made to walk behind in the victory parade of Gaius Marius and then put to death as was tradition.

Numidia again answered to Rome and was subdued until his own father Juba had gained control of the kingdom after the death of his father

Hiempsal, the first-born legitimate son of Micipsa.

His own father had reigned for only three years that had ended with his defeat by Julius Caesar at Thapsus. He was only six years old at that time and sent into captivity and made to walk behind the chariot in the victory parade alongside his father. That was the last time that he had seen his father or his mother in her ailing state after their defeat. His father had tried to create an empire and kingdom like his great grand-father the Great Masinissa. He probably would have succeeded had it not been for the even greater military strength of his greatest adversary Julius Caesar.

Probably due to his youth and lack of parental control, he grew to admire the man who defeated his parents in his incredible power and expertise military tactics.

As a child and into his teens he studied so much that he lost himself in the scholarly world of the written word and grew to admire the Roman's ability in military genius almost as much as the Greek civilization that they had repressed. Like his great-grandfather-Masinissa, he studied the language, art and philosophy of the cultures around him at that time. He buried himself in books to forget the yearnings that he felt for his family and homeland. He escaped through the plays of Homer and the public oratories that he constantly attended and lost himself wearing the robes of the Romans and eventually became one of them inadvertently in his quest to escape them.

When he was younger, he clung desperately to the idea of returning to his homeland and regaining his rightful command that he studied in all of his waking hours so vehemently for that eventual day; for he was adamant that he would be ready with his armory of wisdom and knowledge of all of the cultures around him. He did not realize how fast he had succumbed to their ways in his initial avoidance with being emeshed in the culture of his captive city of Rome. He felt his yearnings dissipate with his all too consuming passion for seeking more and more knowledge and found new ways to allow Octavian to grant him the privileges of traveling to encourage his studies in the world around him and in compiling vast historical resources. He traveled and gathered material for his volumes and had in the interim lost his need to return to his country too enveloped was he in his thirst for knowledge.

However, one day a year prior to this moment, Octavian approached him and requested that he finally return to his country of Numidia to become a king to the now client state of Rome. He was elated at this opportunity and had thus returned without incident, that is until his advisor had returned with yet another word from Octavian that he had arranged a marriage with him to the daughter of his defeated foes Marcus Antonius and the last Pharaoh of Egypt and the legendary Cleopatra VII.

Octavian had even insisted that he had considered her young age in the benefit that she would be easily pliable to lean towards Rome. Juba had not really even given it a second thought until he actually returned to Rome to fetch the promise of his bride and future Queen.

Though he recognized that despite her young age, she had definitely inherited the high spirits of her deceased mother of whose side she only a few years before been deprived of. Thus, the challenge began in earnest as he lay down beside her in the litter on their way to his triremes docked in the harbor at the Roman Tiber.

He felt more protective of her tiny form as she sat entranced in her thoughts beside him and relaxed any notions of suppressing her wild nature. He silently laughed that he would need that in the years ahead to keep him from becoming forever lost in his studies. He hoped that she had retained some of the knowledge that her mother was noted for in her wise rule of Egypt. That indeed would aid him and keep him well grounded in matters of state.

XIV

Cleopatra Selene's bags were added to her new husband's and they were set aboard the ship that would take them to their new home on the coast near the ruins of Carthage in a new settlement there. She grasped her brother's stylus on board and attempted to compose a letter to her beloved family left behind. The sea was too rough for any hopes of that and her thoughts wrenched too much in her new situation for any possible hopes of compiling her thoughts on the papyrus of her lesson book that muffled the cries of her baby sister in the flower that she once held in her tiny hands.

Her journey had taken her through the Roman Sea to the coast of her new home so close to her place of birth, between Egypt and Mauretania. Numidia was a land of fierce nomad tribes of the Massylians and the Massaesylians who were eventually banded together two hundred years before her birth.

A land of bloodshed by the Roman Sword as was her own homeland. She felt a kinship to her new husband in his turmoil's similar to hers. After Carthage was destroyed, Roman interest in it was renewed to the point which they kept client kings on the throne such as Hiempsal and Juba II's father, the first Juba. They were descended from Masinissa who she knew from her mother to have been a fierce yet intelligent leader. She had heard that first Juba, he new husband's father) had joined the cause of Pompey the Great and served as his most loyal supporter in Africae Provincia. Juba had defeated Caesar's representative in this fierce land called Gaius Curio and then assisted Metellius Scipio during the campaign against Caesar. Juba's father was defeated by Caesar in the battle of Thapsus and fell on his sword as the rumor was told. Though her husband told her later that he had walked beside his father in the triumphal parade behind the chariot of Julius Caesar. Caesar had then gained control of Numidia and named the province Africa Nova.

She was told that Numidia was land of fierce sunlight that would tear directly into ones very soul to rip out any essence of the Roman softness that one could possibly hold dear. This harsh environment demanded any weakness to be crushed beneath the lush pastoral soil that permeated their bones as it surrounded them. A land of fierce men who were legendary in their equine abilities so much so that they were more at peace on their horses than they were on land. Their baggage barely made it intact to what was to be her new palace. The tiny queen walked somberly towards her destiny in the dimmed shadows of her new land behind her husband in his tall Roman exterior. She hoped for a glimmer underneath of the vibrant Numidian blood, for that would be interesting indeed.

XV

The palace was situated on the coast near the ancient city of Carthage behind the ruins of the walls that surrounded it that were destroyed over a hundred years prior by the Roman leader Scipio Aemilianus and more recently by Julius Caesar. The ruins dominated the landscape until Julius Caesar had sent colonists to repopulate the area and ordered a new palace to be built for the new client king. Octavian had recently ordered further improvements and the work was steadily under the great Roman speed in progress as her initial footsteps joined into this newly reopened city and her new home. A small land to rule over and to sit by the side of her husband the most learned man of their era.

She had learned much about her new husband on her arduous journey there. In that he was sent here just one year before to rule over his own people and to squelch any possible uprisings of the rebellious and leaderless people on the orders of Octavian. Though she had learned that they were possibly being sent to Mauretania to rule over instead since Octavian had wanted the power over that small land which known for it's vast wealth in gold.

The puppet rulers of Octavian must bend to his cause. Had her husband any feelings over this, she had yet to learn. She did learn, however that he was an inspired and truly accurate historian and cartographer. He would compile many journals and logs of all of the known world around them and journeyed quite frequently for new material to add to them. He was boldly accurate for his era in that most of the prior historians had bent to the wills of their rulers. For Juba II took pride in the truth that he unraveled in his meticulous accountings of the world in which he lived.

He also encouraged Selene in her own pursuits of painfully extricating any truth from the rubbish written about her own mother. She wanted the world to know the truth and inspiration of her own mother. In gratitude she also would research some on Juba's family as well.

For it was rumored in Rome that Julius Caesar was the father of Juba's youngest sister, Aurelia. Her soft curls shone contrast of the dark locks of her parents and added a question as to her true paternal blood. But, then everyone claimed that Caesar was father to half of Rome and of the territories that he conquered. He was well known in his time for his amorous pursuits, surprisingly none of which he could legally claim from his own Roman wives. One of the most well-known was Selene's own brother Caesarion. It was also rumored that Caesar's own close confident and later murderer, Brutus was connected to Caesar through blood as well, through the mother of Brutus the legendary seductress of Rome named Servilia. For it was all the rage in gossip about Caesar and the Servilia, the ravishingly beautiful mother of Brutus to have created his younger sister Tertullia in a torrid affair that was all the rage through the streets of Rome in that age. Servilia even tried to divorce her own husband to marry him, though Caesar would not have any of that in that he stated that he would not marry an unfaithful wife. It was well-known that Caesar had divorced his second wife Pompeia, the granddaughter of Sulla for her being unfaithful to Caesar with Clodius. It was strange how Rome and Caesar noted how the poor Servilia was unfaithful to her own husband with Caesar, and no Roman seemed to give a hoot that Caesar was unfaithful in his own way to his own later legal Roman wives. Strength to the dictator and his paths chosen and let none be under foot or in his way to blemish his name.

So much controversy rambled in that troubled Rome and from its people, that it almost reminded the despairing Selene of what her own blood told.

XVI

About a year after their arrival in Numidia and their trying to establish some type of order with the scattered nomadic tribes, she had received word that her brother Alexander Helios would soon be joining them along with his new wife Iotape the Princess of Media Atropatene who was the daughter of Artavasdes, King of Media Atropatene who was the grandson of the great Mithradates who was connected to her family as well through her mother's side and who was a granddaughter herself of him. She was looking forward to seeing her distant cousin almost as much as she was in seeing her twin, Alexander Helios. She had also received word from him in a characteristic short commentary on the matter.

"My dearest sister and twin,

Elations on your marriage and upcoming birth of your first child! I am most delighted in our fates of being able to meet once again. I bring along with me my beloved wife Iotape who has a will almost as great as your own, for you will surely adore her. I will also have a letter from your friend Antonia Minor with me along with gifts from Octavia and the rest of the family who all miss you so. I will also have another surprise for you as well and cannot wait for the presentation and the look of your eyes. Don't worry, you shall definitely love it!

I also wanted to mention that not long after you had left for your new home, Antonia Major was married off to that monster Lucius Domitius Ahenobarbus. Antonia Minor, your closest friend is at present preparing for her wedding to… I'll save that information for you to read when you see her correspondence in person as per her wishes. I am sure that she will fill you in with all of the latest events that occurred since you had left.

I bid you farewell until we meet in person!

Your brother,

Helios"

Well, that soon put Selene into a rabid frenzy to establish some semblance of order in her chaotic kingdom, at least in their home and hearth and makeshift palace. She ordered the finest tapestries from Syria to adorn and cover the dusty floors of their dwelling and sent out for the most fragrant of herbs for which she would burn in the braziers along the newly painted mosaic walls. For she left no detail to any other. She also had the hidden delight in preparing the chambers for the heir to the Numidian throne. She was elated on how fast the news of her condition had spread to Rome and to the only family that she had left.

She had even paid a visit to the quarters of her husband's cavalry to inspect their living conditions as well. When everything was arranged according to her strict protocol which she had adhered to from the start she finally sat down in her favorite alcove to watch the sun drip slowly over the walls of the palace and into the star-filled ocean beneath her. Colors melted into one another and brilliantly lit up to match the cascade of emotions that she sought to keep under control at the arrival of her brother and his new wife. He long lost connection to the past and to her childhood that was disappearing with each day.

Her marriage, she assumed was better than most in that her husband was always kind and gentle to her and had even encouraged her thirst for wisdom that often matched his own.

She looked back to the first evening in their palace when they were finally able to consummate their union in the rough fortress that it was at that time. She had changed that roughshod fortress into a palace with all of the freedom that she had found herself in as a Queen and not a child captive in Rome. A Queen in her own country to rule over as her mother once had.

She fought desperately to make some sense out of all that her mother had taught her in ruling a country and empire. Though the country that she ruled over was not exactly the empire that her mother ruled over nor even that independent for that matter, she still maintained incredible amounts of power.

Juba was constantly involved with his studies and into the politics of their country and with the orders and wishes of Rome in that they were in reality only a client kingdom and they the puppets of the wishes of Rome. Still the had an advantage of distance and that both of them were not really fierce individuals as their own parents had been and would rather just worry their time with the betterment of the country rather than trying to antagonize Rome.

It was very difficult for her and Juba in gaining any type of order since most of the people had reverted back to their nomadic ways and detested any urban development that had been established by Juba's great grandfather over a hundred years ago.

They had retained to their merit a much better infantry due to the teachings of Roman warfare learned by Juba and his predecessors and had incorporated the strengths to form a better force to lend to the aid of Rome when requested.

Numidians were noted throughout history for their cavalry and their incredible skills with warfare when on horses. They had been defeated in the past only due to their half-hazardous infantry which did not have any order in the centuries past and relied solely on their cavalry to win battles.

Juba had studied commentaries on every battle that he could get hold of, no matter which country that it involved to gain a better insight. He drilled his men constantly when he was not entranced in his studies on everything else.

Due to this, Selene had learned the freedom to do whatever she wanted and had emeshed herself into the research involving everything that she could learn about her parents and had started her own chronicles, since she was not able to obtain those of her mother she had to rely on the writings of others, many who had not even met her and from her own memories of growing up in the shadow of such a great woman.

I

27 B.C.E.

Selene knew that the date was approaching when she would be able to catch site of the ship carrying her brother and his new wife and every morning of that week she had been up before dawn walking the recently plastered walls hoping to view it as it approached the harbor. For the past three horrible days she had to retreat with the sun, when finally on this fourth day she was rewarded with her persistence and increasing apprehension and joy to see her twin once again.

She was about to retire for the evening once again, when she noticed a speck in the distance that she had originally though was nothing, for it grew noticeably larger by the minute, until she could finally make it out to be what it was! In response to her desperate inner pleadings and fervent prayers to her secret and beloved Isis, she heard the horns from the palace call out in entreaty to the approaching retinue of ships bearing her brother at long last! She cautiously ran down the steps heavy with her first child in her otherwise young form to meet the awaiting embrace of her husband who had graciously left his studies to be with her in this moment.

She had not really seen that much of her new husband since their initial days of marriage in that he was so engrossed in his studies and determination to make his kingdom whole once again that he seemed almost to have grown taller since their last meeting. She thought herself silly in this apprehensive musing of this moment since she knew that it was not possible in that he was fully grown at the time of their first meeting. But, alas was more than grateful with his presence silently by her side as they watched the approaching ships to dock safely in their harbor.

By the time the ships were docked in the harbor and the passengers unloaded, she and her husband had just arrived in their respective litters and were placed down softly in wait. The torches cast a somber glow over the people that unsteadily arrived to bow down to them. Tinted in the glow of the evening luminescence they appeared eerily before them. She had observed what she had assumed was her new sister in law by the form she had immediately guessed was her brother being carried by his physician and was bundled heavily in blankets. In Iotape's arms was another bundle which clung to her form blocking any possible recognition from Selene.

She ran to the side of her brother wrapped in a cocoon by his physician who was thus carried due to his being too weak to walk from a sickness that he had caught on board that had grown worse as they approached her new kingdom. Iotape stood a distance from Selene as she rushed to her brother's side with Juba trailing behind her. She gazed into the glassy eyes of her brother and knew that he did not have long to live, that he had probably used the last of his strength to keep himself from dying until he saw her. Juba realized the danger of his wife being exposed in her current state and rushed to softly extricate her from his side and had to nudge her carefully so she realized his sincerity and concern in this matter.

Tears filled her eyes and her body began to tremble and all went dark in the reality of the moment that she had prepared so long for that was all too swiftly taken away from her. All of her hopes and dreams were dashed in such a rapid moment that the ground was unsteady beneath her feet. Her earlier curiosity about the form in Iotape's arms and Iotape herself stolen away just as quick.

For at that moment her own physician, whom she had recently begun to call her shadow grasped the dire situation almost a little too slowly and had to be prodded by her husband—rushed once again to her side to whisk her away from the dock and into her litter with swift orders to hurry the Queen to her palace chambers for her rest.

Juba remained behind to set things in motion for the travel weary passengers and rushed Helio's to the care of his physician and saw to Iotape and the form in her arms which he found out was a small child with golden blonde ringlets and fast asleep.

His slaves placed them in litters with all of their belongings and all proceeded at a rapid pace to the palace gates and into their new quarters. He followed behind the forms of Iotape and the child to make sure that they were alright as he knew that his own wife would do had the circumstances of the meeting with her brother and twin been any different.

It was then that he noticed the form of a small boy that had been sleeping in all of the confusion against the wall and almost forgotten by the people around him. He picked up the boy, not knowing who he was and put him on a cot next to the pallet that Iotape was sound asleep in with the small girl-child tucked safely in her arms.

His thoughts ran rampid with possible explanations on the two unexplained guests but he turned on his heels and headed towards the part of the palace harem that his wife ruled over and to her sleeping side. He felt sorry that he had not been by her side that much lately and wished that he knew what to do and how to comfort her in her apparent distress and the knowledge of the condition of her brother. He just sat down beside her sleeping form that was probably prostrate from sheer emotional exhaustion.

II

Later on the next day, Selene had finally found stable grounds for her thoughts. The potion that her physician had given her had finally begun to wear off. She slowly washed all of her pain away the best that she could from her almost emaciated body that had succumbed to her violent sobs before the potion had taken effect, until she felt whole again. Her slow grounding was added with a small fraction of a hope that her brother would recover from his malady. Though in her soul she knew the truth. She motioned to her attendants as she was dressed in her stola and veils with her toga lined in her regal purple and as her long tresses were at last in place surrounding her tear lined face. Her attendants knew her thoughts which were the talk of the palace the evening before and of their orders to keep her from the side of her brother until the court physician had deemed it safe for her to be by his side.

"My lady, please do not stress from this for you might harm your babe that is almost ready to be born. Please think of the babe inside of you and that your husband was quite distressed over this decision knowing how well you care for your brother…" Bowed her more boisterous maidservant Serian. Confused, though silently acceding to that order she weakly responded to the situation, "Well, what about the Princess Iotape, surely she must be exhausted from her journey and needs comfort in her time of need." Partly in question and partly in demand. "As you wish my lady, after you." Serian's tall and nimble form followed in the trail of her mistress and she climbed the stairs to the outer halls of the palace harem where she had prepared the chambers for Iotape.

III

Upon her arrival to the sitting chamber she arrived to the dim evening glow of the scented oil lamps that had arrayed the room and bathed the occupants sitting in hushed conversation therein. Iotape was sitting in the forefront of the room and had looked up at the sound of her arrival. Iotape was beautiful indeed and had long strait amber brown hair that flowed deftly to her waist and surrounded her form as she gracefully reclined on the large pillows that had filled the room on the softest of carpets that Selene could find for their comfort. Iotape had eyes of violet with long graceful lashes that she knew her brother would have fallen for even if this were not an arranged marriage of state.

Her long and tapered fingers stopped suddenly from their place in soft conversation with the tiny form curled up next to Iotape, which in a rush of newfound glory Selene had recognized as her precious little sister

Arsinoe. Ptolemy Philedelphos from out of nowhere had rushed to his older sister walking into the room. He stormed into her arms, though was carefully softened by Selene holding him slightly away before the impact with her unborn baby. She held him in front of her when he realized what he had almost done. "Why sister, you grown up already! You look like Momma!" She crushed him as close as she could with that inadvertent reference to their mother and the realization that she was all grown up too being close to her fourteenth year. A woman in her world. Arsinoe screamed in delight, "Seeny! Your back!!" and ran to her side and wrestled Philedelphos for the best hug from their big sister.

Selene and her younger siblings rushed their words together exuberantly in a tidal wave of emotion and had almost lost Iotape to the shadows, when Selene rushed to her side with her siblings," Please Iotape forgive me, for I certainly did not expect any of this. Have all of your needs been met since your arrival? Is there anything that you would request of me and my husband, I will definitely arrange it. Please, you are welcome sister to our home." With this she walked over to Iotape who had stood up to receive the blessings of her new sister. Gratefully she sank into the embrace of her new sister. Tears streamed down her face which mingled with those of her sister in their many scattered emotions for both were still very young girls in truth and had just experienced many vast all too grown up emotions in a very short time. For Iotape was only eleven years old herself and newly thrust into a marriage with a husband, that she felt was adorable, though had barely known and on their journey away from all she had known her whole life and family-to try to nurse him from a rapid illness that had struck him from nowhere and to comfort two very young and precocious children who had been trust into her care immediately after her wedding.

Serian took her cue from the moment and rushed to the attention of the younger Ptolemys to scoop them in her arms so that Selene could talk with her fellow princess. She had carried them out of the room to give her mistress some privacy.

"Iotape, please tell me all, for it is so nice to meet someone my own age and a princess like I was" She looked down to the floor almost in respect for her understanding of this princess's lost childhood.

"Your highness, please forgive the circumstances for which we have all arrived to your generosity…"

"Nonsense, all that is mine you are welcome to, for you are married to my other half, please go on." She motioned for Iotape to recline on the pillows that arrayed the room and lay down herself arranging the pillows as a sort of fort from the world outside as one would when a child, which at that moment with a girl close to her age, she felt that she was. When she had finished her pillow arrangement she bent her head earnestly to await Iotape's response and to hear all that had occurred.

"We were married a month ago and Octavia and her brother the Imperator had decided best that we go along with your siblings to your side. Octavia had vehemently pleaded for your cause and had grown sad for your brother and sister constantly crying out for you. She wanted to see you altogether again. She was also assisted in this by your friend and cousin Antonia Minor, whose letter that I have along with some other letters."

She fumbled in her robes and retrieved some scroll that were travel worn. Selene took them gratefully and besieged her to continue.

"Helios is very kind and so handsome, I fell instantly in love with him. We talked since the moment we met at the state wedding to be broken off by his sudden illness. I do not know what ails him and dread that I cannot be by his side, your physician has not determined if it was contagious yet, though I had been allowed briefly to see him this morning. His health is failing rapidly and he does not recognize me at all!" Her eyes clouded at the telling of this and Selene fought to control her own emotions at the telling of this. "Octavia thought it best that your siblings were by your side with the stipulation from Octavian or Julius Caesar as he is called to arrange their nuptials. They will be returned to Rome if you do not heed him when they are arranged." Selene felt a chill at the statement, but knew that she would acquiesce to his wishes, but fervently hoped that they would have a chance to grow some more together before they were taken away to kingdoms far away from her side. She had not even expected this time with them and had felt that that day in Rome was the last that she would ever see them again, yet rejoiced in their stolen reunion in time!

"Hush, that is understood, Iotape, for I had not even expected this time with them and will bend to the will of my superior, for we are only client rulers for Rome and it is their will that we ultimately abide to." She continued, "I wish for us to be friends for I understand all too well what it is like for all that you have known to be taken away so suddenly without any say in the matter. As princesses, we are political pawns and I am glad that you have found such a wonderful husband as my brother and I hope with all of my soul that he is not taken away from us, for we both need him!"

IV

After her meeting with Iotape, when Selene was alone in her chambers she wrapped herself in her blankets and retrieved the scrolls and began to unravel them. Octavia had written to her on the details of her newly arrived siblings and mentioned that she had felt sorry for the way in which they had parted and could not stop worrying over how much they wanted to be with their older sister. Considering all that had happened to them and how desperately she had grown to love them, she acceded to their wishes no matter how that distressed her so. She begged Selene to update her on their progress with all of the details since she truly missed them. She had worked very hard to convince her brother to let them go to her in Numidia and only did it because what they had been through at so young an age. She understood how important a close family was since she had nourished one of her own with her children and the son of Fulvia. She further mentioned that Iully missed her so much and had sent along a scroll from him as well. She read the letter from Iully and reveled in his humor on everything that happened to him in his life. He told her that he missed her goofy ways and how she had always managed to beat in willful debate the undefeated Antonia Minor, when no one else had before Selene's arrival. He was glad that his half sister had finally met her match in Selene and knew that she missed her so. He assured her that he would take good care of both of the Antonia's and of Octavia as well. He had also mentioned that he had become friends with Julia, the daughter of

Octavia and his first wife Scribonia. His second wife Livia was constantly pestering them and sent Julia crying back to her father who was planning on marrying her to his friend and advisor Marcus Vipsanius Agrippa. Julia's husband Octavia's son from Metellius had died recently and rather suddenly leaving Julia without a husband. Her father was fervently working to remedy that before she got herself into trouble. Iully was upset over this since they were only friends and rather upset that his uncle would not consider him as a suitable match for her. He did not like Agrippa in that he was only a commoner and not of patrician blood as were they all, he appealed to her in her royal blood and position to talk with his uncle. Selene quietly knew that she would, but that she did not carry any weight at all with Octavian in that she was too close in relation to her mother, even though she was dead for a few years now. She knew that he suffered all too much from all of the damage that she had caused, especially since she was a woman and knew that Octavian was very reserved about women and felt that they should stay out of the business of men. She silently vowed that she would give it her best try, for she truly loved her Iully as did all of the children under that roof in that short time. Such a short time to have affected so many lives, but she knew that it had thankfully to do with Octavia, the woman she had tried to hate.

She then arrived at the letter that she was waiting most for, the one from Antonia Minor.

"***Greetings sister!***

Oh How I truly wish that I was there by your side! How fast that life travels for us and how short a time that we have to actually be children! I morn the day that you had to leave and knew that I was soon to share the same fate with what my uncle plans for me. He married my sister off to a nasty man by the name of Ahenobarbus, who has red bristly hair and a straggly beard. Poor Antonia! How she dreaded her fate but carried herself like royalty. She has resigned to her villa in resignation to her fate. Oh, the Gods be cursed when they decided to take away a girl's right to chose her husband. Then again as Momma always tells us that it probably is for the best, for if we were left to choose for ourselves, who only knows what we would end up with for men when they finally grew

up! She says that after the glamour of the day-dreamy love wears off, you have to deal with the reality left behind and hope that he is responsible enough not to lose the family fortune and the dowry left for us! And most often those boys that are handsome grow tired of you and look to the next pretty girl they find, leaving you all alone to deal with an empty house full of babies! How sad the fate of some women! I hope that does not happen for me. For I am to be married next month to Drusus. Momma told me that he was in our house when I was a baby when his own mother, Livia was forced into hiding here when her husband Tiberius upset my uncle Octavian. My Uncle forced Tiberius to divorce his wife, Livia when she was pregnant with Drusus and had little Tiberius by her side, so that he could marry her instead! My husband to be was raised at the palace with his mother who my uncle truly loves and raised with his older brother to be his heir after his daughter from his first wife, Julia. So much has happened here and I miss gossiping with you and sneaking into the atrium to listen in on Momma's parties to get all of the dirt from Rome! Livia sends her love and concern to you as well for she is truly a dear and close member of this family. She is ever by the side of my uncle and dotes on him so. He is always smiling at her and stopping sentences in mid-thought to send over a kiss to her! Sometimes is quite ridiculous. But, then I have never been in love. Though I do think that Drusus might have potential. He is kind of tall and awkward though and has pocks on his face, I do not think that he looks pleasant. Though Momma assures me that he is in his worst stage of development and will grow into a man rather nicely. I hope so! I will definitely let you know! Please let me know all of the details when you have your baby, since I am to have them too for Rome, who knows, at this rate, someday, they might even be kings. I believe with the way Rome is—it might just lead to that and we could both be Queens! Imagine that! I miss you with all of my heart and beg that we will someday see one another again!

Kisses and all of that,

Antonia Minor"

She gathered that scroll and all of the others and held them close to her breast and let her soul and heart combine in the cries of despair and joy for too many things in her life.

V

The next day after not hearing word from the physician and she had felt confident about her meeting with Iotape, she found herself wandering the corridors despite the warnings from the palace physician and her husband in her condition. She slowly made her way to the chambers that held her brother in yearning to be by his side as she was through most of her whole life when it was normal and perfect for her. Her slippers trailed against the marble hallway that was recessed by alcoves containing torches since this was in an almost remote section. Her fingernails trailed the walls behind her in her silent walk to some sort of normalcy in her world turned upside down. She greeted the sentries as she approached and knew that it would be guarded since her husband knew her all too well in her desperation to visit her brother who lay prone in his illness and helpless. She had prepared for this moment just moments before in her racing mind by begging to change garments with one of her chamber slaves.

The stiff homespun and repaired garment folded around her form in concealment though her graceful long fingers might have given her status away in that they were soft and unused to toil. She carried a basket in her other hand filled with bread she had taken from her own chambers and made her way ever forward. It seemed to take so long in her mind this small journey, though had lasted all too long before this day in that she had once thought that she would never see him again at all. She bowed submissively to the guards as she made her ever slow progress.

At last she arrived to the antechamber that contained the form of her brother. A waft of incense had arrived by her feet from the room in silent greeting to her screaming soul. She peeked into the room and had found his form alone. She did not know how long that this moment of opportunity would last, so she stole her chance to run into the hoped for embrace of her brother. As she approached his form she had stood back to completely enclose this moment in it's stark reality.

The chamber was bathed in shadows that allowed only a fraction of light in from the outside though a tall arched window that had been covered in drapery. The chamber was covered in heavy drapes probably in an attempt to let the magic of the incense do it's work on his person. She could feel the vibrations of the room in the many prayers in invocations performed there very recently. The torches that were by his side seemed to have left behind the essence of them being recently lit. Her thoughts wondered mutely why he was abandoned seemingly only seconds before her arrival, when the harsh realization struck her with such force that she had to steady her violently trembling body so that she would not fall on her brother as he lay there in the slumber that she had thought that he was in when she first walked into the dreary room. His soul had passed without her being there! She sat in numb horror on a small space beside his body in the cot. It was wrapped in the finest of blankets and robes and his face peeked though them. His eyes were shut inside an empty shell of what was so recently her Helios. Through the robes she had found his left hand closest to her and she grasped it and held it with all of her strength, despite it's emaciated condition and the coldness that seemed to fill the room, she held it truly and reverently. Hoping to catch his soul and knew that it was too late. How could Isis have let this happen again, too many people were wrenched from her before she even had the chance to let them know how much she really loved them. She still desperately needed her mother, now more than ever since she had recently become one herself. She was afraid for all that she did not know and would never get the chance to know.

She had felt before this moment that Helios was left behind with her as her consolation of the events in her life, a gift from the Goddess. When she had left Rome she was heartbroken but held on to the notion that she would someday be able to see Helios and her little Ptolemy and Arsinoe again. For she was traveling as a part of her duty as a princess and valuable asset to Rome. She knew that even had the events in her life had not occurred, she would have still been sent away in this part of her life to serve a husband as it was part of her duty. She wiped away the tear that went along with the thought of her oldest brother Caesarion that should have been the next king of Egypt. Instead her world was shattered and Egypt was no more.

She wiped away all of the fear that she had that her brother might have died of a plague of some sort, which could have been entirely possible. However, no one else aboard that convoy that brought him there had died or displayed any of the symptoms. Only the Goddess knew the cause of his demise.

Just then the physician had returned to the room, his ancient form bent over and startled in surprise at finding her here," My lady, I had just sent over someone to send word to you of this…My heartfelt condolences to you." He bent his head in reverence to the moment and of seeing her there clinging to her brother, her head lost in his wasted form in desperation.

"Why, Asandros, why did this happen?" She implored to the weary and exhausted physician.

"I believe that he had a noxious poison in his chest that had been rapid in it's destruction. After careful observation, I had noticed that there were no signs of leprosy, or any other kind of pestilence that could have spread through the palace. I would have sent for you when I had deemed that there was no fear for you, but he grew increasingly worse. He had in incredible thirst and hunger, though could not keep anything down. His body wasted right before by eyes. I was so busy and had not slept trying to help him to keep some nourishment in him. He was in such pain. I had never witnessed the progression of the wasting sickness in one so young and so devastatingly fast. There was no time in sending word, for I had hoped that after most of his torment he would relax enough to receive some kind of respite or be able to hold something down, even water. Just when I had thought that the worst of it was over and I had felt that there might have been some hope in his gaining ground or recovery and his violent convulsions had ceased, his soul left his body. I am so sorry your highness not to have been able to have you by his side. But it confused even myself with the swift nature of it." With a silence that followed his torrent of words and frustration, he collapsed in a heap of the weary on a bench by the bed and enclosed his head in his hands.

The room had then taken on a more somber perspective and she wearily embraced it to fall asleep in her brother's arms. His arms were still in the prime of youth like hers and his still looked like those of a boy's and would never become strong like their father's. Her soul left the moment to travel to the land of dreams, perhaps a last gift of Isis to her.

* * * * *

...Before her in her mind she observed a vast ocean, stretching out before her eyes. She wondered if it could be the very one that she is sitting beside, though sensed that it was in a very distant part of it. To the right of her fixated vision, she noticed a woman walking beside the shore. Her long amber hair flows out in waves behind her footsteps in the sand. She is looking for something, she appears as if she is lost, though she is not. Behind her a village is burning from waves of ash pouring down from the sky and from the mountain nearby, the smell of innocent blood lingers in the air, as if to catch up to her and capture her in it's destruction. The ash is swiftly engulfing the once pretty sea-side village on the shore in the background. The woman walks idly, as if out of place with her desolate surroundings. She is looking for someone. She calls out, though the ocean drowns out her voice in it's anger. She walks over to a shape in the distance ahead of her gaze. She walks slowly towards it. Her steps quicken to a brisk pace as she reaches the confines of her vision. She stops suddenly near the shape. The woman realizes that it is the shape of a lone figure sprawled out on the beach, still before her. As the vision of the woman on the beach clears, the observation and eventual recognition of the figure, send her form into wails of agony. She runs close to the figure and wraps her form around it, as if in protection. She pounds that prostrate figure, is if begging for it to stand up and talk to her. The figure is that of a young man, bearing an uncanny resemblance to her. The man on the sand returns no response to the wails of anguish emanating from the core of her being. Time seems to stand still or becomes all times at once, as if in rapture of the horrid moment being played out on the shores of the violent ocean. It seems as if the ocean's response to the moment corresponds with that of the mourning woman. The figure of the man lies still before her and is covered with the tears of the woman and the ocean. The figure is drenched in tears and lies still, ignoring the empty pleas of the woman in her sorrow. "The water will be their downfall if they heed

not my words..." This voice fills the picture before her and buries the screams of the woman. Not knowing from whence the voice comes to them. The woman wails on trembling in the throes of her grief. The ocean cries out in agony over the punishment.

The woman then realized that she could do no more and stands up and with a fresh rush of adrenalin rushed back to the city being buried by ash to look for a child in her care and for her lover who is protecting the child while she ran out to find what she had found on the beach...She was afraid that she would fail them as well as the also looked out to sea and saw the many boats leaving filled with the only survivors of her home. Desperately she ran back to find them..."

*****

When she awoke from her trance by the side of her brother, the remnants of her vision were swiftly fading away. They seemed to real, so close to the pain that she was feeling, though could find no meaning for it. For it was not herself that had mourned but I woman that she had never seen before. She felt close to that woman that the vision had revealed to her. Was it some sort of echo of the past, or something that had yet to happen in time? With her trainings of Isis that she held close to her from her mother, she hurried out of the chamber, leaving a confused Asandros in her wake.

She dropped down her concealing garments revealing her royal garb underneath in her wake leaving a confused sight to those who witnessed her flight.

At last in the sanctuary of her royal chamber she made swift progress to her writing desk and reached frantically for her scrolls on divination in search of some explanation for such a vision at moments subsequent to her brother's death. Her soul elated when she had at last grasped the document that she was looking for. She held it out before her knowing that it might contain some reason for what she beheld in her minds that needed an answer. It was ancient and almost falling apart and the inks to soft it was almost lost. Her eyes traveled across the sacred text before her until she found the passage that she was searching for. It read...

"To those born with the sight, visions of great prophesy are endowed to them. To ignore the prophesy would be dangerous and heretical to the Gods. Visions are most brought for to those gifted at moments of extreme stress or solitude. There has been no reason found why extremes of emotions are necessary for this gift to emanate, thus it does.

A prophetess born of this mighty nation was the most valued we have seen by the name of Cleopatra III, Euergetes, wife of our beloved Pharaoh Ptolemy VIII Euergetes. Who was a twin at birth, in which her sister died soon after their birth. She and her brother the Pharaoh, were the children of Ptolemy Soter and his concubine who was a noted seer in her homeland of Syria. The blood of this woman had left behind remnants of her gift to those of her line. A family prophesy of water held forth and told by her of her future generations. Difficult to grasp since Egypt holds it's well-being with water. She had told of a dream of her witnessing the last of their line being all consumed by the water of the universe with each death being on or near water, with the very last of the line ending with not being able to evade destruction by not being saved by the same water that would destroy all of the others before them"

Selene tried desperately to find some sort of reason to those words, but had vainly given up, knowing that it somehow pertained to her and the children that she carried in her womb. Had not the last of the Kings of Egypt been destroyed with her mother. Yet the life of the line lived on and would spread from any children that her remaining brother and sister might have besides her own children. She felt oddly like that prophetess Cassandra, whom no one would listen to until it was too late and all of Troy was destroyed. It would have been avoided had someone heeded her warnings. Cassandra was a twin like herself and she felt a close kinship to her, since her twin was the famous Paris who fell in love with the ill-fated and adulterous Helen of Sparta.

She knew that in their highly advanced and modern era, no one would heed her words either on the destruction of the illustrious line of the mighty and most powerful of all of the Cleopatra's, her beloved and much missed mother.

She decided to watch how her life panned out instead and to silently watch vigilantly her children and siblings and to slyly keep them away from water. When they were old enough she would beseech them to take heed in her strictest of confidences and warnings. She felt responsible as the only one with the power in the preservation of their line.

She still wondered how Helios was affected by the water prophesy, was it tainted water that he had drunk from prior to their departure? She would inquire into that carefully. As to her parents…she knew that her father had fell on his own sword after battle of Actium was lost and they thought they were at peace, when Octavian snuck over to Alexandria and attacked her parent's unaware. She knew that her father was beside the harbor in his tent when all of his hopes for any future were dashed and he ran into his sword, especially after he had heard mistakenly that my mother was dead when he found out that she was sent as a prisoner to their own mausoleum by Octavian.

Her mother, as well was aided on by water herself. This Selene knew in her soul of truth. She could almost see her mother lamenting over the form of her father and hear the echoes of her grief through the palace walls and enclosure in her exquisite pain. She could feel the form of her numb mother after knowing that she could do no more for the man that she loved, when she slowly made her way to the side of Octavian to plead for some type of bargain so that she would not have to walk in his triumph. She trembled with the echo of this infamous moment when her mother knew that her pleadings were deftly ignored and almost mocked. Her mother's essence slowly trod to the temple of Isis by the loud and onerous waves of their rocky harbor and begged the Goddess for guidance. For silently she knew the truth of the moment. For she knew in the recesses of her life and all that she held dear, that her mother was answered by the waves of what she had to do. The waves had told her mother what to do…

With that truth revealed to her and all that had occurred, in a wave of emotion bitter and angry, she violently burst out with her silent torments of fury in her destiny. Alone in her chamber she clutched at her blanket as she threw herself upon her pallet and let herself be enveloped by the waves of hatred she felt for Isis. The Goddess that her mother had been so faithful to and had betrayed them and her. She fervently made the silent vow—as she let no sound of her torment escape her room. She vowed that she would rear her children in reverence to their family prophesy and that they would be educated and not to forget those before them in the line of her mother. They would learn to respect and hopefully avoid any of this. She would make sure that they would be educated in any sacred writings and ancient religions and powers that could possibly save them from it all. For she vowed that her children and siblings would not share her torment at the loss of so many from this horrible prophesy.

She would be especially weary to any twins born to this line, since the visions seemed to correlate with them and gain power. She was pass on the chronicles to the twins in each generation and make sure they were well away of where they came from and what was deep inside of them.

VI

They day that dawned was filled with an omen of blood-red shadows that grew from the earth to touch all of those who were there to mourn Helios and to add his body to the land of the Gods. The body was adorned in her brother's royal toga and the crown of their land of Egypt. Selene' had wanted his body preserved like her grandfather's and laid to rest in a tomb in her family mausoleum, but Octavian would have none of that since Ptolemy had not really ruled at all and was not considered a Pharaoh and deemed that Helios would still be given a traditional Roman funeral. Emissaries were sent in the stead of Octavian, now known as Caesar Augustus to attend. Selene looked on and lost herself to the moments at hand in respect for her lost twin. She was unaware of Iotape standing solemnly beside her and of the of her sister and brother in the arms of her husband to the right of her as she looked on to her brother and watched as the pyre was lit and his body was fed to the Roman Gods in the heavens above them. Her tears followed his essence to the sky as she stood there transfixed and oblivious to time which had seemed to still in respect for her brother.

The sky gradually consumed all of the onlookers and mourners in radiant shades of umber and maroon and at last to the rays of a vibrant day before them. Though all present on that day were unaware of the tragic beauty and held on to the time at hand. Hands searched desperately in silence to those they loved beside them and to almost keep them from the same fate. They held on to their humanness and stood fixed in their fear of their own deaths all to imminent and unknown in the way of the Gods. Their own mortality hoped fervently for more time to have been by the side of Helios, for all present had been touched by his short life in some way or other and all had fond memories of him. Juba had only met him briefly in Rome before the marriage and was touched by the closeness the twins had between them.

Juba leaned close to his new and precious wife and held her younger brother and sister closer to his side and sent out thoughts of love to his wife in this grave moment for her.

I

26 B.C.E.

Three days after that even, Selene went into a premature labor. Despite her age, it went relatively well considering that she not only had one baby, but another soon followed. The whole palace was in uproar over the event and all prayed that she would be fine as well as the heir to the throne. Her body feverishly and violently swayed in the throes of labor and after many hours into the early morning hours a small girl was born and then minutes after another small girl was born to them. The palace rejoiced in that Selene seemed to heal so soon after the deliverance of her first born and twins at that. The first born child they named Jubilla Helia Cleopatra in honor of her brother and the second born was named Selena Antonia Drusilla after her beloved friend. Selene called them respectively and playfully Helia and Tonia.

II

Helia and Tonia were growing fast and the days went by in a blur for Selene who was always with her new daughters. She insisted in their complete upbringing and was content with each gurgle and smile directed from these two inspirations in her life. She was determined to be as good a mother as her own was in supervising every aspect of their upbringing. They slowly helped to wash away the tears at the loss of her own twin and relished her brother and sister and how well they had adjusted to the palace life in her new home of Numidia. Iotape was enthralled on how Selene wanted to be always present in the rearing of her own children. For Iotape was used to the Median way of the tutor and court physicians rearing the royal palace children. She had only seen her parents when young on a few state occasions. Her own mother was one of several royal wives, and she was only one of the twenty princesses.

Iotape had reveled in how Juba insisted that Selene was the only queen for him and that he did not need a vast harem as most kings of that time and even from his own line required. For Juba's own great-grandfather, the great Masinissa had many wives and a large harem. Masinissa had over forty-four sons and countless daughters. There was a political purpose in establishing allied kingdoms with the marriages of the offspring. But, Juba had witnessed all in recent generations on how much controversy could spring from that arrangement as well as civil wars. He firmly believed that way too much blood had been shed in his kingdom and others over the disputes of heirs. He wanted no such thing to occur in his own kingdom. He had enough trouble in trying to get all of the nomad tribes in uniting in his own land than to have to deal with that same thing in his own royal house.

Iotape thought this beautiful, though did wonder about her own fate, now that she had no connection to keep her in this strange and close family. So completely unlike what she was raised in. She had been only one of a number of princesses born to her family and had spent her childhood waiting for that moment when her father, who had barely seen her saw how best she could add value to her family in her marriage.

She had ended up with Helios since she was one of the lesser daughters. He would not have been a king of Egypt, since it was now property of Rome and she would never had been a queen anyways. Though, Helios did have the royal blood required to take her as wife from her family and had funds for which to pay her dowry as well from inheritance, enough allowed by Octavian, provided that he agreed to the marriage with Helios as a benefit to Rome.

Still, Iotape had grown to love this strange royal family that loved each other and had dreaded the moment when they would have to send her back to her father. She had spent much time with Selene and her new twins and the younger Ptolemys to wile away her frustration in her predicament of being in Numidia without a husband.

She was sitting by the gardens on that particular day watching the guard practice their new infantry moves that Juba had learned from Greek documents in the Peloponnesian war. Juba had loved to teach ancient military techniques to his own forces and incorporate some new ones. She felt that he was a very learned and creative ruler and would do well for Selene. She was also aware of the political unrest in Numidia at that time and of how Numidia was in drastic need of new measures in order to unite the tribes that had grown apart in the absence of a ruler for so long. She languished the warm summer sun and her ability to witness this. For growing up she was never allowed to roam freely on her own and had spent most of her life in a secluded harem.

She was so grateful of this new way of life, she basked in the warmth of the sun that had melted into her pores releasing any dreads that she had recently felt. The ethereal breeze was almost nonexistent, but it did not tarnish the joy she felt in life this one stolen moment as she sat on the side. She even held out her hand for a bee that was passing by, oblivious to the sting that might come as a result. None came, while the bee lazily buzzed over the skin of her fingers then merrily went on it's own way. She held her hand over her eyes to shade the rays of the sun and she turned towards the palace. For her eyes had queried a shadowed form of a sentry as he approached her position. He indicated that she should follow him to the palace. Was this the summons on so perfect a day that she had dreaded. She followed the young boy in trepidation of the news.

III

In the palace, it was cool from the strategically placed arches catching any crosswinds to their advantage. She walked on through the tall Corinthian pillars that marked her steps. The marble floors so cool they seeped through her slippers and she tred behind for the news in wait for her. She knew this was big, for she had not been interrupted during the day before like this. They had actually sought her out.

She arrived in Selene's waiting chambers and awaited the summons of the Queen and her presence. She had grown to adore Selene over these past few months with her and to respect her greatly. For she felt that Selene was the only possible match for a wise man such as Juba. Those two will do well in rule together, for they are in complete compliment to one another.

Selene had her hair done up in an ancient Macedonian fashion that complimented her long narrow face and large vivid eyes. Her hair was worn up in a loose and large bun with tendrils of wavy ringlets cleverly arranged to appear there as if by chance. She admired Selene on how regal she had always conducted herself, even in the most extreme and personal circumstances. For her royal blood was always there and obvious to anyone in her presence. Yet, Selene had the uncanny way of looking at a person so completely, that the person would instantly fall into her confidence in her sincerity and genuine interest to those in her presence. That is what set her apart from other royal people, the personable way she conducted herself that all who met her were instantly willing to devote themselves to her and her many causes.

For Iotape knew of most of the causes that Selene worked for. Selene not only was greatly involved in her own family, but was constantly busy in the palace and in the land they ruled over trying to form many alliances for the benefit of Numidia in hoping to band together all of the shattered tribes in the cause for a united Numidia. She worked constantly by Juba's side in matters of state. Juba granted his wife the unheard of almost equal status in dealing with politics. It was more admired since Selene was still so young, but had fast proved how much she had actually retained from her mother in statecraft and instinct.

"Iotape, I hope all treats you well here..."

"Yes, my lady and I thank you immensely for your kindness as well as your husband's." Her eyes shifted down in uncertainty.

"Oh, don't you worry, for I see that you must have an idea as to why I called you here." Iotape assented that she believed that she knew the matter at hand. Selene continued and had reached down to pull forward a scroll that she had to her side that was hidden from the initial view upon the entrance of Iotape to this chamber. "I did not want to bother you with this matter until things were settled. You see I have been in correspondence with your father on the matter of the death of my brother and your husband. You father had initially wanted you back for a further alliance that he had in mind, but..." Selene gazed at Iotape and had let the tension build in the room for a moment before she continued on..." I had written to him of my need for you here at the palace." She had observed the smile brighten the features of Iotape her new found friend and continued. "I had written to him of what a great asset you have been to my brother and sister and my daughters of course. I had also requested that you may stay for a few more years and that you were young and still had plenty of years to still make a profitable marriage for his kingdom. I also mentioned that he could probably find a better arrangement in the interim than the one that he had mentioned in letter to a governor in Judea that has asked for your hand. For in that marriage you would only be a lesser wife. I mentioned that he could search for a better opportunity for Media and to not just take that first offer. He agreed and decided to let you assist me with the children." With that, Selene was elated in the excited reaction she had from Iotape at the news and threw away all formalities and sprang up from her seat to breach the distance and to embrace her new friend and sister. The two girls hugged and giggled at the news.

IV

As the days marched on and the palace life had begun to take on a new shape of contentment, the tides began to turn. For outside of the protected walls there was much chaos and battles fought over borders and tribal leadership. Almost as if Rome meant nothing to them. So much blood was being shed that something had to be done about the matter. Juba had set up extra patrols through the cities and fortified them even further. He had even requested troops from Rome and neighboring cities to their aid in reigning some order.

The royal family was under strict orders not to leave the palace compound upon danger of their very lives. For there was constant threat to end the monarchy in their desire to win back their early nomad life that they felt viciously taken from them over the centuries. The general populace felt that the royal family was merely the puppets of Rome and cared nothing for them. They desperately wanted ancient traditions upheld and not the call to Roman leadership from their King.

Every statue and building that Juba had built in desperation to culture the country was destroyed along with threats towards his and the royal family's lives. Selene was concerned at the constant sleepless nights of her husband and mercurial pace that he set in policy making. Each policy and law made for the betterment of the people was ignored and mocked. She observed the heavy furrows which sprang up on her husband's once perfect and ageless brow. She knew that their rule was waning and that it really had nothing to do with them. The people of this aggressive land simply did not want any kind of leadership to take them from their nomad way of life. It was difficult to get them to farm the valuable grain lands for Rome and other countries let alone themselves. For they did not tolerate order of any kind. Though still in their chaotic way of life, the country had still been the leader in grain and wheat production with it's many inland prairies and vast pasture lands.

The people in general just wanted to be left alone from the demands of the fast encroaching Roman society. For urbanization was truly abhorrent to them and their way of life. She helplessly watched the country slipping away from them and had actually begun to fear for their very lives and for her daughters and younger siblings. She had begun to hear their nomad chants daily, of how they despised her and her husband as the puppets of Rome as they seemed to echo upon the very walls of the palace.

I

26 B.C.E.

In Numidia, Juba continued his studies but still had time for Selene to learn that he was to become a father again-he deftly ignored the angry sounds below the walls of his palace to take care of the business of his families future. Juba was elated at this and then had begun to asses the potential marriages for his children that lay ahead in the future. He thought about the family in Rome that was currently gaining status as the first empire due to the aggressive maneuverings of Caesar Augustus. Though decided that he would have to stay away from them in relation to the connections with his children. He recalled that his nephew Llud was gaining ground in the farthest Roman territory of the Isle of Britons.

Llud was the son of his great aunt Don ferch Matonwy, who had married a major king over there by the name of BelI Mawr. She was the older sister of his father, the first Juba. The Britons could not pronounce the name of their father Hiempsal and she had gone by the name of their mother Matonis. He recalled when he was in Rome of having met her grandson Mandubbracios-the brother of Llud.

He recalled the meeting with this strange kinsman of his from such a far away land. He saw the resemblance of his sister with his long dark brown hair and the beautiful insightful eyes that he had inherited.

Mandubbracios was much older than he, who was still a young child of six and very new captive of Rome since the death of his father. He often wondered since that date if he had shared the same fate as his father, since nothing was heard of him since in Rome, though he had sent out queries. Mandubbracios had told him in that all too brief meeting that he had a daughter named Cartismundua and a son by the name of Prystytwg. He wondered as to the children and their positions at the current time. He should consider them when the children grow older. For he would love to find an excuse to visit that strange and barbarous country and to add information on it in his chronicles that he was compiling.

His attention and reverie was distracted at once when the news came in of the entrance to his chambers of his wife. He followed her form as she graciously entered his area of study. The torches only added to the beauty that she held even in her fullness of pregnancy. Not as large in the latter stages as she was before, he prayed that she would only have a single birth this time since he greatly feared for her safety. He noticed how the dense illumination made her dark hair appear the reddish hue comparable to the sunrise he had just seen this eve. No matter how she felt, she was always elegant in apparel and the ease of grace that she was natural to in such a long line of royal blood. Her intelligence grasped his mind in thoughts so lost in her and her ability to rule well in his place, which allowed his deep passion for studies to thrive.

"Husband, I beg your indulgence on this matter." She bowed slightly in reverence to his station. He noticed how her eyelashes playfully touched the tips of her cheeks so long were they. "Selene, you do not have to speak thus in the privacy of our chambers, what is amiss?"

"I was deeply concerned about the grain rations for our own people. For you see, Octavian has requested such large amounts to be shipped to Rome and naturally we must oblige him in this, though I am concerned how this will affect our people in that it leaves little for us." She continued, for whenever she spoke of state matters, she would lose herself in all of the intricacies of detail, which enabled such an accomplished reign in his absence, "The tribes are constantly mingling with the settlers sent from Rome under Octavian." She would always refer to Caesar Augustus in private as Octavian, perhaps in justice for her mother and showing some resentment still. "What have you to say about that husband?" Juba adjusted himself in his seat and turned to face the many scrolls he had spread out in his studies in rapt concentration on this new development.

"I shall write to him about this matter, for you are aware that I knew him well once during my captivity and later studies in Rome before we met." He continued to say," don't you worry about this matter, I understand how you dread dealing in matters concerning him. Why don't you write to your beloved friend Antonia about this in your next letter to her. That way we will have conquered the matter on both fronts." Satisfied he turned the matter to her condition," How fare you in other ways dear wife, does the child seem ready to meet me, for I cannot wait."

"Juba, do not fret about that, I have it well under control, his royal sisters are just as anxious to meet him". Juba delighted at this gender that his wife used in reference to the unborn child." Could this possibly be a son?" Selene walked slowly over to her husband and wrapped her arms around his wide shoulders and softly whispered into his ear, "Possibly…"

II

Selene glided into her own chambers after a long evening spent dreaming about their empire and the future of their yet to be born child in the loving and tender embrace of her husband. She admired how gentle he could be with her when he was such a large and powerful man. Will such wonders ever cease? In the early hours of the morning she made her way to her own chambers and flopped down upon her own pallet with the aftereffects of their closeness still deep in the air around her. She lay there watching the early rays of dawn seep into the large arched windows to her room and make their way across the floor to greet the dawn. She had taken back the teaching's of Isis much to the dismay of her husband, but nonetheless respected the architecture that she instilled in the city they had created in their kingdom.

Her chambers were veiled in the finest of fabrics found from her birth land of Egypt and statues and carvings reflected the ancient temples that she had visited and admired in her youth, all to vivid in her memory.

Incense burned of frankincense and myrrh as they had in the sacred ancient temples of old. She even had an altar dedicated to Isis, which she had received from Octavia a few years ago out of respect, since most of the items were from her mother.

Her husband was enamored in the architecture of Rome and of course the ancient Greeks and requested that she have buildings commissioned in their new city to reflect this. She had willingly complied for she admired them as well. She also snuck into some of the latter buildings the architecture of her homeland and even had a temple of Isis built over the site of the temple of Astarte in an site near the conquered Carthage.

Her room reflected her deepest feelings and homesickness for her birth land which had left such an imprint on her mind. She watched the dance of the softest of her silks that hung around her bed with the morning wind of the Roman Sea over which their new palace was built. The very new colonized city was steep on a cliff overlooking the mighty embrace of the Roman Sea and rested near the ruins of Carthage in a city named Cirta. Almost as if it was being watched over by Caesar Augustus, he had also sent over many colonists from Rome, probably to report to him how she and her husband fared in the rule given by him of this country. She despised this way of thinking from Octavian, even though this land was rightfully inherited from her husband by his father Juba.

Strangely to add to this morning chorus, sounds added to the delight of the waves crashing against the treacherous shoreline over which the newly built palace was situated.

III

The weeks went by and Selene began to worry about the unborn child in that the time seemed almost overdue. Then suddenly almost as that thought approached her mind, Isis had seen fit to send her the very first signs of it's readiness. Her back became sore and a sudden gush of the life waters had left her womb in preparation for the birth process. Her handmaiden Serian and the physician Asandros had observed this and rushed her willing body to the birth chambers prepared for her.

The chamber was decorated in the style of the ancient Egyptians in that the walls were covered with hieroglyphs on the Gods and Goddesses and the statues of short dwarf form of the Goddess Bes and the grossly large breasted Hippopotamus Goddess Happi. The ominous and grotesque figures watched over her and would have frightened anyone not familiar with the pantheon of the Egyptian. For they only guided and protected her and she knew that they were similar to the ones that had adorned her own mother's birth chamber for all of their births-if not the very same ones since they were received recently from Octavia. She did not have this chamber with the birth of her twin daughters and resented it daily, but had no choice, since the city at that time was so dangerous, she barely had time to request the makings of this room in that she was pregnant so soon after her marriage.

This time she had made sure that she was more than protected as well as her unborn child. Confidently she had given birth to their first son Juba Ptolemy Helios in honor of her twin brother she had still cried over before sleeping. Iotape was present as well as her little sister Arsinoe who was now nine years of age and at an age where she will soon be married. She wanted her sister to see her duty for her family in bringing forth the heirs to their line for their long lost mother, the great Cleopatra.

Arsinoe put up such a brave front as well she should have since the birth lasted only two hours, with a lot less effort than it took to bring forth two. Selene felt exhausted despite this, but elated on the ease and that it would not frighten her sister nor Iotape. But alas, they needed to know the process they would someday have to endure.

IV

A great ceremony was held in honor of the heir of Numidia, Prince Juba Ptolemy Helios. The feast and celebrations went on for a whole two weeks in their eagerness for a male heir born to their decaying nation. Most of the people held vast hope that he would band together the unrest and violence that had become epidemic in this country.

The two princesses who were only three years old had delighted in their new brother and often tried to play with him as if he were their very own doll. Selene was on constant vigil over this. For they were too young to realize how truly fragile he was. Still she entrusted in them a great love for their baby brother that would someday determine their lives, according to her husband. That she would have to change. For she was determined to make sure that her own daughters were the author's of their own destiny and possibly only "guided" by the wisdom of their brother. She was planning a way to give her daughters more power in this male powered world. She looked over her husband's writing on his travels and delved into the cultures of faraway lands and of the one she precariously ruled over at present, searching for some key to help them when they were grown.

She would however teach her daughters the worship of Isis and to determine which one would continue the family chronicles in honor of her mother.

V

On this day, Selene had decided to wander the palace and to try to steal a peek at her husband's latest work in his chronicles. She loved to talk with him about his latest findings. She knew that he was planning to travel along the Roman Sea and to possibly find out the place where his great aunt's family was in farther Briton.

She entered his chamber cautiously, even though she knew that he was busy with the emissary from Judea who had recently arrived along with the emissary from Syria. She let them talk amongst themselves knowing that she would have a full report from her husband later that evening. They refused to deal politics with her and would only speak with a fellow man in matters of state due to their highly patriarchal customs. She allowed that and understood that her husband was a rarity in his treatment of her as an equal.

She lit a lamp on a small table to illuminate her quest. She arrived at his desk and started to move the scrolls remembering where each was originally, so that she could return them to her respective places when her goal was accomplished. She was looking for some sign of correspondence with his family in the province of Briton. She had hopes of this, since he had once mentioned it to her, though it had stopped with that brief connection to his great aunt Don.

She found a scroll that lay almost to the side of the table on the verge of falling on the floor. She scooped it up and started to read the writing in Greek. Thankful for her lessons as a child on this from her mother.

It was a letter from a King of a tribe called the Trinovantes, she read his name as Tenvantius, who was the youngest son of Llud and heir. It stated his willingness to consider a marriage in the future with one of Juba's daughters with his eldest son Cynfelyn Cunobelinios. He had other sons by the names of Togodumnos and Annius. She knew from her own research on the matter since it deeply interested her in in that her husband was considering this; that Tenvantius was the younger son of Llud and nephew of the high king of Briton named Casswallon. Casswallon was crowned the King of CaerLlud who the Romans called CaerLluddein and later Londinium and had recently established their ties there.

She had even heard her father mention this great king of the Britons named Casswallon and of when he was sent as a captive to Rome there by Julius Caesar. She knew that he was also the man who killed his brother Llud and stole the crown from Llud's older son Mandubbracios. In retaliation of that act, Mandubbracios had run to Rome under the protection of Julius Caesar and in a sense brought the Romans in full conquest to Briton under a new curiosity sparked by the son of Llud. They did not like this braggart and betrayer of family and rumor had it that he was killed around the same time as Juba's father was. She also recalled that Llud was the son of BellI Mawr who was married to Juba's aunt. There was the family connection and thus her husband's interest.

She had read as much as she could get her hands on with the matter that might concern one of her daughters someday. She had also learned that the sister of Mandubbracios named Penardun had married the son of Casswallon by the name of Llyr. And they recently had a son they called Bran who was famed for his gentile nature and a King in his own right at such a tender age of five-so famed was he.

Cynfelyn or Cunobelinios was only a very young child at the present time, but he held the promise of uniting the tribes as his father raved over in his correspondence with her husband. Still she found the lineage almost as confusing as her own with the many family connections and murders to attain rule. The tribes were known to be separate but there were many family connections.

For example, Casswallon had two sons Llyr and Andico. The older son Llyr had a daughter that married an Atribite of Gaul who was connected to their tribe with relations to the notable Vercingetorix. Vercingetorix was the famous leader of the Gaulish tribes that were eventually defeated by Julius Caesar. She recalled that all of that had occurred before her mother was born. Yet the Keltoi as the Greeks called them were connected to the mainland of Gaul by marriages, yet they cried complete independence from one another.

She also knew from her husband that Comminos who was a leader of the Atribites alongside Vercingetorix had fled to that same kin tribe mentioned in Briton and later became King of that same Briton tribe on the Island. This same King had a brother by the name of Tasciovanus who became the ruler of the Catuvellauni tribe that is becoming almost as powerful as the Trinovantes tribe and a force to reckon with.

She wondered at the fate of the heir to the throne the prided first son of Tenvantius, little Cunobelinios. When Augustus hears of this child he might just swoop down to gain opportunity in raising him. Especially since he might gain some information in this correspondence with her husband about the fate of his children and the possibility in endowing their fates in marriage.

Having gained the information that she needed she rushed to her own chambers to prepare a plan in which she could delicately bring up the situation with her husband.

VI

She was unaware of a presence that slipped into the room behind her to gather some information to bring to his master Caesar Augustus. He also made sure that the papers were returned to their original position. Publius Cloinius was sent to Queen Selene under the guise of a palace servant and was able to travel about the palace in ease of his mission in bringing information to his real master in Rome.

Publius was small of stature with a notably large nose. Despite his common origins in being the son of a freedman he quickly rose in the ranks of the palace servants when he was noted by Caesar Augustus for his incredible and detailed memory. Augustus wasted no time in getting close to this servant and in giving him gifts that rapidly bound the young otherwise unnoticed man in his service.

He was so common in appearance that he was able to travel about the palace of Numidia virtually unobserved in his searching for information. He tunneled his goal and remained unswayed by the rulers and clients of his true master Augustus, who was semi-divine.

He quickly memorized this information on the possible marriage alliance of the heir to the barbarous kingdom of Briton with the houses of Ptolemy and Juba. He knew that Augustus would relish this information and would require it fast so that he could move against it. For if those two powers were to unite, they might be able to gain enough attention between the two farthest sides of Rome to surround it and possibly conquer it. He did not really know too much about that farthest Roman conquest or about it's people. But he figured that they would have to be powerful enough for the King of Numidia to consider them for his daughters.

Soon after finding this information, the absence of Publius was virtually unremarkable in that he was not really considered in the life of the Numidian Monarchy in the great scheme of things. For he was only a servant.

For this was one of the great advantages that Caesar Augustus had over all of the illustrious Kings of the East, was that he was first and foremost just a man. When most of the Kings and Queens of the East had been raised in that they were the descendants of Gods and Goddesses and that palace servants were to be seen and not heard and virtually inconsequential in their daily life, only that they were to answer for the needs of the royalty. Caesar Augustus lived as close to a commoner as possible in his simple way of living. He was like his uncle Julius Caesar in that he would often sit beside the common man who grew to admire them greatly and fight valiantly beside them both faithful to the last. Caesar Augustus often befriended men of common lineage, such as Marcus Agrippa and noted them for their talent and not their lineage.

VII

In Rome, Antonia was reclining on her couch for the evening meal with her mother and dear friend Livia. Antonia was adjusting well to her new marriage with Drusus, the son of Livia from her fist marriage. After the last three Ptolemy children had left to join their sister with the wife of Helios. Octavia had joined her brother in the palace that he had built on the Palantine. Antonia Minor had joined them as well since her new husband Drusus had been raised in the palace by her uncle who had recently received the title of Augustus, signifying his semi-divine status and his namesake—Julius Caesar was fully deified, it made sense.

Antonia had missed her sister who was married before her to the straggly red-headed barbarian. She did not like him one bit, and hoped her sister fared well. Her sister had sort of cut them off from communication. They would see each other at family events at the palace, but her real sister had left the face that looked out at them all. The older Antonia's husband was none other than the son of Gnaeus Domitius Ahenobarbus who were of the reputed and ancient Domintian family. The legend of the family was that the Dioscuri, Castor and Pollux had made a promise of protection to one of the earliest members of that family at the battle of Lake Regillus over the Latins over four hundred years ago. To prove the power of their word they placed a hand of the black beard of their client, the earliest member of that family and turned it red.

Antonia was especially worried since the members of that family were noted for their cruelty and hostility towards others and she feared for her sister. The marriage was made due to the alliance between both of their fathers. His grandfather had served Antonia's father well at Actium and had helped their father loyally as an officer and further assisted him with the political spoils after the treaty of Brundisium when he received the governorship of Bithynia. He joined her father in the Parthian War against the pirate Sextus Pompey with the Governor of Asia Furnius. Due to his loyalties and ties with Antony, he had to flee Rome and was offered a position on the staff of her father and his mistress Cleopatra. However he had an illness which soon after proved to be fatal and just prior to had left the side of their father and went over to Rome and the side of her uncle Octavian, now Augustus. Probably seeing it as the lost cause that it was and wanted to save his families place in Rome since he had left a son after him, who was Lucius.

Lucius Ahenobarbus was the father of Lucius Ahenobarbus and Gnaeus Ahenobarbus. Both of them extremely cruel. Lucius Ahenobarbus had married the Elder Antonia, though Gnaeus was still rather young had shown early the family traits and was known to have killed three of the family cats. Rumor had spread around Rome over that one. She had questioned her sister on the matter and her sister responded that she would not be surprised if it were true. She only knew that the cats were missing and they were found in a trap that young Gnaeus had claimed was for killing bears. She would have thought that sad and rather cute in his attempt to catch bears, but admitted reluctantly that the child was a loner and very peculiar. Antonia wondered about the child even though he was only five. There were too many odd things occurring around the domus of her elder sister.

Antonia knew a lot about Lucius her sister's new father in law as well. He had conquered the Allobroges of Gallia Transalpina and served as consul. He had married Portia who was the sister of Cato Uticensis. His daughter Portia had married Julius Caesar's friend and later murderer Brutus. Cato was his ally due to that marriage against the triumvirate with her uncle Julius Caesar and Pompey and tried everything to oust their power and to bring back the ultra conservative ways of the ancient Roman republic. When Lucius was a praetor he proved himself a worthy adversary of Julius Caesar and had later on threatened to terminate Caesar's control over Gallia Transalpina, which had been pacified by his father. There were many verbal battles in the senate between Lucius Ahenobarbus and Julius Caesar and even a time when he tried to remove the powers of Caesar to allow Pompey to crush him politically. However a conference was called instead which was later called the conference of Lucia. They reconfirmed the tenants and the shared power of Julius Caesar and Pompey.

However war did eventually break out between the two of them and Ahenobarbus took over Gaul. Ahenobarbus headed north contrary to the orders of the great Pompey and fought Caesar in Corfinium, where he was defeated. Julius Caesar pardoned him as he was noted for of his enemies, and as a result Ahenobarbus immediately rejoined the cause of Pompey and played a major role in the siege of Masilia and took command of Pompey's left wing at the battle of Pharsulus where Lucius the father in law of her sister Antonia Major was killed.

Antonia Minor sat on her couch and picked at the food offered to her by the delicate palace slaves at her evening meal with Livia and her mother. She was not that hungry at that meal despite the lack of appetite that she had lately. Her mind often wandered to all that was occurring too rapidly with her family. The recent elevated status of her uncle as semi-divine and of all of the constant palace intrigue that only grew with each day. Her mother looked tired and missed dreadfully the younger Ptolemy children and dreaded her cold actions towards her favorite friend Selene in preparation of her wedding.

She looked over to the couches where her mother and Livia reclined and at their rapt attention to a conversation whispered about some important palace matter or other. She did not care to participate it though, she had other matters on her mind. She was too much of a worrier and had missed her soul-sister Selene. Things had been too quiet before she had met her and had dramatically changed to the opposite since her sister left Rome. She knew her mother missed them all as well since she no longer had any smaller children to look after, which was one of the main reasons why she moved in with her brother. The halls of her mother's once busy and loud domus were ominously all too silent for her mother, especially after her last two children had left to lives of their own.

She held in her silken purse that she carried everywhere the copy of her latest letter from Selene which announced the birth of her son. She was elated when she recently discovered the she was pregnant with her first child and fervently wished that she had her friend back for advice. For it took a few months to receive correspondence from where Selene now resided and wanted fast answers and the kind that you could not safely put in a letter.

She felt her almost perceptible stomach which carried new life and the next generation of her family. She knew her mother anxiously awaited the birth of her grandchild and doted on Antonia with all of the rare delicacies the palace could offer in food to pamper the babe which grew inside of her.

Inside the chamber that they all were eating in muted silence a loud noise burst in which promptly ceased the hushed conversations of her mother and Livia. For into the room stormed Julia in one of her tirades.

Julia was Caesar Augustus' daughter from his first wife Scribonia and was in almost every aspect a princess or thought herself to be anyways. For she was constantly granted her every whim by her father. The sun rose and set by her according to her uncle. She entered the room and immediately demanded the attention of all of those in it to her latest cause. Her blonde hair was fumbled and clutched in her dainty hands in dramatic futility. "I cannot believe tatta wants me to stay married with your son Octavia when I love Tiberius and Marcellus loves that dainty Portia! Why do we have to put up with all of it Mother" She bent down to her step mother Livia in exaggerated supplication. "How dreadful, do you think I look convincing enough to tatta to appeal to him again! The wounded look always got things done before." Livia giggled and grasped Julia closer to her side," You silly little actress. You know how conservative your father is. You truly know how much he values the ideal ancient Rome where women just stay at home and wash the feet of their husbands…" She trailed off to continue on the original trek with her stepdaughter, "but no matter what he always has your best interests at heart. So just be a proper Roman matron and give your family some respect and just abide by his wishes. Just drop that idea that you have in your pretty little blonde head of yours and go back to your husband, he is not really all that bad you know." Livia looked at Octavia for some sort of intrusion,

"He is my son dear and you know he cares very much for you." Octavia responded hoping that Julia would just take the matter elsewhere, for she was busy in an interesting conversation with Livia and wished to return to it.

Antonia Minor took the cue from her mother's unspoken plea "Julia, tell me how was my sister when she came to visit you and Marcellus last ante Idus in the month of Julius?" She leaned forward and beckoned her palace sister to join her and to drop her latest dramae of the moment. She really cared for Julia and understood her nature for it was truly simple. For how could she help the natural doting nature of her father, who has not had any further children from Livia and had begun to accept that there were not more to come either. So all of her uncle's attentions were devoted to Julia and to the son's of Livia from her former husband Tiberius, Tiberius the younger and Drusus who was born in this very palace. He had dotted on those boys as if they were his very own. The boys' father the elder Tiberius was still fuming over the matter that had occurred years ago in which his children and wife were taken from him.

Caesar Augustus had never forgiven him for proposing to the senate that the assassins of Julius Caesar be rewarded. For her uncle never forgot something of that magnitude and stored things of such matter in his mind to strike at a later time. Her uncle was like a cobra in that way. He never struck when people thought he would, it was always when they least expected it. Like how in later years he just happened to fall in love with the wife of Tiberius and demanded that he hand her over to him, pregnant and all. Caesar Augustus raised Tiberius' two sons instead.

Her uncle also struck in later year for the ridiculous notion that Tiberius had for raising a slave revolt in Campania to undermine him. For Tiberius had to flee the country for that last event and actually sought out Antonia's father in aid of the matter. Due to the treaty of Misenum, he was allowed to return to Rome with his wife and the young Tiberius. Upon his return was the time when her uncle fell in love with the intelligent and haughtily beautiful Livia, who sat in the room with her. Since Tiberius was so graceful in handing over his beloved Livia, Caesar Augustus took pity in him and allowed Tiberius to visit frequently and to take an active role in raising his sons. The young Tiberius even gave the funeral oration to his father when he died thirteen years before.

She felt bad for Tiberius who was obviously desperately in love with his young wife Vispania Agrippa who was the daughter of Marcus Agrippa, the closest military confidant of her uncle Caesar Augustus. She knew that her uncle had plans to send young Tiberius to the East to assume command there and that Julia was trying desperately to stop this with anything in her power. She used all of her famous theatrics hoping to assuage her father to null that command and to grant her the hand of Tiberius instead. For she was way to mercurial a wife for the muted and conservative Marcellus who was too much like his father, her mother's first husband.

At the current time, Tiberius was the first in line for the throne that Augustus was all too soon being given by Rome and who was fast abandoning the ancient republican ways. A monarchy was all to real to them at the moment and the beginning of an empire was at hand and her family controlled the strings.

Antonia Minor knew of how powerful her mother and Livia were in the way things were being run and in their influence with the greatest man in Rome. She sat there silently next to Julia, while she was probably planning another desperate scheme to make her life more interesting and in observance of her mother and Livia now back into their conversation like school girls they giggled to each other over one thing or another. She sat there and brought Julia's attention to them and they both sat there staring at the two older women intently.

The two older women reclined into each other with couches so close as they dabbled at their pastries and walnuts. Their watered down wine still topped their glasses neglected to the words passed between them. Still Julia and Antonia stared at the women wondering when they would be observed. To no avail, they continued in their plots and schemes for the betterment of Rome.

"Antonia, how is Iully doing? Where has he been lately?" Antonia was frazzled for a moment, not expecting that but knew of their friendship anyways.

She also remembered that before even Scribonia, Caesar Augustus was first married to Claudia, the daughter of Fulvia by her husband before her father Marcus Antonius with Clodius. Still she responded absentmindedly to the query put before her by Julia on one of her favorite brothers that she was raised with, even though he was only her half brother through her father. "Oh, out and about the senate and his studies. I haven't seen him much lately." Julia continued ceaselessly "well, what about the wonderful princess that you had at your domus for awhile... The daughter of Cleopatra, what was her name?"

Antonia was glad for this respite in Julia's fascination of men. She believed that if Julia did not hush her weird fascination with them and had muted her relationship even in friendship with them, it might come back to haunt her sometime in the future. Her uncle and Julia's father was growing more powerful in Rome by the minute and was desperate in setting a good example for his beliefs in family starting with his own domus, crowded though it was.

"I just received a letter from her, she mentioned that her son was born on the solstice and he is beautiful. She said that her daughters who are now three years old look a lot like me and resemble the Antony side of the family! How wonderful for her. I wish that she were here to help me though, pretty soon it will be my own turn. Oh, how I wish my own tatta were here." She sadly turned her gaze down, since her own father was never there for her at all. For her father left her mother Octavia when she was six months pregnant with her to be by the side of Cleopatra. She found out in later years when she finally met Cleopatra Selene, that Selene and Helios were only a year older than she if even that. She supposed that she should have hated Selene and what she represented. But in the way of her soul she could not. Instead she embraced one so similar to her in that Selene looked so much like her in that they both resembled their father in most of the exterior attributes that were notable in the Antony family. They both had the same dark brown hair and hazel eyes and were tiny for most roman girls. Their father on the other hand had all of those characteristics, though was larger in muscle and strength than most of the men in Rome. She assumed that the Antony women were well noted for being petite in stature. Selene had told her that she was actually tall compared to her own mother.

Antonia Minor continued for Julia who sat in rapt attention. "Selene mentioned that it was glorious being a Queen and that her husband was very quiet and was engrossed in his studies on geography, botany and in the compilation of an encyclopedia that would rival the works of Strabo, an historian from her native Alexandria. Selene has every confidence in her husband and explained in her letter that he was extremely well educated and he in turn had full faith in her ability to lead their country in his absence." Antonia Minor reveled in that story by her sister overseas living a fantasy life that she as a Roman could never have. Though might just be possible, but for her children possibly, not her. She knew that Rome was quickly becoming a monarchy. She really dreaded the tossing aside of the values that her homeland held so dear for four hundred years. She and her husband Drusus loved the old ideology of the republic and secretly did not like that road that Rome seemed to be traveling towards, though agreed that just in case, they would go along with it and support her uncle in his cause, however quietly on the sidelines.

Drusus had told her once that he had actually admired the tyrannical Cato to a point, in that if he was not so radical in the presentation of his ideology in the preservation of Rome and it's senate in calling Julius Caesar a tyrant as horrid as the ancient Kings-he would have sided with him, had he been around at that time of course. He read fervently on the issues presented in the senate and had admired many of the works of Cato, though was not as radical. Drusus was very similar in personality to her uncle Caesar Augustus. That he never struck when most people expected him, he would always bide his chance. Though Drusus was even more of a sidelines player and was more prone to observing all of the tyranny surrounding him. He would carefully choose sides and remain faithful to them. He loved the ancient Rome and it's idea of the republic, though had also seen the reality that Rome was in dire need of a change. If anyone was to be a ruler of Rome, a king… the only man that he could find able to do this was Caesar Augustus as he was fast on that road to becoming a king. Antonia praised her husband's wisdom in this matter and on many others for she felt him very astute on the matters of the senate and could almost predict directions and matters and saw patterns that few had before or since.

Antonia continued her description of Selene, carefully choosing the parts that she knew that Julia cared most for. For it was obvious that Julia had envied her friendship with the strange and pretty foreign princess. She knew also despite what her own father was responsible for, secretly wished that she were a princess herself. "Selene mentioned that her sister Arsinoe was becoming quite a lover of fine fabrics and was fast emptying the royal treasury on her quest for the rarest of imported fabrics and had requested that Selene restore the ancient dye factories of Corinth that had the secrets of the famous Tyrian dye. She mentioned that though Arsinoe was still very young, she had somehow acquired one thousand pairs of silk slippers which she would change several times a day and Selene had sworn that she had not seen a pair worn by her younger sister more than once!" She must have raised her tone for just then her mother jumped into her relations of the lost princess to them. "Why Antonia, Selene is much more than that and you know it! And Arsinoe is still very young. Selene is just spoiling her like she was as a child, for that was all she knew as a child." Antonia looked at her mother and gave her a look trying to secretly explain to her about why she was bringing those things up. Fortunately for her Octavia caught it and immediately comprehended it and decided to let the girls continue the conversation, silently priding herself in her own daughter's grasp of a situation and conversation at such a young age. She had taught her well.

Antonia continued her soliloquy about her departed friend for the benefit of the jaded Julia. "Selene is very happy in Numidia and mentioned that the weather there is always summer and the breezes from the ocean by her palace are simply divine. She is also renewing her studies in the temple of Isis to become a priestess like her mother was. She has learned so much of the ancient Egyptian language she can speak like an ancient herself! She had taught me a few words, like how the ancient Egyptian word for her country was Kemet for the Black soil of the Nile!"

Despite her all too grown up condition on the impending pregnancy, she prattled on about her half sister to her cousin with the glee of a young girl that in reality she was. Though true to the time that she was born to and her status as an important Roman matron, she was well advanced in maturity and was well skilled in conversational arts and quickly grasped all too well what her important cousin wanted to hear to keep her rapt in attention.

For Julia was captivated by her cousin's noble connections and dreamed about a life as a princess in the mysterious East. For she had always admired the notorious Cleopatra and grasped desperately for any story told about her and thought her father silly in his hatred of the long dead woman. For she had learned that she was a great ruler and had done much for a woman in any time, she was extremely powerful.

She hated her father's twisted and ancient ideologies on woman and the hearth and all of that babble. For she knew where the true power of women lay and was learning fast how to use it, much to the dismay of her stepmother, who was all too quick to catch on. For her tatta was still oblivious of her true nature and she wanted to keep it that way.

"Antonia, don't you wish that you had been born a princess and wonder why we were not by fate?" She turned her dreamy eyes towards her cousin waiting for the answer that she loved to hear of late, "You, know dear cousin, that at the rate that things are going, you may soon get your wish… just be a little more patient, there is talk in the city that they are planning to make your father Emperor and to abolish the republic. For more had been annexed to Rome along with Numidia, Egypt and recently Pamphilia, Pisidia, Lycaonia and Galatia. And Julia, don't forget your father's Praetorian Guard that he has established…" She let this trail off for Julia to lovingly take the bait. For she knew all too well her cousin's interest in men and knew that Julia would make some excuse to leave and to find the location of them.

"Cousin, tatta told me to stop by and pick up something for Marcellus that he needs for the senate tomorrow." She smiled with her whimsical dimple dotting her elation at the changed subject to something that she could take immediate action in and jumped up with all of the grace of Aurora, Goddess of the dawn and the divine herald of the day with the brightness of her theatrics that she added to every occasion. She always ended any dilemma in brightness and really was child at heart and though she dreamed of being a princess, she had always loved the underdog like her father and notorious great-great uncle Julius Caesar. She watched Julia gracefully nod to her stepmother and her aunt Octavia in respect and glided out of the room to her new endeavor.

"Antonia, that girl never ceases to amaze me in the dramae that surrounds her. She had better quell her fascination with the stronger gender and stick to her own hearth and home or it will soon catch up to her and possibly lead to a disgrace with her father with all of his ideals. It would also be in her best interest with me and my own influence to stay by her hearth by the side of my son where she belongs." Antonia quickly chimed in in defense for Julia's whose essence still clung to the room where they all sat, "Oh, mother, you know all of her affairs are imaginary and she is true to Marcellus. She is a very close friend with Iully and you know how kind he is and not of that type at all and would not associate with any other of that type either. Julia is just bored, especially with Marcellus so much older than she. And remember that marriage was of your choosing and not hers. She just has normal emotions about what she, nor many other have the fortune to have, a marriage with true love. We are all innocent victims in the world of men. I have been one of the lucky ones with my marriage to Drusus in that we actually get along, you even had a taste of that before my father with the elder Marcellus. You should understand that all too well with what happened with my own father. He was never there for me and you know it. Yet, I do not let that get in the way of things, I just accept them for what they are and realize that now is not the time to wage such a battle that cannot be won." Octavia beamed with pride at the wisdom of her very young daughter.

Livia finally found the chance to add in her own piece in this conversation after listening on the side, "Yes, we all know too well the role of a woman here. We can only sit by the side and hope that our men-folk who have the paterfamilias make the right decision with our own future. Also, heed you that we are all the fruit of wise decisions made by our fathers in that we sit here today in a world that is fast rising to an empire. We will now be in positions, though silent, of great power in our influence. The only thing that we can do is take advantage of that and to instill this wisdom in our daughters as I know that your mother has done with you Antonia" She glanced at the still young and awkward Antonia in the early months of her pregnancy that was just beginning to reveal itself to the world. "Use your influence and power wisely, hopefully Julia will learn her lesson. For when she is older and has lost the beauty of her youth, her theatrics will find no sympathy." Octavia nodded her assent to this.

"Antonia, tell me more about the letter from Selene, how fares she in her rule?"

Antonia Minor then bent down to take out the letter that was concealed in her pouch, "Oh mamma, I do miss her so and would love to see her new daughters and son. It must be difficult to play the mother for not only her own children but to her little sister and Ptolemy as well. She had also mentioned prior to his arrival in Numidia to Cirta, Helios had taken ill and had died just a few days later. Oh, how I wish that I could hold her and tell her as a best friend should, that everything will be alright!"

Octavia left her couch and trod across the chamber to the side of her daughter to be by her side. For she too felt sorry for Selene and the younger children and her tears had begun to pour forth in remembrance of poor Helios.

The poor boy was destined for disaster just because of who he really was as the son to the great Cleopatra and her own brother's enemy. He should not be dead but alive and at the side of his twin sister as the possible heir to Egypt, should it ever be broken from Rome. She also feared for Ptolemy, Arsinoe and Selene and often believed that they were in danger as well. She hoped that Selene had enough sense to play well for her brother for her and her families' safety.

Octavia knew that the marriage to Helios was planned due to his dalliance with Helena, against the wishes of Octavian. She watched in horror as her brother had gained knowledge of the news of his plans being destroyed with the son of his enemy taking up hearth with the Gallic princess and heir to Vercingetorix, Helena-who was now reduced to living in squalor in the Roman Subdura. He raved on for days and finally decided to haste his planned marriage for him with Iotape the princess of Medea from Syria. Helios did not even know about the son that was born from that union with Helena and Octavian made his sister promise upon her very life not to inform anyone, especially Selene or Helios. She held close that secret waiting for the day when she would be better able to speak with her brother on the matter.

Though she also knew that Numidia was in constant warfare and had recently begged her brother along with Livia, after pleading her case on the safety of Selene and her family. The matter that she was discussing with Livia for most of this time. She urged her brother and Livia to take Selene and the children out of Numidia and to give the rule of Mauretania to Juba instead. For Mauretania was too large to be controlled as a colony by Augustus and was still sitting vacant since the deaths of the two prior rulers Bogud and Boccus. There were two separate territories ruled separately by each and after the last of them died it left a territory too large to be controlled by only one man. So, she suggested that her brother give that territory to Juba and to exchange it for the much smaller territory of Numidia. Caesar Augustus seemed to like that idea and was in the process of putting it into action. She hoped that in the interim Selene and the children would be safe and survive it to rule the larger territory of Numidia. After that the conversation between her and Livia had drifted to Rome and its rich and never-ending supply of gossip.

The three woman sat together in the chamber the food barely touching their lips looked very different in their ages and status, yet all shared the similar trait of being all too valuable to Roma Dea. They had learned to adjust to their positions in life and all have served their husbands well which had eventually served them well and aided any personal cause that they may have.

For Caesar Augustus valued the ancient virtues of the republic and bowed down docily to the perfect Roman matrons that each of these women represented too well. They all knew that he would listen to their pleas and to work for their causes since they were good representatives for the Rome that he wanted to present in his fast rise to a leader of an Empire.

Part three

I

25 B.C.E.

Selene and her husband vainly tried to stabilize the fiery province of Numidia to no end. Octavian sent a messenger with orders to cease their rule in Numidia and to head for their much larger kingdom of Mauretania. Selene was relieved in that they could hardly leave the palace confines without vast armies for their own protection from the various uprisings from every direction. The people felt that Juba II was not an able ruler over the nomadic roots of the people of Numidia in that he was way too Roman for their taste.

So, after a precarious and turbulent last year of their reign in Numidia they stole into the night and balmy air to their new kingdom of Mauretania and let Octavian—Caesar Augustus as he was now called have the unstable country of Numidia for himself.

II

When the climate turned rocky and dangerous she knew that she was finally in their new homeland. For Mauretania was known for it's harsh landscape and jagged mountains and rocky coastline. The warlike tribe of the Maurii roamed it's environs. Two hundred years prior Rome had only slightly became aware of the Maurii and it's small kingdom with the Punic Wars and then the Jugarthine War had increased it's curiosity over this dangerous landscape. King Bogud had joined in the civil war of Caesar and Pompey on the side of Caesar. Since none of the Maurii would claim rule over the whole of their country, Augustus hoped to gain stability when he installed Juba II to the throne.

So, she and Juba assessed their situation on where to begin. They were to bring culture and prosperity to a land and to bring it together. Roman laws for order and her Greek upbringing would assist in the culture part of it. For she immediately sent for scholars, artists, sculptors, poets and musicians to populate their new capitol. For she felt in her heart that they had a much better chance of succeeding here in their leadership and was wondering why Caesar Augustus had decided to give she and her husband another chance. Were they just an experiment to him or did he actually have knowledge of all of their accomplishments in Numidia, despite the harsh conditions of the people. In her biological animosity with Caesar Augustus, she probably would never learn that answer and had accepted the situation for what it appeared. Let it be.

III

It was an ordinary day, like most others. The wind was blowing fair as usual through the large and ornate arched windows of the palace looking out over the sea that the Romans claimed was all theirs. Their stay in Mauretania had been much better as far as treaties made with the local tribes of the Maurii and their acceptance of the rule of Selene and her husband. For after the wars caused between their two rulers Boccus and Bogud, they welcomed a peaceful respite, unlike Numidia where they had fled almost for their very lives. The nomadic tribes of the Numidians were all too content with their constant aggression towards one another and now they could turn their attention to the Romans who were the complete opposite of them. They resented Selene and especially Juba in their all-too-Roman ways and now they had to deal with the actual Romans in leadership in her and her husband's stead. Well, that ought to be interesting for them. She had thought that she and Juba were making a little progress in bringing art and culture to those people, when the worst of the rebellions broke out all over the kingdom. They had sort of witnessed the proverbial calm before the storm just prior to the real blood shed, which actually approached her palace walls.

Well, that was another chapter in their past and they were all adjusting well to this new climate to the east from where they once were. Juba had built an extremely large study to accommodate his rapidly expanding collection of what he called his study material. Selene had even approached him on making his collection public to the people in a sort of smaller imitation of the Alexandrian Library. Juba thought she was sweet in that suggestion, but brushed it aside, for he loved to hoard all of that information all to himself and was ruthless in it. He wanted his collection perfect and complete before releasing it over to the public-such was his pride in his scholarship. She just let him be when he was in that scholarly mode of his and understood all too well the tunnel vision that a writer would have to cocoon himself in in order to sort through all of the research to weave out what was important or not.

She had conducted serious research of her own in the compilation of the chronicles of her own life and her mother's in order to give the public a more accurate view of the reality kept from them. She had started it due to all of the slander that Augustus has published including lurid caricatures of her mother seducing her father that ran rampant through Rome and branded her mother as a common harlot. She was also repulsed on the works of Cicero who only had one meeting with her mother and had felt that he was worthy enough to judge her mother. For she knew that Cicero was only sandal licking his minion Augustus.

That she understood, but wanted to have an accurate portrayal and would constantly look around for people who personally knew her mother, which was more difficult, though it had prompted a correspondence with Livia of Rome and Octavia, the woman who had she and her siblings captive for a few years.

Their letters were joyous and kept her in touch with Rome and the mood of Augustus, which allowed her to better serve her country and her husband in matters of state. She liked to know which direction the wind was blowing in politics.

Her husband had left the rule of their country in her hands since he had every confidence in her abilities, while he sailed around looking for new plants and cultures for his journals. She jokingly called him her Odysseus and she his faithful Penelope. Which in reality sort of scratched the surface of their relationship. They hardly spent anytime together after the birth of their son, Juba Ptolemy Helios, but it was not even thought of, just accepted. For they were both very independent and had full faith in the abilities of the other. She had done her duty in giving him his heirs with the added gift to him of ruling his people affectively so that he could pursue his real delight in compiling his encyclopedias of botany and the world's cultures.

She thought it odd in how much he prided himself in being a true Roman, more so than the Roman's in Rome. But in reality, he was more Greek in his ways. In a way much like one of the earlier Ptolemy's of her own dynasty, before wealth and power corrupted them in the later reigns. The earliest Ptolemys were Greek in origin and did not forget that in their love of the arts, philosophy, science and mathematics. They balanced their power and knowledge beautifully. In the latter reigns, that balance was reversed since they grew too confident in their rule and began to tip the scales of their learning for their own pleasure at the risk of the declining kingdom and unrest of the people.

She learned a great deal from the early reigns of her own family and her husband's as well as watching very closely what was going on in Rome. She had the unique ability to use the wisdom attained in her studies with the implementation in the land in which she currently ruled over.

She kept careful watch over Rome and noticed how Augustus, as he liked to be called was actually impressing her with his wisdom in government. The people of Rome wanted a King and wanted to get rid of the Republic. She noted how carefully he avoided that, yet set himself down in control so cunningly. She had heard that he was in the process of reforming the old laws of the Republic that had become so tainted over the civil war years from the time of Sulla.

She compared the two in that Sulla had been an Imperator as Caesar Augustus was and had tried to reform Rome and it's laws as well. After Sulla had defeated Mithradates, he declared himself Imperator of Rome and began vast reforms to the courts and laws of Rome. He strengthened the senate and weakened the tribunate, which had increased the number of magistrates to better administer the provinces attained. The people of Rome were not ready to go back to anything that resembled the tyrannical Kings of old and Sulla voluntarily abdicated as Imperator and the republican constitution functioned the way it had prior to the upheaval. Even to this very day, they were shouting the doom of Sulla and his dictatorship, yet placed Octavian in a place even more powerful than what Sulla had during his reign. What a land of contradictions.

She knew that they greatly valued their idea of a Republic as Julius Caesar was famous for lamenting. Yet, her father was not one to hide behind a false curtain to the public and admitted that monarchy was just fine for him and that most of Rome felt that way as well, they just would not let anyone else know about it, especially their fellow countrymen. He was not afraid to hide how he truly felt. He mentioned that Rome desperately needed a King since the time was ripe and bred such people as Julius Caesar and Sulla. He felt that Sulla was doing a good thing, before the people had to jump in the way and destroy all that was starting to reform Rome for the better. For he had told her when she was young that Rome hated the idea of change and especially in actually admitting it. The basic Roman believed that the idea of the ancient republic was hailed so much that it was beginning at that time to almost appear a legend and probably did not exist. For at the time of her father, most of the constitution was jaded and changed so much that it was grotesquely altered and left little semblance of the ancient republic. But, he added, a "True Roman" would never admit this and would live life as if they were actually living under that original constitution, yet deep in their hearts they wanted one wise man to rule over them and to have the power to change the way it had become.

She had observed how the Romans were reacting to Augustus in the present day, almost the complete opposite. She also recalled that they had done the same thing to Julius Caesar in practically begging him to become king, as they were with Augustus. Her father probably would have been in the same boat as Augustus was in at present, had he played the game the way the Roman's preferred. Yet, he was the type of man that refused to hide how he truly felt, no matter what the position that it politically put him in.

Though Octavia, or Augustus, was weak in appearance and was rather Greek in his effeminate ways with his chest illness that kept him from actual military combat. He represented the most Roman of ideals and was fast gaining popularity with them. The view of the people was becoming obvious in that they had deified Julius Caesar after his death. For they had tried during the course of his life, but were cleverly thwarted in their many attempts. Yet, she noticed that Augustus was wise in the way that he gradually took on honors presented to him by people so desperate for a monarch—and used it to the best advantage in what he stated was only for the people.

He used the powers vested upon him to the best advantage for the people in re-instituting the ways of the old republic. He was politically becoming a monarch and kept it that way to better implement his changes for the betterment of the people of Rome. For she had felt that he was obviously concerned of someone else taking over the reign of the empire of Rome and running the way of the tyrant. The people were in such a malleable state that she thought all the better to make his so called changes that she was carefully keeping a close watch on in the way it would affect her and her husband's rule and their kingdom.

She also noted that the people of her own country were at that all too pliant state that a monarch would best be able to work with. For the monarch who had much wisdom in matters of state and with the situation of other cultures, would be able to use that valuable knowledge to possibly create an empire.

She saw that Augustus had seen this matter for he was taking advantage of this, as was she with her own people. She also saw the wisdom in keeping monarchs under his control and letting them lead countries, rather than sending over Roman citizens urbanized, to lead over the colonies and provinces of Rome. Especially in that she and Juba, as well as some other client Kings, were left to rule their own country after having been duly Romanized. They would in turn take their knowledge attained from being raised in an open captivity with them in their rule and also have the loyalty to Rome. For Juba was raised from a small child in Rome in a captivity given to Royals and was even given an education comparable to the patrician children of Rome. Prior to Julius Caesar, most people that were conquered where killed along with all of their offspring.

Julius Caesar had changed all of that and actually pardoned those defeated instead of killing them at the triumphs in the old way. This may have been his downfall in that it freed all of those who opposed him to gain strength in being in the position to alliance themselves with other's pardoned with the excuse of ousting a possible king. Yet, In the end, she had observed that it also ended up in gaining more notoriety for his being that all of Rome cried at his death. They had even deified him regardless of his wishes.

Selene had thought about this and other kingdoms and monarchies, as well at the Greeks democracies and oligarchies, where a few people would rule over the polis' instead of one. With all of this knowledge in her studies, that her mother had mentioned was very important in establishing any kind of rule. She quickly ascertained which way would be the best for her people.

Juba gave her full control in this, especially since he was constantly agreeing with every idea prior to, and he thought better for her to implement them herself, and let her use his name. She was almost at the point where she just used her own with some of the latest buildings that she had commissioned in her new city that she called Caesarea. She had told her husband and Augustus that it was named for him and the Caesar family, though, in reality and in her own soul—it was for her oldest brother Caesarion. She knew that Octavian had him killed, though there was no proof. He was responsible in that act, as he was in everything else—he found someone else to do the dirty deed. He sat back and found the right person for it.

Caesarion was definitely killed for who he really was. The only political threat to Rome in that he was the only world-wide recognized son of Julius Caesar. For after the death of the first Caesar, the people desperately wanted a king of sorts, though even then they would not let it happen, especially with Cato stopping everything Julius Caesar did prior to that in political attacks. Even after Cato fell on his sword, the people of Rome were aggressively crying out for a one person rule. Augustus probably rightfully feared that the people of Rome would have latched onto Caesarion, despite that he was not born of a Roman Dominae and rather a Queen of the mysterious East. That last bit held the influence of the wives of the important people of Rome, for they had resurrected the Temple of Isis in Rome after her mother's actual visit. The people of Rome recalled all too well the visit that the Queen of Egypt made and were in their own subliminal way intrigued by all of the pomp and splendor of the East and their own secret cravings for monarchy. They would have begged Rome to Unite with Egypt in rule under Caesarion.

In looking back as a mother and not an adoring much younger sister, might not have been that good. His personality was the type that might have vigorously latched onto the rule and with the strong ideals of his father would have radically tried to adjust the constitution of Rome in adoration of his little known father who was away much of the time on campaigns. Even gone for as long as eight years when he was subduing the revolts in Gaul.

Yet, Caesarion would have quickly exhausted himself and have probably abandoned any good that he created in the Roman way of reform to pursue other interests at the expense of others left in the wayside. For most of him was true Ptolemy of having been raised in the most sumptuous court in the known world. Everything was handed down to him from the position of his birth. He was not his father, who was known to sit beside the common man and eat the same food and endure the same harsh treatment of the ordinary soldier that made him legendary and much adored by his troops. For Caesarion's father had a humble upbringing in that most of the illustrious fortunes of his family were lost and his mother actually had to make a living by renting out a subdura and had even grown up in it as it was located in the worst and busiest section of Rome.

For that humble beginning was what Augustus tried desperately to emulate, though he was raised in wealth. However, he was very observant and saw the value and devotion of that which it had created in the people of Rome that would try to make him divine as his great-uncle Julius.

Caesarion never had that and never understood the value of being humble. For Caesarion had every advantage. He was the first born son and made Pharaoh when still very young. He was Horus in human form and treated as such. For mother encouraged the spoiling of her children.

It only took the humble heart of a Roman matron to be able to give her the introspection to actually see this and the value of being humble in the years of her captivity. For Octavia was a lot like her brother in that she stood behind the action for the most part mainly because she was a woman; Augustus due to his physical frailties. But it gave them the vast powers of observation and learning the best time to strike when necessary and for the best of their intentions.

This could not be learned in the royal luxuries under the roof that she was raised in, but had to be learned only from being in both places to gain that insight that had proved valuable in her present rule.

She had known secretly in her heart that Caesarion was dead, though kept the naïve and sisterly hope that she would someday meet up with him, since there was no funeral pyre as there was with Helios. She never told her brother how much she cared for him and worst of all, never said goodbye to him. There was no closure at all, which probably enabled those little rays of hope to sink in to torment her.

Well, let Augustus take the reigns that were all too available for him now. Hopefully he will do what is right for Rome. For she was beginning to see what he was actually doing for them and her ill feelings for him were starting to fade in anticipation as to what he was going to do next.

For in reality, she was his client ruler. But secretly, she watched him in avid curiosity and possible admiration in his ability to grasp so effectively the rule that the people of Rome were practically throwing at him. He was actually handling it more than capably and decided that she would learn from him and apply it with her own people as she saw fit.

I

23 B.C.E.

The day had dawned slowly wrapping the tendrils of emotion through her soul as the rays struggled to catch up with the day. She glanced out through her window as the brilliant auburn hues lazily adorned her sill adding to the veined texture of the marble imported for the palace from Carthage. She had woken up early that day, though was unsure as to why. Before this spectacle of the Gods she lay awake for most of the evening over some apprehension. All of the cells of her body were restless and awake, so finally she rose from her feigned slumber to answer to the call of her body. She put on a finely woven light robe that she had recently acquired from a caravan that hailed from Tadmur in Syria. She was delighted with that caravan's contents especially since there was correspondence from Antonia and others from Rome. She was desperate to hear if she was a mother too.

For Selene blossomed in her new motherhood. Her twin daughters were identical in everyway and were soon to be four. She so loved how tiny and perfect they were. Her son little Juba was fast catching up for he had just celebrated his first birthday and was already toddling along ready to wage battles for her. She spent more time than was usual for a Queen and especially a Ptolemy. She supposed a lot of that had been from her mother's hands-on raising of Selene and her siblings. Her mother and father both, were the types of personalities that would not let anyone tell them how to do things.

She recalled her mother discussing this with one of her nursemaids why she raised her own children. Her mother had mentioned to the confused wet nurse that was hired for her little sister Arsinoe, that the services were not required since she as Pharaoh had decided that she would be the sole person to give her children milk. She insisted that her children have only the best and not second rate. She further told that poor woman who tried to slink out of the room at that time, that her children were very important to her and that she would be there completely in raising them. She continued to tirade to the woman that her milk was from Isis herself and her children would not have other than her own, as the others before the youngest child that she was arguing for. For her mother was the only one to teach them every step in their learning how to be proper rulers, that it would not be tainted from wrong teachings. She ended this tirade by stating to the bewildered woman that it was very important that her children love one another and be completely faithful to each other as those children are in a common household.

Looking back on that moment Selene understood her mother's vehemence on the issue and of why she fought against the normalcy for rulers of that time. Her mother was raised with bloodshed under her own roof by her own family members. Her mother had dreams of creating the largest empire the world had ever seen and she wanted to make sure that all of her children would be loyal to her and each other. She wanted to leave them a legacy. Unfortunately there was a power much greater than hers and when unleashed ended up in her downfall and of the loss of the legacy that Selene would have inherited.

However, she did see a great wisdom in her mother having the sole power over her children. Though eventually there were others in the nursery, but as assistants when her mother was busy administering the kingdom. These people were carefully chosen by her and never had complete control of the royal children and none more than the other. Their time was very limited and always Selene's mother was more often seen with her own children by her side in administration.

The only downfall was in my mother's belief in her own immortality that we were so attached to her, we were completely damaged psychologically at the loss of her. Our world was torn asunder in great heaves, none of us had ever recovered completely and she feared that none of them would completely. For their mother was the center of their universe, so uncommon among the more august of individuals that it was considered by others to be obscene. Yet she turned her back on the unusual way that she raised them and went on with her life and in being there almost always for her children as her mother was for them.

For if, she would have lived, her children were made by her an unbreakable unit. For when it started to break, the remaining pieces held together steadfast and stronger than before from survival.

Due to the laws in the Roman world and culture which seemed to envelop all, woman of the culture were distant in raising their children. They kept a safe distance especially soon after birth, for with the complete control that their husbands had with the paterfamilias, there might be the possibility for the baby to be left exposed to the elements if the child were for some chance not to please the father. The mother could do nothing if that fate was decided as her child was ripped from her arms to be left outside to the elements. There also was the high mortality rate of the young children who died very young. Not to mention that added woe if the wife should be divorced by her husband, the children would end up with him to raise and she erased from the picture with no recourse.

Romans and other similar and conquered nations had laws very similar. Also, with the paterfamilias, the father could choose to sell his children and wife into servitude or slavery for debts that he had incurred. And to complete that cultural norm, for the latter occurred more often than not; the paterfamilias gave the father or male guardian complete control over the lives of his children until his daughters were married off and became the property of the husband. But the father could decide while they were still under his control to end the lives of his children, if they had disgraced the family name and honor.

Selene had understood why most women chose to have others raise their children and remain a safe distance. For they wanted to protect themselves from any pain they may experience from any of those things occurring with her offspring. For when one actively participates in the raising of her children, they do become a great weakness. But, to establish an empire, one had to overlook the weakness and look to the complete picture and make sure that nothing would happen to the children.

In reality any of those things could happen to her since her husband was so completely Roman and adhered to it's principles and customs. But, he was so emeshed in his studies that he let her rule the kingdom and nursery as she sought fit. For he had no reason to complain and she did not feel that he would take on the custom of taking on multiple wives since he was so addicted to his studies, he really did not have much time for that. Plus, he had explained to her of the time when he was very young and still in the palace with his mother and his father's wives. He mentioned that he had abhorred the way his father's wives were constantly fighting amongst themselves for favor with his father; and he recalled in revulsion the petty political intrigue, that came to naught upon the death of his father. He never found out what happened to them, nor to his older brothers who were fifteen and twelve at the time they were defeated and sent to Rome. Selene assumed that they might have been killed, since they were too old to gain the habits of Rome as seemed to have been one of the motives in keeping Juba, due to his young and tender age-perfect for molding into a puppet king for the later use of Augustus.

However, neither she nor Augustus planned on Juba in being so much of an intellect with more Greek tendencies then Roman in his constant quest for knowledge. She genuinely felt that she got the better end of that deal and languished in her power. Though she was always sure that all of her actions would be to please her husband and that she would not slip up to inflict the dreaded paterfamilias.

She ruled well and adored her freedom in raising her children in that the servants and slaves listened to her. Mostly since her husband was mostly unavailable, and also because she was Queen.

After her mind burst with thoughts as it almost always did with her almost crippling analytical mind. She was dressed to meet the demands of her day.

For today she had planned an outing with the children to a small pond that was built in the town's new park that she and Juba had built and was finally completed in the old Greek style with Corinthian columns that had been rescued from the ruins and destruction of Corinth. She had even imported some statues to adorn the gardens from Athens. She and her husband admired the ancient ruins of Greece that had dotted the known world. Instead of letting them perish to the elements as they most often did, her husband had set about collecting them to add to the building of their new capitol of Caesarea of Mauretania. She wanted her children to bask in the marvel of creation. She felt like a sculpture with a new work of art, waiting in anticipation to show what she had worked so hard to create for future generations. She languished in the delight of being able to explain to her children why each sculpture was chosen and what it represented and where it was from and even about the arrangement of the whole park so that it faced the sun as it rose over the cliffs above the harsh ocean that bordered their new homeland.

She completed dressing in her newly acquired garments and stole out of the room in the frenzy of a new day with her children. She strode purposely into her children's sleeping chamber. At the sound of her presence into the room her children were instantly by her side in anticipation of the surprise that she had planned. Drussi, Tonia and little Juba were all too glorious to behold even in their tiny dawn soaked and sleepy eyes and morning kisses aimed at her. She first scooped up little Juba into her arms surrounding him in all of his little baby pudginess and deep joy. Tonia and Drussi followed suit and scrambled over each other for the best place in her embrace. She so loved mornings with her babies. All the problems in her kingdom and the world ceased in the cocoon of love that she had created in those first moments of each day.

She bade her favorite servant who slept by the edge of the room to await any attendance upon the needs of the sleeping princesses and prince should they wake. Cilia was chosen over all of the others in the palace due to her keen intelligence and devotion to Selene and her children. She simply bathed in the glow of her mistress and her power and was amazed at how much a part in her charges lives that the Queen paid her own children. For she was there whenever Selene was not. "Morning

Domina" whispered the sleep weary maid to her mistress. Cilia promptly rose and attended to the dressing needs of her young charges.

"Morning Cilia, will you check to see that everything is ready for our outing later on this morning. Make sure that all is ready for the surprise that I have planned." The little ones squealed in delight over this, for they had always loved surprises from Mamma. They ran around the room with newfound energy so normal in ones so little, excitedly chirping over every little thing that entered their fresh and inquisitive minds. "Mamma, Drussi swept wif my dolly a' nite. She has at give it back a me!"

"Did not! Momma! Jubbi hurry up." Chimed in Tonia, always fast to respond to the quips of her older sister by two minutes. It seemed to Selene that possibly Drussi was always aware of being the first born and was eager to defend her position. Though little Tonia was all to eager to let her sister know that she was not far behind. They might argue often as was common amongst siblings, but they had a bond like only she as a twin could understand. They were even developing their own secret language. Little Juba was always taking the world at his pace. She joked to her husband that he might be like Augustus in that respect and saw that he might be developing a conqueror's mind. Of course it was way to early to make any kind of assessment on the personality of her son at this point. But it was fun anyways to try with every nuance noticed in that she was such a big part of their lives. This was something radically missed in the lives of other royal women that she would never let go of her love for her own children.

Her babies were also especially musical much to her delight. She loved to believe that they had inherited that from her grandfather Ptolemy Auletes, the notorious flute player would shake the foundations of the palace Bruchion in the endless playing of his latest compositions. Drussi and Tonia were singing a song made up for her while they changed into their miniature toga's bordered with embroidered desert roses in crimson set against the stark whiteness of it. She made sure their togas of youth were embroidered in that they were not so staunch as they were in Rome and austere, but held a taste of whimsy that she could get away from so far away from the city principalis. She added it also since her children were rarely seen in public and it was her own special touch that she added as their mother. Cilia had embroidered most of the borders herself and Selene though she was exceptionally talented and patient to compose such works of art on something that was not meant to be whimsical in any way. Such was the vapid mode of dress of the Romans. They had tried to emulate the Greeks, but had succeeded in making it more staunch and regal rather than flowing in artistic sense as the Greeks were known to garb themselves. All their clothes from sculptures were beautifully flowing and only attracted the human form underneath, rather than the Roman way of hiding the human form in humility. The Greeks were proud of their bodies, while the Romans sought to hide them in heavy drapery. That might be the accepted mode of garb, but she would add her touch in as many ways as she though fit for their position and distance, they were able to get away with it.

"Goin to da pawk, goin to the paaaak" the twins chimed in unison as if they had practiced it for days.

"Don't worry little ones, Momma will take you, but after your lessons." Juba hobbled in on his unstable chubby legs and did his own little dance for her with his big sisters. "All right babies, just hurry up and do your best and we will be on our way." The lessons that she had them do was more of having them learn how to write their names. She was getting them familiar with hieroglyphs which they thought were very pretty in that they looked like animals and flowers. She made it into a game. She also believed, as her mother taught her that a child's mind was like a sponge, willing to absorb everything presented to it. She recalled avidly how her mother had always addressed her with adult terms and let her sit beside her when she attended to business, explaining everything to her and her brothers and later Arsinoe would be brought into watch as well.

For most of the day except for one hour in the morning and two hours after midday, when her children were either at nap or at their first lessons- they would always be in her presence. She even gave them special duties so that they could help her and not get bored.

While the children had their lessons, she made sure that all of the preparations were complete for the outing that was planned for that day and gathered her sister Arsine who was now eleven and showing signs of potential beauty. Her hair was very long and naturally curled and hung down freely around her back in rivulets of golden sunshine. Yet, Arsine had been mostly raised by Selene in the years that she remembered and hung on to every word and action of her oldest sister in constant dotage and admiration.

Ptolemy Philedelphos was now thirteen and ready to don his toga of manhood in which a ceremony was being prepared for next month. She so wished that she had the advice of her father in this. Juba had to do most of the work in that matter in that he was raised in Rome and had his own ceremony put on by Augustus himself. When her husband was a captor, Augustus had raised the children of the conquered kingdoms as his own in his residence on the Palantine Hill in Rome. That was where her husband had most of his education, except for his later studies in Athens.

And the lovely and shy Iotape who had fast become another member of the family of Juba and Selene who was now sixteen years old and had assisted Selene in most of the matters with the children.

All of them were eager for this day, for it had been awhile since they had an outing due to the inclement weather that had been pouring down on them for several days. This was the first day in almost a week, where it was so beautiful with temperate winds.

After the lessons were over, Selene gathered all of her charges with several slaves in tow to carry the litters through the streets filled with the royal charges. Several guards were posted in attendance as well for the world they lived in was constantly filled with threats from many directions. Though, Selene had made sure, like her mother that none of the treats of her and her children's lives came from her own household. She vowed on this and continued this until her death.

Through the newly paved streets of her city in resemblance of the streets of Rome, they traveled to the outskirts to the destination she had chosen as her new Greek Gardens. Through arched tunnels of trees they made their slow progress at the pace of the slaves and though rows upon rows of Greek Doric Columns and sphinxes she had commissioned throughout her new city. For Selene loved the architecture of the Greeks almost as much as she favored her own homeland with the brilliant colors painted on the mud brick and stone buildings. The many bright hues stood in stark contrast to the almost severe white of the Greek architecture, yet Selene had arranged it in a way to enhance each other rather than compete for magnificence. They had passed the granaries, the shipyard and then past the treasury and her replica of the Museon that her mother so loved during her life as well as the great library that was at that time just a skeleton in progress of the great structure that she had planned. All of her collected works were stored in the treasury in a vault way below until the building was completed enough to open it to the public.

The love of administration and learning of the Great Cleopatra had surely found it's home in her daughter with all that she had planned for the great city which she and her husband now rule over by the name of Caesarea. She was also planning a new city to be built further west in their province on the ruins of a much smaller Town to be called as in antiquity Tingis. This new city was in the very beginning stages of planning, though it was located in a very strategic place geographically and would be a great seaport town one day. This city was located at the Pillars of Hercules and almost touched the coast of Hispania at Baetica near the city of Gates there.

The day was growing more and more bright with each step closer to her chosen destination. Selene purposely left all of them wondering where the outing would be. For Selene loved to surprise people, especially those whom she loved. She would never reveal her plans until at the destination or when the surprise was revealed. That way in her extremely complex life, if plans should change due to her politics and rule or even for some inauspicious reason such as omen predicted by her soothsayer, she was able in the allowed flexibility of her mysterious suspense that she often led the others to, to be able to change those plans to an alternate, unbeknownst to those she was lavishing something or other on whom she loved.

Though on this day, everything had gone perfectly according to plan with out her needing to attend to business elsewhere and to have to postpone this day. It seemed almost as if the weather had changed for this day in that it was destined to happen. Despite her sleepless night and the ramblings of her soothsayer of an omen to occur…

She lay in her litter soothed by the steady, yet relaxing pace of the slaves who carried it with her twins wrapped in her robes beside her with a firm grip on little Juba who on many occasions, tried to jump out of it. Those thoughts of apparent woe were lost to her and faded away with each step towards the rest of her day and the plan ahead.

With each attempt in the flight of her son, she grasped him a little tighter, though not too tight and told him that he must cease in this, for it would make the ride even longer! He was so much like her in the matter that she always hated traveling to her destinations. Rather, she would love to fly there and skip the actual means of travel to get her from place to place for it took up too much valuable time in exploring places and meeting with people. This trait she had also shared with her husband and definitely little Juba was wriggled in her tight and reinforcing grip of his chubby baby body.

The twins in her litter were almost motionless near her restful body and peeking through the curtains of the litter to see everything they could. Soaking up the sights of their small journey like ambrosia and gathering it for a three-year -old's analytical skills, fast becoming more like their mother's.

Drussi, had started her little game with her sister and would tangle her tiny fingers into the unsuspecting wavy hair of her little twin sister. This in turn would cause Tonia to turn on her sister and grab her hair in turn in her own fingers. Selene watched in wonder at this interaction which would cause horror in most other children that age, but was possibly the way in which her twins connected. The late morning sun snuck into her litter splashed in sunlight from behind the curtains to weave soft intentions of a beautiful day into her daughters hair as it touched the rays that poked in from outside by the constant peeking from them.

She understood the little games of connection that her twins played for she had similar games with her brother when very young from the times she and he shared the same elaborate cradle that their father had carved for them. She still had this cradle, which was found and later given to her by Octavia.

This cradle was a blending of Egyptian and Roman carvings of the Gods and Goddesses paying homage to the contents within. It was carved in wood from the faraway forests in the coveted Cypress of Syria near Damascus. It was so beautiful it was worthy to carry future kings. Though Helios never had the chance for his own children to sleep in it.

As she watched her children play with each other's hair and little Juba had finally ceased his struggling and fell into a deep baby sleep, she thought about her beloved and greatly missed twin. She tried to block him out and focus on other things, which was difficult enough. She recalled the joy that she felt and her immediate connection when Iotape had presented her with the journals her brother had kept in order that his life was preserved when he became the famous general like his father, as he had often dreamed of when they were very young and last together as siblings. He had even had a silver stylus made for her to give her in that he had obviously seen that she had taken his in memory. He was always thoughtful of her in the littlest ways. She hoped that her daughters would be that way to each other.

At last they arrived. Time seemed to have finally stirred from it's slumber on the journey there with all of the emotions drudged up from the abyss of her ponderings. Yet to the present moment she had at last arrived with the sudden stopping of the litters in procession at their destination. She gave the awaited word and all of the other royal children climbed out in anticipation to the sight that she had picked in her new gardens. "Momma, so pwetty" Exclaimed Tonia in rapt delight for she had noticed the small statues of the childhood deities of Cupid and his friends that were at the very entrance of her great gardens. Little Juba had climbed out in the careful way he was learning to navigate on his chubby baby legs from the litter to the place that his sister's had already run to in their excitement. Iotape and Arsinoe had begun to wander around as well in delight at this haven that Selene had created that was atop a small hill against cliffs that fell away to the beautiful ivory cliffs that touched the waters in splendid sky blue.

They all finally observed the tent that Selene had set up with a small feast fit for her royal charges. In reverence to the prophesy that she had always kept in her mind, she had made sure that there was a fence constructed around the edge of the steep drop-off. She had wanted to create a place that would meet the sky above in that it was the highest spot in the city beside the location of where their palace stood. Yet she made sure that the area was safe enough for her still very young children. The tent was set up and couches were placed there especially for all of them and a larger one from the palace in which she could sit with her three young children and help them to eat. For they were still very young and little Juba had a tendency to throw his food when he was done eating. She even made sure there were musicians to dance and sing to them of the many adventures of the Goddess Isis in the quest to find the pieces of her beloved Osiris as stolen and broken apart by her hated brother Seth.

Her children loved it when she had the stories of her homeland recited to them and little Juba especially delighted in any of the adventures of Osiris, which she had planned for them to watch that day as well. This was one of the ways that she had connected her own history in her children's lives. She also knew that Arsinoe especially loved this tale as well and that Iotape was unfamiliar with the legends of Egypt.

As they moved into settle onto their couches in preparation for their meal, the older ones present settled in decorously while the younger three had to be fetched up by Cilia who had joined them for the reason in helping Selene to keep the children by her side. For they were apt to run on every occasion they could. The twins would often try to take something from their little brother in tandem, while he had tried with all his little might to catch up to them and retrieve whatever they had of his. This day, however at the delight of such a warm and sunny day, they just ran all around in the pure delight of this new place before them and in being out with their mother, who all too often of late had pressing matters which took her away from them.

Finally they were gathered by the persistent Cilia and placed beside their mother. Selene had told her children that they each would have a turn to pick out from the tables prepared for them exclusively anything that they wanted. Though she told them that they could only choose a small bit, for the food left untouched would go to the palace slaves as was custom. As she explained this, the official food taster, in the view of Selene had tasted each and every item. When this was done, he motioned to her that all was well. Then Selene took little Juba by his tiny hands with Drussi and Tonia in tow to the tables.

The table was laden with all different types of delicacies for the royal palates with such items as shellfish from the beaches below them, tiny fruitcakes in a mint sauce, crabs cut in half and stuffed with herbs and bread crumbs, fruits of every kind imaginable, especially their favorite pomegranates and even the dates that Tonia loved. There were many things to choose from for this special occasion of showing this garden to her children and charges before anyone else in the world saw it. She had to choose a little bit of most everything because little Juba wanted everything. The twins had chosen their food and pointed out each item that was scooped onto almost overflowing plates of gold that shone in the sun almost blinding them. Drussi had wanted another plate brought over just so she could see her face in the smoothness of her reflection that she had noticed to her delight. Selene motioned that each of her little children should have an extra plate for this as well. She noticed the many fresh sea muscles that Tonia had put on her plate and that Drussi had followed suit. It was almost as if they were of one mind to fit how identical they looked to almost everyone but their Mother and those who knew them best. For Drussi had favored her left hand, while Tonia had favored her right hand. Besides Tonia had the chubbier baby face over her sister. And Tonia had a small dimple that Drussi lacked on her left cheek. Those little differences would set them apart for those who knew them well. For they loved to play tricks on the servants slaves who attended them.

At last they were settled to eat their meals. Her sister and Iotape and Ptolemy had chosen their food and had joined Selene on the couches that she had placed in a circle so that she would be easily able to converse with them. The bowls were brought around to each one of them filled with jasmine scented water to wash their hands before beginning their meal and a linen towel offered to each in turn to dry their hands. Basking to the soft music that she had chosen to soothe her children so that they could eat in peace as they all reclined in the Roman fashion to eat their small feast.

Selene recalled that in Rome, the women and children would sit on stools beside the men who ate on the couches. Though she would not allow that so far away from Rome and bid all of the royal family to eat from couches.

She first helped little Juba with his chosen delights and was busy paying attention to him, when all of a sudden her head turned out of instinct to the rapidly turning blue face of her daughter Tonia. The tiny face was increasing fast and choking off her airway. Drussi with her plate untouched stared in silence at her sister. Selene threw off her plate and screamed for Cilia to grab her other two children so that she would be better able to attend to her daughter losing her air right before her. She grasped the small body in her arms wondering if she had choked on something, trying desperately to get out that food item. Tonia's face was turning almost a deathly green while her eyes suddenly clouded over in delirium. In panic all of the other slaves and servants were running around and trying to extricate the small child from the desperate mother who clutched her daughter trying to save her life.

Even after it was apparent that the small Tonia was dead, Selene fervently clung to the reality that her child still might be saved. The lifeless body was loosing the greenish color of the sudden malady that had seized the life out of the child. Selene was still trying to get the life back in her daughter and the normalcy to return. All others stood still, not knowing what had happened, since it occurred in only a few seconds of time. Selene was now shaking Tonia upside down to get some imagined piece of food out of the airway. It was apparent at this point that it was not food, and to all old enough to witness this wondered if it was poison. Yet did not think that it was possible since the food taster was still standing and stopped in time as the rest of them to this sudden breach of peace on a such a beautiful day.

The color of Tonia's face was rapidly returning and to it's normal size again, when Selene had stopped in her mad quest to get the life back for her child. In the naked reality of the moment, Selene must have known that it was too late for her little Tonia. Drussi sat still as the marble statues that played in ignorance around the state of horror that held them all on companionship.

Iotape then rushed to the side of Selene and Arsinoe followed suit, while Ptolemy gathered his little niece and nephew and made orders to rush them back to the palace to contact Juba. Selene sat there with the golden painted ceramic plates crashed to the ground in her frenzy and battle to save the life of her young daughter. She looked down on the sweet face of her Tonia which was now looking more like she was in a soft slumber. The color had returned though not to the usual vigor with flushed cheeks, but rather a shadow. The eyes were wide open, which were promptly shut by Arsinoe to give her sister the vision that she was looking at her daughter in sleep and not in the reality before them of Tonia in death.

Selene entered a dream state at that moment probably to save her soul from the moment before her in her closeness to her children. The weakness of such that her mother had mentioned to her was lost in her delirious state that she was cradling her live daughter in her arms. She refused to let anyone take her Tonia away from her body. Others around her had tried noting the state that Selene was in, but to no avail, Selene held fast to her child cradled so desperately in her arms and in turn had enveloped herself around the still child.

The other's decided that it was best to follow the suit of Ptolemy in taking the other two children back, and to just gather the Queen with her child in her arms to take her back to the palace.

In the litter Selene held the body of her small child as if comforting a sleeping or sick child. She touched the soft curls of dark chestnut that crowned her daughter's face. And twined her fingers into her daughter's that were so small and delicate. She folded her body around that of Tonia's as they made their slow progress towards the palace. Tonia was growing cold in her mother's comforting hug, but Selene was oblivious to it and refused to let it touch her. She sang the little girls favorite lullaby of the Goddess Nut in spreading her body over the heavens in comfort and in holding in her body all of the stars of the sky. An ancient tune that was taught to her by her own mother.

When they reached the palace, Selene fought in anger to keep her child in her arms like one possessed. "She will not be taken from me! I am her mother and with me she belongs! Don't you touch me!" Her screams echoed in the vast chamber which brought Juba to her side. He collapsed over his wife to try to stop her mad ravings in keeping the still form of her child. "My love it will be alright! They need to take her way to get her dressed. For her clothes are dirty!" He whispered soothingly to comfort his wife in her shock. It worked for Selene's muscles had relaxed enough for her to loosen the hold that she had on Tonia for the servants to take her away for funeral preparations. "Make sure that she has on her lavender shift with the pink slippers that she loves!" Selene then stood and brushed herself off and slowly walked a few feet and then without warning collapsed from an exhaustion that had suddenly crept over her. Asandros was there and had gathered the bereaving Queen into the arms of his servants to be taken to her chambers.

Asandros knew that Selene was of solid character, though feared that she might slip into a sort of madness due to her closeness with her children that he had warned her about. He also set into motion his assistants who would help him in finding out the cause of the death of the little princess, for he set about an investigation into the matter for the ease of her parents when they came to and wanted answers.

II

In his chambers after he had given Queen Selene a sedative, he had peered at the small body of the little princess who appeared as if in sleep. Such a shame, for such an innocent to have such a dreadful fate. From his accounts of those who witnessed the event, he found out that the little princess, Selena Antonia Helia was eating shellfish when all of a sudden her face turned green ad swelled up to three times the size. Jubilla Drusilla Cleopatra had not touched her shellfish prior to that moment nor anything else on her plate. Others had eaten the same shellfish and they were fine. It seemed to him after examining the princess that she had a violent adverse reaction to the food. He had heard about this malady from other physicians, though he had not seen it since his younger days in his education at the Museon in Alexandria. After looking at her body in death and with all of the interviews that he had conducted he had arrived at the conclusion that this princess had suffered the same fate. He also knew that sometimes the person would have had to have eaten the shellfish prior to the reaction in order for the body to determine it as poison for the next time that it was eaten. He also determined that the other princess and the prince should avoid anything prepared from the sea to avoid similar adverse reactions in them. Thus, he had not seen such a violent reaction in one so young before. Yet all of the signs for this were there in his examination, for he had also found nothing lodged in her throat.

At the conclusion of his investigation, he reverently wrapped the small form of the princess up to cover her face, since it was beginning to haunt him as well. Such a pretty young child. He hated when the little ones were taken from life to suddenly and especially from a mother who so loved and cherished her as the Queen obviously did. This was one of the reasons that he had begged Queen Selene not to establish such close connections to her young. More often that most, they were taken away soon, and also in marriage, the royal children would soon enough be leaving the warm protective nest that Selene had built for them into the cold harsh world. Would his Queen follow them? Certainly not, for she had her own kingdom to run.

As the princess was taken away he had to sit down and reflect on this and to try to bring his professional self back into the picture to help the grieving parents. In other cases he often told the parents left behind grieving that that it would be alright, that they could always have more. But, he knew that in this case those words would fall on unhearing words and only anger his Queen in her closeness to her offspring.

III

Days had passed and Selene would not leave her room hoping for her child to be brought back to her. Oblivious to the world around her. She could not even leave to see her daughter's soul lifted up to the sky at her funeral pyre, nor hear the words recited by her husband and brother in oration of her funeral. She would not accept the idea that her baby Tonia was dead. She thought that if she prayed hard and deep enough to Isis, she would return to her and try to cuddle by her side in her sleep. For little Tonia had loved to curl in her mother's arms leaving the nursery at night.

Drussi would be on one side and Tonia on the other. They had their own pallets to sleep on, but the two of them would in unison sneak into the chamber of their mother to be by her warm side. Selene would wake up, since they were not as quiet as they believed that were, but pretend to be sleeping whenever those sweet nights occurred and when they fell asleep, she would make sure the blankets would cover their tiny forms close to hers in slumber.

This evening she had woken up to one little body besides hers cradled and looking for comfort. It had shocked her into the present and the tears that she had held back for an eternity had begun to flow desperately down onto her little remaining daughter, Drussi. She grabbed Drussi and held her in an eternal body hug as she wrapped herself around her daughter. Her loss met up with her soul which she tied onto the form of her daughter so close to her. "Momma, when is Tonia coming back? "

"Oh, baby…" And she rocked her little daughter to sleep with her tears flooding down.

Part four

I

15 B.C.E.

Eight years had passed since that horrific event and still Selene imagined that her lost daughter would be returned, as if she were only away. Her grief had faded so that she was able to wrap it deep inside of her, yet still remained as strong as the moment that her daughter's life had slipped away from her in her arms.

So much had occurred since then. Selene was still in control of the kingdom while Juba was busy in his studies. The other city had been completed and they had spent time at both palaces frequently. Most just to escape anything that reminded her other her lost princess, her little Tonia. Whose memory was perfected and sharpened in her mind. She had a statue commissioned that resembled the little cherished princess so exactly, Selene could not bring herself to see it when it was erected in her mausoleum for several years. She had inscribed the lullaby of Isis on the tomb with orders that it would be sung every evening at the sight of the first star in memory of her daughter.

In the years that had passed two marriage contracts were made for her remaining prince and princess after much investigation on the other countries they would soon rule over.

Selene had chosen for Jubilla Drusilla Cleopatra to marry Cunobelinios, who was the grandson of Llud, the leader of the Cassi or as the Roman's called them the Catuvellauni tribe in Britain.

Llud was the older brother of the legendary Vellaunos who was referred to by the Romans as Casswallon or sometimes as Cassivellaunos, which was in reference to his tribal name as the Smiters of Vellaunos which would be interpreted by the Latin tongue as Cassivellaunos. There was a rich history in them and they worshipped the mother Goddess who was similar to her Isis. A woman was valued in the tribes, which was the main reason why they were chosen by Selene. Leadership was chosen by the lineage of their mothers and the connections to the tribe. However, in this particular case, Cassivellaunos was crowned the King of a merchant settlement that the Romans called Londinium and the Keltoi called Lludein in honor of their King Llud who had conquered the Island and subdued the tribe into his family leadership. It was rumored that Casswallon had murdered his older brother Llud for the throne.

For Casswallon's sons had not gained the throne, as it was passed on to the sons of the brother that he had allegedly murdered. His own sons died young and one of them left behind a boy named Bran and called the blessed by many even as far away as her own land-so legendary were his healing powers.

For she had learned through her studies on this faraway land that she would someday send her daughter to the descendants of that the very first ruler to that land was Beli Mawr, the same man who had taken to wife the sister of Juba I's father named Don of the Royal Numidian House. Together they sailed away to the far reaches of the known world and found a wonderful place in which to bring up their children. She is referred to in history as Don ferch Matonwy and is now looked upon as the mother of their tribe and revered as a Goddess. Together they tried in vain to unite the many tribes scattered there under one rule. They had three sons and one daughter named Ahrianred who, as legend points out had hair as bright as dawn. Her beauty was legendary and caused many battles to be fought over by the hands of her brothers and kings of the land in which they settled, she was most importantly a brave warrior who helped to cease the battles. Selene was impressed by this fact about Juba's aunt and only intrigued further studies on her and her children.

Finally one of the son's of Beli named Llud with the help of his mother's forces, was able to restore order to the tribes and was named the first king of the city that he created that the Romans now called Londinium. For the name was truly Lludein in honor of their family settling there and establishing that they were the true descendants of Troy, from one of the son's of Paris, the legendary Prince of the City, the son of King Priam.

Llud had taken the hand of his sister Ahrianred to keep the line pure in the spirit of the ancient Egyptians and other ancient dynasties, unknown to this strange new world. Yet after ten years of rule, his youngest brother, Casswallon had killed Llud and was crowned in his place to rule over the tribes united.

Nennius, the middle brother was horrified that he was so quietly passed over in rule, that he ran over the Romans to seek their help in getting the throne back for him that should rightfully have been his. Don purposefully passed Casswallon over in favor of her youngest son Llud due to Casswallon's true nature that was venomous from birth and felt that her youngest son, Llud had rightfully earned the throne with his good and honest nature.

Nennius was also known to the Romans as Affallech Avarwy Mandubbracios. At the death of his father, Beli and of his oldest and youngest brothers, Nennius finally assumed rule over the tribes; though they divided over the feelings towards the betrayal of Nennius. For Nennius had brought their secluded interest to the ever grasping attention of the Romans. Julius Caesar led an expedition to the farthest south corners of the island closest to the conquered Gaul and set out an expedition. At that time, he decided that it was much larger and too turbulent to try to subdue and had too much on his plate already with all of his other conquests, that he left the island to explore at a later date. This later time never did arrive, much to the delight on the Britons who thought that Rome gave up for good and continued on peacefully with their way of life and of worshipping in their groves.

After the mysterious death of Llud, Casswallon had gained the attention of his mother who prided herself on her sons and daughter in the battle skills against the Romans, that she had taught them. He skillfully maneuvered her attention from her oldest surviving son Mandubbracios and never ceased in reminding her that he had betrayed them to the Romans. He gained her attention in matters in her older son's absence.

Casswallon, before assuming leadership from his mother had earned her further attention when he had successfully retrieved Fflur who was the daughter of Mynach Gorr, a minor chieftain under them. For she was abducted by a Gallic prince named Mwrchan. He had landed with his troops of over 61,000 men and defeated the Romans in battle without a drop of blood shed on their way to retrieve Fflur, which he did successfully.

He had crept up in the middle of the night with his invisible cloak and whisked her to safety without battle. That was what really impressed his mother. For though she was a warrior, she abhorred bloodshed. And to win a battle without it made her happy in that when her husband died, she gave the throne and rule over the Trinovantes to her youngest son due to that very reason.

When Casswallon had retrieved Fflur, it was not so easy getting back to Briton and their homeland, for he had to remain in hiding. Comminos, the brother of Mwrchan and leader of the Gaulish tribe of Atribates was angered by this betrayal to his family. Comminos was also battle strong after having recovered from his battle wounds from the losing battle of Vercingetorix against Julius Caesar. After having recovered from that he was eager for new battle and used it as an excuse to lead forces in pursuit of Casswallon in order to retrieve his brother's lost daughter Fflur, whom he was betrothed to marry.

Comminos had chased Casswallon all of the way back to Briton and had managed to persuade the Atribates tribe there to rally with him in pursuit of Casswallon. The Atribates of Briton were angered at all of the homage they had to give Llud, who was one of the three main kings of that Island the Romans called Britain and they called Pryttain. They joined him with little persuasion and even made Comminos leader of their tribe since their prior one was old and unable to rule and he was childless. The

Atribates were as much willing for battle as was Comminos and wanted to bring their tribe to the forefront with legend. They set off in pursuit of Casswallon who had again returned to Briton and even went so far with her as Rome, where he fell in love with the splendor of it and admired the buildings in stone and the columns. He found a home for he and Fflur in a small village outside of Rome and lived together as husband and wife in handfast for almost a year.

Comminos with his Atribates eventually caught up with him and waited for his guard to be down. They spotted the magic cloak by a rock on the river where it was set down so that Casswallon could bathe. Comminos took the chance and ran into the house where Casswallon and Fflur dwelled. Fflur took one look at Comminos and fell in love. Together they fled back to their Island of Pryttain and returned to rule over the tribe of the Atribates.

Casswallon was angered by this and the loss of his magic cloak which Comminos had stolen with his wife. He set out in pursuit of both of them and followed them to Pryttain. Casswallon had returned to his tribe that he had assumed the rule over given to him by his mother after the mysterious death of his oldest brother Llud soon after his return. His mother had found out of the trials of her son with Fflur since she had sent out emissaries to follow them and to check on their welfare. She welcomed her son into her arms and pushed aside Nennius Mandubbracios Avarwy, since her favorite son had returned to her and together they planned a way to win back the heart of Fflur from Comminos and to retrieve the magic cloak passed down to him by his father before he left on the expedition.

Mandubbracios was very upset for prior to the return of his brother, he thought that he would gain the throne having assisted rule with his mother after the death of their father. But upon the return of his brother, his mother had seemed to have forgotten all they had done together in rule. His wife Ivora was very upset as well that her husband would be passed over since she was setting herself up for rule and had flourished in the idea. With her husband and much persuasion she had convinced her husband to go over to Britain one more time and gain their help. Her children were still young, just babies. The oldest Avarwy was looking more and more like his father, though only six years old. She left them in the charge of their grandmother Don, while she went with her husband to Rome to seek help in attaining the throne for the rightful heir, Mandubbracios.

However, when they arrived and sought the aid of Julius Caesar, he was angered by the pathetic countenance of this weakling and betrayer prince and ordered his execution. Ivora was spared her life, though was banished from Rome. However, Julius Caesar was intrigued by the information about this virtually untouched country and wanted to see for himself what it was all about. That was the reason he sent over an expedition, in order for him to gain knowledge. Due to his current political situation and having to devote more of his time to Rome, he abandoned the idea of returning there to a later date, which never arrived. Julius Caesar hated betrayers to families and was appalled by this Mandubbracios and his nagging wife. He was especially repulsed in that Mandubbracios was willing to pay him 3,000 pounds of silver for the betrayal of his own brother. He did keep the money though for his waste of time.

Selene had heard the rumor that Casswallon had killed his brother Llud by wearing their father's invisible cloak and stabbing his brother while he lay by the river in a nap. She was not sure how much of this was true and believed that it could have been created by their brother Nennius Mandubbracios out of anger. Whatever the case, Don favored Casswallon over his older brother Nennius, she must have had her reasons.

Don and her favorite son had devised a way to win back the heart of Fflur. Casswallon set out for the land of the Atribates where Comminos dwelled with Fflur. He was in luck for when he arrived and scouted out the area he found his love by the river crying. He went to her side and inquired why. She responded by falling into his arms and explained that the true nature of Comminos was horrible and that he had stolen her with lies and that she was truly sorry. For when Comminos returned to Pryttain he locked her in their lodge and beat her into submission. She stated to Casswallon that she truly desired to be with him. She mentioned that for all the good he had done, she would reveal to him the location of the magic cloak that Comminos had stolen from Casswallon. And to prove her love for him, begged him to let her find it and bring it back to him.

Casswallon waited and was rewarded by the return soon after of Fflur wrapped inside of the magic cloak, which she used to hide herself in escape from her tyrannical husband. Together they fled back to the Trinovantes and established a happy rule together. She soon after gave birth to Llyr and then Andoco.

Upon the death of Casswallon, their oldest son Llyr had assumed rule over the tribe for three years and he had married the daughter of Llud to intertwine their tribes. The daughter was named Penardun. His only daughter was married off to a prince in Gaul named Divico and under Roman leadership. After the death in battle with the Atribates, Andoco assumed the rule over the tribe, though the domain was lessened and he called the tribe Catuvellauni that he now ruled over.

Andoco left no heir and had died young.

After the rule of Andoco for three years upon the death of Llyr, the rule was then passed on to the youngest child of Llud named Tenvantius. For Penardun was pregnant with her son Bran at the time of her husband Llyr's death and in her grief of her married daughter lost to her as well as her cherished husband had left the tribes to live far away from the politics of court life in her own refuge by the sea in the southern-most part of Briton.

Penardun lived peacefully with her son named Bran, the grandson of Casswallon. For her son, Bran was noted among the wild people by the sea as being blessed with divinity as revealed to all by his fair face.

However, Selene considered Bran way to young for marriage with her children and was reinforced when Penardun had written to her that she had already promised him from birth the daughter of a Wiseman from the land of Judea named Joseph of Arimethea. For Joseph of Arimethea had a daughter of about the same age as Bran by the name of Anna. Penardun in later correspondence with Selene had felt sorry for this. Penardun had further mentioned that she had no other children, though suggested that Selene and her husband should try with her brother Tenvantius who now was ruling over the land that she left.

Selene had reestablished the correspondence that her husband had abandoned due to his latest expedition. And wrote to Tenvantius. She was further advised by Penardun that she should try to stay away from her brother Nennius Mandubbracios who had betrayed them and had a son named Avarwy who was proving to be as conniving as his father was.

So Selene established a faithful correspondence with Tenvantius who had informed her that he had three sons and the oldest of which was studying in Rome at the request of his grandmother Don, by the name of Cynfelyn, though the Roman's called him Cunobelinios. He sent praises of the valor of his son and would think that the granddaughter of Cleopatra would establish a fine line of Kings and Queens to rule over their land. For he had heard of the legends of Selene's family and already knew of her husband and their own connections to the family though him. He also mentioned that she should stay away from his brother who had been killed by the Romans and his children, who had been exiled and had set up rule over a tribe that was known as the Silures in a Rocky land far from them.

He affirmed his good relationship with his sister Penardun and of her holy remaining son and kin.

Selene had then taken all that she had learned and approached her husband about the idea of going to Rome to see the young prince Cynfelyn to make the final decision. She had also wanted to see her half sister Antonia Minor who was now well established in her marriage with Drusus. She further assured her husband that he could visit his benefactor Augustus and visit with him. They could use that visit to also reassure their position with Rome in that there were recent rebellions by the Maurii tribe and they needed the assistance of Rome to help quell them.

For those reasons and the wisdom of his wife. Juba II agreed to the voyage and decided to bring his daughter and son along as well in that they, though young might benefit from the visit. She thought of that visit in retrospect for it occurred four years from her current musings on the situation and led her to the current time in her life.

II

When Juba and Selene had gone to Rome, it was four years after the death of Tonia. Since then, Selene had emeshed herself in politics with her son and daughter by her side to leave herself little time to think about it. Drussi at the time of their visit to Rome was then seven years old and showing signs of great beauty. Her hair was by the year, showing more and more signs of red in the dark brown. Juba the Younger was only five years old and would not stop his running and even was beginning to outrun his own mother much to the delight of their father. Her brother and sister came along with them for the journey and to see those in Rome that they had missed. Arsinoe was almost past the accepted age of marriage and Selene had to start considering this, though dreaded having to part with her. She was already fourteen and the matter should have been thought of before this, though Selene put it on the side since she had grown too attached to her young sister with the summer blonde hair. Iotape would also join their entourage along with Asandros and Cilia and many others assigned to assist them in the voyage and their stay in Rome.

Many things were accomplished in that long ago voyage to Rome, Selene thought in retrospect. For upon their arrival, they were immediately put up in the palace on the Palantine where Augustus was residing with his wife Livia and his niece Antonia Minor, her husband Drusus and his sister Octavia.

She had many mixed feeling on Augustus. Partly from her loyalty to her mother and part in her own observation on how he creatively ruled Rome and how he was with his family. He had also taken the young prince Cunobelinios under his wing. For he admired the brave young man's approach and request for help in his education, forgetting that it was he who had taken him from his own home long ago. And Augustus was further flattered that his family considered Rome. Selene noted that Augustus made the world that he lived in to suit any possible mistakes that he may have made to shield himself from any guilt. This she realized was all too human and humored him in his reality as did everyone else.

When Selene and her family arrived in Rome, Augustus was forty one years of age and well contented in his peaceful marriage with his wife Livia. Though they did not have any children of their own, he had accepted Livia's sons from her prior marriage with Tiberius under his wing and tutelage.

Selene had also found out that Cunobelinios was truly the son of Penardun who had been born to her and Llyr prior to their hand-fasting being completed in a year and a day, thus he was adopted after his birth and raised by her uncle Tenvantius. Selene understood why Penardun had pushed Cunobelinios on a possible marriage relation with him. She had closer connections in that he was her first born son. Selene understood this and was especially pleased when she had finally met him. For he was much older than her daughter at eleven years of age. She still deemed that there would be a favorable marriage, to take place when her daughter had grown some and again after meeting his mother-aunt Penardun to talk with her personally on the matter along with meeting the present rule of Pryttain, Tenvantius.

She and her family were very much impressed with the wise, yet soft-spoken demeanor of this man to be her future son-in-law. He was tall and very fair and had towered over the Romans with grace and style. He was not pretentious in any way and had shown she and her husband the proper respect due to their position. For Selene had an uncanny way of looking at the whole person and saw though any façade. She sensed great potential in this man and wanted to seal the bargain of marriage of he and their daughter. Cynfelyn, as he preferred to be called had further assured her that Jubilla Drusilla Cleopatra would rule equally by his side and fight along side him as well in equal valor. For her lineage was considered in the marriage and greatly admired amongst his tribe, especially with her connections from Juba's Aunt and his great-great grandmother revered as a Goddess to his people.

After they were satisfied with Cynfelyn, they decided to visit with Augustus and Antonia Minor and the others whom she had been in faithful correspondence since the day she left Rome.

Antonia ran into the arms of Selene and together they giggled like young school girls. Antonia was eager to catch Selene up on all of the gossip of Rome. As they were giggling, in sauntered Livia's son Tiberius with his adoring wife beside him. "Hello girls. How are you Selene, or should I say your royal highness!"

Giggling all the more and forgetting her age, she responded, "Oh, Tiberius, here time stands still and I am just Selene to you and others here who took such good care of me and my brothers and sister. Besides, you are almost a prince for the care Caesar Augustus takes of you and the position Rome seems to be in." Forgetting her candor in memories of Tiberius when she lived with them, she spoke frankly.

Concerned, Tiberius whispered, "Hush girl the walls of Rome have big floppy ears. Besides Augustus would have you flogged with any mention of Rome mixed with Royalty for you know as well as I how much he favors and intents to restore the old republic?" He winked at Selene to complete his sentence. Vispania Marcella his wife and daughter of Octavia giggled at her playful husband and the recourse between him and the Queen of Mauretania. For Vispania was a very devoted wife to her much loved Tiberius and grew sad when he was not around. She had recently given birth to their first-born Drusus named in honor of her husband's brother and wife of Antonia Minor.

Selene looked back with delight in those conversations with her second family in Rome and the joy they brought her and recalled that in a loving way Tiberius had warned her on further mention of Rome and Royalty. She understood him and was later very thankful in that.

She recalled that while she and her family visited in Rome she had learned the many things that Augustus had done and how well his family spoke of him. She though it simply amazing in how he only wore robes homespun by his sister, daughter, and niece in establishing the traditions of the old republic.

She had observed the many constructions throughout the city and wondered at his reasons for establishing citizenship to a wider area than Rome. She saw his wise administration skills as well as his excellently delegated tactical maneuverings to men very worthy of command under him. She had also noted that upon the death of Marcellus, the son of Octavia, Augustus had married his only daughter Julia with a commoner who had risen high in Rome by the name of Marcus Agrippa who was constantly seen by his side. For the couple already had two children by the time of her visit four years ago, a son named Lucius who was two and a newborn daughter named Julia. She wondered as to why Augustus had chosen someone of common birth to establish his future lineage when he could have had the pick of the known world for his daughter. She in later retrospect assumed that he had chosen Agrippa due to the type of person that he was hoping to add new blood to the future empire of Rome. It had also cemented his love of the common person in Rome, who were far outnumbering the patricians. She later gave him credit for this in the result that it had. Though she did not see it at that time in her youth.

She had also recalled her meetings with Julia, the daughter of Augustus and felt almost sorry for her in a way. She had guessed rather perceptively that she was under the complete control of her father and had not married the man she truly loved. For she had noticed the sparkle in Julia's eyes when Tiberius entered the room. Though naturally in her role as observer and outsider to the palace had noticed that Tiberius had entertained no such thoughts on the attentions of Julia and only had eyes for his wife and newborn son. Apparently he was oblivious in her adoration of his, as was Vispania Marcella, Octavia's daughter and his wife. For she basked in the glow of attention from her husband.

Selene wondered what trouble this would cause at the time, especially in how Augustus doted on her so. For Julia was so lovely, it was understandable. Especially in that Julia had given Augustus his heir.

She also noticed the way the Tiberius and Augustus interacted with each other. She sensed some kind of tension and wondered if it had any root in Augustus now having a grandson and his being pushed out of the position as heir. Especially since he was only a married connection with Augustus in his marriage with the daughter of his sister, Octavia from her first marriage prior to Marcus Antonius. Tiberius, in blood was the son of his mother and loved greatly by his step-father Augustus.

Selene watched the dynamics of this family and felt sorry for them, since she saw a lot of possible trouble in the future for them in the way they interacted with each other.

She recalled that she had also found great joy in her visits with Antonia Minor who was well content in her marriage with Drusus. Selene felt sorry for the elder Antonia, who was in a miserable marriage with a loud and boisterous man named Ahenobarbus, due to his red beard. Antonia mentioned to her that she was worried for her sister because his temper was becoming legendary throughout Rome and of his acts of cruelty. Antonia had told Selene, that Lucius Domitius Ahenobarbus was so cruel that when he was as Aedile four years ago, he ordered the censor out of his way brutally and the censor at the time a Lucius Plancus was an old man. Also he was reprimanded by her uncle Augusta for his animal shows and gladiatorial fights that were too bloody and repulsed him. He was rebuked by her uncle, but still gained honors for Rome despite all of it. She felt for Antonia Major and prayed that her own children would find happiness in their marriages. She knew that she would feel responsible if they did not.

Selene did not want a Roman marriage for her children because the women were not treated as equally as they are with the Keltoi. She wanted her daughter especially, not to become property and to be appreciated as she was by her husband Juba.

III

In looking back on that visit to Rome and what it had ultimately accomplished left her husband well pleased with her diplomatic skills and in having it look to the Romans and especially Augustus as if it was all her husband Juba's idea. He later revealed to her that he was very much impressed by her skill. For she knew well the thoughts of Augustus and how he hated the rule of any woman, especially the rule of her mother. So she made sure she had reached his mind through his wife, sister and niece by the uncanny way of gossip among woman in mentioning carefully in conversation that Juba had inquired after Cynfelyn due to his kinship with the boy. As much as she loved the woman, she knew that much of what she stated would later be revealed to Augustus. Not spitefully, but in normal dinner conversation in later evenings after their leave from Rome.

She never forgot the slander he threw on her mother, that only grew worse as the years passed by after her death. Though she also found out that all of the women in Rome secretly admired the valor of her mother and she was great-fully taken into their homes in avid curiosity as the daughter of such a powerful Queen of Egypt.

She had also seen how Octavia had softened over the years on her feelings over Selene's mother taking her husband away from her. For Octavia was genuine and gave no ill thoughts even when in her household towards the children of that woman. Though she understood the early trepidation on her meeting up with Augustus after all of the years that had passed since her mother's death. She knew that he still had feelings over the matter. After she and her husband had a few audiences with Augustus, his feelings had actually softened quite a bit about her especially, partly due because of how he had grown to care for her husband while he was under his care and the many years of study in Rome. Augustus had even approved of the marriage plans of their daughter Drussi with the Prince of the Keltoi, Cynfelyn, or as Augustus referred to him as Cunobelinios. He had admired the young man and how well adjusted to Roman life he became. He noticed great skills in him and felt that he would make a good future leader when back in his homeland.

Selene recalled that Augustus was very impressed when her and Juba's children were presented to him. Selene made sure that they all had very Roman garb during their visit and left those moderations that she had her children wear with the embroidery, at home. For she had assuaged rightfully in Augustus' favor in all things of the ancient republic that he was trying to restore. They impressed him with their fine manners, he even had them both on his lap in a short time. Her mother would be rolling in her grave had she known about this! But Selene had also noted that he was just a man who loved to dote on children, almost more so than being the great leader of Rome. Augustus presented she, her husband Juba and children with fine gifts and asked if her could help them in the matter of finding proper marriage negotiations for her brother Ptolemy and sister Arsinoe.

After careful consideration and a few months later after their return to Mauretania he had found some possibilities. He had suggested a prince in

Media for her sister and a princess of Damascus in Syria whose family was descended from the dynasty of Sumer and Babylon through Hammarbi, so noted was her lineage. Selene thanked him for his consideration in the fates of her siblings and responded that she would look into the matter. Which she did fervently. She also looked into Medea for her own son Juba Ptolemy as well.

In her inquiries on the matter she had found out that there was a princess available for her brother in Medea by the name of Iotape, who was the younger sister of her brother's wife Iotape and from a higher born Queen named Drusilla. However, upon their arrival to meet with their father Tiradates I, branded as a rebel King by the people in how he ruefully usurped the power from Phraates IV.

IV

The land was now in uproar and Augustus was trying to maintain control and had sent Agrippa over to quell the uprisings and struggle for power between Phraates and Tiradates under the Parthian control. Augustus sought in careful negotiations the daughter of Tiradates named Julia in honor of the daughter of Augustus to prove his alliance with Rome. Augustus wanted that Julia to marry the son of Selene and Juba for Mauretania to cement his position in Rome. Tiradates of Syria had also acceded in the marriage of his daughter with the brother of Cleopatra Selene, by the name of Iotape of Medea and the daughter of his first wife Drusilla.

A few years later upon their visit to Syria under Parthian and Roman control, she met up with the possible future family of her son and brother Ptolemy. Her brother's wife Iotape was again with them and ran to greet her half sister with the same name. Selene recalled how close they became. She had met the formidable Drusilla who was the first wife of Tiradates, one of his fifteen wives. She sat by his side and Selene wondered if this woman was of the same character as she, for she had observed how the mighty rebel king Tiradates consulted with her on almost all matters. She had found out that his number one wife, Drusilla was descended from the

Seleucid Dynasty that had established rule in Syria from the conquest of Alexander the Great and from his famous General Seleucid who started her noble lineage that had ties with the family of Cleopatra's mother in the many times both families were intermarried. Selene instantly established a warm friendship with the powerful Drusilla in their family connections, for they were really distant cousins in that Cleopatra VII, Selene's mother was the daughter of Mithradates Granddaughter who became known in the Ptolemy Dynasty as Cleopatra III. For Drusilla informed Selene that her family had Cleopatra's, Berenice's and Arsinoe's in it as well as the Ptolemy Dynasty. She had married her husband and helped him to get the throne from his uncle Phraates, when it rightfully belonged to her by blood, even after the Parthian conquest of her families lands. Her husband was also the King of Armenia over the ancient lands of Babylon.

Selene listed to how Drusilla recited the history of her family and wondered if all of the great empires were connected by blood. For it seemed to her that after a family or dynasty was conquered, the leaders of the line would marry into the old line of the land-thus establishing a blood kinship, perhaps to stave off possible rebel bands trying to gain control of leadership by blood. The bloodlines of the new would enhance any weakened blood of the prior dynasty in making it strong.

This gave Selene another reason why she wanted to attach her daughter to the Pryttain tribes far in the outreaches of Rome and why she and Juba were carefully considering marrying her brother and son into the Parthian dynasty before, also it was added that they were in good standing with the emperor Augustus which would assure their survival. She however, did not like the harem structure that they had in the satrapy they visited under the leadership of Tiradates. For she had also found a possible match for her sister Arsinoe with much sincere trepidation. Though Arsinoe mentioned that it was okay and was assured that she would be well treated by her new prince and given status of first wife due to her bloodline. For that, Selene had no doubt in, though did not like it all the same. She hoped that possibly Arsinoe would do fine with her all too subservient nature. For Arsinoe was very shy and reserved and found no pleasure in leading things, she was well content on the sidelines. How unlike her mother and herself was her younger sister. Though Selene felt that it probably had to do with the very little influence their mother had on her since she was so very young at the time of her death and of how much mothering Arsinoe actually had from Octavia with her Roman matron ways.

Selene did like the idea of the re-mixing of blood lines of the Archimedean Dynasty of this family from their direct decadency from the great and legendary Kings such as Darius I and Cyrus. For they were legendary in their wars with Greece in the Peloponnesian War. She had loved to read stories about that period in time. How strong her future descendants would be with such strong bloodlines with connections to all of the great houses in the world! For she and Drusilla were in concordance on that idea.

They had stayed over there for a year and made strong connections with the family, when they finally had to return to their own country. They brought with them Iotape for their son Juba Ptolemy.

They were going to leave Arsinoe with them for Drusilla's older brother, Antaxes. However, a few days into the preparations for their return voyage, Antaxes was on his way to the palace when he and his party were attacked by a rebel band in which Antaxes was killed viciously by a hidden rainfall of arrows. The city went into deep morning on the incident and for the future King, for Tiradates had bypassed his own son in favor of the brother of his first wife Drusilla. The rebel war band was opposed to this and thus had destroyed any possibility of it. Antaxes was lead to the underworld into the God Baal's ever waiting arms with splendor and his body was set on a Pyre in a Temple of that God. For Drusilla was formally a priestess of Astarte and had read the funeral speech of her brother and had donned the priestess robes in mourning for the brother that she cherished after the unexpected loss of her beloved daughter Iotape.

Selene had felt dreadfully sorry for her newfound friend and left with a confused Arsinoe and the rest of the entourage with her son's new wife Julia. For they also mourned the loss of Iotape who had secretly loved the brother of Drusilla Antaxes and had taken her own life to follow her prince. Iotape had plunged with purpose from a Ziggurat that her family in ancient times built in honor of the Goddess Astarte; the same Goddess that her mother had left her power and kingdom behind to worship in solitude and mourning for those whom she loved most.

How horrible for such a tragedy to tear apart such wonderful people. She held back her tears for she really adored Iotape and felt sorry for her brother Helio's wife Iotape at the loss of her newfound sister with the same name. Tiradates had deemed his older remaining daughter Iotape too old for marriage and sent her to the temple of Astarte to try to get his wife back.

Regretfully, but understanding the rule of the girl's father, Selene and her family poured many tears over the loss of their own Iotape, who they had grown to love in the years that she had been with them.

A confused and bewildered Julia joined them and cried at the abandonment of her mother. Julia was such a tiny girl and very fragile. For she had been raised in seclusion in the royal harem and had never seen the faces of any men, but immediate family. She stood over to the side and watched her new husband, Juba Ptolemy from afar in vivid fascination. She responded gratefully to her new position in the household of her new family and understood all too well her duty as a princess. Selene had hoped that she made the right decision.

For upon their return from that voyage Juba again went to his infamous study to delve into his newfound knowledge he had gained while over and the many manuscripts he had obtained. For when there, Tiradates had been delighted in the interest that Juba had in learning more about the Phoenicians knowledge in geography and astronomy. For the Phoenicians were the settlers along the coast of Syria who had mixed their blood with the Canaanites. Together they had attained vast knowledge and great fleets and were well known to the present era in their travels and superior knowledge of the seas. The Phoenicians were later conquered since they had never really formed any unity as a whole nation. After the Phoenicians were conquered, they left behind a vast source of information in geography that even Julius Caesar had referred to as well as Sulla; which had never been fully interpreted nor understood to this very day. Her husband welcomed the challenge to comprehend the masters of the seas. Tiradates had not much interest himself in the ancient charts and could make so sense of them. He gave several of them to Juba for his interpretation and good faith. Juba was delighted and had set to work upon his return, fifteen scribes in their interpretation of the lost language.

V

She had even increased the intervals in correspondence upon her return, for prior to their arrival in Rome, the letters were rare in reaching her and she was busy as well. Though after her departure and renewed friendship with Octavia and Antonia Minor, as well as with Tiberius, the letters increased to a renewed vigor and still do the times of her reflection on that matter and how she arrived at the present day four years later from their visit to Rome.

In her last letter from Antonia, Selene read the following,

"Greetings sister,

For at last I am pregnant with our first child. Drusus is elated. Already it seems as if it were only yesterday when you were last here, your face is so clear to me. Drusus and I have not been able to get with child due to his many campaigns for my uncle Augustus.

Tiberius sends his love to you for he was really impressed with how you turned out. He is now battling the Keltoi tribes in the Alpines. We are all very proud of his successes in subduing them.

My uncle and Livia still have not been able to have their own children, so he adopted his grandsons by his daughter and Agrippa, Gaius and Lucius. You remember Gaius, who was named after none other than Gaius Julius Caesar himself; well he has grown into quite a character following in the shadow of my uncle. However Tiberius has been very upset about this in that he had been traveling on campaigns for the glory of Rome and in his absence his favor goes to that of child of five and a baby of two years and still in swaddling at the time of this letter! Understandable the feelings

of Tiberius. Though what would he expect as he is only from the blood of my uncles wife, and boys are Augustus' own grandchildren. Livia has been upset at my uncle since and tried to meddle with the affairs of Rome. Tiberius had even served as the Governor of Gallatia and then this. Well, I need to remain neutral in this matter as the tension grows around here.

Uncle Caesar Augustus has reformed the constitution of Rome and it has gone remarkably well. He still refuses tactfully the crowns offered him and serves as consul. He also accepted the honor of Princeps Civitas which is his being regarded as the First Citizen of Rome and makes him politically almost as powerful as a King.

The air is thick with anticipation to see if he would actually accept even one of the crowns offered him. I know he will not bow down to this, no offence intended in this and your station. For he is a very frugal man and wears only the robes spun by myself, his daughter and Livia in respect for the ancients of the Republic which he is desperately trying to restore. He tells us that he only accepts the honors that enable him to do this without usurping kingship over the people. For he knows as well as I that he is the best man with his influence to actually have a chance at doing this. Though he is constantly fearful of someone stepping in to take over his power and to send Rome into Tyranny. Therefore he is extra diligent on whom he chooses as successor and makes sure that all potentials are raised with him under his careful guidance.

His influence is well excepted by all of us since he does have great wisdom. I pray fervently to Goddess Diana with all of her might that she may grant great listening skills to little Lucius and Gaius of Julia. For it seems at present that the future of Rome may be in their tiny hands.

Also, between you and I, Selene, I sometimes understand why my uncle passed over Tiberius at the birth of his grandchildren-despite their blood connections. In putting that last reason aside, I have noticed tension in the relations of my uncle and Tiberius before the birth of young Gaius. Even though Tiberius was given his toga of manhood several months earlier than the norm from the power of my uncle. But, it seemed that Tiberius is of his own mind and my uncle is probably nervous that the republic will not rest that well in the hands of Tiberius who had all too much the influence of his own father before his death several years back. Now he has the assurance of the complete raising of his grandsons under his own roof and careful tutelage.

Well, that is Rome, once again for you. My fondest blessings on the marriage of your son and new daughter in law. How is she, is she as bold as her legendary mother Drusilla?

Sad news on that point, for after you left to return to your home there is were rumors that Drusilla had died of an illness a year later. For as a priestess of Astarte she became the mistress of Baal in the form of the Goddess Astarte and would stand in the name of the Goddess to become a temple prostitute. For they believe over there that the temple priestesses were in the very form of the Goddess and on holidays all of the men in the city would line up to pay their holy "respects" to their Goddess. Any children born to the temple were considered Goddess-born and reared in the temple. Why would she willingly send herself to this cult?

Anyways, other than that, please tell me how you fare in the great scheme of things in this world? How are negotiations with Tenvantius and family going. For last I heard, Tenvantius had died two years ago and Cunobelinios had returned to take over leadership that his father left behind to him. Is Drussi still pledged to him? Let me know, Sorry about Drusilla. For we know as women that she must have had her reasons for this.

With all the love in the world,
Antonia Minor"

Selene had to force all of the patience that she had to recover from the blow of learning about the temple of Astarte. She had not known about this. Her heart reeled in love for her newfound friend Drusilla, for she had not heard from her since they returned, nor from Iotape, which she considered very odd. She will have to convince her husband to send an emissary to find out the fate of poor Iotape, a victim of her father's will. Though she knew that Iotape was only sent to retrieve her mother from the influence of the temple. She had no idea that it would have been that dangerous. She certainly had no idea whatsoever of the role that a priestess played in the temple. She thought that it might have been similar to what the priestesses of Isis were in their legendary powers of healing and dream interpreting. She had mistakenly thought that Iotape would have been in good hands in taking up residence as a priestess. For all of the needs were met of the temple priests and priestesses from the people.

She was also baffled as to how Antonia did not know that until that visit she still had her brother's former wife at her residence. For it was not the norm in matters, usually they were sent back to live with their former families after the death of their spouses in such a situation. She was equally surprised that she had neglected to mentioned Iotape in letter's to Antonia, for Iotape had played an important role in her dedication to her and Juba's children.

She was also a bit upset in the way that the information was presented to her by her sister Antonia in that it seemed a bit like a juicy morsel of gossip to pass over dinner with the local Dominae. But, she knew in her heart that Antonia did not truly know of the extent of her relationship with Drusilla and of Iotape or she would have been more subtle in informing her of this.

VI

The days passed and Selene knew that she was more than negligent in making the final preparations to take her daughter to be with her betrothed husband on the other side of the world to the Keltoi. She knew that her daughter was at the ripe time for starting her own family as she was herself and almost with child at her daughter's tender age of twelve. Though she had dreaded the separation. She knew that it was the way of things. She also felt that her mother would have approved of this match and found it rather amusing that the great Caesar Augustus had consented of this as well as the match of her son and his new wife Julia of Syria.

Selene would have to complete the travel arrangements to set sail for the next week. She had just received an urgent message for her on the death of Tenvantius, which had occurred two years prior, and the succession of her future son-in-law with out incident. Her daughter would go as she did in entering her household as a Queen. Though her daughter in her own right and armed with all that she had taught her might succeed her own husband since the tribe was very matriarchal and the mother's line was most often first considered in rule over the tribes.

For she was in her position of power only by the grace and good will of her husband who had every confidence in her ability to rule so that he may engage more time in his studies. She also knew that Juba had made sure that he was present on the voyage with their daughter as well as she. He wanted to gather information on the kingdom which was so far away and felt that the writings in the last generation in the time of the emissary trips of Julius Caesar, may have been a little tainted for the glory of Rome. Though he was very Romanized himself, he insisted on the truth over the glory of any one culture or another. He was quite eclectic in where his thirst for knowledge led him. He was hoping to stay for a few months in the lands of the Keltoi, what they called Pryttain to assure the safely of his daughter and for enough time to answer all of the questions on their culture so that he would be able to add them accurately into his cultural encyclopedias.

Selene, on the other had wanted to also possibly find matches over there for her sister and brother as well. She also had the hidden notion, that over there they would be better able to watch over her daughter so far away from her.

She renewed her vigor in completing the necessary travel preparations due to her horrid emotions taking over in losing her only remaining daughter. She had also received the urgent request from Cunobelinios in that he was now king, due to his father passing away and he urgently requested his betrothed queen beside him.

Selene was impressed with the eloquence in which he had stated his request. She felt that he had definitely shown great knowledge and skill earned from his education in Rome. She further thought that her mother would have definitely approved of this man for her granddaughter and thought it rather odd in how the man who helped cause the destruction of her parents was also approving of this match with definite genuinely good intentions. She had made sure of this with her own research on the political front and the situation of the Keltoi and the way in which her daughter would be treated over there. She wanted to make sure that her daughter would be able to use the knowledge that she had taught her, instead of being locked away and being used solely for breeding purposes as most queens in this part of the world were treated.

She was extremely fortunate in how her husband let her rule over most of the kingdom in his stead. For he was such a scholar and had every confidence in her ability to take care of the people and their children. He had been raised by Augustus in Rome and had been inundated in academics which had eventually taken control of his senses. However, in his studies and own observations he had respected the power of women and their ability to gain power. For he had read of many such powerful queens and knew that Selene was not the type to take the kingdom away and had actually made most of her policies appear as if they were his ideas, when they were solely hers. For both of them knew the conservative view that Augustus had on women and how much he despised her own mother just because she was a woman who had gained so much power that he felt it was a tragic abomination to her gender. Augustus felt that women should be at home raising the children and spinning and weaving the wool for the family to wear as the ancient women of the republic did in the days long past. Yet, he held the belief that he held the power to bring the old glory long lost back to his people. Selene and Juba both knew that Augustus also had more power and ruled most of the world and could take everything away from them as well and the downward turn of his thumb.

As long as Augustus saw that the kingdom was being run efficiently and by Juba and they were relatively quiet on the world front and stuck to their own domains in rule. He left them alone. For they knew that he was more than generous to them both in that he had taken away the kingdoms of both of their parents and their very lives. They were raised and treated well by Augustus and his sister, as all of the children have been who ended up in his charge. The captured children of his enemies were treated as fairly and generously as if they were his own. He was a very good and reliable correspondent and would send them letters asking how things fared over in Mauretania and with themselves. She knew that it was genuinely out of concern for over the years a sort of repose had grown between she and Augustus and there already was one with her husband, since he had spent many more years under the wing of the powerful Imperator.

Augustus had even been over to see the new Cities they were building and had informed them on the condition of their old capitol of Cirta they had abandoned with their very lives in Numidia many years before. He informed them of the constant battles and destruction to all of the fine buildings they had built prior to their leaving and that he often wondered if the tribes would ever find any peace at all.

In that meeting when Augustus had last visited them; Selene recalled that she had observed the Imperator carefully and sat to the side while her husband and he dominated all conversations. Augustus had responded and reacted as if Juba was his own son of a sorts in that his pride was noticeable to all who were in their company. Augustus was impressed with all that her husband and done (she smiled at this but said nothing, knowing her position in his eyes) and of his many writings and compositions and of the development of his encyclopedia. Augustus had mentioned that he had also had that very dream of traveling and compiling information on all of the known cultures of the world, but his ill health kept him from traveling from most of the places and his adverse reactions to food in that he would spend many days in rest in recuperation after a banquet. He felt that his body perhaps responded differently than most as a result. For he also had a reaction to shellfish and avoided them aggressively. This she feared was shared by her long ago lost daughter Tonia. For she recalled that her father was a cousin of Julius Caesar and thus Augustus was related to her through the Caesar line. She was not aware of this family trait at the time, many years ago when it could possibly have prevented her daughter's death.

Selene had observed in his visit that for his age of forty-two years, he looked remarkably well despite his odd habits. But they must have worked for him. She had observed that he still had a full head of rather duller blonde hair than she recalled in her youth. Also that he would often not eat at the evening meals when everyone else did, but would eat when he was hungry and very sparingly at that. For his diet was much more simple than one would assume for his stature and power and for the immense wealth that he possessed. He would jokingly tell her that he wanted to eat the simple fare of his ancestors and that he was no better than anyone else that he ruled over. Why should he have better food, just because he was more advantaged than most. She knew that he had brought over his own chefs to make sure that his diet was simple. Probably knowing the excessive tastes of the average king and queen and their retinue. Her physician mentioned to her that his diet might really be due to some blood disorder that he could have, for he noticed some of the signs in that his left eye was failing him and that he was numb in his extremities. He had told her that Augustus' physician was very wise in this. For he further mentioned that if Augustus would consume too much in sweets, his body could go into a coma and that he could possibly die. That was why he would have to recover from any overeating and why his body would react so adversely to it. For his body could not break down sweet foods as the average person did. He had also observed that Caesar Augustus also had a breathing problem that would become aggravated by dust and humid weather and had rightfully predicted that Augustus had to cut his visit short due to his body's reaction to the humidity. He had told her that the chest would expand to a point where it was difficult for him to breathe and again, he could die if he did not have such a wise physician.

Selene wondered if due to his excellent care under his own physician Micantros, if that was his reason for granting citizenship to all doctors. For the wisdom of this man was definitely keeping Augustus alive against all odds in his careful diligence over his charge and the Imperator knew it.

Unfortunately such good laws are oft corrupted by all of the quacks and charlatans taking up citizenship by calling themselves doctors. These ridiculous people in becoming citizens were allowed to receive the grain dole that Rome had established from the rule of Julius Caesar. She knew that Augustus, in light of that had to limit the number of citizens since everyone seemed to be freeing their slaves so that they would not have to pay for their food in that the grain dole would take care of them. This created a great problem, especially when Augustus widened the citizenship to outside of Rome into all of the Italian Province around them.

So the Caesar Augustus, Imperator of Rome would have to find a way to make good again a generous concept that had went bad. He succeeded in this in that he limited the laws on the freeing of slaves in that they could not free more than three. Also, he had to reconstruct the whole of Rome into more feasible districts to better keep track of the people and had reinstituted the census again. For some people were taking advantage of Augustus' generosity in claiming the grain dole of those deceased and not logged in to city records. Thus the reinstatement of the census to keep better track of all of the live citizens of Rome.

His careful administration and meticulous attention to detail, a character trait that Selene shared with him, had helped to resolve most of the problems with Rome that had developed over the civil wars that had been fought in Rome for the past fifty years that had led to the decline in government that Augustus had to face. However, with all of the newly conquered territories brought to Rome by his predecessor Julius Caesar—it was peaceful at long last. For Augustus did not seek out new territories for Rome but rather wanted to deal with what he had. This enabled Augustus to deal with his own people and to the rebuilding of Rome to its former glory days before the many years of civil war in the times of Sulla and Julius Caesar.

She had learned a lot from that visit a few years ago in which Augustus had assisted them in helping maintain good relations with Cunobelinios, since he had been practically raised under his roof as was Juba. Therefore, Augustus had many fine things to say and felt that the boy was purely Roman and not barbaric as his roots were. Naturally Juba and Selene did not say a word to this in response, knowing their kin ties with his tribe and great grandmother.

Selene wondered if Augustus was like this at the time that her mother had to deal with him and wondered why they hated each other so much.

Though she knew that most of it was because of all of the power her mother had of how unnatural Augusts felt that was for a woman, any woman. He seemed to be oblivious to all of the women, even his own wife and Selene knew for a fact that they were anything but timid. He seemed to be living in some idealized fantasy of the old republic that he adored so much and had tried to emulate in every aspect of his life with the power of his rule.

She did not like the way that she had to hide her power and remain in her husband's shadow, but understood the times all too well and took the words of wisdom from her mother so ingrained in her life of, "Choose your own battles, know when to fight and when to plan." Since she did take that advise to heart, her rule was relatively peaceful, especially in her own home. For she let her husband take credit for some of her works and the rest was from them as a couple. Only she and her husband knew who was really behind all they she had created in his and their name. He truly appreciated her and how he as a person was able to thrive in what his soul most craved for. Juba was always showing his appreciation in showering her with many fine and quite unusual gifts.

Though his visit was short, she had gained a lot of insight on Augustus as a person. She knew that he was quietly assessing everything in his own wise mind. For in all of his cosseted treatment while young due to his many illnesses, he had read a great deal and prided a person's education and encouraged those in his own family to share his love for reading and gathering information. Selene could definitely relate to that. Though she knew that her mother in contrast to the Imperator had ruled entirely by her heart and love for her father. Unlike, Augustus who was the type of person who waited, his stare would send shivers up a person's spine, for you knew that he was gathering knowledge on his opponents and would use anything, so meticulous and penetrating his gaze, for his own victory at the advantageous time.

She recalled that he was the type of person to not eat whenever anyone else did, but would eat sparingly throughout the day and sometime ate late at night, when he was often up walking about, going over some matter or other. He very rarely sat or lounged on the couches as was the norm for the august citizenry of Rome and it's domains, for all other cultures were fast to emulate the people of Rome in architecture and style and way of life. But not their ruler. His dress was simple and homespun and his hair was certainly a matter in itself. Selene was told by the palace hair servant, that Augustus drove him mad in that he kept trying to get up for some matter or another and was even writing on the occasion of his hair grooming.

Selene was very keen in her observations and had also thought that was definitely the type of person who made a great leader, for she had recognized the traits in what her mother and others had mentioned about Julius Caesar. Possibly a genuine leader who would gain any type of power at all, was the type of person who made it their obsession and took very seriously their rule, so that it encompassed their whole lives. For she knew personally all it took to rule over their large territory of Mauretania, though Augustus ruled a much wider and vast area than their corner of the world. She knew that, despite her reservations due to her families' history with him. She knew that Augustus would succeed very well and was impressed in that he was handling it in a very politically astute way. He had known that Rome was in desperate need of reconstruction and reform to the original and ancient ways of the republic that had become way too tainted and neglected over the many years of the civil war. And what most impressed her was that he had very accurately sensed the whole mood of Rome and how best to make the reforms. Yes, he was very clever indeed.

While he watched them, she returned the same secret study of her own and took notes and locked them away in her mind for any possible later use. She also made sure that their physician Asandros talked extensively with the physician of Augustus Caesar and made serious notes of his own.

VII

She had received a letter from Antonia Minor that had brought her up to date of the situation in Rome in the way that only Antonia could see things. Antonia had informed her that finally she had her first child and named him Germanicus Julius Caesar and called him Germanicus. Her husband was doing well in his public career that he had started about the time that Selene was last there with her husband in Rome when Julia had given birth to her daughter Julia from her husband Agrippa, the third child born to Agrippa after two sons named Gaius and Lucius Caesar. Antonia mentioned that at the time of her letter her husband Drusus was in Gaul with his brother Tiberius working in order to stabilize the barbaric territory now in Roman hands She was expected to join her husband over there soon in a villa that was being built to her specifications.

Antonia had mentioned that she was worried for Tiberius being pushed aside by Augustus for his two infant grandsons, as if everything that Tiberius had shared with Augustus was for naught. Though she further mentioned that all worries of Tiberius were pushed aside when his beloved Vispania gave birth to a tiny little boy that was named Drusus in honor of his brother and her husband. Antonia stated that Vispania appeared frazzled since little Drusus was not taking well to her mother's milk and cried constantly and rattled the walls of the palace.

Antonia related that her second son Tiberius Claudius Drusus Nero Germanicus, whom she shortened to Claudius—was almost a year and thriving well and walking though wobbly on those chubby baby legs of his. Selene laughed at this and recalled when her Juba Ptolemy was the same age and an earlier walker as well.

She noted sadly there was not any mention of the rumored ailments that seemed to plague her younger son almost worse than Antonia's uncle Augustus, which he was known to have conquered successfully and hid well from public scrutiny.

Was this from Antonia and Selene's father, those powerful and early walker genes? She also found it amusing when her son was almost in the position to rule in his own right, Antonia's second son was just learning to steady himself on his legs. So odd, how things turned out for them. She and Antonia had hoped that their children would have been the same age and playing together. Now it seems that one meeting a few years ago might have been the only one.

Over the years her friendship had grown strong with her beloved half-sister Antonia Minor and she knew that on many occasions Antonia had to plead for things to her uncle on her behalf.

Antonia had also informed her that her uncle Augustus had adopted his two grandsons Gaius and Lucius as his heirs since he did not believe that Livia could have any children from this marriage. Gaius was six years old at the time of her letter and Lucius was four. Antonia was also upset on how soon Agrippa was married to Julia after the death of Marcellus and that it still shone on Julia's face. Julia confided in Antonia that she felt her new husband was rather crude due to his common birth and was angry at her father for it, though did her duty in producing heirs, which seemed to Antonia to appear in rapid succession. She also noted secretly that she had sensed that Julia had feeling's for her brother-in-law Tiberius and wondered as to what course in fate it would play out. She further mentioned that at the time of the letter Julia just gave birth to her fourth child a daughter by the name of Agrippina who was adorable and Antonia doted on her with all of the golden curls around her tiny newborn face. She told Selene that she would forward her new address to her son in Mauretania and had wished her love and luck on their journey so far away.

VIII

Alas, her ruminations had to end for the reality of her planning for months of the retinue to bring her daughter, a bride to her husband to such a far away land of the Keltoi-was finally ready. She had made careful instructions for the rule of the kingdom to be placed in the hands of her son Juba Ptolemy and his new wife Julia of Syria. They would be gone for a year and felt safe and this decision, should anything happen to them. If anything should happen to them on their journey, it would be by the will of the Gods alone; she knew that she had nothing to fear from her son as her ancestors had from their own families. She had loved her son well and felt more than capable of his ability to rule in her and her husband's stead while away. She also had other's watch over them and felt confident that their country was not facing any adversaries outside nor treats from within. For despite all of her parents' feelings on Caesar Augusts, Rome and it's territory was in relative peace and the civil wars that had waged for so long had all but ceased and all of those opponents were dead by the time that Augustus was first made Imperator. All of those men who had killed the glorious Julius Caesar were now dead. She had felt well secure after this visit that they were all in good hands, especially since Augustus had wisely utilized this time of peace to restore order, rather than to divulge in any amusements as past leaders were known to have done, thereby squandering the treasury to almost depletion on many past peaceful occasions. She could learn much from this man and sometimes wished that her own husband could have taken a liking to politics and administration, it would have lessened the burden somewhat that was laid precariously on her shoulders alone—it seemed.

Sometimes, she felt the heaviness of all that she alone did under the guise of her husband in even the daily maintenance of the palace, let alone the rest of their territory. Sometimes, she would for a very brief moment wish that she was like a normal queen and just worried herself with wearing and purchasing nice gowns and jewels. But, then, she knew in her soul that she never could have been that type of woman. She had learned way too much and had even more than she wanted to do with her life and had even more to say.

Part five

I

Wedding Voyage to Britannia 14 B.C.E. through 12 B.C.E.

Drussi was all too eager for the voyage, which was apparent to all those in witness that she had inherited her father's love of the open sail. For both would gloriously revel on the deck each time the sails were hurled out in their splendor and when the rowers, well paid, would be able to relax under deck. The rowers were not slaves and were trained for this position. For it was a great skill and much needed, especially in a time of war, when the rowers precision was a required skill along with their strength and endurance. They even had their own guild, which was in one of the higher echelons of the trade skills.

Drussi in all twelve years of her glory insisted that her mother drop her childish nickname and that she be called by only her full name of Jubilla Drusilla Cleopatra. Selene responded that she could call her whatever she wanted, though compromised by calling her Jubilla.

She watched Jubilla standing by the side of her father one day. They both were enchanted as they had kept their small fleet close to the shoreline. They both would carefully observe all that lived on the shores and would talk rapidly about the many cultures they had observed. She was getting to be almost as tall as her father, for she had already passed over the height of her mother. Jubilla was tall and slender with dark auburn tresses, for the brown seemed to melt away with their sunny climate and her love for the outdoors. Her father had taught in her a love for botany and she had many samples of her own under close study in her chambers. Her hair came to life in the sun and hung down in soft waves down her back, since she always hated having it bound. Though adhered to the torment on state occasions in that it was proper Roman fashion.

This little girl was in all observance a woman and ready to have children. For she had promised her daughter that she would be present for the birth of her first child to make sure that if it was a daughter, she would be properly initiated by name and inheritance to be priestess of Isis, like her mother and down the line.

She adored the way that Juba was paying fond attention to their daughter. She knew that he had not done much of late due to his studies and gathering all that he wanted to find out from the druids. He was explaining all of this to their daughter as was his way of bonding. For Juba always forgot the ages of his children when explaining something to them that interested him. For always after they would have to run to her for the children's version of their father's lessons.

Though, now, that bridge was no longer needed. For Jubilla was grasping every word that her father had told her and was even asking very enlightening questions of her own. She could tell by the expressions on his face that Juba was very impressed with his daughter and had even looked over at Selene and winked at her.

Arsinoe was under deck nursing her horrid reaction to the sea. For, which Selene was under deck as well to add comfort, leaving the deck to her husband and daughter. The sea had behaved rather well for them in this voyage and hoped that their return one would prove the same. Her sister and brother were rapt in conversation and would use this time together to make sure that Jubilla would know all that she could about her mother's homeland. Selene sat silently and listened and added in items occasionally, that they could not remember since they were too young when their parents had died.

For Jubilla had grown up in the kingdom of her father, and though Mauretania was not their kingdom originally, Numidia was only next door and they had been there on a few occasions when they would try to rescue some of the ancient treasures from destruction and to bring them back to Mauretainia for preservation. Jubilla had also been raised by many people who knew her father's family and it's history very well.

Selene was so busy that she had not told her daughter as much as she probably should have, though she had told her that she was the one chosen to carry on the words of her and her mother for future generations. For she was the first born daughter and equally blessed since she was also a twin. She had given her daughter the crib that her own father had carved for her that was so elaborate and made Jubilla promise the crib would be passed on to the daughter who was chosen for this privilege.

She had every faith in that her daughter would write to her, though also knew that due to the distance, it might be only one time a year that she would be able to hear from her daughter, if even that.

They had sailed past the Roman Sicily and past Etruria. They had to travel on land through Narbonesis and Lugdonesis and to the coast, where again they would sail to the coast of southern Pryttain and then again by land to the untouched by Roman lands of the Trinovantes tribe, where her daughter would rule as queen.

She and her husband and all of the family used this time well in doting on Jubilla and teaching her the ways of a woman and wife. Naturally her husband would not tell her the secrets of woman, he would tell her all that he could about his studies and in this they bonded at last.

Selene would take some precious time with her daughter alone and then make sure that she was well armed with the knowledge that her mother would have passed down to her before she died. She was thankful in this moment that she had taken the time to learn more about her mother and the Ptolemy line and was able to pass this information down to her daughter. For had she not been born inquisitive and hidden in some dark harem, she would not have had the opportunity to gain the information that she had easily passed down to Jubilla. She was thankful to have a husband who firmly believed that no one should be kept from knowledge.

Though, naturally Selene secretly thought that there should be that love for knowledge but with an equal balance and proper utilization of such if one were born to rule. She made sure that her daughter had this balance. As every mother who loves her children, she made sure that her children would learn from the mistakes of her self and her mother and all of the women of her line. This knowledge she would pass on to her daughter with love. She would give her daughter the legacy of the sun and moon that her mother, Cleopatra VII had created in her womb. She also made sure that her daughter knew about the prophesy about water and had copies of the ancient text that she had deciphered from in hieroglyphs from one of the earlier Cleopatras. For her daughter was another Cleopatra in this wonderful powerful line of women.

She knew that her daughter had all that it takes to be powerful in her own right and would shine in this culture that fully embraced and worshipped the powers of women.

As they neared the land, they were forced to travel by mule and horseback through the treacherous mountains of the Gaulish Alps in a steep and precarious pass. Each night her husband and Jubilla would compare observations to a scribe so that it would be properly laid down for his return.

The culture of Rome was fast encroaching the domains of the Long-Haired Gaul settlements that were primarily of agriculture. They had noticed the Roman roads suddenly appearing before them to lead their way even further into the domains that were losing way to Rome. They noticed vacant fields and animals adrift and neglected wandering about as the ground became more level.

There were very few settlements of the strictly Gaulish round-houses surrounded by well tended fields. More often than not, they had observed cities springing up on almost every elevated space they came across in their attempt to emulate Roman urbanization. All of these cities were bursting with energy and many colors. Some men that she knew were definitely Gaulish with their very fair complexions, had donned the toga and had shorn their prided beards and for all appearances were almost as if they were in Roma Dea proper.

She did observe some genuine Romans in administrative capacities, though some were of a mixture of purely Roman coloring and dress with the unmistakable height that the Gaul's were noted for. They were much more boisterous a people in these settlements and were notably gregarious of mood for the most part. They extended their hospitality to this Royal entourage and heaped upon them vast amounts of mead and beer and the occasional and prided Roman-like vintage wines. For Gaulish versions of Italian wineries were appearing all over the country-side of the ancient chalked cliffs of the valley with the large river of that region. She could not pronounce the name of it when she was told. Endless rows upon rows of grape orchards dotted the landscapes. She had heard that inside those chalk cliffs people had lived since the beginning of time and even to the present day with sometimes even large and luxurious villas carved deep inside of those very steep cliffs made primarily of Limestone.

There were also many messages to give to their cousin tribes in untouched Pryttain that were given to the entourage to take over with them. The tribes had an extensive communication system amongst them and their incredible ability for horsemanship and their speed of travel. Message of this entourage had preceded them to each city along their path to the coast.

Celebration was endured along the way in the most important of the villages in which they arrived. For the farther they traveled the further from the influence of Rome they became. In each city where they were eagerly accepted, a guard was given them and a guide along with even more messages to impart to their Island kin. Many had already settled there who had escaped persecution from the defeat of their hero Vercingetorix in the time of Julius Caesar. The people, many Atribates had settled over in Britain, where the brother of the leader Comminos had established himself as king with Rome behind him. His grandson now ruled that area and people had fled the tribal area in Gaul to settle in the untouched area of Pryttain in this generation.

They were in constant communication with the Island kin and were jealous of those lucky enough in distance to have received no hint of an invasion from Rome. For as they approached the middle of Gaul, they encountered a vast and terrifying river that they had to cross, which took them through the edges of mountains that seemed almost as high and endless as the other mountain range. They had entered the Pyrenees mountain range. This lead them to the lands of the vastly sloping vineyards and mentioned.

So incredible in it's majesty that Selene was in constant awe. For she had grown up in Egypt, which did not have any mountains nor hills that even compared with either mountain range encountered thus far.

She and her whole family had also encountered snowfall for the very first time. Juba was elated for he knew what it was from his many studies of lands around them and even knew that you could hold it together in your hands and with the heat to make a ball out of it.

Everyone had long left behind the clothes of their climate and even Juba had abandoned his Roman robes for the much warmer trousers worn by the local tribes and the very warm woolen cloaks that were incredibly woven in many bright and vivid patterns. She observed that the weaving had definitely surpassed that of Rome. Though she wondered if they would surpass Egypt's fine linen in transparency with the great skill that she noted in the heavy cloaks that they all donned in many colorful layers.

Selene had begun to collect many items of jewelry which had impressed her greatly in how artistically precise these people worked their gold and silver. Intricate spirals, mazes and swirls would disguise faces, animals and leaves in the many patterns that were divinely graceful and complex.

The long-haired-Gauls were an extremely vain people and grew more so as the distance grew larger, eventually leaving any domination and control of the Roman culture that swept through the large land in the years since the great conquest to those closer geographically to Rome.

The people bathed daily and all wore their hair long and with great pride. Some had hair the color of such fantastical red or gold, it almost reminded her of the styles of ancient Egypt when it was dyed with henna and seen in the temple friezes thousands of years old. Though she did not believe that that particular dye was found in this harsh climate. These people were adorned in colors in a greater array than she could have possibly imagined and the men worried over their hair as much as the women. Juba thought it ridiculous with his short-shorn hair in Roman fashion.

The villages were very neat and organized and the people worshipped amongst the trees. She marveled in this having erected many great temples of her own and recalled those incredible ancient ones before time was recorded in her homeland. All of the cultures that she had any knowledge before the strange ways of the Keltoi, were of them of worshipping in tall and grandiose temples. This was truly a new and delightful concept to her.

She and her family soaked up all of the information that they could to better assist Jubilla in the people that she would rule over. For they were told that the land of the Trinovantes was similar in their own and was completely untouched by any influence of Roman culture to take away the ancient traditions they held.

The closer to the coast and to the country that her daughter was to rule over, they were more celebrated as the kin descendant of the Goddess Don who was worshipped as the mother of Kings and great Queens. Jubilla reveled in this in that she knew that Don was in fact her great-great-aunt and they did share actual kinship. She was also shown drawings and carvings of Don as well as pottery that represented her image. This image repeated was of her with flowing red hair that was legendary. They pointed out that Jubilla had a softer and darker version of the Goddesses' hair.

Much of their knowledge of the people that the Greeks' called the Keltoi, were biased in their observations so they had to rely on their own. The language was difficult to understand for it differed drastically in each tribal territory that they passed. Though the main points of conversation were understood, the subtle intricacies were not.

Arsinoe had secretly told Selene one evening that she thought the men of this culture were glorious and tall and were all majestic even the old. Even the women were taught in the skills of war and battle and were great chariot drivers and rivaled the men in the distance they threw the spears. For the women of the Keltoi were taller than the average Roman and people of the cultures that she was most familiar with such as the Parthians, Judeans, Syrians, Egyptians and Greeks and so forth.

These people held themselves with fierce pride and were definitely far superior to them in height and she felt as well in their skills shown in their weaving as well as the jewelry that they all wore, including the men. She was a little disappointed in how some of the Roman control had arrived here in that the tribes were beginning to become patriarchal and were losing the lines of their mother's. She hoped that it was not the case where she was sending her daughter. Jubilla was her and her mother's hope in conquering the glory that was deep in their blood though in latter generations repressed by the powerful sway of the Romans.

In a ruler's point of view she felt that it was very wise in mingling the blood with those they had conquered. She knew that Julius Caesar and Augustus and all those Romans before them had sent over retired troops to settle and marry into the cultures that they had conquered. She had seen great evidence of results of this in her travels thus far. She had already seen the mingling of the Roman blood with that of the Keltoi, even prominent on the outskirts of the territories closest to Rome and close to the coast.

The land journey had slowed their dramatic and swift progress by sea and had finally reached the coast, though they had to winter there to wait for a safe crossing. She also used this time to send word to the Pryttain tribe of the Trinovantes of their arrival and to arrange a guide for them. For their knowledge from Rome had ceased to this point and all they had to guide them at that point geographically were very obscure references by purely Roman sources. She wondered how close in content they were. For they had explained how barbaric the Keltoi were and they used human sacrifices and would burn them in trees and large wicker carvings. She found this to not be true at all.

As, usual Selene would take that information from the source and had considered who wrote it. For the Romans, as her own personal experience was still feeling the bite, would neglect the truth for the glory and power of Rome and often made it seem as if every other culture were crude and barbaric, unlike the superior culture and traditions of the Romans.

She also wondered about the knowledge gleaned from her own mother; that Julius Caesar would often consult with a druid who he had taken back to Rome with him. This man was incredibly knowledgeable in astronomy in relations to the calendar that he had improved upon. For in Caesar's time, their calendar was completely out of sync and had to be drastically updated. So Julius Caesar consulted Chaldeans, and the works of the Phoenicians, as well as this druid. She knew that the druid had oft consulted with Julius Caesar and her mother had even met him on one occasion.

So, if Julius Caesar kept a druid in his confidence and consulted him with the calendar, how could she find validity from the words of those only out to make them look like dullards and too fond of drink.

Though she did notice also that the Keltoi were very fond of beer and mead and even imported wines and did drink to excess on celebratory occasions, though were often busy in farming and in their own lives to establish any kind of danger in habit. There was never a time when people were considered to have had enough of drinking, though they would completely look down upon those who would overeat. She thought this interesting in that the Romans, unlike Augustus, were fond of eating often to the excess and would even have to vomit during the course of the meal, so that they could have even more. They even had a room in them most august of domiciles for this purpose called the Vomitorium. This definitely repulsed the Keltoi who considered it a taboo.

These people had a strict way of living and every dispute was dealt with fairly. For fairness and equality was viewed by everyone and adhered to vehemently regardless of age.

Within tribes, Selene marveled on how harmonious they lived. Though she found it strangely familiar in how they battled amongst each other. So like Numidia at that! She had learned they had always been that way and that it would never change.

II

The ocean that they wintered by was so unlike any large body of water that she nor anyone else in their family had seen in their lifetimes. It was so turbulent and gray, in dark contrast to the bright and vividly dressed people around them.

They all hovered close together in warmth around great bonfires built outside the dwellings and smaller ones within that led to a hole in the great round-houses ceilings, each of the dwellings were all nestled close together. The houses were big enough for several families to sleep side by side. Though Selene and her retinue required a whole house for themselves with all of the rowers and people they brought along on the journey.

Bards would travel from house to house with their incredible satires and bawdy revelry with loud music in accompaniment. Though they had beautiful and sad dramas as well with extremely long verses. She was incredulous on how much each bard seemed to have memorized and all seemed to be lines with great lineages of the leaders and of great heroes and heroines of their people. She was enraptured on the spells cast upon her soul with the telling of them.

The storms seemed to last forever, but were almost forgotten with the spells of enchantment passed by these gregarious people with their love of song. Jubilla was growing to love these people and Selene was happy with this thought, though knew that there would soon be the time when they would have to part. That is, after she saw her first grandchild! This child that she could not leave for home without. She knew that her son and new daughter-in-law were too busy to start their own family with all that she had left them with in their absence. She made them promise to wait for her return, so that she may be there for the birth. They agreed eagerly since they, in their youth were reluctant for this added responsibility to take out without wisdom from their parents.

It seemed to Selene, Jubilla, and Arsinoe, as if all of the Gods had unleashed their fury with them with each blistering wind that throttled the walls of villages in which they slept for the winter. This hardy group of people assured them that it would end and that it was normal for them. They armed Jubilla with knowledge on how to deal with the harsh winds when she would go to her new land to live.

The days were dark and dreary and soon even the celebrations of the bards had ceased to make way for the preparations of their winter solstice. A time most celebrated in that it also marked the beginning of the spring. Which Selene still had serious doubts and started to even hate the ice which she was originally fascinated by which seemed to be everywhere and over everything, including her hair when outside. She marveled in how they could gather any energy without the light of the sun to inspire their energy.

III

The entourage for Jubilla could not gather the intricacies of the meanings behind the celebration since there was a language barrier, though they were becoming familiar with some phrases and words to assist them.

She recalled that the Romans celebrated a special day called Saturnalia which occurred around this time and started the beginning of their new year. It was in honor of the Roman God Saturn. It celebrated the fall of the old father-God Saturn to be replaced by the new god and son Jupiter. In Rome the whole month was officially devoted to the celebration at the Kalends before the month of Janus.

These people with their own feast day, brought in a huge old log from the year prior and used it to light the new log newly cut of a giant tree that Selene could not recognize-she was told that it was called the tree of Yule. This added a delightful and balmy fragrance to the air of their round home. They had decorated their homes in evergreens from the forest, since it seemed to be the only thing that Selene had observed that was still green at this time of year. Many herbs that were gathered and dried were then put into the pot on the main fire and their scents wafted through the air. Songs of a different sort were sung and the people seemed to even exceed their vigor from drink from the last celebration that they had encountered here.

All of the songs in each of the houses seemed to blend into one and tried to outdo one another on noise level. Selene and her family wished that they even knew some of the words since it all seemed great fun.

Outside great bonfires were lit in a clearing in a grove of Oak and they were invited to attend some of the ceremonies welcoming in the new sun God and sending out the old sun God. They had difficulties pronouncing the names, but they tried and the people of this tribe were delighted and covered them in warm embraces like children learning a new song.

They stood in the clearing along all others who had gathered in which she assumed was everyone in the village. A druid officiated along with his retinue of five Bards and five Ovates or Seers. This occurred in the darkest of nights that Selene or her family had ever witnessed. You could hardly see anyone and had to arrive at the area clutching the clothing of those in front. Down winding pathways they all walked though a heavy wood to this site. The woods were made darker in that the trees were bare, but had further blocked out any light from the stars. All knew the solemnity of the occasion and even the children were oddly hushed reverently for the moment. She was impressed by this though felt a charge in the crisp and cold air that surrounded her.

When they had all finally arrived to their destination, Selene stood there in the building anticipation that the druid had created by waving a space in the center with his flaming wand. Her hair felt as if it had frozen to her skull though deeply wrapped in layers of cloaks given to her and her family. Her feet were well secured in layers of wrapped soft leather, though her toes still felt the pinch from being unused to this cold climate.

The moon above them had begun to rise and cast an ethereal glow upon the fresh snow that had covered every indiscriminate part of the landscape. Selene felt as if she were not on the earth but in some strange chamber of Osiris' realm of the underworld. She assumed that this was what the underworld probably was most like in the stark nakedness and crisp cold that would wake all one's senses to each and every moment with such precision and reality.

Time stood still for them and seemed out of place, when all of a sudden the druid's wand came to a rest on a huge pile of wood in the center. Upon lighting it a glow came to life immediately bringing all of the forest to life with the rapid pace that it had caught within the protection of the grove and the clearing that they were all transfixed in awe. For two other bonfires were lit as well slowly creating a cradle of warmth to those standing quietly in the clearing. The shadows cast from the naked branches above them danced ethereally in the snow around them and covered their still and transfixed forms with movement.

For slowly, a note a struck on a string instrument glided to their ears while low sounding drums began to beat and ominous pace. The bards started to chant and then the people slowly were taken away with the movement and began to sway in the ancient rhythm of the forest which seemed to correspond to each beat of the drum.

The crisp and untouched snow was feeling the pressure of many dancers whose cloaks began to flow in unison to the rapidly increasing pace. Faster and faster the people began to dance until they were twirling in somewhat of a frenzy as if intoxicated. Though Selene knew that they were not due to the religious significance of the occasion. There were several punishments for that. For it was taboo for drinking of any type of liquor at any religious occasion and that all must attend.

Selene found herself being lost in the mad music and pulled herself away from all that she knew and was familiar with. She felt every cell in her body responding to all that was around her and encode it to some familiar place deep in the memory of her blood. She briefly noticed that all in their retinue including Juba and her daughter and even her siblings were responding the same as she. She lost them and became emeshed with the people and almost lost who she truly was, so powerful was the music and words that were uttered that eve. She felt something primeval awaken in her that night and was lost in all of it. A strange aroma came from the fires and permeated all of those who danced through the spaces in between each fire and around the edges of them—that all concept of time was lost while the scent of the ancients filled her bones and clothing. She even found that she had taken off some of the layers of clothing and was oblivious to any possible cold and all seasons appeared one. She last recalled dancing around in her simple shift that she had underneath all of the heavy garmets, that she had worn on the warmest of evenings back home. She felt at one with everything around her and the people, though most of them towered over even her husband who was tall amongst her own people and culture.

These people them appeared like trees in swaying with the music, their skin as white as the snow. She was mesmerized and enraptured in the sweet intoxicating beauty of it all.

Her mind was mixing up times before her, so realistic was the memory of the soft and warm River Nile sand beneath her feet, that she fought hard to erase the reality of the snow of the primeval forest that she was in. She could see her body become the same as it was when she was only nine years old and suddenly the illusion became reality for her.

She swayed in rhythm beside the graceful flowing movements of her mother who was head priestess in this ceremony. Her mother's form was blocked out by the intense rays of the sun with her arms raised high to the sky in praise of Sobek for this ceremony. Priests danced along with them, their heads hidden by the ceremonial crocodile masks in reverence of Sobek at the temple by the banks of the mighty Nile. The Sun peaked through the mighty and ancient columns casting in shadow all of the worn sacred texts that adorned the façade and walls around them. Bells chimed and the palms danced in the heat of the sun. Her tiny form attempted to appear as expert at the dance as her mother, who smiled down at her with her beautiful eyes the color of the sand of the desert mixed in with the leaves from the palms, so magical were her eyes to her small daughter who danced beside her to the beat of the drums, sistrums and bells that seemed to emanate from everywhere, though Selene could find no musicians. It was so magical she could even smell the henna on her mother's fingernails and in her hair. The scents mingled the incense that burned all around them with the sweat of the dancers and her mother's own scent mixed with jasmine. Helios was even there and winked at her since she was much better in practice at this very complex dance and he let her know that he was constantly out of beat and trying to hide it from their mother. His hair shone in the sun—so dazzling and beautiful. The warm sand scorched her sensitive skin so used to the slippers that she wore in her palace. But her mother had told them that in dancing with the Gods, one must be barefoot in supplication. She also added to them that it was easier to feel the magic of the earth's response to their devotion in their feet. Selene in her youth felt it then for the first time. The response to the earth of the moment and the reverence they were dancing to. The power of the universe surrounded them and made her feel so small and insignificant in the grand scheme of things, though safe with her mother's hand holding hers and her brother on the other side. Two halves with the creator of both between them. Little Selene felt the magic and power of her mother flowing through her veins very strong for the first time and cherished it to learn more from the moment.

The music grew louder and louder and she swayed becoming only one of the dancers, suddenly her mother's hand was lost to her in the excitement and she fought frantically for it to stabilize her emotions that ran amok. She ran and ran and called out to both her mother and brother, who only seemed to be slipping away from her and becoming lost in all of the other dancers around them oblivious to her plight and frenzy. She ran and ran, not seeming to get any closer to either of them, but still seeing their forms. She called out to them and they only smiled at her and danced on and on and on. Her tears started to flow in the frustration of seeing her mother and not holding her hand, her brother was only smiling at her and dancing, getting farther and farther away from them. Her hands stretched out and she cried even harder in her desperation. The warm sun was dazzling all around her and she was growing tired from all of the dancing and her emotions becoming so unfrosted. She collapsed in a heap and her tears poured out.

IV

When she awoke the next day she had found out that most of the people had slept for most of the morning and those that were up were preparing for a feast to be held that very evening. Her head was spinning and she heard her husband and daughter both snoring heavily under piles of cloaks by the fire in their round house. How she arrived there, she could not recall. She knew that she did not drink at all, though her head felt heavy and the world seemed still unreal to her. It seemed as if she were on the edge of a dream, though a happy one. Her body was tired and weary from excessive use from all of the frantic dancing that she could barely recall. It was all getting more and more imperceptible by the minute and ever the more hazy to recall in any detail.

V

The days wore on and soon it seemed that the Gods were perhaps relenting in their fury of snow and storms and they were soon notified that they would be able to start to plan their final part of the voyage to Pryttain.

She had noticed one day when it was finally warm enough to sit outside for a decent amount of time that her daughter Jubilla had the same idea and found her sitting on a log watching the farmers prepare the ground for planting. As she walked over to the form of her daughter she noticed how glorious her hair was in the sun and how it seemed to dazzle all those who noticed her daughter. Her daughter's hair was the color of some of the autumn leaves that dripped over the beautiful and strange landscape here that seemed to be in constant change.

This was utterly alien in concept to Selene who was used to the serene and almost unchanging landscape of the Nile where she grew up and to the barely perceptible changing climate of Rome. Though Rome did receive snow during her visits and stay in captivity, it was only just a powdering of it and the trees had lost their leaves and had changed in the fall just prior to the winter in yellow and brown tones, not the extraordinary array of colors that were displayed before them so far up north. She was even told by the natives of the area that it would only increase in color the further north one traveled.

She felt the weather here truly exotic and more deadly in winter than what she had ever experienced. The winds were furious yet truly spectacular to watch in how completely everything was covered in such a brilliant white, that not even the fine linen of her homeland of Egypt could produce.

Her daughter's hair was the color of the fall leaves that brought such delight to Selene that she had collected as many leaves as she could to surround her sleeping quarters inside. They eventually grew too stiff and broke apart when touched, but the colors on the leaves had helped her during the cold and long winter months in this strange new land.

She slowly walked up to her daughter, hoping not to disturb her too much, but was unable to hide the sound from the forest crunching beneath her fur lined sandals. Twigs crunched mercilessly underfoot and her presence was known and had broken the reverie of her daughter.

"Drussi, can I sit beside you?" Drussi had motioned her hand to a space beside her on the log. "Oh, Mamma... I'm so scared." Her long dark eyelashes were downcast at this last utterance and her formerly straight form slumped to her mother who gingerly sat beside her growing daughter. She put her arm around her daughter and whispered, "I know...I felt the same myself once." And together they sat side by side at the field coming alive before them. They were off in a distance and those that walked by respectfully gave them room for they had sensed that they needed space to be mother and daughter. They watched the trees before them struggling to burst out in bloom and the grass throw off the dew to create more life. The birds called out from everywhere surrounding them in a celebration of a renewal of life and the mother and daughter sat side by side in the next step to their life.

VI

Alas came the day when Jubilla had to take the final step to her destiny and in growing up. They left the village and proceeded across the mighty sea on a voyage that had been rather short in duration compared to everything else they had endured along the way. They gave the village gift for their hospitality and loaded all of their belongings in the many boats prepared for them and finally had the word from the chief druid that all was safe for their final crossing.

Upon landfall they observed the vast cliffs of white above them and had been greeted by the first tribe of Jubilla's soon to be new homeland. They stated that they were kin of her husbands tribe and had been sent notice to welcome them until he could be notified and arrive to gather his bride and her family who had traveled so far. They had informed the weary travelers that they were of the tribe called the Belgae and they also were related to the tribe who kept the voyagers over winter to make a safe crossing.

Selene was grateful when all of the introductions were done, and she was shown into a carved out dwelling lined in the softest of furs. She sweetly sank into oblivion and had hoped since the night of it's occurrence to catch the image of her mother at a time in her life she desperately craved her advice. She wanted to hear from her mother that she was doing right in sending her daughter so far way from her home, especially since she heard the muffled sobs at night from her daughter the closer they were. Everything was so strange and foreign to them, though knew their hospitality to be genuine and true. They all insisted on being separate tribes, though they all seemed similar to her in their boisterous personality and love of life.

Most of them traveled and their homes were temporary, though stayed within some invisible boundaries. She had even observed in the villages over here and in those which they had passed, the walled enclosures that surrounded the village main with age worn and new sculls woven within. For the walls used as enclosures were mainly made of woven branches, though were very sturdy.

She had wondered about them and had thought that they must be the victims of human sacrifices that some Romans had mentioned in writings of these strange people. Though found it rather odd, since in her time among them so far, she had not witnessed any sacrificing more than of a bull at the fires of mid-winter solstice. She further recalled that before the fires were lit it started the ceremony of walking every single herd creature through them for hopes of fruition and a bountiful harvest. Again a bull along with some chickens were slaughtered. They were prized and eaten by the Chief of this tribes that called themselves the Belgae. This she witnessed in anther celebratory day that they called Beltane. A holiday noted for its fertility rites.

It was all happening so fast and so much was completely alien to her that she found it difficult to make any sense to any of it and wondered about the skulls peering frightfully out at them as they entered the clearing for the dwellings.

It was all the more difficult when these people seemed to have no apparent sense of time as they did with their culture. There were no names or markings for hours nor weeks. The only time kept was by the druids and chief leaders. The leaders of the tribes kept the days by how many there were after each phase of the moon and that way kept track of the planning of the celebrations. The druids kept time recorded for the people in meticulous detail and would travel to each village to tell them the exact time of each celebration. She had found no evidence on how the druids kept this time, for it appeared unrealistically accurate, even more so than the water clock that she had in her chamber in her palace back home. She was very amazed at this fluency the druid had with time.

It was also rather confusing how the Keltoi seemed to blend all times with one. They believed that the past and present are the same and that Gods walk the earth in their power and as they once did when time began. That death was the same as life and air the same as fire. She thought she understood when looking at their art, she noticed upon closer observation that the spirals were more complex than what they appeared initially and more often than not to have words, faces and animals hidden inside. Reality was oblivion and oblivion reality. Which seemed to explain why they did not fear death. As one druid had remarked to her, how was she to know that she was not really in her death, that all that appeared real in this life was only in response to how she lived in her last life and just added to each lesson that she had learned before? Very interesting perspective.

VII

They were there for possibly a few Roman weeks when at last she finally noticed the ground heaving from the weight of many chariots led by horses of a large retinue. Selene was forced from her reverie to walk over to where they all appeared to stop. Juba had appeared in the fore of the crowd that had gathered beside the chief of this tribe called Drennedd. Drennedd was a large man with flowing gray hear and braided beard. He wore a large golden torc around his neck with elaborate patterns. His arms heavily adorned with many golden and equally intricately carved bracelets. His leather trousers were finely made and of a deep yellow. His cape in many colors all woven together with a great broach that wrapped around a large red brilliant stone that collected the rays of the sun. He looked so regal next to her husband who had donned his heavy almost white as snow Roman robes for this occasion. Her husband stood tall and bold and almost reached the breastbone of the colorful leader who stood tall beside him.

The riders when they arrived lifted their large bronzed arms up to the heavens in greeting and supplication to the leader of the tribe. One of them, finally got off his dappled gray horse at the allowance Drennedd. He was taller than most of the men present and wore the robes of a leader which were finely woven and equally colored as those of Drennedd. His hair was long and golden and hung down around him with braids interspersed throughout. His hair reminded Selene of a horses mane. He seemed to tower even more than all the men present, herself mixed in with the crowd. His hair then caught in brilliance from the sun and he seemed as powerful as a God in all of his glory. His skin was bronzed as if even in this harsh climate he had spent every moment possible outside in it. His boots were fine auburn leather wrapped around in intricate patters with lace and seemed lined in rabbit fur.

He loosened his cloak and took a few step over to Drennedd and gave him a large embrace, "Thank you Sir Drennedd in taking this fine family into your village's notable hospitality." He smiled and turned to face Juba, who appeared rather comical in his small stature against these giant men who surrounded him. Yet, Selene was proud, his confidence gave her husband more height in the fine way he carried himself. "And your voyage your highness, I pray treated you well." He spoke this in the most eloquent Latin that there was with no trace of an accent. So strange to hear such fine elocution in one who would appear to the average Roman as a barbarian. She knew instantly from this that he was the man who would marry her daughter, the notable and now king Cunobelinios, or as he liked to be called Cynfelyn. He nodded and all of the others in his entourage dismounted and approached the clearing to make formal introductions to all. She had noticed in her confusion the gaze of her daughter wrapped firm on her husband to be. This was rather interesting mused Selene and wondered if it was a crush or genuine adulation. Then she noticed Jubilla rapidly fixing her hair to emulate as best as she could the proper Roman fashion. Selene smiled at this and looked over at Juba, who also seemed to have noticed.

Cynfelyn's guard had made all of the arrangements for the last part of the journey so that they could all get to know each other. He brought over some beautifully carved jewelry for Jubilla, her mother, and Arsinoe and some of the other ladies in their entourage. He also had beautiful cloaks as gifts for all. Her husband thanked him for his generosity and the hospitality of his people and passed out gifts from their family and then they both wandered off to discuss the preparations to the lands of the Catuvellauni, and the Trinovantes that he now ruled over.

The women were left alone to sort out who was to have what. Selene took a moment and watched her daughter's eyes follow the forms of her father and especially the fine muscled form of her husband to be as they left the clearing strewn with fine gifts.

VIII

The next morning at daybreak, they all set out. Over the most wild and untouched landscaped they traveled in a northerly direction further away from where they had initially landed. Selene was beginning to regret sending her daughter so far away from her own homeland and knew that it would be on very rare occasions when they could actually see each other again.

Again on horseback they rode on though valleys and forests that all seemed to blend together to Selene and confused her in her maternal misery. There were wagons this time to load all of their things they had needed for the journey. Juba was riding beside Cynfelyn talking rapid to him about all they had encountered and about the goings on in Rome, Mauretania and the rest of the world. Two leaders, two great men. She wished that daughter would find even half of the happiness that she had with Juba.

The landscape before her was wild and untouched yet beautiful all the same. The small villages along the way were well into planting by then and were singing to the rhythm of the winds. The sun catching the Keltoi people's long and decorated hair while they worked.

Selene and Jubilla marveled at the abounding happiness of the new people so different from their culture. To the world that she was most familiar, stress was a normal part of it and people would die in the face of it sometimes. Baldness ran rampant, though she saw no sign of it here. Even the elderly seemed young and strong to her and all would participate in the planting, even the royal and privileged. For she latter learned that it was considered holy to plant for the well-being of the tribe and all must take part or suffer the just punishment of the Gods. The chief especially had to take part in this for he or she was responsible for feeding their own people.

Everything was based on fairness with these people, whom she was beginning to think were far from simple in just the short time that she had made their acquaintance. She had also learned that most of the tribal chiefs paid homage to her new son-in-law and that he was a high king here and recognized in Rome by Augustus. For he was considered most holy in that all things of import were by the number three. He was the third high king of the land after his father and before that, grandfather. Thus, he was all the more revered amongst his own people and already the subject of legends. Selene even recalled hearing a few of the songs in the village over the sea where they wintered. She was not sure what they had said—but thought that it might have been about him. She was affirmed in this after speaking with her husband Juba, who had attained an almost fluent grasp of the strange language and dialect that she could not make any sense of at all. He had an uncanny ability to make sense out of sounds that to her sounded utterly foreign and unintelligible and even grasp it enough to be understood in it as well.

The only thing that Selene had difficulty with was the lack of the grand palaces and architecture made of the finest carved stone and marble that she was so used to her whole life. She was used to vast covered spaces and cavernous halls surrounded by tall stark white pillars elegantly carved in the palaces she had spent her whole life in. The Roman might abhor the idea of anything relating to royalty, yet they surrounded themselves in elegance in imitation of the Greek architecture as did her own family that started there.

But here, the houses and all dwellings were very small and people slept in close quarters to each other. She wondered how her daughter would fare over here with that and if she has even noticed in the times that her eyes ceased it's amazement and constantly locked gaze on her new husband.

The villages were bustling with activity in preparation for the harvest. The air was vibrant with life and was starting to reveal itself everywhere in brilliant hues in the lush greens of the leaves to the bright and rampid colors of the flora that was completely unlike any that she had ever seen. She knew Juba was collecting samples and seeds to take back with them and inquiring them all about the various new forms of plant life they passed on this journey.

They spent the evenings in makeshift camps that were set up with the ease of soldiers, yet warm and cozy enough with the close sleeping quarters and the piles of furs they were wrapped in for the evenings. Some of the furs were from creatures that she had not learned about, yet were as warm if not more so than what she had knowledge of.

They had learned the identity of two men who were most in the company of Selene's son-in-law. They were the younger brothers of Cynfelyn. The middle brother was thin and had long wavy hair and his clothes were not as well kept up as his eldest brother, though he seemed at home on the saddle and was diligent in the care of his mount as well as those of his brothers. His name was Togodumnos. He had not spoken much to them on the journey thus far and stayed off on the side lines—yet close to his brother and always in sight of the horses.

The youngest brother was revealed as Annius and he was the smallest of the two, yet still taller than the average Roman and very slight of build. He was quick to answer and spoke almost as fluent Latin as his oldest brother and was always the first with a quick and clever response. He was the one who drew forth most of the laughter on their journey and made it much easier for the now weary Selene. They both seemed completely devoted to their older brother who was ruler over the people.

Even if her new son-in-law was not born to leadership, he was the type of personality that led men naturally with his careful observation of the world around him and his quick response in times of danger as well as many other qualities that were fast becoming eminent to Selene.

They had traveled northwards through the lands of the Belgae and then the Atribates. When they reached the borders of the lands of the Catuvellauni, some of the men in their entourage bid them a safe rest of the journey, until they were at least within sights of the territory that their daughter would rule over.

IX

Finally, the men of the Trinovantes started to add an extra bounce in their pace for it seemed to Selene that they were nearing the borders of their homeland and territory. There was even a twinkle in the dark blue eyes of Cynfelyn as he requested that Jubilla lead her horse next to his as he explained to her the area that she would rule with him. Jubilla's small Bay mare was put into a trot to catch up with her new husband and their voices filled the rest of the journey.

Selene and Juba trotted behind them and smiled at the ease in which their daughter and her new husband seemed to be getting along. For prior to that Jubilla had remained in the background admiring her new husband from afar in her shyness at the giant that she was to marry.

For though they were married in contract and have been since she was very little, the nearer they reached her new homeland—the more reality seemed to catch up to Jubilla. During the journey, Selene had explained to her daughter her duty with as much detail as she could provide on the matters which she would need to know very soon. She had taught her daughter the secret knowledge of women and how to use their powers well on their husbands.

Jubilla was shocked yet very curious and wondered if her new husband had felt the same way about her for she was only twelve years old and her new husband was a man of sixteen. The years might be a burden to them now, but her mother had told her that as they both grew up together, their ages would seem as nothing in the great scheme of things. For her father and mother were separated in many more years than she and her husband. She wondered how they both got along in the beginning and when it started to get easier for them.

X

Jubilla glanced around at all the wonderful new sights before them. At last they entered a great clearing on the edge of the thickest forest that she had ever seen. Inside the great clearing people had gathered from almost every direction to see their new queen and in preparation for the marriage feast. The druids present to officiate were in dressed in their finest of the purest white robes that she had ever seen, even more so then those of the stingy and boring Romans. The colors of the villages surrounded them and flowers were strung up in every available space for they were only weeks away for the proper time to conduct most weddings on Mid-Summer's Eve.

The closer they came to the center of the clearing she had looked up and noticed more buildings around her with elaborate carvings adorning the facades and painted in marvelous colors. She heard wind instruments and soft drums as they approached the clearing and children arrayed in flowing dresses and wreathes surrounding their fair flowing hair with tiny flowers greeted their new queen and heaped upon her endless garlands of flowers in the most unusual colors. Her mare walked along countless petals that covered her path and her husband smiled down at her eyes that were soaking in everything that was occurring. She felt joy and extreme happiness from each of the villagers and admiration at the sight of their king of two years and his new wife, a Goddess from a land so far away.

The villagers had heard tales of her grandmother and of her being a priestess of Isis which was very similar to their Goddess, Brigit. She was a triple Goddess of fire and smith craft as well as poetry and motherhood and childbirth. She was the daughter of the Dagda. They had just associated the attributes of Isis with that their own and familiar Goddess and had embraced their new Queen because of this as well as her relation and kinship to their Goddess, the mother of Kings-Don. They had also noted her hair revealing the legendary bright red hair of their beloved Goddess Don in the red of the autumn leaves, though of a lesser shade.

This was the largest settlement that Jubilla had seen so far with it's flourishing trade in pottery, weaving, and she had even glimpsed a silversmith shop with fine jewelry on display out front. Though the settlement was made of wood, it was large and bustling with excitement and busy activity that would rival most of the cities that she had seen in her life made of marble and stone.

The fragrance of the many flowers strewn about were dizzying with the singing and joyous utterances in this language that she was only beginning to grasp. The sun poured down on her and suddenly she felt utterly and completely alone and searched desperately for her mother and father that she knew were somewhere in this crowd. So unfamiliar were her surrounding she felt every bit a child at that moment.

Cynfelyn had glanced to the side and noticed the apprehension of Jubilla and made the fastest speech that he could to his people and bid his wife to bow to them and he rushed her to where her and her families new quarters were to be for their visit. For he knew that Queen Selene and King Juba wanted to be present for the birth of their first grandchild. He had a separate clearing made for their loving quarters and new longhouses built for them which he had hired the finest carvers to adorn their building.

He went to extravagant measures to insure the comfort of his parents in law from Mauretania. Their assigned buildings were filled with the finest of furs from his land as well as some from the far reaches of civilization, including the soft white fur of a large and ferocious bear that dwelled in a land of snow all year round and was extremely rare.

The buildings were all surrounding a beautiful garden that modeled after the gardens he had observed while he was studying in Rome; complete with a running fountain that contained the waters from a cold spring. He had workers erect large murals, though could not import artists from Rome or anywhere that was familiar with the Egyptian or Roman pantheon. The Gods that adorned the building were his and most familiar to his people. In their completion, they could actually almost out-shine in quality any that he had seen in Rome due to their colors being much more prevalent and brighter. The scents of many different species of thyme wafted through the air when a person walked upon the paths of the gardens in the center of the buildings. He had even imported carpets all of the way from Parthia, for they were renowned for their exquisite workmanship the world round. Even in the living quarters, which were grand and spacious for his people and what they were used to, were separated by finely woven drapery in the famous bold purple dyed in Tyre. The columns were made of the rich and rare Cedar much in demand from Syria and were carved with the bold patterns of flowers wrapped around them.

Cynfelyn was very pleased with his accomplishment and was rewarded for the reactions of the wedding party from Mauretania and especially how his new wife's amber eyes lit up in wonder.

XI

Over the next few days the weary travelers from Mauretania were settling into their new home for awhile and getting to know the people of this settlement which they had learned was called Trinovantum and was further the capitol of the land of the Trinovantes tribes. Jubilla and Selene had also learned that the rule of the Catuvellauni tribe was being offered to her new husband by the right of inheritance and after the wedding was planning on establishing a capitol there as well.

The villagers were elated to have another excuse for celebration which glowed on their rosy cheeks to further betray their enthusiasm to the foreigners and the ever inquisitive Juba. Juba was fast appearing the regular among the druids camp on the outer reaches of the vast and sprawling settlement. For they had extreme knowledge in astronomy, plants, and seemed to have most of the ancient and now lost knowledge of the civilizations older than theirs of people known as the Picts and Jutes. Juba was fascinated with their knowledge and even more so that it was all memorized. For druids believed that writing only encouraged laziness and told him that the proper training of a druid was nineteen years and that there were many levels. They were mostly the people that kings referred to and had knowledge and precedence of all of the laws and administration of such in their land. The druids further told Juba that most of them were not allegiant to one tribe or king, that most traveled from tribe to tribe with sacred immunity in their entourage of wisdom. Most often the retinue would contain various levels of Bards who composed the ancestry of the tribes and bold deeds of the heroes, while the Ovates who traveled along with them as well, had the knowledge of things of the other realm, for they foretold the future for those wise enough to listen.

Juba soaked in all of this knowledge imparted from the wise druids and knew that they had known much more than he could possibly imagine. They had further informed him that all worlds and all times were one and that is why their warriors both men and women did not fear death, as most other religions did. They told Juba that the souls of their ancestors and descendants walked in the same path as people who appear in life as Juba knew of it.

The druids had also explained to Juba that the Gods and Goddesses of their people were one with the land as well as the people that they ruled over. To keep them happy, would be to keep the people in the most material realm happy. They treated their bodies as temples and homes to their Gods with respect as well as other people.

When Juba had inquired about the sculls that he had noticed in the walls around the settlement, the wise druid named Bellinos had informed him that they were the sculls of the enemies of this tribe and that the people kept the skulls in admiration and deep respect of the defeated. Juba had learned that Bellinos was also known as the Arch-Druid and was the highest ranking in the whole of their lands. For he had assigned most of his time to the young King Cynfelyn, as his father had to Cynfelyn's father Tenvantius until the time of his death.

He had accompanied young Cynfelyn while in Rome and had known Julius Caesar as well as his adopted son Augustus. Bellinos was nearing his eighty-seventh year though felt as if he were a youth of sixty. So full of delight was this great wise man that he attracted Juba to his side immediately, especially with the wise man's elegant and patient responses. Juba had felt in the Arch-Druids' presence as if her were a young boy of sixteen and basked in his awe often forgetting that he was a well established King.

Bellinos adored this fine young king before him and loved his thirst for knowledge, so refreshing from the stuffy men of Rome who were inclined to believe their race and religion superior to all else in the world. Though Julius Caesar and his nephew Augustus had shared this thirst that he had also noticed on this fine man who was the father of their new Queen. He felt that Cynfelyn had chosen well in her due to her blood connections as well as the power that he felt in her and her elegant mother Queen Selene with her honey blonde tresses always kept up around her face reminding him of the murals he had seen of the Goddess Aphrodite while away in Rome.

The daughter, though as elegant as her mother, had a wilder personality that her mother did not possess. The old druid watched the sun catch the red on the young girl's hair and it reminded him of Don, the mother of Kings who had a more brilliant hue of red. Perchance this new Queen possessed some of that quality brought over so long ago from her kin who his people had deified as the Goddess Don. He saw untamed fire in the child's eyes and in her hair. This would be a great Queen who would create another line of Great Queens from her womb. Yes, Cynfelyn had chosen wisely and it helped their cause that the Roman King Augustus had approved of this match as well. For he further saw in her eyes that she would be essential in creating the seed that would fight back the Roman invasion of their beloved lands in years to come. He had also noted that she carried the approval of a sister Goddess Isis in her being. He read much of the Egyptian religion from where this girl had sprung from in his travels. He knew that though her line was only a mere three hundred years old, it also was deeply emeshed from a princess of the line who was the daughter of a high priest of their God Ra and of the royal blood of Pharaohs past to the beginning of time. Maternal blood was very strong in power in this bright young girl he saw walk around her new home in wonder.

He noticed with a giggle that the girl had responded to Cynfelyn's request that she wear her hair down, unlike the other women of her people. Jubilla's hair was long past her waist in long rivulets that created a river of chestnut red in currents down her back. He knew that Cynfelyn had greatly admired this and was always caught by the observant druid watching the sunlight in her hair take on new life. He giggled at this and recalled all too well the vivid red of her great-great aunt's hair that he himself had loved so long ago. He had promised her that he would watch over her family after she left this realm and kept that vow sacredly to his soul.

He adored the many visits of the girl's father and recalled many others over the years which were rapidly becoming all the same to him in his later years. Sometimes he confused Cynfelyn with his grandfather Llud or his brother Casswallon. Maybe they were one and the same and his soul was telling him this.

He had noted the altar to Isis that Selene had built in an old potter's shed for her and her daughter. For Bellinos knew that she was fervently passing on all of her knowledge of this great Goddess to her daughter. Bellinos saw a lot of Cleopatra VII, whom he had met one time in Rome long ago, in her daughter and granddaughter. The hair was the only thing different of the three women. For he recalled that Cleopatra VII had hair as dark as a raven against the purest ivory skin. Her eyes were shared in her granddaughter. With piercing strength to lead armies and the wildness to fight well for them. This seemed to have been passed over in Selene who had clear blue eyes and hair the color of honey.

Bellinos observed that Selene had the grace of a thousand years of great Queens, and had observed a wilder form in her daughter in her youth of only twelve summers. He sat back in his time of rest watching those in the settlement and in how history was mixed with his present and all those who played in this scene before him. How long would he last to teach this man who will lead all of these people? Would he be around long enough to impart the necessary advice to a new advisor of equal merit to be chosen in the Arch-Druids' stead?

The shell of this life was wearing him down in not being able to keep up with his mind as clear as it once was. For he saw now how the worlds of the past collided with that of the present and how the future walked beside them as well. Before, when young he only saw it in the mist, yet now it was loud and clear before him.

XII

Jubilla was escorted around Trinovantes by the younger brother of her new husband named Annius. He was the second most knowledgeable in the Latin language and was assigned to teach her the language. He made the lessons so much fun with they way he made words for her to remember silly to her in her native Latin language. For she was picking up her new language in a rapid pace and was told by her mother that she had inherited her grandmother's ability to learn languages that must have passed over her. For she had to be pulled away from the rest of her family due to the rapid pace that she was learning. The rest were taught by Andocos, one of her new husband's fiercest and most noble of warriors. Yet, he also had grasped the Latin tongue enough to teach the basics to the royal family of Mauretania.

He had noticed Arsinoe, the sister of the Queen with her summer blonde locks and quiet demeanor and had taken a liking to her. Though he never assumed that she would notice a fumbling soldier such as he. She seemed as graceful as a swan and had an elegant neck to support such lovely tresses the color of ripe summer corn.

For Andocos was the younger son of his family and his mother and father had no special merits to add to his namesake. Yet, he was fierce in honor and loyalty and felt that he had earned his place in the royal guard due to his hard work. For he was not even noble enough to have been fostered out when young. He was tall and gangly and his arms and legs were longer than the norm, though he was excellent with a spear which had gained the attention of Cynfelyn. This princess before him was like a Goddess, he dare not let her know his true feelings towards her, though in his heart he knew that he had bound himself to her safety for life no matter how she felt for him.

He spent his mornings giving lessons to the royal family and he felt confident in his teaching abilities due to the reaction and fast pace they were learning. Andocos was a little hurt when Jubilla was assigned to the prince, though understood since he had noticed her fast pace at learning had actually made her a little bored when the others were straining to keep up with her grasp of the Trinovantes dialect.

XIII

Cynfelyn would sometimes join Jubilla and his brother with lessons and hold up flowers for his brother to teach his new wife the meanings to, until Jubilla with her concentration broken, had scooped up all of the petals and flowers strewn about her in such fury and threw them at him. They all ended up rolling on the ground in giggles. He left the clearing in admiration of her temper. Very good at that in her not being daunted by the people. She would make a great leader, for she knows how to get attention and to earn their respect!

Cynfelyn walked back to the clearing and noticed Juba in rapt conversation with his Arch-Druid, who was like a grandfather to him. He was glad for that and contented decided to walk back to the main settlement to oversee all that went on in his brief absence.

He walked over to where many booths were being set up for the celebration of the Summer Solstice and Mid-Summer's Eve. For it was extra-special in being the sacred time for marriages which only added the good fortune for he and his bride. For it was also the beginning of the cycle of their year.

This was a good year for them and bountiful, for it had already produced two hay harvests which were being gathered as he walked around. He was hoping for a good winter barley and winter oat crop that would be harvested soon after the solstice celebration. For he had already noticed great signs of this in the fields allotted. For these crops would tide the people and animals well into the cold winter months when all of the other foods prepared would have been depleted. Winter seemed so far away from them all at that moment to Cynfelyn.

Plenty of herbs were being gathered and stored for the winter such as Borage for rubbing on the skin before battle for strength, and Marjoram, whose leaves were crushed and used as a powerful painkiller with the flowers being set aside for dyeing their colorful purple patterns in the finely woven wool. He noticed the other dye plants being gathered as well and prepared for it's use. The woad flowers for blue, madder for brown, and the vivid green produced from the flowers of buckthorn berries that ran rampant through the village. Cranberries and Bilberries were being gathered for the feast as well as many delights from the river banks such as freshwater clams and muscles which melted on his tongue. For their settlement was on an estuary of the mighty river that led to the town of his father and grandfather to their city named CaerLlud after his grandfather who founded the city.

He left CaerLlud to start his own city for it was prophesied from his birth that he would be the founder of his own cities in the lands of the Catuvellauni and the Trinovantes lands.

For after all of the celebrations, he would send over an envoy to establish his claim and rights. He knew form his sources that they were currently battling over the true leadership rights over the Catuvellauni territory and had fractioned it's strength, made it all the more vulnerable for attack.

The scents of the summer were so strong and vibrant he breathed it all in as he walked along in pride of his new settlement. He had carefully picked practically every board that sheltered them all from the cold winter months. He had even helped to put each one in place. He firmly believed as was taught by his father that a good leader must do everything well and not to put himself above any job that he expected people to do for him. That he must sleep beside them in battle and die beside them as well.

With this valuable lesson and the implementation of it, he had earned the pride and love of his warriors male and female alike. For all were equally fierce, sometimes the women were more so for the Goddess Brigit often entered their lithe forms in battle to lend them her strength and valor. For his female warriors belonged to a sacred guild that would only allow those born from warriors to enter and though a matriarchal line only. They were only allowed to retire when they had their first daughter, who would enter the guild after them. It did not matter how many sons were born to them. They were noted to chose only the noblest of warriors for their consorts, as he was one himself last year for his lead ranking warrioress Ceridon, who had given birth to a son who breathed for two days and had died. His soul still ached for that lost child and welcomed Ceridon into his ranks again and noted that her valor was even more fierce than before, almost in an angered response to the death of her first born.

He was fearful that this would affect his ability to sire children with his new wife, though held it close to him. Maybe those of his were not as strong as his father's who had produced three sons and three daughters. Only time would tell at that.

He did know that his wife was a twin and had lost her sister when very young. This, he knew was a trait in a woman with a strong womb and that would carry many fine children. For to have twins was sacred to his tribe and all were revered. His wife especially since even her mother was a twin. He prayed fervently to his favorite God Bel the sun God for whom his great-grandfather was named for and now worshiped in confusion by his people. For he was the father God of all of the lesser Gods and his great-grandfather had fathered lesser Kings. So he supposed that they both might be very similar. For his greatly loved Arch-Druid had affirmed this and told Cynfelyn not to bother the people with details on whom they worshipped. For they all walked the same world and all times were one.

As he walked around he found a lonely old wheat grinder busy with the remnants of the last harvest. He requested that he might sit beside the old man, who gratefully and reverently allowed Cynfelyn room beside him on his bench. Cynfelyn picked up a long stone and began to grind next to the old man who had his own well-worn stone working fervently into the pace he was at before his honored guest arrived and joined him at his lowly task. Both King and wheat grinder picked up a beat to the distant drums and were making fast progress. When a young fair-haired child picked up the basket containing the fine powdered grain for the bread, she noticed in admiration and praise of the great man beside her uncle as none other than the king. The great king did not even notice the girl, but kept on working beside her uncle. If it were not for the difference in the clothes they both wore, one would have though they were father and son-so close and in perfect unison the rhythm they set together deep in their work. After her initial wonder the little girls went back to her chores being used to the strange ways of her king. She recalled during her lifetime of seeing him as his father did before him toil among the sides of the lowliest of workers with equal respect. He was well loved by his people for this humility and natural curiosity he had for every trade of his people. As she walked along in a hurry to get the newly ground grain to her mother for the Solstice bread she stumbled upon a small rock in her path which was followed by one of the royal princesses that arrived recently at her village from far way at the end of the earth. This princess scowled at her for being in the way of the pretty white stone that was thrown into the path before her.

XIV

Arsinoe ran after the pretty stone that she had found in the morning while checking on the laundering of her travel clothes by the river bank by the village women. She had noticed this stone when she was trying to balance upon the many round stones that dotted the river bed down stream away from where the old women were beating her clothes upon the rocks to dry in the warm summer sun. She had watched them for awhile in avid curiosity, since never in her life had she witnessed how her garments were cleaned, nor had she even cared before.

She had woken up early and inquired of one of her slaves as to the whereabouts of her favorite soft summer gown she had purchased while in Syria that was gold like the sun around her that morning and it reminded her of the dress. She was told the whereabouts of the launder-women by the river. When she inquired of the women of her dress she was shown it and was told that it still had to be dried from the sun, though it would be ready when the sun was low in the sky near the last meal of the daylight.

Since there was nothing more to do, she just found a spot on a smooth rock that was just large enough for her to sit upon and to stretch out her legs. She had taken off her sandals and placed them on the rock beside her and stretched out her long winter white legs and wiggled her toes in greeting to the morning sun. How wondrous it felt to just sit all day and to do absolutely nothing. The lessons had been abandoned for the busy preparations of the celebrations that were fast approaching. She was finally getting used to their sense of time here. For their day did not start with the entrance of the sun, like theirs did, but began with the end of the day at twilight and included the whole day after until the next twilight. They were very careful of the twilight and dawn and called them the "Tween Times" and told her that it was the time of day when all of the worlds can be seen. When the past and future walked in the present. They were very careful and had so many taboos concerning this time that she was rather confused over it all. It was almost as if she was on a different world and wondered if she would ever go back to the one that she was most familiar with. She wondered if the reason why her sister had brought her to this place at the edge of the world was to marry her off. And with each prince that her sister introduced her to, the truth of the matter was all too apparent to her.

She found this place overwhelming to the senses and did not like it at all. The men were like Titans and were loud to her in everyway. She was very quiet and prone to introspection in all matters and did not appreciate the company of loud people. She would rather find her harp, which could not be brought along with her on this voyage, which she missed dreadfully. Where she would bury herself in the music that she created. Selene encouraged this love of hers and hired the very best of Greek instructors for this. She had also learned to develop her voice as well. She would rather read poetry for hours until nightfall. All of this was strange and hard to grasp so far away from home. Her soul cried out for it. She sat there on the rock for what seemed to her as hours when she glanced down into the clear water of the stream and noticed the prettiest rock, so piercingly white it reminded her of the color of the Greek Doric Columns of the palace back home. For she had very little memories of the palace in Egypt and of her mother. She held her fine embroidered linen gown close to her body while she bent forward to retrieve the small rock.

It was so perfect in shape an almost perfect oval and it was the size of her thumb in length, yet very flat. She held it in her hand and felt an electric pulse from inside the rock. She was glad that this rock was close to her in that she had never learned how to swim and she knew that she would risk it just to reach this beautiful and powerful rock. She turned the rock over and over in her dainty and soft hands. Wondering if she should have something carved into it.

She stood up and put her sandals back on and started to walk back to the settlement, since she knew it would be awhile before her dress was done. Slowly she walked and at the same time she examined the small rock that was certainly growing on her in the soft beauty of it. Oblivious to her surroundings that she had not noticed until too late the beautiful white rabbit that had crossed her path in the corner of her eye. She looked up at the rock when it was flying from her grasp as it tumbled onto a path that had crossed hers and a small girl that was walking along was just about to step on her treasured rock. She scowled at the little girl and made her way after retrieving her rock to the buildings where her brother Ptolemy was. Maybe he would know where she could have it carved.

XV

Arsinoe saw her brother's concentration in what he was doing and thought better than to bother him over the matter of her rock. She decided to wait for that evening instead and hopped away.

Ptolemy was busy learning the arts of the spear and enjoying practice with these fine warriors. He marveled at their technique. He found it amusing at first when the women were allowed to join in practice with the men. His amusement was turned rapidly into respect when he was beaten in his stubbornness in wrestling with three different women. He was amazed at their incredible strength and skill. For most of these mammoth women were much taller than he. He was told about their cult and that each of these women were born to heroes in battle. For only the strongest were allowed in both men and women to join the elite warrior ranks of the king's army. The women were especially fearsome on horseback which they seemed to be morphed into during practice. How mighty must they look in battle, with their long ice gold hair flying in the sun of battle. He supposed many men were lulled into the vision and killed gruesomely by the illusion.

He had learned about the chariots which had virtually disappeared on the continent with the long-haired Gauls. The people of Pryttain had chariots that held two people, one with a spear and the other to lead the horses, yet would fight in close quarters in combat. The chariots were made of what appeared to be extremely light-weight wood that was woven almost like baskets, yet here it was demonstrated to him, the incredible strength of the wood and durability. He was told that to weave it, it had to be wet to ply into shape, yet when dried it was tough as the black wood of the Elder tree. The chariots were led by two horses that were much smaller than the horses that he was used to, though very muscular and very solidly built. Their mane was longer as well and the coat thicker and more rough. Though the horses could race and possibly outrun any of the horse breeds that he was familiar with. They seemed to have an uncanny intelligence and were treated with great respect. He had come into contact with the prince named Togodumnos this way. For the boy was rather shy, though his face lit up and became animated in the mention of one of his horses. He had had gained that this prince was the master of the horses and had earned the totem from his patron Goddess named Rhiannon who reminded him of the cult of Epona. For he had learned from the other warriors that the prince was part horse and would never truly fit into the world of men. It seemed to him that he spoke better the language of the animal of his Goddess and that every horse responded to him more than any other person. There was a legend told to him that the price was born the same day that the most prized horse Maidenlove went into fowl. That the price would not take the milk of his mother and someone had suggested that he have the milk of Maidenlove which had resulted in nourishing the boy the Queen thought she almost lost.

Ptolemy thought this story interesting, though wondered at the validity of it. For he had noticed with his better grasp of the language how the people loved to tell tales even when not needed, but for the pure joy of it. Everything, it seemed to him had a small tale inside.

He had grown to admire the warriors of the king and met up with four of his finest whose names were; Andocos, who helped to tutor his family, Dias, Rues, and Sego. They were all very large men who towered over him yet gave him great respect for his rank as prince and the brother of their new queen. They were very patient in showing him some of their battle skills and even in taking him out to some of the local mead houses. For they were very boisterous people and loved their mead and beer after a long day at practice. In this respect Ptolemy thought them all equal for he felt the same and joined in heartily.

After a few days in the company of the warriors, he had noticed that one of the smaller women was most often in the midst of things. She was actually smaller than him. This perked his interest since it was a rare thing for them in this land of giants. He wondered why he had not noticed her before. For she was very beautiful and had the most glorious red hair that he had ever seen. Her hair was wound tight in braids for practice and tied neatly in colored leather laces. Her legs were long and shapely in her trousers of the softest of leather and her short cloak wrapped around a tiny and perfectly womanly shape. He was suddenly intrigued and sought her out.

"A flower for you fair maiden." He bowed and elegantly extended out his hand to her that held vivid orange flowers with dark brown centers. "Your highness, how gracious and deeply appreciated, but I would rather wrestle you than have some dainty flowers to adorn my hair. Though I have to admit they are my favorite. Do you know what they are called?" Ptolemy glanced down in horror at his mistake in thinking that this fine warrior would be like the other women that he had known and would go for something "dainty:"

"Well, I will tell you, they are called "Black-Eyes" since they are the image of the eyes of the horse Goddess Rhiannon and contain her powers on Mid- Summer's Eve. It is told that if a maiden wears them in her hair the wildest of horses could be tamed by her, but only on Mid-Summer's Eve." She continued for the power of her speech had enraptured Ptolemy and all he could do was just stand there helpless feeling like a little boy at the power of her personality. "Though since I believe that you genuinely did not know, nor were trying to test me…I will wear them, that is if you will be my dance mate at the fires tomorrow eve." Ptolemy was completely stumped at the boldness of this tiny girl and almost stuttered out a yes to this unexpected turn of events.

"Do not worry prince, for you will not have to wrestle me for the honor either!" With that she spun around placing the "Black-Eyes" in her dazzling hair and skipped off to join the others near the fire for the mid-day meal of bread cakes and garden greens. Completely caught off guard he could not think of where else to go but to the building where he knew his sister would be assisting his niece with the wedding preparations that would begin at sun-down tomorrow.

He arrived at the building and found his sister looking at the cradle that she had brought over to give to her daughter. He recalled when Selene had her own three children in the cradle so long ago. He saw his sister tracing the delicate carvings that seemed completely foreign and from another world here. He was about to tell her of his strange encounter when he noticed the tears falling on her cheeks and decided that he should leave her alone to her grief. For seeing that cradle brought back memories of both twin little princesses inside so many years ago. He silently left the room and decided to approach her about this later on in the day, possibly at the meal served at days end.

It was funny how the hours and precise times that he was used to most of his life had no meaning here and how he was actually getting used to their sense of time and thought that with the closeness to the earth in which they lived, that it was much more reasonable.

XVI

Selene sat beside the cradle that her father had carved for her and her twin brother Helios. How could such a beautiful thing that had caused so much joy in the reason of it's creation bring about so much heartache and pain from the memories invoked. Still, it was the cradle that was made for her and her mother with the promise that her daughters and theirs should be placed in this in the generations to come. She made Selene promise that it would be passed on to the oldest daughters of this line.

Yet, it made her brother and daughter appear before her in her mind so clearly, she could almost touch them. Her little Tonia with all of her curls lost to her forever. For so long she held on to the belief that she would run through the door and slip under her covers at night. It seemed odd to get used to just one tiny body beside her at night rather than the two. She never did get used to that, even long after when Jubilla grew too old to sneak into her room at night.

She did not think that she would ever heal from the loss, it might fade to the back of her mind for awhile, but the smallest things brought back images so loud and clear before her. Sometimes she could smell her baby Tonia's body beside hers or sometimes hear her giggle in the wind. She imagined that she would look very similar to Jubilla had she lived to this age.

However, to Selene, Tonia was forever the tiny little girl who giggled at the slightest things. Her voice grew softer over the years, but it was never lost to her. Never.

After the loss of her little Tonia, so fast was she ripped away from all of their lives—she always slept with Drussi and little Juba after that. Her husband could not bring himself to approach her for more children due to the look in her eyes. He had eventually learned to fill his time by burying himself in more studies and research.

Her fingers traced the patterns along the sides of the beautifully carved cradle. The summer breeze sending to her the fragrance of the summer flowers. None of them familiar to her. Her thoughts suddenly jarred back to the present and the idea of how her Drussi was leaving her, as was her duty as princess.

She had spent many hours with her daughter on the journey and here in preparation for the celebration that would begin on the morrow. She gave her daughter all of the wisdom that she had wished that her mother would have been able to give to her on her wedding night with Juba. Octavia gave her the secret woman's knowledge prior to her wedding. She cherished Octavia for that and had kept in touch with her over the years as she had with Antonia Minor.

She was thankful for any piece of knowledge on the situation at the center of the world as Augustus called Rome. For Rome was a very busy place, very similar to her own city Caesarion. However, this place that her daughter would rule over was busy in a very peculiar way. The scents of living were much stronger here so far away from all that she was familiar with, though not in a necessarily adverse way. For she thought that perhaps most of these scents or some similar would be back home as well, though probably blocked out by all of the marble that surrounded the city, blocking out the sky. She was so used to it, she never gave it a second thought.

So many things were blocked from her in the everyday process of living that was normally in very plain view, one could not help to notice and even take part in life here. She thought it rather invigorating and hoped that her daughter felt the same about her new home. She knew that her daughter would be a fine leader and hopefully even learn the arts of battle here. What a wonderful thing to allow the woman to take a part in battle, especially when there was meaning to it.

She giggled at the thought of her self in Keltoi war gear and her hair all in disarray and screaming to scare the enemy. It would be a great way to get rid of some pent up hostility. That is without all of the blood and gore that was usually a big part of the whole battle scene. Then again, she recalled hearing that after a Keltoi warrior woman gave birth, her time in the army was over if it was a daughter.

Since Selene knew all too well the reality of war and had lived in the results, she hoped that her daughter would give birth to a daughter as soon as possible after the ceremony. Then she would be able to go home in peace knowing her daughter would be safe and out of the way of battle. She loved the smoothness on her fingers of the cool dark wood of the cradle and had traced many patterns by now and the time her mind had wandered. So much time to spend here just in being alive, it was joyous to her. For back at home, she would have had several meetings to attend and buildings to plan, among many other things. She absolutely lived by her precious water clock to keep such an animated schedule adhered to. Here one was not needed. Everybody helped one another and she had learned many things herself.

They had slaves here but only for a period of years and to repay debts. They were treated much better than anything she had observed in her whole life. She knew that her daughter had much more to learn about this place than she ever did about Numidia and later Mauretania. For they were very much in the Roman world. This world was so diverse and unique and so alien to anything she had raised her daughter with.

Though she had noted that her daughter seemed to be catching on with the new language at a more rapid pace than the others in the family. Her daughter's cheeks were constantly rosy and her whole being lit up when in the presence of her new statuesque husband. She hoped fervently those feelings would last long after she was gone and retuned to Mauretania.

Arsinoe seemed to have found her niche with the Bards and their version of the harp called a Lyre and had even learned rudimentary skills on the many wind instruments they had in this culture.

And her brother Ptolemy was constantly observed in the company of the warriors. She rarely saw the two of them lately.

Juba was constantly by the side of the Arch-Druid Bellinos and had lately exclaimed to him his jubilation in finding some of the long lost properties of some herbs for medicinal use. He was also intensely excited about the new astronomy that he was learning from the Druids. Selene could almost see the look in his eyes, wondering why he was not born of this culture and to have the knowledge of the Druids, that had been lost for so long. Juba had explained to her that it seemed that the druids had a knowledge similar to that of the Phoenicians and early Greeks in so many of their mathematical and scientific concepts. He also explained to her his frustration that he had not brought over enough Fannian Paper along with him on this journey to attain some of this knowledge. For her husband raved about that type of paper that was lightweight and very easy to obtain, which he did in bundles and used for his notes on research. He vented to her one evening that he simply did not think before that these people had even half of this amount of knowledge in things that he was interested in. Juba was so appalled at himself for misjudging this culture that he was becoming absorbed with.

Just then, her husband had filled the building with his presence. "No need to have taken that cradle out so early Selene, it would only bring you heartache." She looked up from her broken reverie and responded quietly as if to try to preserve the solemn state of the moment, "I know, it just called out to me." Without explaining further, for they both knew. Juba sensing that there needed to be a radical change in topic, exclaimed, "Selene, they are making some wreaths for the celebration and are desperately seeking your wisdom in the matter, though are too afraid to ask." Selene, loving to feel needed again stood up and brushed off her light purple linen gown of the tears that only she could see and walked to the side of her husband and out of the door. She thought to herself how wonderful to have a husband who knew exactly what to say to her.

XVII

The sun from the day was slowly ending it's weary course across the hazy summer sky to reach it's place of slumber for the eve. The rays of the sun danced lazily across the green hills dusted with puffs of sheep and vibrant life-filled fields of the crops that surrounded the settlement. As if to bring the attention of every person living there and in those smaller settlements outside the main settlement and new capitol. All living bodies responded to the call of the beginning of a new day in this upside-down world of the people of Pryttain. Trades were finished up for the day and people started flooding in from all around to witness this magical and special day before them. For it was the Summer Solstice, on the longest day of the year, the day perfect of the wedding ceremonies where most people invoked the year-and-a-day rite that was called the handfast. In this ceremony lovers would be united by an officiating Druid of their connection for a year-and-a-day to each other as a couple. When the time was up they could go on with their pledge and continue the bond. For the only way it could be broken was to return to the spot where they made this hand-fasted oath and under the witness of the people of their tribe and the Druids, the woman would walk from the spot towards the north and the man would walk from that spot where they were handfasted towards the south of the circle of protection.

There were so many intricate meanings of Mid-Summer's Eve to the Summer Solstice that Selene and her family were trying to make sense of it all. This was the beginning of their year when their old God would die and the New God was to take over. A time of new beginnings. When the houses were swept out with special vigor in getting rid of the old to have a good place for the new to take hold in their life.

This was the time of year that had the day that was not a day, in that it was mystical and belonged to the realm that only the Druids could see into. The symbolism in this with all of the details was even lost to Juba who was only learning the very basic of knowledge from the Druids and had only penetrated the very surface of their knowledge. That which they taught to all of their people in just their way of living.

Juba was extremely frustrated that whenever he spoke with the Druid in his learning sessions, he was not allowed to write a single thing down. For the druid had told him that writing only encouraged laziness of the mind and that the knowledge of his people could only truly be taught to those people with minds open enough and strong enough to be able to hold such knowledge. He did not insult Juba in mentioning this, he was merely stating a fact of his people.

More people had started to arrive, more people than Selene thought had even existed on this very large island at the very farthest known place on the earth. She was amazed as were the others from her family. They were all in their finest. Selene was arrayed in the High-Priestess garments from the temple of Isis in a very ancient pattern with her ceremonial diadem with symbol of the cobra above her third and sacred eye. Bellinos nodded at her and beckoned her to join his side in reverence to her priestess status. She had let go of the grasp of her daughter and husband to join the ancient druid to where the other Druids, Ovates and Bards gathered in a grove on the outskirts of the capitol.

While Selene joined the company of the druids, Arsinoe and Cilia had rushed the now very nervous form of Jubilla to complete the final wedding preparations. For their ritual was to be held prior to all of the other weddings that day.

Ptolemy and Juba just stood there not knowing what to do when the much appreciated appearance of the two princes Togodumnos and Annius had arrived and started to explain all that was occurring before their eyes.

They had pointed out all of the brides that were gathered to the side and being lectured to by the druid high-priestess chosen as the mother Goddess figure for this celebration as was her duty. And then to the tall dark-haired figure of his uncle Avarwy, the leader of the Silures who had arrived for his duty to stand in for the old-king in the ceremony, since the father of the new King Cynfelyn had died. There was a grievance going on between them in matters which would be brought up at a later time. But all were to be put on hold by the order of the druids. Avarwy was explaining the duties of a good husband to the grooms gathered on the other side and far away from their brides. Bards assigned to this event accompanied them both as was tradition to further enhance the ancient lessons for new husbands and wives.

Togodumas' eyes were glued to the back of his uncle watching him carefully while his younger brother explained the event to their guests. Annius pointed out that every item of food that was prepared on the many and endless tables overflowing with unusual delights, had sacred meaning and were prayers to the people for their bounty and for a good year as well. He explained that everything had many meanings, and none at all. His winked at this, for he knew that he was confusing his two guests. He further explained that there was to be a play that evening before the actual event that would take place in the stones outside of the grove in a place that all would walk to in the twilight of the evening. The actual beginning of their day and celebration.

He explained that they very little hours of daylight and soon the people would be led to the plays would be shown in the sacred groves. At the actual time of twilight when the day and night were one. The Druids would light the bonfires under the stones where all of the people would gather, the plays would commence to explain it all, for only the Druids and Bards acted in them since they were sacred teachings of the ancients. Then the sacred wedding of the King and Queen would commence and to precede that would be the rest of the hand-fastings. It all would end with a feast back in the town that would last all day. He told them that it was strictly prohibited to partake of any type of food or water by any until the time of the feast at the end. For as they looked over at longing at the tables off to the right of them, they were being covered in hides and guards were set about them.

Suddenly horns sounded for all to gather to join them in the clearing of the sacred stones. He had noticed Jubilla, Arsinoe and Cilia running out to join them and the throng of people who suddenly appeared around them in every direction. A young druid of lower rank had whisked Jubilla aside and explained that she was to come with him for her final preparations for she was to be wedded first in the most secret of ceremonies. Her father bid acceptance at this and gave her a reassuring kiss on her rosy cheek and sent her off with the druid.

The princes accompanied Juba, Ptolemy, Cilia, Arsinoe and the others along with the rest of the village on a path that was flanked on each sides by all of the warriors of the tribe holding candles made of ash and animal fats supported by wide shells. As the sun was dipping in the sky, the many dotted lights were a comfort to the family as they made their way along the wide well traveled path to a smaller path which led away from the grove and farther away from the settlement in a westerly direction. The whole village had broken out in song as soon as they left the boundaries of their main settlement and capitol. They were all joyous and sounded merry and full of hope.

As they walked even further the summer sun was losing it's power over the people, yet were guided by the many lights that dotted the edge of the path before them. People of all ages and ways of life had joined in to celebrate. The brides and grooms way ahead of the procession were surrounded by Bards blowing their trumpets and flutes to accompany the songs that sprung forth from the people in an endless supply.

In listening Juba could not tell when one song ended and when the next began, the tunes and patterns would blend and then form something completely different from the last without an obvious break. So complex did it all sound that he was amazed that even a little girl walking next to him that could not have been older than three knew all of the words, her tiny voice drowned out by all of the others, but her lips in sync with those of her mother beside her.

Over hills and through a forest they walked until they reached another clearing where inside in a large circle were many stones that appeared ancient to him. Tall and touching the sky, they appeared as if they were frozen Titans from a long lost culture. He had seen smaller versions during their journey through long-haired Gaul. But none with half the glory as these, nor as ancient. Before they approached the sacred clearing he was quickly told by Annius that these were not the largest magic stones, that there was one that was the most sacred of all that was further to the south. Juba was amazed since it seemed to him that Annius had read his mind at that utterance. Yet, again everything seemed magical the closer they were to the strange monument of stones.

As soon as each person entered the sacred space, their voices hushed until all had entered and it reached an eerie crescendo of silence that surrounded them. When the silence was complete, it continued until a slow drum beat began and the Druids took up a chant similar to what he recalled from the Mid-Winter celebration in the other village, that seemed far away to Juba at this moment. He then noticed the feeble figure of Bellinos guided by that of his wife appear to the center of the clearing. How beautiful she looked in her Egyptian-priestess robes. The white flowing robes of the Arch-Druid blew mystically as if the soft wind around them now was all the more fierce by their power. He looked over at Selene who joined the druids in their chants with a chant that he knew was in ancient Egyptian and probably just as old as what was uttered by the Druids and Bards that had joined in.

Suddenly the sun sank into it's final descent and the all of the colors had melded into darkness that surrounded them completely. Bellinos uttered a word and the five bonfires that surrounded all of the mystical personnel had sprung to life in passionate enthusiasm. The wind added to the power of the flames. Bellinos threw powder into the fires and they suddenly danced with the life of sparkles of various colors.

Bellinos called over to Cynfelyn and his brothers and other family members to enter the forefront of the crowd and to Juba and his family as well. Selene went out to the side of the circle and retrieved her daughter and beckoned Juba to assist her. Arsinoe and Ptolemy were placed in the front near the princes of the tribe.

Bellinos stood tall and proud, one would think that he was as strong as a thirty-year-old rather than his true age. Selene took on the glamour of her Goddess and was regal, beautiful, and ageless beside Bellinos.

A broom handle was placed on the ground and Selene took her husband's hand and placed it on his daughter's and she led them both over to Cynfelyn, whose hands were held by his brothers. The bride and groom, king and queen were led to face one another and their hands were placed upon each other's by their family. Bellinos entered the space and whispered words that sounded more ancient than anything that Juba had ever heard before, out loud he called for the God and Goddess to witness this union and to guide over it for a year and a day and for this life and the next. He then took out two chords. One braided by Jubilla and the other braided by Cynfelyn. He wrapped the chord loosely around the entwined hands of the bride and groom. He assisted them in walking over the broomstick once and then back to where they originally stood.

Bellinos and Selene led the newly married couple over to where there were two tall chairs and bid them to sit and to watch over the rest of the proceedings. They did this and sat together side by side with one hand each entwined in the others by the chord of their union.

Now all of the brides were gathered on one side of the clearing while the grooms were gathered on the other side, while Jubilla and her husband Cynfelyn officiated. Each couple was then brought together and the chords were loosely placed upon their eager to be martially bound hands. There were twelve couples this year and each was given their proper ceremony by Bellinos.

When all were complete the music began and all began to dance wildly about the fires. Children running around throwing flowers off of the branches they carried on the newly handfasted couples. Flowers were thrown up to their king and queen and three tiny little girls with hair so blonde that it was almost white presented their queen with a garland of the brightest blue flowers of Borage for courage and strength that were woven into a crown to be placed upon her amber red curls that hung down past her waist. She smiled and accepted her crown and bowed to her husband who assisted his queen in placing it upon her head. All of this was as clear as day from the brilliant light of the bonfires. Though the shadows danced around to add magic to this eve.

Selene wove in and out of the crowd until at last she came upon the entranced figure of her husband to join her hands with his. Plays were set up in small booths telling the story of this eve in different intervals around the clearing at the time most were dancing. The children gathered hungrily to watch the many plays and puppet shows. She wondered why the plays were held after the ceremonies rather than before as she and her family were told. But then again thought the better when she recalled that to the Druids and the people of this land-all times were one and did not mean much in the order of things. She joined the rest of the people on this powerful eve.

This seemed to last hours, yet there was a strange youthfulness added to the older bodies that evening that gave a special long lost vigor to their step.

Suddenly the event turned again and all of the people had started to head out, dancing to the path that they had arrived at towards the village. Children were gathered by their parents and the king and queen were carried out in their tall chairs. People as they were led out of the cirlce sang even louder and grabbed all of the flowered branches and threw up and all around petals that danced lazily all around them bathing them in new-found life. It appeared to Ptolemy as if he was walking through a warm summer snowstorm. His nose hungrily picked up the many scents foreign to him yet all the more delicious than anything that he was used to.

Someone must have gone on ahead, because the closer they came to the village the louder the scent of the food was. The singing became more aggressive in a merry way and even ribald in hidden suggestion, to fool the ears of the youngest of children.

The paths before him were lit up as before by the lights that all of the warriors held. A welcome sight in the darkness of the forest and even in the open land along the rolling hills.

Drums, horns, stringed instruments and an odd harp music played on through the night and the people all around him almost broke into a run as they approached the village for the hunger forgotten in the ceremony was very strong in all by then.

Juba along with Selene had finally found her brother Ptolemy just as they had approached the village food tables. It was well lit up by torches by then and all were now ordered in to line up for their fare. Selene and Juba had found a niche under an Elder tree that blocked out the light of the stars that were now bright up in the vast and endless sky. Arsinoe then found them for they had designated this spot before on the advice of Annius who had informed them about the confusion of the rush to the food tables after the celebration by the sacred stone. They were glad that they were well warned of this. As they were resting and talking all at once on their observations, Annius pushed aside the branches along with Togodumnos, Drennedd, and Andocos loaded down with food and heavy brass goblets of mead and beer. "Alas, dear friends I find you here. But not to worry, we have brought you all some wondrous delights from our humble land for you to sample. We made sure that the best were chosen especially for you."

Arsinoe came to life at that and uttered thankfully," Oh thank you all, please join us here." Juba and Selene nodded. Juba added, "Yes, many thank you's sit here and join us."

"Yes, please do!" Exclaimed Selene.

"Why thank you" Stated Annius who took the lead in setting out all of the delights before them on a cloth in the middle. Togodumnos sat beside Selene and smelled of horse as usual which she politely tried to ignore, yet found it difficult in how overpowering the smell was. Arsinoe was oblivious and dove right into the with as much enthusiasm as the others. She glanced at her sister with the disapproving look of their mother. Hoping that she would remember her manners as a princess of the Ptolemy line and to make them proud. It was silly, yet angered Selene when she was arrogantly brushed off with her sister's fervor in the many foreign delights spread out in front of them all.

"Andocos, may I speak in Latin?" At his assent, Juba continued, "tell me about the meanings of those songs that the druids were chanting in the circle, they did not seem to be similar to your language. I did not recognize any of the words." Juba questioned Andocos who had tutored the royal family as he was pausing between bites on a large leg of mutton.

Andocos wiped away the savory rosemary scented juice with his sleeve. "Oh, yes sire, you see those words are only known by the Druids. An 'tis told to us that it is a language so ancient 'twas believed to be the very first language and only known to Gods and Druids. We are used to that language and of never knowing the meaning for we are only simple folk and live by the land. The Gods speak to the Druids and they need that language to relate to all of us."

Juba seemed satisfied, but Selene grew perplexed at this odd notion of a sacred language. "In the land of my birth we spoke the language of the Gods, though it was lost by the average person over three hundred years ago. But, it seems rather recent to have lost a language that you tell us that your people never knew and only the Druids... Why?"

Annius noticed the confused look of his fellow soldier and decided to rescue him. "My lady, for 'tis known by only the Druids on that matter, though I know that Bellinos would be the best person to ask on that matter. Maybe the people preferred their own language so that they could hide things from the Gods so they wouldn't get into trouble in their mischief." He laughed at this and was joined by all those sitting on the crisp Mid-Summer's Eve under the Elder tree.

On the other side of the clearing sat Jubilla in wonder over the moment. Beside her observing the crowd carefully was her new husband Cynfelyn. His eyes caught the attention of the icy stare of Ceridon. He knew in her highly opinionated way of looking at things, she would take his marriage to Jubilla as an insult to her warrior blood and a slight over their lost son. He would have to watch her carefully.

He also recalled the official presence of his Uncle Avarwy and had in advance chosen carefully on his most skillful and quiet of warriors to keep a close guard on his and the party he arrived with.

Cynfelyn also looked over to the Elder tree and had observed his bride's family in rapt conversation with his most notable warriors. He could not hear any words, though had noticed the careful dotage that was being paid to Arsinoe by his loyal warrior Andocos. He would have to do something about that. He scanned around the crowds for a possible wife for the brave warrior and close friend to hopefully veer him away from the young and oblivious princess. He did not want any feelings to be hurt potentially on this matter, as he knew there could possibly be, if he were to let this continue. For he and Juba had spoken on the possibility of Arsinoe's marriage. He just needed Selene' opinion on the matter.

Voices of satiated hunger and friendly chatter permeated the village main. Torches shone welcome over the celebrants, while the stars danced gracefully in their brilliance up above. Children had begun to find spots in the folds of their mother's and grandmother's gathered skirts to sleep. The older children were now running around the tables in a game of catch. Selene looked up as she leaned against the back of her husband at all the sights of this peaceful village. Her husband was deep in conversation with Annius, with the occasional comment of Togodumnos and Andocos. Ptolemy had stood up and walked over to where the other warriors had gathered near the strong woven fences of the animals who sat on benches and on the ground in enthralled conversation with beer goblets clanking in the evening breeze. She had found where they had placed the tall chairs of her daughter and son-in-law and had noticed that Cynfelyn was observing all while Jubilla slept peacefully leaning on his shoulder. It was then that her glance reached his from up above the slowing din and he glanced over at Jubilla and he winked. Selene giggled silently at that and smiled at her new son. She felt her daughter was now in good hands and she was enjoying the peaceful bliss of warm comfort and the large shoulders that were perfectly comfortable and she closed her eyes for just a moment, though unintentionally fell into a deep satiated with life slumber.

XVIII

After the Solstice celebrations were over and the cleaning up had begun reluctantly by the people who dwelled in the settlement, Drennedd approached Cynfelyn one evening. He approached the long house where the royal couple shared lodgings while the new palace was being built under the specifications of the new Queen Jubilla and her mother. Off to the side of the present residence Drennedd observed the beginnings of what was soon to become a Grecian Style Villa. It was elaborate for the land on which it sit upon. He knew that it would be soon the grandest building ever to grace the area as any other that he had been to. He had not traveled much in his life for his time in rule was mostly being spent in keeping the Romans interested in the mainland and not on the island.

For Drennedd took great pride in his lands being well protected. For if his lands were conquered by the Romans, from what he had learned they would be a mighty force to reckon with and he knew that with all of the inhabitants on this island, there would not be enough to hold off when they were hit with a full scale invasion.

He and Cynfelyn worked together in this matter. For Cynfelyn had the knowledge of the Romans and had even studied amongst them for several years, though took back with him a great store of information to protect his people. For eventually the Romans had recognized Cynfelyn as one of the three great tribal kings of the land in his being a direct descendant and grandson of the great Llud, King of CaerLlud, his city at the end of the great River Thames.

From what he had learned from Cynfelyn, they needed to keep the Romans uninterested in their land and to feel that there would be nothing for them to see over here or worth for them to conquer. For he dreaded the day when their land would be overrun and turned into cities as those lands who belonged to his kin over the sea, whom the Romans called the Long-Haired-Gauls.

With those thoughts heavy on his mind, he entered the main dwelling of the newly married king, Cynfelyn after being admitted by his guard and chief warrior Andocos. The large burly blonde bear of a man with the heart of a kitten, was one of those who were accepted into the ring of his king that he was utterly loyal to; tipped his head at Drennedd in honor and bid him to enter. Drennedd walked in long strides with a purpose over the table of the king set in the far corner of the room, lit in this late hour with additional oil lamps he brought over from Rome.

XIX

The bon fire in the center of the room added the warmth needed on this extra cool summer evening, though did not set enough light in the corner where the King preferred to work at his accounts. He passed islands of furs of court lingerers, followers and relatives as they lounged and listened to the soft music of the lyre played wistfully by a young Bard. As he approached the corner of the large wooden structure he noticed that Cynfelyn was bent down and looked dazzled by something that he was reading. Those around him in the islands of fur were oblivious to the workings of the great king. He noticed his young wife to his side going over some paperwork as well.

Just then Cynfelyn noticed the presence of his friend and fellow leader. "Drennedd, welcome and have a seat to rest your feet my friend." He bid a servant sitting off to his side almost hidden in shadow to bring some wine and cheese. "How fare you this fine summer's eve?"

Drennedd bowed and softly exclaimed, "'Tis glorious indeed, such a shame that the duties must keep one inside. 'Tis crisp enough for the soul to wake indeed, almost feels like Autumn approaching…" His deep voice chuckled.

Cynfelyn nodded, "Indeed, though I prefer to spend all the time possible with my lovely wife. Though this eve I am teaching her about the land that she now rules over. We are going over boring import and export records and such necessities, that need to be learned. "

"Aye, my liege, I know those onerous duties that rulers must face and would bid you continue, though I do have a matter that needs to be discussed, would you have the time soon my liege, I do need to head back to my people so that I may attack my own boring books. I don't trust that the scribes have kept up with such while I was away."

Just then Jubilla looked up and approached her husband, "Darling, why don't you attend to the chieftain, I think that I understand this and may be able to take care of a few things on my own. When you return, you can look it over to make sure." She bowed to him prettily and let her long black eyelashes touch her rosy cheeks.

"Then it seems that I do have time after all. Thank you. I won't be long."

"Do not worry, I am a big girl husband." Her giggle sounded cheery in the lazy hall and Cynfelyn bowed to his wife and wrapped his arm in the arm of his fellow chieftain leading him out of the hall through the islands of lazy courtiers in their fur laden islands. "Like boats we sail Drennedd through a Sea of Sloth!" Bellowed Cynfelyn in laughter as he and Drennedd made their way through them to the entrance of the large hall.

Outside the sky was brightened by infinite numbers of stars and a rising waning moon that cast it's glow shattering the extra cool evening for this time of year. The two men made their way through long intricately carved wooden longhouses and through the circle of the new wooden structures that he had built for the family of his new wife. They made their way through the labyrinth of other such clearings in this settlement that would lose oneself easily if they were not familiar with all of the pass ways through, for there were many dead ends and twists and turns and paths between the clusters of longhouses and the traditional round-houses of their culture. Some of the wealthier nobles were trying to emulate in wood the Roman style and had started to surround their gardens with the wooden dwellings. The gardens were not ornamental as the Romans from what he had heard about them, but every inch of land in all of the settlements that he had even known of in this land including this one, was completely used for some purpose or other.

Drennedd's capitol settlement and government seat was much smaller in size, though he knew of the trend of the Roman fashion and noticed how the wealthier citizens tried to add that to their homes. Some were even importing marble and artists to carve it.

Too much had occurred since the visit of the Roman Julius Caesar, he was deeply concerned and thus wanted this meeting with Cynfelyn. Maybe he would allay his fears on the matter.

They approached a clearing on the top of a hill which had a wonderful view of the settlement and even the scent of the fires inside the dwellings in cooking their evening meals. Cynfelyn had sensed correctly Drennedd's need for urgency and privacy.

Together they sat, Cynfelyn spread out his cloak over the summer grass and stretched his long warrior legs out before him and bid Drennedd do the same. Drennedd was a large man and it took a little longer to adjust the large and older body down on the ground. For Drennedd had fought many battles and some beside the father of Cynfelyn as comrades. Some of his wounds had started to bother him more so over the past few years. With a grunt he was finally sitting beside the new King.

"Drennedd, what is on your mind?"

"Your liege, I am concerned with the ever advancing interest of the Romans and even in the people of this nation in their curiosity over the luxuries of the Romans. I had received notice from one of my scouts that Augustus is planning an expedition."

The two men sat in silence while Cynfelyn pondered over this matter. He had heard of this and when he was in Rome he made his people out to the Romans, as simple with nothing of interest. That was the only instruction that his father gave him before he was fostered over in Rome. For he was sent there in friendship, though his father had gained great concern when Julius Caesar came over under the reign of his grandfather.

He had learned wisely to always know his enemy. When he went over to study in Rome he had met the Great Imperator Caesar Augustus and had attained in careful observance that he was a man who had incredible power over a much larger territory that his family ruled over and limitless amounts of forces at his disposal. He did genuinely befriend the man and promised to himself that he would not do anything offensive against this great leader. He merely went to Rome to obtain information to see how much they needed to fear this strange new possible threat.

He was fearsomely right in assuming Rome a great threat due to all the territories that they conquered and subdued, even their own kin in Gaul.

Cynfelyn had feared this news, though knew that it was inevitable and would have to be dealt with. He would send correspondence over to Rome and to Augustus. He took great pains to ensure Rome that they were a small nation and very simple with only farmers, though nothing that Rome would need. He did though maintain a steady trade on the homespun warm brightly decorated cloaks to Rome and it's many territories. Pottery as well was exported to Rome in great demand. The cloaks from his homeland was becoming quite the rage over in Roma Urbana in it's fine craftsmanship and practical warmth. He had to install more workers and Shoppe's to keep up with the demand.

He turned his head towards Drennedd's and thought out loud, "I had sensed that this was coming. I am going to send a letter to Caesar Augustus and inquire the best way that I can on the matter. He might be just sending out envoys to look into our lands and not actual armies of conquest. For the most part I feel that information about us is mainly used in entertainment, for they have great plays in huge stages built out of marble for that purpose and are all the rage over there. However, I am a little concerned about the information on our people that King Juba is gathering. For he had been in constant company of Bellinos."

Drennedd's eyes looked up inquisitively on that. Cynfelyn noticed, "Though do not worry. He has no ill will in this, he just seems to have an unconquerable thirst for knowledge. Besides, Bellinos makes sure that in his learnings on our people, the king is not allowed to write down one iota of knowledge!" He winked at Drennedd on that and they both heaved in laughter on that one. For they both knew that the nobles of the Roman culture were well versed to write and read. Drennedd recalled that prior to the arrival of the royal family from so far away, Cynfelyn had issued a decree for the protection of his people that all reading and writing materials were to be hidden from the view of the visitors. This he assured his people would keep important knowledge from escaping even inadvertently back to the ears of Rome. And he recalled that Cynfelyn also assured his people that they had plenty to battle over with in this land and did not have the time for battle on the outside.

Cynfelyn lay back to look at the stars and to contemplate this matter further with his older companion and fellow leader. He had absolute trust in the loyalty of this fine warrior and leader who fought beside his father. He knew that everything discussed would be retained wisely and implemented with his own people upon his return.

"I will send over some information bands out to the Roman lands as well. We will definitely have to reconvene on the matter when it is gathered. Hopefully before the moon of Mabon of this year. After the second harvest there should have been enough information on this matter gathered to be able to set forth some plan of action. I just want to make sure and not raise the curiosity of the Romans any further. For we definitely do not have enough to fight off even half of the forces that I have observed over there. The only way we could gain some way would be to fight the way of the ancients in small skirmishes and in ambushes. Their forces are mighty and numerous, uncountable and everywhere. They build roads made of finely cut stone over all of the lands they conquer. Which I have to admit are a wonderful way of keeping armies from getting idle and rebellions from starting. You need to keep the soldiers busy. I keep them busy in hunting parties, information gathering missions, as well as the numerous squelching all of the numerous mini and petty rebellions that break out constantly all over this island over ridiculous matters. To unite these people against a force as mighty as that would be almost impossible. Though I am trying my friend. I have been gathering the druids to help in uniting all of the tribes in case it comes to all-out war with the Romans. The going is very slow on that matter though, since most of them believe that we are the fiercest fighters in the world and are unconquerable. They have made up tales that Julius Caesar took one look at us and fled in terror! Most of them have not even set one foot upon any of the land at all across the sea and yet feel that they are experts of the matter concerning possible Roman invasion. They parade like peacocks over their fierce powers. Yet I have seen the might of Rome and the skill and intelligence of King Augustus. He is one to be watched carefully and guaranteed that he is doing the same thing as us." He paused for a bit to let it all sink in and realized that there was nothing more to say on the matter at the present time and saw that his older friend agreed and decided to let the matter rest.

"I feel that it is also high time that you are married, my friend, for it had been four years since your Naishedd has passed, may she glorify the halls of splendor and come back soon" Cynfelyn stated respectfully on the soul of Drennedd's wife who had died in childbirth. He tred this matter lightly, though had been thinking about Arsinoe on this matter after Selene had approached him on this matter after speaking with Juba. He had been meaning to bring up this matter sooner, though found it difficult since he knew that Drennedd missed his wife and the lost son. He had a house empty of children and heirs and was growing rightfully concerned since his years seemed to be catching up with him. Drennedd desperately wanted a wife. The loss of Naishedd occurred four years ago, though it was still fresh in his mind. He felt honored that Cynfelyn would bother with his welfare.

He continued, "I was thinking of the princess Arsinoe…" Cynfelyn looked inquisitively at his friend and waited for his response on the matter.

Drennedd finally responded after grounding himself considerably from his wandering thoughts, "I would consider it an honor that you would think of me for this noble woman from afar. Was her mother not a warrior herself?"

The king was surprised that Drennedd knew this piece of information. "Why yes, in fact she was and a great queen in her own right. Her name was Cleopatra VII of a line called the Ptolemy's, who have ruled for over three hundred years. She had led great fleets of boats against the ruler of Rome Caesar Augustus. She even had a son by the name of Caesarion, the son of Julius Caesar…" He had heard so much about this man from his father and how he was brutally murdered on the senate steps. When he was studying in Rome, he had even walked upon the area where this man was murdered by the men he worked beside. One of his murders was even his best friend. His father had told him to take that incident as a valuable lesson. That even your closest friends and confidants could eventually turn on you when there is too much power. For Cynfelyn had this occur in his own family when his grandfather Llud was murdered by his own brother Casswallon. "This woman was also a priestess of a Goddess named Isis that is similar to our Warrior Goddess and Earth Mother Goddess. Her other daughter Selene, wore the Robes of that Goddess on our solstice celebration."

"Aye, I recall that, they looked so different from anything that I have ever seen. Is her sister trained as priestess as well, or in the ways of the warrior as their mother?" Drennedd inquired.

"Nay, I think not. For when they were very young, Arsinoe was only four years old, they were defeated by the Roman King Caesar Augustus." He pondered on the matter. For he had also heard somewhere that his wife's father was also a captive of Rome as well. Though the king was rarely seen out of the company of his Arch-Druid.

"Is a shame, though she is very fair and beautiful. She seems to also be displaying an interest in the Bardic arts of the lyre. Have you heard on that matter liege?"

"Drennedd, is there not a haven in your lands for arts such as that? Maybe when all is said and done, you can send her there and possibly have her trained as a warrior as well? Though I feel that she might be getting a bit old for that. You best be getting her with child soon on that matter as well. Though think what her blood would do for your line?"

"Aye, on that matter, lets find some beer, for this summer's eve is making me rather thirsty."

"Drennedd, everything makes you thirsty for beer, especially for imported Gaulish beer!" The two great men walked towards the smaller settlement off to the side alongside a small grove of Apple trees towards a tavern that Cynfelyn knew had the best ale and a friendly breweress named Alesia who told the most interesting and ribald tales.

XX

Selene tossed and turned all night and wondered if it was due to the new delight she had found in this strange land of what they called apples. They were small and bright red and were very tangy and rough. Though she found herself craving for more and more. They reminded her on their supposed sacredness of her beloved and sorely missed pomegranates. For both were jewels of the earth. The apples that she had were the last ones from storage and the new ones would be arriving at the end of summer before the snows came. Though they were dried, they seemed so sweet and she could not have enough of them. She wished that she could introduce them to her favorite pomegranates though. She was happy as well due to the reactions of marriage that her daughter had. She had also observed her new husband's careful attention paid to his new wife. Selene thought she saw the signs of her daughter beginning to bloom with motherhood and hoped for it to be true.

She also observed the looks of friendly envy from her sister on the marriage of her niece. Arsinoe had been visiting the Bards of the apple grove very often, though she knew that she needed to approach her husband on the matter. Selene also observed the careful diligence that Andocos paid to Arsinoe. He followed her everywhere in gallant protection, never daring to overstep his bounds. She needs to be a mother on her own and it should have been dealt with sooner. She was afraid to lose her sister in a sense, though knew that it must be so. She also had the assurance that her daughter would be looked after by her own family when Selene had to return to her Mauritania to rule.

She lay on her cot and tossed about with a stomach ache. Oh how she wished that she had her Asandros her for her for he had the most awful tasting concoction for this, though it seemed to work a little faster than the one she was given here.

In body turmoil, through no fault but hers in overeating she continued to toss, though was comforted that her little sister would now be taken well care of. For earlier that day she had approached her husband and then her son Cynfelyn, when he had told her that he would in turn approach Drennedd on this matter.

Drennedd was a very large man, though she had sensed a merriment about him that overshadowed a loss. He must have lost someone close to him. Drennedd lived a few days travel from here in the southern part of this land, she recalled when they traveled through it and found the lands mountainous and wild and very beautiful. Besides he was a good leader of his people. For they as well valued the power of women and regarded them well. For the only princes available for marriage were too young and of the type that locked their wives away in harems for breeding purposes only. She felt that was too dismal a fate to place on the blood of Cleopatra VII. She knew that though these lands were almost foreign to her mother and father, they would have approved.

Finally the potion was taking affect, she felt her self slipping into a slumber and had promised that she would be more careful in the future. For they looked at her as politely as they could in her new found passion for dried apples. Though she found out later that the Keltoi tolerated little those who overate. Though they cared not on drinking to excess. For in Rome, she would have been looking for a vomitorium and then would return to her seat to indulge some more. At some houses in Rome, she recalled small bowls placed under the couches for this purpose, for when they were too lazy to walk over to the area designated for expunging the body of excess. Though, on the contrary, they watered down the wine frequently and Caesar Augustus would not even allow the women under his roof to drink wine at all, in the ways of the ancient and respectable. Ah, to have a vomitorium would have been nice and would have avoided this most inconvenient stomach ache!

Juba, had watched the torments of his wife and had been the one to tell her about their view of food here. He also told her that she was more than welcome to indulge in their beer and mead! For he loved the way she softened when she had even one of their warm dark beers steeped in herbs. For he knew that she was all too used to her watered down wines as a child and later in her freedom during her marriage. He recalled her expression when he had inquired as to her favorite wines that he should send out for their palace. She was like a little school girl in her giggles since she was not allowed to indulge at the matronly Octavia's house.

He also knew that his wife had a great taste for sweets. She had loved the ice delicacies brought down form the mountains to Rome when visiting and tried unsuccessfully to emulate it in Mauretania.

He felt bad for his pretty wife, though she did look rather adorable. He held her close in this soft and barbaric luxury of sleeping quarters with his wife. For he dreaded having to go back to their cold and large palace where she had her own chambers. Though he missed greatly his study and his fingers itched to write something down. He had gathered and carefully dried samples of the local flora and fauna and tried desperately to attain the oral knowledge from the wise druids Bellinos.

His thoughts drifted at the relaxation of his wife in his arms besides him and though about his daughter. His daughter was a wife now and a queen like her mother. How the circle of life turns. He felt sometimes that it turned so fast that he would fall off. For he wondered how much time that he had lost in the other world of his studies. For his wife seemed to be only growing more beautiful and her wildness that he met in his young girl bride, had softened to the wisdom of this woman beside him. Her honey colored curls escaped their Romanesque bindings. He found one in his fingers as his wife slept and held it to reflect in the light of the fire in the center. The color of the honey that she loved to put on everything. He chuckled at that to himself so as not to disturb her slumber.

Arsinoe would now be settled in as well, though he would have preferred prince Lardicois from Parthia, though Selene had thought long on the matter since all had that had happened with Iotape and had fought him adamantly against the matter. She would not have her sister locked up in a harem, nor sent to a temple of Astarte if she angered anyone! He knew that she still grieved over the loss of her new found friend Drusilla and would blame herself if anything happened to Iotape.

Before they had left, he sent out a search party with instructions to them to return Iotape and to report to him immediately. He had heard nothing so far on the matter.

He had also observed Ptolemy who was constantly in the company of the warriors here. He had not told Selene this, but he was worried about him. He had a sneaking suspicion that he might not be safe for much longer from Augustus. He had also inquired of Cynfelyn in confidence of the family of Ahrianred, the one that he knew to have caught the eye of his brother-in-law. He had found out that she was of an ancient line of the warrior elite. That her line was from the leaders of the old race of the Picts that ruled the land before the Keltoi conquered six hundred years before. For he was told about her height being a characteristic of the ancient people, though her hair was a vivid red and usually braided as to the traditions of the warriors. Cynfelyn had also mentioned that she was a cousin of his and shared his great-great-grandmother Don's blood through one of her sons. For Ahrianred's family and warrior blood was strictly matriarchal and was not allowed to be diminished according to the ancient warrior code of the women's house. She was also not allowed to marry, though was able to choose consorts to father her children.

Juba was amused as this, though dared not show it to his host and son-in-law. For he knew that they were completely the opposite of his very chauvinistic brothers in Roman territories. He was an exception to their general attitudes in that he respected the power of his wife and her wisdom. This was more than normal over here in recognizing the power of women.

He found their ways very odd, and was trying very hard to memorize enough of it to bring home with him when he had the luxury of his study and writing materials! At this though he drifted off to sleep beside his wife.

XXI

They day had dawned in the full glory that only the wilds at the end of the earth could produce. Ptolemy was fast becoming enamored with this land and the strange warrior beauty who he could not get off his mind. He did not even know her name! She was the only woman who had gained his interest from the arts of war and the battlefield. Not even his designated wife who had died, in what seemed like years far away in Syria. He felt bad for her, but she did not love him either, she had died for the man whom she truly loved.

He knew that love rarely entered the game when born with his blood and family connections. Especially when a man was to rule. But he did not even have that to look forward to! With one sweep Caesar Augustus had taken his rule and throne away, along with his father who he desperately wished were around to teach him some of what he had learned while in battle beside Julius Caesar. He also understood that according to the Roman tradition that Juba emulated well enough, that he was the paterfamilias now, being the oldest male relative. Ptolemy had to wait until his union was chosen by his sister and her husband.

He knew the position that his sister was in and had learned to hide his true feelings and motives, since he had recalled the words of his oldest brother Caesarion, "Choose your battles little brother!" This was stated to him over and over again on all of the chaos that he had caused in the very little remembered palace in Egypt.

Growing up the younger prince of a kingdom that was taken away from him when he was barely old enough to remember had been rather difficult for him. When older he had learned to bury himself with every type of martial art known in the world. This was even encouraged after he came over to live with his sister. For Juba found some great teachers on battle tactic and the most diverse arts of war imaginable. He learned from the lands of India and Parthia and even from the writings of every famous battle fought. He had read on the battle tactics of the famous Achilles of Sparta and of the Hannibal, as well as those of Alexander the Great and many others. For Juba had taught him that a great leader must not only know how to physically fight, but he must learn how to plan the battles to the best advantage as well and that included reading about almost every battle ever fought. Ptolemy was grateful for this for it had also kept him from dwelling on the reason for his growing anger.

For as he grew older, the more impossible it was for him to be able to get a chance to fight against King Augustus. Though he feigned friendship, and that very well had to be convincing to all even the careful scrutiny of his sister—he seethed upon meeting the man who stole their families legacy.

He was grateful to learn even more of the arts of war in his visit in this land that was slowly growing on him. The more he was around these fierce and proud people, the more he was beginning to feel a part of them. As if he had a destiny after all.

All was forgotten when he was in the presence of this incredible warrior Goddess! He ran over to the warrior barracks to find out her name. He was also eager for today they were going to learn how to carve one of the spears. In his delight at nearing the barracks, he collided into his sister who was equally in the throes of a daydream. "Arrrch, are you alright?"

"Oh coarse I am you ninny?" Screeched Arsinoe, whose perfectly ordered curls were thrown into a small disarray at the suddenness of her collision with her older brother. "Where are you off to in such a hurry in such a cheerful mood?" Smiled mischievously at her older brother. For she had wondered if anything could possibly take his interest off of the battlefield for even a small moment.

"Oh, sorry about frazzling your fine gown sister, but I am on my way to learn how to make a Keltoi spear today!"

"Ach, not to worry brother, there is plenty more where this came from!" She grimaced at that remark, since the dresses that she had brought over were fast becoming worn due to being beaten on rocks! She had worn a pretty dress that she had purchased at the celebrations that was a vivid blue with swirls on the sleeves and apron. She knew her brother was teasing her in jest and had probably even heard her complaining over her dresses to their sister the other day. "You and your battle love, I was beginning to think that possibly you have finally found a lady love" She stated the last in Latin since there were many people about on this early morning day in their busy activities.

He responded in Latin, "You know sister, that if there were a Lady Love, the only chance that I would have to marry her would be with the approval of the King of Rome!" He giggled as if he had stated something funny to his sister.

Arsinoe responded, "Don't worry, you will find a way… You always do, let me know all about her later". For she was wise and knew what he was trying to hide from her and the family. She bid goodbye and parted off with a skip to her step. For she too had found someone who had taken her breath away. She knew that she would never be able to have him in marriage. Though wondered with some small wisp of hope that she might just have a chance, since she was well past the normal marriageable age.

She had found a Bard by the name of Sion, who was teaching her the art of music on the Lyre. When he played her soul was in rapture, she felt as if her very heart would melt from the fire within! He was very patient with her.

She ran off to watch his magical fingers on the instrument sing to the Gods. His long delicate fingers were unusual in one so fair. She fantasized on how beautiful their children would be and as she ran from her brother began to plot a way that she could approach this subject with her sister and brother in law, Juba. Her blonds curls leaving a trail behind her as she strode off towards the Bards quarters.

XXII

Selene had found her sister as she was heading towards her Lyre lessons to the Bards round-house. She knew about this musician and felt that her sister had a childish crush on him. It was up to her in their mother's place to find a suitable match for the youngest of the Ptolemys. She was reassured when her inquiries were answered by her husband when he had told her that the marriage would be set for a week from thence and that it would be by contract by Roman laws to be followed by a ceremony by the Druids. She was pleased at this and had set out that morning to approach her sister before she would make a fool of herself with the musician.

"Ah, Arsinoe! I am glad that I have found you. Would you please walk with me a minute, I have something that I need to discuss with you." She noticed the shadowy figure of her sister's watchdog Andocos to the far side and nodded to him. He understood and left them alone.

For some reason her heart started to pound deep in her chest at this and nodded. "Selene, how does it fare? For soon you will be a grandmother!" She giggled to her sister lovingly.

"I feel as ancient as the wind." She started to giggle with her sister, but stopped so that she would not forget her mission.

"Arsinoe, Juba and I have arranged another marriage for you." She quickened the pace of her words so that she would not stumble on sentiment, for she did truly love her little sister. "He is Drennedd, he is wise, and fair and a great warrior and leader of the Belgae people. You will be a queen in your own right beside him and revered by them." She stopped and looked at the chalky features of her little sister.

Her shock was sudden and overpowering. Yet, she knew that her sister had found a better match than she could expect back home for her. For a lot of the men in rule over there did not want to be connected to a daughter of the harlot Cleopatra, as she had heard people whisper about her mother. She knew that they would keep her locked inside a harem if she were married in the east near her homeland and place of birth.

"Fine, sister, I will prepare for this." She stated with the sudden clarity that reality could possibly bring to a moment such as this.

"I am sorry, for I know that your heart probably lies elsewhere."

"No, sister, just a silly crush and will end this moment. No need to worry. I must go to my lesson now, if you permit me to."

"As you wish sister, though would you play a piece for me this eve?"

"Of course!" With that she hurried back to the path to her Sion.

How foolish of her to think that she would ever be able to follow her soul. Her sister would never be able to let her join the Bards in apprenticeship at this point and abandoned the idea as well as she headed towards her Lyre lesson.

XXIII

Jubilla was going over the many records of the settlement that her husband had written in meticulous Greek and Latin for her perusal. She had noticed that the lands were well maintained and that his armies and people were well supplied and fed. The land around her was prosperous and was beginning to have a flourishing trade in pottery and in the cloaks exported to the Roman territories.

She loved the fierce determination and pride of the people that she ruled over. Their music was as captivating and as complex as they were in themselves.

She was worried about her mother though, for the look in her eyes when she gave her daughter the cradle that her father had carved for her was soul wrenching and almost made her cry. She knew that her mother had thought about her twin more often as of late due to the possibility of her having a child.

For she was not sure though she felt that her menses were a few days later as it were. For she would wait a week or more to make sure before she told anyone. She held that knowledge close to her and prayed for it's truth.

Though it did make her a little fearful, she would make sure to raise her the way she was by her mother. She would have this babe constantly by her side as her wise mother did her. Though it make the necessary parting in life the more difficult due to this unusual closeness. She did not know how she would react to this inevitable conclusion in her life when her family had to leave.

On the matter of her aunt being married to the chieftain named Drennedd she heartily agreed with her husband, though in a way felt bad for her aunt. Though he was a good man, she knew that her aunt pined after someone, for her face shone with the truth. She now saw her accept the contract and formalities of the wedding and went gratefully into the arms of her new husband, though she saw the tears being held back and her heart jumped at this, though went back to the reality of life that a woman must face. The Lyre seemed sullen for the joyous occasion of a wedding, and wondered if there was some native reason for this that she was not aware of. It had already been a week since her aunt Arsinoe went to her lands with her new husband. Her mother was visiting there to settle her aunt and was due back any day.

She brushed the matter off and went back to her business of securing some debts of cattle owed to them by the Catuvellauni tribes that they had failed to pay. She and her husband were working furiously on what to do about this matter. For it did not bode well, the longer he stalled in retaliation. He was at present at the warrior barracks.

She decided to find her husband to discuss further the matter over the cattle with him, when on her way she thought she heard voices in the trees up above her.

She looked up and heard a shusssssh and a giggle. The leaves rustled a bit then and suddenly a ripe acorn landed by her feet. "My what large squirrels live in this tree!" She picked up the acorn, having spotted the form of her uncle in the tree with his mysterious lady friend. Her red braided hair impossible to hide in the lush greenery of the trees above.

"Hello down there Drussi!" Called a joyous Ptolemy from up above. With that he climbed down to stand tall before her looking like a little boy whole stole a treat from the kitchens. "Lady fair, 'tis safe for you as well!" Just then two tiny little feet came down and landed perfectly besides her uncle. Though small and slim, this woman before her looked powerful and held great strength, for her muscles were well defined in the warrior's leather garb. Her braids once neat, now in disarray at their sport in the tree above. Though Selene, wondered what one could possibly be able to do so high up in the tree! She might have to ask her husband about this. In the merriment of the moment she giggled and blushed at that last thought to herself.

Oblivious to his niece and her embarrassment, he introduced his friend. "This, my fair and noble niece and royal highness is the fair Lady Ahrianred and your distant kin as well."

"A pleasure to meet you. I have heard about your great battle skills and are very much honored by my husband and the people of this tribe." Seizing the opportunity to play matchmaker since her mother was not around and her father forever busy, "Will the two of you join my husband and I for dinner this eve?"

Ptolemy looked at Ahrianred and at her smile responded, "We would be delighted."

"Thank you your highness" chimed in Ahrianred.

"I am sorry, for I must run off to find my husband for I have a matter to discuss with him." Both bowed and off she went to find her husband.

She found Cynfelyn sitting underneath the shade of the fading summer sun reading a note on leather parchment. His long legs stretched out before him, while his eyes squinted at the lettering.

He looked up when he had heard twigs crunch at the approach of his new wife. He would have to teach her how to walk silently around especially in the forest-then again though the better of it with a smile! He had made a mental note to contact Bellinos to teach her some of the rudimentary arts of war, for her survival. For lately there had been peace and no rebellions that he had to take care of, though be knew with the fierce nature of his people, the silence would not last for too much longer. For he was reading a report from one of his scouts that had just arrived sending him this information written in Latin lettering in their language.

"If he continues to write this small in everything he sends, I will have to send him a tree to write these reports on" Cynfelyn bellowed almost to himself, though received the giggle in response that he needed to hear at that moment.

"How fares my mighty and fearless husband?" Jubilla smiled.

"I am only fearful of the writings of Davidd, the scout who writes as if to fit every word of his thoughts in a report to me into the smallest of places. I am going to have to send him some papyrus for him to write on!" He smiled and put the leather parchment aside and beckoned his new wife to sit beside him on the soft summer dew soaked grass underneath the grasping willow branches that made the tree appear to Jubilla as if it were weeping. She placed her tiny body next to that of her warrior and king husband and made herself comfortable. He wrapped his arms around her had held her close.

"So, lovely wife, what matter of import brings you to seek me out?" Jubilla felt his smile reach her soul with those words.

"Cynfelyn, I have found out who my uncle has been pining for up in the apple trees today!" She giggled and before she gave him a chance to respond, she continued, "and I invited them to sup with us this eve!" She looked up into his bright blue eyes and found merriment in them which led her to continue.

"Her name is Ahrianred and she is a warrior like Ptolemy! She is the only thing in the world that had ever taken his interest off his studies in battle tactics and such. Do you think we should approach my uncle on this matter?"

"Now Drussi!" He had taken on very well to her childhood nickname as called lovingly by her family members. "You know very well, that we have to discuss this matter with your parents, they may have arranged someone else for his hand."

"I know for a fact that they have not, why just the other day my father had brought up the subject with my mother and I do not believe that they had reached any resolution at all on that matter!"

"Fine, then for dinner this eve, your mother should be back by then from staying with her sister. I am sure that she would love to hear about this!" Suddenly eager to get back to the warriors, for matchmaking did not interest him one bit and he was eager to see the new shipment of wood gathered for the fences around the sheep that had been broken down recently by the wild boar. He was glad only one of the sheep were killed and even more glad at the idea of that wonderful boar on his table. Though still the fences needed to be repaired.

Sensing that her husband had matters that he needed to attend to she had also decided to wait until their meal that eve to bring up the matter on the stolen cattle. "Well, I will let you return to your business, though am counting the hours by shadow until I can kiss you again!" With that, like a child she jumped up and ran off giggling towards the main settlement road, perhaps to wait for the caravan of her mother so that she could scheme further. He laughed and pretended to get up to run after her, which only sent her running faster away from him. When he bent down to retrieve the almost forgotten report.

It had read that two of his warriors were recently killed while guarding a caravan headed for the boats of the Belgae lands and to Rome for trade. The pottery that it carried was shattered and destroyed and useless in trade. These brigand bands were starting to act up again and he was determined to set about more patrols in the area to prevent this. He further wanted to find out which tribes were responsible for this act, he suspected the Silures were behind this latest ambush.

He found his wife adorable yet very wise from what she had learned from her mother. He hoped that with this woman they would found a mighty empire.

XXIV

Selene had returned from sending off her sister to her new husband Drennedd, who she felt was the best possible solution for her sister. She knew that her sister could be rather reckless at times, and Selene was genuinely afraid that it would lead to her little sister's destruction. Arsinoe tended to jump rather than wait out for the right moment or chance. That was why she was very surprised at her sister's reaction to the news of her marriage with the leader of the tribe of the Belgae.

She had barely spoken the whole way down and knew from their conversations while there, that Selene would come down for her as soon as possible to be there for her first child, if she was still in Pryttain by then. Selene assured her youngest sibling that she would be there anyways prior to her leaving the Island for her home. Selene was always dependable.

She had observed the happy façade of her sister and both knew that nothing could be done to change anything in her destiny. Arsinoe would be very happy, Drennedd was a good man and obviously doted on his young bride, she wanted for nothing. He made sure that she even had her favorite Lyre teacher Sion sent down to tutor his young wife in the bardic arts and was even enrolling her in the school. It was obvious to everyone that Arsinoe just did not have the aptitude for any of the warrior arts at all. Though she did reveal a hidden skill for the Lyre and her voice was beginning to show some real promise from her instruction. Drennedd was very proud and the people of his tribe had followed her everywhere in admiration of her beauty and graceful Goddess-like ways and demeanor. The children placed petals on her path in front of their new Queen so that she would not have to step on the dirt with her dainty slippers and would carry her Greek fashioned robes that she had adored wearing over the Roman or the new clothes of this land.

Selene laughed for her daughter was quite the opposite of her dainty and exquisite aunt. Her daughter was like a summer storm that came out of nowhere, completely unpredictable, though ended with a brilliant rainbow. For her daughter preferred the native garments of the land in their brilliant hues and spiral patterns in all colors. The colors only made her daughter's red hair appear more bright rather than subduing them against the plain Roman garb that she was forced to wear when young on state occasions.

As Selene made her way back to the settlement of her daughter, she reflected on how much had occurred while they were there and wondered how her son fared under the leadership of his advisors that she had assigned while away. She made sure that with each of her advisors, they were assigned various tasks that depended on the assistance of the others. Her husband was very proud of her decision in that matter. This way the power was equally distributed and no one would want to take the power away from her husband. She had worked out a very complex arrangement for this. She even made sure that Kateiran was available to her son as advisor.

She was also very eager to hear news of her son in that he fared well himself. She had sent over her first correspondence a few months ago and knew not to expect anything from there for a few more months. She knew that her husband missed his son as well and Jubilla, though she loved her new life and in being treated like a woman, sometimes missed her old life of when nothing was expected of her in her youth.

Growing up is a huge weight for one to bear, especially one born to rule. The responsibilities were far too numerous to count and you were really only a piece of the puzzle owned truly by the one with the most power.

She had taught her daughter this and a little on how to play the game to win. She also knew that her daughter would have to learn most of the game herself and to take a few losses as well. For she sometimes felt that no one could possibly have taken as many losses as she in one lifetime and still be in the game. Sometimes she even wondered why she even played, but knew that she really did not even have a choice in the matter, for she was her mother's daughter and was born into this horrid game of power.

Sometimes one would glide and sing blissfully in the winnings and other times one had to learn to lick the wounds sustained no matter how much they festered, and get up to play again.

She wondered as her body swayed in the rhythm of the horse that she was on over valleys and rolling hills of crops as far as the eye could see. She wondered why she was not born the daughter of a simple peasant. For in reality, were they not the true winners in this game. She saw how the daughters born to simple farmers had their choice of whom they were to marry for the most part. They grew up, were raised, then married and eventually died in the same place surrounded by their family and later grandchildren.

Will she even know her grandchildren at all? She knew that her mother's family was mainly married into each other close in the line, but for the times when a princess was married into the line from Syria, they most likely never saw their family again.

Her husband wanted them both to have mates from out of the family. She had an idea that her husband had the sacred Roman abhorrence to close kin marriages and kept it from her out of respect. He wanted stronger blood ties. Selene understood and partly agreed. Though she wished that she could have her daughter by her side and her sister and brother and she knew in her hear that she would gladly trade all that she had for this luxury, if it were an option at all.

It was amazing how the average person seemed to envy her and her family in their royalty, but really they had the better life. She also understood all the more on the downfall of her mother's idea of raising her children close to her.

For if she was not attached so much to her children, she would not have even made this voyage with her daughter and risked her kingdom to be with her until the birth of their first child.

However, her mother had planned on the marriage of her and Caesarian and Helios to Arsinoe. She knew that had her mother lived she would have probably had another daughter for Ptolemy to marry as well, keeping in the tradition. So in reality-had their life not been ripped asunder from their known traditions-she would have been by the side of her mother until her death.

Selene knew that the conception of her first grand-child was soon to be made known, for she had observed the signs in her daughter and would probably have the affirmation when they arrived.

XXV

Ptolemy was simply under a spell by his warrior enchantress and could not spend enough time with her. He felt her return in that emotion as well and could read it in her eyes. The world and time with it seemed to stop when they were together. People around them were swept away with the two lovers in wishing the same for themselves or recalling when they had that same reaction and emotion as well. All those around them knew that it was much more powerful than a simple reaction to the opposite sex, that it was much more, almost ancient. As if the two lovers were fated to be together.

XXVI

By the end of the day the settlement was finally made aware that the wagons and horses of Selene were approaching with the weary travelers. All ran about in preparation for their return.

Juba, so entranced by watching the two lovers of Ptolemy and Ahrianred was swept away and ran down to the field to pick the brightest flowers that he could find for his wife. So much had happened in such a short time that he felt like a school boy again with a crush. He was eager to have his delightful wife in his arms and cherished the moments sharing such close living quarters with her. He knew too well that his time with his daughter and his wife's family would soon end.

He had gained a lot of information from the ancient Druid and stayed up late at night trying to memorize everything that he had learned during the day. He could not wait to put his scribes to work upon their return.

He had just finished a long day this time by the harbor and watching them build a flat-bottomed boat. He was amazed on their technique and skill. He was even asked to assist them and enjoyed every minute of it.

When he had received notice of his wife's approach he was covered with caked on mud and his trousers had a large tear on the side. He gathered all of the flowers that he could on his way to the buildings to change into his Roman garb for her arrival.

Cynfelyn saw his dismay and realized too soon what it was. "Your highness, If I may. I have a toga inside that had barely been worn, you look in need of fresh apparel."

"Thank you so much son." Cynfelyn led him into the royal enclosure and had a servant retrieve the garment. The look of delight at his being saved from the scrutiny of his wife was amazing. Cynfelyn chuckled to himself as his father-in -law was inside changing.

XXVII

As Queen Selene approached the area where she was welcomed after her journey, she had noticed her husband in a freshly cleaned toga, which she felt unusual for this time of day with her husband. And then she noticed the mischievous look in her son-in-law's eyes. She tried to hide her stifled giggle. For her husband had always been a lost boy when it came to his studies. His servants and she would have to remind him to change and bathe and even to eat whenever he had discovered something new, so engrossed was he in his studies. She knew that she would find out all about it this evening after she bathed all of the travel grime off of her.

She was assisted off of her horse by her husband and her brother, while Cynfelyn sent out the servants to prepare a bath for her in the small bathhouse that was recently completed in the Roman fashion. When she heard about the completion, she was ecstatic at the news, for she felt that she was too old to be bathing daily in the brook outside the settlement. Her body was craving the warm waters heated underneath that her son-in-law had explained to her months ago at the time of his inspiration. He named the baths after his wife in her honor and they were a gift to her. He even had a special room commissioned for the use of the royal family only. The other rooms of hot and cold water were open to the public.

Jubilla was by her side at once placing a soft cape around her mother's shoulders made of the whitest of rabbit fur to keep off the evening chill that was rapidly approaching, a small sign of the autumn season and of the first harvest that was soon to be brought in.

She smiled at her daughter with a look that told her that all was well with her aunt. She had truly felt that her sister would be alright and was reassured by her sister's happiness when she left her to her new home. Though something bothered her deep inside. Was her sister truly happy, or was she only playing her part in this whole matter that a princess really did not have any choice in. Whatever the case may be, the path for her sister was chosen. It was up to her sister what she would do with it from now on. For she truly believed that each person had a major role in the hand that destiny would reveal to them in life.

It was really up to them what one should do with the good as well as the bad that was placed in their path by the Gods. If lessons would be truly learned or ignored. Whether one wanted more out of life, or found pleasure with all of the good in their life and in others.

She knew that her sister was pampered and never recalled their mother due to Arsinoe being only four years old at her death. Her sister was raised mostly by Octavia and then herself to the best of her ability. She felt responsible for her sister nonetheless and wondered what it was that she was missing when it regarded her sister.

Selene looked at her daughter and said in her eyes so that only her daughter could see, that she knew and smiled. Jubilla blushed for she knew the powers of her mother. Selene then looked at her husband who reminded her that very moment of what he must have been like as a small boy, for the toga that he wore almost dragged the ground, she guessed at once that it was one borrowed from her son-in-law. He passed her some meadow flowers and held out his arm to escort her to dinner that eve. She smiled and walked by the side of her husband.

In the weariness of her travel by horseback, which she was only just getting used to, she had noticed the absence of her brother. She followed the new King and Queen to their banquet hall newly carved out of the darkest wood from Numidia, the place of her daughter's birth. For Cynfelyn had surprised her with it and had it imported for the new hall to be completed for his new bride. Selene had spent a few evenings with them in this hall and was still amazed at the beauty of the carvings and had always found something new each time she looked at a particular pattern that she thought she had known at her last visit.

The wood came alive with carvings of flowers that she had not seen anywhere or in her travels and assumed that they must be from the Keltoi underworld and "Tween Time" visions of the druids. For when a fire was lit in the hall and the oil lamps were lit from hidden niches on the sides, it made the room come alive and all of the carved flowers seemed to dance to the whimsical and enchanting tunes played by the Bards in the firelight's shadows.

There were large tables placed around the hall with one side open. Hunting dogs sat by their master's feet waiting for any scraps. Amphorae lined the walls for Cynfelyn was a wealthy King and had many things imported to grace his table to impress his guests. There were benches for the guests to sit upon and elaborately carved chairs for the royal family with Jubilla and her Cynfelyn in the center of the table in the middle that one could see directly upon entering the hall from the large oak doors. The roof was of thatch and tightly woven with an opening in the middle to catch the herb scented smoke of the fire in the center of the hall. She sat to her daughter's side while, Juba sat to the side of Cynfelyn in the places of honor.

As the people were being seated, she had noticed the running forms of her brother and a lady guest in tow. She was tiny and had the brightest red hair that she had ever seen. Though the girl was clearly winded as was her brother, she had noticed about her an air of confidence and power. She saw how her brother was attracted to this very enchanting woman or girl, she seemed ageless; and her brother was drawn to her tiny form like a moth to a flame. She smiled as they approached their seats as shown to them by servants at the high table beside Selene. Besides Juba was Bellinos and two of his lesser Druids. The Bards were in the front of the room on the platform by the door adjusting their instruments.

There was the usual confusion while all was being readied for the feast at the end of the day. Most of the time, the hall was full for the evening meal with as many people as could find a place at the table of their king. Some people would wait for a few hours to guarantee themselves a seat.

Which was why Cynfelyn made sure that this new banquet hall would fit everyone in his capitol with room for more.

Selene was not aware that this was the largest banquet hall ever built in this land. For she was used to the grandeur of large dining halls, for her mother's palace of Bruchion had four of them and all were almost twice the size of this room, though carved in marble rather than wood, and two of them had fountains.

As Selene gathered her freshly donned garments around her in comfort and settled herself on her cushion she glanced over at her brother to her left and found his eyes locked into those of the small lady beside him. Her daughter whispered to her, "She is Ahrianred, Mother…" and smiled. She had also noticed the nudge from her husband to playfully hush her from gossiping with her mother. She giggled with her mother at that, which had then gained the attention of Juba who looked inquisitively at his brother-in-law.

XXVIII

Introductions were made and scrumptious delicacies were heaped on their plates. Normal fare for the people of this land, though still rather new to Selene and her family. Jubilla and her family had already explained about her not being able to have any shellfish, so Cynfelyn made sure that the meals did not include them at all, so that his young wife would not be tempted. For it was difficult since they were also proud fishermen for many centuries and had prided their skills. He made sure that no fish were stuffed with shellfish either as was also normal in that and sauces. He would take no chances with his wife that he was fast growing to love.

Cynfelyn had known about the love that was growing between Ptolemy and the warrior Ahrianred and approved of it. He felt that both were from noble houses. Though he wondered how Ptolemy would stand to being only a consort. For he knew the nature of the Romans and the Greeks and similar cultures of that area in the world and wondered if the Egyptian prince even knew of this yet. For according to the matriarchal traditions of his land he was only the consort of Jubilla, before he was King. Though the technicalities made it the contrary in reality.

His people knew of her royal blood and of the power of her name of both her paternal and maternal lineage and approved of it for their king when he was still very young. He was truly glad to find that he was attracted to her as well and sensed that as she grew, her beauty would grow even more. For her mother was still very beautiful herself and he noticed how her father would glance at her across the table as the mother and daughter were rapt in conversation. Cynfelyn wondered if Juba was only beginning to notice the beauty of his wife for he looked like a young boy with his first crush. He noticed that Selene was oblivious to the attention being paid to her by her own husband, and observed that her gaze and his wife's were focused on the two practically entwined heads of Ptolemy and Ahrianred.

Warmth permeated the long and spacious chamber, while delicate and soft oranges and yellow's surrounded the room in dance upon the diners. Their voices muted by the thick dark elaborately carved wood of the hall and the sound of the Lyre wafting around them.

Ptolemy noticed that his family had observed his attentions to his lady love. For he did not mind. He wanted this precious and fierce warrior for his wife and the mother of his children. He knew that he should inquire about this at the dinner for he had playfully avoided any glances they were constantly throwing his way for his attention, especially his niece. He was having fun at the moment, knowing that they were only waiting for his word.

"Delphos, your family seems to know of us, what think you on their opinion my love?" Ahrianred whispered seductively into his ear at the table. Virtually unheard from the other guests since they were for the most part engaged in their own conversations, while he sat for a moment to reflect. Ahrianred playfully called him Delphos to shorten his full name of Ptolemy Philedelphos. She despised the long eloquent speeches of court and shortened everything. For she had a very abrupt personality and only liked things short and sweet and to the point. No long and eloquent court conversations from her, for she hated the subtle intricacies in which he was discovering were a great game of these people. Where even one word could have many hidden meanings, both hidden and obvious. He loved the blatant speech of his lover and delighted in even that for her voice was very deep for one of such tiny stature.

"Ahrianred, do not worry one bit about the opinion of my family on the matter, for I am a man and have even donned the full toga into manhood several years ago…" He trailed off, noticing the expression in her bright dark blue eyes.

"I am not afraid of anything they might think, I am curious, is all. Your sister seems to have a great part in any marriage connections as well as your father. Do you think that they would not accept you being only my consort. For you culture…"

"Wait, you mean I am to be only a consort, I thought to take you for a wife, the mother of my children." Ptolemy was jarred from his reverie that was until that moment lost in the room and of watching the people around him in rapt conversation. He felt extreme comfort in just being with Ahrianred. They did not have long conversations at all and sometime just spent hours by each other's side in the bliss of their company and in silence just gazing at each other. As if words were too simple for the love they possessed for each other. Yet, this was something that he had not thought of at all.

Selene from across the table on the other side, had picked up disturbing vibes from her brother and his love beside them. Her conversation with Jubilla had ceased for the moment while she focused on her brother in conversation. Jubilla had picked up on her mother and had scanned the room to follow the gaze of her mother. Selene noticed this and whispered to her daughter. "We should continue our conversation, for it is not any of our business."

Jubilla acknowledged this and struggled to find a topic. "Mother, after the baby is born, I have decided to travel with you to visit with Arsinoe and to see you until you journey home."

"Hush, darling, do not worry yourself about our goodbye at all, for the babe inside of you is still very new, you have not even told your husband about it."

"I was waiting until the waxing moon a few weeks from now, to make sure that the babe is safe."

"Very good. Now this dish in front of me, what is it, it is simple delicious…"

Ptolemy was staring at Ahrianred, oblivious to everyone else in the long filled chamber of people around them. His voice started to rise, though not so much to disturb the other diners. "What ever do you mean, I just thought…"

"That is it my Delphos, my love, you assumed the cultural norm for your people. Our ways are different. I am from a long line of women warriors. It is the line of the mother that counts. Though you must also understand that I am also very choosy about the blood that intermingles with my own to create the future of my line. For you are the finest warrior that I have ever seen. "

"But, I had heard about that. Do you know how careful that I must be as well in that I am the only male heir left in my generation to the Ptolemy Dynasty."

Soothingly, she continued. "I understand, though will you ever return to your lands?" Ptolemy nodded negatively.

"It is tradition that the women of my line choose only the bravest of warriors to mix with our blood, though it is also tradition that I may also have more than one consort."

Ptolemy's face contorted with a growing rage over this. For he had the Roman sense of possession when it came to his women, especially the woman that he choose to marry. For no one until Ahrianred had even made him remotely interested in them before. "I had no idea of this. Perhaps I should look elsewhere for my wife, for it is important that there be no doubt to the paternity of the children from my line."

Ahrianred continued, undaunted by the growing rage of her love. She was unfamiliar with the ways of the people from so far away from them, the Romans and the Greeks and such. That she could not comprehend the meaning of his anger. He should be honored that she chose him. For no other had attracted her in so many ways as he. She had even decided to plan her family with this man, this great warrior, with his battle tactics to foreign to her. She had learned much from him to improve her own skills and was elated with each meeting and encounter with him. "Do you not understand the honor of being chosen, for my line is very old, much older than yours?"

"I do, though I will not share you with any other." With those words he stood up and hastily left the table and sought out the comfort of the deep woods and the sanctuary of the groove behind them. He needed to be alone.

Cynfelyn had noticed the disturbance of raising voices between Ptolemy and Ahrianred and guessed that he knew the meaning of them. Ptolemy was too Roman in his ways and he understood them having spent a good many years in study there. He had also correctly assumed that she had just informed Ptolemy that he was to be her consort. He admired both of them well and considered them to be of his finest in warriors and did not want to lose Ptolemy. He had been searching for a way to keep his skills and knowledge of battle with his people and to not return across the sea with his sister. Yet, he joyously welcomed the fate of love, how it snuck up and bit one when you least expected it. For in Ahrianred, he had found a way to keep Ptolemy here with them.

He had encouraged the meetings between the two and even put them together in training squadrons to ease their relationship and for them to have the most contact possible. He did not want this to change and understood that the powerful passions of love could easily be turned into the powerful passions of hate, so fine were the two lines when immense feelings were involved. He bade his leave from the table from his wife, who had also noticed something amiss. Jubilla went over to the side of Ahrianred in the empty chair of Ptolemy, while Cynfelyn sought Ptolemy who was making rapid pace in his anger.

"Ptolemy" He called out to the shadowy figure ahead of him. Ptolemy slowed his pace and looked up at Cynfelyn. How he wished that he could be in his place and rule over Egypt, the country he was born to rule, though was in the control of the Romans and gone from their line forever.

His anger dissipated when Cynfelyn had produced a horn of dark ale from under his cloak that he had taken from the dining hall. A smile lit up his face. Ptolemy returned the mischievous smile and reached out for a swig. For he had grown to love the brewing skills of these people and shared their hatred for the Romans who were fast conquering the world.

The two men walked together in silence until they reached the space of the grove. The brightness of the full moon's rays peeking through the dense summer foliage of the large and ancient Oak trees that made a corridor as far as their eyes could see.

Knowing that Ptolemy wanted to talk about anything other than what had occurred in the dining hall, he found another subject. "These trees are older than the first people who walked these lands, they say that they are older than the small folk who dwelled the lands before the time my family came into rule."

Ptolemy was barely hearing any words but those of Ahrianred in his head.

Sensing this after the long interval of silence, he switched tactics.

"Enough of that, I will stop the excrement of trying to divert your attention and get the main point of my presence this evening. I sense some anger with you and your lady friend the warrior Ahrianred." He looked into the eyes below him of Ptolemy.

"I need it to stop. At all cost you are to get along with all of my warriors, there must be complete camaraderie on all matters and anything that you do not understand or have a question with is to be brought up with me and I will decide the matter."

"I understand your liege, though I was meaning to ask the Lady Ahrianred to be my wife."

"I see, are you familiar with the traditions of the female warriors of her clan and especially her line?" He saw the blank look mixed with that of anger and continued with his explanation.

"You see, Ahrianred is the first born child of Lyei who was the first born child and daughter of Rhiannon and so forth through the time of oblivion. She was born to a great and noble women warrior line and it must be kept pure at all costs only mixing with the finest of blood. There is much that you need to learn about our people, if you should wish to stay amongst us. For Ahrianred to even consider you as her consort is an honor indeed. For I was chosen as consort to a great warrior by one with a lesser lineage than that your Ahrianred, and I was extremely honored at that, though she had a son who died soon after his birth. I never would have been her husband in the way that your culture provides for that station. We do not lock our women hiding them from all the world. They are valued members of our culture and their lines must be respected as our own." Ptolemy's shoulders slumped at this, Cynfelyn though that he was possibly beginning to understand and guessed that he knew the reason for his disturbance at this knowledge.

"Also understand that though they do have the right to chose more than one consort, I know that Ahrianred had not chosen any before you and I doubt that she will chose any even after. For the look in her eyes tells all. This I know from my wisdom and as your King."

"I understand, you really think that I should not worry on her choosing another man besides myself as consort? For my line is also very old and it is necessary that the blood be mine only in the future generation."

"Yes, though her line has been here before any of the Keltoi, as you call us, have ever walked these lands. She is of the older race called the Picts, that is why she is so small unlike, others here." Ptolemy nodded in understanding of that.

"What is more, Ptolemy, is that you truly do not have a land to rule, through no fault of your own in reality. I would be honored if you would stay here among us and to remain here, whether you choose to consort with Ahrianred or not. Though I guarantee you that your sons and daughters will be of the finest warrior blood in the known world." He noticed Ptolemy drifting. "I would be greatly honored if you would chose to stay here and you would be welcomed as one of my greatest warriors of the most noble of blood. I would find the most noble of ladies to marry you from the Keltoi people."

"I would have none other than Ahrianred." He fiercely stood his ground on that matter.

"Than you must respect the ways of our people and understand our traditions. For she is worthy of the highest of honors so old is her bloodline. I honestly think that you do not have to worry about her choosing another consort."

He continued, "Though I do feel that you must keep your feelings in check and not let them hinder your performance in any way be it in practice or in battle. If your love for her should prove to be too distracting, I will terminate your relationship with her. For I will not have any of my warriors thinking of anything other than their duty. The life threat to yourself and other's who rely on you would prove too great."

"I understand Cynfelyn, I would have no other but Ahrianred and will learn as much as I can about her ways. For I can never return home. I honestly have nothing there for me. Here I have honor, duty, and have found the only woman who means something to me. I appreciate your consideration in finding another partner for me to take to wife. But, the feelings that I have for her are too strong and cannot be ignored. I am in your land and will live by your ways."

He stood taller then and faced Cynfelyn as squarely in the eyes as he could due to their height difference, "Though understand that I do have a very honorable line myself and possibly someday would want to visit along with Ahrianred, to show her my own roots and the kingdom that I should be ruling right now if it were not for Octavian!"

Cynfelyn realized that Ptolemy was a very passionate man in his love for Ahrianred and hatred for Caesar Augustus. Though he greatly admired his skills and knowledge of battle skills. He also understood that during the time of peace at the present time in the part of the world that he came from, he was also untried in battle. He would work carefully on his emotions and hoped only that it would come out to enhance his skill in battle and not to hinder it.

"I would suggest having a talk with Bellinos, for he knows of all of the legal intricacies of the female warrior clan. He may be able to assist you with any questions that you have on the matter."

"I will take that advice and seek him out on the morrow."

"You forget, unlike your sense of time. The morrow has begun with the sun setting."

"That is true my friend. There is much for me to learn in your ways. I am growing to love this country and the fine traditions you have here."

Cynfelyn smiled at this and the two men sat there in silence on the large branches of a fallen oak tree that had fallen in the storm the evening prior.

"I will have to get some men out here to clear this tree and to plant another." He stated almost absentmindedly. The crickets of the night chirped as if to make a point at the maintenance of the sacred grove where the two men sat deep in their own thoughts.

XXIX

The months passed by with the winter that soon followed to when they were winding down their soft Spring with the immanent birth of Jubilla's first-born child as they were approaching the Summer Solstice once again. Wondrous was the significance of this omen.

The Queen with the autumn red flowing hair was large and full with child. Selene knew that her daughter carried twins as she did. She felt it in her soul and wondered if her mother would be there in spirit to assist her in this birth of her great grandchildren. So fast was life passing Selene by, she knew that her time here would soon end and she would have to leave her daughter to run her life on her own as she once did at almost the same age.

She knew that her daughter would not have any problems for she was strict in her diet and ate all of the foods the healing women prescribed to her. Selene wished that she had brought with her Asandros, but felt that he was better needed in watching over her son, to keep him out of trouble due to his youth.

She had received two letters in the time that she had been here with her daughter from her own son. She was very pleased with his progress and growth. Though he still sounded like her little boy that she so desperately wanted to hold close to her and to tell him to stop growing so fast.

She had also received faithful and honest letters from her trusted Kateiran, who told her in depth of the court issues and of the strong personality being slowly revealed of her son's wife Julia. She could tell that he was concerned about this princess who was slowly rising in Selene's absence. He assured her that he would monitor the princess closely.

Though as with her daughter, who was soon to be a mother on her own and was already the mistress of her own home now. She knew close to her heart that it was her duty to make sure that her babies grew enough to lead on their own. That she was only there to give them wings for them to fly as she had been. She made sure that her children had very strong wings that were stitched tough with her love.

Cynfelyn had handfasted the two loving souls of her brother and his lady love Ahrianred. The two were always seen together and rarely apart, so involved with each other they were. It was magical just to be around the two of them. She felt in her heart that theirs was a love immortal that few would ever experience in even one lifetime, nor perhaps in many lifetimes. She felt that their love would be the main focus of legends long after their bodies turned to dust.

She had even heard from her beloved sister Antonia who had told her that she had given birth to a fine son named Germanicus. She had sadly told her that Agrippa died, who was the husband of Augustus's daughter the lovely Julia, and that Julia had given birth to their last child four months after by the name of Agrippa Posthumus. She had mentioned that Julia was the mother of five children from Agrippa and was still rather thin and hardly tainted bodily by motherhood. For Agrippa had Divorced his prior wife Marcella, who was the daughter of Octavia from her first husband, so that he could marry Julia on the wishes of her father.

In reading the letter form Antonia, Selene reflected on how many lives were changed and shattered by the whim of Augustus and his daughter.

Antonia had also told her of how her uncle made Tiberius divorce his loved and cherished wife Vispania to marry the precious Julia. Selene had suspected that Julia had a thing for Tiberius. Interesting, she thought on that information. Tiberius must have been livid since Vispania was pregnant with his second son at the time! Just like his own father. Selene felt sorry for how fate had treated Tiberius in his closeness with Augustus. She wondered how Livia was while all this was going on. Probably the devoted matronly wife that Augustus admired her so much for on the outside. Yet she knew how powerful this woman really was and suspected that Livia had a great part in all of this.

Selene thought about the mighty man the Caesar Augustus, who was excellent in state matters and in planning his beloved Rome, though seemed to come up short when it came to the emotions of his family members, excluding those of his doted on and spoiled daughter Julia. He seemed to bend over backwards in doing everything to please his only child. She did serve her duty for Rome though in finally giving her father the male heirs he desperately wanted And could not have from his second wife Livia. For now he had plenty of male heirs and in the process had pushed Tiberius aside since he was not truly of Augustus' blood only of his wife Livia. Tiberius probably would have been a good leader if given the chance to grow instead of constantly being pushed aside in favor of his blood heirs. For if Augustus died while in the office of Imperator, his heirs would inherit his role.

The Imperator Augustus still insisted that he was not a king and only a leader to his people so that they would be better able find their way out of the chaos that was created during the long years of civil war. He only wanted them to be a republic again. Though Selene wondered, how it was a republic, if his heir would inherit. Was not a republic a right to rule chosen in vote by the populace? She observed the tendril of a monarchial power slowly descending over Rome to their inherent and steadfast oblivion. She smiled over this.

She sat this beautiful day with the brightest of blue skies that she had ever seen, by the side of her daughter. They sat on Roman style folding chairs under a large Maple tree relishing the shade of the huge green leaves. She and her daughter were finding shapes in the clouds like children and giggled all the while. They were observing a small practice for the tournament for the spear throwing competition. The tournament was to be held on the day of the New Moon.

A loud cheer from the practice field went up and broke the reverie of mother and daughter sitting peacefully under the tree. Selene looked over to the area of the sound with her delicate long fingers shading her eyes from the noon height of the sun to view the cause of the commotion. She had noticed that her brother was taken up on the shoulders of two large men from the group and they were making way towards the two Queens in repose. Others crowded them as they made their approach.

They placed down the elated Ptolemy when other's crowded to tell the tale. "Your highness" Glanced the warrior named Dias, who was flanked by Rues, Sego and Andocos. "Your uncle is surely the finest shot we have ever seen. For he hit the bulls-eye thirteen times in a row!".

"Such excellent marksmanship and an honor to have among us." Chimed in Andocos.

"Worthy of the hand of Ahrianred, whose record he just beat." The giant men guffawed at this. For somewhere primeval in all men, was the sense of power over women.

Jubilla giggled at this and called out to the huge men winded from their elation and practice, "Well, Ahrianred will just have to try harder!" All joined in with jubilant laughter for the day was holding up as a fine summer day, easy to break with play. She continued and sensed their mood. "Well, warriors" for there were four warrior maidens among the ranks for this particular practice session, as well as Ahrianred, whose face lit up at her mention. "Why do you not all break this practice session and test the temperature of the baths, for I think I am in need for a swim!" More laughter accompanied this while they scooped up Selene and her daughter to place them in the litter that Cynfelyn had made for his wife in her condition carved in Apple wood, the most sacred of woods to enhance the spirit of their unborn child and to ease her burden. The warriors fought playfully over who was to carry the two Queens, for it was a genuine honor, though the mood of the day filled everyone with laughter. For it was warm from the rays of the sun, yet the wind made the day perfect to endure.

Andocos, Rues, Sego and Dias were chosen and prior to their picking up the litter, they grabbed the laughing Ptolemy and placed him inside as well. Selene and her daughter laughed. They were being carried down the path towards the main settlement and when they were carried close to the trees that lined the path, Selene called out, "Halt a little close to that Oak tree for a minute." Which they obeyed cheerfully. Selene reached out and pulled a long new branch of oak leaves and wrapped it around the head of her son in Roman fashion of a crown. "You will always be of the blood of Kings and my honored brother, even without your many talents!" The men guffawed at this and poked playfully at Ahrianred who only giggled in response. Selene blushed at this and the litter resumed the path ahead of them.

The men and women picked up joyous war songs, which she knew that she had her brother could barely understand. She looked over at

Ahrianred whose glance was cemented into the litter at Ptolemy who was returning her gaze feigning luxury like a Roman senator in repose. Jubilla giggled at her uncle whom she adored.

They arrived at the new bathhouse of imported marble and noticed that the mosaics that her daughter had styled to represent the Gods and Goddesses of her own land were making great progress. The artists were at high sun break and under the shade of some trees nearby in hushed conversation.

The men and women of their entourage rushed on ahead to check the temperature for the two Queens, for they were all too fast becoming accustomed to the tradition of the baths brought over from this family from far away. The four that were carrying their precious cargo, lightly lowered the litter to let the occupants climb out.

Cynfelyn had arrived on hearing of his practice session breaking up and wandered over to see what was amiss, when he observed the joyful mood of his warriors with his wife and mother in law. He quickly joined in with their contagious mood and called out to the two Queens, "Halt, for the way to the bath must be prepared properly so that you do not soil your dainty feet!" He grabbed some wild roses from the bushes outside the baths and plucked at the petals making a makeshift carpet to place their silken slippers on leading to the main chamber of the bathhouse. They giggled and proceeded into the bathhouse with Cynfelyn in tow behind them. Ptolemy scooped up his Ahrianred and carried her ran on ahead.

"The water is perfect!" called out Ahrianred from deep inside to where the warm baths were.

All the restless warriors with the two Queens dominated the newly constructed baths for the rest of the afternoon along with their king, a later member of this lazy summer group.

Andocos mournfully joined in the camaraderie in bold attempt to hide the loss of the princess he was honored to protect. Cynfelyn ran over to him and plunged him deep into the waters that surrounded them in play. Andocos in turn grabbed hold of all of the water around him and heaved his powerful arms creating a large wave that engulfed most of the bathers around him in laughter.

Ceridon just stood by the side near the clothes her eyes on the form of her new Queen. She was paralyzed with the envy in which her Cynfelyn had ignored her prior advances and found only happiness in the eyes of his new Queen. She was mortified in his refusal to his being her consort. For with the ways of their people he could have a Queen and still be her consort. She could not understand him. He had denied her bloodline for this foreign usurper. He had crushed her honor. She then backed from the room unnoticed by the others and made her way outside. She could no longer endure the pain of his refusal and had decided to seek better blood for the line of warriors she so desperately wanted to fill her womb. She was still numb from the pain of the loss of her young son. She would look to better pastures for a fine warrior who would appreciate her lineage. She had thought of the Silures tribe and decided that she would look into this. For she had noticed the eyes of Avarwy scanning appreciatively her lean and battle-hardened body unblemished by her childbirth.

XXX

Jubilla awoke with a start from the depths of her slumber to meet the sharp sounds of the darkened early morning. The late summer chill filled her bones as the warmth of the furs around her no longer met their duty. She was not sure the reason for the suddenness of her completely wakeful mood when all else was deep in sleep. There seemed to be no sound at all but her curious breathing and that of her husband sleeping soundless beside her and occasionally tossing the furs about.

The blackness was entire, even where they slumbered close to the evening fire stoked occasionally by a servant. Not as necessary as would be in the darkest of winter months. The servant was a small boy in light slumber beside the fire who lazily slumped back against the post nearby. All other occupants were deep in the land of slumber themselves and their noises muffled by the loud nature soliloquy outside the large round-house where they slept while their new palace was being constructed. They were waiting a final shipment of marble imported from Athens in the purest of white granite that was reputed to have been used on the Pantheon.

Jubilla had spent months finding the best artists of her new homeland who had the most eloquent plans for the paintings and murals that would be later set off by the stark white, pink and coral colored imported marble. She had learned a great deal as well about the local legends and of how some of them were somewhat similar to those she was raised on from Greece and Rome and even ancient Egypt. She wondered vaguely with the contrasts and comparisons, if possibly there was an original religion before any civilization where the legends must have sprung from, a sort of master and creator Bard that was the genesis of all legends and religions. And later they were adapted to the cultures which were founded from these early tales and stories of Gods and Goddesses.

She sat straight and tall in bed not knowing any reason for her sudden wakefulness and wondering why the oddest of thoughts were entering her mind at this very dark and early hour of the morning. For she was wide awake and it seemed as if every sense in her body was working overtime and extremely acute, almost as if it was waiting for something.

Normally if she woke so late at night, she would get out of bed and wander about to look at all of the new creations she and her husband were planning. She would also wander over to her new herb garden that she was soon cherishing more than most of the beautiful garments and luxuries that she had been raised with. It was amazing how incredible it was to witness such a life force from something so small as a seed. Then to water it, weed around it and nurture it to eventually reap the fruition of all of that hard labor in the growth of the plant. Sometimes she even wept when she knew that the plant would eventually die the yearly death before being put to sleep for the long and cold winter. They would fill the gardens with manure and hoe the garden to mix the soil and then cover the whole plot with the glorious colors of the autumn leaves. In this way the soil would retain the nutrients and be ready for new growth in the Spring. She would lament her lost herbs in that event. This was the second time that she would be doing this and she was looking forward to each and every process of the garden and the joys it brought her in each stage.

She mourned all of her beautiful and very useful herbs of her first garden plot the very first time that she had learned about this process from the village wise woman named Elena. Elena was ancient and ageless at the same time. She was covered in ragged garments probably homespun years ago when her fingers were more nimble, though had become threadbare through the many years of use and numerous washings. Cynfelyn had told her that this woman with the whispery voice was the most knowledgeable in the area and had taught his own mother and before that her mother the arts of the herbs and the properties sacred to them.

This art was almost unknown to Jubilla in her youth, especially those of this area and climate. Her mother had taught her a few things about herb lore for the plants native to her area, though mostly for ceremonial use. Such as making incenses and such.

Elena had a small round-house of her own close to the royal palace quarters and would always be seen no matter what season looking over her own garden and also the small garden of her Queen.

Jubilla believed that the wise old woman had the patience of the wind and was marveled by all of the knowledge that this woman had. She had even seen Bellinos visit with this woman often for advise as well as the other Druids. She had observed the two ancient figures bent over from age in animated conversation on many occasions, to almost take on new life when the discussion veered towards the topic of the many healing properties of herbs. Debates were picked up with uncanny accuracy and most of the intricacies of them were lost on the confused Jubilla who was sometimes in the fury of their heated debates, left invisible to them on the sidelines.

She thought of the seed of life deep inside her womb and how her body grew fast to protect it. How her stomach would toss and turn with life waiting to burst forth. She felt such fierce love for the babe, or babes inside. A completion of the love she felt in material form for her husband and king.

This sharp morning was punctuated with these thoughts and many others which fought to wreak havoc on her new greatly acute mind. Though still she sat straight in bed not daring for some reason to get out of the warmth of her fur cocoon to seek her solace elsewhere.

Her husband mumbled something barely audible against the increasing growing sounds of the nature so close to her and the round-house in which they slept. The crickets were full force then, possibly waiting to greet the dawn with joy. Possibly. The creaks from others sleeping around her in huddled cocoons of comfort in various areas around the glowing embers of the fire whose glow played wistfully on the sleeping form of the room non-discriminately.

Even the small boy fire attendant seemed to suddenly sense that the fire needed stirring as time seemed to stand still in the room. Jubilla observed as the small boy was lulled from his light slumber to stir the embers completely almost breathing new life into them and then his body slumped back into the state from which it was briefly roused in duty.

She smiled at this and wondered why, as usual she was the only one so loudly awake at this hour. Of course she had no way of knowing which hour it actually was, since her water clock was long deemed useless here in this land without time. She was getting used to their much grander view on time rather than the preciseness in which her culture looked towards time. She was born to a culture that was constantly finding new ways to keep accurate time schedules and learning new ways to determine an accurate ways of finding it. It almost seemed to her as if it actually minimalized time in itself-instead of glorifying in it as the simple Keltoi do. They had sun clocks and water clocks and mathematical equations handed down from the wisdom of the Greeks in order to catch and note almost each second and not letting anything escape.

This culture on the other hand could care less for this meticulous time keeping. They cared more on the phases of the moon and then the sun. The year, contrary to the one that she was raised on began in the height of Summer on the longest day, rather than on the bleakest day in winter and the shortest which was usually in January according to the calendar established by Julius Caesar. Though in the later years after his death, was not kept up as in his life at the implementation of such an ingenious calendar. Prior to that calendar, the months were completely out of sync with the seasons of the year. Her mother had told her all about this as described by her mother before. Though before they left, the months were slightly coming askew again and she knew the calendar would again have to be revised and kept in better order, if the Roman people were to be happy again.

The peoples of Pryttain based their whole year on the wheel of life as they called it and in the seasons that they represented. It was based on the story which evolved at the beginning of the year in which the old God battled the new God. This occurred in the height of Summer on the longest day of the year. The new God would win this battle and begin a new cycle of life with the crops and harvest which ran the loves of these people who were first and foremost farmers.

The defeated old God would stand aside, while the new God assured the progress and harvesting of the new seeds that grew in the ground. The ground in which they grew was represented by the mother Goddess, who had three forms as well. The Maiden; when the ground was broken from sleep and planted, the Mother; for when the ground grew new life inside of her with the planting and growing seeds to nourishing plants; and eventually the Crone; when the earth was harvested and bare and served it's purpose in nourishing the people of the land that worshipped her.

The old God stood on the side and was used in the fertilizing of the life-force in the Godess' womb; and after the harvests would die. This occurred during the second harvest and was celebrated on a day called Samhain, in which all of the people would honor their dead as well and leave out food for them. This was the eve on which the realms and other dimensions in which old and new souls traveled at will, would be most seen and often contacted for advice, since the veil was thinnest. Food would be left out for those family members departed from this material realm.

For the average Pryttain believed that generally the spirit world walked side by side with the material world and that eventually all worked together side by side, though the material world generally did not see the spiritual world, except possibly on that eve of Samhain.

The new God then reigned supreme in the heavens and in the cycle of things. The wheel of the year would turn more and eventually came to be the shortest day of the year celebrated as Yule to these people, for at this point of the year the Goddess who was impregnated by the old God during the Spring Equinox on their holiday of Beltane was in full term of her pregnancy. It was Yule in which the Goddess gave birth to the new God all over again. The new God was then deemed old and waited his turn for Spring Equinox to perform his last duty and after be noted as the old King by the time of the start of the new year.

This cycle was repeated year in and year out. All of the days were determined in their accordance with the solar and lunar holidays. The hours were not noted by any people except for the Druids. The average person had no care for the details of the days, only their own responsibilities to equate with the major holidays. They also cared greatly for the observable phases of the moon and based everyday matters and tasks on them.

When the moon was new and not observed in the sky it was a time best used in planning new projects. The Full Moon was generally noted to be the best time for celebration and rest from all arduous tasks. The women especially would honor this time since it mainly coincided with their menstrual cycles. A woman was considered the most powerful at this time of month for she was with the cycle of the Goddess and the Goddess was most in her in this lunar cycle of the woman.

Contrary to her culture from which she was raised, when a woman was considered most dirty and often ignored by her men folk. Husbands would sometimes make their wives sleep in another chamber so he would not have contact with her in this time, in his ignorance of lunar ways, only repulsed him. In some cultures, she had heard, such as the one form which her son's wife was from, the women were completely be kept away from the men in everyday contact.

She had learned from the wise women of this culture that it was also due to the men being only afraid of the women and had sought only to make her weak in having them ignorant of their most valued time in her closeness to the Goddess.

Men in this culture always had the women by their side and knew most of the ways of women and were not afraid of them. Though they had learned to respect the women who were especially in synch with the Goddess and to obey any whim during this time or fear the all too known wrath of a woman upset during this time.

He body was learning the ways of nature and had also began to keep time with the Goddess in becoming in synch with the Full Moon to reap her full power. Though soon after her marriage, she found out that they soon ceased and she knew in her heart that she was to bear a child.

When she informed her mother, who had already known with her own Goddess powers from Isis. Elena had told her all of the ways of the Great Mother and had taught her own mother much as well. Her mother was also often in company with the wise woman and the two would compare herbal remedies. Selene would teach the woman about the herbs native to her own land and would learn the ones which would serve similar purposes that grew here. Her mother had taught the wise woman about the philosophies of the Greeks, Philistines, Sumerians, and others whose cultures were lost in that day and age. Elena seemed to know some of them, though were called different names since they had been passed down to her orally and not from the writings of ancient scrolls as had her own mother obtained the knowledge in the libraries of Alexandria and later her own which her parents had brought and created anew in Mauretania.

Her thoughts were collecting in stunning accuracy on the meanings of time and the year. For she had inherited her mother's ability to accurately reflect with an objective view all of her learnings and them to compare them with other things learned in her search for knowledge.

For she also knew that her mother was the chosen one to carry on the words of her grandmother for future generations and that she was chosen by her mother to carry it on to the next generation, so that the knowledge of the mothers in the family would not be lost to the world dominated by men.

She realized that all of the knowledge of her grandmother and then mother would not be ignored, but greatly nurtured here. Which she was beginning to realize why her mother had coerced her father to marry her so far away from home. She knew that it tore at her mother's heart, though she also knew that her mother wanted her to flourish here in a culture that was friendly towards women and their ways and would not be smothered as they were in the all too consuming culture of the Romans and their chauvinistic ways.

Her mother was wise in conforming to the ways in which her world was lead in that she had no other choice. Her mother taught her to choose her own battle and to know when it was right to fight and when it was wise to lay down your spear and to admit defeat. For in admitting defeat, they would still be alive to fight another day and to pass on the knowledge to their daughters.

Her mother greatly despaired in not having the actual words of her own mother the great Cleopatra, for which they both were named. She constantly searched for them for they were lost upon the death of her mother. Which is why she believed that her mother had not died by choice since she was not notified as to the whereabouts of those cherished scrolls. Her mother promised that she would receive them when found.

Her mind was swimming with so many things which had suddenly came to an abrupt and powerful halt, for now her purpose for waking at this time of eve was becoming clear. For suddenly a gush of waters had escaped her body. Her time as maiden had long ended and the limbo was over, for her time as mother was to begin.

XXXI

Selene was pushed by an invisible force as the Goddess called her from her slumber. Tearing her way from the long hallways that she wandered as a child in the now far away palace of Bruchion. For prior to her wakening, she and her brother were running in the halls trying to escape the ruthless callings of their nursemaid for breakfast.

The sleek coldness of the polished marble that touched their tiny bare feet as they ran seemed so real to her as was the smell of the incense that burned in the oil lamps that lined the statuesque corridors.

Her gauzy childish gown trailed her in her flight, her tiny hand entwined in those of Helios in time beside her. His youth lock swiftly trailing them from his shaven head. The two of them giggled as they ran, knowing that they would find trouble with their mother finding out of their disobeying their nursemaid. Yet the twins were oblivious to this fact an on they ran. Thonk thonk…thonk thonk… their dainty feet touched the floors at their rapid pace in daring escape.

Suddenly the familiar incense emitted an utterly alien scent as they made their rapid progress through the vast corridors. The guards they passed were almost as faceless as the Gods in the temples. Turning into new corridors, which strangely resembled the one which they just ran from, yet knowing in their youthful souls that it was new and not the old paths which they traveled.

Yet, that new incense was strangely familiar, though not of this time in her life. Reality was slowly jarring her to the present and just when she recognized what the scent was...apples—she woke with a start by the urgings of her husband beside her. He looked worried and was calling out to her. Her mind in desperation urgently tried to ignore the ranting of her husband to return to her play with her lost brother. The apples were not from her past, for they were her present. Then it dawned in her mind like the arms of Nut who made the sky with the stars in her breast. The present—her daughter.

At the realization of this she practically jumped out of her soft lightly furred coverlets and almost in her sleep dazed mind expected the bed to have been raised as in her own chamber back in the palace in Mauretania. Her feel almost did not recognize the closeness of the ground so suddenly was she jarred from her sleep-clouded bliss, that she almost caused injury when it met with the wooden planks so fearfully close to her. Juba laughed deep from his belly at the escapades of his wife and assisted her and their servant in donning garments on his wife. This was usually the task of her slaves and servants from her whole life, though he, in the vigor of this new land and culture was sharing in this task and preferred it for himself in such close quarters. For usually they would joyfully end up taking apart all the work they had done and end up in furious lovemaking under the privacy of the many furs and cloaks that covered their sleeping area. For privacy as they have known it their whole lives was virtually unknown here. Where all was done in the perfect view of people of any age, with nothing at all said about it.

Juba was so unused to this at first for women were mostly kept to their own quarters and their beauty regimen secret to all male eyes, except of course the eunuch or palace female slaves which assisted them in this. Yet, here it was nothing sacred. For the Keltoi or Pryttain people did have their vanity and rigidly adhered to ways in preserving it, though out in the open.

He gathered the colorfully woven robes of his wife in her skillful way that she had adapted from their own daughter in mixing the drapery of the Romans, though rather that the stark whiteness with the borders his wife fashioned in defiance; the robes were completely colored and spirals were interwoven with faces of animals and people reminiscent of the wild people of this land. Though both mother and daughter preferred the robes they were so accustomed to from life experience, as did he. He did occasionally witness his daughter while busy at work in her garden with a shorter garment that reached down to her knees and gathered at her waist with a cloak of equal garish color wrapped around her and gathered by a broach, elegantly carved in gold from her husband.

He knew from his wife, though she normally preferred the long flowing robes of her culture, colorful though they were; had laid them aside for the occasion of her daughter's giving birth a garment more utilitarian on this occasion.

It was placed upon her and in her haste to be by the side of her daughter, insisted on tying the gathered waist herself. She wanted to complete the rest as well. She gathered a long scarf to adorn her head from the chill of that time of eve and had placed upon her feet the sandals she had adapted for this terrain, which had studs on the bottom for traction and were padded with leather for her support. Her handmaiden laced them up while she checked her herbal contents for the third time that she had prepared a week ago for this occasion. She mumbled out loud as she did this while having her sandàls laced. "Motherwort, Bloodworm, Basil, Thyme for fever, Hyssop and …Oh, I forgot the mint!"

"Selene, I am more than sure that Elena would have all of that."

Oblivious, to that, though it had surely struck a note with his frazzled wife. "Oh, Oh, you are probably right. I am so nervous, what if something happens to her? What if something should happen to the babies!"

"Darling, nothing will happen…babies, you mean…"

"Of course I do, do you not think that I would not recognize that more than any other?" Almost not expecting an answer, she continued, "She will have twin daughters, just as I did." Her face for a brief moment looked far away. "I could not tell her, for I did not want her to worry. Not all women survive such a birth and I wanted nothing that would cause her distress of any sort."

Her sandals were finally laced and she braced herself and stood up to join the servant who summoned her. She looked at her husband before parting. "Juba, will you please find the cradle and have it ready for her? Have someone bring it over as soon as possible please…?" She then ran off to join in the biggest day of her daughter's life thus far.

XXXII

A special hut was built for Jubilla for her to give birth since she was the Queen. There was a smaller round-house built especially for this purpose already in place on the corner of the settlement for all of the other women to use at their time for birthing. This gave the women peace during this process away from the other cycles of life. It also gave the other women of the village a focal meeting point for them to assist them in any way that they could. This hut as well as the newly constructed one was next to that of Elena, the wise woman and herbal specialist. The Druid priestess was summoned from Bellinos to assist in the birth as well as the female Bards to soothe the Queen in her pain and to help her with the natural rhythm of life.

Mothers had gathered to witness the birth of their Queen's first child and placed fragrant herbs in newly made garlands to adorn the hut. Jubilla was carried to the hut from her sleeping quarters by a litter carried by the mothers of the tribe as was their honor and right to witness another mother into their secret society and arts.

The royal birthing-hut was completely covered in soft white rabbit furs which would collect the birth blood of the Queen. Incense was added to a fire in the center of the small round hut. Selene had requested that of Frankincense and Myrrh since her daughter was made priestess recently of Isis and this was sacred for their religion as well. How odd was the scent of ancient Egypt mixed with those of the land here, yet strangely they began to mingle as one.

Selene entered the enclosure by moving aside a leather door cover fastened to the top of the opening. She joined the forms of Elena and Brigit, the Arch Druidess. Brigit was about forty years old and had endured the vigorous nineteen years of initiation as any Druid had done. She was deemed in a ceremony four years prior to be the Arch Druidess from the words of an Ovate for she was also sacred in that she was conceived at a Beltane ritual in sacred ceremony to her mother who had birthed her on Yule. For she was sacred from birth and her powers extreme.

Elena and Brigit had met with Selene to discuss the sacred women's ritual of birth on a few meetings prior to the date in which they stood at the present time. Together the three wise women melded their knowledge to assist the new Queen. The village women waited outside and passed the time in song. Ancient songs, Selene and Jubilla were told. Ancient songs from the original women to this land as they were brought forth from where they came from over the sea and mountains in a place far south of here, in a land of desert and a large River from which all women sprang from.

Their voices rang up to the skies in high unison melting with the arms of the birth of the sun. The warmth of the Summer day spiraled into the small roundhouse to assist in the arts of the three mothers.

Jubilla lay there helpless to the life force which sprang from her body and carried her to a place in her life that she had never been before. She was excited and yet very afraid for she had heard of things going wrong. Though somewhere deep inside of her she knew that nothing would go wrong for her this day and she would see many other births from her womb to bring forth it's life to further nourish this tribe which she was High Queen to.

As her body took on strength she knew that she did not possess but had learned was the strength of the Goddess to assist her, she writhed about. The pain becoming incessant, and still the women had told her that it was not time to push as of yet. More and more together her bodies contractions became and pulling her with them. The women outside were singing louder and louder and children were now asked to leave or to still themselves for the moment soon to come.

As if the outside world and the inside world were one, the women outside had ceased their song to start with the pounding of many drums which had began to pound the life-beat to her own body. The mothers beside her told her that it was now time to push. And push with all of strength she did. The women outside chanted, "Push, Push, Push!" In unison with her body. Jubilla did not know nor even cared how the outside and even the women inside knew how her body was reacting to the forces of nature. She was busy bringing forth life. Her mother had pulled her to sit up for the final moments and with a flourish and great relief of pressure one life and sprung forth from her womb. Elena delicately grabbed this first daughter of hers to make way for the contraction and a half which brought forth her second daughter so close behind her sister, which was deftly caught by Brigit.

The twins roared with their reaction to the harsh cold world and to the bold new colors that stood before their tiny wiped clean eyes. The twins used their eyes for the first time and bellowed out their dislike. The muted noises that soothed them to slumber often was now loud before them and unfamiliar to them. The only thing they were familiar with was each other. Soon they were placed by cold hands onto the breasts of their mother, whose heartbeat they quickly recognized. Their hunger and frustration was encompassing their tiny world brought hopelessly asunder, yet they ere slowly being lulled into peace by the beat of their mothers heat. When each were placed to a breast to suckle the warm milk of their mother an ancient knowledge overcame them for their very survival.

Outside the royal birth house, when Jubilla expected rejoicing, there was a soft lullaby sang by the mothers outside, in which the three mothers inside joined in. For Selene had been taught the words which she had never learned to understand.

Selene had originally planned to give her daughter the ancient Egyptian custom of birth for her daughter as she knew that her mother would have insisted on. However, after discussing the process and of hearing of the birth process used for the women of this culture, she relented to their ways in being prominent.

For she felt somewhere deep inside of her that their way was probably the oldest way of all and was probably lost to the people of her own culture. For did they not mention to her that the very first people of this land came from over the sea and the mountains, over which she assumed might have been the very same that she had traveled over to arrive here. They had also mentioned that their original people came from a land of vast desert with a large River, from which all life sprung forth. It sounded so similar to her own birth land of Egypt that she hoped fervently in her heart that this religion was an older and perhaps more preserved version of the ancient Egyptian religion before the world of men had corrupted it. The words to the ancient's song sounded remotely Egyptian. It possibly was. For the women who sang this song had lost their meaning generations long before. She loved the way the drums reflected uncannily the contractions of her daughter and even the appropriateness of the lullaby instead of the joyous and loud cries of elation normal at a royal birth. She felt that it was much more comforting to the new born babies. New furs were brought inside and placed under the new mother and her newborn daughters, while the old and battle worn furs were brought outside. The women gathered them and had placed them in an elaborate carved granite box created for this purpose. The mothers would place all of those furs inside with each successful birth after burning the battle covered and bloody furs and gathering the ashes. This was a women's special sacrifice for the Goddess. She would fight the oldest battle known to bring forth life in the image of the God and Goddess. The small tomb would be placed at the woman's sacred mother alter in her home to sit beside the hearth which she was in charge of. Only the mother who shed the blood in battle could offer the sacrifice of the bloody furs. For they were placed aside for Jubilla to do just that.

Elena sang forth a song of the moment for the mothers in the hut watching the mother and her newborn daughters in the blissful joy of life.

"May the seasons of Life reward you,
Daughter of the Sun and Moon
May the Moon forever bless you
May the sun forever warm you and your own
Your daughters born on this day the third set of twins

The third set of twins to adorn the house of the great mother Ptolemy
The Great Queen of Egypt
The Great Priestess of Isis
Mother of the Sun and Moon"

This song of the twins was picked up by the mothers inside including Jubilla and then joined by all of the women of the settlement camped outside. For this was the birth song of the princesses and would be sung at their wedding and then at their funerals as was the custom of their land. For each child had a birth song unique for each of them. The two princesses shared this mighty and powerful song that mothers from all around sang in the joy of their birth and the health in which all of them, mother and daughters emanated with such fierceness and determination.

The men began to arrive at that point for only at that time were they allowed to witness the secrets of the women's mysteries. Juba rushed to the weary side of his wife and Cynfelyn found his wife and his new daughters.

Tears sprang forth from the old father's eyes in his remembrance of a similar moment so long ago. He recalled all to vividly his first time in seeing the tiny forms of his Drussi and beloved Tonia. He had pushed all of those memories that contained his long lost Tonia to the farthest corners of his mind in his inability to deal with her loss. Selene had guessed the cause of her husband's dismay in this moment of joy. For it was not their age at all but the memory of Tonia. For these two were so much in appearance to their own mother's birth despite their tiny tufts of wispy birth black hair. That wispy hair would soon fall off to be replaced with hair so blonde it would appear almost white. Selene and Jubilla were told that it was how fair the children of this village were at birth by Elena. For the children of these giant people were very fair that had surpassed even that of her sister Arsinoe's with her summer blond sunny locks of curls. The children's hair often appeared so light that it appeared almost white, though later grew darker and thicker. For the younger they were, some were even born hairless and some with only very wispy fair hair that seemed to take forever to grow.

Selene hoped that her daughters would have her and their mother's thick wavy hair instead of the ultra fine and too delicate hair of the children of the village. Though very pretty to look at and even made the children appear to her as fairylike. But she cherished brushing the long curls of her daughters even in their very young years, so full was their hair from the very beginning.

Selene wondered which hair would replace the baby hair they saw now that adorned the tiny twins heads. Juba pulled Selene close to him," Let us give the new parents some privacy with their babes and seek some of our own as well my love."

"As you wish." The two of them linked their arms together and made their way out to the path leading out of the village. For the day at this point was past the highest hour of the sun and was heading towards the time of the twilight. The two of them walked in silence.

Selene was thinking of the fact all to clear that they would have to return home, for she missed her son dreadfully and was content that her daughter would fare well in this new life of hers.

Juba, was thinking of the days of Tonia, which all of a sudden so long neglected came rushing back to him in torrents of un-solaced grief. Selene was jarred from her thoughts to observe the look of pain on her husband's face. She felt the cause of this in the way that women do and rushed to find privacy for his pain by her side. He went with the urgings of his wife for he knew that he could not ignore this pain so long denied to himself.

They found a place by the side of a small brook with a large flat rock beside it, on which Selene beckoned for him to sit with her. Like a mother she held firm her husband's weeping body close to her breast. She sheltered him so that he would mourn their lost daughter.

She knew without him even saying a word for the very image of their new granddaughters reminded her of that very same moment at their birth. It also brought forth the image of the tiny pyre that was burned with the form of Tonia. Her soul's flight to the sky above them. She wanted to preserve her body and place it beside the body of her mother and father in their tomb. Though Juba mentioned that it would only cause anger from Caesar Augustus who they were greatly indebted to, for he hated the practice of the ancient Egyptians in that ritual.

Selene recalled also the pyre of her brother as well and abhorred the custom of the Romans. Angered over that until her meeting of Elena, who had explained to her that it was similar to the customs of her own people as well. They believed that in burning the bodies of those who died it was only enabling the release of the soul at an easier pace for it to better walk amongst them in the spiritual dimension.

For Selene felt the contraction of her husbands sobs heave forth from his powerful body in the silence of his sniffled sobs, She knew he was healing from the torment and pain over his daughter's death that he never allowed himself to face.

She had felt that there must be great truth to what Elena had informed her, since she did often feel the spirit of her brother and daughter close to her when she was in the Tween Time of sleeping and wakeful states. She felt their strong and powerful essence beside her very real in those moments. While her mother and father's image was fading with the years like the scent of Jasmine after leaving the room where it once filled. It trailed behind her in life leaving a weaker essence over the years. Unlike the harsh and powerful scent of her brother and sister which reached her before she was fully awake. How odd.

She tried to explain this to her husband, which he politely requested that she not speak of that to him. For he was a man of science and refused to believe in a thing that he could not see, touch or analyze. The spirit realm was alien to him and would never be reached in his all too logical mind.

Though at this moment, she knew that the memory of his daughter so long ago lost to him placed in a trunk in the farthest corner of his mind, which had long since been covered with the cobwebs of distance and neglect-had finally been breached. She felt for him more than ever in this moment for he seemed all the more human to her and their bond was made solid in those moments of his grief.

Juba's body writhed in agony recalling the guilt that he had felt in that he was never as close to his lost Tonia in her life as he was to his Jubilla in her later years and especially in that journey. Anger at this only made the pain more intense. For he was angry that he had not spent more time with Tonia, that he did not know that he had to. For his father had never spent much time with him before his father was killed. For his father had fallen on his sword before the young Juba even had a chance to even know him. Nothing was passed down to his son of the family. He had learned the most information about his own family and lineage in his many years of captivity in Rome. He had learned some of the things one would learn from a father—from Augustus. For Augustus was the one who had the celebration and arranged the ceremony for him to adorn the toga of manhood, as his father should have done for him.

Juba was angered in that he should have learned of his pain of his father's example and had tried to do the opposite with all of his children. Instead of that he had buried himself in the only thing that he knew, his studies and search for knowledge. He did not know how to be a father.

Selene had helped him on this voyage to finally approach his daughter. Selene had mentioned that he would be a good father in just sharing with his daughter conversations on what interested him the most. He was extremely jubilant when he found out that his daughter had shared the same interests as he. How sharp and intelligent she was! He could not wait to find out about his own son. Would he share the same passion for knowledge as did he and his sister, Drussi?

For he also realized with a start that little Juba would not be little by the time of their return and would soon be donning his toga of manhood. He wanted to be there for that and to plan it. He would not be remiss ever again in his being a father.

He was angered that he never did this for Tonia who was a tiny bundle of joy and ringlet curls in her life. She was brought to him on occasions of state when he paraded his children for his subjects, but he would returned them to their mother and palace servants who knew more of their care than did he.

He did make the most of his time here with his new-found relationship with his daughter. He would often seek her out with each new discovery of the plants and culture of this land and debate every aspect of it with her. He began to look forward to those discussions and his days began to depend on them.

Selene had told her that Jubilla would be very busy now with the twins and the discussions with her would have to be put on hold. He reluctantly agreed, though fervently wished that there were palace servants to take care of the needs of his twins so that he, as king could enjoy the conversations he was beginning to cherish with his own daughter with her meticulous and very intelligent outlook on things.

His sobs started to wane and he collapsed beside his wife in exhaustion over the power of repressed emotion. Selene collapsed from the long hours beside her daughter in the birthing-house. She had folded her body inside his and they both lay on the sun drenched summer rocks softened by moss in the needed slumber of exhaustion.

XXXIII

After the celebrations of the Summer Solstice, the preparations for the return journey began in earnest. For Selene and Juba had to return to their Mauretania to assist their son who had ruled in their stead for two years.

Wagons and chariots were loaded while others were commissioned to meet them on the other side of the channel in Long-Haired Gaul for their final part of the journey home.

Juba had gathered all of his dried herb samples and was repeating madly to himself, so that they were fresh in his mind to write down as soon as he was able to attain writing materials. For his had long since been depleted in correspondence with his homeland. He was helping the men to secure the ropes which held all they would take back to them in supplies for their journey as well as the gifts from Cynfelyn and his kingdom.

Selene was visiting with the two princesses who were sleeping side by side in the cradle that she had given to her daughter. The cradle looked so foreign in it's new home, yet strangely in place. Selene also noticed with glee that the beginnings of bright red hair was forming on the heads of the two princesses who were named Drusilla and Cleopatra. For only the mother had the honor to name the daughters while the fathers named the sons. The mother playfully called them Silla and Cleo in her special way.

Jubilla and her mother sat on the ground by the side of the family cradle. Selene had a copper bowl with gathered fresh water from the brook, placed securely on her lap. For she was going to do a mother's reading for Jubilla on the fates of her two daughters. Jubilla was asked by her mother to touch the water and to sprinkle it on the foreheads of her two daughters and then to place some on her own forehead. Jubilla did just that at the request of her mother and then placed her hands on her own lap. Selene glanced over at the mother, her own daughter and then to the tiny redheads of her granddaughters, Cleo and Silla. She traced the rim of the copper bowl with her finger and softly chanted as her own mother had taught her and she alike had taught her own daughter. She traced the rim three times. And reached into a pouch by her side and placed in olive oil scented in Frankincense and Myrrh for this purpose. She placed nine drops of oil into the bowl. The sun ahead was ignored as she slowly stared at the patterns created at the oil's mixture with the water. Swirls and Spirals formed in the bowl, her vision misted over while concentrating in the reaction. Her mind picking up responsive visions from her third eye. She saw two little girls with hair the brightest red that she had ever seen in her life, running in play by the banks of the brooks where she had retrieved this very water in the bowl vibrant with visions of the future. They appeared to be about twelve years old, for the first signs of womanhood were observable in the small tunics they donned in play. Their hair shone fiercely in the summer sun. The birds hovered all around them and the air seemed alive with tiny yellow butterflies that surrounded them the while. A hand reached out from behind the bushes clad in the gear of a Roman soldier. A soldier weary, had heard the noise from the young girls and had hidden behind the bushes deep in foliage to stalk out his prey. The hand grabbed the red curls of one of the girls, the other stood paralyzed in fear for a brief moment and then ran screaming back to warn her tribe of this horrendous act. This warning vision had emanated the reaction of such on the contours of the older Queen and mother's face. For Jubilla jumped up from her warm summer gaze at her tiny daughters and uttered, "What is amiss mother?" Selene was startled out of this and the vision faded. She would not know what had occurred, was her granddaughter saved or not? Part of her did not want to tell her daughter, though knew that she had to from the look on her own face could not be concealed at this point from her knowing daughter.

"Drussi, you first must understand the family prophesy of the twins. All in our line will achieve greatness, though must avoid the water for it will only bring death to us all."

Jubilla was forcing every cell in her body not to react to this, but held firm to sit still to await the wisdom of her mother. She nodded for her mother to continue.

"I have brought along with me for you to have the words I have deciphered from a prophesy that was passed down to me. As you know Helios died by the sea from an illness caught while on ship to live with us, and then Tonia was killed by her reaction to creatures from the Sea. Which is why you are not allowed to eat any shellfish of any kind, nor have ever learned to swim." She saw the rapt attention of her words on her daughter's face and gained the strength from somewhere deep inside to continue. "Please be careful not to let your daughter wander alone over, by the side of the brook without proper guards." Jubilla knew the wisdom of her mother's visions and took careful heed to obey them.

"Also, you know that upon my death, you will receive my version of the scrolls that you will continue for all of our daughters. In this age of men, though far from here. It would be forgotten without this. I also have seen that someday generations from now the world of men will conquer all of the secrets of women and we will be their property as they practically are in the world as conquered by Rome. Keep this knowledge safe and make sure you know which of your daughters will receive this honor in turn. For you will have one more as well as many strong sons with Cynfelyn. I have dreamed of this, Elena and Brigit have only confirmed the validity of them with their own similar dreams. Do not let your daughters wander without guard. For the Romans seem far away now, they look to this island with thoughts of owning it. Maybe it will not happen even in their own generation, but still the fear is very real. For the future generations of your daughters will have to fight to protect their very own gender from being erased and subdued in the world of men that I return to. I am very lucky to have your father, for I could have easily been lost in it myself and kept in a harem in competition with many other wives. But your father had been true to me and of all of us. I will try to visit you before I breathe my last on this earth, but know that our palace is always your home." Mother and daughter embraced, knowing that it was finally time to get back to their own lives.

XXXIV

In Mauritania, word was received by Juba Ptolemy of the return of his parents from faraway Keltoi lands. On this particular day, he was celebrating his thirteenth birthday. As he reclined on the couch beside his young wife Julia, he would appear to one who did not know the boy personally, to be of a much older age due to the calmness unusual in a youth of only thirteen. He had hoped fervently that his father would return to rule in time for him to don his toga of manhood. It would mean a lot for him to have the presence of his father at this time. For he had known that it meant much to him in that his grandfather was not there at all for this. Only the man who had practically murdered the man in his stead, Caesar Augustus. Augustus might well have pushed the sword into both of his grandfathers and grandmothers for that matter. For all he had done to destroy them all, his legacy. At least he would have a kingdom to rule, unlike his poor Uncle Ptolemy, who constantly raved about his lost Egypt and family.

He had learned much about the famous Caesarion from both his mother and uncle. Though his uncle Ptolemy and aunt Arsinoe were very young when all of the events occurred which brought history to this very moment and eventually led to the throne upon which he sat for his father.

He would miss his sister Jubilla, for they had been close as children in that there were no other children in the palace for them to play with. They were practically separated from all others in that they were royalty, also in accordance with their mother's fears of losing another child. They were also most often by the side of their mother growing up while she ruled the kingdom, when he had learned much of the course of administration of the kingdom.

He also had heard about the marriage of Arsinoe and Drennedd in correspondence from both of his parents. His father was a very ardent letter writer. Of which he was grateful. For he had learned more of his father than he did when residing in the palace before their journey north. For most of his childhood which was fast coming to an end, his father had spent much of his time with his studies in his vast personal library, or out on expeditions in search for more knowledge. His mother would maintain the kingdom in his stead for most of the time.

He vowed to himself that when he came of age to rule, he would be the one who did most of the work. For he did not inherit his father's unquenchable thirst for knowledge. His thirst was for battle as well as the acquisition of the finest garments of the known world. Both off which he would not have any until his toga of manhood was worn. Also it was a time of peace in Rome and it's many territories, and there were no battles to be fought, other than keeping the borders in line.

Juba wanted desperately for his father to come home to see a man sitting on the throne and not a child that he called his little Juba. He was not little any more. He had a wife, though mainly in name, for the marriage would also be consummated at the time that she had reached her full flower of womanhood as Julia would call it almost mockingly to him. All he could do was wait until he was finally allowed to assume his full roll as husband and then begin to produce the heirs for the continuation of this kingdom so that it would not end up in the hands of Caesar Augustus.

At the present time there was nothing to fear in that. For Augustus was using the time of peace wisely in reviving the old constitution that had fallen into disarray during the many years of civil war. Augustus was bringing back the glory into the state of Rome and doing a fine job of it. He was not out reaching for more territory as Romans were mainly known to do in their quest for conquering and blood. Instead he was learning how to deal with what he already had. For Rome already had a vast amount of territory under it's possession and the citizenship mainly went only as far as Rome itself. Augustus did extend citizenship to all of Italia, which quelled even more possible rebellion within the territory. He implemented many other changes as well which stabilized his lands.

Ptolemy admired and hated this man at the same time. He could not tip the scale entirely either way. For he admired his great skills in statecraft and was learning from all that he was doing with the constitution. Though he could not neglect to note that the man did everything in his power to destroy his grandparents besides cause their actual deaths. Though he darkened their hearts enough to have caused them to fall in their last thread of honor on their own swords from all the pain caused by Caesar Augustus and his horrid campaigns against them and all that they stood for.

He wanted to be an even better administrator than Augustus was and had studied all that he could in statecraft in order to do this successfully. He also watched him very carefully and watched the results of each new law enacted and in every move made politically. He had further read all of the published works of Julius Caesar and of his campaigns in glory. He could not wait until his uncle Ptolemy returned for when he was made ruler, he would put his uncle in charge of the whole army with his battle skills and knowledge of war maneuvers.

As he thought about all of this while daintily picking at the seeds of his pomegranate, he glimpsed over at his wife in her own leisure beside him. Her raven tresses were artistically gathered to resemble those of Aphrodite in her ancient glory, in the style that his wife most favored. Her eyes covered by their long thick dark ebony lashes. He loved her eyes, cold and light as the ice that topped the mountains of Syria, her homeland and place of her birth.

He admired the way in which she rapidly adapted his customs as her own and she was even beginning to lose her accent to take on the classic and sophisticated elocution most seen in Rome, to where she had never been. She had learned this through the incessant teachings and her ardent absorption to fit in to her new culture.

For it was all the rave in court to speak as if one had just strolled from the gardens of Rome, rather than where most of it's citizens were located in it's far reaching territories. For one had to call his young wife Domina and not just the royal highness as was customary of this land. For Julia had acquired a love for Rome and everything from it. She would have nothing in her suite that had not been made in Rome itself. Even her food and wine had to be imported from there. She would not let anything from outside of that city touch her delicate taste buds at all, or the palace would hear of it and nothing else for days, such was her temper when irked.

Ptolemy found her tempers rather amusing in that she was still a small child of only ten years old. He did have to pull her aside one day and tell her that soon she would be a queen and her tempers would not be tolerated by the people. For he reminded her of his own mother's graceful and tolerant temper. This had set her off on such a tyrannical temper that she would not talk to him for three days. He had learned fast never to compare her with his mother.

He could not wait for his parents to return. Especially since Julia was continually taunting him about them having to become parents. He had promised his mother and father before they left that he would wait until she had reached of age of when he would don his toga of manhood. Sometimes, though he just could not endure her tantrums as all.

Julia sat there quietly and dazed off in the distance. He was not sure what had caught her gaze, and questioned her about it, "My princess, what ever interests you so?"

She turned her attention to her husband and rolled her eyes. For she could definitely not tell him that her gaze was lingered on the guard standing by the fountain of their dining chamber. That would be rather funny if she had though. But decided politically not to. For she was not queen yet and had learned from her mother and the other women in the harem where she as raised that one could not trust anyone with secrets such as that. It could even mean their own lives if caught by their husbands.

For she had recalled a day when she was only six years old when her own aunt of only fifteen years of age was caught talking about her feelings about one of the guards of the palace. It had reached the words of her husband, a valued soldier in her father's army. He had all of the women in the harems witness what could happen if the thoughts of wives began to wander.

She recalled the last time that she had seen her aunt was when she appeared in dusty rags her hair wildly trailing about and catching in the wind of the courtyard where they all had gathered after a month of captivity in the palace dungeon. Her aunt was kept in confinement and kept alive only for this moment and valuable lesson to the women of the palace harem. Aunt's hair had lost it's luster and barely clung to her scalp on an emaciated head in which her sunken eyes had been dulled as well. So was the life lost behind them prior to that moment from her confinement. Her hands and bare feet were skeletal with her gown filthy and ripped that had barely clung to her gaunt and blue tinged body. Even her lips were blue. Her whimpers were barely heard over the formal allegations and reasons for her being there. Julia recalled being held close to her side by one of the palace women of the harem. Her own mother was not one for closeness to her own children or others for that matter.

He aunt stood there shackled by heavy iron chains to a post in the center of the courtyard. After the words were read the executioner swung out his large plain curved scimitar and cleaved off her already weakened and starved head for all to see. She viewed the scene with morbid curiosity and wanted to see what would happen next, of they were going to leave it there to rot, or if they were going to take it away. Her maidservant was repulsed at the act, though hid her reaction, though Julia knew, she could sense it. Julia was wondering why it did nothing for her. Julia looked out at the woman who was rushing her back to the harem quarters and very boldly inquired, "Slave, what do they do with the heads? Do they burry them or let them stay out there to rot?" The woman did not answer her and only rushed her back more urgently at those words.

She did find out later though, they had left her body to rot there and placed her head outside the womens' quarters for a lesson to be learned. She had stared at the head on a spike for hours on end, watching the birds pick off the flesh and poke out the eyeballs. She watched the crows fight over one eyeball and the victor pecking to death it's rival for the bloody share. The blood had dyed the spike a dark purple. The hair on her head was taken of in patches in the birds conquest for a share. She did not resemble her aunt at all after even two hours upon that spike. It had only gained her morbid curiosity in the effects that death had on people. She was greatly encouraged to conduct her own experiments in the future and could not wait until she was old enough to do so.

Upon reflection of that early lesson she had only learned that one had to be very careful and to play their part well so as not to be caught. Still the thrill of being caught doing something she ought not to do, only encouraged her and built up adrenalin rushes. For she had learned many ways as a child after that to be naughty, though play the part of a polite and respectful princess that she was.

Even after she had heard about the death of her mother who had run to the temple of Astarte to mourn the death of her stepson and daughter. She found her mother to be very foolish and would not run away when a challenge in life faced her. She would fight in all the ways that she was learning.

She loved the way her husband was kept busy in his lessons in statecraft. It only gave her more time to wander her palace freely, something that she was never allowed to do as a child, nor her mothers either. She spent her entire life before marriage locked in sumptuous suites away from the world of men and anything unpleasant, The lesson was hard learned from all of her harem mates inside.

She basked in her newfound freedom and had learned everything that she could about the palace and the people over which she would soon rule. She even watched the soldiers in practice and had developed a strong desire from deep inside her that she could not control her feelings that were becoming very powerful in her very young body.

She knew all about sex and had seen the many ways in which the harem women were pleased when their husbands were away. Such was not kept secret from any of the children. For sex was nothing to hide, nor be ashamed of as were the Romans and their squeamish ways. They might have hid their women away, but unlike the men from where she was from, she believed the Roman men to be ninnies in bed. This she could only guess about since she was too young to even know any of the true feelings for herself. She had tried in vain to engage her young husband to play with her and to discover their bodies. She had to rely on the palace eunuchs for that. She had soon trained no more than ten palace eunuchs to please her in the ways she wished. This she had learned from her mothers and aunts for they had done the same.

Ptolemy was so oblivious to the many desires of his young wife and would soon learn about them when he felt the time was right. For he was just beginning to enter manhood physically, and she still had some time to go. Though she was already mastering the woman's secrets in alluring men as prey for her many wishes and whims.

She realized that her husband was trying to gain her attention. She batted her eyelashes at him as she knew that he liked, "Nothing, Juba, nothing at all. I was just thinking on how delicious this pastry is, from Rome no doubt?"

Ptolemy had learned long ago it seemed to not tell her otherwise. "Of course."

"Juba, will you be meeting with your Calvary on the morrow?" At his nod of confirmation she inquired, "May I perhaps join you, for I would very much like to see how they have managed with the new Syrian maneuvers that they have learned from that retired Calvary commander that I had brought over with my retinue."

"Why of course. I had never known you to have an interest in battle maneuvers? Anything that I can do to make you happy."

She smiled at that and had continued to pick at the grapes in her plate, when her interest was suddenly diverted to the seeds of her husbands pomegranate that he was delicately picking out one by one to taste in turn. She loved pomegranate seeds in their squishy contents of sweetness mixed with a sharp tartness that bathed her sensitive tongue. She could not get her own, but sought out those of her husband's who noticed her desire and rapt attention. He then reached out to give it to her to finish. She giggled and finished them with full vigor like a cobra in the craftiness of conquest.

XXXV

Arsinoe was only beginning to adjust to her new home and situation. She was made a queen, though under the realm of her niece and Cynfelyn. Her husband was the Chieftain of the tribe of the Belgae. She found her new home cozy with an incredible view of a fierce and hungry ocean. The wind soared across the frothing waves in a scream which would penetrate her soul. She had learned about the Silkies which were reputedly the ancient people who inhabited the vast island which was her new home. These Silkies were people of the ocean who were donned in the form of a seal by day and by evening during the Full Moon would in turn don their human form. They were magical creatures in which the people of the tribe that she was now to rule over, had taken on as their own ancestors due to intermarriage with them long before time was recorded.

The people who lived by the sea were incredibly talented fisherman and preferred to dwell in small round-houses scattered in niches of the rocks throughout the steep cliffs. The houses were themselves made of the stones from the cliffs of the purest of white and were hidden to most from view if one were not familiar with this area. The cliffs were ominous and practically touched the sky, though graceful and majestic.

The Belgae were famous fishermen as well as the women. They used the seaweed for almost every possible use imaginable, such as for kindling when dried, for garnishment of food and nourishment as well. There were also countless medicinal uses for the many different types of seaweed. She had always thought that sea weed was just that a weed and of no use. Arsinoe was amazed at the various uses and incredible value it had when one knew the properties of each kind.

The small houses were nestled a good distance from each other, though there was some order to it, which was still incomprehensible to her, though it was explained to her on many occasions.

Each house was separated from the others by winding paths along the rocks, concealed from the view of the ocean. From the tops of the cliffs, if one were to approach by mainland, there was absolutely no trace at all of any settlement whatsoever underneath them. Only the barely perceptible whiffs of smoke that emanated from down below, which the local people had planted the tallest of tress as close as they could to hide most of the traces of their hidden abodes.

The paths from the settlement in twists and turns finally led down to the many beaches where the docks were built of the lightest wood that she had ever seen. They were plain and again they were concealed mostly from view by rock pilings and brushes interwoven among the lengths of the docks.

Arsinoe was greatly impressed at her husband's ability to conceal so well their dwellings from possible attack. This she had soon learned was a great possibility due to the invasions of small parties of the mainland by roving Roman bands bored with the subjugation of the people of Long-Haired Gaul, the kin of the Belgae.

Though most of the Island people who called themselves the people of Pryttain did not believe any such attack from Rome was imminent in their future, her husband and his own tribe that he ruled over were all to aware of their need for preparation should that inevitable day arrive.

They had moved their original settlement into the carefully concealed abodes on the sides of the cliffs due to the devastation from the latest attack by a lonely and bored small group of Romans. They were tired and frustrated with their share of plunder from Long-Haired Gaul and of the pittance which they believed should have been more for their share of battle under the command of Julius Caesar. They wanted more than the lands that they were given for service and wanted to brave the temperate channel to see what they could find across it.

They arrived during the rule of Drennedd's father who was Leiwallyn, who was the Chieftain at that time and the cousin of Casswallon. The settlement at that time was peaceful and had only seen during the past several generations ships arriving for trade, though there were a few in attack mode. None of which ever made it that far, due to the great naval skills of the Chieftain and his villagers and those in the surrounding area.

On this particular occasion Drennedd was only three years old and had three older sisters. His mother was very quiet and did not talk much, though was very loving according to her only son. His father was constantly out at sea it seemed to the memory of Drennedd when recalling his youth to Arsinoe.

Drennedd recalled the day as if it had only just occurred. He told her that the mists rose out from the sea that morning as usual for that time of year when the harvest were all in from their crops a good distance from the ocean. The fires were stoked for the cooking to be done that day. He recalled that his sisters were out gathering the last herbs from their garden to be tied up and stored for the winter and his father had left before they woke to bring in the last of the soft shelled catches before the winter broke and the sea creatures would grow their hard shells for protection.

He was left under the care of his aunt who seemed so old to him at the time, in his being only three and a lot of work. For he would constantly run off on whoever was caring for him. On this particular occasion he had left the shady spot under the Oak tree while his aunt's attention was diverted to a loud noise that came from the direction of the sea. Drennedd had stolen his chance and left running out towards the bushes of ripe blueberries, looking for any that had not been harvested. He plopped himself down and proceeded to stuff as many as he could in his small cloak that his mother had made for him for the cold winter months ahead and was still clean and smelled of her and of the many herbs which hung down from the roof in their cozy round-house made of clay and tall grasses interwoven to harden and form a thick clay that would seem to Drennedd as if the houses were all made of the stone that linen the vast cliffs over the ocean below their village.

He sat there in the bliss of childhood engorging himself in blueberry juice, oblivious to the sounds around him. He was startled from his reverie to his aunt calling for him and had decided to crawl into a tiny opening amongst large rocks that bordered one of the crops.

He giggled to himself and hid. For he knew that he would be in deep trouble when found and probably get a trashing for his disobedience. His aunt continued to cry out to him, sounding oddly desperate. The noises from the sea were getting louder and louder and by the time they had reached the village he had peeked out through the minuscule opening to see what was the cause of the strange noises he was starting to hear all around him. He saw strange men whose skin appeared to glow brighter in the sun which reflected off of them and had large feathers attached to their heads. Some carried large swords unlike any that he had even seen before. He could not understand what was occurring for he had never in his life seen nor heard of such men in the most whimsical of tales that he was told as a child by traveling Bards.

His aunt had called out to him and he had noticed that she was joined by his sisters and mother who continued to call out to him and were more frantic in their desperation to retrieve him. He was frightened and he did not know why. Though he was more frightened of them catching him. He then noticed their attention was distracted at the approach, of which he learned later were Roman soldiers. One was ahead of them and had looked tired and dirty from his climb up the sides of the cliffs and walks through the treacherous pathways along side the oceans. They looked more like men, though were very oddly dressed. He thought perhaps they were Gods due to the way they glowed under the sun.

Drennedd wondered if his aunt, mother and sisters had felt the same way, though noticed their hesitation and how they started to walk backwards away from the strange men who were bedraggled in appearance.

The soldier closest to the women barked something to the men who were lining their escape route towards the village hiding place that was carved out of rocks and hidden. There was no alarm that had sounded and all of the men were out fishing. One soldier grabbed his youngest sister and had ran her through with his spear. He reached out for his other sister, who had broken out into a run. Two soldiers from behind grabbed her and proceeded to take of her homespun dress and raped her and began to pass her around to the others. Some more men were still arriving. The bloodlust filled their eyes and soldiers had gathered most of the women, children and elderly people from the village at this point and led them to an area under the Apple trees filled with the fruit of the harvest waiting to be picked.

A frenzy of horror and bloodshed began after the two young girls were impaled on spike that were stuck in the ground, a grotesque reminder to all those frightened women and children left. His youngest sister was barely five and her blueberry eyes were stilled forever and had looked out to nothing. Drennedd was stunned and too afraid to move from his hiding place.

He had told Arsinoe that the events that had occurred subsequent to that were so rapid, he still wondered to this day, if it had ever really occurred at all.

The soldiers were tired and drunk, fatigue had only accentuated any emotions they had. For the men began to bark back at their leader in defiance and proceeded to ransack the village and setting fire to each and every dwelling. They started to throw swords and spears and arrows darkened the sky in target practice on the women and children and elderly of the village. And as if that were not enough, proceeded to even attack the lambs, sheep, cows and few horses of the village. Blood spilled everywhere and darkened the ground with their hatred. It seemed almost as if it would never end, for frightened Drennedd stayed put in his hiding place protected from view of the soldiers with easy prey. The sickening sounds of the squirting blood and the begging and cries for mercy wrenched and tore at his soul. He wanted desperately to get out of his hiding place to be a man to protect him, though he knew that he would be no match for these men, when he was only a small boy of three. His berry-stained chubby baby hands covered his eyes for most of the gore and had not seen the actual deaths of his mother and oldest sister. He peered out again from his tiny fingers frozen in terror to see their mangled corpses lining the paths of the village. His mother lay beside what he knew was the body of his oldest sister by the dress that she wore, since her head was missing and her hands as well. Her dress was in tatters while her naked body lay bent and exposed to the Gods as well as that of his mother. He noticed that his mother still had herbs clenched in her grasp, the last of the Basil from her small garden plot which she would use to add to the meat dishes that she would cook for flavor.

The soldiers sat amidst the bodies of all that they had so ruthlessly taken away from him. The bodies of the only people that he had known, those that had raised him, those that had played with him. His grandparents were among those all crumpled and barely recognized by the child Drennedd who sat stunned and fixated as if a statue so great was his fear.

Those that made any noise at all were stuck by a sword or spear or any sharp item they had closest to them. His own cousin Tarydd who was only a year older than him and would often play with him, was lying face to the sky with his eyes wide open impaled to the side of the barn with a spear. His tiny body hanging limply under the sharp cold glare of the fading day's sun.

The men soon wearied of their sport and began to look for mead, beer, and had even found the stores of wine amphorae in the root cellars on the outskirts of the small village. In their quest they ruthlessly stepped on and over the many bodies of all of the people that young Drennedd had ever known in his short life. They grew frantic for alcohol and in their quenched bloodlust, they spilled great amounts upon their shiny body armor which had mixed with the congealed blood of those innocents slaughtered on this sunny Autumn day.

They sang in a language that he had never heard and ignored those cries he heard growing fainter and fainter, begging for help or mercy. He heard a baby's cry that suddenly stopped. He could not see that wide of range from where he was huddled beneath the large rocks on the side of the field. He smelled the pungent smell of death all around him.

He felt he should only crawl deeper inside, yet was strangely paralyzed in his horror and grief. The sickening stench of burning flesh had taunted his nose, he knew not from where this came and why. He did not recognize the smell and had only found out later.

The hours passed and it put him deeper into his daze at the fright that held him rooted in place. The singing of the soldiers grew less and less. Until suddenly, he heard further shouts, which was the battle cry and grief of the men who had returned from fishing to find the grotesque site that befell them. Drennedd could not recall much from that, because the sounds were even more horrific and loud. He heard the loud crashing of steel and screams and grunts of pain as if to punctuate the silence that surrounded the bodies of the women and children that he had known his whole life.

He must have fallen asleep, because he awoke to hear the sound of his name from his father and uncles. It was in the darkest hours of the night when the goblins come out to play, though with the desperation of his father's voice he ran out from where he was hiding into his fathers large and welcoming arms. His father dripped of blood which his tears were fast mixing with the adulation of finding his only son unharmed.

He was told by his father that all of the men who had killed the women of the village were dead, his father pointed to him the large bonfire of which their bodies were thrown into after the heads were severed to hang up on pikes on front of their village in warning. The skulls, when picked clean by hungry vultures, would be later bleached and then added to the wall that surrounded the village. This was customary for his people since the skull of the enemy was considered valuable in that it contained the power of their enemy. It was also a way in battle to keep track of how many were slain in battle for recognition.

Thus, Drennedd grew up with his father's renewed vigor and determination to make sure that there would be no further attack on their village when unaware-ever again.

Leiwallyn made sure that some of his men stayed behind to guard the village and had also been the one to suggest moving it to a more concealed place. They made temporary shelters until the village appeared that Arsinoe saw in her time.

There were only three women who had survived that vicious attack and had been so used viciously by the invading men, begged for death. Of which the Druid named Taleiddyn had concocted drinks of a nightshade that would give them death after slumber. Swift and painless. So fervent were their prayers for death.

The men eventually married the women of the tribe of Belgae from across the sea which were their distant kinsmen. They had forged a new bond with them as a result. The Belgae across the Sea would keep them in check of the doings of the Romans on the continent. Thus, a warning system had been created rather inadvertently by the men's desperate intermarriage with the women from across the Sea.

Arsinoe had arrived to a peaceful village that had suffered such pain that it was constantly a reminder even in the houses where they lived.

She had also learned that her husband was a very powerful man, a power that he had gained in later years from the large army that he recruited to his cause. He was extremely influential and very charismatic. His village might be small and the abode in which she and her husband dwelled; yet he was in charge of such a large army, that he was known as a force to be reckoned with.

She had learned a lot about her husband in the months spent in his village. He was a humble man and would not accept praise without complaint. The death of his father ten years prior had still caused him grief as well as the death of his wife. For when he loved, he loved deeply and completely. He valued how difficult it must have been for his father to have raised him on his own. In trying to keep after a rambunctious son at the same time as having to take him along with him on fishing expeditions to sustain and nourish his son and his people.

He had devised the plan of creating a new village partly from distracting him and others from the overwhelming pain of grief and the guilt of not being there to protect their women and children, but also to keep them and all busy. He wanted to give them a reason for life.

The Bards sang that it was a lesson to be learned, as Drennedd's father wisely projected this to his people that were left behind.

The village they created hidden in the depths of the steep and treacherous cliffs was amazing to Arsinoe, for there were winding paths that would lead nowhere and to everywhere. She wondered if she would ever learn about the many intricate ways of getting around in it, though understood all too well it's main purpose.

Her slippers, though worn from use and the constant washings of the streams of the Trinovantes brook, were very inconvenient for this type of habitat. She had been given by her husband tough leather straps to tie around her feet and calves that had were insulated by soft doe fur. This prevented her from getting scrapes from any falls on the rocks. Since she did not consider herself nimble in anyway, she had fallen on many occasions. It was difficult to adapt from one who was raised with large and winding corridors of polished marble that would span an eternity, whether in Bruchion, Rome, or in her older sister's Mauretania. She was used to a much grander living.

Though princess through and through, she did not complain, but accepted her lot. She did miss her Lyre lessons, which had to stop for a while so that she would grow accustomed to such a strange and unfamiliar way of life.

Her husband was sought out by many people for advice and judicial matters from all of the surrounding territories and other villages had adapted their village format of hiding amongst the cliffs in protection for themselves.

On a few rare occasions when she would walk inland, she had come across many abandoned villages and had observed men in training out in the fields that used to be crops. The only remnants of those villages were the unending stone walls that had crumbled from neglect and the abandoned shells of houses whose roofs had long ago toppled in from no one there to repair them.

The people of those villages who had survived had escaped the notice of that small war band, and fled to seek out protection from Drennedd's father, who had created a small army of his own. The people gave up their farming and combined forces with the other villages around to sell their ocean's bounty for trade for the crops which they had abandoned to gain the time to train an army for protection.

For they had learned when attaining willing brides from over the sea, that the Romans controlled large armies and that if they should ever reach so far as either of the territories, they would be a force to be reckoned with. The force that had found and destroyed the village of young Drennedd, was only a very small group of soldiers who were only looking for sport.

Drennedd had learned more from Cynfelyn when the two met upon Cynfelyn's return from his studies abroad and in Rome. Cynfelyn had explained to Drennedd the real threat of Rome, which most of the land of Pryttain ignored. The rest of the Island felt that Julius Caesar was a coward and had weaved their Bardic tales to illustrate the way in which he came over with his men, long ago, had taken one look of the people they called the Keltoi and fled for their very lives. Cynfelyn had urged Drennedd to not believe a word of this, and had explained the real fear of them. Drennedd knew from experience the damage that only a small group of uncontrolled men could cause and still felt the pain.

Drennedd was a good man and very simple in his tastes. His home was small, though made luxurious with the furs and finely woven carpets from Persia that lined the inside. She had even brought with her a few fragrant balls incenses to burn in her oil lamps brought from home, which Selene had given to her for her wedding gift so that she would have a little taste of home.

Arsinoe knew of the goodness of her husband and had tried many times to not think of Sion, the Bard who was training her on the Lyre. Though his vision tormented her, made all the more worse when he offered to join them so that she may continue her studies. For it had become apparent that Arsinoe had exhibited a natural talent for the Lyre as well as her propensity for all forms of music, along with her celestial voice that would pierce the heavens above to torment one's very soul.

Though her lessons ceased for a time in order to better adapt, she still felt incredible longing for her fingers to play across the strings to rip at her very being in the delight that it caused her. The elation that she felt next to her beloved tutor when in practice was overwhelming and had felt that she should also devote more time to her good husband.

Drennedd had patience for his young and eager wife. For she was eager to learn all about him and his people and would listen patiently to all of his ranting of the past and would invite discussion of his dreams and what he hoped to achieve with his army in case of an attack by the Romans. For they both shared an equal hatred for Rome. Her in the death of the mother and father she barely knew at almost the same age that Drennedd was when he lost his mother and sisters. Such an impressionable age to have left such fervent marks upon their very existence.

This was one of the reasons why she agreed to marriage with him, even though it took her further away from her niece. She understood his feelings towards Rome. She and Drennedd did not like the way that Cynfelyn abhorred the ways of the Roman in their city dwelling ways, yet in the same breath commissioned things to be built in his very settlement which emanated all too clearly his feelings for them. He agreed and sought out an alliance with Cynfelyn and bowed to his greater authority, though still he had too much pain to endure due to even a few of the Romans whose influence was fast encroaching upon the territories of Cynfelyn and neighboring tribes. Drennedd refused to let his people live like the killers of women and children that they were and despised all things Roman.

Though he allowed his wife to have some of the things from her home and culture. He even understood her language was Roman and taught her fervently the language of his own people and the main dialect of the people of the Island used in trade. He begged her not to utter one word in Latin, especially after her sister left to return to her niece under the care of Cynfelyn.

Though his passionate hatred for all Rome was powerful, he reigned it in wisely and used all of the knowledge to proceed with caution. He felt it more tactical to distract Rome from the shores that he found himself protecting with all of his armies force and might. Cynfelyn had warned him the real damage that could be caused with any interest from Rome. For, Cynfelyn warned, even in their small forays into their land would bring great danger. For they would return to warn the others and in turn would warn their leaders and eventually Augustus, who had the power to send over vast armies.

Though Cynfelyn had mentioned at the last tribal meeting in which all of the Chieftains and lesser kings met to discuss the situation under the leadership of the Arch Druid, Bellinos; he had mentioned that at the present time Augustus was relishing the time of peace and kept his attentions on creating a better rule for his own people. For Cynfelyn knew that the tribes would not fathom the idea of a constitution, in all the complexities of Rome, in their laws being known and administered by the Druids in their oral tradition. For the people of Pryttain could not possibly conceive anything written down as being law. They felt that the laws should be as sacred as the wind, ever molding to the wills and ways of the people. To write such things down would be taboo. The Druids enforced and interpreted the vast laws that the people of his Island adhered to. But it all boiled down to a strong and healthy stew of respect towards others, good deeds, and good will. The intentions of one's actions was looked at and interpreted by the wisdom of the Druids in the legal administration for any civil disputes that often broke out among so passionate a people.

Drennedd was a large man and very powerful of build, though Arsinoe was soon comparing him with his totem animal of a bear. For he could be very protective and aggressive when those he loved were threatened, yet he was loyal and kind as well and very fair in his dealings with people. She considered that he was also very warm to cuddle up to during the coldness of the ocean winds that tore through the stones of their home, as if she were cuddling against all of her furs that she had been given to keep her warm in this climate. He was slow to walk due to his hulking figure, though was sharp of mind in his ways of coming up with what she felt were very ingenious ways of punishing the wrongdoers. Their punishments would fairly fit the crime and very rarely if ever, had to be overrode by the Druids authority or Cynfelyn's. For they had even adapted some of his most common punishments in their own administration, so just they were.

Arsinoe had also watched in admiration the beautiful baskets woven by the women and girls of the village. They were of all sizes and had many uses. All were water-tight, so finely were they woven. The colors of various grasses and thin branches were added together in clever patterns. Some of them were dyed from the many plants in the area adding vivid and bold statements of the artists.

They were a large people and tended to be rather plump since they had abandoned their crops and farming ways, those that dwelled on the cliffs for protection. Those that lived inland preferred to mind their endless flocks of sheep, goats and other animals adapted to the treacherous and steep hills and cliffs that were scattered along the coast for a great distance inland.

Their women focused most of their talents for color in their beautiful basketry, while their clothes were simple and dull in color. They sang with almost everything they did and had a genuine joy of life. Their well-being was contagious to Arsinoe, who was learning some of the songs for herself.

They were also great cooks of everything caught from the sea. The meat of their diet consisted mainly of mutton, wild boars that hid in the depths of the forest that seemed to cover this whole of this great Island, young lamb, and cattle which was mainly gained from trade for their usual over bounty of sea creatures due to their uncanny talent for procuring such large hordes with each expedition along the coast. They did not travel far out to sea, but stayed rather within main sight of the land, where they found more than enough to feed their own people as well as extra to use in trade with the surrounding tribes.

Arsinoe was learning the meaning of contentment. A completely different emotion to be expected from living a lifestyle so absolutely alien to what she was accustomed to. For her to sit under the vast colors of the canopy of Oak and Elm trees and others which she did not know the names of, with the sun sprinkling through was complete peace to her. There was no stress of any kind living like this with such peaceful people.

Still she prepared her settlement for the eminent visit of her older sister before she left for the main continent on her return home. She wanted her sister to be assured that she had found a new life that was suitable for her.

XXXVI

Selene dreaded this day, and of having to leave her daughter and first grandchildren in a home so far away from her. Yet, she knew in her soul that this was the right decision and would reap only favor for the future of her line, far away from Roman eyes and ambitions. She knew that it would be only a matter of time before their lands in Mauretania would be added to the purse of a future ruler of Rome. She wanted to stop by in Rome to better assess the conditions there, if they were to have a possible monarchy or not. She needed to know where Mauretania stood in all of this debris and political fallout from the civil wars. She also wanted to see her loving confident, sister and closest friend. To be able to cry into her arms at the loss of her daughter who was now grown with a family of her own. She knew that Antonia was the mother of two very young sons and possibly would not understand. She knew for sure that Octavia would understand her pain and that she would be well received by her.

All of the animals were loaded for her journey home and the feast especially prepared for this day was now another memory to add to her list of impressions and travails of her life. The day was new and beckoned her to begin the first steps of her journey to her own home and her rule that she was absent from for too long. Juba was like a wall hiding any pain that she knew he felt on this day. For he had finally had the time to get to really know his daughter and then he had to say goodbye to her and to the grandchildren that she knew he adored deeply.

They were all there to bid them a safe journey. Bellinos, Jubilla, Cynfelyn and the twins, each with a shock of bright red hair who gurgled in the loving arms of their mother and father. The top warriors were there; Andocos, Dias, Rues and Sego. Ptolemy chose to stay here and to assist Cynfelyn and to be by the side of his love, Ahrianred.

Selene looked at all of them as if to preserve their images in case she was not able to make a visit back to this land so very far from the land she ruled over with her husband. Juba locked his arm in hers in bid them a final Goodbye, since he knew that his wife could not find the proper words to utter.

Juba assisted Selene onto her enclosed wagon, while he mounted his Bay Arabian that Cynfelyn had leant him for the first half of his journey. Cynfelyn had imported some to breed with the local wild sturdier breed of his lands. He wanted to create a taller and durable breed for his war chariots in battle. He had taught Cynfelyn some of the basics of the horsemanship of his own people during his stay, and he knew that the King preferred the ride of that particular horse, similar to his own that were stabled in Mauretania. Juba had promised to send over some more horses for Cynfelyn to breed upon his return.

The official parting ceremony had occurred the evening prior when all that had to be said was said, whispered, elated or sang in verses created for that day for the King and the Queen of Mauretania who had forged their blood with the blood of the land that they gave their daughter and sister and brother to.

The carriage was sturdy and normally used to transport vegetables and pottery to local markets, though was especially adorned for the comfort of the Queen. It was filled with the many furs from this land such as rabbit, fox, bear, wolf, any many others that Selene did not learn the names of.

The faces of those she loved dearly and had grown to love and admire were fading into the distance as their slow heavily laden baggage train made their monotonous progress in the late Summer mud filled roads. The faces grew smaller in the distance until the bend of the road when they were gone to her altogether.

Her wagon was one of many in that entourage, as well as soldiers for their protection which surrounded them, carrying their spears, and swords. Her husband ahead of her at the lead next to the guide who knew the swiftest route of travel to their destination of her sister's settlement in the southern most part of this land.

This wild and unsettled land was so completely different from anything that she had experienced in her life, yet she had admired it deeply for them being so untouched by civilization and the ways that she knew and was raised in. She wondered if in fact it was a better way of life. She pondered over this tremendously, since she had sent her daughter here to live as well as her sister.

She did observe how well her daughter was adapting to the people and their ways and had even begun to sound as if she had been raised there. She was comforted by Cynfelyn's adding some buildings of marble to the settlement in helping his foreign wife adjust to the vast differences in culture. The bath houses were an enormous boon when most of it was completed during her stay. She knew that her daughter would add wonder to that settlement and would help in making it a grand city for them to rule in. She was amazed on what was accomplished in her short visit of almost two years.

When they had all arrived it was a modest settlement of round-houses with thatched roofs and long wooden structures that dotted the hills and was surrounded by a deep and penetrating forest. By the time that they had to leave a large part of it was cleared away to make room for the buildings and roads that would be added to the grandeur that it was becoming. The streets were slowly being paved and the structures were being made into stone and some of them with a Roman flair to them with their columns and gardens. Mosaics were being made and peristyles and arbors created to bring a little bit of Rome to the people who dwelled so far away from it.

Industry was urged into the area for pottery, sculpting and other artistic trades. Though she knew that Cynfelyn loved the beauty of the architecture of Rome and Greece and Persia, she knew that he had wanted to mix it with the talents and culture of his own people. That was why the mosaics and sculptures were created to resemble their Gods and Goddesses and incredible legends where everything morphed from animal to person and then back again. It almost reminded her of the Gods of Egypt in a strange way. They Egyptian pantheon had Gods that took on animal forms such as Horus as a hawk, Anubis as a Jackal, Isis as a cow, Sobek a crocodile. Even Serapis a Greek addition was part bull. That was a heavily worshipped cult in the time of her mother. For her mother had worshipped often at the temple of Serapis that was located in Alexandria, with Julius Caesar by her side.

She wondered if perhaps their religion had found it's roots with Egypt or the other way around. She had observed that the people of Pryttain had a religion which seemed to her untouched and pure. Unlike her own that was supposedly kept pure in that the temples of Egypt that had allegedly kept the same traditions for thousands of years. Though it seemed to her as of the people in this land worshiped something much older and even more untouched by time and outside influences that Egypt had plenty of. Egypt was a land that was conquered many times in it's history. They were conquered by civilizations in almost all directions; the Hittites, from the north east, the people of Sumer from the same direction practically, the people from the west of them that she had ruled over briefly from Numidia, and from the south from the land of Punt and the end of the cataracts of the Great Nile River. The River Nile made them wealthy very early on in the beginning of recorded time and others sought too often to have the riches themselves.

Yet, unlike most lands that were conquered throughout time, they kept their way of life intact. The conqueror only became absorbed into the intoxicating and powerful way of life and mysteries of the formidable Egypt. Most other cultures when conquered took on the ways of life of the people they were conquered by. The only culture which gave something to Egypt who conquered them were the Hittites who brought with them the chariot, which was perfected by those whom they conquered.

The people of Egypt had lived a lifestyle that had been the same as those who breathed the same air thousands of years prior from the first Dynasties and the times of the Pyramids and before. They practically wore the same clothes with very little change. So perfect for the climate in which they lived.

The only change came when her ancestor the first Ptolemy, a general of Alexander the Great had assisted him in conquering Egypt and later inheriting the rule over such. The Dynasty of her family created over three hundred years prior had adversely kept the ways of their homeland rather than the past conquerors of Egypt. They lived and learned and spoke Greek in their time of rule, until her mother had changed all that.

Her mother had seen how the Greek way of life was not helping her family and had decided to revert back to the Egyptian ways of living and worship. Besides, her mother had related to her how similar the Gods were of Greece in Egypt in personalities. It would not be as difficult as it would seem.

Perhaps due to that Selene was able to look as cultures seemingly opposite hers and was able to find some common link and even the admiration of them.

She had felt that the people on this land worshipped something far older and pure than all of the religions of the cultures that she had ever learned about in her studies an research. For these people worshipped out in the open and did not hide their prayers under tons of marble and vast columns and subterranean chambers cut out of cliff faces.

Juba had explained to her how advanced the Druids were in mathematics and some of their theories were more found than the ones that he studied in Greece. They had incredible knowledge in astronomy and in celestial matters. He was greatly impressed with their skills in recitation and memorization and felt it was most revealed to the people in the great recitations of the Bards, though he knew that it was much deeper than what was outwardly seen by their people.

Selene had found a peace in her short time here that she had never experienced before. She felt the people were simple compared to the many intricacies of the court life that she was accustomed to; though had a better grasp of the more complex aspects in life.

She could not understand much of the complexities of their belief structure, and fought to find some common grasp for her to hold onto and to understand them better. For she could not understand how they believed that all of the worlds were the same, in that the past was the same with the future and present. That the world most observable was the present. But that it all locked into place and connected in some way. She had felt that this was a better mystery explained by a Druid to her, but soon gave up. For she realized that it was too much for her to grasp at that point in her life. The average person understood this and lived it as well and made wondrous and colorful works of art to emulate this belief.

They accepted her and revered her in her place as Queen, though had not sought to understand her as she did they and their ways. She realized that these people were very content in their lives and needed no other things to confuse their way of being. She was strangely jealous of this and wondered why her own mind constantly craved for more knowledge of other people and cultures. Of how she was constantly trying to find out why people acted the way they did and lived the way they did. She wondered why people made some decisions over others and chose the paths they did in life. They told her they accepted it and that it was the way that it should be. Not wanting to know any further as did she in her hunger for knowledge.

She was elated when the Druids never turned her away or her questions. They answered her many seemingly endless questions on everything that came to her mind. Clouding her with even further complexities and creating vast mountains of further inquiries. They smiled at her in this curiosity. Bellinos had informed her that he believed that she had an ancient soul and would absorb attained knowledge as a sponge, and in the last hours of her life would find the connections of all that she had learned. For he told her that this life was one of her souls last lives and that her questions had been asked by many lives before this one. She was in the phase of her soul that was gathering any debris not learned from prior lives and would finally add all of it together and to reach the final life force on this material realm. Bellinos had told her that the soul travels in many lifetimes until it attained enough knowledge of being, when it would finally end it's search and enter a realm of eternal light that was in all times. He told her that signs of this eternal light could be found in the stars above them.

She was amazed whenever in the presence of Bellinos and knew deeply that she would miss him. She knew that with him and Cynfelyn, her daughter was in good hands and would be well taken care of. She smiled inwardly as how like a child she felt when in the company of Bellinos. And of how like a doting parent he seemed to her in his patient responses in perfect explanation of her ceaseless inquiries. He always seemed to know the answer to her queries. She would search her homeland to find another advisor to assist her upon their return.

The clomping of the horses and occasional snorting was not noticed to Selene as she sat back relaxed on her homeward journey in deep reflection.

She trapped the image of her granddaughters in her mind's eye as well as images of her daughter and new family. Tears trickled down her sun dappled cheeks and windswept hair unbound over her shoulders. She was unaware of this and went over everything that she had experienced with her daughter to block out any further tears and trying to concentrate on the happier moments together.

She knew that her brother and sister would be happier in this land as well as her daughter. She wished ardently that she was not the one who made of these important decisions sometimes. What if her daughter found out that she no longer wanted to live there and that things were not as peaceful as they seemed. She would be unable to contact her as easily as if she had been married into one of the Dynasties closer to her home. Selene knew that she had done what she and Juba felt was best for their only daughter.

She also noticed that Ptolemy was well content with Ahrianred and it seemed as if a weight was lifted from his shoulders in finding a home here. She knew that he had a difficult time back in Mauretania and probably held hostilities hidden deep inside against Augustus. In case that was so, she felt it better for Rome and her family alliance, that he was safe and far away from causing any harm in the farthest reaches of the known world.

XXXVII

After a very uneventful journey south, they had at last entered the realm ruled by her younger sister, Arsinoe. They had passed through lands of rolling hills, dark and formidable forests and through treacherous mountains and steep elevated passes. It seemed as if they were lost and wondered at the skills of their guide, when suddenly the lands evened out again and they could tell by the presence of Sea Gulls that they were headed in the accurate direction and nearing the lands of the sea and southern most tribes.

The Belgae scout sent out a blast from his horn to notify those in the settlement of the approach of the travelers to their realm. As if from nowhere at all, people materialized in order to greet the large travel retinue of the King and Queen of Mauretania at their approach.

Arsinoe, upon first hearing the horn from the distance was sitting quietly by the side of the expert weaver of the village. A young woman in her forties with hair as white as snow, braided neatly as the baskets that she wove. She sat there doing what she loved most out of life. For Hadwinna truly believed that she reached a spiritual plateau when she was at work making her beautiful and intricately adorned baskets, woven in with only the materials that she had chosen with her worn hands. In the act of weaving her works of art, she would often enter the spiritual world and was considered for her great talents in prophesy as a Master Ovate. He fingers were as knarled and narrow as the baskets that she wove. Every whisper upon her work was a prayer to the Gods, such was her talent and skill. Deftly she wove out her dreams so that all could enjoy them and sing of the future while at work.

Arsinoe loved to visit the wise woman and more often than not, sat by her side, when not ruling by the side of her husband. For the woman drew her into her shell of knowledge, patiently guiding the princess in the ways of her new land and people. Hadwinna had taught the art to this pliable young woman who sat still beside her. For she had long ago resigned herself that she would have no daughter to pass her knowledge to, until the arrival and connection she found with her new queen from so far away. The woman appeared to Hadwinna softer than the harsh land that she had found herself in. She pitied this young girl and found herself as drawn to her as the young woman was to she. She loved that she had ears to hear of her lineage. For Hadwinna was a widow, her husband had died years ago, and she had not found another to even compare with him. She missed him so much she was too afraid to even mention his name, even to herself, less she wanted to find herself drowned in her own tears of pain at his loss. With each season and year passing, she wove until her fingers could not feel the pain anymore. She never did have any children and lamented that fact all too close to her heart. And yet, out of the mists arrived this woman, this queen from a land so distant, she could not even imagine what it looked like. It was incomprehensible to a simple woman such as Hadwinna, of the huge buildings made of marble and the great sea that stretched farther than the eyes could see. She could not understand a land where it never snowed, with trees so alien that her mind could not even grasp it.

Yet, when she wove her heart onto the palate of her creation, creating nothing from sticks carefully gathered and grass, dried just so, she felt her art taking on new levels when this young woman was beside her while she worked steadily away.

Prior to her arrival in the village that she had married into long ago, brought over the ocean from the land of her birth; she had felt that her days would end soon, that her life was soon to end on this earthly plane of existence. Yet, Arsinoe brought with her a strange renewal of the life force in the weaver. For she felt that her life's reason was finally here at last. For when she was at her side her dreams while weaving were more clear than ever before in her life, even before when her husband was alive and love seemed new and fresh as each basket that she wove.

On this particular day she was sitting as usual by Hadwinna while she wove. On this day she had chosen to weave the pattern of her dream the evening before. The colors that she had chosen for this were from the dyes of the land and of the weeds of the sea. The colors were of every shade of blue to represent the great ocean that she had seen, perhaps the same that Arsinoe had explained to her. She knew not. Hadwinna chose fine dried grasses dyed in the many blues as the medium in her weaving. She added the dried stalks of herbs to represent the concept she felt broken by the great waters in her dream. She knew not what the concept was yet, though knew that it would play an important part of this princess' young life. That something was to be torn asunder from a decision that she was to make. That the sea would shift in it's course at the reaction. She knew that water, for her was also a curse and that it was played upon her very soul until she had found a way to avert this fate for this young princess that she was growing to love dearly as if she came from the waters of her very own womb. She knew that this young girl would be one of the many great legends that sprung from a mighty Queen's womb.

Arsinoe, distracted looked up. "Hadwinna, do you hear that? It is notice of the arrival of my sister. Come let's greet them!" Hadwinna observed that Arsinoe's eyes sparkle as she obeyed what her young ruler bid and sat up stiffly from her work. She placed down her grasses that she had lined up for order of use and placed a long piece of driftwood to weight it down, so that it would not be disturbed. Both of them stood up from where they were sitting with legs crossed. The younger one hopped up with more ease than her teacher who stretched out the cramps that she was long used to, though barely tolerated all the same.

"Hadwinna, I will have Taleiddyn prepare a poultice for ye aches, It worries me so, that ye do nothin 'bout it."

"Your highness…"

"Hadwinna, you know that I care greatly for you. "

"Arsinoe, worry ye not 'bout the pains I bare. I hold 'em them fer the greater cause." She smiled while looking skyward, for she had a great sense of humor, "Besides it comes 'long wit me chosen trade, ye know that fair chile. Are ye goin ta come by on the morrow to show me your progress with yer Sion?"

"The Lyre! Hadwinna… The lyre." Blushing furiously, for she could hide nothing with this woman that she was growing to love as a mother. "I have even composed a song for my sister when she arrived. Now hurry, you silly woman. She will have been here and left for home, if we continue in this conversation. I need to be there to greet my sister. What kind of hostess would I be at that?" Laughing the two women left the enclosure of stone where the weaver lived. Deftly the two woman climbed down a narrow path to meet up with the frantic pace of the other villagers. At reaching the top and most level land, they had mingled with several others with children running all around them to greet the large wagon train surrounded by Trinovantes guards. Arsinoe knew that at last her sister had arrived. She could not wait to hear how her niece fared with her first birth. Hadwinna called out for Arsinoe to hurry and to not worry, that she would catch up soon.

Anxiously she arrived to the place where all the others had gathered and found her husband greeting the weary travelers. She had found Juba first and hailed him. "Juba, you look wonderful. How does it feel to be a grandfather!" Her eyes beamed in her face as she spoke those words to her brother in law.

"Why, Arsinoe! It feels tremendous! She had twin daughters with hair as red as a sunrise. The glory of it was astounding! You look well yourself!" He called out in return, He moved closer to her side, which was difficult with the confusion of all of the people who came to see to the arrival of the guests.

At last by her side, he spoke softer. "How are you doing princess. Is all well with your new husband? Will I have a niece or nephew soon?"

He smiled so sweetly that she could not possibly take offence at his brashness, and whispered to him, "Your highness, we are trying, though nothing as yet." She looked down and Juba offered his arm, so that he could escort her to her sister who was looking around in all directions as she usually did when arriving at a new place. He always found her childlike curiosity amusing and it endeared her all the more to him. He at last found her and led his sister-in-law over to his wife who looked a bit frazzled, though still regal at the same. For she had insisted on wearing a Grecian style stola and a long flowing gauzy cape due to the intense heat of the day they awoke to. Selene appeared as if she was a flowing bird in her wispy and sinuous gown like waves in clouds, if that was possible. Her hair was askew in her elaborate plaited coiffure from the wagons heavy movement in travel. Yet, he admired on the way how despite the hardships of the travel in this strange land, his wife still appeared very regal. He loved that talent that she had, in no matter what conditions they would face-she appeared as if a Goddess had arrived in any place she walked. For he knew that she must have struggled to gain her composure to appear just so under the travel conditions and the heat of the day. Arsinoe looked magical as well and continued to wear the Roman drapery of which she was still accustomed to and seemed afraid to abandon. Her robe was homespun from local wool and was impressive in that it was much more sturdy and of a better quality than those purchased in Rome. Yet, she made it look oddly in place, here in her new village that she ruled over with her husband. She glided over to him seemingly from nowhere, so ethereal was her sister-in-law's presence. Her hair was even lighter, if that was even possible and glowed in it's summer glory. He always felt protective over her and had expressed genuine concern to her plight. She had reassured him that he worried for naught. Juba felt assured at Arsinoe's response and demeanor as well as her quick step to the side of her husband as Drennedd guided her over to her sister. Drennedd trailed his young wife and seemed to hang on her every word.

The two sisters eyed each other and then very elegantly walked over to greet each other. Juba and Drennedd were left standing to the side, while all eyes followed the two woman who appeared as if Goddesses in their midst. The heat and scorching intensity of the fierce sun was forgotten for a moment while all people stopped to witness the two sisters collide gracefully into each others arms in squealing delight. Both were very fair and petite, yet long legged and graceful, daughters of the Goddess Cleopatra VII. It was all too evident in their demeanor that the two sisters were not of the material realm. For both had faces as smooth as porcelain, and fingers and feet soft as if they had never known strife of pain nor a hard day of work. The people around them were not appalled by this at all, for it seemed as if the two women were more magical to them. Their eyes both shone bright in contrasting colors of deep blue with specks of yellow. They were of a different people and not of this land. Yet their blood was more than needed to give their rulers in future generations a requisite added strength for the years soon to come, as had been predicted by their weaver and Ovate Hadwinna. She had told them not to fear their new ruler and queen, for she had the blood of great women flowing in her veins. That any children born to her would protect them and their ways. Hadwinna had told the people to honor their new queen and princess from afar, for she witnessed great things from children born to her. Though some felt that it was odd how Hadwinna never looked anyone in the eyes upon the prophesies of the offspring of their new queen Arsinoe.

Hadwinna had not told anyone about the other dream that she had in which she foretold that Arsinoe would make a very important decision that would affect her life on this spiritual plane. She had greatly feared this decision, yet knew that Arsinoe had to make the decision herself when the time came and all was revealed.

Hadwinna finally caught up with her favorite and stepped in place behind her and witnessed the two women embrace. She felt incredible power between the two. She knew that the older was a priestess of a Goddess that she did not recognize and felt drawn to her. For she had learned about their mother from Drennedd, the leader of her people. She admired his decision in choosing Arsinoe as his wife and mother of the children that she hoped she saw in her dreams. She wondered if it were wishful thinking, then again thought the better of it and watched all around her in their reunion of sisters from afar. She looked over at Drennedd and was further hurt by his ignorance of her form. There was a time long ago when she was important to him.

XXXVIII

Arsinoe helped Selene in setting up camp and in giving the instructions to the servants as to where everything would be placed for their visit. "Selene, can you not stay longer."

Selene looked into the bright blue eyes of her baby sister and stated simply, "You know that I have to return to my people, for I do not know how much longer little Juba will be able to hold off any potential threat to the throne. For he is only a boy."

"I realize that and do understand, though can you not just pass over Rome altogether. For it will still be there for you to visit another day." Selene laughed knowing that her sister was trying. Both knew that Selene was extremely busy in all of her administrative duties and knew that the visit did have to end. Still, Arsinoe hoped that the fates might bring about something that would keep her sister close by her side. She knew that it could not be so and accepted it. But she did have fun making her sister laugh, for she almost reminded her of days so long past when she was so little that it was at the beginning of her memories. Of a time when life was simple and they all used to laugh often. Or that is how her mind had arranged things for her to cope with on a level that she could understand mentally.

For Arsinoe remembered when all the cares in the world that she ever had to face was on what color to wear and what scent to trace across her slippers as she walked endless marble corridors with no thoughts to trouble her but on the latest entertainment for the late meal of the day when all were gathered in one of the large dining halls.

Since then, even though she was such a small child, Arsinoe had too much unwrapped before her of the stark reality of life. For she adored the days remembered in Egypt and those in Rome under the doting patience of Octavia and then later under the wings of her older sister in a similar world of Numidia and then Mauretania. She had grown accustomed to her life being simple. Of not having to make any decisions that her sister had to struggle with, nor duties of any kind. For she had spent a great deal of her life without meaning. A figurehead. Known to all as the daughter of the Great Cleopatra and the sister of the Queen of Mauretania. Nothing was expected of her. Even the marriage that had been arranged for her prior to this one that had not occurred after all. For she was glad for that first marriage not panning out and in secretly knowing that she would have been confined for the rest of her life in a harem and probably voted out by another wife. This she would have accepted as her fate, had it occurred. Though it did not. She had resigned her to her life of having no meaning and was even becoming accustomed to it as well. Until the news of this voyage was first known to her.

She accepted the invitation of her sister to join her in seeing her niece off to the King of the Keltoi, and went along since there was nothing better to do at the palace.

She felt it rather amazing how a few words and later footsteps could so completely change ones own destiny. For now she felt that she had a destiny at last, a meaning to her life. For she had discovered her passion for playing the Lyre and the rapture that it entailed when she was lost in the reverberations that would echo in the chambers of this land so very far away and different from anything that she had ever known. She knew that initially Selene had dreaded letting her go to be married off to Drennedd and to a land which did not appear to fit her well.

Yet, each step she made in this new life took on a whole new meaning to her, for she had found her home at long last. Even if she was not destined to be a great ruler. For had nothing ever occurred in Egypt and her mother still lived. Arsinoe, would have been married to her older brother Helios, while Selene would have been married to Caesarion in the tradition of their family in tune with the ancients of Kemet.

The two sisters continued on arranging out all of the garments of Selene for the wash as they became lost in their own thoughts and in the safety of each other's company.

XXXIX

"Your highness…"

Arsinoe looked up to see her old friend and protector, Andocos and smiled as his large form filled up the small doorway to her hut. "Oh Andocos, it is wonderful to see you again…" She sat up from sorting out all of the gifts that her sister had given her that lay strewn about. She was sitting there dreading the organization of all of it and recalled wistfully the day when she had slaves in every room to do all of this. She smiled at how different her new life was and of how much she had to get used to.

"I had not seen you, dear friend in all of the confusion earlier." She looked down shyly at the jumble around her on the soft furs. She did not want to lead Andocos on she knew how he felt about her.

"I just wanted to let ye know how I fell about some things…"

"Andocos, you don't…"

"Shhhh, I know. I understand that one so fine as ye can never fell the same for me and I accept. But, I want you to understand that I would do anything to held ye, if ye should eva find the need… Please send word, if ye need me. Sion can also find away to get word to me, for he is also a great friend."

"I don't know what to say…"

"Say that ye will accept your highness, for I place my sword and bare hands at your disposal, should anyone try to harm ye."

She stood transfixed at the soft deep words of this kind man before her. She understood and was thankful for his most noble of intentions.

"I must warn ye your grace, that things are not what they seem in reality to all others. I fear for ye. All alone out here. I know things… I worry for ye greatly. Ye cannot tell a soul of this visit, only Sion-for he senses somthin' amiss…Trust all you can with Sion, though no one else-there is somthin afoot that I cannot place…please heed my words…Here-take this and send it to me-shall you find the need of my protection" He held out to her a small smooth white pebble that had the Druid's writing of Ogham carved into it. "It says seek and ye shall find…"

He looked down to the floor at his large feet as if the words had finally left him. Then suddenly he turned and left the hut so suddenly that it appeared to Arsinoe as if he might not have been there at all.

Selene had been satisfied that at last her sister had found a home. She found the way in which Drennedd doted on Arsinoe and was comforted on the decision she had to make. Her husband in his usual way was gathering knowledge from the fisherman of their trade. It was amazing how close he became to each person that he spoke with. People would hang on his every word and strive their hardest to please the unending curiosity of this intense King.

The village was simple and the people here were very warm and accommodating. She had even noticed Sion, the Bard from her daughter's settlement at peace with these people. She wondered if he would stay with her for long to help her sister adjust to her new home. She hoped that he would.

She had met with Hadwinna, the skillful basket weaver of this settlement and had commissioned many pieces to take back in trade to Mauretania and to adorn her own palace.

Selene and Juba had stayed for three weeks, though had to bid a further farewell, in that they had to make it back to their homeland before winter and rough seas.

Thus, Arsinoe and Selene parted with tears streaking beautifully down their sun glistened cheeks, clasping each other as if the world would end at their separation. Juba had to actually soothingly distract his wife so that they could part. "The winds have finally picked up, we must make haste to greet them." To Arsinoe he added, "Please keep in touch, I have left you some parchment so you are not able to make excuses!" He laughed to ease the moment and final parting of the two sisters.

Selene followed her husband onto the heavily laden boats that awaited them, "Please send word when you need me for anything! Never forget our parents dear sister! Never forget Helios, Caesarion, or little Tonia! I love you!" She fought frantically lest she cause a scene to keep herself from collapsing in choking and incoherent sobs. For it was at that moment that she knew in her heart that she would see the last of her baby sister.

In that very moment in the mist of time, the Druids teachings became reality to her when Arsinoe was no longer a young woman, but a tiny little three year old girl with ringlet blonde curls surrounding a halo of innocence and youth. Her chubby baby hands waved out to her as she climbed onto the boat and not the delicate hands of a woman who has traveled the world. "Seeny, don weave me! Seeny!" She heard her sister cry all over again as if lost in time. Selene caught in the fervor of her emotion's lost memory stalled in her step and almost lost her footing. She felt the firm grasp of her husband jar her back to the present and to hear her sister cry out in her adult melodious voice, "Selene you will always be in my songs sister!"

XL

The journey to the seven hills of Rome was uneventful and healing in a way. Bringing Selene closer to what she was familiar with most in her life, almost took away some of her pain at the parting with her sister. She knew that she would see her daughter again, though not when or even where. She just knew. But with her sister, she knew that it would be her last visit. She cemented the memory of her sister in protection and was slowly brought to the very outskirts of Rome, so lost had she become in her thoughts.

It seemed whenever one traveled to a place, in the beginning everyone was talking fervently and at a rapid pace in their anticipation and excitement. Yet the return was always filled with silence, as if to reflect all the knowledge and experience in life they had gained in the adventure now over to return to the continued existence of a life familiar.

The reality of her surroundings seemed to wipe away her fears and to place her experience of such an alien land into a cocoon deep in the recesses of her mind. The marble homes set on terraces on the wide hills swayed any dismay that she felt inside. She welcomed the familiar that was very healing to her at this time in her life. For soon she would be able to cry to her hearts content into the arms of her half sister and closest friend Antonia Minor.

The bustle of the great city seemed overwhelming at first, so far away from their everyday life for so long, she had almost forgotten the urban way of life so normal in her world. Wagons groaned in the weight of many diverse contents, one was even stuck on the side, with the driver shouting obscenities to the horse standing mutely to the side. People of all kinds filled the Apian Way almost to overflowing from the city and away. Litters dotted the way held by slaves carrying their burdens. Curtained in a cocoon of protection from the filth of the view outside. The road was large and accommodating to many kinds of traffic and seemed almost worn from excessive use. Wagons tred carefully along over the many bumps and jars in the cobblestone pathway. At this point in their travels they hired litters for their better comfort in travel along the Roman roads. For it was much better than to ride in a wagon and also more acceptable to their status.

They had passed over the Apian Way which was lined with the tombs of the many August Romans in many states of repair. Some deeply adorned with flowers of all kinds, some crumbling in the decay of neglect.

Selene had decided to close the curtains in her litter to try to keep the smells of the city refuse from reaching her nose, which was crinkling up in distaste. She had missed already the healthy air of the country and had realized for the first time in her life how detestable were the smells of Urbana in all if its glory. Unwashed bodies at close quarters assailed her senses and the many smells of the market place which she realized they were now passing, intermingled with the manure of the horses and mules used in transport that practically clogged the main roads to the city.

Finally they approached the domicile of her patron and half sister Antonia Minor that was set above the din of the city on the Palantine hill adjacent to Caesar Augustus' vast palatial domicile.

She had decided in her state of extreme fatigue to keep her litter curtained until their arrival. At the time the litter came to a complete halt, Selene realized that she must have dozed off briefly. For the noises of the main part of the city were somewhat muffled. She opened her curtains and found an older Antonia rushing out to greet her. "My sister! You must be exhausted from your travels! Hush before you say anything, I have arranged everything for your comfort. You are to rest and then join us as soon as you are fed and well rested. For I want to hear everything about your trip!"

She placed her finger upon the protesting lips of Selene's to silence her, "I do not want to hear anything from you until you rest! I miss you and want you in top shape so that we can talk, for I miss you so much! There is much to tell you as well!" Her eyes were lit up and Selene in her present state of exhaustion obeyed her half sister and let her self be led to her quarters. She had even noticed that Antonia had arranged for a large tub of copper to be filled with steaming water in which rose petals daintily sailed on top of the miniature current. Antonia smiled and placed her hand up over her lips to silence any protest from Selene and quietly left the room for the two slaves that she had left behind to assist the tired queen. Selene gratefully sank into a thermal bliss, relishing her senses to inhale the fragrance of the petals that she knew were from Antonia's garden. The travel wounds and pain began to slowly slip away from Selene.

XLI

The dawn broke with astounding accuracy into the small spaces shuttered against the evening chill. The air in the chamber in which Selene slept was malignant with suspense of something, though she could not place her finger on it. Some event was going to occur which would alter the very foundations of her whole being. She felt this as she woke shielding the sun from her eyes as it pierced into her sleeping chamber. She sat up in bed and gathered her Roman formal garment of stola and robes in the homespun acceptable fashion of Augustus's conservative realm.

After breaking her evening fast with delicious olives picked from a grove to the south of the villas where she was staying, she had inquired of a servant as to where she could find his mistress.

She was then led down a winding and dark windowless corridor and then out to the very center of the domicile. She found her friend reclining on a pillow clad couch in the center of a courtyard filled with a luxurious and very plush garden in summers end. The leaves on the small newly planted trees were turning a lovely bright yellow. She knew her time would be short with Antonia as well if they were to have favorable seas on their final homeward journey to Mauretania. She could not put her return off for another year. While lamenting the shortness of her visit, she resolved herself to make each moment with her closest friend count.

Her eyes scanned the elegant courtyard. It was simple, though she knew it was very costly with prepared with excellent taste. She noted the finely executed murals that adorned the exterior walls of the elegant domicile that surrounded this oasis in the greatest city in the world. There was a small pool made of marble in the center with a statue representing Neptune the God of the Sea in full splendor. The murals on the walls portrayed famous scenes from the works of Homer and Virgil. She knew that this was probably commissioned by Antonia, for she loved the performing arts almost as much as her famous uncle, the Imperator of Rome.

"Selene! You look well rested!" as the roman matron left the luxury of her friend who entered her sanctuary, she rushed over to where the queen of Mauretania stood taking in the oasis in the center of Rome. The serenity was overpowering to her senses and the reality of it struck her deep in her heart. Both she and Antonia were growing older and they were no longer the young children that they were when they first met years ago here in Rome after the death of their father the famous Marcus Antonius.

"Antonia! It is wonderful to see you again! I cannot wait to see your two boys and finally meet your husband Drusus." They collapsed into each others arms forgetting all of the years which stood since their last meeting. Both women melted from time as if they were little girls of only ten years old. For that was the moment in time when the friendship was formed between two sisters, it only seemed to only set the base for future occasions.

"Please sit down, would you care for refreshment sister?" She lounged down on her couch leaving room for her sister Selene to lay down beside her. "I love to come here to get some peace from each day, and like today, to gather strength to face the day ahead. "

"It is beautiful, you have excellent taste."

"Thank you, I only mentioned what I would like to feel when sitting here and the artists and sculptors brought it to life, life which I can reflect on."

"Selene, enough of the formalities, how are you truly doing? I cannot imagine how you must feel with Drussi so far away from you and everything else that you have been going through, my little boys are so little and yet I am so attached to them I could not bare parting with them."

"Why is it always the daughters that leave! For I was so much more in synch with Drussi than I ever could be with little Juba, who is no longer little anymore" Both of the women laughed at that in memory of the boy that he was.

"You will have to find another pet name for your son, Selene."

"That I will indeed. He is wonderful though and I truly miss him so. Perhaps it is because, I know that he will always be at the palace. I knew from the beginning that my time would be short with Drussi. Perhaps that is the reason why I made sure that I knew her so well." She rolled her head back and searched her eyes to the clouds as if waiting for their response at that. Antonia knew that she was not meant to answer that. She knew that Selene needed someone to listen without judgment.

Selene continued her speech in a whisper, "What does this all mean in the great scheme of things? Why is it that the daughters have to leave the sides of their mothers? I made sure that the chances of that happening to Jubilla were rare in researching that culture. For it is a matriarchal society…" Her voice trailed off and Antonia just sat there listening to the pain in her sister's voice ad she whispered of her heart.

Selene continued, "Could you believe that my own brother choose to be a consort to a warrior maiden? He chose to give up his namesake for the love that he felt for this women. I admire him so much for that and I hope that she treats him well. He accepted the conditions of her lineage." She went on to explain the warrioress' great lineage and of how the daughters born to the union would be greatly revered through future generations.

Antonia rolled her eyes in rhapsody and romantic illusion on that beautiful sentiment of the great Ptolemy prince. Her husband was kind, though locked so completely in his male orientation and preferences that she just might well been his breeding mare and nothing else. She was his figurehead and trophy to show off to his troops. He was on campaign in Germany at the time and was not known for responding to her ceaseless letters. He would pat her on her head whenever he returned from his tours of duty and then take her into the bedchambers for her to perform her marital duty for the state of Rome. She could only imagine what it must be like to have someone truly love her for who she was and not the bloodline that she would give to his seed. She wistfully envied Ahrianred and her valiant lover, who practically gave up a kingdom and the only home that he knew to be by her side. She thought it equally romantic how Selene had described that the woman was a warrior as well and would fight beside him in battle. After Selene left she would commission that the two of them forever to be carved out in marble to add to her dream sanctuary in this courtyard away from her humdrum reality and duties for the state and for Rome.

Antonia loved her two little boys and daughter Livilla, only weeks old; though she rarely saw them. The nurse took care of most of their daily needs, while she lounged in the domus unless summoned by state or to attend the chariot races which she loved on the Circus Maximus, or the plays performed in the lovely theatre productions. She would entertain on behalf of her husband Drusus, many of the notables in Rome such as his brother Tiberius and Julia.

She had Julia over a lot lately since the death of her husband Agrippa a few months ago and would arrange to have Tiberius over as well. Julia pleaded with Antonia and anyone who would listen to speak with her father for her to marry Tiberius in her stead. Antonia knew that something would happen soon to that matter since she knew her uncle was tired of her wailing over her Tiberius. Tiberius was still married to his love Vispania and doted on her completely, blinded by all else in the world. She had tried to explain this to the besotted Julia, but she would think of nothing else and did not care what the repercussions would entail to her and to Tiberius.

Antonia knew that Julia had feelings for Tiberius even while Agrippa was still alive and hated that her father had forced her to marry such an old man, as Julia often called Agrippa in secret conversations to Antonia. She told Antonia in confidence that his hands were course and rough like a commoners. Antonia felt sorry for Julia in a way, but assured her that she would do all that she could to assist her in this, though she warned Julia of how Tiberius might react to this maneuvering of his life as his own father's was.

For she knew that Tiberius had never forgiven Augustus for destroying his own father's marriage so that Augustus could marry his mother Livia. Antonia knew that Livia had moved on in her life years ago over this matter and accepted her path in life and had earned the respect of Rome for it. Livia was always by the side of her husband Caesar Augustus and supported his every decision. She also knew that the woman had considerable sway with him in turn. So she had convinced her mother, Octavia to side her on the matter, for the possible political reasons of the match. In truth, she was sick of hearing of the complaints of Julia about Tiberius being married to that ugly viper as she would describe the poor Vispania. Antonia really did not think that anything would result of her queries on the matter with Augustus, and was appalled that the reasoning from her and her mother with Livia as well, only brought forth a reality. For the very next day Augustus ordered Tiberius to marry Julia to further cement the succession of the inheritance.

Tiberius had no choice at all but to agree with his orders, for as he stood, he was backed further away from the position of inheritance by the children of Julia which were Gaius, Lucius, Julia Minor, Agrippina and Agrippa Posthumus, only and infant. Tiberius, as argued by the conniving Livia, and Octavia who held great power with both Tiberius as well as Augustus; would have a closer grasp to inheritance with the children that he would have with Julia. Livia was Tiberius's mother and had a charisma and power on just about everyone with the way she would extract even the smallest of things in any argument to sway anyone to her cause or side of an issue.

Octavia was just plain bored with her life and wanted to have something which would perk up her gray days lounging in state. Besides, Octavia could not stand the little chit Vispania, even though she was her very own daughter. She knew that her youngest daughter Antonia would be the one to bring about an empire with her charming ways, great intelligence and even with the extremely powerful people who were attracted to her and her company. Octavia had given up on her daughter in gaining any power in her extremely matronly and plain ways. She loved her all the same and realized that Vispania was only a reflection of herself in life. Of what could happen to a woman when you just sat around and accepted the fate that befell you without a fight. Antonia was her daughter who would fight and make sure that she was a part of history, rather than just letting history happen around her.

Antonia reflected on all of the women in her life and in the ways a small word could shape a destiny, for better or for worse. How kingdoms and empires could be created and destroyed just by the influence one made with people. She knew how Octavia felt about her as well as Livia. Though with the fast reaction of Augustus on her argument for Julia, did not know until then how much sway she truly had in life with the powerful people that she was surrounded by.

She admired Selene more of all of them and in the way that she did not meddle into other peoples' lives as a woman was forced to do in Rome out of sheer boredom if nothing else. The woman of Rome had very little influence in front of the scenes and knew that most of the power and influence came with their conversations and persuasions in dining halls and between the sheets with the men who could actually do something about it. Most of the woman just lounged in the sun, occasionally spinning as Augustus liked to see them do. For she would send her work to be done by slaves when he was busy in state matters and present her uncle with robes that she assured him were really woven by her. She laughed at this.

Selene looked up from her reverie. "Something amiss?"

"No, I was just thinking on how my uncle actually thinks that Livia, Octavia and I really weave his robes instead of the slaves that really create them in our names. He lives in a fantasy world and expects that we should become as the ancients in the time of the great republic. That is what he is trying to create with all of his sleepless nights, 'The Great Republic, Act II'. Honestly, with all of the modern marvels that we have to make life easier and the excellent prices for obtaining talented slaves on the market. I do not know why he thinks that illusion of his!" She tossed her head back in exaggerated laughter at the thought of her antiquated uncle sitting on a marble bench feeding the birds mocking the position of the Greek sculptures of the famous stoics, that he wished to emulate.

Just as both of the women were laughing for the joy of it, a guard entered the courtyard in the full regalia of the praetorian guard that Augustus had commissioned a few short years before for his own protection. Augusts had feared another assignation attempt as had occurred with his predecessor Julius Caesar.

The laughter died on their lips, for they knew that a guard sent from that elite guard was there on business. The sharpness of that late summer's day was only made the more dangerous and dissipated any further fun to be had by the regressed giggling women.

"Domina Queen Selene of Mauretania and Domina Antonia Minor, I have come from the Imperator Julius Caesar Augustus with official news to elate to you." Both woman just sat there frozen on his next words. Not waiting for their response, he continued, "There sits in confinement a boy who names himself Ptolemy Helios Marcus Antonius, with claims of being the son of prince Helios of the client state of Egypt. His August presence awaits your decision on the matter and your presence in council on the matter forthwith." The steely words of this man in the formal

Roman garb made the words appear all the more ominous to her. Antonia just sat there in rapt fascination, feeling the adrenalin rush of something exciting that was about to occur in her boring life as matron of Rome.

Selene in her trained capacity as queen to meet the demands and protocol of any court responded after collecting her breath that had seemed to evade her own lings. "Why yes, of course."

Antonia chimed in since she was in due course the matron of this domicile and as her duty as hostess, elated to her nearest attendant slave hiding in the corners awaiting her summons, "Yes, indeed, summon the litters for transport to the palace immediately." Which was still quite a walk which would have given her time to collect her thoughts. It was only that she and the other Roman of national status had promised Augustus that they would only travel by curtained litter and to avoid walking the streets without suitable escort and carefully concealed, being that they were also women was an after thought.

Antonia and Selene shared a litter carried by eight slaves down the winding paths over the hill towards the gates of the palace with the guard in the front of their retinue. Here they would be able to get to the bottom of the matter.

Selene was practically exploding with tension. How could this be? Only his own twin could possibly guess at the paternity of this claimant to her families' name. She assumed that it could be possible. Helios was fourteen before his sailing out to reside with her and his own death shortly thereafter. His son would appear to be at least fourteen years old. The same age as her beloved Jubilla, a Queen far away from the lands she was raised.

Antonia practically memorized how many steps it would take to reach the very gates of her uncles palace, since her own mother stayed there in a suite along the west side. Finally they were led to a chamber, which Antonia knew to be the formal meeting chamber.

When the litter was stopped, the curtains were pushed aside to allow Selene and Antonia to exit. Both women entered the room to face Caesar Augustus. Selene felt that his age was finally beginning to show as well the tension of all he hoped to create that lined his deepened brow with worry.

His eyes had lost their glow which women in his youth admired and flocked to. For in his youth he was very handsome it was reputed, though smaller than his great uncle, or father by adoption, Julius Caesar; who was a giant among men as well as his great height.

Augustus beckoned the two women to sit upon two folding chairs by the couch that he reclined upon. For women were not allowed to recline on couches when dining with him, but to sit matronly as was proper in chairs in the custom of the old republic, which he never ceased to imitate in every possible way.

Antonia shot Selene a look to comply with his orders. Selene technically had the upper hand with her status and should have been the one telling him to sit in her presence. Though in reality she knew the precarious position of her very throne and knew that it was owed to his great mercy in sparing her life. For in reality and in the ways of the ancients, he could have killed her and her siblings along with her own parents after seizing the kingdom.

Through it all, she held her head up to him in pride. Augustus beamed out looking straight at Selene, "My you have grown into a beautiful woman Selene! A very able ruler and Queen as well. I made the right decision when I sent you and King Juba to Mauretania. I am very proud of you! You remind me of your mother. Not quite in looks, for you are definitely the more beautiful. I think it is the power that she had in those incredible eyes of hers. She could break mountains with a look from her very eyes. Come closer. No, they are not even the same color. Yet they are hers truly! "

He waved at her to sit after briefly inspecting her eyes. He continued, "You have done well as a mother, your two children married. How does Jubilla fare with her new husband. She is a Queen as well?" He continued on for a while in this manor, practically having a conversation with himself. Adding each question without even waiting for a response. Tagging on each sentence just to evade the calmness of the air in the room. Antonia knew her uncle very well in his later years. She had clued in Selene on their ride to the palace about the way in which he would bedazzle each person with his tirade of endless words. That Selene should just respond emotionally and sit quietly while this lasted. Antonia had felt that her uncle did this due to his age and was possibly getting a bit feeble. For Selene had recalled a much more quiet and calculating personality and was unprepared for this.

Selene saw this outpouring of words for what it truly was. His way of toying with the emotions of his subject. He would toy like a cat to a mouse before the kill noting each reaction every word out of his mouth and watched as each word sank into his victim of his word kill. He was extremely astute and observant.

For in response to her assumptions of the great leader of Rome, he had ceased his words to let them sink in. Taking this for what it was, Selene sat there patiently, while Augustus studied her. She felt the many violations of his unwavering gaze.

Punctuating the moment of silence, his voice boomed in the room creating an echo that bounced against the coldness of the pink marble that surrounded them. "So, Queen Selene, what do you think of the matter? Shall I bring the boy in for your inspection? Or shall I have him executed as an imposter? What use would a child conceived in a moments folly be of use anyways." He summoned the guard to get the boy upon reading the reaction in Selene's seemingly emotionless face.

Selene was made all the more cautious at his extreme ability to read even her hidden emotions.

As they waited, Augustus continued, "He was brought here in response to allegations that his own mother the potter's daughter was the one who poisoned your brother Helios causing his own death. His mother was taken ill and had revealed her plot on her deathbed two days ago. Thus we have taken into custody the boy. We were noted of the plot since it was overheard by the landlord Clodius Pisenum, who is a notable owner of many slums deep in the Subdura. I have confidants throughout his many lodgings that report to me reliably on many matters.

The source of the matter is honorable, though the actual situation brought to light is here for review. I ask your opinion on the matter since you would know more than anyone the true paternity of this boy. Thus solving one question in the matter. The rest would be under investigation."

Selene thought about what Augustus had just stated and wondered why anyone would have killed her beloved brother and twin. He was so young when he died, only fourteen years old.

She could have done many things with this knowledge. It was not as if the boy would attain the kingdom of Egypt. That issue was moot. She wondered if this boy wanted the wealth of the family and his paternity? Illegitimacy had not kept people from obtaining power in the past. Some were even given rule despite this fact. Her own grandfather, Ptolemy Auletes was illegitimate, though made king after his uncle, the legitimate son of the ascendancy was murdered for the death of his own mother, the legendary Berenice III. Ptolemy Auletes ascended the throne after the puppet king had failed, his own people placed him there, needing a continuation for the line. For planned in marriage or born to greatness unplanned, it did not matter. What truly mattered was the actual bloodline. Which she knew would be instantly revealed to her. Antonia sat by her side in silent witness.

Why was Augustus granting this to her? She wondered. Her thoughts were cut off as the young boy was brought into the room chained and surrounded by guards. He appeared a shadow in the great room that he now found himself in. His garments were not the formal robes of the roman elite, they were the garments of a simple merchant. Homespun in truth, not like Antonia's mockery of her uncle's wishes and dreams. For in front of them stood tall and proud before them, striving to wipe away all of the signs of deep mourning that he was wrenched from to stand before them. They were clean despite their simple fashion and well tended. Selene could even make out the careful mending of an able seamstress. He was taller than her brother, yet his eyes were hers and her father's as well as her cherished twin's. The pale yellow speckles surrounded by a sea of deep blue. Eyes that would capture the soul. The color of Marcus Antonius, that Antonia shared as well. Though the shape of them was the deep almond whimsical and challenging eyes of her mother. He was well nourished though a bit on the thin side, probably due to his simple status attained from his mother. He was well cared for and wondered if he had inherited any of his father's talent in writing or his thirst for knowledge, especially of military tactics and the like. She recalled that her brother wanted desperately to be a famous general like his father was as well as Julius Caesar. So much flooded back to her as she looked into the eyes of her own twin. This was indeed the son of Helios. She did not bother to hide her reaction from Augustus. For he had accurately gleaned it from her demeanor and wordless stature.

For the boy did greatly resemble his own father, though taller, having perhaps inherited that from his mother who was a Gaul and a freedwoman in the service of Octavia as a potter who was noted for his extreme talent in his artistic creations with crockery. His daughter was talented as well, though expressed such emotion painted onto them with her fine brushstrokes that her's and her father's work was well sought after throughout Rome.

Augustus and Antonia both recalled the woman in the service of Octavia. "Your mother's name was Helena, was it not?" Antonia uttered into the dead silence of the large and airy chambers. Her inquiry echoed throughout.

The boy looked up stunned at being addressed by so August a noble, the famous Domina Antonia Minor, his words stumbled out of his mouth. He felt like a small school boy caught at some mischief. Why did they want to know this? "Domina, yes… My mother…my mother was Helena." His tongue practically tripping over his words. He could not believe why his words froze in his mouth. They were all staring at him. What was the matter? Had he done something wrong? He was taken from his mother's bed as she died, his mourning so intense he had not thought much on the matter until this moment. His mother was the only one who cared for him, the only one who looked out for his welfare.

His grandfather died only two years before. His grandfather died in misery of coughing fits until his weary and exhausted last breath. His mother had died of hope lost. She had told him that he had a destiny to fulfill. That he had the blood of kings in his veins from his father. She told him everything. Of how she fell in love with the foreign captive of Octavia and he with her. He would pick flowers from the sacred gardens of the Dominae that they served, not caring if he was caught. He told her of his family and of his great family name, Ptolemy, which she in turn gave to him. They were both children when they met, yet their hearts had found one another in the harsh cruel world. His soul understanding hers. For her own father told her that her mother was the daughter of the great Vercingetorix, the leader and hero of their homeland.

Helena and Helios would lament the twist of life and how they were caught up in the intrigues of the paths the Gods had chosen for them. Helena made sure that her son knew of his whole lineage before she let go of her last labored breath to end her journey in this life. She repeated over and again of her family and of how they ended up in Rome. She left his father's side a mystery to him until the evening that she had finally let go of her struggle in life.

Helena told Helios that she was born in slavery to her mother who was captured after the defeat of her father Vercingetorix. Helena's mother was left behind with her mother being of the age of two at the time. Her mother was unable to fight due to her nursing her younger brother. Helena told her son that her mother's mother was murdered after she was passed around to the soldiers after her children were given to the safekeeping of a young Druid that was kin. The man ran with the two children of the legendary Vercingetorix through the mountains in flight of the pursuing Romans. The infant boy, had perished in the flight due to the hardship of obtaining milk for the infant's nourishment. The druid fed the feeble child with milk stolen from goats and cows along his treacherous path, suckling the boy with a cloth drenched in milk. This painstaking labor was to no avail, for the infant boy was no longer able to gain any nourishment. The young and very patient Druid continued his flight to bring the children as promised to their dying mother, to her mother's homeland on the great island across the sea to the lands of Llud. The young Druid had kept his promise until he was finally caught while sleeping in a warn barn he had broken into. For her mother being only two had somehow managed to break free from her tie and wander off into the house of some Roman settlers. The Druid had a great fear of her straying off to danger of many kinds, even to the wolves they heard loud in the forest each night. He had to tie her to his side while he slept. Helena's mother was mischievous and had figured out how to undo the tie that saved her life and gave the Druid enough confidence to fall asleep.

He sang to her and played with the little girl who was named Maeve, the Mother of Helena. Nonetheless, the little girl was noticed by the Roman matron and her husband who had settled in the area to bring civilization to the barbaric tribes upon the orders of Julius Caesar.

Helena told her son that the Druid and her mother were sold into slavery and not long after, the both of them had ended up in the household of Octavia and Marc Antonius. Maeve had fallen in love with a Greek slave by the name of Aristotle, after the tutor of Alexander the Great. Though Aristotle never became the great philosopher of his namesake, he had instead held the great talent of making elegant pottery. His art created out of clay for tools of a common purpose had inspired his mistress Octavia, who had encouraged his talent. The work soon became sought out in Rome.

Octavia freed her favorite slave Aristotle in great admiration for his incredible talent, along with his wife, who had served her well.

Upon earning their freedom, they were given enough money to set up a shop in the Subdura and left to make their own fortunes. They had soon acquired enough money to purchase an Insulae of their own and to become landlords. Maeve and Aristotle had lived in comfort and bliss in the life that they had made with their great talent. This life was even more enhanced when Maeve gave birth to a daughter who soon revealed the ability and great talent to paint any image into the pottery made by her father. People came from places they had never heard of to purchase their pottery. The rest of their money was received from those who lodged in the Insulae gave them a good and decent life. They were even able to purchase a slave for the cleaning of their own comfortable apartment in the very top floor of the insulae that they owned, as well as a slave to care for the little Helena.

Helena told her cherished only child that she would slip down all of the rickety stairs every chance she got to work by the side of her father. He finally let her stay and let the slave in her charge, tend to other matters, thus allowing his daughter to work by his side.

Helios recalled each word that his mother repeated to him the events of that day that their life had changed forever. She told him that she was twelve years old and by the side of her father, painting some of his latest ceramic plates. Her colors would blend perfectly with each perfectly sculpted angle and curve into the clay that he created out of nothing. It was too late when the news of the fire had reached them on the ground floor of the Insulae. Her father was climbing down the stairs having just visited with her mother. The fire came from nowhere and had almost consumed her father with the rest of the building. He called out to her throughout the blinding smoke that enveloped the building threatening it's imminent demise within seconds.

He finally found her not noticing until too late the board that came crashing down from above to trap his arm in smoldering ash. Helena pulled her father out of the building and stumbled under his weight until he could finally run on his own. He had burned his right arm severely in that fire and had never gained full use of it. His talent lost along with his wife Maeve and fourteen other people that were accounted for by their families.

For the fire was finally brought under control, by the trained workers as commissioned by Augustus, in his noting the tinderbox of the many dilapidated structures built throughout the overpopulated Subdura. He created a fire brigade of people who ran chains of buckets to put out any fire that would break out in the city. He had commissioned this fire brigade in his attempts to save the whole city from being destroyed. This had saved the city from destruction on many occasions, but could not prevent the lives from being lost due to the shoddy construction of most of the buildings in that part of Rome and being so close to one another. No one knew the cause of this fire.

Thus, Helena and her father were forced to rely on her talents alone. Being only a small child, Helena was forced to seek assistance of the Domina Octavia. The wonderful lady had taken her into her own home and provided her and her father with shelter. That was when she first met the children of the great Queen Cleopatra, and especially her oldest surviving son, Helios.

The last part of that great tale that his mother had told him was only revealed to him on her deathbed, thus finally establishing his paternity. His mother was kind, though held great bitterness at the lot of life that she was given. She admitted to her son that she was angered when Octavia had sent her away to live in squalor, upon learning of her condition and of Helio's grand plans to marry her. Octavia, would not even hear of it and had told her not to forget her station. Octavia quickly arranged the marriage of a princess named Iotape for her beloved Helios.

Helena was left alone and forced out in the streets while the lady Octavia still sheltered her father under her roof. Her father was angered at his only child, the bitter Helena. Helena had to find work in the only way that she could care for her and the child of a prince that grew inside of her. She was taken in by a Brewer in a local tavern and brothel.

Helena had told her son in her last moments the reason for her bitterness and anger. For she had permanent lines of rage embedded against her fine high sculpted cheekbones. Helios could not recall his mother smiling not even once for any reason at all. She was a good mother to him and cared deeply for his well-being, but never smiled and rarely spoke to him except to tell him of his great matriarchal lineage.

Helena whispered to Helios that as she worked for the tavern that took her in she would steal moments away and find herself looking into the fence surrounding the domus of the Lady Octavia. There she witnessed her Helios in the rapture of his new wife. For it seemed to her that she was forgotten by him after all that he had promised. For it was obvious to all who had been in the presence of Iotape and Helios that they were besotted in each other's love for one another.

So many emotions clouded her weary and exhausted mind. To be so abandoned for no good reason had wreaked havoc on her soul. She told her son that eve of her death, of how she snuck into the ship stores and had poisoned her Helio's favorite treat that was loaded for the journey. She knew that he could not resist pistachios and had always taken great care to label his own rations of them to show all how he greatly coveted them. She saw the label on the sack that contained the beloved pistachios of the father of her son. She opened the sack and sprinkled the fine powder in a generous amount all over the contents of the bag. The tied the bag neatly and shook it fiercely as to mix it all in. She knew not what the powder contained, only that it would cause him a slow and agony filled death that would resemble a mysterious illness. She had paid a month's worth of wages carefully horded under her pillow for this purpose, so blinded by hatred was she in her grief of lost love and being tossed out alone to face the angry world.

The smiles of her child's father ripped her apart further each day until soon after when word of his death had begun it's rounds in the city. She had heard from traveling merchants at talk while ordering a round of beer one stormy evening. She relished servicing each one of them for a week of their pay. For in her extreme youth she was well sought out and highly recommended by the tavern owner. From that day forward, she told her son, was she able to finally live her life. After a few years, she had finally earned enough to finally leave the tavern owner and the brothel to set up a small shop on the outskirts of the Subdura. She raised her son close by her side and hid her past life until her very last breath.

Her son had no memories of his early years in the brothel where his mother worked, but only in her lovely and honorable care as a storekeeper. He knew of his grandfather who often came down to visit in his later years, who had always called him Helios. His mother always called him her little prince. Helios never made any connections, even during his school days when he had learned of the downfall of this great family by the brother of woman who had owned his sister as a slave in her household.

There he stood in a magnificent chamber that reached the sky. The pillars were elegantly carved in the Greek style and hung forlornly in his presence as if asking him his own fate.

"Boy, come closer." Augustus told Helios. "It is amazing, is it not?"

Selene did not know how to react about the murder of her own twin brother and to his very close likeness standing before her.

"He looks exactly as my brother did when he died so long ago, only taller." Selene whispered in amazement at looking at her twin almost as if he rose from his tomb. He very essence was strong in the room and surrounded her senses almost bringing her back.

"Do you have any family?" Selene inquired of the boy in Latin so eloquent that he almost did not understand it at all. For he had been raised hearing a mixture of many different languages, and knew the Greek in which the noble people spoke in front of him, seemingly to mask what they were speaking of from the rougher type of people that he in appearance came from.

He nodded negatively. “I am alone, for my mother has just died.” The words did not sound right coming from his mouth, they sounded odd, as if someone else had spoken then. Yet he knew the truth of them and could not stop them. It was the first time that he had actually spoken those words since her death, almost as if he feared that it would make it reality.

Selene’s heart reached out for this boy who resembled her twin too much though hesitated on the accusations of his mother, “If you have nowhere to go, you are welcome to join us. My husband and I live and rule over Mauretania.” Helios bowed to this fine lady and felt that she would be safe. He assented to her. Together they walked out of the room after the approving nod of Augustus. A litter awaited them on the steps of the palace, where another one to carry the lady Antonia followed close behind.

“My lady! The Imperator summons you once again, please haste!” Selene bowed to her nephew and turned back up the white granite steps to face him once again. She had hoped that this would have been the first step in her journey home, but alas, she must again bend to the whims of this man.

“Selene, please sit for but a moment…I have something that I must speak with you, for I had hoped that you would have brought it up sooner in this meeting with your brother’s son.” A simple chair was presented for the Queen of Mauretania to the side of Augustus on his ivory encrusted chair or state. She was lower than him in that his chair was raised due to his lack of height, even to her.

She was curious as to what he would have to mention to her that could not have been brought up before with others in presence. For now the room was bare, but for the two of them. Servants and slaves having been sent away.

“Do you truly understand the significance of my finding out the existence of this boy? “

”I thought he had come to you.”

"I often wondered what would have happened, had your mother not died. We were true enemies in life, yet, we both had much in common, even then."

"I…"

"No, let me finish… you see, I had hoped that we would have had a chance to get to know each other over the years and you have been all too quiet in your responses."

She began to move uncomfortably in her chair, he put his arm out to her form. "Please understand, I did not kill your parents. Rather, I had sought to punish your father for his abandonment of the republic and your mother for luring him away from my sister and his Roman wife. They were greedy and wanted more, much more than Rome could have given them. I suppose that I was greedy as well on those days. For I was still rather young then. I was only eighteen when I had inherited all from my adopted father, Julius Caesar. "

"Caesar Augustus, I have thought about the way things have turned out for years and have often wondered on the true nature of my parents. For when we are young, we tend to idolize them and to make them into Gods in our childlike innocence. But much wrong was done to their memory in your literary slander, though the author, Cicero had been long dead…"

"Yes, I have often tried the same with my own parents and have seen my children do that with me as I age, with all that I have created."

"At the expense of my parents and of my families kingdom!"

"Hush, little one!" So soothing was his voice, and even in her later years as a mother of grown children, she felt oddly comforted by his tone of voice and demeanor. She had not felt that she had any resentment built up in her over the years, but suddenly it grew powerful and hungered to be uttered forth to what her mind had created as the author of it's torment, the destruction of her family and lineage and the deaths of her parents. She felt young and tired and truly wanted to believe this man, this man who knew her parents well, who played such a vital part in their lives ending.

"I understand all that you must feel about it all, but it is all cobwebs now. Only we are left to view the events and the evidence that has fallen into decay."

"The decay had only made every event in my life scream out loud for some sense to the death of my parents. For they were truly wonderful people, my mother was an excellent ruler. My father might have been, but had his own daemons prying at his gate. But, most of all, they were good parents, I have learned much from them in the raising of my own children, if not from the whispers of her memory and no true advice from her."

"Yes, but were they not truly destroyed by their feelings and emotions, rather than myself? Think on it, please. I have tried for many years to make this up to you and your husband, the deeds done in my youth. Every action had been well orchestrated and well maneuvered, with each risk that I took, there was a greater goal in mind, that which you see before us and that which you go home to, when all is done."

"But what do I truly have but to return to a puppet kingdom ruled in reality by Rome, I would have been the Queen of the independent country passed down in lineage from my mother."

"Do you honestly think that it would have turned out like the play you see in your mind? Have you not noticed the uncontrollable movement of fate and the small roles in truth that we really are playing? Your mother was ruled by her emotions. She chose well in seducing Julius Caesar to her kingdom and plans, yet she was too young to have his soul completely to her alone, for she had to compete with Rome. She did perfect that passion and beauty to an art by the time of her meeting with your father, but was it as wise of a match as she had with Julius Caesar. As you have seen, it was not. Had they met under different circumstances in another time without their responsibilities and royal connections, the story would have played out to the perfection of your dream. The perfect family, the perfect lovers. Yet, the time was not right for their love, your mother's responsibilities as a Queen of a great land was not meant to have a love that would bind her from her role and her rule as her love for your father did. He was rash and did not plan things out carefully, and your mother's love blinded her in his silly dreams. Rome was not ready at that time for a king, and the reality of it was that your father would not have made a good king at all for Rome."

Selene shifted even further in her seat, as people often do when confronted with the truth. She sought desperately to hide from his words. For her dream world was collapsing right from under her and this man, though ineloquent in his presentation, was filling her with reality, the reality that she had dreaded to face in all of her years. "What about your sister, how did she fit into this master scheme? My father was forced to marry her in an alliance between you and he years ago."

"Yes, it worked temporarily, but you know what later occurred. The love of your father and mother. It was not meant for this time, it was not meant for them. For it caused their very deaths. You mother could have lived on and eventually brought Egypt in the prosperous direction that it was heading at that time before Actium. I actually approached her before her death hoping that she would forge and alliance with me. Even though I had not truly resigned to a woman in a place of rule, yet, she had that talent and despite my misgivings towards her sex, I saw what powers that she had. I hated her and loved her in the same breath. I have never gotten over her death either. For it did not seem to fit well into my life. Her death left a shadow, yet a yearning to know you, for I see so much of her in you."

"Did you love my mother once?"

"I suppose in a way I did, but what could I do, I was married at that time and had started my dream of bringing Rome back to the ancient days of the Republic and an adulterous affair had no place in the great plan I had for Rome. I merely wanted to be by her side. For we would have made a great force to be reckoned with. But I was also young and rash in those days, with headstrong values that caused a lot to unfold as a result of it. For when I married Livia, it had caused an avalanche of regret from her sons, and their father Tiberius. Even when I tried to dote on my daughter Julia and to give her her hearts true love, Tiberius. I did not stop to think that it would do to Tiberius and his love for his Vispania, how it would come to crash upon my daughter in the wake that ensued like a tidal wave of loss."

"What really happened with my mother? Did she kill herself?"

"That I truly do not know. We found her in the mausoleum with her two servants Iras and Charmian, all were dead."

"Her death plays in my mind so often, I really have forgotten the truth of it. I did not think that over the years, I had harbored any ill feelings towards you, but it seems as if it did, deep down inside. I suppose as we grow older, the only true lesson that we learn through all of the lessons in life is that we truly do not know anything at all. Are we all just pawns of the Gods and of the fates they dole out for us?"

"I often wonder that myself, for even though I rule over much of this material world, in the true story of life, I feel helpless, no matter how carefully I plan everything. For more often than not are the hidden agendas revealed after the climax of events unfold."

Selene nodded at this. "So now I return to my rule and you to yours, will we ever gain any thing from all life has taught us?"

Augustus only whispered to her, "Only that we truly know nothing at all!" They both laughed at this.

Part six

I

1 B.C.E. to 3 C.E.

Julia dreaded the loss of her figure due to her necessary duty of being a future Queen of Mauretania. She gave birth to a very small boy who was named Ptolemy of Mauretania. He had curls of burnished gold to fit his royal status. He will be a charmer, that one. She made a promise with herself to return to her normal figure again as soon as possible. She had ate very little while pregnant so as to not upset her figure, thus the low birth weight of her son.

She really had little use for children and made sure that he was cared for with a suitable wet nurse of calm disposition. Within a week she was up on her feet again and back to her usual visits among the warriors in training. She kept her liaisons a secret from the royal family and was proud of her many accomplishments and the naiveté of her doting husband.

Selene was worried that Julia spent little time with her first born son and understood that her own ways were especially unusual for women of her status. She accepted it, though was upset all the same. She always had her children by her side, despite her very complex schedule. She made sure that her children learned the correct procedures of state and sought constantly to make it interesting for them, especially when they were young.

She had observed that Julia was very shy in her presence and never sought her out on questions pertaining to the rule of their country, which after her own death, she would assume as the reigning Queen of Mauretania. Julia seemed constantly in the shadows more often than not in avoiding the very presence of Selene. There was no proof of this, other than her own very active imagination and instinct. She had tried on many occasions to engage the especially beautiful girl in conversation and had made a point to invite her to many of the state visits which she performed during her reign as Queen. Yet, she felt that Julia would only entertain Selene, and had desperately sought to be somewhere else.

As the years passed, she did not press the issue and just felt that it was just in the nature of the princess. She also wondered on her many absences and was told that she had a delicate heart and would often seek rest after a busy day.

She had felt secretly sad for her son in the attitude of his wife, especially relating to matters of duty, which she always seemed too ill to attend. Ptolemy was completely infatuated with his wife and oblivious to her many quirks. He had an excuse for her on every occasion and saw no fault. He praised the very ground on which she stood, when she was not reclining of course. Thus, Selene was civil to her daughter-in-law. She was also very thankful that she have paid special attention to teach her son how to rule the kingdom more effectively. Though he was mainly interested in battle tactics and warfare, as was her long lost brother Ptolemy, far away across the seas with his love Ahrianred. She wondered at his fate. She had not received a correspondence from him in over a year.

II

Julia wandered silently down the bluish tinged marble corridors that seemed to go on forever. She found all of the turns that counted and knew exactly where to go through the darkened halls that led her deeper into the palace confines. Her tiny slipper-shod feet carried her happily towards the meeting spot of her latest sport. She had solicited the attention of a gladiator named Hermes due to his incredibly rugged and blunt exterior.

His mind was pretty much devoid of any serious thought which intrigued her all the more, for she did not like much of a challenge and preferred them to be as easy as she was.

The seasoned gladiators were a favorite for her attentions in that usually they were very numb due to the constant jolts in the head during the mock battles which they managed to survive. The newly trained gladiators were too much for her to endure, with all of their constant whining on freedoms and of families left behind. She lavished them with promises of their freedom until she grew tired of their sport and then moved on to the men who had taken the most in beatings, since they had very little conversation, their will having been beaten out of them long ago. They were basically shells of humans and more like beasts. She preferred their animal instincts and raw hunger for pleasure. She was their sole conqueror and they submitted to her in every one of her requests, no matter what it was, so wrapped under her power and too weak mentally to resist any battle.

"What are doing here Julia?" Startled, Julia let out a gasp followed by a bowed posture to her Queen Mother, Selene who seemingly appeared out of nowhere.

"I, ah, was just wondering where my husband was, have you seen him your highness?" She meekly uttered quickly composing herself.

Selene had noticed the hungry look of her daughter-in-law at the gladiators and had hoped that this was just a phase. She put it into her mind to have a talk with her son and husband about the roving eyes of the future Queen of Mauretania. "Julia, he is in the arms room awaiting a shipment from Crete as you well know, I would hope that you would soon be there to assist him and to learn more about this kingdom that you will someday rule."

"Why yes, sorry." She almost stumbled as she rushed from the presence of Selene and almost ran into the arms room to be by the side of her husband. She hated that woman and could not wait until she could drop her role as the simpering princess. Yet, the time was not right for that, even though she had given birth to a son, she knew her husband wanted more children and she had to oblige him and that it was her true duty after all was said and done.

III

Selene wearily reclined on the couch for the evening meal lavishly set out before them all. Around her sat her husband at her closest side. He was looking even more handsome to her as the years progressed, if that were even possible. His dark hair streaked with white at his temples. His features more firm in serenity and the many years of peace in their kingdom. There had been rebellions, though nothing that was not quashed within days after their inception and very few fatalities. "Husband, what think you of Julia"

Juba in all of his refinement and placid ways was startled by his wife's inquiry, "Julia, what of her? You must have some reason for this question, knowing you…" He laughed, for she would always keep him on his toes, with her many curiosities, he liken to often indulge in them when he was not traveling and gathering information for his extensive encyclopedia's that he was working on diligently.

"Well, she just seems to be interested in men who are not her husband…I was just worried for our Juba, that is all."

"Well, it is not as if there is any great love between them, for it was a marriage of state, as you and I have been."

"Yes, but ours turned out differently, for we are happy, are we not?"

"Yes, my love, but their love will grow in time, she has only been here a few years, we are now happy grandparents from both of the children"

"I understand, but she worries me, she does not seem to be who she really is…I can't place my finger on it really, I just have this feeling that something is going to happen between them."

"It would hardly be surprising if they had no feelings for each other, for their marriage is for the greater good and not really for each other. I understand how you feel Selene in that he is your son, but it really matters on the lineage for this throne that is created by them. They are how we carry on our families and create alliances. You really must understand the real picture and not what your heart tells you."

"Yes, I know… we all have our duty. But, I sense that she will not be careful with hers, that Ptolemy will suffer because of it…"

"What does it matter really? We will just have to find a concubine for him, someone for him to vent his emotions."

"It is truly not a fair plight for us women. For we have to remain loyal to our husbands for the validity of the line, while the husbands could stray and plow other fields."

"Yes, but your children will inherit the line and rule, while the other fields tilled will only rot in time."

"Do I have your love, husband, your heart?"

"Does it matter that much to you? Are we not content?"

"I suppose the woman in me wants to know."

"Would I have let you rule as freely as you do, if I did not completely respect you and admire your intelligence…"

"Yes, but your love, not that it really matters…"

"I long for you, for your beauty is still great if not better than before, softened in time…"

"Yes, but your love…"

"Do not all of these things make up love? Do we really have the right to love? Our stations in life are great, but reality has us only the pawns of our kingdoms that we rule—we might not be allowed to love. Can we not just accept what joy that we have been allowed to have by fate?"

"I suppose that we really have no choice do we?"

IV

Selene had been kept informed of all of the many events in Rome by her precious Antonia Minor in many correspondences over the years.

Antonia mentioned that Augustus ordered Tiberius to divorce his beloved Vispania to marry his daughter Julia, for which he had no choice but to submit to the Imperator for Life's will. She described the miserable wedding, of how elated and blind the poor Julia was to the true emotions of her husband forced into marriage. Though his head was held up high in his bold façade, Tiberius walked solemnly in the procession that led him further away from the ostracized Vispania, powerless to do any thing about it. His son was sent to the court and taken away from his wife's death grip to be raised in the palace, never to set eyes on his mother again.

Antonia lamented the fate of Vispania and wondered whatever became of her after that event when her husband and only child were taken away from her life.

Julia became pregnant soon after, though miscarried. This, as related by Antonia, had put further restraint in their marriage and drew Tiberius from even civil relations with his wife. And Julia realizing all too late that Tiberius never returned her love and devotion, had sought it out from others and began to cause scandal at court with her many affairs, becoming more and more blatant by the year.

Antonia even suspected that their beloved half brother Iully was seduced by the wanton Julia, the Imperial Princess of Rome. For though she had given birth to five children by Agrippa in her prior marriage, she had still retained her slim figure in which she had chosen to adorn herself in robes of silk, eccentrically worn only by temple women of ill repute. However, being the only child of Augustus, it was quietly ignored.

Though she knew that her uncle had often spoke to Julia and begged her to cease her behavior and to behave like a proper wife to Tiberius. Julia had told her father that she wore garments of silk to attract her husband who was becoming more and more an illusion to her in his many absences from their villa which looked over the slums of Rome in a hubris reference to their plight. Though living far above, they still had the same problems of the masses that were all crowded below them in the vast subdura.

Antonia told Selene of the great funeral for her mother the year after and of the birth of her son Tiberius Claudius Drusus Nero Germanicus in Lugdonum in Gaul. Her youngest son. Of her constant worries for his welfare. He was slow and drooled and ruined many gowns. It grew so bad that she had sought out a nurse for him and his seclusion from matters of state which she attended most frequently for her uncle. As he grew older, she was slowly drifting away from her son and made may excuses not to attend him. She felt that he was growing into a monster and could not tolerate his very presence, blaming herself as the cause of this malady which only grew worse with his years.

Selene was especially thrilled that their Iully had seemed to abandon his affair with Julia to finally wed Marcella, the Younger, Daughter of Octavia from her first marriage with Marcellus. The couple seemed enamored with each other, or so everyone thought.

Antonia had sent a letter relating in somber tones the death of her husband Drusus. It seemed to Selene that Antonia was very matter of fact in relating the incident to her in the letter. Antonia had related in her letter of how she grew to love her husband over the years and of the wonderful children he had given her. She had mentioned that while her husband was en route to Rome, when he had decided to return for a brief respite before proceeding on to Cherusi after his victories in the lands of the Chatti. He had fallen from his horse and fractured his leg. Tiberius was sent to his side by Augustus, though he died soon after. He was finally laid to rest in the Campus Martius. So little on paper to her, yet so much between the lines was said on that succinct description of the death of Antonia's husband.

Selene and Juba had followed the campaign of Drusus and his brother over the years from a safe distance all of the way in their protected section of the world in Mauritania. They recalled how Drusus had embarked his public career by serving many campaigns in the Roman provinces. He had joined his brother Tiberius in a war against the Reatians, who had pushed their way out of Noricum and had further threatened parts of Italia and Gaul. Tiberius and Drusus crushed their advance and embarked on a general invasion of Raetia. After two years, Drusus then advanced on to the barbaric lands of Germania. For in the following four years he not only reached the notorious Elbe and Rhine Rivers but had managed to dig a canal to the Rhine and sailed through it to the Roman Sea. Which finally brought him to his final successes during the year of his death achieved at the lands of the Chatti and Suebi, despite the thunderstorms and portents of ill omens of the campaign of the consulship that he was pursuing that year. His victory in the regions brought him further on against the Cherusi. However, due to the many warnings and bad omens that had occurred he stopped his campaign there to return to Rome to be by the side of his Antonia. The fall from his horse occurred on that trip towards Rome.

Selene knew that Drusus was probably the better loved of the two brothers, over Tiberius by the people of Rome. In the letter Antonia swore that she would never marry another, so great was her love for Drusus.

Selene knew that Antonia would have to appeal to her uncle Augustus on the matter of changing and old Roman law that demanded that all windows remarry. This law was called "*The Lex De Maritandis Ordinibus*". She was elated when she found out later that Antonia had succeeded in persuading her uncle of her wishes.

Tiberius was rising fast in Rome, first as counsul and then he received tribunate powers in the office of *tribunicia potestas*. He was also noted as the visible heir to the Imperatorship in the all too apparent youth of the Imperial grandsons and children of Julia from Agrippa, of Lucius and Gaius Caesar.

Antonia explained to her favorite sister Selene, that she understood why Tiberius eventually retired from public life to his private villa in Capri along with his astrologer Thrassyllus. He had informed her in confidence that he was tired of playing the pawn to Augustus and despised what he had done to Vispania who had died a few months prior alone and by her own hand. They had found her body floating in the murky waters of the Tiber one gray dawn in the bleakest of winter evenings. His heart left Rome that day and he sought sanctuary from the life that everyone wanted him to lead. He was also angry on the constant toying of his status as heir by Augustus, who was constantly changing his mind on that issue as the clouds above changed their shapes with each passing wind.

Antonia wrote to Selene of how she had to deal with how upset Augustus became with the absence of his stepson Tiberius from office. She had to deal with his constant mutterings since Livia was too busy with her own schemes for the survival of her son's status in Rome and made sure that he did not lose his good status with her husband.

V

Ptolemy relished each moment with his love, Ahrianred and of their fragile time together on this earthly realm and in this era. He picked carefully each desire chosen on the path years ago, almost in another time it seemed to him. So very long ago, when things seemed normal to him. In the years that have passed they forged a new life together. He chose to drift away from everyone's chosen plans for them and to forge a new life with his Ahrianred, a woman with her own destiny.

He had learned about the many traditions of this land about the taboos and geis one was given at birth in order to survive this harsh and unforgiving climate. They had left the kingdom of Jubilla and Cynfelyn long ago and had drifted to another island far to the west of where he started this journey with Ahrianred. In the new land they decided to use new names for each other. Ahrianred was called Brigit and he was called Lleu Llaw Gyffes, a name chosen by his Brigit which meant that he had a steady hand. This name was more than useful when it came to their chosen profession for survival, of hiring themselves out to the kingdoms independently for their skills in battle. Ahrianred had chosen the name of a Goddess that she had worshipped before battle in homage to her honor.

Their new life was adventurous to say the very least and the adrenalin rushes soothed his wandering soul and kept his love by his side. They lived in a constant state of excitement, which was trebled with the birth of their first son Gwyngyngwn and then for the son that followed Gwanat. Those were their names of dedication in ceremony. The first name meant *the white one triple blessed by the Gods*. They were called Madron and Mabon by those closest to them.

Madron was the first born and most powerful and most cherished by their mother. For she blessed him with not the usual one geis, but three to compliment the power of his sacred name. The geis were logged down in the sacred Ogham writing of the Druids and then placed in the vault underneath the most sacred of worship sites the Great Stones of Henge on the main part of the larger Island. After this was done, they had left for brighter horizons and places distant and headed for the cousin Island to the West called Tara, with an even fiercer people and even more untouched by Roman occupation and interest.

Brigit gave her first born sons geis of inhibiting power that she felt added further protection for this cherished life in such a strange and foreign land in their travels. The first was that only she could arm her son, the second was that only she could name him and the third was that he could not marry a human woman. The first was due to her long and established line of powerful warrior women and of the special sword that she handed down to him when she found out that she could no longer have any more children after their second son was born. This almost destroyed her since she was determined to have her much needed daughter to carry on the line. Ptolemy wept for her, though was secretly elated that he had two sons.

The second geis was a break from the traditional norm of her people, for prior to that only the Druids had the power to name all children born, especially sons. This swayed their power to her.

The third and final geis, upset Ptolemy, but she wanted to prevent him from incurring a broken heart, from any woman who might try to take his heart away from her and to attempt to attach themselves to the new family fortune that she and Ptolemy or Lleu Llaw Gyffes had accrued in their travels and in their becoming legendary in their undefeated skill in battles.

With his tactical talent and her pure talent, they were almost completely undefeated and had acquired vast riches and had build an enormous hall for themselves gilded in gold. The walls were tall and foreboding to any who came upon their dwelling with the heads of vanquished enemies staring empty to those from the vast heights and widths of this enclosure, almost in challenge to any further callings to the famous family of warriors.

Lleu Llaw had argued vehemently to no avail with his consort's prohibition of their son's marriage to a human woman. She was like a wall and unperturbed by any debate on the subject. Thus, the book was closed and he could do nothing about it, unless he incur her wrath, which he chose wisely not to do.

Their second son, Mabon was left mostly under his own tutelage while Brigit worked closely with Madron. The seasons passed and the boys grew to be strong, talented and well educated in all ways known in tactical skills. He would often hire him and his son's out for the use of Cynfelyn, who had respected the distance that he and Brigit had chosen from the court life. Lleu Llaw cared nothing for anything even resembling Roman life, so harsh was his hatred of them, Cynfelyn respected that and called upon him when needed.

He and Brigit never left each other's side for a moment so close were they tied in soul and time, they felt they would die, if even if a slight part of their bond was severed in any way. Their love was legendary and many ballads were composed for their love for one another and of their constant companionship. For it was well known that she had never chosen another consort and never would, so completely satisfied was she with her foreign prince.

He was mysterious to all who met them, since he resembled none of their people and his origin became a mystery as the years passed. Their love grew more powerful.

Then came the day when their oldest son brought home to them a princess from the land of Tara named Bledeudd who was as fair as any with hair even more red than his fair Brigit, if possible. She had told them that she was not born of a human mother, nor father and was raised by an old tribe as an orphan and May-Begotten Child. For her mother was a High Priestess of the grove of flowers and her father a God. When conceived, it was legend that her mother was under the power of the faerae and had not been in her human form at the time. She was magical from her first footstep into their vast domain in the way that she did not walk, but rather floated. Her voice was musical and a pure delight, which warmed their very souls after the blood they all spilled in hired battle. She added music to their silent hall and her charm soothed them all and made them unaware of whom she really was.

She was welcomed into their home and became a member of their family, though sat home in wait all the while they fought in the battles which earned them fame and even further fortune.

Brigit was enchanted by her son's chosen lover though forbade him to marry her nonetheless, for she could only be his consort. This he accepted, so close was her beloved Madron to his mother's wishes, he feared to test her will. She also added a further geis for his protection. She stated that Madron could only be killed if he had one foot on the side of a water bucket and the other foot on a goat. This sounded hilarious to Ptolemy Lleu Llaw, though he had learned long ago, to keep his tongue silent in respect for the woman he loved most on this wild and rough world in which they lived.

Brigit, Lleu Llaw and their sons Madron and Mabon went out on many battles and Bledeudd stayed home and kept the fire burning on their hearth in wait for them. Their fame spread to every corner of the earth and their services well sought out. The flower maiden Bledeudd was equally legendary in her enchanting ways and had left their son defenseless against her many charms and convincing ways.

The halls were filled with her laughter when they returned though the cradle still remained empty. Brigit was hoping to become a grandmother and to perhaps have a little girl in the household, to teach her warrior and Goddess ways to. But it was not meant to be.

While they were absent on one of their many battles, Bledeudd had enchanted a lover by the name of Gronw, who was hired by them to tend to their war stallions. He was beautiful for a man and possessed a genuine talent for husbandry in all of their livestock as well as the horses. He also had a secret ambition for power which was hidden in his quiet demeanor, unbeknownst to the warrior family. For while they were away, he stepped in to seduce the flower maiden Bledeudd and had enchanted her as she enchanted other's with his tales of power and of how they could easily attain them.

For his chance came upon hearing the news after the most recent battle. Brigit and Lleu Llaw had both fallen in battle to their deaths. Brigit was thrown from her chariot and was crushed by the wheels and Lleu Llaw had witnessed his life fall apart in that very instant. He had then, in anguish looked to his sons to continue the battle and jumped with his chariot to her side and cradled his beloved Brigit in his arms. He had breathed his last when a stray arrow pierced his heart, which was already pierced by the death of his Ahrianred- Brigit.

Madron and Mabon returned to tell the eventful day and the dusk of their parents lives and the battlefield which embraced them into the depths of legend with their valor and love for one another.

Madron returned to tell his consort that she was to become his wife in every sense of the word and he took her to his bed that evening and spent his fury at the endless bloodshed and the lives lost of his parents who cherished him. The loss of his mother was eating at his soul turning it bitter with regret and anger. He took this out on his flower maiden Bledeudd in the tangle of his emotions. She cried as he took her selfishly and passively into his bed, having no choice but to allow his anger upon her fragile body.

While he slept after every drop of his essence was drained into her in his boiling hatred, she cursed him and vowed to seek vengeance upon what he had done to her. For her laughter had finally ceased on that evening. She sought out the forgiving and loving arms of her lover Gronw, and he embraced her fully without malice, only love-or so she thought.

She and Gronw conspired a way to kill her new husband. For that very next evening she called upon him while he had a few drafts of mead and his head was spinning with passion she knew was meant for her. She tested him and called him to a dare. She asked for him to stand with one foot on the side of a water bucket in mock hubris of the geis he was placed with in protection. Madron did that willingly, since he adored his wife and aimed to please her. For he also had doubts about the superstition that his mother was ruled by. He also requested that the skin of a goat he placed under his other foot, to complete his faith that he had in his wife.

"See that no lighting strikes me dead, no hand reached down from the skies above to slam the life out of me!" Screamed the mighty and fearless Madron.

"Dear husband, you are right! Your power is supreme! But, what about this!" As she uttered that last cry heard by Madron, Gronw leapt out from behind a screen with Madron's own sword in his hands and ran the prince through his heart. The blood came forth in torrents and the illusion of safety and benevolence crumpled with the warrior hardened body of the fearless Madron. Lying in a pool of the blood that seeped out from his heart, he looked at his wife and lamented his anger and with a smile joined his mother in the greatest hall of all that only belonged only to the Gods.

Thus, this family slipped into legend and into the tales of passing bards. Ballads rang forth through the primeval forests turning the mortal warrior family into legend and into Gods.

VI

Far away in the settlement that prospered under her husband, sat Jubilla a Queen of the Roman Britannia as recognized by them, like her own parents. So far away from any Roman domination, they had much more freedom to rule as they pleased. She and Cynfelyn had grown in peace and prosperity under their rule and justice. Their tribe of the Trinovantes grew large. She had given birth to several other children after her first twins Silla and Cleo. For after them came her other daughter Leanydd and then her sons Cyllin, Caradawc and Gweiryth.

Cynfelyn was raising them to rule over his vast tribal population and would be granting them further rule over the farther territories soon. Bellinos had long ago died and had joined the Gods and Goddesses of legend.

The brothers of her husband were gaining their own fame and had long ago earned their trust in rule. Togodumnos became legendary in his fine breeding of a new horse to grace this far island. The Romans sought them out for their own stables as well as all of the surrounding kingdoms and tribes. Annius had proven a fine warrior and able administrator. He was teaching his skills to his young nephews.

Her twins were preparing for their weddings as well as her new foster child, Alanya who had come here when she was only six, from her aunt Arsinoe. Alanya was cherished as one of her own daughters and had shown an interest in battle skills.

Jubilla had sent her third daughter Leanydd to the Island of Mona for her training as priestess. Her daughter Silla was in fervent training as warrior and learning new tactics along the side of her brothers. Cleo was more domestic and was enamored in the Roman Goddess Vesta and about the hearth and fire. She informed her mother of the many similarities of that Goddess and of the many Pictish Goddess' who names were lost to Jubilla.

Only five years ago their rule over the Trinovantes tribes were extended to rule over the Catuvellauni tribes as well. The Catuvellauni lands were long ago conquered by the Romans under the leadership if Julius Caesar in the time of Casswallon, the father of her husband Cynfelyn. Casswallon then transferred the leadership over to Mandubbracios, of whose son Dubnovellaunus later inherited the rule over the Catuvellauni lands and then his son Addedonmarius was being groomed for the same rule, of which he would eventually become a puppet to the Romans. Cynfelyn wanted to prevent any further dominion over his island and in a final rebellion took over the advantage of the lands being open for invasion. For Dubnovellaunus went to Rome in order to pay tribute to Augustus. Thus Cynfelyn rushed in with his troops and captured the capitol Canovis which contained the first Roman settlement called Canivum, which was set up after the invasion of Julius Caesar many years ago.

She was very proud to learn that her daughter Silla and Arsinoe's daughter Alanya played a major part in that battle and returned to her nest unscathed along with the eldest of her sons, Cyllin. Cynfelyn beamed with pride and with tales of the valor of their family in the battles that brought with them the added kingdom of the lands of the Catuvellauni along with the Roman settlement of Canivum. She was so grateful to see them all unharmed and found it difficult to let her daughters and cousin face the blood streaked battlefields in which they thrived. She wondered if this were all from the bewilderment of this strange new land in the fierceness of the women that it bore.

Drennedd had only recently requested the return of his daughter, Alanya for a judicial matter to be settled, and Jubilla was fervently waiting for the girl's prompt return.

She could definitely relate to her daughter Cleo and her matronly ways and sought to find her a suitable husband and had even written to her mother to discover that she had a cousin that her mother had found and brought back with her to raise in Mauretania upon their return journey many years ago, it seemed to her almost a lifetime ago. In her latest correspondence with her mother she agreed to the son of her cousin and daughter bonding in marriage and had also received her husbands blessing's on the matter. For the young Alexander, the son of her Uncle Helios was due to arrive by winter.

As she thought about all of the pressing matters of court, she heard drift across the dusty leaf covered roads the sounds of music drifting out to her from the grand music hall. The strings of the Lyre caught her and called out to her as they always did, they brought her fiercely back to the present and to the place that she now called home. She got up from her writing desk after rolling up the latest correspondence to her mother to be sent out on the morrow and went to find out the meaning of the solemn words that called out to her. Into the grand music hall she found herself, in a refuge from the oncoming winter chill. The echoes of color long lost from the leaves that covered everything, preparing a blanket of protection from the fierce winter chill and snow soon to come. The darkness was pierced from the light that crept outside from the hall. She found herself walking over to her seat by the side of her husband and companion in life, her Cynfelyn. Her seat was empty, yet warm from the presence of his favorite black wolfhound Loki, named from a God from an even farther people from winter lands far to the north. Loki, got up reluctantly from the swish of his master and let his mistress take her seat. Jubilla arranged her multi-colored skirts decorated in swirls and forms of animals from bright colored dyes.

The words finally grasping meaning to her and she deciphered them reluctantly. It was about her uncle Ptolemy. She had not heard from them and their fine sons in at least five years. Yet, this seemed to be in answer to her plea for information on them. It was a ballad as sung by a traveling Bard. She noticed that all of her husband's finest overlords were in attendance this evening. She observed Andocos with his wife Nissa along with Rues, Dias and Sego in all of his loveable gruffness. They were caught up in the pure talent of the traveling Bard who came to regale the latest news of the lands and those around them.

"I have a tale to tell, of love, of betrayal, of the Gods and a fair Goddess. A Warrior family. A family that now dwells in legend and in song…

Ahrianred, fair maiden was she,
Carried a spear in her hand and forged it well.
Found a lover from across the sea
For side by side the many battles they fought.

Daytime brought their love afresh,
Nighttime sealed their lovers pact.
A Timeless love,
A boundless love.
Reunited souls in a timeless dance…

Together they wandered the land for battle,
Arms entwined—a souls hungry bond.
Seasons passed and stronger their fate molded to each others.

To this union a hope for a dying land renewed
Two sons born to Ahrianred under the rays of the moon.
The second to care for the land-Mabon.
The first to keep it safe-Madron.

A long warrior's line to end or to begin.
The silver wheel turns weaving time before.
The silver wheel turns weaving yarn to knit.

Knitting the future, knitting the truth.
Her spear laid down in slumber,
While her lover protects the hearth she cares for.
While the warrior queen sings delight by the moon in full.

Weaving threads of life together,
Destinies entwined from the womb.
Geis she whispers for their path,
To protect each of them from harm.

Only your mother shall name you,
Only your mother shall arm you,
Never, young son, marry a woman of mortality,
To break your precious heart.

The twins grew to boyhood and beyond
And learned to carve a spear.
By their parents they rode a golden chariot,
Through fields and driving snow.

Along came a maiden so fair,
Who lured away Madron.
Ahrianred cried a river of tears that day
That drowned the flowers in the fields in her pain.

Her lover tried to console her breaking heart,
Taking her in his soul to mend.
While Mabon, not vexed at all,
Only continued to toil away at field.

Madron was sore and lured away,
By a love that promised him security and peace.
To the arms of Bledeudd he went in passion,
In fields of flowers they lay alone in their bliss.

Bledeudd, a maiden of flowers and magic was she
Whose hair of red shone brighter that the deepest sunset
and glory of blood-soaked battlefields.

Of flowers and prayers and moonbeams
Was she born.
Raised in forest under the dewy leaves,
No mother to call her own.

Outwitted was Ahrianred by Madron's skill,
He had found a wife not human to care for his hearth and fire.
Thus her son and his lover wed,
Under a canopy of golden Oaks in a forest grove.

And still Mabon worked on,
And still the years did turn,
The silver wheel spun,
A destiny to be won.

Bledeudd had a secret,
Untamed as the northerly wind,
Of her secret lover named Gronw.
He secured her under his spell.

Ahrianred heard of her son's lament.
And thus, another geis was blessed upon his weary mind and soul;
"To slay Madron… impossible,
Though only if one foot to a bears back,
The other on a water vats edge-precarious!"
Thus, elated, Madron could live in peace.

Bledeudd and Gronw conspired,
And whispered plans of woe.
While Madron blinded by love fell prey to her lure.
Gronw ran him through in the moment well planned out,
The spear carved for this deed did strike true, and Madron was no more.

Ahrianred cried a river and called out for her chariot.
In the winds she screamed in fury,
And she caught the lovers sly.

In a web she wove,
Captured through their lies.
Ensnared for all time in shame.
Ahrianred sings out their crime,
While Mabon hands her an axe.

Her lover by her side,
Shared her pain in torrents.
Together souls do mend,
And life begins anew,
While Mabon prepared the land.

Mabon gave them happiness,
Though no wife shared his fate.
Childless he died during a winter so foul.
Ahrianred saw her woe and mistake.

Alone in the world by her lover's side.
Her womb ceased the call to life for her.
Her scarlet hair mellowed to snow.

Her lover by her side,
Spear heavy to hold.
A hollowness by her hearth,
Her selfishness paid in price.

The silver wheel turned and spun the last time.

Alone without embrace,
Desolate in sorrow.
So cold her destiny's end and final breath"

Jubilla let the words sink in and formatted the truth from the tale. She understood most of it was garnished to mean all times at once. Her aunt was made a Goddess whom they called by her name and was also referred to as the mighty Brigit. She knew of the geis bestowed upon her oldest son, not a twin as in the tale. Though all of them were warriors and she and her uncle, Ptolemy, she could not recall his warrior name-had died in battle. That tale should be told, she felt that it was more important. Of a love immortal. They never reached old age in reality and had attained vast riches from their hired service in battle. They were also at the famous battles over the lands of the Catuvellauni and won by her husband seven years ago. She understood all the same the Bard's need for poetry and mock meaning in words. The elegance of his tale will live on immortal through all time. She still wanted to speak to him of the famous love her aunt and uncle shared and of how they died, perhaps that would make another great epic tale to be told by fire on winter evenings to avoid the chill of this harsh climate and of the lives they faced. Perhaps…

VII

The fire was dazzling the memories of Arsinoe, of how this fateful moment had arrived. The many roads she had traveled. How her destiny came out and bit her ferociously.

A knot burst forth from the fire, exploding further torrents to the forefront of her mind. The scenes of her life rushed by her as the log crackled and threw off their delicious autumn scent to comfort any past choices made.

Her hand reached out tentatively for its comfort, for her Sion. Together they sought the refuge of the deepest forest. Overhead the statuesque Elms and mighty and majestic and ancient Oaks stood sentinel over their flight, as if guarding them or possibly in silent judgment over their hearts.

Sion's hand clasped her's close and held it to his chest, covered in the furs of the wolves-whose voices pierced her soul in the evening hours.

Taunting them on their journey's eventual demise. Their bodies weary, their souls were tired from choices made that placed them in the present and ominous danger.

Why must true love have too steep a price, she wondered enchanted in the smoke of the fire. All her life she faced her duty, without complaint as a soldier faced his mission. She looked at her chosen path only and never truly swayed.

Her love for Sion was pure as was her destiny. His chaste companionship compelling, yet perfect. She was too afraid to consummate her desire with her soul's cry of completion. He respected her position, her bloodline, to even ask for any more than her friendship. His aura reached out to her from the very first meeting, so many years ago. He knew with her rusty grasp of his native language and culture, that this princess from far away was his destiny. He would do everything in his own power to protect her and to teach her the ways of this new land for her understanding.

Sion praised the very core of all that he was in being allowed to witness the purest and most melodious rapture in song emanate from the petite and fair foreign princess. He praised her talent. He even went so far as to plead the Arch Bard's permission to nurture this pure musical talent. For he also discovered her natural aptitude and ability for the Lyre and flute as well. She had soon surpassed his own talents.

He begged the Bard Circle of the Eastern Realm for him to train her in their ranks and secrets.

His world crashed down in the realization of her imminent marriage that was her duty in her being a princess of royal blood of Egypt, Mauretania and even in the power of Rome. He pleaded and begged all those in power and had even sought the aid of Bellinos, the Arch Druid. But, alas, that battle was lost for him.

In a most fortuitous boon, he was requested by none other than her betrothed, Drennedd—to accompany his new bride and he and to continue her lessons in song and music. For she had also won the heart of Drennedd, the leader of the Belgae Tribe, with her enchanting Goddess-like voice.

Elated, he joined them farther away from all he had ever traveled in his life prior. He followed the calling of his heart and destiny and made her life, his own in a way. The only way that he would ever be allowed.

Her worries became his, as well as her many joys. Though he dreamed of her rapture and fulfillment. He became her closest confidant and friend. He lived on the lonely side of her life, looking on and yearning for her.

He watched her grow into a woman in every aspect. When he initially met her, she was already twenty years old, though like a child with her sheltered and naïve upbringing by her older sister, the Queen of Mauretania. Having suffered the trauma of losing her parents at a very young age, she barely recalled them at all. Her sister, Selene had raised her and stood as the role of her mother to her orphaned little sister.

His soul melted for this exotic princess. Her blonde curly tresses glowed with sunlight and touched his very reason for life and of remaining by her side in torment. For she belonged to another, a very powerful man and leader of a tribe in the southern most part of the land in which they lived.

He fought for her in everything, even so that she could find meaning in her life and possible reason for the way things were.

When Arsinoe gave birth to her only child, her cherished daughter Alanya Cleopatra, he cherished the dark-haired fairy princess as if she were his own.

He found comfort in Hadwinna's sage advice to Arsinoe and bonded with her as well, fitting in the abandoned mother role of a sister far away past the farthest seas.

All seemed magical for the first few years for his Arsinoe and her new family. Then came the day that Drennedd brought home another woman to be his wife. She was younger and though to be even more beautiful, a princess from the Silures tribe by the name of Elena. She was as crocked and rocky as the lands that birthed her and treacherous as well. She was dominant and willful, unlike the precious and soft natured princess from Egypt. Elena wanted to rule as the main wife and to oust the older Arsinoe and her young daughter Alanya. It was she who suggested to Drennedd that Alanya be fostered out.

Drennedd was held powerless under the spell of his younger wife and followed her advise in all matters and in all of her selfish suggestions.

Sion felt helpless as he observed the laughter fading from the once brilliant blue eyes of Arsinoe as she was being cast aside along with her daughter Alanya.

The horrific events soon emanated when Elena soon gave birth to a son, Drennedd. Sion knew the chieftain Drennedd took Arsinoe against her will to produce more sons. And when that failed, the bruises followed. She hid them with care under her dim smiles and lies to reassure him in his persistent questioning.

Elena ruled all, while Arsinoe stood quietly in her shadow, giving up the last of her hopes and dreams. Even her voice was muted in her pain. Her songs almost completely ceased, especially when her only child and comfort, her precious Alanya was sent away for fosterage to her niece Jubilla. Jubilla was now the Queen of all of Britannia as accepted by Rome and their Imperator Augustus.

He heard her last song in a soft musical whisper as her daughter, then only six years old was sent away from her nurture and protection. She had sang a lullaby to her daughter to ease the journey and to probably comfort herself with the ways of this new land. Sion's soul cried along with hers in silence, for she needed his strength in this world that was closing in against her.

He observed Arsinoe spend more and more time with Hadwinna, the weaver and prophetess, a long ago Ovate for the order of the east until she faded into obscurity in this far away village by the edge of the sea. He noticed how, Arsinoe as well faded almost into the shadows herself and become lost in the weaving. Abandoning her song and music. Yet, he still was there for her friendship and comfort. He held her close, while she cried over her loss, over her life, over her duty.

He sent offerings to all of the Gods and Goddesses for his strength in keeping him from kissing her, from taking her into his arms and into his deepest passions that he felt for her. He knew that it could not hold out any longer and even tried to hide from her, where he wept bitter tears at the Gods who sent him this sweet torment.

He had even considered on many occasions jumping off the steep cliffs that were always there mocking him. Screaming of his chaste relationship. The waves below beckoning him as he knew in life he never could.

Yet, she would always find him with her needs, her overwhelming needs that would conquer his own. Her pale form beckoned for his pure and loving embrace, his truthful words that soothed her horrors.

A few days ago was one such evening when his desires had found him. For he sought his haven to gather his strength. The full moon covered the steep drop below him. The waves in angry violet crashed sadistically against the jagged jaws of the narrow harbor far below. The roar of the waves ripped with sharp teeth at his very being and meaning of it all. Calling him, cajoling him, taunting him to escape her and his love that was overpowering his every thought and losing his fight in control.

A twig snapped, a form stood silent in witness to his turmoil. There she stood, as if his soul had reached her somehow. She was covered in wispy Roman robes. A silken cocoon of ethereal beauty. Her long summer gold curls danced around her in response to the windy place where they stood.

Without words, their souls collided and finally their physical bodies. An end to his torment, his fervent prayers answered at last. Lost and then delivered. So pure and full of passion, time stood still for them. Their embrace eternal. Realizing the heavens in their full glory. All questions were answered—yet many more were created.

Knowing what could happen to them if discovered. Risking it all nonetheless. A twig broke, their flight began. Not knowing who it was who could have betrayed them, not caring. They ran, with hands entwined. Their destiny realized at last.

Connected in fate, they ran along the coast for awhile. Living off the land and in each others embrace. Risking all. Knowing their doom would soon be delivered to them. Sealing their fate.

Though the embrace on the cliff brought to them their demise, it was pure and innocent. It was more. It was all of Arsinoe's dreams realized. Her soul had found it's very completion in the fullness of his embrace. Her body met his in perfection. To an observer the embrace was more. The illusion of two perfect hearts joining in the obscurity of a life of completion denied them for so long. More was felt than the reality. More was implied from simple observation.

She lamented silently in their flight all that she had left behind. A daughter now old enough to have children of her own. Her soft delicate child who resembled the insubstantial dreams of a fairy in her ethereal demeanor. Destined to be cherished and loved. The visits over the years were enough for her to see the way her daughter was flourishing under the care of her niece Jubilla, who was a mother on her own several times over.

She knew her Alanya and Jubilla's twin, Silla were close friends and allies in mischief. The responsible other twin, Cleo kept them in line and in their stations as princesses.

Her great nephews from Jubilla, she barely knew. The daughter left some time ago to become a priestess. The sons of Jubilla and Cynfelyn were becoming fierce warriors like their father, along with Silla.

As for her brother Ptolemy, he and his love had become famous warriors in their own right and almost disappeared from their lives many years ago. Rumors of their life drifted to her in song from passing Bards, though with nothing of substance. She missed him fervently, yet was also angry that he shut his family out of his life-as if they never were. She had given up crying for him long ago.

For her sister, Selene who was diligent in her correspondence, her love for her was like the tough scrolls upon which they both wrote to each other. Endurable and as real as the words written on them. Yet, she longed for her sister's embrace. Selene wore the fragrance of Jasmine that she most recalled in the faded memories of her real mother. The reality of her childhood seemed almost a dream to her in her life that she now lived. So far away and ethereal. It seemed almost to Arsinoe that her mother's embrace would reach her through each of her older sister's hugs of comfort which she so desperately needed at this time in her life.

Through her present travails-she longed for some connection to her safe and native land of her birth and past. Of a time when she was protected from how ugly life could possibly be.

She was glad that Selene led a happy and contented life, she deserved it. Selene, like she, had done her duty. She married in contract, gave birth to heirs, none that would threaten Rome. Selene was lucky in that everything she touched turned to gold and sparkled for the world to see, yet not enough to threaten the eyes of Rome. She smiled genuinely at her sister's well deserved fortune.

She never let Selene know the truth of her declining life and position. Perhaps it was pride. Perhaps she knew that Selene would cease all of the good that she was doing far away in Mauretania and rush over here to be by her side and to pursue her enemies. She might have also been afraid of her sister actually telling her that she could do nothing about it, due to the reality of her precarious position and throne to the power of Rome and Augusta. She knew deep down inside that she feared the latter the most. Arsinoe knew that if Selene would run to her aid and safety, it would be a grave mistake. The political situation that it would create, could possibly shatter any illusion Rome had of Pryttain or of the land they called Britannia. They felt the land of the Keltoi in the farthest reaches, too unstable with inside political battles and strife, to be tamed. They felt it far to unstable to settle or to conquer, as this would bring them over to their peaceful shores that her husband faithfully guarded. She knew that it would be an easy invasion would they choose that path, and so far, they were safe from them at present.

So, in the correspondence with her sister, she kept her life on papyrus safe and simple to protect her shores and her sister, most of all.

As they sat by the fire in the only place in the world that had allowed them a brief peace, both voices slowly rose up unison to the ballad of the sea and it's protection and of the branches that covered them in hiding.

The twig that snapped was followed by another that brought the two lovers from their song to the present in which they sat and to their predicament.

The branched parted to reveal the slight figure of Hadwinna who had followed them. "Finally, I have found you both!"

"Do join us please, for you are like a mother to me...", chimed in Arsinoe. She had moved over from her close position from Sion to provide a space for her beloved Hadwinna. Her long white hair frazzled from the journey to find her precious charges cascaded feverishly in the ominous light of the fire. Her garments were frayed and dingy from her flight from the village by the Sea to find them.

"How did you find us?" added the startled Sion to this ancient woman and weaver.

"Had ta leave the village at some time or 'nether, did I not? I was afeared some ill would hae become ye without me wisdom." She cackled to the brilliantly starry evening above them, peeking between the canopy of great Oaks that surrounded their solitude and hiding place from the events of the world.

"I am so glad that you are here, for I would have dreadfully missed you."

"Do ye lovers know that they all be out looking for ye? Drennedd hae even left empty the bed of Elena to seek ye lovers out, for he truly repents the way he tossed ye Arsinoe aside in his reckless yearnings for that evil woman. He was startin' ta see the illness in her and wanted yer truly ta understand."

"I had no idea, I have always done my duty, and where has it brought me? I have tried to be the proper wife, yet he tossed me aside for one who was much younger. Does our child matter not to him at all?"

"Hadwinna, we have never been lovers in the flesh only in our hearts. She is untouched by any but her husband, this I swear!" Cried out Sion in his desperation.

"But what does it truly mean, when all of this be judged. Ye should not endure no' other embrace, but that of ye husband chile! What were you thinking, Arsinoe? To have thrown all yer hard work away for somethin' that can never be? Ye own daughter'll be sought out and destroyed as will ye both and she will be deemed illegitimate and not worthy for future reign! And all for somethin' which would be over in one minute!"

"I had not thought of that, truly, it was only an embrace!"

"Yes, but yer souls be both connected and erased everythin' else in the world with that one act! Ye should have kept him to yer dreams. Now ye foolish girl have brought yer Alanya into this, an innocent."

"It was I, who lured her into my arms, wise one!"

"Nay, it was the both of ye! For years I have watched the love grow between the two of ye and tried to prevent it's fruition, to no avail, For I walked into it's wrath on that cliff!" Her anger was growing, causing Arsinoe to jump back a little bit from the full onslaught of her words.

"Don't' you realize what jeopardy you have placed your husband in? They sent out troops to find yer daughter at yer niece's settlement. Alanya would have been a fine warrior, adding to the glory of yer family name. But all of that forgotten with a kiss, that should n'ver have occurred!"

"But, there was no kiss, only in our souls has that come to be!" Arsinoe cried in exasperation to the dire words of her beloved mother weaver.

"For too long I have waited for Drennedd to notice me and to seek me out. For I have a lineage as noble as you, though I was passed over due to the emptiness of my womb! I have seen ye mock at being the perfect wife to him, not really caring how it affected him! How ye actually were hurt that he would seek out 'nother wife, since ye had ignored his pleas in yer marital bed. Ye were actually slighted by him! I comforted ye dear Arsinoe and had hoped that ye would see the error of yer whoring ways, but ye have not! Yer selfishness, sees no bonds in this life. For all was lost in your determination to be with Sion. Yer Alanya, but a shadow to your feelings for Sion!"

She was practically drooling in her seething contempt for Arsinoe and had then turned her wrath on Sion, "And ye find Bard ye be, who played the mute in all of this, was secretly fanning the fire to her dreams. Has any of your training rang true. Ye have no part in her life and never will. Now because of both of you and yer selfish desires, ye both will be a part in the end of all of this, ye two will be the main act. Ye lovers two who could have kept yer feelings aquiet deep in yer souls, have opened the floodgates of wrath! Actions have consequences! Do ye both not see this, no matter how little!"

Arsinoe collapsed in the reality of her impending doom. For no sooner had the old woman spoken had the forest come alive with the voices of the warriors of the Belgae who had entered this clearing being hailed forward by none other than Hadwinna.

Arsinoe had sent out the day before her pebble given long ago by her friend Andocos for protection in her plight. She had found a small runner to pass the stone north to her niece's tribal lands. She initially had hoped that it was the army of Jubilla and Cynfelyn. Her hopes and prayers to Isis in vain and she faced the reality of her heart and the consequences.

Sion and Arsinoe were led brutally over to the side of the clearing. Elena and Drennedd had arrived to mete out the fate of the doomed lovers before them.

"Let it be that no one should mock the King of the Belgae, you belonged to me woman and to no other! Let your crimes be paid in full with this. Let their embrace be their last!" Five men had grabbed the trembling Arsinoe and her Sion together with arms entwined against a large oak branch that was placed in between the both of them in their ghastly embrace. Voices arose from the distance.

"We have the other one sire." The form of their daughter Alanya was then brought over to her mother and thrown into a heap before them all.

With surprising coolness, her father looked at his daughter as if she was a deformed piece of meat brought to him for inspection. He looked her over and looked at one of his men to the side who came over to the princess and swiftly cut her throat from one side to the other. "I deem her illegitimate!"

Arsinoe was too shocked to grasp the fullness of the situation that unfurled mercilessly before her. Did it not matter that they had never kissed? Did it not matter that Drennedd had killed his daughter, and no one else. He just stood there as if nothing had happened. She even had begun to doubt the reality of the event herself, but felt the tightness of the ropes that bound her to her love, to her soul's completion. Was any of this worth it in the long run? The wood was being gathered and placed at their feet, she knew her destiny? Would her sister understand? She had only veered slightly from her duty. She never really did in the flesh. But her mind held vast dreams of his embrace and of his kisses and of their bodies becoming one, over and over again. The smoke wafted to her nostrils and the heat lapped at her feet. She was numb in the embrace of her Sion and he was numb in her embrace. Their eyes met for one last time as the fire began to swell and to embrace their forms into happy oblivion.

Annius, Cynfelyn's brother stood behind the warriors of the Belgae with a smirk spreading over his face and in his hand he held tightly the intercepted pleadings of help in the form of a small white pebble with strange undecipherable writing around it. He tossed it into the ashes of their foolishness. Maybe this will inspire his brother into action. The warriors of his land were growing fat with too much peace-they needed something to fight for.

VIII

"My dearest Antonia,

How I long for the sweet innocent days of our childhood, when reality was kept far from us.

I have recently learned the news of the horrific fate of my sister Arsinoe! My beautiful sister with the summer blonde curls. My baby sister, whose innocence will remain in my heart forever! For she had been executed along with her daughter and her alleged lover by her husband one month ago. The information had been sent to me from Jubilla. Jubilla wanted to gather an army against the Belgae in retribution and had asked me for advice. She was greatly upset at her foster daughter and Arsinoe's daughter being torn away from her teachings in becoming a warrior and of being deemed illegitimate. She had not known that Alanya would have been found guilty of something that was done before her birth! You know as well as I how true that could be from the Roman rule. How many families had been ripped apart and destroyed for the sins of their fathers. I wish she did not have to learn this lesson so harshly of the rule of men.

I will never know the truth of Arsinoe and Sion, since she mentioned nothing of him in her letters to me. I thought her life with Drennedd was fine and comforting to her. I feel partly responsible as if I had sent her to her death. But, how could I have known what part fate would play out for her and what plans the Gods had in store for her life and her daughter's. I never had the chance to meet the girl and wondered what she may have looked like. Had she the warrior heart of my mother? Did she have the Antony eyes that we have, sister? She was only thirteen years old. As for my sister, her life was based on duty always making those in charge of her life in obeying the life chosen for her. Did she die

hating me for sending her there? I thought her life would be so much better with their ways that tend to give women an equal voice.

I tend to doubt an affair as alleged to have occurred between the two of them, since she was so adamant in doing what was right and her duty. She took her role serious and would not have done anything to jeopardize it. She would not have risked the life of her daughter, for any fantasies that she might have had for her Bard.

On the other hand, I do believe that she had passion for her music, and possibly it was played out in the form of her trainer and Bard. I hope that after all that has happened, she found some happiness in her reality, which she never found important enough to tell me.

As for the rest of life in Mauretania, Julia has given birth to a fine son, Ptolemy of Mauretania and is expecting her second child soon. She worries me, I hope that she does not do the same to my son, for her heart seems to wander as well. That does not bode well for a princess.

Juba and Helios had fast found a common love, travel. The two of them embarked on a two year journey which led to vast discoveries of uncharted lands along the west coast of this continent and past the pillars of Hercules in the lands of Hispania, with some islands discovered. He brought back five small yellow birds that sing gloriously and like none other that I have heard before. He called the lands the Islands of the Canary, after those delightful birds. He had also discovered many new forms of plant life to add to his journals.

As for my brother, he just seemed to drop off the face of this earth, for nothing has been heard of him and his love Ahrianred except for in songs. There is a delightful ballad written for them, which I will enclose. Who knows the truth behind the words, for the rhythm played along is marvelous and dreamlike. The Keltoi have a way of making ordinary mortals into Gods, as is in the epic lyrics dedicated to my brother and of his life.

Jubilla is the mother of a small tribe of her own. For the twins only look alike, according to their mother and are as different as could possibly be. For Drusilla was in training as a warrioress along the side of her doomed cousin, Alanya. Cleopatra is preparing for a marriage. For I will be sending over my brother's son, Helios for her to wed. The moon and the sun will connect with their union! Her younger daughter Leanydd is in training to be a priestess, while her sons are proving to be great future warriors! Her husband Cynfelyn has created a great rule over that land and a fathomable troop of skilled warriors to serve as overlords under his rule.

How is life in Roma Dea? How are your fine sons Claudius and Germanicus? I believe that Germanicus will soon be donning the toga of manhood, how fares Claudius? Is he almost ten years old by now? And your little girl Livilla, she must be a darling! You must also send word of Tiberius and Julia and how their marriage fares. How many children does she have now? And her son's Lucius and Gaius, are they ready for the rule after their grandfather?

Please send my love to Livia. I am waiting for a letter from Livia, it is her turn to write. I truly miss the letters from your mother. She was a wonderful writer and I do love the stories that she had to tell of life in Rome, she makes life there seem wonderful and fun.

Will you be planning to visit soon with your children? If not I will stop by on the way to bringing Helios' grandson Alexander over to Britannia. Alexander was born from my twin brother's son Helios and his wife, Berenice from Macedonia. Helios and Berenice have lived here in the palace with all of us. Alexander is a joy to us all and I believe truly looks like his namesake and famous ancestor, Alexander the Great with his beautiful golden locks that his mother refuses to cut in any way. Such vanity will not come to any good for the boy, though so far he is untouched by it.

Tell your husband that I am sending along some marvelous pottery from a local tribe to adorn your villa, along with some purple dyed cloth from Tyre that was sent to us from Julia's family.

With love,
From your sister,

Queen Selene of Mauretania"

With that she sealed the scroll and bid the nearest slave in the shadow of her chamber to take it out to one of the ships in her harbor heading out for Rome. She had a few things to settle before taking her leave with her brother's son to Britannia. She was planning to leave within the month. Slowly she stood up and began to walk out purposefully towards the nursery to see her fine grandson and to check on the condition of Julia, for she was preparing for the birth of her second child, after which, Selene would leave for her last journey to Britannia for a while. She would not be as long as the last time and would stay only for a month or so to make sure her grandchild Cleo was settled in with her soon to be new husband, Alexander.

Alexander was growing into a fine warrior with a lust for travel that her husband had tried to give to their son. Juba III was fine in staying within the boundaries of their kingdom and burying himself in judicial and administrative duties, perhaps almost too much. For she had noticed Julia often alone and wandering around on her own throughout the palace. The woman had no interest in Mauretania or her children for that matter. She noticed the absence of Julia from way too many important functions. Ptolemy never complained about that though, and mentioned that it was probably due to his spending so much time with the countries accounts. His love of battle displayed in his youth was forgotten in his lack of use, since the reign of Augustus had brought about an end to the civil wars that Rome was filled with for so many years since long before her own birth or her mother's for that matter.

As she was walking along she almost stumbled into the disarrayed form of her daughter in law, Julia. "Julia, you should be resting in your condition, let me help you to your quarters, please. I was just heading there."

"Mother Selene, I am fine and am on my way to an important matter that must be attended to."

"There could be nothing important, but rest, for you carry the heir to Mauretania, you need your rest, for there are only three moons left until the birth."

Julia was frazzled, for she desperately wanted to be in the arms of her gladiator lover, rather than to be talking with this incessant woman. For her form had barely changed much despite how far along she was in her pregnancy and she wanted to take full advantage of this. "I realize that, but I had promised the cook that I would give him my mother's recipe for heartburn that she would hide in a stew. I do not like the remedies here. I would only vomit them out."

"My dear, let me take you back to your quarters and I will have a scribe transfer the information and then send it to the kitchens for that dish." She placed her hand on Julia's arm and she turned to flee the scene. Selene had wondered about her daughter-in-law and of her true motives of her apparent need to flee her company.

"I really have to go! I need to speak with the cook about it since I do not want it to take so long!" She was desperate, for she was panicked that her form would catch up to the stage that she was in pregnancy and was fearful that she would not be found attractive to her young gladiator that she had so painstakingly chosen, due to his lack of speaking their language. He was from farther Gaul and if he were to complain about their affair, he would not have been understood. For she had half forgotten the ability of Selene to speak this language from her journey fourteen years prior.

"Nonsense, I will take you to your quarters myself." She grasped Julia tighter now in light of the situation that she was trying to prevent. For any slight to her son was a slight to herself.

"Selene, I am a grown woman and can take care of myself. I am tired of your trying to take over my life! I can handle this myself and would appreciate you to unhand me to handle my business by myself!"

"Julia, first you must understand that I care only for the welfare of my family and I am sensing that you are on an errand which will render harm to it. I do not for one minute believe your motive as stated to me earlier. I feel that something is amiss in your fabrication and wonder if it affects my son and your true feelings for him. I must insist…"

"My feelings for him? Since when was I consulted in my feelings on our marriage. I understand it is my duty to obey the command of my father and for what I must do as a princess, prostitute myself for the alliance of your country and my homeland. But, that does not mean that I have to agree with it, besides…"

"I understand all of that, I had to face the same prospects myself, for I never chose my husband either…"

"You ramble on old woman! You have a husband who loves you and lets your rule by his side—or rather let you rule for him. I never will get that chance, for your son dominates everything. Besides, he hardly has time for me and is a horrible lover at that!"

Selene was mortified at what this strap of a girl was saying about her son. She had always wondered about her and her way of hiding her true personality under her shy and apparently false recessive personality. She was rendered speechless at the tirade that was bursting forth from this girl, completely unexpected.

"I am tired of having to depend on the affections of the eunuchs that I have trained as my own mother did. For my own father hardly had time for my mother with all of his wives. True, I am only one wife to your son, but he is always busy with boring matters of state. I really do not care about this paltry country and of being a puppet ruler to Rome! Your son has his own lover as well, for his lovers are men! He is repulsed by my body and only comes to it as a form of duty! I am beautiful and young still. Do not worry, both Ptolemy and this child that I carry in my womb belong to your son, for I took careful measures to assure this…"

"I cannot believe what you have told me about my own son! How can I believe you now!"

"Believe what you will! I do not care! I am going to my lover who does find me attractive. You have nothing to worry about his seed gaining anything on my already plowed fields! I am very cautious on this and assure you on the validity of your grandchild. But stop condemning me on finding affections from a man, because your son is repulsed by me and only does his duty!"

Selene's grasp loosened on Julia in the shock of the revelation about her son. She had no idea. She wondered if she could still find fault in Julia and in her wandering ways. Looking for love that she would never receive from her own husband. She watched as Julia ran away from her presence down the long and seemingly endless marbled halls. Her form growing smaller and smaller to turn down another corridor and out of her sight.

Still, she stood there numb from shock. She had to confront her own son on this. She did not worry about the paternity of her grandson for he looked too much like her own husband and little Juba at that age. She fervently hoped for the sake of Julia that the child that she carried resembled Juba III when born.

On thinking of those matters so new to her in comprehension, she did not hear the approach of Kateiran, her slave who had been with her since her leaving Rome for the marriage of Juba so many years and adventures ago.

She looked up from her reverie into his deep blue eyes. So handsome. She hated the way that fate had made him a slave and she a Queen. She wondered which Gods laughed over this. For she always had a fondness for Kateiran and had sought out his advice on many matters in the past and admired how he was always right and loved his strong objectivity on all matters. She felt that he would have made a wise ruler.

She had cried over his story on how he was the descendant of Vercingetorix, same as her nephew Helios from his mother's line. Kateiran was taken away by a wandering band of Romans while he was in training to become a Druid. Kateiran knew of many healing secrets from herbs native to that area, they would often compare notes on the similarities of plants and of their many different names and properties.

She felt weak in her recent knowledge acquired from the flighty Julia and looked up to Kateiran for advice on this matter. She bade him to sit down on a bench in the hallway where they stood and she then related what she was told.

"My lady, for the truth hurts does it not? If real life was not so interesting and full of hidden turns, for what purpose would fiction serve if not to lighten the burden of the truth so that we may handle it better?"

"I had not thought if truth quite like that..." Her eyes downcast as if to hide from any further truths that might catch her unaware. For she had already had her fill for the day.

"So, you have heard about my son, Kateiran? Does he truly have male lovers."

"Do you really ask me for that answer. Think on him and all you know about his ways. Julia is a beautiful woman, a trifle cold perhaps and selfish. But what princess is not sometimes, even yourself…Besides neither of them chose one another. Their lives were planned from their births. No one consulted them on that matter at all. They might be royal, but they do have hearts and souls that need to be fulfilled. You know the answer about your son, he is Greek in more ways than in just the way he dresses." He paused to let her inhale this.

"I am surprised that you have not chosen lovers yourself, my lady…For you have that right. As long as your issue is from Juba only, there is no reason why you have not chosen someone to warm your beds on chill evenings. You and your husband have separate quarters do you not?"

"Kateiran, surly you cannot suggest anything of that…I simply cannot even think about it."

"The truth sometimes hurts a little too much, but it is what it is, the truth. Do you think that your husband only seeks you out? And what about his many voyages, a man has his needs…"

"Enough, I cannot bear hearing any more about this! Juba loves me and is not that sort of man. "

"He is a man Selene. And you as a woman have been spending way too many evenings alone waiting for his summons. Your youngest child is a father of his own now! You are still in your childbearing years, if not almost at the end of them. Why has he not called you to your bed in so many years…" His tone gentle and understanding. Selene found it difficult to find anger on him and sat quietly in contemplation of words she had not even uttered to herself. She blushed at the realization of Kateiran by her side speaking to her in confidence. Something a normal slave would not dare to do with a mistress. Yet, he was more to her and wondered why he had not left her years ago when she had freed him. He had stayed by her side and acted as advisor. Much to the ignorance of her own husband. She dared not tell Kateiran that she had dreamed of him on those many lonely evenings, and of their being born to different stations in life. She accepted her fate wearily over the past many years and had always retreated to her cold bed. Longing to be found attractive again by Juba, anyone.

And here was Kateiran telling her that her husband did not come to her bed because he had found others, perhaps younger. For she had served her duty and provided the heirs necessary for the continuance of rule over Mauretania.

She understood Julia and wondered why she was not as adventurous as she. She was not even as adventurous as her own mother, who had won the hearts of two very powerful Romans and succeeded in turning the tables of time. Her mother had followed her heart, why she could not was bothering her just then.

Kateiran noticed the moral conflict that his mistress faced and watched the many emotions that crossed her beautiful face, even the blush that covered her slender neck. He wondered at this and understood it at that moment. For he knew why he stayed by her side.

He reached over and placed his fingertips along her jaw line and brought her face to his. He kissed her full lips softly, pleadingly and felt her body stiffen in response.

"I cannot… Please, Kateiran… I need to handle the truth right now, please understand." She looked up and noticed a guard all too quiet standing in the doorway closest to them, yet in the shadow. Would news of this get to her husband? She hurriedly stood up and ran back to her quarters. She must find a way to speed up the journey to Britannia to visit with her daughter and grandchildren. She needed to be away from Kateiran, where she knew her heart would never let her have peace by his side.

Berenice then slipped from the shadows with even more secrets of this wild and exuberant family that she knew she would take to her grave. She loved the shadows, they often revealed much information, some she did not even want to hear. Though due to her all too quiet demeanor, she never had anyone to talk to about it. Her mother-in-law was always too busy and Julia was too preoccupied, and the men, well… that would never happen. Her husband Helios was constantly away on matters with the King and her son, well, he was too small to talk to on matters of import and when he would be finally old enough, he would be taken away from her. Most often people forgot about her, so she preferred to live in the shadows of the vast palace environs and fall even deeper into her silent world in the solitude she was more than used to.

IX

"My dearest sister,

I have some dire news to relate to you. For Julia's sons are both dead now and the rule of Rome will go to Tiberius. First Gaius died of an illness and then a year later Lucius died. Two illnesses to heirs of the rule does not bode well with Rome. Livia is all too quiet with this, for people suspect her of some part in this, though there is no proof. For both were rather sickly from birth.

Tiberius has left Rome for his villa in Capri, much to the dismay of my uncle who is livid over the matter. He wants to train Tiberius for rule. Yet, Tiberius would have nothing to do with his stepfather. He is angry at him for forcing him to divorce his beloved Vispania to marry Julia. After Julia gave birth to their stillborn son, he left her and Rome. Julia has ran savage at the abandonment of her husband and is seeking love from everyone. The rumors fill the streets of Rome of her scandalous behavior. I fear for our half brother Iully, the son of our father and his wife Fulvia, for he has fallen to the charms of the wayward Julia. I fear greatly for his safety. For Julia's behavior is destroying her own father, he will have to set an example for Rome and he might have to bring her down, and all those associated with her!

I congratulate you on the birth of your granddaughter, Drusilla! I hear she most resembles your mother with her raven locks and charming eyes! Let us hope that she has the personality and the sense of adventure of your mother as well! For I believe our lives so boring compared to those led by our parents!

As for my mother, she had died over a year ago and am sorry that you have not heard about it. Rome celebrated her as a matron from

the old Roma Dea and was admired by all and many men had cried over her pyre, while gifts are still being placed upon that spot. Alters have been erected by many wives of Rome, hoping they will be as faithful as she in her duty to Rome and her husband. I still miss her and her advice dreadfully and hear her voice and what she would say when I search for her advice and guidance. Now we both are motherless. What a fate for anyone to have to bear. For now I truly understand your plight in having to lose your own while still young. It is even a wonder why you even spoke to us in the first place.

How is your family doing in Britannia? You must be anxious to visit them. For I had heard about the delay in bringing Helios over there. My heart cried for you and I wish to hold you close. How could Juba have chosen a new wife at this stage in his life? Glaphyra. I hate to tarnish this letter with her name. Is she truly so young? I had heard that he was devoted to you. I am truly sorry. I am glad that my husband never did that to me. For he blamed me on the monster that I gave birth to, Claudius. He stammers and drools and stutters like a baboon. He is s disgrace to our family and has been sheltered from all public view. He even limps and has the falling sickness. Germanicus, my elder son blames me for this and stated that it was due to the allegation that I had an affair while pregnant. Only you and I know the truth of that as well as dear Drusus, may he rest well with the Gods! Livillia, on the contrary is growing into a raving beauty and we are planning her betrothal, possibly to Drusus the Younger, Tiberius' son from Vispania. Young Germanicus is on campaign in Germania and is planning to leave to Gaul on matters which I care not.

Fondest love,
From your sister,

Antonia

Post script. I had not sent this letter off as soon as it was completed for I felt there was more to write, and it was true.

My uncle Augustus, had sent word to Tiberius just prior that he was adopted as his heir along with Agrippa Posthumus, the last son of Julia and Agrippa. Tiberius in meeting with my uncle that last time was forced to accept his brother Germanicus' son Germanicus the Younger as heir over his own son in the line of succession after him. Such was the public outcry in Rome on that matter of surprise.

Also, my uncle was forced to banish his own daughter, his cherished and spoiled Julia to Rhegium an island isolated from the mainland and away from causing scandal in Rome. He also added to his will that Julia would not be allowed internment in the family mausoleum."

Part seven

I

12 C.E. to 16 A.D.

The ominous halls of the palace of Mauretania were bathed in the gold of the setting sun. So quiet was it's appearance that it would seem almost as if it sat in tranquility and peace. Such was not the case. For trouble brewed along the shores of Mauretania with the local tribes in the land. They abhorred the rule over their kingdom with a king they felt ignored them. It was all too apparent that the rule was mostly done by Selene and her son, Juba III. They felt that it was time for a change. They wanted the rule to go to the leader of the tribal kings to the grandson, though illegitimate of Boccus. Boccus the Younger led a fierce band of illusive warriors who adhered to the non-Roman ways of old. They wanted to oust this family from Numidia who tried to rule a country not theirs by right of true succession.

Boccus the Younger had led many small rebellions that were easily subdued by the ruling family over the years, though was saving the best for this quiet evening.

He took the God of the sunset as an omen for the good and felt that the Gods were with him this time, for once. Over the past five years, the small attacks were stopped and the royal family felt that the threat was over. How wrong they were. He looked over at the palace that was built over the ruins of lands owned by his family before their defeat. How garish the Egyptian and Greek styled palace looked, as if trying to tame a feral land with what they viewed as civilization. The walls were large and daunting in their simplicity. The columns seemed ominous of the lands they tried to emulate. Lost civilizations in their time. Both dominated by Rome. Though, to the best of his knowledge, Rome had never created anything new on it's own, only borrowed the great ideas of Greece and made a wreck of them. Losing the grace and flowing form lost in their cubist ideas. Making rough the forms meant to be soft and graceful, hardening them to their Roman logical minds. His own land of Mauretania was free flowing and bright before the dull colors of the Juba and Ptolemy lines tried to simplify them in long columns of white marble imported from far away to dominate his land with their culture.

He was told by his uncle after the death of his father, that the palace that once stood there was made of wood from the large and majestic trees that stood further inland in vast jungles. Various colors long ago adorned the high and imposing walls and told the stories of his family. It was all burnt down and this garish display from the new ruling family held ground. These upstarts from Numidia and Egypt who invaded his land on the orders of the great Julius Caesar's heir, now Imperator and growing old.

He turned to his men as they lined the surrounding hillsides and coast in battle formation, "Wait for my orders. I want to see the oil lamps lit. We strike by the first rays of the moon." The men laid down their weapons, sparkling against the setting sun as they did so. Their painted bodies and dark glistening skin almost blending with the colors of the dying sun, now bending lower to sleep. He knew that tonight was the first of the full moon's evenings and felt it graced his mission.

Selene lay down among the various colored pillows to read her letter just received from Jubilla. She felt in her heart that she did not want to truly read the contents, but knew that she must. She felt that these were the last chapters in her long life of fifty two years, and somehow she must participate in them. She noticed the date and realized that it took almost two years for her to receive this letter and hoped that all fared well with her daughter and her family.

"Dearest mother,

I write to you with great tears that blind my soul. For now I truly understand that pain that you had faced with the loss of your daughter and my sister Drusilla. For I write to you about the loss of my own Drusilla, my beloved Silla. It almost seemed as if she was doomed with her name from birth. For she mocked it, she truly did. She entered the warrior school and excelled in her battle talent and tactical skills, much like your brother Ptolemy, may he rest with the Gods. For I have not heard much about him, nothing but silence for many years.

As for my Drussi, she was the top in skill for the women warriors and had learned so much, you would have been proud of her. For she was glorious in her warrior garb with her long flowing flame colored hair, she painted herself like the Pictish warriors of old in purple with menacing designs very symbolic to my people.

For on the day of her death, she was summoned into battle and even led them all on her gold plated chariot that was carved with magical Ogham prayers in the sacred writings of the Druids. Her chariot was blessed. I saw her ride out, how wonderful and powerful she looked with her long beautiful hair trailing out behind her. Many men sought her hand in marriage, but she would never take any-for she was truly married to battle! Like the grand Goddess Morrigan of our people or the Roman Goddess Hecate or Athena—she looked fearsome. I felt safe knowing that she and her warriors were protecting our people.

That very evening I was greeted by my sons, Caradawc, Cyllin and Gweiryth carrying the mutilated body of my beautiful daughter. They had bound her wounds and fixed her hair in braids for the matron that she would never be. My soul has not been the same for me since, even though I still have another daughter who will soon be a mother, the exact likeness of her valiant warrior sister.

How did you learn to move on mother, all this pain overwhelms me. I feel as if I will soon be lost in the labyrinth of despair for I am too tired to do anything but cry and hold my other children close.

Silla was murdered by Roman butchers who had camped out on the coast and were probably just bored, there were no orders from Rome on this, I assure you. I fear that there will be many more such battles, soon to come, when they realize how wonderful it is here, so far away from the rest of the world. They will try to seize the sanctuary as their own and will not stop at that either, I fear. I know as long as Augustus rules over Rome we will be safe. But with the next ruler, we fear and have nothing to do but wait.

It has taken me so long to write this to you and will probably take awhile sending it to you. Almost as if it makes the reality of her death the truth when it is put down on papyrus.

My husband was recognized by Augustus as the official ruler of Britannia in ceremony, whatever that must mean, since he had been that all along in name. But still, it gives us more clout against the many neighboring tribes here. He is a just and able ruler over his people. He makes me very proud. Each of my sons rule over neighboring tribes that my husband had conquered and they all are doing fine with wives of their own. I am a grandmother to three boys and two girls as I write this to you, yet sometimes feel as if I am still a child in the palace far away in Mauretania. I remember all of the stories that you have told me about my grandmother the legendary and greatest of all of Cleopatra's. I have told them to my own daughters.

I cannot wait for your visit with your brother's grandson, Alexander. The story you have told about his father was so tragic. He must be well loved if he is anything like your twin brother whom you lost so many years ago. I wish I knew him. But fate handed be another place to stand in time. Will I meet his wife Berenice from Macedonia. How wonderful to be joining two children who have such legendary namesakes, Cleopatra and Alexander. The people here only have a small understanding of the powerful names of the future bride and groom!

My Cleopatra fervently awaits her prince from Mauretania, and I cannot wait until she becomes a mother! For Leanydd cannot have children, having taken a vow of chastity as a priestess in serving the Goddess. Though she will be present at the time of birth for Cleopatra. She is much older for her first marriage than you or I have been. It is a shame that the waters have not been calmer for a safer journey sooner in years that now.

How is Julia and Juba, my brother. Do their children resemble their father at all with his cowlicks that never stayed in place. I still remember that. He will always look like a silly little boy to me and I will never forget how many of my sand castles that he had destroyed with his slingshot! I do miss him so! Send my love to my beautiful niece and nephew.

Also send my love and a large hug for my father. I am forwarding some beautiful antique weapons that were recently uncovered by some ancient warrior Druids of this land. There is mystical Ogham writing engraved in the Iron. Cynfelyn feels that there is another metal as well mixed in them for it is not familiar. The local Druid mentioned that it could be the metal of some meteor that fell hundreds of years ago.

It is odd, the weapons held by Druids, for all the people know about the Druids of our time, that they are great soldiers of peace and never actually chose one side or another in a time of battle. They might stay with a leader for a while, but never have any in all known history, ever taken up arms in battle. They have only been known as advisors, whom even the kings and rulers bend to in their great wisdom-except for the recent find, which changes every known preconception of their history.

Mother, please come soon to visit, for I need you!

Love always,

Jubilla,

Queen of the Trinovantes and Catuvellauni tribes of the land of the Pryttains whom the Romans call Britannia."

She held the now wrinkled scroll that she had read over and over again. The weapons were sent over to her husband to review and display. He loved to collect rare and vintage weapons no longer in use. She saw them being gathered into the arms of several slim ebony youths with delicate care.

She decided that it was time for another visit to the living quarters of her son's family.

II

She arrived to see her husband Juba with his grandchildren Drusilla who was now twelve and Ptolemy who was thirteen, going on fourteen and soon to don the toga of manhood.

"Grandfather, I want a ceremony too! I need one for becoming a woman! Because Momma told me that now I am!" Drusilla chimed in, innocently, to the blushing face of her grandfather who just sat there in mystification.

Selene felt that this was the perfect opportunity to break into the conversation to save her husband any further embarrassment over woman's things that he cared little about and certainly did not want to know about his own granddaughter! She kept her amusement to herself out of respect for her husband though and proceeded to enter the room with a change of subject. She entered the chamber loudly almost knocking into the eunuch by the door who frantically tried to appear not frazzled at the sudden appearance of his mistress. For he was also enjoying the position that his king was in.

"Oops, sorry." Chimed in Selene, making her sudden appearance known in the chamber.

"Children, how are you? I fare that all is well in here. Drusilla… Have I told you that your grandmother has a surprise planned for you for next week. Now that you are a woman and all. But you must not bother the men about this. For if you want to enter the secret society of women, there are many secrets involved, that men must never know! Are you truly ready for this?"

"Oh, yes I am, I have already chosen my dress…"

"Sssssh! Men in the room!" She looked over at her son Juba the Younger and his wife who tried to hide her chuckles as she lounged elegantly on the couch eating her end of the day meal by the side of Berenice who was quiet as usual. She winked over at Julia who covered her finger to her mouth and looked at Drusilla in mock conspiracy.

"Secrets Drusilla! A lady must know when to keep things from her men!"

Juba had found this chance to stride across the room to where his son and grandson sat who only looked more bewildered at the game that the women were playing.

He noticed that Helios was no where to be seen. "Has anyone seen Helios"

Everyone in the room nodded negatively, with the exception of Berenice who responded so quietly as to seem a whisper, "I believe that he is checking on that latest shipment of cloth from Tyre as you had requested my Lord." Juba nodded.

"Why am I always left out of things Tatta! It is my night, for I will be a man!" Cried Ptolemy to his father who sat with a heap of scrolls on his lap after finding an empty dining couch, while his food was left to sit cold on his plate. He had just received some work from his personal advisor who had slipped it by his side as usual just after Selene had entered the chamber.

"Ptolemy, let the women have their secrets, we will begin planning this event on the morrow! Not another word about it!" He winked at him while putting his work aside.

Ptolemy shrugged his shoulders at a battle lost and ambled over to where his sister sat. For he knew by the tome of his father's voice that the adults were going to discuss business matters which he felt truly boring.

"Where is Glyphra!, someone summon her now!" Juba irately questioned the guard closest to where he was reclining.

Selene's joy was momentarily waned at the mention of his second wife's name. "Husband, she had been locking herself in her chambers again—I had tried to gain her attention earlier this day. I am sorry." She looked down before sending a quick look over to Drusilla.

He grunted at that, "Something must be done about this-I am thinking of sending her back since she is useless here."

"Juba, may we speak of this some other time…"

"Selene, I do not care who hears this, I only married her, so that you may have more time doing what you do best and to give you an excuse to stay away from my chambers. It is rather lonely for a man."

"Tatta, please talk about this when I am not in the room" uttered Juba III who rolled his eyes at the thought of his parents duty together.

Ptolemy took his cue and felt the same about his grandparents discussion. He wondered why his grandfather had to discuss this in front of everyone. "Drussi, tell me did you see that cloth brought in from Cathay? I heard that it was made from worms!" He looked over at his sister, hoping to gross her out.

"Ummmm yum, maybe I should eat some of this cloth—I love worms!" Ptolemy was dazzled as always by his younger sister's bravery and quick wit. He was constantly trying to repulse her and she only asked for more. She truly was amazing! She should have been the son, for nothing frightened her. She would be a warrior, if only their father would let her. He would tell her along with their mother, that it was unseemly for a princess to bear weapons. She was not angered by dirt or anything, it seemed to him. He was a lot like both his mother and father in the fact that he was constantly in meticulous dress and in the latest fashions, without one hair out of place. Where his sister came from, he would never know. Only she looked the very image of his legendary great-grandmother, Cleopatra VII. He knew that when his sister grew up, she would rule over men, rather than their pitiful attempt to rule over her. He would love to see them try, for he tried to be her protector, even though she really did not need any. She let him try anyways. The adults voices droned on in their matters that little concerned him while he tried to interest his sister in the latest shipment from Syria and lands farther east in the lands of mystery. He wanted to see them someday and to travel farther than his own grandfather had.

III

"Juba, must you please see the seriousness of the situation! At least, Younger Juba, convince your father the direness of this.!" She looked pleadingly at her son and then up to her husband, who seemed all too content as of late.

"Mother, the last attack by the band was two years ago! They were all destroyed. We have nothing to fear!"

"Wife, why must you always find something to worry about!"

"Because that is what women do, they worry! I have learned that all times of peace are not always what they seem. Besides it had arrived to my attention that some weapons have been stolen as recently as one month ago. The smiths have been busy forging new weapons and not for us? I have checked into the matter. Not one order has been placed by anyone in authority in this family in over six months. Yet the forges burn! For whom are they burning? I have told you before and I will repeat this information…"

"Mother, I have heard you on this matter before, on Boccus the Younger. He is only legend. There is no proof that a son of his even existed! The forges are being fired for the new shipment of horses recently received from Macedonia."

"That is what they will have you believe. But truly, my son and husband. Why would the forges be running all through the evening hours as well. There were only forty horses sent over. How many shoes have been forged for them, millions by the heat of the fires that burn!"

"Mother, surely you exaggerate!"

"Selene, this matter can be looked into further, for you have brought some things to the fore that should be examined carefully. I hope it is to put the whole matter to rest? For all we need to face is something even remotely similar than what we faced as children." All heads bowed at this realization and how precariously they held their rule. They knew their situation was granted by the kindness of Augustus and could be taken away at any time. The air seemed tranquil from the direction of Rome, so the threat had to be from somewhere else. They knew what Juba and Selene faced. They knew how insecure their rule truly was.

"Selene, do not upset the children with this!" Volunteered Julia.

"Since when are you concerned about your children Julia, you are hardly ever in this chamber! Besides, I have always involved my children and yours as well in matters of import that concern this family!"

"I understand, but you are disturbing the digestion of my grapes with all of this talk about potential bloodshed." She smiled at this, of which Selene found humor in this antic.

"Besides, they are too busy ignoring the boring adults and talking about the latest fashions!" Added Selene. All heads turned towards the two children, at which the tension of the room was released.

"Children, you must retire to your sleeping chamber for we all have plans to make on the morrow!" Selene looked over to their nurse to bade her to lead the children out of the room for the evening.

"Always taking over the role of mother Selene!"

"If you would only do so yourself, you see how tired they were!"

"Ladies, please, we have matters to look into. Now lets all retire for the evening." Pleaded the tired voice of their King. All heads bowed and each went about readying themselves leave of the chamber.

Boccus the Younger, outside was patient. Other felt that he was perhaps too patient. He looked over to his next in command Lepi and told him, "Back off the men, we will wait until they return from the voyage. I know that the King from those lands is giving them a large tribute in weapons-I want them."

"But, sir…why not when they leave, surely the time will be more fortuitous at their absence."

"On the contrary-the guards will be tripled, as they have been so already while they prepare."

On the side Cian looked troubled, but needed to intercede, "But sire, the men grow restless, they need the blood to flow. Some will rebel if they have to wait any longer. Lepi nodded in assent.

Boccus growled, "That is why I am the leader and no other! For do you not realize that there will be more confusion at their return and the weapons will be easier to gather for us to use against them."

"Yes, out stores are still low, even with the infiltration of their own arms. We have received four hundred new recruits just the other day from a village just south of here by a days march."

Cian nodded at the two powerful men and understood the wisdom of Boccus, even if it did mean that he would have to wait. He would calm the men and give them new reason. For this new plan was much more stable and seemed almost too easy. He agreed that that guards had doubled with their journey almost over night and now had no problems in waiting, for he truly believed that the reign of Boccus seemed almost too ripe with this new twist of events.

IV

Selene was in the Winter of her life and with each step, her body felt the curtains of her life starting to fall. She had all of her scrolls carefully packed to be passed down to her daughter before she left to return to her daughter's new home. She gazed at the cedar trunk that contained them. She knew the cradle would be passed down to her granddaughter and the daughter of Jubilla, to Cleopatra, the remaining twin. She knew her family history would be safe, so far away from this virulent part of the world. She wondered what role her granddaughter Cleopatra would play in the great scrolls of history. Would she be like her mother and play a major role, or would she be like her half sister Antonia Minor and play a minor, but very important role in giving birth to greatness...As for her part in life, she was thankful in any part that she actively played part in, for she was lucky that her husband had allowed her to do so, which was very uncommon in a world dominated by men. She was grateful for even having known her mother in all of her greatness and of course her father, even though it was only for a brief time in the whole of her life. So short, yet those memories remained untarnished among the later memories, along with the whispered dream of the feeling and scent of her daughters and son asleep beside her so long ago. Such was life, the impressions that were made and created with each breath and step made, to become history and forgotten as the ages fly by. These things she made sure to include in the history of her family to be passed down.

V

The voyage was long, though passed without incident. She had brought with her Kateiran, her favorite servant, and Cilia, her companion—the nurse of her children over the years who had stayed by her side and preferred not to marry but to remain in her service. Juba, her husband was also along for this voyage and to bid a farewell to Alexander who had been almost constantly by his side in his studies and travels as was his father Helios, the son of her cherished twin of the same name. Her granddaughter Drusilla was also along for the voyage to see her family that she had never met, while her brother Ptolemy remained behind to watch over the kingdom while they were away along with his father and Uncle Helios and the quiet Berenice. They were not going to stay as long this time and had planned to make the best of this visit. She knew that she and Juba were growing too old to make any further voyages.

She was rather reluctant to leave Mauretania in the hands of her son once again, though he did need a chance to prove his skill. Helios and Berenice were very faithful to the throne and would keep it secure while she and Juba were away.

"Selene, Do not fret dear, those left behind will be fine!" related her soothing husband who had almost snuck up on her in her reverie. She was sitting on a wagon in which was erected a canopy for their comfort while traveling the treacherous and unpaved roads of the northeastern-most part of Britannia. They had arrived in the later part of summer and the heat was pounding down on them despite the shelter of the woolen canopy above their heads. She was surrounded in pillows and was leaning on the side of Juba. She had felt as if she was really in a chamber back home and he had walked up beside her, so sharply was her mind wandering. He had startled her as if he was not previously by her side. She giggled in response. "I know…"and continued to wander.

Finally a party of Pictish warriors in full battle gear had arrived to meet their traveling party in inquiry. They were fierce with long flowing hair that seemed to follow the hidden winds on this very hot day. They were men and women of miniature height and appearance. Blue and purple paints were painted in profusion on their strong battle shaped bodies. They would have frightened her had she not recognized that these were the colors of her daughter's tribe. The dust settled as her long travel entourage had ceased it's pace. Their faces appeared dangerous through the settling dust, as if they were daemons from the underworld appearing through ominous clouds.

As all were staring at each other, she noticed a very tall warrior that seemed to lead the others in command by gestures hidden from her observance. Because all of a sudden the warriors al disembarked their chariots and steeds to surround her weary party.

"Hail, Roman travelers, what brings you forth through our lands. You fare a far way from the new Roman colony in the lands of the Iceni, Thy party travels through the realm of King Cynfelyn." Spoke one of the tallest of the strangely clad warriors who had stepped to the fore and had approached the wagon that carried Selene and her husband who were dressed in the travel stained white robes of Rome. Their diadems glinted from the sun along their brow distinguished their rank as royalty, which was why the leader of the band addressed them, rather than a herald or Bard.

Selene recognized this and looked at her husband, who had started to stand up. This had taken a moment due to his age and stiff bones made worse from the long voyage and damp weather of this climate. The humidity did not suit them well in their old age. Juba II looked regal and stood tall and proud despite the close quarters of the wagon and his tired bones had responded to the request of the bold warrior that was looking him over from head to almost toe.

"I am King Juba II of Mauretania, come forth to bring my great-nephew Alexander to wed Princess Cleopatra, Daughter of King Cynfelyn and Queen Jubilla of the Trinovantes and Catuvellauni Tribes. I am traveling not to stay but to witness the ceremony and to bring tribute to their family." He had stated bluntly, finally recognizing the warrior for some relation due to the bright blond hair with flaming red streaks that donned the head of his own daughter.

The warrior had stepped forward to reach out for an embrace from his grandfather, "Then I welcome ye grandfather, for I am Cyllin, the eldest of yer grandsons and heir to the throne of me father and mother, whom you seek visit with. Please join our party, for we were sent out to protect our borders and had hoped to meet yer party. We offer our service and protection."

Cyllin was tall and noble underneath all of the fierce warrior paint and matted hair. Underneath the red glinted brow his eyes sparkling had added promise to their meeting. He reached forward and Juba II and his grandson embraced for the first time. All around them cheers rose through the fields and more warriors came forward to greet them that were hiding in the brush by the side of the muddy road to curiously glimpse the strange foreigners with robes as white as the late afternoon sun in brightness. The gold on their brows gleamed in the sun and relayed their rank and nobility to all around them who had never left their homeland to see people from so far away.

Cyllin added, "My brother, Caradawc wishes to greet our family as well…" He motioned to two other boys who stood by his side off to the side of the crowd, waiting their formal introduction. Caradawc had the manner of his father and looks as well. For he was well muscled and bronzed from an outdoor life, smaller than his older brother, though rougher of build. His blond hair much brighter than his father's shone from underneath the dried and matted paint and had already started to chip away from the heat. His hair shone like starlight, thought Selene as she admired her second youngest son. She felt then as she witnessed him embrace his grandfather and then look over at her for the same, that he would achieve greatness in his life in rule, though felt herself shudder as well for some ominous future that was lined up for him. She prayed that Isis would only send her good thoughts for her grandchildren, though knew that she would receive all that was for her to be known about them, regardless of the circumstances that the future might allow them.

All of them blended together and headed through the broad lands of the two united tribes to the home settlement of Jubilla and Cynfelyn.

They crossed the end of the farming plains and then entered a bright forest of trees that she was told as Birch, with the magical white bark in which faeries dwelt. It seemed magical to her. These trees almost appeared to her as if they were made of silver. So tall and regal looking. Such a fitting tree to surround the dwelling place of her daughter and her husband and the land of her grandchildren.

"Cyllin, was this not the site of their settlement? What has occurred here? Was there a fire?" Selene looked around as they approached the charred ruins of the site that she was sure their settlement was, but was confused. It was obvious that there was a fire here, though it looked to her that it had happened many years ago due to the amount of new growth and small trees that fought for space along the ruins and grazing goats that stumbled hazardously among the fallen marble columns.

"Aye, my lady Queen grandmother, for though speakest the right and true of the matter. There was indeed such a fire that laid ruin to all ye see around you. For I was only a boy of four at that time. Though be assured that no one was injured in this. All was picked up and moved to the north of here on the hill and highpoint yonder. Much better place for my father to watch over and protect us."

Cyllin smiled at her in assurance. "A flower for you my grandmother, for tis' called *the Lily of the Valley* and was brought over here by our cousins and kin from the land you call 'Long-Haired Gaul'"He giggled at the sound of the stiff Roman words that dotted his musical language. He was also impressed that his grandmother had retained enough of their language to converse with him from a trip that occurred long before his birth. He felt a bond forming with this strangely dressed foreigner that he knew to be his grandmother. He recalled how fondly his mother had spoken of her as if she were a Goddess with all of her magical powers that she sent them to sleep with in relating her many adventures that occurred long before he was born. He noticed her warm smile in return and knew that she felt the same.

"Cyllin, where is your sister and brother, are they not warriors as well?"

"My lady grandmother, you will have to wait till we arrive to meet them. For Leanydd is out hunting with father for wild boar for the wedding feast, and Gweiryth is completing his fosterage and will be meeting with us for the wedding."

"Did you mention that Leanydd is hunting wild boar?" She giggled at this, and then Cyllin understood.

"My this makes me think of a modern day Goddess Artemis!" She smiled.

"She is an excellent hunter and no one else has beat her skill in this, she is probably giving tips to me father as we speak!" At this, they both smiled.

Selene, felt thankful again at her choice of sending her daughter so far away. For where else could a woman hunt beside their men folk as in the ancient days of her own culture, almost before history was written. Leanydd reminded her of the ancient Greek woman warriors called the Amazons. She silently wondered if perhaps the Keltoi woman were from this lost and ancient group of woman. For no one had matched their hunting skills as mentioned in legend.

She noticed that her husband was in rapt conversation with Alexander and Cyllin turned over to join in conversation with them after nodding slyly to his grandmother.

Caradawc then jumped into his place. "Grandmother, you are even more beautiful than legend has written, or what my mother had related to us!"

"Caradawc, it is wonderful to finally meet you. For the words on papyrus, could never do justice for such a fine and noble warrior such as you!" He blushed at this and humbly looked to the side.

"Would you promise to tell me about your parents someday, before you return home." He tried to change the subject. His humble manner endeared him to her as well as the brash behavior of his older brother.

"Of course, I will answer any questions that you may have for they were incredible people, your great grandparents—you are worthy of them and they would have been proud to see all of you!"

Caradawc grew even more embarrassed, though was drawn in curiosity to all that she had witnessed in her long life. He was a collector of history and wanted to know all of it. He already knew of his father's family and their valiant origins and the mystery surrounding their throne. He had even placed a stone in remembrance at the site of the town established now referred to as CaerLlud or referenced by the Romans as Londinium.

Selene then changed the subject, "Are you an historian like your grandfather?" She could tell that this had finally reached through, for his blush seemed to change into rapture. "Aye my lady grandmother. I have learned to write in your language for it is easier to chronicle all that had passed in this land. The Druids would have me whipped if they found out about this. But I wish to save it all for my children." She saw the glow of his enthusiasm on the subject.

"Would you relate to me the history of the family that my daughter has married into and created such fine warriors with?" Selene graciously inquired of her grandson.

"You may be certain of that! As I would like to hear more about the birth land of my mother and her family that she was born to to add to the chronicles. My sister Cleopatra helps me with this task. For she writes as well. We both write in Latin and in the Hieroglyphs of Egypt as well as Greek."

"Such talent. I am very proud of you as will your grandfather be, who had spent his whole life in creating a very extensive history and geography of the known world, with all of his travels."

Cyllin joined in on this and looked at his grandfather, "What an incredible family we have been fortunate enough to had been born to. It is noted though, that the writing talents of my brother and sister must be kept from the zealous ears of the Druids. For they tend to dominate the skill of writing to themselves! Our mother had taught them how to write as you probably know, and my father as well!" He smiled and somehow the traveling party grew quiet in reflection as they entered even deeper into the land of the Druids in respect for their power.

"I am eager to meet my bride to be, brother! For I might be meeting my match!" They all ended up in laughter over this. Since it was well known how studious and brash that Alexander was. Alexander had hopped out of the cart at that and joined in the marching pace of his cousins Cyllin and Caradawc. They both welcomed him and placed their arms on his shoulders. Alexander lifted his toga to better march with and forgot the dust as it dirtied his once white toga along the winding and muddy path that meandered on ahead of them. He was eager to be accepted into this family as he was from the one he was leaving. He was conscious of his small height next to his large and powerfully built Keltoi family members and recalled that he had Keltoi blood as well from his own mother. He hoped that would heed him well, even though his own family on that side was long gone and subdued by the powerful Romans. His sandals collected the first pebbles of this strange new land and he knew that he would have to don another footwear for his future comfort. For he vowed never to be carried in a litter again. That he would walk in pride beside his brothers in this new land where he would meet his bride.

VI

Horns sounded from the trees upon their arrival and many people ran out to meet the wedding party. Jubilla ran faster to greet her parents, for she had waited patiently by the side of the road that led to her new settlement that she had made sure was carefully line with gleaming white Corinthian columns that were now sparkling in the fading sun of the day. She ran to the side of the wagon that held her parents and called out to them, her skirts flying with purpose.

"Mother, father" Her stature as queen forgotten as she ran to catch their embrace. She felt like a little girl again. She had not realized how much she had truly missed them. She was almost startled when she realized that their age had shown and their weariness. In her mind they were forever the age that she had last seen them. Even in the letters of her mother, she recalled the scent of jasmine and snuggling close to her mother. She had also seen the small ghost of her long lost sister in a brief moment as the sun sank lower into the depths of the sky. The long shadows cast by the towering pillars of white marble were now covered in rich scarlet and orange hues and hid the form of her baby and twin sister along the side. She noticed the startled look of her mother in that embrace where her sister was revealed in the corner of her eye. She felt that her mother saw Tonia as well.

At that moment the Bards began to play in the foreground at this time of a family reunited from far away. Selene did see her daughter, as if hiding behind the columns and noticed her daughter's reaction to it as well. She had then fervently looked around the area for her brother Ptolemy and Arsinoe to be somewhere near as well.

As all were greeting each other and the introductions made, both formal and personal, Cynfelyn had mistaken the look of disappointment on Selene's face to mean that she must be weary.

"My lady and Queen, come you must be weary." He reached out to grab hold of her arm to lead her to the quarters that were prepared for them. Juba had followed them as well as the rest of their party.

"All has been prepared for your arrival. The ceremony will be in two days to coincide with the feast of Lammas, our first harvest." The wise and noble King Cynfelyn led the weary travelers to their beautifully prepared quarters that he knew had surpassed their original quarters at their first visit.

It was then that Selene had noticed a small and sprightly young girl that reminded her so of how she looked at that age. For she had long curly hair the color of honey, as hers was before it had turned white and her eyes were of the same ice blue as hers once were with green flecks deep within. She wondered if this could be the noted Leannydd.

"Lady Queen Grandmother, I am Leannydd!"

"My word, child, how could you be any other than a child from this family. For you look as I did so many years ago. It is wonderful to finally meet you. For I have heard so much about you!"

"Leannydd! Do not bother your grandmother! See to her quarters and make sure that nothing is left out!" And off she went in a flash at the command of her mother who joined her husband in leading her mother in the walk that was slowed for her pace. Jubilla had looked over and noticed how Cyllin and Caradawc had surrounded their noble grandfather and were rapidly in conversation with him. This all seemed so wonderful, almost as if in dream. The scent of her mother reached her heart and she wanted so to be a little girl and to snuggle by her side. But now she was a grandmother as well. For after her mother's rest this eve, all of the family would be at the feast in their honor before the wedding feast of her eldest daughter.

"Jubilla, it was fine about Leannydd" She had reverted back into the familiar Greek spoken often in her youth to her children.

"Oh mother, How I miss hearing you speak thus! Leannydd means well, though she has the gift of gab and you definitely look as if you need some rest! You will thank me for that, for one must have all the strength to catch up in any conversation with my little bird! She can sing endlessly with her whimsical words and stories!" She giggled.

Selene was thankful, as much as she wanted to hear her granddaughter speak, she was also bone weary and her body could no longer hold itself up any further, due to all of the unused to exertion in the latter part of the journey. She barely noticed the large and spacious quarters where they were to retire for their stay.

VII

The shadows had cast such darkness on the buildings before them that the lights of the torches that were being lit, barely revealed them in her weariness.

She sank gratefully into the volumes of pillows adorned in the softest of silk that she knew were imported from her part of the world. She did not even notice the color as she fell into a deep and grateful sleep in the arms of her daughter.

Jubilla lay down with her mother's small figure in her lap in slumber. Her mother's hair had turned completely white she had observed as she quietly removed her veil. Though wrinkles had evaded her mother's fine features, they were still high featured and proud. Her mother might be in the evening of her life, but she was still regal and beautiful. She knew her mother had not lost her joy in life, for she felt it in her words. Her father lay on the pillows with his back facing them.

She was amazed that they could still handle such a long and arduous journeys at their age. She was proud of them and was glad that she was their daughter. It was wonderful seeing her parents again. For that life seemed so far away and faded to her. Though with seeing them this eve, it was all brought back to her in incredible precision and detail, even her little sister.

VIII

In the banquet hall, the younger members of the traveling party were promptly sent to finish the evening properly. Helios was ushered forth by Cyllin and Caradawc. Finally Cynfelyn had arrived after leaving his wife's parents to their tired slumber, he walked arm and arm with a young girl.

The bawdy humor of the younger crowd stopped for a moment when all eyes in the room glanced upon the reaction of Alexander's first glimpse of his bride. For by the side of Cynfelyn, walked his nervous daughter with the brightest red hair imaginable to him. His eyes were instantly drawn to her as was the anticipation of the rest of the room.

"My daughter, Cleopatra, I present to you, Alexander, son of Helios and Berenice, who was the son of Helios of Cleopatra VII, Queen of Egypt and Helena of Gaul who was a descendant of the legendary Vercingetorix, Leader of Gaul." He paused to let the whole room grasp the importance of the lineage that his daughter was marrying into, of which he was proud that he had married into. Such powerful blood would flow in their veins!

He looked down at his nervous daughter. "She will sleep in her quarters this eve and in the morning I will meet with you both to discuss the purpose of the handfast for which you will both be bound, if you so choose."

The mystery hung thick in the air, for Alexander was not familiar with the "handfast as was mentioned by King Cynfelyn. He wondered if it were some sort of test. He quickly forgot his curiosity as he gazed at her. Her red hair was brighter than any that he had seen before and her eyes were of the darkest of emeralds in their brilliance. Her skin was golden-brown from a life outdoors. So different from the Roman beauties who spent their lives locked inside under the protection of their fathers.

The hall was silent, not that he noticed, so rapt was his attention to every detail of his bride to be. Cynfelyn had noticed the look upon the face of the nervous boy and decided that it was the right time to leave the hall and prepare his daughter for her own sleep. He briskly turned his heels and along with his daughter in tow walked out of the hall as sharply as he walked into it.

Startled out of his reverie, Alexander uttered softly, so only those closest could hear, "Was that a vision of Aphrodite or a dream!"

"Young prince, for that was only your soon to be wife!" Added the mischievous Caradawc from behind.

And then added Cyllin," That is, if she accepts the handfast, after a year and a day!"

Alexander turned around in horror at some possible complication. He looked at Cyllin and Caradawc, his face as white as the columns around them in the vast pink marble inlaid chamber that served as the new banquet hall.

"Oh, brothers do not scare him! Have some mead! You have nothing to fear, for I glimpsed that she might have taken a liking to ye as well, dear Alexander!" Leannydd placed a large wooden goblet of warm foaming mead into the trembling hands of the young golden-haired bridegroom who eerily resembled his ancient namesake of legends and who stood transfixed at the spot where her older sister once stood. She had heard that the original Alexander the Great had conquered most of the world by the time he was thirty-one years old. Here was this boy who appeared frightened and timid. Let us hope for the sake of my sister that he gains some backbone!

It was then that the hall chimed with life and the music began to play. The Lyre rang joyously through the dark hours of the evening, while the young reveled in the celebration to come and of a family reunited.

The young travelers forgot their weariness from their journey and joined in arms in the bright and jubilant dancing steps of this new and mysterious land that had embraced them so completely.

Kateiran watched the next generation and stared into his mead. It stirred memories deep inside him to be among people who were probably kin to him.

Just then Togodumnos noticed the Gaul's reverie and joined him and together they sat side by side in silence watching the youth. He cast a weary eyes at Annius who stood in the doorway and went loudly over to join the young in play. He glanced over at Kateiran and they both felt sad for this prince who never seemed to grow up and watched him try to find his youth again.

IX

Cynfelyn had summoned the young and eager Alexander along with his daughter for his fatherly duty and discussion of the ceremony they were about to take part in.

"Alexander, the handfast is an ancient tradition in our land that is honored and valued for it's timeless tradition."

He spoke in Latin for the complete comprehension of the boy, which he and his wife had taught their own children for future diplomacy with Rome. He noted the curiosity that was ripe on the young lads face, and soothingly explained that Cleopatra understood well their conversation. He was charmed by the amazement and slowly warming comfort of his face. For Cynfelyn knew that it would have been worse had the two been brought together without a common language, though he knew all too well how common that was among the royalty who married for political alliance.

He continued as if unbroken by his thoughts, "A traditional handfast ceremony usually occurs on Midsummer's Eve, at the time of the solar Equinox. Though since you have traveled from far away, it has been changed to the upcoming celebration of our season's first harvest in celebration of Lammas. You will both then make a promise to live together as a married couple for a year and a day. After that period of time, both shall return to the ceremony to continue the union which will last for this life and all of your other lives, or you will choose to terminate it. The result on that day must be in complete agreement with the both of you. If any child should result of this handfast time, it shall be the both of yours and to be raised by the parent agreed upon. If the union should terminate, you are free to return to your home in Mauretania with out any hard feelings from any family involved. "

He looked at the face of the young golden-haired boy before him as he was striving to ingest all of this information and nodded his head in agreement to the terms laid out before him.

"I wish you both all the best of luck and am looking forward to a further alliance with your family. Your children, should any be born from your union, will be equally blessed in such a royal and ancient lineage. Am I to understand correctly that you are a direct descendant of the noble Vercingetorix, young man?"

"You are correct, for my grandmother was of that lineage from the defeated land of Gaul." He bowed his head in remembrance of such a mighty tribe and lineage that were kin to these people who have kept the traditions of his people alive.

"Father, I feel that we will last for eternity in love, though not in memory, but rather and a daughter will be born to us who will fight off the Romans from our shores and she will live on forever long after we all are gone. My part in all of this is to give birth to greatness and that only..." Whispered Cleopatra, her hair alive in the sunlight that streamed in from the windows high above them, almost as if in blessing to her wishes.

Cynfelyn smiled at his daughter, "I hope so my dear, though you have only met..."

"But, I feel that something great will come of us being together. Something that will help our land..." Such revelations were almost unheard of from this daughter. Cynfelyn paused for a moment to grasp what she had whispered with such confidence. For he would have expected something like that to have been uttered from the lips of his daughter and her twin who was a priestess-warrior who was killed shamelessly by the invading Romans, though not from this daughter who he had thought all too worldly.

Alexander just sat there in silence.

"I will ask your mother about any revelations that your sister may have written down pertaining to this, for I feel that some truth may have been uttered by you." He stood up briskly and turned and left the room alone to the both of them to seek out Jubilla on this matter. For his curiosity had been reached in the tone of his daughter's voice and he knew that his wife was the daughter of the priestess of Isis and perhaps with her mother, the both of them could make sense of his daughter's prediction.

X

"Jubilla, what do you think of what Cleopatra had mentioned today?" He uttered after the strange declaration of his daughter that sounded so like their lost daughter Drusilla, almost as if she had taken over her sisters' form at that moment.

"It was meant to be heard, mother, will you divine for us? Will you find out if a child of greatness will be born to them and if they will be together for eternity?"

XI

Selene missed the humor of her brother's grandson whom she had brought over a few months ago to her daughters faraway lands that she ruled over. She had a very uneventful journey over there and delighted in meeting all of her grandchildren and even her great-grandchildren. The wedding was delightful and Cleopatra looked glorious with her fire-red hair that hung down in marvelous curls down her back. Her eyes were almost purple it seemed to her and magical. Her granddaughters skin was so fair, almost ivory in color with bright cheeks with a sprinkle of freckles across her nose that gave her an ageless look.

She recalled how astounded she was at her own daughter's mature beauty. Though her reddish auburn hair was dulled in gray, it still sparkled with her hazel eyes beaming out at her as if time never passed for them.

Alexander looked marvelous and was almost more handsome that she recalled of her own twin brother so many years ago. She lamented his faded memory. But it was renewed when she looked at his fine young grandson. She was proud to learn that both the bride and groom were well suited for each other and had almost seemed content as her own daughter was with her husband Cynfelyn, who had become a fine ruler on his own.

The settlement was much larger than when she had seen it so many years ago, with lots of imported marble and fine bathhouses. Tall colonnades of Greek styled columns bordered cobblestone roads in the City proper, as it was now called.

Her grandsons were handsome and strong and made her equally proud. She wished that her own mother or father could have seen what they helped to create. She felt confident that Alexander would be happy there for he was well received.

All of this she thought about, would not erase the very different life that she was assigned to. She knew that soon she would have to begin the composition of the last chronicles of her life. For at her last visit, she requested that her daughter give the famous carved cradle from Marcus Antonius to her daughter the newest Cleopatra. She felt it justice that the cradle would be passed down to a grandchild from her and her twin brother's son. She knew that a child that would sleep in that cradle would inherit the legacy of the sun and the moon. Who knew what wonders the world held in store for that child? For nothing was revealed about it as of yet.

Slowly she separated from the rest who were busy in a conversation that she did not care for in the main dining chambers and sauntered towards her own lonely chambers. She knew that her husband would be going to an equally lonely chamber, since his short lived second wife Glaphyra had left him while they were away with Alexander in the lands of Pryttain, she did not produce issue from her short union with Juba II. Glaphyra slipped out in the quiet of the night. Not another word was heard of her, nor mentioned of her either. For she knew that this would only hurt her Juba.

She had grown fond of him over the years and had even learned to forgive him that slight. One thing she had learned was how unpredictable life really was.

It was then that she heard something. The barking of dogs ceased her wandering thoughts. Whatever would they be so frantic about. Then they stopped altogether. The silence seemed all the more frightening to her.

She gathered up her robes and ran as fast as her arthritic legs would carry her to the chambers of her grandchildren.

On the way, she heard the screams and smelled the smoke from fires being lit everywhere. Carpets and screens and other flammable objects were being set afire as warrior nomads ran through the palace. Their own warriors had only recently been aroused from retiring for the evening, and she heard loud sounds of battle all around her. The acoustics of the marble walls were loud and mystifying, for she could not tell from which direction it all was coming from.

She at last came upon the chamber of the children who sat beside their bed with the nurse huddled in a state of panic. For their safe world had been turned upside down.

Selene recalled this all too vividly from her own life many years before. Scenes from her past clashed with the present, fighting for sanity. Calmly she grabbed them all along with their eunuch Toronius.

Just then, Julia came around the corner to find her children. Her hair was frazzled and her face pale. She looked as if she were the undead.

"Julia, come with me, children, Now hush! Have you your slippers on? Good." She led them through the corridors, carefully listening before proceeding onward. Julia was in the very back of them. Berenice had then joined them to follow behind the children before their own mother.

Suddenly one of the nomad warriors grabbed Julia and their children's nurse Ursula and with a large scimitar, he hacked off their heads one by one, as if were only a game for him. The children screamed, causing more warriors to head in their direction. Selene grabbed a torch from the wall, and with the children in her arms away from the grisly scene in front of them—set fire to the wall hangings above that warriors head and then to his own headdress of brightly plumed purple feathers. He screamed in fright, the burning flesh trailing them in their flight.

"Please, you must hush, save the crying for later... We are warriors now. We must be very quiet and find that place your grandfather built in case this happened...". Berenice grabbed onto the silken garments of her new charges behind their aged queen, who had seemed ageless then with her quick and confident steps.

"But what about grandfather and Tatta! What ab..."

"Hush, nothing about that now… They know where it is. We must haste!" She prayed that no one would hear even the stifled sniffles from her grandchildren and that the rest would soon find them.

She made her way cautiously towards the room near the docks made of marble. Her husband had constructed it for that very use, but it had remained unused and virtually forgotten. She wondered if there was any food stocked in there, should they have to hide out for awhile.

On they frantically walked towards their destination over the bodies of those fallen in this rebellion. She had noticed the body of her own son, but turned the children's heads away from the sight. She passed palace servants and women being raped and then mutilated and tried desperately to hide it from the children whose lives she would fight to her own death to save.

They ran on, and almost seemed oblivious to all of the carnage around them. Their silken robes soiled after dragging them over bloodied corridors. Their slippers worn in their flight.

At last they reached the secret room. She hurried them along the tunnel underground that led to the secret room. She was surprised to find a small light emanating from within. She wondered as to the fate of Helios and the quiet Berenice of Macedonia, for they were nowhere to be seen. In their flight, Berenice had somehow disappeared from their group along with her trusted eunuch Toronius.

He seemed almost peaceful sitting there by the light of a small oil lamp. The only glimmer of light in the whole room surrounded outside from all of the gore and sounds of death.

"Husband, do you know?"

"I do, come children, there are blankets. I fear we must sit here for awhile. My forces will be arriving at first light."

They all sat in silence stunned at what they had just witnessed. Yet, both had recalled a similar scene of even equal devastation. They knew they would be able to comfort these children, for no one knew better than the both of them what it was like to lose parents in bloodshed to recklessly.

Selene decided that she had to plan the marriage of Drusilla as soon as possible for her own safety. For she did not truly understand where this battle would lead them. She had thought about Judea, on looking towards the family of Herod for her daughter.

When all of this was settled, she would seriously look into this matter of her granddaughter's safety.

She then moved over to her husband Juba and both of them cradled Drusilla and Ptolemy in their embrace. Her tears were silent and only glistened her eyes, but the pain was deep.

Too many people have died. Two of her own children, her sister and brothers and not to mention her parents. She never really liked Julia, only tolerated her, but felt deeply for her grandchildren to be raised without their parents, her own son! She would try to comfort them as best as she could! Juba, as if reading her mind nodded at her, telling her he agreed with her thoughts and continued to stare at the entrance in silence that was agreed upon throughout the hidden chamber.

XII

"Greetings dear sister,

Congratulations on the wedding of your grandson Ptolemy, the heir to Mauretania! Talk is still wandering through Rome on the splendid ceremony, none other has been seen in this province of even half of the grandeur reported. Well done!

I am sorry that I was unable to make it, due to my son's campaign here in Germania. The weather did not permit our safe travel and I have been trying to recover from a wretched flue that has been lingering for over a month!

Rome has been in an uproar since the death of my uncle Caesar Augustus. I had heard that at your last visit to Rome, he had even tried to make amends with you. You had never mentioned that. I know that his first love was for Rome, but I still think that he often

wondered as if he could have probably made different steps in attaining all that he had in the beginning of his career, earlier on.

He had never gotten over his animosity towards your mother, though I know that he sometimes wished that he could have known you better. Upon his death bed he had uttered an actors cry as to the closing of the curtain on his final act. His whole life was a play that was never thought to be written. He wondered through most of it, if his role might have been played much better, had Julius Caesar taken rule instead of he—had not that vicious murder ever occurred. His last words as relayed to me, make me ponder on my own existence.

I often wonder what life would have held in store for me had I been born a man. What shape would my destiny have taken, would I have had any control on the reigns of destiny? You are so lucky to have more control in the grand scheme of things, than I could have ever hoped for. Were we born lucky or truly cursed? They have even deified my uncle as his predecessor before him—the legendary Julius Caesar. I do not know how you must feel about that one.

Since Tiberius has taken reign in Rome over the offices of my uncle, he seems almost a different person. Not the young boy, we once knew so many years ago. Upon the death of my uncle, Tiberius feared for his very life at that time and was perhaps waiting for orders for his death which was reputed to have been on a boat passed by the orders of his succession of the Imperator rule after the death of Caesar Augustus! I am not sure of the truth of that, though it would actually have seemed very likely at that time!

I had heard such sad rumors on the fate of my uncle's beloved Julia. It was well known that Augustus had placed her in banishment on an island far away from Rome due to her scandalous behavior. But when Tiberius took over control of Rome, it was rumored that he stopped her food rations until she eventually died a grueling death of starvation. How sad! For all of her faults and rash judgments, Julia had never done anything to truly deserve that kind of fate, if there is any truth to that! Julia's daughter Agrippina, that spoiled wretch recently gave birth to a son whom she named Gaius Caesar Augustus Germanicus by her husband and my son Germanicus, so now I am a grandmother, finally! She has my son wrapped around her little finger and he is so blind to it! The baby is glorious and I see great rule ahead for him in the future! She is pregnant again and I sense that it will be a girl! The men on my son's campaign have fallen in love with the darling boy with bright blonde curls, they call him Caligula or "Little Boots".

I also want to congratulate you on the betrothal of your granddaughter Cleopatra, Jubilla's oldest daughter with your grandnephew Alexander! Have they any children yet?

Are we entering the final stage of our lives dear sister, for I feel as if I have many more to go! I am not ready to leave the stage as my uncle was fond of saying.

Despite all that has ever occurred in the history of things in our lives, would we have been given the chance to have such a wonderful friendship had things turned a different page to history? I wonder if we would have ever been given the chance to meet at all?

So much we have been witness to in our lives in the great history of Rome I feel almost privileged to have been given this chance by the Gods! I am truly thankful that we have met and have found so much in common. Had you not been my half sister, I would still have loved you!

Your correspondence warms this dreary weather where I am so far away from proper civilization. I live precariously through your many adventures and active life. While I can only play a minor role for Rome, as the wife and breeder to it's future rulers. I suppose that is good enough, I should not complain any further.

With love,

Your sister,

Antonia Minor of Rome and Inferior Germania"

XIII

Mauritania had returned to a place close to the peace they once enjoyed before that brutal attack that had killed her only son and his wife. Helios and Berenice had found some shelter and had survived.

Selene had promptly sent word to their son on the news along with the horrendous news of the attack. She wondered if she would have any energy for any other battle should it occur again.

She gazed over at the decaying heads of Boccus and his battle-mates in the fading sun of the pristine white towers of their palace whose peace was so shallowly disturbed. All were gathered up soon after and beheaded in a great ceremony led by her husband Juba II, with the tear filled faces of Ptolemy and Drusilla after the pyres of their parents were lit the evening before.

Helios and Berenice stood silent as if captured in sculpture at all of the events before them. Selene held on to her husband as if in fear of falling even deeper into her pain. All could sigh at the events and how quickly Juba II had gathered his forces in harsh vengeance on Boccus and all who followed him. It occurred too fast, it was still whirring before the mind of Selene.

Jubilla and her husband had made a voyage with their children to pay tribute and final respects to her brother and had only just left. They were here too short a while for Selene. She used all of the strength that she could muster to be a proper hostess to her family from afar. All events occurred as if in dream sequence so surreal to her was it all.

Selene felt in her heart that it was to be the last time that she would see her daughter, she gave her explicit instructions to open the scrolls she had brought with her at her last journey when she brought Alexander to Cleopatra to be wed. She wanted to complete he final scrolls on the true history of her mother, which she intended to start this very evening.

"I am Queen Cleopatra Selene of Mauretania, the mother of Queen Jubilla Drusilla Cleopatra of Britannia who married Cynfelyn, King of that land and of Juba III Ptolemy Helios who married Julia of Medea.

Many grandchildren have been born unto me and have lived to carry on the legacy. A chart of them will be added to this final document of my life.

I have lived through the grandeur of the mighty Egypt under the powerful rule of my mother Queen Cleopatra VII and her consort Marcus Antonius of Rome. I have paid tearful witness to their downfall under the young rule of Octavius who after the death of his great-uncle the noted Julius Caesar, became Imperator of Rome and was later known as Caesar Augustus. He formed an empire from his rule and grew up to bring Rome to a peace that it had not seen in over a hundred years of civil war.

My mother and father had suffered from his slander and attacks and finally succumbed in defeat to his brilliant battle maneuvering to subdue their power which he perceived as a threat to Rome. No one will ever know if my parents would have been successful, since they died in honor so many years ago.

They left behind their children who were raised in seclusion from the world and the brilliance of their love and devotion as parents.

Cleopatra VII was a devoted and loving mother and wife. She had given Egypt back it's former glory lost by her father by her excellent rhetorical skills and more than able leadership over her country and genuine caring for her people. She was noted for bringing back pride to her people on their magnificent history of the land on which they lived. Greek culture was displayed fervently beside the Egyptian glory.

Her children were Caesarion, who was reported to have been executed by Caesar Augustus as well as the brother of Marcus Antonius who faithfully served his brother in alliance. This occurred soon after the legendary defeat of my parents after the battle in the harbor in Alexandria. Caesarion was the son of Julius Caesar and considered too great a threat for the young Caesar Augustus.

Her children from her second consort were the twins named Cleopatra Selene, myself and Alexander Helios. Alexander Helios had a child through a Gaulish maiden named Helios, though was married soon after to Princess Iotape of Syria. He died from an illness upon arriving at the new homeland of his sister from marriage to King Juba of Numidia. No children were born of that marriage.

Cleopatra VII also had a son named Ptolemy Philedelphos who married a great warrior princess named Ahrianred of Pictish decent of the faraway Keltoi land of Pryttain. They became famous and legendary warriors and have disappeared from historic record. They had two sons. The first named Madron who married a flower maiden named Bledeudd, who later killed him for her alleged lover Gronw. They had no children from that union. The other son of Ptolemy and Ahrianred was named Mabon who settled to an Island to the west and no further had been heard of him.

Another daughter was born to Cleopatra VII and Marcus Antonius named Arsinoe who and married later on in life to King Drennedd of the Belgae tribe. She was executed along with her daughter Alanya for alleged deeds such that I do not believe are true of her. She had died along with her Bardic teacher and friend Sion.

There are songs and legends on the fates of the youngest two children of Cleopatra VII and few know the truth, not even I.

Though having known them in life I believe that only good deeds emanated from those youngest two children of my famous mother.

My mother was not a whore, but a woman of great charm and powerful communication skills. She had the power to calm all with her steady and logical voice and plans. She was a patient teacher and I owe all I have done for Mauritania and Numidia prior to that from all that she had taught me.

The men of Rome do not approve of any woman having power to rule. They feel that women are too ruled by their hearts and do not make strong leaders. For I feel that there might be a little truth in that today, though I would have greatly fought that when much younger. Though reality and my own life experiences have changed that a bit.

In retrospect, my mother could have perhaps defeated the then young Octavian, had she been less swayed by her heart and my father. For he was a very brusque man and was not known to think things out carefully. Which I believe was his downfall. My mother was blinded a bit by her love for him, which had overlooked many of his faults.

My father meant well, but was too rash in his actions. While Octavian was very similar to the legendary attributes of the Egyptian cobra, who would wait for the right opportunity to strike. Few have survived the strike of the cobra, such a ruthless killer was he.

Perhaps the world would have seen a completely different ending had my mother chosen the more powerful man in this epic battle between Egypt and Rome. Perhaps I would not even exist to write this truth on my mother.

So much was destroyed in his slanderous writings on my mother, that she never forgave the effective battle strategy employed by the young Octavian that she knew and despised.

She was powerful and passionate and would have been very dangerous by the side of the latter Caesar Augustus.

In the later years of his life I have had the opportunity to speak to him on a few occasions and knew that he felt sad about the way that things had turned out and the actions performed by him in his youth.

For after the deaths of my parents, the children of Cleopatra and Marcus Antonius were raised under the roof of the sister of Octavian, the legendary matron of Rome, Octavia. Octavia was the Roman wife abandoned by my father to be by the side of his Egyptian Queen and love. He had married Octavia in a political alliance in the brief time when he and Octavian shared the rule of Rome after the death of Julius Caesar.

Octavia had raised her children alongside the children from her husband's mistress and prior wife before her, as well as her own children from a prior marriage.

This woman was noted in Rome and loved by all as being the famous matron mother of Rome in her generous ways with all of the children who grew to love her despite the history that brought them all under one roof, innocent of it all.

I am very proud of my children and all they have done. I want history to know that I also had a daughter named Selena Antonia Helia, who was the identical twin of Jubilla Drusilla Cleopatra. She was adorable and tiny and we all loved her dearly for her mischievous ways and smiles that have only grown stronger in my memory over the years. She died at the age of four and left a deep gap in our hearts. My Tonia!

How easy it is to write of those I have loved in my life and how curiously difficult to write about myself and my own accomplishments. This was my intention at the beginning of the chronicles, to let my children and their children know of the powerful blood that flows in their veins. A very odd trait for a princess to be humble, but alas, that I am. Perhaps my daughter will continue this, though far away from the land of her birth.

I suppose the reason why I cannot speak of my own accomplishments is due to what I have witnessed in my long life. I have been the subject of great power and incredible wealth that I was born into in an very ancient lineage of extreme nobility.

Yet, I have also been just a child, lost without parents to protect her. Alone in the world at the mercy of another. Knowing that it was customary for Romans to kill not only their enemies and all related to them as well, no matter how young. I sat there alone, for many evenings waiting for my last, wondering why it never came.

I was confused, yet grateful in my youth that Caesar Augustus, or Octavian as my mother called him with venom, had set a new precedence with us as well as a few years prior with my own husband. He had let us live, which was almost unheard of in the bloody history of this part of the world. He even married myself to Juba II the son of a King that was defeated by Julius Caesar. Julius Caesar had let my husband live, for he was only three years old at the time of the defeat of Numidia.

We were both thankful for our lives and knew that each moment was granted against the wills of Gods, but by the mercy of men, Roman men. Roman men who had defeated our parents and had taken away our noble birthrights and added it to the glory and ever expanding empire of Rome.

We were children then, though still were grateful for each moment granted to us, and even for the kingdom that we were given the freedom to rule, though as client to Rome.

There was so much peace in the lands that had seen over a hundred years of betrayal and bloodshed. Caesar Augustus had devoted his time in improving the Roman constitution and in improving the ways of his people.

It was very difficult for myself due to personal history to admire such a man, though it slowly caught up with me over the years, so slowly that I did not realize it.

Would my parents have done the same, had they been the victors and not Rome? Would they have worked so hard for the people?

Perhaps the people of this world are a bit better in the long run, since Rome is a Republic and eventually ruled over by the people. Which I know was what Caesar Augustus had tried to restore to his people. He wanted the glory of the ancient days of Rome, after the kings were destroyed.

My parents on the other hand did fall prey to the power of a monarchy and my mother was considered God on earth as Pharaoh.

Then again, after the death of Augustus, he was deified as well. This would never have occurred during his lifetime. For it was well noted that he only took on offices because he knew that with those offices he would better help his fellow countrymen. It would have been much worse for the people in Rome, had any other man held the power of those offices, like perhaps even my own father.

I loved him dearly, though I do not think that Rome and all of it's vast empire would have fared as well had it been under the rash rule of Marcus Antonius. From all accounts, he seemed rather immature to look towards the feelings of his people, nor to listen to any advice from them either. He was very stubborn in his ways.

The man I had vowed to my mother that I would hate, seemed a better choice after all that he had done.

My parents had taken their own lives, though I would have argued different in my youth and have in the earlier chronicles. Though as I have aged and have witnessed many occurrences in history and the effects of the policies written during the rule of Augustus. I have learned to observe from a different perspective.

Had my parents only lived longer, would there have been many more years of war?

Alas, I have only what has truly occurred in history to learn from. I can surmise and wonder the "what could have beens" in life, but for what purpose? I suppose it does help in my personal reflection of things and in giving myself a better understanding and a better grasp on the things that I have had to survive. And that is it.

I am sorry for so many reflections on such great people, but I did feel it important. Perhaps in the future generations will better understand the idea that great leaders in life are human and will err as well as create a great many good deeds to be left behind if they be able.

All should be viewed in a person if we are to truly understand them and it will perhaps enable us to better see ourselves. In working with and recognizing our faults makes us better to battle what life would send at us. Maybe you will be better prepared.

For I know that the histories of these remarkable people will be tainted by those who wrote them and for whom they were written. I want the world to see these brilliant people that I have known in their real and human light.

In further retrospect and consideration, I often wonder if all of our words will ever carry on at all after all of our glorious buildings have turned to dust. Will only our follies be remembered after all is lost.

So, I leave these words of truth for my daughter, Jubilla, Queen of Britannia to carry on and to bring forth to all of you. Not that my son and his children are not worthy of this, they are. I feel that the truth will be well guarded so far away from this part of the earth and all of the political struggles that are fought on this ground.

The descendants of the house of Ptolemy and Juba will live on to carry the truth forward to the next generations. The Roman ways are killing the ways of the Goddess and destroying any power that women may have yielded over the many past millennia's. I sent my daughter away from all of this, so that she may keep any power and learning I have taught her from my mother and hers before and be still able to give it to her daughter, so that she may continue this legacy.

The legacy at the time of this writing is as follows:

1. Cleopatra VII married Julius Caesar of Rome and begat Caesarion who died in battle when Egypt was lost to Rome.

Cleopatra VII then married Marcus Antonius of Rome and begat twins: Alexander Helios and Cleopatra Selene and then Ptolemy Philedelphos and then Arsinoe.

2.A.) Alexander Helios loved a Princess of Gaul named Helena and begat Helios. Alexander Helios then married Princess Iotape of Syria and died soon after. No children were of that union.

Helios was sent to Mauretania and raised by Cleopatra Selene.

He married Berenice of Macedonia and Begat Alexander who was married in Britannia to Cleopatra, the daughter of Jubilla, Queen of Britannia and Cynfelyn, King of Britannia.

2.B) Cleopatra Selene, Queen of Numidia and then Mauretania, married Juba II, King of Numidia and then Mauretania. She begat twins named Jubilla Drusilla Cleopatra and Selena Antonia Helia. Selena Antonia Helia died at the age of four. She also begat Juba Ptolemy Helios.

3A.) Jubilla Drusilla Cleopatra married Cynfelyn, King of the Trinovantes and the Catuvellauni of Britannia. She begat twins Drusilla and Cleopatra. She also begat Leanydd, Cyllin, Caradawc and Gweiryth.

Drusilla was a warrior of her tribe and was killed away by Roman soldiers during a battle.

Cleopatra was married to Alexander of Mauretania and the son of Helios and Berenice of Macedonia.

Leannydd is a priestess of the grove and an experienced wild boar hunter.

Cyllin married Charydd of the Silures tribe of Britannia and they have two sons by the names of Sion and Cynfelyn.

Caradawc married Sera of the Belgae tribe of Britannia and have two sons by the names of Bran and Caradawc.

Gweiryth is not yet married.

3B.) Juba Ptolemy Helios married Julia of Syria and begat Ptolemy of Mauretania and Drusilla of Mauretania.

2C.) Ptolemy Philedelphos of Cleopatra II and Marcus Antonius married Ahrianred of the Brigantes tribe of Britannia. Most of the knowledge gained of them is now legend and the truth has not reached my ears to this date. They were mighty warriors and fought many battles together. They both died completely in love with one another.

They begat two sons by the names of Madron, also known as Gwyngwyngwyn who married Bledeudd. The other son was named Gwanat or Mabon.

It was sung in halls across their land that Bledeudd had outwitted Madron and killed him for her lover named Gronw. There was no issue. Ptolemy had used the warrior name of Belatucados Gwyn among other names. There are many versions of the legends of them as famous lovers and warriors, so famous were they throughout the lands of Britannia.

2D) Arsinoe of Cleopatra VII and Marcus Antonius was married to King Drennedd of the Belgae tribe of Britannia. She begat Alanya. It was reported that she was killed along with her only daughter Alanya for her allegedly adulterous affair with Sion the Bard.

I know my time here on this earthy plane is at it's final turn and so I write these words to my children and to theirs. May the mighty Isis bless her children of the House of Ptolemy of the lost land of Egypt . May the lands that have blended with the blood of this house only enhance it's daughters and make them strong.

The words of this scroll tell of a family and the legacy to be continued to the end of time. The trials recorded are only brief excerpts of their wondrous lives. May the truth prevail and be known. Do not use your lineage as an excuse for wrongful acts, but use it as strength and encouragement to do honorable acts in the name of the blood which flows in your veins. For the Great Mother will always smile down in love on the children of her powerful womb."

Cleopatra Selene wearily signed her name and added the seal of Mauretania. She laid out the carefully woven sheets of papyrus to dry. They would then be bound and sent by ship along with her diadem for her daughter Jubilla. The tears slid down her cheeks knowing that she would not be able to deliver these words herself. Though she knew in her heart that they would be well taken care of.

She had made sure that Jubilla had not lost the art of writing, even though her new culture forbade it. She had made Cynfelyn promise to her that the scrolls that documented her families truth would be well taken care of and that the chosen successors would have the knowledge of writing to carry on the future truth for the unborn generations.

She had made Cynfelyn promise and to make sure that the chosen daughters would retain the knowledge necessary before married off according to his wishes. She would never have let Jubilla marry her Cynfelyn if he had not made this promise to her. She corresponded regularly to keep up her daughter's skills, as well as for her own peace that her daughter was well taken care of so far away from her.

As her days drew to and end, she felt that all of her family that she would leave behind was safe and well taken care of to the best of her knowledge. She had sent out scouts to the far corners of the earth to retrieve information on her brother Ptolemy Philedelphos and her sister Arsinoe and her daughter.

She had Bards come all of the way to Mauritania to sing to her of the tales of her brother and sister and their families, though brought no real proof of what could have occurred. She knew Jubilla was possibly keeping some information from her about her sister Arsinoe so as to possibly not to upset her.

The body may grow frail with age, though not the mind. The present may not be as recalled over the all too clear past deeds in one's life. She could barely recall what she had for her morning meal. Though she clearly could recall in all too vivid detail every word spoken by her mother so many years ago. It was etched in her mind. As well as the sound of her young daughter Tonia's sounds while asleep beside her. She recalled in bright details her wedding day and all of the days spent waiting for her husband to return from his many journeys in research pursuits.

When young, she was full of opinions and visions of what she wanted out of life. Then life happened. It may have occurred to slowly for her to truly grasp the reality of it when it struck, but it did. In the process, her dreams were changed and she realized that opinions could be altered with what life had actually put on her plate. She remembered all too well of feeling almost indestructible when very young, that nothing could stand in the way of her view and beliefs. That changed as well, when she actually lived them. She still had those views, only softer now and more allowing of life's demands and lessons.

As she sat there waiting for her papyrus papers to dry, she did not hear the respectful foot steps of her cherished companion Kateiran.

"My Lady, why are you waiting for those scrolls to dry?" He smiled at her and his voice was soothing to her tired soul.

"Oh, I really do not know. I suppose every minute I wonder as I sit her, if I should add more to them. Should I have mentioned my thoughts and deeds as well? Or would that be too brash?"

"Only you know the answer to that one." He lowered his eyes in thought on that matter and let her continue.

"It seems as if my life was very inconsequential and not worth mentioning. I really wanted to accomplish so much more. I wanted to gain back Egypt for my family…" She let those last words trail off and Kateiran just sat there knowing how deeply she had tried with that and knew she had almost melted away with that failure.

"You have done great things with your life and you know it. Your children know it. Juba let you rule this land in his name. It might go down in the history books as being his accomplishments due to the way the Roman's like, but your people know in their hearts who loved them and who has brought this country to the peace that we have had for many years. Juba had been too busy with his research and the writings of his chronicles to care about the people. Though he had someone care about them in his name. That is your duty in this life my Queen."

"I realize how lucky that I have been, but my mother did great things in her own name and in our own land! This land is not even the land of my husband's family. It was given to us under the kindness of Rome and of Augustus. Who even knows how long our family will keep this land? How will Tiberius be with my grandson, Ptolemy who will soon be the King of Mauretania for Juba does not have much longer to his life as well. For he has ten years over my sixty eight! Will Tiberius even let my son rule here? He may give it to his son to rule over and then all will be lost in this part of the world.

I even worry how Ptolemy will rule this land, he is more interested in his fine imported garments and in the Roman games to truly know what this land needs after we are gone. I worry, Kateiran…"

"You mustn't worry, for you have done much to carry on the power of your family and wisely too. For only in those lands far away will your daughters and her daughter's power be allowed to grow. In those lands you chose wisely for over there the lines of the mother are valued as well, if not even more so than the lines of the father. There your precious Isis is still worshipped, under other names. But she is still honored!"

"I realize that, but…How long will it be before Rome reaches over there to destroy all of it like they have here. People in Rome and now most of the youth here no longer worship the Gods and Goddess of old. They are looked upon as mere superstition. They might be adored, though only as one would a reckless child, none are taken seriously here. The ways of Rome have taken more to the politics of the land, rather than it's creations and origins and great mysteries. The Romans feel they know all of the answers and no longer look to the heavens. The attitude is destroying our daughters who will only be the breeders of Rome and it's cultural ways. I want my family safe from all of their nonsense!"

"Oh, Selene, you know as well as I that we are only small players in the world plan. We have our fates and destiny that must be fulfilled and we walk our chosen paths." She let his familiarity pass unnoticed as she had for so long now, since she no longer truly cared any more for all of the new politics or old ranks of status anymore.

"I do not feel that way. I had always felt that I could do something more…"

"You have, even Juba will tell you how grateful he is for all that you have done. Who could have predicted how powerful Rome would have been in it's true influence on people. You were the only one who has even come close and have protected those you could from it."

"Over the years, I have also realized that not all of Rome is bad either. Augustus has done many great things. He made a few mistakes in his youth and the future will have to deal with them. But, he had done many things that will benefit Rome. And even possibly Mauretania, if it is eventually swallowed up in the future. He had brought faraway lands together in communication with his vast road system. Because of that I may communicate with my family far away. Though it may also bring about their being enveloped into the great power of Rome in the end. I have sent letters to Jubilla and Cynfelyn to warn them of this possibility."

"Kateiran, have I ever told you how much I truly appreciate all that you have done for me?"

"I do not believe that you have…" He winked at her, for she may not have said it precisely in words, though he always knew in his heart. They had an unspoken appreciation for each other. For he was the only one who has truly been there for her all of these many years. Juba had meant well, but was all too consumed with his voyages and discoveries and all of the numerous volumes of history, and geology in his vast encyclopedia that he has created for the world. Juba had compiled all of the works of the ancients from the many libraries of Rome and even from Alexandria, for Selene knew of the secret chambers where the most ancient texts were hidden. He compiled that work and elaborated and proved some of those theories as well as developed some more and further enhanced them as well. He had also found treasures from lost civilizations and kingdoms, thought to have been lost. This treasure was kept from the hungry eyes of Rome and hidden safely on an Island that he had discovered and visited frequently to replenish with new finds.

Kateiran felt sorry for the neglect of this beautiful and wise Queen. He would put himself to sleep each evening in the safe world that he had created in his mind where he could be allowed to love her freely. He had hoped for in the final years to be together. Though he realized his dreams of youth were never to be breached with the reality that he was forced into by fate. He looked at her eyes and her tired soul and felt that it was the time to finally break his silence.

"You are tired?"

"That I am, I have lived my life and know that soon I will be at the side of my parents. For I hear them calling me in my dreams. Tonia is there along with Helios and my son little Juba looks as he did when young. They all look the way I most remember them. In those dreams Caesarion is holding my brother Ptolemy's hand and Arsinoe looks as she did with her summer golden locks and tiny hands reaching out for me. Perhaps the legends about them are true? That they are no longer on this earth, but are waiting for me to join them soon? There seems to be no age or time, but all meshed into one and the same."

"Perhaps…"

"I always wanted to live a long life, but I believe that it is much harder because I have had to live with those I love and to have parts of me destroyed with each of their deaths."

"You were not destroyed with each death, you were made stronger. You are only given out of life what you can handle. Each hardship in your life has been a lesson and has taught you well. I have seen how much you have grown. You have raised your children to be great rulers and they have taught theirs well in stead and from your words."

"You have always been there for me, why? You could have left when I gave you your freedom, why did you not return to Gaul?"

He sat down next to her on the couch and was silent for a moment. He wondered why she had not asked him of this sooner. "Perhaps you already know…"

"I think I do… But I am not sure."

"Gaul is not the same anymore. As you know it is like Egypt now, only a province. My family is long gone."

"But, you were young enough to create another."

"I knew I would not find my true soul mate as I have with you."

"Why do you tell me these things, when they could never have been or ever will be?" Her anger flushing her pale and finely wrinkled face.

"Why do you tell me these things, so that I may suffer? I have no choice and never have. I was not allowed to have a choice in life. I had a duty to fulfill."

In a softer voice she added, "I never wanted you to leave. I would have been empty completely had you left."

"Myself as well. For with you I have found my home. Maybe in our next life, we could be together."

"I fear that we never will. But have to live with the torments of love in front of us, yet never be allowed to do anything about it. That is our plight. That is my misery! You should leave this chamber now, so that I am left to toss and turn all night for a life that should have been and never will be, ever!"

He bowed to her and saw her life slowly drain out of her to a peaceful pose on her couch. Once outside, he summoned a servant to place her on her bed in her own chamber and started to gather Juba and the rest to her bedside.

He dreaded that he had to tell her his wishes and wondered if it only sped up her last moments. Though deep inside, he knew that it did not. It had to be told. For he saw the beginning of this process as she laid down her stylus. The same silver stylus that she had taken from her brother so many years ago in remembrance of him when she was sent off to marry Juba. A stylus that had seen much use over the many years that had written down her travails and triumphs.

XIV

On the last day of the life of Cleopatra Selene all were gathered in her chamber to bid her farewell on this earth. Juba II, Ptolemy the heir to Mauretania and his sister Drusilla.

Her body was weak and placid. The chamber of her room was filled with incense and Jasmine plants at her request in memory of her mother who she was about to join.

"Grandmother, I hope you are proud of me." Stated Ptolemy to the small form on the bed.

"Oh, my dear Ptolemy, I will always be proud of you, for you make me smile, you have the gift of laughter and remind me of my own father. I am so glad that he lives in you!" He seemed rather upset at this. For she did not know how torn he was in his feelings for Romans who had so much control over his power. He did love their games and bet frequently on gladiator events and other arena events.

Selene had caught this hidden reaction and wondered about it.

"Grandmother, I do not want you to leave! I want you to choose a husband for me and to be there for me!"

"Drusilla, I will always be there, even after I am gone!"

She looked over at her husband, "Juba, you will make sure that she will marry Azizus, will you not? We have discussed this."

At his nod, she was assured. She brought her eyes over to Drusilla, "Darling, you have the spunk of my mother and I know that you will have a lot to offer in your life and I wish so much to be around to see it and to offer you advise, I can only watch silently from above. Azizus is the King of Judea and will treat you well. There is a new force over there, that is led my a prophet from Nazareth. Perhaps his teachings will guide you well. But never forget your trainings as a priestess of Isis, for she will truly guide you and save you. You are the great-granddaughter of Isis on earth in the form of my mother, wear it well and walk tall in pride my dear child!" Tears began to trickle down Drusilla's alabaster cheeks.

"Juba, you have taken good care of me and have allowed me more than I could have ever wished for. I thank you." He nodded and placed his delicate hand over hers that was growing so cold as was the room around her.

She felt like it was winter in her soul and the room began to darken. The last thing that she saw was upon her left forefinger. It was the ring that her mother gave her that was passed on from mother to daughter from the time of the ancient pharaohs of old. Her mother had told her that the ring was made for the daughter of Nefertiti who was the wife of the Pharaoh Ramsees II. It was made of silver, the tears of the Goddess Isis and was formed into a lotus flower with the stem that wrapped around her slender finger. The bud opened up and on top was a transparent stone polished to clarity with what always looked to her as if the stars glowed inside with all of the colors known in their world. The inside hieroglyphics were long since worn down, the she recalled that her mother had told her what it once said; "To my daughters with Love eternal through the sands of time." This was passed down to all of the daughters and would in turn be passed on to her Jubilla along with the scrolls that dried in the other room.

A thought had entered her mind just then of when she was a small girl along the side of her mother in her glory as Queen of Egypt. She recalled so vividly that day when her mother had shown her the new family tomb just completed. She could even smell the freshly painted walls all around her. Her mother had bent down to her and had told her, "I believe that no matter what happens in this life we will all return to be together in the next. No matter what happens in life, we will always be together…" He voice was so vivid and her form so close, she could almost reach out and touch her.

A light appeared ahead and seemed to surround the hidden form of Kateiran behind the curtain in the corner of the room. She saw his aura began to fade as the room closed in on her in cold darkness.

XV

The scrolls had finally dried as the body of Cleopatra Selene was being prepared for her embalming in the ancient Egyptian tradition. This was done in accordance with her final wishes and fervently promised by her husband who had always wished that he could have been a stronger husband to her. He had loved her the only way that he knew how, though he knew that it would have never been enough for her.

The scrolls were then sent of to their daughter far away along with the ring that she wore, after he made sure that copies were stored in his secret vaults of his families treasures. He saw how close Rome was to his door and knew that it all could be taken away from him at any time. He made sure that his descendants were well taken care of and a certain select few knew of the location of his families true treasures.

His grandson Ptolemy knew, though was forbidden to touch it until all was lost in this kingdom. He hoped that it would never have to be used. He had also told Jubilla about the family treasure.

The treasure contained sacred family heirlooms and works of art and family chronicles as well as copies those told by his wife. He had searched Egypt in Alexandria and Memphis. He had traveled to Rome, Macedonia and Numidia to make sure that all was safe where the world would not loot it and melt it down.

His own wife had done much to improve their countries economic condition with trade and agriculture and the prosperity that she had brought her in his name.

He silently and gratefully bowed down to her wisdom in those matters, for her mother had taught her well. Their city was flourishing in commerce and was well known for it's cosmopolitan ways. People had come from all over to settle here and to learn in the universities that she had built. She had set up temples for the Gods of Greece and Egypt as well as Rome and their land became a center of worship as well. Even the new religion of Gnostic teachings was spreading it's impact here.

The streets were lined with tall and graceful marble pillars that were open to the gentle rays of the sun that always shone brightly here.

He knew he contributed to this treasure as well and had finally completed his encyclopedias in over five hundred chronicles of modern world wisdom that ranged from plants, to cultures with all knowledge compiled form modern and ancient texts and from his own observations. He had finished his life's works and purpose and was grateful that his wife had kept his birthright intact and flourishing. He realized that he had never told her how much he appreciated her and all that she had done for her. He tried to, but his words had always stumbled and sounded silly to his own ears, so they were virtually left unsaid.

Even in the end of her life, just prior to it, he had found out the truth of what happened to her brother and sister. He could not bring himself to tell her. He felt that he was truly a failure as a king, let alone a man. He could not even tell his wife something that she had been trying to find out on her own. He did not want to upset her. Yet she had the right to know.

Three years ago, he had told her that he was exploring some islands to the very west of their lands, in un-chartered territory. He had found something far from here, but that was years ago. He had lied to her then.

He initiated that voyage so that he might find out some information on them that was better than the songs that had been sung to them from Bards. He wanted more than just legend, he wanted the facts.

He had even recruited his nephew Helios to come along for this and swore him to secrecy. For he wanted to be able to return to Selene with something other than her dashed hopes.

He sailed over to Britannia and had even endured a shipwreck along the way, though all were saved thankfully. He had kept this knowledge from his daughter and had only informed Cynfelyn of his plans. He did not want to worry Jubilla or for her to inform her mother.

Cynfelyn even lent him the use of his own men so as better to navigate the land and to find the facts. He took along with him Cynfelyn's brother Annius and his two overlords Andocos and Sego.

The search led them to the northwestern part of Britannia and then to another Island even more wild than the land of Britannia. They ended up in the wild rolling lands with the brightest greenery that he could possibly imagine and eventually to the halls of Tara.

They finally met a warlord and leader named Connail who had told them that he had fought along the side of Ptolemy who he had repeatedly called Belatucados of Gwyn. He had described the lord of Gwyn as a talented warrior who had come to his land seeking his fortune along with his wife who was of a noble Matriarchal Pictish Warrior line. He related to them how they always fought by each other's side and their love was sung about. Their battle skills were deified by his people and their love was immortal.

The great war lord Connail had misted eyes when relating the tale to his enthralled listeners. Connail was a large man with ivory skin and the blackest hair he had ever seen. For he told them that he was the remaining son of this man some time after their initial meeting and after several horns of mead. The resemblance to his brother-in-law was almost lost in the brightness of his garb and long braided hair with matching braided beard and long curled mustache. This man before him was young though wisdom shone brightly through his eyes.

Juba then realized that the man had uncannily guessed who they were in that he was staring vividly at Helios in apparent recognition from the beginning.

Connail had at last told the wandering band that he was called lovingly by his parents as Mabon and he was not originally a warrior as was their trade. He had become one due to his life's circumstances. He was a farmer and had kept his familie's land which they had earned through many a victorious battle. He had tilled the land and had silently watched while his brother was doted over by his parents for his valor in battle and while he was wooed over by Bledeudd, who eventually killed him so that she could be with her lover. Connail told them that this all occurred after his parents were slain in battle.

Under his long sleeve that he rolled back was a design that was tattooed into his skin. Juba recognized the writing as hieroglyphs, which dazzled him even further.

"This was written in the words of my father—"Mabon the son of Ptolemy Philedelphos, Prince of Egypt and son of Cleopatra VII, Pharaoh and of Marcus Antonius, Roman Imperator."

He further related to them, "The same was inscribed on the arm of my brother. On the other arm I have this of my mother and of her great warrior line written in the language of the Druids in their Ogham writing."

He continued, "So you see, I left my lands eventually and came out here to continue their legacy. I have won my place in the hall of Tara and have become a King here. My line will endure the sands of time long after my death in their honor." His pride was evident and well earned. He then went into his round hut and came out with a long sword. He handed it to Juba to inspect in relation to his tale. It was large and of Roman design and rather old. Inscribed in Roman was the inscription: "Marcus Antonii" in Latin. Juba had wondered if his father had ever told him that it was the actual sword that his grandfather had fallen on after the defeat of Actium.

He knew that he could not take this home and that it would always be on the body of this great man. He wanted to tell Selene about him. For he knew that from this man, would be a great line of Kings and they would be safe from harm so far away from the dominance of Roman power. This man was definitely whom he purported to be. For in his fashion of shaved beards and faces, he could almost picture this man in a toga, so proudly was his head held.

The man left them with a dagger that his father had carved that was on his person. He told Juba that he had instructions that this was to be given to his sister, though he never knew how to contact her. The dagger was beautiful and made of bronze and filled with swirls and elaborate writing. For hidden in the depths of the Keltoi design were words in hieroglyphs which he knew not the meaning of. Only Selene knew how to decipher this.

He left that proud man with sadness in his heart and further pride was earned for the family of his wife and their great valor. He made sure that the dagger would be interred with her in the tomb of her parents with his guilt.

He continued his journey carefully eastward and south to the shores of the lands of the Belgae. There he came across a woman by the name of Hadwinna. This ancient and decrepit woman was living alone in a hut in almost complete seclusion. She reluctantly told him the story of Arsinoe. She would not utter one word of it though, until Annius left her vision and went far away outside. After much debate, Annius agreed to the terms, Juba would let nothing stand in his way.

The woman was nearing her last days and wanted a sort of cleansing of her life's regrets. For she wept as she told him of what she had done. And all for the love of a man that she could never have. She looked over at where Annius stood and after what seemed a long while told her story of the events as they transpired.

She had related that Arsinoe came to her and had been practically taken under her wing, as well as her friend and teacher, the Bard Sion. Both of them were incredible in their talents in music. Her eyes seemed to gaze distantly at the heavens outside of her filthy hovel in retrospect. Juba patiently listened.

Her crackly voice looked at him and inquired, "Do you know why I tell ye this old man?" He nodded.

"This for the wrong that I done for lass Arsinoe! I hae prayed to the Goddess Brigit for vengeance, that life will battle my soul, for I hold it out to her mercy for what I have done."

Juba sat patiently listening to the babblings of this dilapidated woman and endured her rabble. He felt compelled to hear her story.

"She trusted me and I let her down. I saw how much they were meant for each other, her and Sion. She and the Bard could do nothing bout' it! Twas their fate. I don twisted their stars! Sit wif' me hansom man" she beckoned to Helios who stooped over her putrid cot.

"Tis not oft in me life I had the chance to be wif some burly man, please the ol' lady will ye!" He hesitantly agreed after looking at the pleading face of Juba.

"Now, Arsinoe came to me and learned the arts of basketry and of the prophesying, she had the gift ye know! She sang with the Goddess in her eyes and was possessed with her power. My Drennedd don see this and fell in love wif her. He was meant for me!

"This vermin named Annius came from far away and beckoned at me. He prom'ssed many jewels for me. He told me to con'spire with him to convince Drennedd that Arsinoe twas the lover of the Bard named Sion. I friended them and held their con'fidence in my hand. Drennedd married 'nother lass named Elena when he was supposed to marry me! Annius promised me and betrayed me! I was filled with hatred and anger over his lies and betrayed Arsinoe, who I once looked at as my daughter! I gave her up to Drennedd with her daughter. Annius brought Alanya over to Drennedd himself!

I saw Drennedd kill Alanya and called her the daughter of Sion and then be burnt Arsinoe and Sion all tied together on that stake over there in the clearing. I never specked it to happen. Just thought they would he banished and I would have him for myself!

"I 'cided to live and die here near the reason for her death and to mourn over her til I died! Twas all me fault. She was shameless and innocent. They spent every moment of their lives together in my company! Their eyes searched 'chother but their bodies kept to thyne own music and songs!"

Juba was angered and understood the punishment this woman had set out for herself. He knew that Annius must have heard what had transpired and he had secretly hoped that the man had fled.

After the woman had related her story she had silently died with a smile on her face. Possibly she had waited until someone had listened to her. He would never know. For he then left her stinking hovel and walked outside to where the others had gathered under the unseasonably balmy sun. The heat hung around them in rivulets he recalled which made her body smell all the more. It seemed to him as if she was already decomposing at the time he had met the strange and ancient woman.

He looked over at Andocos, Sego and Helios deep in conversation, and at the others in their search and information party and then over to the spot that she had described to him that was almost hidden by the overgrown shrubbery and a fence elaborately designed to shelter it from wandering eyes who would happen into her territory, secluded though it was.

He searched in the heat and had found a latch partially obscured from view. For the design had grown in and was covered with the corpses of roses past bloom. Their once pink blossoms gone in this autumn enclosure. Years had grown into this creation he knew must have been woven in love by this woman in her years of retreat for her crime to her beloved Arsinoe.

He opened the latch and went inside. Overhead he noticed the fading autumn leaves drop and fall from the balmy wind. He was now in a cooler spot, guarded almost entirely from the elements in her finely woven shelter. He walked around and looked at the center of this round enclosure.

In the center was the charred remains of a post that was broken in half, perhaps by the elements before this shelter was erected in love. Rocks were carefully laid about and arranged in size winding from the entrance of this shelter to the center at the exact location of the pole.

The ground long since lost most of the remains of the people who burned here. For only a few pieces of coal were found and what appeared to him as bone fragments. The rains had washed away the crimes of Hadwinna long before this shelter was built.

He had no idea why, but he then bent down and started to search for something. Something to bring back to his wife. Proof that this was truly her Arsinoe. Then he found it. By a sparkle in the sun. Something was hidden under the carefully weeded faded summer grass. He placed his hands on it and he found a ring. He knew that it must have been thrown by her before the fire reached her, for it surely would have been melted along with her.

He wondered if perhaps she wanted someone to know her fate. For in the grass, hidden under a rock, he knew was carefully placed there by the old woman, was a ring. The ring was gold in the design of a scarab. It was the ring that he knew belonged to Selene from her mother. For to assure himself of this, he looked inside to the inscription, which he knew were the hieroglyphs spelling out Cleopatra VII. A tear fell down at that moment for he knew that he could never tell his precious Selene any of this. He placed the ring safe in his trouser's pocket. He had to abandon his toga in order to travel safely in the Keltoi lands, so that he could gather information. He was thankful that he had recalled much of the teachings in the language in his initial journey to this land from the ancient druid named Bellinos, who was the Arch Druid.

He kept the ring and decided that it along with the dagger would be placed along with his wife in her families' mausoleum, safe from breaking the heart of his wife. He knew that she lived only in hopes of seeing them again. That she had blamed herself for sending them over there, especially if any harm befell them. Which he had unfortunately found out had. He would write about the truth and decide how to seek vengeance on Annius. The truth would be with the rest of his families' security and would only be revealed when the time was right.

He knew that he further could not do anything about Annius, for he knew that if he informed Cynfelyn about the duplicity of his brother, Cynfelyn would rashly seek vengeance for the betrayal of his wife's family. Juba was nervous about that since he was not sure of the stance that Rome would take in all of this. He was afraid that Tiberius would take advantage of this battle amongst his client kings and probably swoop down and conquer Britannia. He knew that this land did not have the chance to defend itself against the force of Rome. He also knew that Mauretania, despite all that his wife had done for it, could not stand up against them either.

So he kept his knowledge to himself and did not even tell Helios about the latter found information. He made Helios promise not to tell his aunt of the matter for the possible political repercussions that it would cause. He felt that he was avoiding an avalanche of war, should any of this information leak.

On their way back, he had observed the flight of Annius and of his horse safely in the distance, probably wondering how Juba would handle this matter. The man seemed to grow bolder as he realized that a pursuit was not to occur and had tailed him even after Sego and Andocos had returned to Cynfelyn.

He had observed the smile glow on the face of Annius hidden behind shrubbery on the shore as he rowed out with his men to the trireme anchored out in the harbor. He saw that Annius held up something that he had around his neck. It appeared from the distance to be a smooth round pebble that almost glinted in the harsh sun. Juba wondered at the significance of that act by Annius.

Juba did not know the heart of Annius, he could only guess. And his guess was only partly right. For Annius had joined the band initially to prevent the knowledge of the fate of Arsinoe and Alanya from ever reaching Juba II. His hatred of the foreign king had only turned to admiration of how this ancient man was deeply persistent in finding out the truth for his wife. He had slept in tents beside this man for a few full moons and had learned much from him and of how he felt on life. This man was more of a scholar than a king and nothing to be fearful of as he had originally thought. He had ended up in feeling sorry for this man instead of fearing him. He had planned on killing him, though it did not bear fruition due to the fear of his brother finding out.

Instead he followed him and had admired how fast this man picked up languages over everyone else that traveled by his side. He also admired how this great king had not only learned about the new lands visited but wanted to know their ways and honored them.

Annius had around his neck an amulet made of the pebble that he intercepted during that fateful demise of Arsinoe. He made it as a sort of reminder of a family that could not possibly take over his land. He used it to give him power and strength.

Though as he grew to know this man, it had earned him a different meaning. For it became his shame to wear. Of how he leaped without truly knowing why. Had he researched the situation with more ardor instead of just stumbling with his youth's fanaticism-he would not have done the deed at all!

He eventually let the king follow the clues gleaned along the way without hindrance. He knew that upon learning of the truth of the matter he would be a dead man. He was not ready to die. Instead he would leave and try to bring out some good from this situation. If there was any to be gained at this point so many years later.

He was even tempted to wait on the side and to try to kill the king, but decided against it-in that all would eventually lead to him.

He made haste and ran back to the side of his brother hoping to find a way to argue with him for his life, now that the truth of his part in the matter was learned by Juba II and his men.

However, on the way his horse stumbled and it was at that moment that a shadow stepped out from behind a tree to face him. The sun in its late stance had cast a glow around this form that blocked his path and obscured the true identity of this stranger.

The horse had run off, while Annius tried to extricate him from this predicament. He fumbled in his confusion while the form only stood motionless like a spider drooling over the prey caught in his web.

"So you have come to atone for your wrongs prince?"

"Come hither out of the shadows where I can see you clearly nameless voice!"

"Why, did you do the same for Arsinoe? You hid from her and others the evil deeds you had done that have tarnished her name!"

At last Annius had freed himself from the tangles of the branches that were laid in the path for his fall. The trap made all too clear before him. His apprehension only increased his fear. Who was this person.

He felt angry that in his thought's flight while on his horse, he did not observe so simple a trap laid out before him. His determination and selfish escape had again got the better of him.

"How do you think she felt as her daughter was murdered before her very eyes, and all because of the lies that you had whispered to Drennedd!"

"How think you on where your lies led that plight for the princess?"

Annius squirmed under the tyrannical unknown voice of his assailant. For the voice was vaguely familiar and he knew that the person tried to alter his voice to hide his true identity from him. In the anger of the stranger's voice-it fell upon him as a judgment from the Gods, so merciless was the deep voice that cried out to him of his misdeeds!

He felt this person was truly cursed by the Gods and felt his blood boil under the insanity that emanated deep into his pores from this person who stood under the deep shadows of the sun.

Who could possibly have known of his part in all of this? He had told no one. He had only wanted his brother to have a reason to fight the Romans. He wanted to stir some trouble amongst the tribes, since his brother and family were growing too weak from inactivity. He did not truly appreciate the peace that his brother had brought in his reign until very recently.

"Did her innocence mean anything to you? She was so beautiful so talented and would have made a great ruler. And her daughter a great warrior! And you tore it all to shreds! And only for your own selfish reasons!"

Annius was desperate now, for in his panic he now realized that he was immobilized by his broken ankle. The adrenalin had hid it from him until that moment and only made him shudder.

"I know not who you are, but know you this and heed my words—I meant nothing and was foolish in my youth. I had only wanted the army to have reason for a battle!"

"Silence! You must pay for the error of your ways!"

"I beg of you to know the truth on this matter!"

It had slowly occurred to him that this voice could possibly belong to Andocos, for his words had sounded out in a small glimmer that this person had once loved Arsinoe. He had felt sorry for the large warrior, who had refused to marry and remained alone even long after the rumors of her death had reached them.

The realization of this knowledge crept up on him and his mind worked overtime in hoping to find a way to get him out of this trap.

"Stranger, I beg of you, please consider my plight! I had not known what could have happened. I would gladly have turned back time. I had only thought that they would have been banished. Never had I thought that they all would have been killed. I had seen it with my own eyes!"

The stranger finally came out of the shadows and bent down over the trembling Annius. He reached out with his knife and severed the warriors neck while retrieving under the cascading blood the amulet around his neck. The affirmation of the identity of Andocos only brought to Annius his death.

Andocos bent down over the pathetic form of his prince and took the leather cord that was holding a stone all scarlet from blood. The stone was the message that he had never received. The message that was intercepted. The events never would have unfolded had he received it.

He had always suspected this, but had prayed that it was not true. Instead he followed Annius over the years in search for the truth. What he had found was that the intercepted stone was only the very surface of this man's deceptions.

For this man was capable of many horrific things. He had followed him with his own eyes and stood transfixed at the excessive cruelty that was hidden from all with his light and humorous exterior. Cynfelyn had no idea of the reality of his brother and probably chose to safely ignore it or to guard it more closely. For Cynfelyn believed to know your friends, but to keep your enemies even closer.

Andocos kicked dirt on the corpse of his fellow soldier in the contempt that he felt from this man. Of all that he had done to cause dissent in the land, and all because he was bored! How selfish and immature this prince was, how lucky that he would never attain rule were they all now.

He dragged *the Prince of Lies* as he had come to call Annius to himself over the years to the edge of the road and then over to the side of a steep embankment that led to the murky waters of a stinking swamp. Perfect place for *the Prince of Lies* to fester and rot un-honored by his Gods as it should be!

With a skip to his step and a whistle he gathered the reigns to his horse and headed back to the settlement to his Queen and King. Along the way he kept kneading in his hands the connection to his soul—the white pebble that he had finally received. Justice at last was won. May his soul find hers' in other lives and may he save her life the next time so that her voice will join other worlds such as hers' did his. For he was her faithful protector. His love for her was pure, he would have done anything for her and understood her love for Sion. He knew that she was innocent of the crimes that she was murdered for. For she was a Goddess to him and could have done no wrong for she lived forever in his heart and soul.

* * * * *

After Selene had died Juba II faded even further. For he had not even told her about her brother or sister for that matter. He was too ashamed for his weakness, especially how he handled the deceitful Annius and the fact that he could not challenge him on the matter. He could not wipe away his face in that last moment that he saw him by the hut of the horrid old woman. The man gloated at the cowardice of the King of Mauretania. Annius could see it in Juba's face that his secret would be kept from Selene.

XVI

Jubilla knew nothing of her father's visit to her lands and would have riled the dead out of underworld, had she found out. Especially since he had not bothered to see her at all, nor her family. But she never knew.

The day that she had dreaded had finally arrived. For a ship was reported to have sailed into their harbor. It was from Mauritania. She had not received notice of this, so she knew that it was not good news. Her mother would have told her if she was planning a visit.

The messengers had finally arrived to her chamber bearing a large crate. She knew what was inside. She was afraid to open it. For it would make it final. Perhaps if she let it sit until she was ready, she then would open it. She saw the look in her husband's eyes and turned away. She then ran out into the woods far from any sign of their settlement and growing capitol city. She ran until she had no breath. For she wanted truly to turn back time. To when she was safe and in her mother's arms so long ago. She ran until she could no longer hear the busy sounds of life in her new home. For she was always a princess of Mauritania in her soul of souls.

She had grown to love her new home and her wise and brave husband and to cherish her children and her grandchildren. She knew her world would shatter when she opened the box. She felt like the Greek Pandora that her mother had told her about so long ago. If she opened the box, all of the world that she knew would collapse around her.

She could almost see her mother clearly in her mind, even among all of the blueberries that had surrounded her in her place that she had collapsed upon in sanctuary. She picked some, so as to not let that part of her world in. The tangy taste assailed her taste buds and unfortunately started to bring her mother even closer to her rather than what she had hoped by trying some.

"Momma, I do not want to open that box!" The tears assaulted her and captured her soul in wrathful torment. For she had already opened the box in her mind, no matter how much she had tried to run from it. It followed her anyways.

She wanted desperately to go back to where she was safe. Of a time when her mother had long hair that covered her in sleep, by the side of her little sister and brother, who were now as lost to her now as she knew her mother was.

Her new home was exciting and new and completely foreign to her. She wore dresses that would have seemed utterly alien had she walked the streets of Rome of her homeland of Numidia or Mauritania. In her crumpled form on the ground, completely unrecognizable as a Queen, she sniffled back her tears and gazed at the necklace that she had under her dress, in her bosom. It was a medallion with the inscription that her mother had made for her for her wedding, so that she would not forget where she came from.

The chain was silver, for her mother told her that the metal was once sacred to the pharaoh in that it was considered the tears of the Gods. The medallion was huge and bore inscriptions in hieroglyphs and in the picture writing of the royal house of Numidia. The writings stated the same thing, "Never forget your home and family, our blood flows in yours" She held it up so that it glinted in the sunlight in hopes of blinding the reality that she knew she had to face.

After some time, she eventually composed herself and regally returned to face her legacy. For she opened the box with her family all around her. And in it were the scrolls and the ring that she knew was on her mother's finger as well as a silver one with a wide band that she was told came from the step-father of Marcus Antonius with the family name of Cornelius inscribed inside. The scrolls she collected as an extension of her mother and the rings, her flesh.

She placed the ring on her finger and looked over at her daughter Cleopatra who sat mutely on the side in anticipation. Cleopatra bowed her head in response. She knew that she was the one who would wear it after her own death and carry on the legacy. No words for that had to be said. Leannydd accepted this with grace and Jubilla was proud of her younger daughter. In the box was also a letter from her mother which she would read later. She knew that it was her personal version of the legacy scrolls. She made a vow that she would relate them regally in her own memoirs of her family, because she knew that her mother did not have the heart to write about it herself.

She was very proud of her mother and all that she had done, though she knew that her mother had always compared herself to her legendary grandmother, the last Pharaoh of Egypt. She knew that her mother blamed herself for not retaining the land back for their family. Her mother had done more than enough in that aspect, but it was beyond her and not the right time. Her mother was blameless in that matter. She then found at the bottom of the crate the famous diadem that she knew was worn by her legendary grandmother. For it gleamed in the firelight and was polished to perfection. Hieroglyphs covered the rim in precision telling the story of the Ptolemy line as handed them in power by Alexander the Great from the first Ptolemy of Macedonia. In the center was a cobra hooded in protection of the head that it covered. Her children and husband gasped in awe at this, for never had they seen such a snake in their own land. She held in her hands the symbol of the Pharaoh of Egypt that she knew her own mother felt not worthy to wear herself. She also knew that her mother was always afraid to anger Augustus, even after it did not matter any more.

Her husband seemed to have read her mind for he whispered, "Try it on love, for Augustus has been dead quite the while!" He had a mischievous grin on his face and was beaming with pride and she carefully placed the crown on her head. How odd it must have looked in her completely alien and Keltoi garments and wild tangled curls of faded red.

"Mother, you truly look magical and powerful!" Cried out her son Cyllin in amazement at his mother. They all ran over to her and surrounded her with love, for they had all grown to love their powerful grandmother and they all felt a great pride for their mother who looked like a Goddess. For her hair seemed to have in that moment taken on the luster of her youth when the crown was placed on her head, with the ring of her mother on her thumb where it fit.

The tears streamed down her face, especially in the comfort of the embraces of her children and her husband.

XVII

Antonia Minor received the news and felt a part of her soul being ripped from her. She had lost her lifelong friend and now she had no one to confide in. She cherished the visits they had with each other though few in number and went over to her small study and began to pour over all that she had received in correspondence over the years from her sister. They were just words now, just parts of a person who no longer existed! She missed her sister dreadfully and wondered what she was to do now.

Rome was becoming a dangerous place with the actions of Tiberius at his villa. She avoided it with every excuse that they would muster. Her son was safe for the time being since he was safe on campaign.

She did not know the reason for his drastic change in personality. He grieved for his loss over his love Vispania and endured for a short time the relationship and forced marriage with Julia, the daughter of Augustus, until she was finally banished and later died of starvation when he stopped her rations-as was the rumor that ravaged the streets of Rome.

Soon after she learned of the death of Cleopatra Selene, word had arrived of the death of her favorite son Germanicus. He had died mysteriously while on campaign in the Germanic tribal lands while trying to subdue some of the rebellions over there. His wife, Agrippina grieved and came over soon after to cry on her shoulder and was looking for comfort that Antonia could not find herself.

Agrippina was all alone now with nine children. She was by his side when he died and had confided in Antonia that she believed that it might have been poison, though had no evidence of such.

They both sat together in the study of Antonia Minor on a rainy afternoon.

"It feels as if the heavens are opening up to let in my dear Germanicus." The tears began anew and slowly slid down her fine porcelain features. Her blonde hair was un-coifed and hung to her waist. Antonia reached out to her and felt empathy for the young mother.

"I feel that way too. He had so much promise. You may stay here with your children if you would like dear. They need their family."

"Thank you Mother, but I do not feel that I would be safe here."

Antonia leaned closer to discus the items that brought each other near in the strictest of confidence. "I agree that the situation here is not very stable." She lowered her eyes and looked around. She dismissed the servants who waited in the corners of the room.

"I feel that Tiberius or Livia may have had something to do with this."

"Livia…She would never."

"Think about it, Livia is a different woman now. Think about how her son had inherited the power. Tiberius was not the son of Augustus."

"Yes, but he married Julia, your mother."

"Though look how soon she was forgotten in her exile after her beloved Tatta died! He stopped her food supplies! He had your brother executed for his alleged affair with Julia! Your Iully!"

"Hush, Agrippina! Besides, it was not Tiberius who had him executed, it was Augustus. Besides, Iully was almost flaunting his affair with her it embarrassed Augustus. He really had no choice in the matter. He was the laughingstock of all Rome, his daughter was made out to be a whore!"

"Was she really? I mean, she should not have had those affairs, but everybody does."

"She was careless enough to have flaunted it under her father's nose! And Tiberius was bitter because Augustus, your grandfather, made him give up his wife that he truly loved for his "spoiled daughter" Julia."

"My mother was not spoiled, she was just doted upon by her father—she was his little girl." Whispered Agrippina with furrowed brows.

Antonia continued, "I realize that, but who has a choice in marriage. I was very fortunate indeed to have actually loved my husband and to have received his love in return."

"Yes, you were very lucky as was I Antonia! Very few woman have that choice, especially woman who were born to men in power, for all we really end up as are their pawns and have to go where they send us. You two had a rare kind of love and it is a shame that it had to end so early!"

Antonia continued to assuage her daughter-in-law, "Your love as well ended early, ahh the plight of true love amongst all of the rubble of the Republic! But, you have nine beautiful children from him! Even your son whom the soldiers call lovingly *Little Boots*, He is the most cherished of all! All of Rome loves him! He reminds me so much of the Julii line that flows in our veins my dear. He will be a great leader someday and quite attractive to the ladies with his golden curls and long lashes over those fatally deep blue eyes."

"Oh, Mamma! He is precious, but he needs more guidance from his Tatta! I curse the air that Livia and Tiberius breathe! I know that they had something to do with this and I will publicly announce it. I want the world to know of their treachery!"

"Be ever so careful! You know that the more trouble that you cause, you will eventually receive that dreadful summons we all fear and may even end up banished yourself like his own wife!"

"Besides, why do you think that Livia had something to do with this?" She inquired.

"She is too much in the sidelines and had powerful ears listening for her, she always has."

The all too knowledgeable Agrippina continued, "Don't you wonder about Marcellus who died so long ago, that was her doing, all of Rome knows of that, though no one had the gall to say anything to her husband at that time, Augustus."

"Also, what about Gaius and Lucius, my own brothers? Think about it, her precious Tiberius was looked upon as heir after the death of Marcellus, but then these two were born. All of that grooming came to naught when they both mysteriously died. Livia was present at the villa at the time when Gaius died, apparently from a fall from his horse while out riding. Who was with him at that time, but a servant of Livia's. My mother always wondered about that and warned me about Livia. She was too quiet to not have been involved. The woman is very wise. Now look who sits upon all of the power of Rome…her son!"

"I understand that dear, but don't you think that you are being rash in your opinion of Livia, even with all of that evidence presented. My own mother Octavia, did wonder the same thing though. But like all of Rome behind closed doors, she had no proof either. Marcellus was her own son from her first husband. She sat here on the couch long ago with Livia over when he died, I was still very young then. But I remember that Livia cried over him too and was here to comfort my mother. I remember it well!"

"Lady Mother, I have heard about that, but did she not come over here to comfort you as well just yesterday about my Germanicus, your son! She dare not show her face at my door though, for she has known how I feel about her. I refuse to hide my feelings about her politics! She wants to bring Rome back to the monarchy and destroy every Roman ideal of the old Republic days that my grandfather had toiled away many of his years in rule in bringing it back to his people."

"Oh child, do I know the history of Rome on that matter!" She slowly giggled at memories of her great uncle and all of his great visions that he had for the people when she was a lot younger and his visions more prominent.

"Agrippina, I recall a time when he had ordered all of the women in the palace to weave all of his garments and their own, like the ancient days long ago. He not only wanted the Republic restored to it's glory days, but he wanted us all to look like them too!"

"You cannot be serious on that! It must have been quite silly to see all of this family in wretched homespun! The horror of it!"

"Yes, quite ridiculous and thankfully he ceased pestering us all about it as he grew older. He realized how itchy the homespun was. He believed in practicing the morals and codes that he enforced and understood that he could no longer wear them and would not be setting a good example! All of us royal woman rejoiced at that and promptly burned our spindles and looms and set out at once in ordering much finer cloth for our gowns."

Her eyes seemed lost for a moment in thinking back to those days of a much different time, "Though I have to admit that all of us were very close, for we all had to learn how and helped each other while we spun and wove the cloth and put them all together. We would take turns visiting one another for the company while were worked as a team. Men would never understand that. Since then, we have been living separate lives and rarely visit, unless for state occasions."

"Livia is a monster and I will stop her, I refuse to allow her near my own children, she has tried though I have to give her that."

"Yes, she was the type of woman who never rose her voice and in soft tones would receive the world on a platter from her ceaseless, though very tactful persistence in all matters. She is very clever. It seems that unlike most people, age has only sharpened her wits. I feel as if I am much softer now in matters. There would have been a time many years ago, when I would have made my feelings known, but there has been too much death—and many close to me. I am very tired."

"Well, I will fight those battles for you! You know I Will!"

"But be careful that you do not find yourself banished or worse my daughter, tread very carefully around Rome! It has too many ears as you well know!"

"Do you know that Tiberius and Livia are trying to set up his own son from his first wife as the next heir?"

"I realize that, but Rome will have nothing to do with that and you well know it. Just let it pass. Your own son Caligula is too well loved by Rome, especially it's soldiers and he has the better bloodlines."

"I just cannot sit here idly and watch them get away with it all. And the thought of Livia pretending to mourn the very man she has killed with her merciless hands, it makes me ill."

"Agrippina, you have no proof of that…" She leaned closer, "Do you?"

"It is all circumstantial, as is her way. She is known for her association with her slave Nirces. Did you know that he used to be a Druid in Gaul and he is well known for his skill in herbal tinctures. I would not have put it beneath her to have somehow managed to convince him that the potion she had sent him would cure his relentless cough. I know it was tainted! He thought I was being silly when I had warned him not to drink it. He had passed the very next morning after vomiting up the little food that he had eaten!"

"I had suspected something like that, do you still have the vial that contained the potion daughter?"

"That I do not, for it mysteriously vanished, like the other potions sent to Gaius and Lucius, I have heard…"

"That is true. So you see there is nothing that anyone can do about it."

"I hate that beast, I do not know what my grandfather ever saw in her!"

"He saw what all men see, he was oblivious to the rest and probably did not care. For she was once a very beautiful woman in her own time."

"But her wretched existence and all of the wrongs that she had committed to better her family have caught up with her looks, she is old and wrinkly now!" She giggled at the thought of the older Livia that she knew well.

"We all will be that way, if we are lucky enough to grow that old. With the way things are in Rome, not all will have that fortune!"

"I know…Did you hear about the latest atrocities that her son is committing in the name of Rome?"

"Oh Agrippina, I am too old for gossip."

"No, you have to hear this! He takes the wives of his provincial governors to his own bed and the worried husbands are too timid to stop this! He had made his villa into a brothel and had even sold some of them, despite all of the protests of the husbands—he has sold them to his soldiers for sport and puts the money earned in the treasury!"

"Oh you cannot be serious of that? I cannot even imagine that he would do such a thing!"

"It is true! What about your own husband, his brother. With what happened and all. Can you now believe how cruel this man could be when he murdered his own brother!"

"He did not do that Agrippina. Now you are being ridiculous. I was there the whole time of his illness and there was no potion from Livia or Tiberius for that matter. He had not healed properly from a would and there was nothing that I could have done for him. I stayed up until he died, It was horrific, but natural." How am I supposed to believe anything that audacious about Tiberius. "

"How not to. I am sorry about that, I just assumed."

"Your assumptions might get you into trouble. But no matter. Rest assured, not he, nor anyone else for that matter had any hand in my husband's death years ago."

"Again, I am sorry."

"And about Gaius, did he not die the same way too, from the complications of a wound that had not healed properly…"

"Mother, I do not know. I was not there. It is just all that people are talking about behind closed doors."

"Well it had better stay that way for their own safety, especially if what you are telling me is true, not even the woman are safe from him. He has turned so dark since the time his Vispania was taken away from him. He had even dared to hold her in a chance public meeting, before he ruled and while he was married to Julia! He had become reckless since he married Julia. Especially since that marriage had not produced any children. Why not elevate his own son from her to his power? I understand why he wants to do this. The lines of succession were made open by Augustus, it was a wise move that he made in doing that."

"But, I do not understand why anything had to happen to my Germanicus, Tiberius even adopted him on the request of Augustus when he was still alive to succeed him after his death."

"Tiberius was forced to pass over his own son from Vispania for my son, I wonder about the whole thing now! It seems as if Tiberius is still bitter about things that occurred so many years ago and is playing out his anger!"

"He is doing a poor job in trying to imitate Augustus as you well know. He was not believed by the senate when he tried to refuse the Principate powers, he looked pathetic when he tried to turn them down."

"Yes, and I heard that the senate inquired at the mock refusal of Tiberius, "Then how is Rome to be lead without a leader". How insipid of him, he tried to imitate Augustus with his pathetic acting and appearing gracious, he needed those powers. How foolish! At least Augustus was genuine. We all know that Tiberius and Livia want a monarchy and only play at restoring the republic!" Antonia reclined back on that note and stared out at the window in reflection. For she feared where Rome was heading. She agreed with Agrippina in wanting to restore the old republic as her uncle had tried and almost laughed at the pathetic attempts of Tiberius in playacting the old republican. It was never genuine to his nature.

From his birth on, he was raised around power. Livia had made sure of that. She secretly despised her worst assumptions on the true motives of Tiberius and the death of her son. It was too clear to Antonia to be true. She did not want to see it, though it mocked her openly. Now that Germanicus was dead, Tiberius was free to adopt his son from Vispania, especially since Julia was not around to stop this.

On his deathbed her son had accused his murderer as Calpurnius Piso, the Governor of Syria. She knew all too well that he was close in alliance with Tiberius and Livia. Too much screamed at her in this matter. Though she feared greatly for Agrippina, she did want to see this matter resolved and the murderer brought to justice. She knew that Agrippina had brought back her son's ashes to Rome and she knew that Agrippina had the confidence to voice her opinions. She secretly cheered for this young girl and her confidence.

She had to keep still on matters though, for her own safety, for Tiberius' son Drusus was to marry her daughter Livilla soon. The preparations had been put on hold to deal with this sudden tragedy that befell her household and brought her daughter-in-law to her domus.

"I have some advice for you daughter, you have a lot of children to protect, tred carefully in Rome for your own sake! I care about you too much to have anything tragic happen to you or my grandchildren. The gossip will always fly around Rome. Be careful what you repeat! And I do not believe one word about that brothel gossip you have mentioned, despite any suspicions that I may have about him. Do not forget that I have known him a long time. Though I am worried about one thing though—he believes that people are born to their nature that they display, he does not believe that people will change with time! I feel we are only seeing the beginning of the dark days of Rome! His prefect Sejunus is rising too fast and almost has the power that Agrippa had over my uncle. Sejunus is merciless and is trying to gain the ear of Tiberius on those who seek to betray him. I worry for the children of Rome!"

"I will fight your battles, do not worry on that account. And yes, I will tread ever so carefully! You rest and be here for my children, should any of this get out!"

"That you know, but please be careful!" With that the two woman embraced. One full of vigor for life and justice and the old ways of Rome and the other with the same vivre, yet too tired and weary to battle.

Part eight

I

Britannia 19 C.E. to 22 A.C.E.

Jubilla had continued her mother's correspondence with Antonia and had begun her writings to Agrippina at Antonia's insistence. Her mother believed that it was wise to be informed on the doings of Rome, especially for the protection of their own lands since they held the complete power of most of the world.

She had just received a letter from Antonia Minor about Tiberius reinstating the *"maestas"* or the treason acts of Rome. These laws enacted several families to be placed under house arrest for the alleged treasonous acts against Tiberius. It seemed to her that Tiberius was becoming paranoid in his rule and was lashing out at everyone.

She was especially dismayed to learn that he had placed Antonia's daughter Livilla who was married to Drusus, the son of Tiberius and Vispania-under house arrest.

Antonia had explained to Jubilla in the latest letter that Tiberius' prefect Sejunus had attempted to seduce her daughter while married to Drusus under Tiberius' own roof. When Drusus tried to complain to his father about the atrocities of this man, Tiberius would hear nothing further on the matter and threw him out of the house.

Antonia had mentioned that Drusus was as hot headed as his father and had been trying to get the man out of the power of Rome, for he saw a shadow of Agrippa in the man.

Agrippa was a common man who rose to power by the side of Augustus though becoming his most important advisor. His power was secure when he married Julia, of which Agrippina was one of their youngest children. Drusus saw that this Sejunus was trying to emulate this man in having the same common roots, and nothing more. Agrippa was wise and valuable, while Sejunus was a power monger. Drusus hated how his father was blind to the conspirings of this man. People were dying under the accusations brought forth from this common man! Tiberius was tired of the ramblings of his son and felt that Sejunus was worthy of his rank and wise as well. So to complicate matters further, he only placed his son and family under house arrest and not immediately to death as Sejunus insisted. Antonia stated that in that matter alone did Tiberius show any wisdom in dealing with this whole situation.

Jubilla was thankful that she was so far away from all of the drama in Rome. She was also thankful that Tiberius was too busy with matters on his home front to seek out further expansion of his empire and looking to her lands for it. She had tried to keep this letter from her husband, but he had found it and had approached her on the matter late one evening.

It was bitter cold outside, though there was no snow, which was unusual for this time of year. She knew that despite the dwindling light of the loud crackling fire, her husband would glow even more in his rage.

"Jubilla! How could you associate with them! Your mother did because they were family. But it is dangerous there now and your mother is gone."

"They are my family as well, Domina Antonia Minor is my Aunt and Agrippina a cousin of mine!"

"I realize that but could you keep their troubles away from me. It angers me so! They are so barbaric and I know they cast weary eyes on all of this land and want it someday for themselves."

"Yes, but we are safe now. The letters assure me that they have too much to deal with over there to worry about us!"

"Is that so dear wife? Do you know that there have been parties arriving more frequently to our shores in hopes of settlement? Why just one such party arrived in CaerLlud to set up camp! I had sent out men to look into it and they put up a quiet and unassuming front in their intentions! But I know what they are up to, and do not forget that I was brought up in Rome and was educated there, so I can read that pathetic Latin writing of theirs!"

"Dear settle down, there is no reason for worry. I understand that and have hid nothing from you."

"Yes, I realize this, but it angers me to know that you write to those barbaric people. Besides, Antonia and Agrippina might be safe, but their sons and family members are not. One might get wind of us and come over here to investigate. They will come over to try to take what is ours and I will be ready for them!"

"They know nothing of us really and feel that we are no threat, for you are recognized as King of all of this land."

"But in reality it is not the whole land and you know it. They do not realize how large this land is. True that we rule over a few territories. But I would feel responsible that your writings would give any true information to the wrong people as to destroy our welfare."

"I understand, I will stop the correspondence if you wish under those issues that you have raised and I am truly sorry."

"No, do not stop it. Most Roman men would not care to look at the correspondences of their wives and believe them too trifle for their notice. I, on the other hand am wise to the power of my wife and only have to worry. Besides if you stop the writing abruptly it will bring us more to their attention. Just continue as always, though play us down for their ears for our own safety. Never mention details on this land and all we have to offer. This way you can find out still what is going on in Rome. I agree with you, though on a different matter, that it is necessary that we keep abreast of goings on in Rome, for our own safety. Information is good. Get that information, though disguise it well my love!"

His eyes twinkled and he plopped down on her carefully and covered her in her embrace by the glow of the evening fire in their sleeping chamber that was now gloriously empty since the children were all grown and in their own dwellings. Both of them were still young enough to make up for all of those lost years as a couple with children always around them in sleeping and waking hours.

II

"Is everything loaded?" Cried out Jubilla and she watched in dismay as the boats by the shore were filled to beyond her imagined capacity. She was heading out to Mauritania to visit her father. She had heard from her niece Drusilla of his rapid decline. She feared that he would not last much longer and Jubilla had desperately wanted to be by his side. Along with her for company and protection were her sons Cyllin, Caradawc and Gweiryth and her daughters Leannydd and Cleopatra and her new husband Alexander.

Alexander was along also to visit his parents and the home that he grew up in and had missed dreadfully. Alexander was not doing so well in his adjustment to this culture. Jubilla and Cleopatra worried for him. Cleopatra meandered up to her side and together they watched Alexander's pathetic attempt to appear as busy as all of the other men genuinely were in loading the boats. Their muscles gleamed in the early spring sun in their exertions.

Leannydd was among them as well, for she might be small, but she was very strong. Despite her priestess training, she wanted to participate in life more than most women who chose the life of a priestess. She was constantly a part of the hunts, especially for boar and made herself always available for any physical assistance that was needed. She was constantly in competition with her brothers on that matter. Jubilla almost chuckled at the comparison that she made against Alexander with his pale figure and pampered lifestyle.

Jubilla was constantly after her sons to treat Alexander better, for they made great fun of him and were constantly playing tricks on him, much to the dismay of their oldest sister, Cleopatra, who was mortified and knew her brothers all too well. She was constantly protecting her meek and quiet husband from her brothers unavailing assaults and pranks.

Jubilla noticed as Cleopatra eyed her siblings wearily for any new trick they had in line for him. She chuckled at this and knew that Cleopatra would grow to be a fierce protector of her family.

Togodumnos had then snuck up behind them and seized this opportunity when all were distracted to place his arm subtly though harmlessly around the lower waist of Jubilla which startled her.

Too ashamed of her brother-in-law's actions and not knowing how to read the truth of them, just yelled out instead, "Cynfelyn, is my herbal chest packed, should any one take ill, I want..."

He brushed back the sweat from his brow and glanced up at his wife with a bright wide smile, "No worries, all of that is safely tucked inside. You may want to get some new supplies, when you stop on the mainland along the way though."

"You are so thoughtful husband" She inched away from Togodumnos and then went over closer to her husband, "Would you need any help from me, I still have some muscles left in my old age!" She smiled.

Her pulled her close and spoke softer, "Aye, that I know only too well my vixen, no fear though all is done. You have the most difficult part of all in charting this journey of yours. Let us hope that your father's maps ring true."

"They are I assure you of that!" She cried, almost in defense.

"Lass, I mean no offence, I only worry. You know these boats are not that fit for deep ocean travel. Make sure you hug those coasts and be wary of pirates!"

"Julius Caesar vanquished all of them, the seas are safe now."

"Now, though not completely. I have heard that some may be acting up. You do have enough of my men though for protection. Remember that all obey you and my orders. All of you must hide your rank and appear as merchants. The woman must hide that they are women!"

"Hush husband, no fear on that, you know how much us girls love to dress up and a have chance to wear trousers for everyday, it is so completely appealing to us! Especially on horseback! Though I do love the freedom that we have in our gown a little more. Still it will be some fun for us all!" Her smile faded when she saw the look on his face.

"Juby, please heed my advice. Even when you are in Rome, we must appear poverty stricken and simple"

"I am aware of that love."

Just then Togodumnos strolled nonchalantly over to them, "This cannot be a quarrel, the lovebirds, unheard of!" Jubilla rolled her eyes and bowed out to check on her family that she was leaving for this voyage for another goodbye, "I must say goodbye to the grandchildren, Excuse me brother." Both men bowed as she made her way.

He leaned closer to his brother, "Cynfelyn, please reconsider. I would love to join them so that I may be of better use to you. I have many ways of extracting information." His eyes were shifty and his graying handsome looks hid well his true meanings as always, though his brother was always somewhat suspicious of this brother, it was only dimmed by the suspicions that he felt for Annius, whom he had not heard from for too long. He never found any proof though of anything amiss-just no word at all.

"Togodumnos, you know my answer. Besides, your presence is much more valuable here. I need some help in taking over the Silures territory, it needs a lot of work with them fighting over territory and rule. Now is our chance. You are one of my best warriors and only you have the great skills needed to tame that new heard we had just brought in from the far northern lands. No brother, I need you here."

Just then they noticed the presence of Andocos who was always a very quiet man was always on the sidelines, though spoke very little. "Cynfelyn, do you worry about her, so far away. It is dangerous in that part of the world."

"Yes, I worry, but not for her-for any who try to get in her way. I just hope they understand how important that it is to keep a low profile over there."

"Why should they have to hide how truly fortunate we are and how successful you are, you are recognized King of this land brother." Spoke up an eager and obviously upset Togodumnos.

"Again, I warn you Togodumnos, not to be so rash in this! We have not the strength to battle them yet, you have almost grown as restless was

Annius. I want to attention drawn to these lands until we are ready to defend ourselves! We are grossly outnumbered at the present time!"

"I understand this, but…"

"I am the King, not you Togodumnos! Be careful you remember that!"

Andocos gave his liege Cynfelyn a reassuring look, while Togodumnos stomped off. "I do not know what has come over him lately-it is so unlike him in nature to be so brusque with anyone. All he has ever cared about was horses until lately. I do not understand. Though I do understand your caution and am completely in agreement on that matter. I am going to talk with Jubilla before she leaves to make sure that she returns with some of their fine horses for him, that might distract this new temper of his."

"Wonderful idea. Cyllin has orders to look into their chariots to see if ours need any improvements, though he will be the one you should probably speak with on the matter of the horses."

"Aye, that I will." Andocos then left Cynfelyn to seek out Cyllin as he was completing the final phase of loading the boats.

"Cyllin!"

"Andocos, what brings you here, are you offering your help…A little late though, most is done."

"Oh, that… I will leave the hard labor for the young. I do not have the strength that I used to have so many years ago. I came to you of other matters. You know how my elbows bother me. I am sorry truly that I cannot help you with this."

"No, do not worry of that. I meant no offense."

"None taken prince. Will you be sure to look into those matters we discussed the other night?"

"Yes, of course. Though I do not see why you worry so. Our chariots are superior in all matters as are our horses. Perfect for them. "

"No, I have heard about the superior battle capacity those Arab horses have, they are much larger and faster than what we have native to this land. Their chariots might be different, but never underestimate the power of other lands. They have the same motivations as we do. Mauritania is known for some of their superior fighting capabilities and I want you to learn them from your family members. Plead ignorance and work with their pride, but take this information back to us."

"I understand. You know that if any ill should come from the Romans our way, they have promised assistance."

Caradawc had been listening and chose this moment to interrupt, "Warrior Andocos, would I be sent over to Rome as father once was for studies. Would they leave me over there for that?"

"I, like your father do not feel that the it is wise for that, Tiberius is too unpredictable, unlike Augustus was. Your father has taught us that their ignorance and pride would be our greatest weapon someday."

"He is wise, you both best heed his advice in all matters."

"Yes, but he grows old and forgets things, his mind does wander…" Mentioned Cyllin.

"No worry, it is only because your mother and you will be so far away from his side and he wishes that he could be there to protect all of you. He is like that when he worries.

"You are probably right on that account sir. I will go find mother to make sure that she visits the boys at my wife's mother's house. For I forgot to tell her that they would be there today." Cyllin then ran off to find her.

"I will miss you Andocos! Watch over my father will you!"

"Have no worries on that matter lad!"

Andocos meant what he said to his prince as he watched him walk away from him. He worried about his king and felt as he were a brother had so many years been lived by his side. He knew him well enough to recognize some things that bothered him greatly in regard to his health. He had noticed that his brother in arms and king would break out in a sweat, which he tried to hide from all. Most of them were fooled by this. And Andocos fervently tried to protect them all from this as well. He was rightfully worried that Togodumnos would do something to try to seize the power from his brother. He would make sure that it would not happen. For he knew the truth of Annius' disappearance and feared that somehow Togodumnos did as well somehow. How else to explain his sudden change of personality. Perhaps the horses no longer interested him, since now he saw a possible future leading the people after Cynfelyn, with nothing in between.

He was the peacekeeper of this family and Cynfelyn knew it. He knew when to bring things up and when not to. For Cynfelyn was a wise and just ruler and served his people well, but his sons were not ready to take over should anything happen to him. He decided that he should run after Cyllin and beg him to stay behind, just in case, for he was more ready than his uncle Togodumnos was. And he feared justly on that account. For only he knew of the true duplicity of the change in his personality and his actions.

He did not fear the ghost of Annius warning his brother. For he knew that Annius had caused trouble with Drennedd over Arsinoe and had caused her unjust death along with her daughter. For he knew Sion. He felt the man was noble and would never had brought Arsinoe into the situation that she was accused of.

He chose not to bring up the truth of that matter with Cynfelyn, because Cynfelyn would have stormed over there and sought vengeance. That would have brought Rome over so fast, he dared not think on it.

He wanted to make sure that Cyllin would be here should Togodumnos try anything if Cynfelyn's health continued to weaken. He picked up his pace and knew that Cyllin would heed his advice.

III

They arrived on the docks of Caesarion and felt as weary as their guise of poor wool merchants. All of the royal family of Jubilla were gaunt from their sea rations and the abuse of the sea as they were tossed about close to shores. They had avoided any attention from pirates and were thankful for that.

Drusilla, in long flowing robes had run out to the family that she had not seen in years, except briefly and graciously welcomed them. She looked over at her aunt and was amazed how regal the woman looked despite her age and the harsh voyage. She still held herself with pride and even though she trembled at first to the steady shore, she walked with purposeful strides over to her niece and nephew.

Jubilla at once felt a rush of homesickness and the days of her youth when she saw her niece in the silken gowns of azure that made her eyes glow. She missed wearing clothes like that and of a climate where she could wear them as well! She knew her brother would have been proud had he seen the beauty his daughter had grown to be and the confidence revealed how much of an influence that her mother had in raising the young girl. She knew that she would soon be sent away to her new home with Azizus. She felt sorry for the girl, though both knew that it was the way of the world for princesses.

Then Jubilla observed Ptolemy, he was dressed in silken robes of the brightest purple that she had ever seen and his black hair hung in precise curls around his head with a narrow golden diadem. He sat under a canopy with slaves fanning him from the late morning sun. She tried to stifle back a giggle at the sight of him looking so gaudy and pretentious.

She knew her father could not be there to greet them due to his ill health and felt sorry for that, though understood. She looked at her children to make sure they were respectful to their cousin Ptolemy of Mauritania, even though he looked quite feminine to them and their culture, he would be the next ruler of this land. She felt sorry indeed for Mauritania and knew that her mother would have been upset. She wondered how much longer they would rule the country with this jaded child under it's rule.

They all made their way back to the palace over the steep cliffs overlooking the sea. She marveled at all her parents had accomplished while she was so far away from them. She felt sorry that she had only made one prior trip back to visit, especially since it was so long ago. She almost expected to see her mother running out to greet her and her family. A tear slid down her cheek as she brushed it away. Drusilla looked over at her and noticed. She smiled at Jubilla with confidence and seemed to have read her thoughts as she cast a sidelong glance over at her brother. They shared a litter and were slowly brought up to the palace gates.

Her children were amazed at what they saw before them. Never had they seen such a glorious city before under the full splendor of the brilliant sun. For at the time of their last visit, it was under the stars of the evening when they arrived. They had all stayed inside in safety for that brief visit years ago. So many people clambered about the pace that it was dizzying to them who were brought up in a strictly agricultural society. The marble gleamed in the sun everywhere they looked and towered over them lining the main road to the palace. The statues were a mixture of the Greek and Egyptian styles and the temples of many unheard of Gods dominated the streets that they traveled. Market stalls were bustling and loud. People of all colors and from so many distant lands surrounded them. Gold was everywhere and even on the statues.

As they approached the main gates, Jubilla observed a temple dedicated to Augustus and then another one dedicated to Tiberius with a statue being brought in for worship. Her face blanched at this. She looked over at Drusilla.

"Tiberius demands that we worship him as a God like Augustus. We have no choice in that. Remember that we are only client rulers to Rome. We have our freedom, but it is not complete. We are lucky that he is mainly busy in Rome and Capri and that he leaves us alone for the most part."

"Lucky indeed, though I understand. You do know the story of my grandmother the great Cleopatra VII?"

"Yes, I do. By heart. My grandmother and your mother made sure that I did, she would tell me all about it after my own mother died and I took to sleeping by her side for protection. She would tell me everything about her. My grandmother planted Jasmine all over the palace to remind her of her mother."

"Yes, I remember now. Though I have always associated the Jasmine with my own mother, since she had it planted everywhere. I have not smelled it since —well, it has been a long time. Too, long!" Just as she uttered those words, the smell of Jasmine greeted her senses and filled her with an overwhelming longing to see her own mother. She almost felt like a little girl and wanted to run and hide behind her mother's soft and silken gowns.

Living so far away from anything that was even vaguely familiar had made it easy to block out her homeland. For she had no scents to remind her of anything that she had left behind, nothing familiar at all. Now it all came rushing back to her in a torrent of emotions. Drusilla placed her hand on her aunt's and sat silently while they were led inside to the palace main in the litters provided them.

Leannydd looked up in wonder at all around her as well as the others. She had never in her life imagined anything quite like this. She wondered how her mother could have grown up in a place as glorious as this. It was so completely opulent with treasures everywhere. Gold and silver gleamed out from every possible place and the people, no matter how poor wore the finest woven clothes of the softest of colors. The trees were tall and had long leaves that swayed gently in the ocean breeze. The heat was rather stiffening, even though it was late summer, though there were slaves everywhere, some with no clothes on at all who were constantly fanning those fortunate enough to have a canopy to sit under.

She was amazed at the people as well! They were of all shapes and sizes as well as colors. The people from this country seemed to have finely bronzed skin with bright black hair. Their garments were in a dizzying array of bright colors. There were also those people with skin so dark it appeared almost black, they were very tall for the most part and some had no hair at all! She did not know if that was the fashion of where they were from or what. She looked to her side and realized that Cleopatra was equally amazed at all of this as well and could not hide her reactions. She giggled at this.

Finally they were all placed down and led out of the litters. Alexander came over to them and to his wife Cleopatra. Leanydd realized how completely Alexander fit into this alien lifestyle. Now she understood.

Caradawc came over to all of them who were gathering and exclaimed in hushed tones, "We did not have to hide our poverty, we could have just worn our normal clothes to have the same effect." His bitterness was plain for all of them who knew him well.

Drusilla seemed oblivious and came over to them. "I will have the servants gather everything so that you may all rest. We will dine together as a family at the twelfth hour."

She sensed the confusion in their eyes and was thankful that Jubilla had joined them just then, "It is the Roman sense of time. They count hours from the sunrise. Unlike our culture where they do not keep track of time, everybody here relies on it completely."

Caradawc rolled his eyes, "What is "hour"? What does it mean?"

"It is a period of time. There are minutes and seconds and hours, they are parts of a day. I will teach you all about them, so that we may be courteous in their land and respectful of their appointments." She looked over at Drusilla who seemed confused.

"Drusilla, in our land, people do not keep track of time like we do here."

She laughed at the state of shock in her niece's eyes at that, she knew that Drusilla could not even fathom this. She found humor in that and happily recalled old Bellinos trying to explain the whole Keltoi attitude towards time and her equal reaction when told to her so long ago upon her arrival.

"I will leave you all to this and see to everything else and that you are well rested for the festivities that we have planned for you."

"Drusilla, you know that our presence is to remain low profile, do you not?"

"Yes, Aunt, we will keep it as low profile as we know how."

As she watched her niece walk off, she rolled her eyes and knew that their ideas of low profile were completely different. But she knew that her children would have a wonderful visit here all the same.

IV

Everything was familiar to her and as new and polished as it looked when she was small. She followed the many corridors to the sleeping chamber of her father. She could not wait to see him.

She had not bothered to change into the traditional clothes of this place in the world. All of her travel weariness had left her with the birth of a new purpose. A renewed vigor had propelled her forward. She did not care to be led in state to see her father, all formalities were not considered in her trek to see him one last time.

She had guessed correctly as she arrived at his chamber. She was amazed that she had recalled the correct layout and direction to his chamber.

The familiar scent of the priestly incense greeted her senses while the past came rushing to her from all directions. She went forward in only one direction, to the side of his bed.

The smell of Cypress and Frankincense enveloped her being and almost transported her back to the bed of her uncle Helios who she had met so briefly. He had finally returned to the side of his sister, her mother, to be taken away by a sudden and strange illness.

The room was dark which made all times seem one to her. The priests were a motley mixture of Roman, Greeks and Egyptian in religion. She knew that all fought for favor with her father in his treatment. She almost smiled at the thought of each of them groveling to her father and trying to convince him that their ways were the most proper and fortuitous in healing him. She knew that her father did not really care about which one would allegedly heal him, he was probably made worse in his condition from all of the competing clamor for his attention and the cacophony of treatments that were ceaseless though necessary.

In this part of the world, it was political as well as spiritual in the priestly realm. They each in turn fought for favor from her father so that they may receive some sort of compensation for their temples.

She looked over at her father and had to fight hard to keep the tears from building up in her eyes at his weakened condition. For he had always appeared strong to her and in her memory was vital and brave, not this frail old man who lay so still and helpless. Though he had the same eyes, just softer. She wanted to run over to him and bury herself in his once strong arms, but she knew that this was impossible due to his condition.

Instead she stood rooted in that spot, the priests and priestess in the room were oblivious to her presence. Their long flowing garments moved the incense in swirls throughout the chamber and her father looked out towards the window and the stars longingly. She knew that look. She knew how much he dreamed of being strong enough to complete his travels and work.

He had done so much in his scholarly pursuits which had filled his whole life. She was proud of him and felt sorry for him. For she, had inherited a bit of his wanderlust and was very upset that she had not traveled in the past as much as she had intended. But, her mother had ingrained in her a strong sense of duty to the people that she ruled over and that took the first precedence, while her dreams of traveling took the back corner in her busy life.

She moved closer to his side and just sat there looking down at him. How odd, she though that for most of life, he was the strong one and she ran to him and her mother for all of her childhood trauma's to be healed. She recalled her father grabbing her up and lifting her way above his head. If she fell, he would hold her up high and yell at the offending object that caused her fall, such as the carpet, or even the floor itself. Her tears would be forgotten as he would yell at it, "Bad floor! How could you hurt my precious little princess!" He would look at her, tears forgotten and turning into giggles as he would ask her seriously, "Should I have it arrested for treason?" She would giggle and respond, "No! Tatta!"

Now, he just lay there looking so small and helpless. His once thick black hair hung limp and lifeless and was a soft gray in color. She moved closer to him and placed herself by his side on the bed and curled up in his arms. No words were necessary at this time. It was all said in that moment. It was now her turn to be strong for her father and she was thankful that she had the chance to be here for him. She cried silently that she was not able to be here for her mother, but knew that she could not control the sands of time. She was here now for him. She knew that he was thankful by the look in his eyes.

She was proud to be his daughter and lamented the fact that she would soon be on her own in this world. She had her husband, who was strong and would protect her physically from all of the world that she had to face. But her parents probably symbolized for her the spiritual and emotional strength that she had clung to in her youth. She was afraid to face the world so naked and without protection.

She did not know how her parents did it. Her father was only three years old when he was left to a strange place with his parents taken away from him and her mother was not that much older to her recollection. She knew that she did not have their strength.

It was then that Juba looked up at his tormented daughter and spoke softly to her like the whisper of autumn leaves that she was familiar with in her new homeland, "Daughter, we had no choice." She was stunned at his ability to read her mind and looked questioningly at him.

"I know what you are thinking, for your mother had thought the same way as you. I know she worried about you being alone in this world after we were gone...But your mother and I will always be there for you in your lessons learned when you were a child. All of that stays with you forever. My parents have been there for me with the foundation in life that they gave me, even though I was so young. It had allowed me to stand strong and proud."

Tears misted her eyes and she fought for composure, "Tatta, I am so scared. How can I face the world without you! You are my champion!"

"Oh, silly princess, you have a much stronger champion now for you. Besides you have made a new home for yourself in a very different world and I am very proud of you. "

"Tatta, I know, but now it is my turn to take care of you. Just relax, I am here for you now." And he did. In her arms he fell asleep.

V

That evening, all of the others had gathered in the smaller more intimate dining chamber. The family of Jubilla found it odd to lounge on a couch rather that sit among benches and eating from a large table.

The room was large and airy with tall windows overlooking the harbor and the torches that lined it far below. The lighthouse cast an aerie glow over the small houses that crowded the harbor and belonged to the merchants and their families. Again statuesque marble columns in the ancient Egyptian fashion with the lotus blossom tops touching the ceiling adorned the room along the sides of the windows and possibly for support. It was so artistically done that it was impossible to tell. The room was of marble blocks polished to a fine sheen with a top border reminiscent of ancient temples with the hieroglyphs artistically rendering some ancient tale. There were small sphinxes carved to guard the ominous entrances into the room. Priceless and obviously ancient statues of mysterious Egyptian Gods stood sentinel to the oblivious diners.

Leanydd stood in wonder as did the others who entered the hall that evening. The oil lamps that hung from the ceiling cast a comforting glow for those who were to eat in this room. Gweiryth was amazed that his mother had been raised in such luxury, he wondered even more about her for she had never mentioned this to them.

Caradawc was horrified and felt nothing but contempt for such blatant disregard of things made honestly and with care that he believed was so prevalent with his own culture and was obviously lacking here. He stifled a grimace for the sake of his mother and respect for her family. He did not want his homeland to be anything remotely like this.

Caradawc was repulsed on how the slaves here were treated, far different from his own peoples use of slaves. Some seemed to have been slaves for many generations and knew nothing else. While in his own land, people would become slaves or sell his family into slavery to pay off debts. Eventually they were freed after paying off the owed amount and their name cleared. From the small amount of time that he had been here, he found out their world was completely different that his own and he did not like it one bit.

Drusilla had found out from one of her slaves the whereabouts of her aunt and decided to have the meal at the regular time for her children and to help them learn a little more about this land. She decided to start with the customary dining custom.

"I would like to tell you a little about the dining customs here. For example, we sit on couches, more often two people to share a couch. You may all be seated. That couch at the end of the room will be for my brother who is the heir to this throne. He will be here shortly. Please be seated." She smiled and watched them all torpidly wander about the room to finally situate themselves. She noticed that Cleopatra and Leannydd chose to sit together while Alexander sat down beside Gweiryth. Caradawc sat alone and she decided to sit down next to him. She approached him and he nodded assent to her unspoken request.

When all were seated she continued in Latin, which she knew all understood from their mother, "While we wait for my brother, I will tell you a little bit more. You will notice a small low table where the servants will place your food." She looked up and all of the heads in the room turned to observe slaves who had been almost invisible before enter the room with trays laden with all sorts of delicacies. All of which were completely alien to them and their taste buds. The aromas assailed their willing senses with anticipation. Drusilla noticed this and smiled with pride.

As they began to place the delicacies on the small tables beside the couches accordingly she continued, "The servants are holding out to you small silver bowls, they have rose scented water in it for which you may dip your hands prior to the meal."

Leannydd's eyes went up at this curious custom and willingly dipped her fingers daintily into her small bowl that was held out before her by a small child who was naked except for a small skirt of golden cloth. He was as dark as the deepest night and his eyes shone bright with mischief. His head was smooth and hairless. She thought this child was adorable as he tried to appear still like a statue and very serious at performing his duty. She smiled at the child and caught a glimmer of a smile that he desperately tried to hide. She looked around the room and all of the others did the same.

Drusilla continued, "Next the wine will be served, it is customary for the ladies to have watered down wine as is prudent and proper, while the men may have theirs watered down or not. The meal will not be served until Ptolemy arrives."

Drusilla noticed their expressions at this, when Leannydd chimed in whimsically, "It is not absolutely necessary to water ours down as well, for I can handle the effects quite well. "

Caradawc, Helios and Gweiryth tried to suppress their laughter, for they knew well their sister's ability to handle her liquor from their famous tavern visits after hunting. They stifled their laughter out of respect for their host. They also knew that Leanydd hated wine, though was trying to appear the proper lady here. Their eyes sparked at her feeble attempt.

Still Leannydd continued, "Would you perhaps have any beer or mead for my brothers?" Their laughter then burst forth at this, for they knew what she was trying to do. Then stopped while Drusilla sat meekly unable to comprehend the gist of their laughter.

Gweiryth decided to speak out then, lest their hostess take offence, "Domina, we mean no offence, it is just that our lady sister here is not used to such formalities, for she has been well acquainted with winning many such beer contests back in our homeland. We are very proud of her!" His grin spread from ear to ear while in stark contrast to the face of Leanydd whose cheeks had filled with the ripe blush of mortification.

Drusilla realized what was going on here for she had a brother as well, though she loved the camaraderie that all of the children of Jubilla showed for each other and was secretly envious of that. For her own brother felt entitled and preferred to do things without her and considered her of little consequence in the scheme of his life. She let out a giggle to participate in their joy and looked over at Leanydd with a friendly jealous look in her eyes to let her know that she was lucky to have such loving brothers. Leanydd and Cleopatra understood the look given them by their cousin and understood, and then suddenly Ptolemy made his appearance into the room.

With an artistic flourish the crowned prince entered the room. His feet bare with small anklets of gold. Cleopatra observed that there were even rings on his toes. His silken garments were changed from that bright and gaudy purple to a deep forest green. She had never seen such a rich and gorgeous color before. The silk was so soft and pure it seemed to float around his tall slim body with grace and further accentuated his poise and performance for all to see.

Cleopatra knew that this was a man who was used to all eyes being on him in any public and personal function. His head was bald like the pharaoh of ancient times now, she realized that the long black curls she had originally seen on him were only an elaborate wig. She thought this rather amusing as well did her sister Leannydd beside her for in their closeness to each other she felt her sister trembling to keep herself from laughing. She nudged her sister to hold her place in respect for their hostess and host of this great house. Her sister's eyes glazed over in the new seriousness.

Ptolemy of Mauretania had compelling eyes that drew the attention of all around him. They were large and almond shaped with long and gorgeous eyelashes that appeared rather feminine. His eyes were elaborately painted in the darkest of kohl, again in the fashion of the ancients, yet fantastically modern thought Cleopatra. His arms were well muscled and trim, unlike her brothers who had large and husky bodies that were very powerful. She wondered if this man was as quick as he looked. She wondered that he probably kept fit for his looks only and never had to lift a weapon in his life, for he seemed to have many willing slaves for that.

Cleopatra was amazed at the appearance of her cousin, yet was strangely attracted to him, she realized that he was used to having this affect on people and it seemed to her that every motion that he did, no matter how small was for the affect he had on others, as if it were all acts in a play that he willingly performed for all eyes, loving to be the center of attention. She found it difficult to take her eyes off of him, for he was so beautiful, almost dreamlike in a fragile yet virile way. She knew that beside her, Leanydd had the same reaction to his sudden and artistic presence in the room. She looked over at Drusilla who rolled her eyes behind a small fan that she had pulled out from behind her gown. How clever thought Cleopatra. Again she fought to stifle a giggle that was fast erupting.

Cleopatra noticed that of these two siblings only their beautiful eyes were shared. For Drusilla dressed in the tasteful and subtle garments of the Macedonians in a flowing one piece silken dress of a brighter green that reminded her of summer grass back home. She had her eyes lined in the kohl, though it only accentuated her eyes rather than put them on display as her brother's were. Drusilla's hair was long and cascaded down her back in the darkest of black curls that had almost purple highlights in them when the lamplights shown on it. Both of them had eyes of the most deep hazel with golden flecks and deep green and brown in them. She found them both to have beautiful eyes. Both had long tapered fingers that had probably not seen a day of work in their lives. Drusilla had elegance and class while her brother had the same, but with a flamboyance that would draw the attention of crowds to his command.

All of them had been freshly bathed in the largest bathhouses that they had ever seen and were amazed that they were private and only for the use of the royal family. Their own bathhouses were a smaller version and were shared by the whole village. Their clothes were easily abandoned since all were found impractical for this warm and humid climate and were each given long silken toga's to don during their visit. The leather wrapped boots were replaced with the softest of slippers that made them glide across the softly polished floors of this large and never-ending palace.

Cleopatra looked across the room at her brothers and her sister beside her in their new clothes that were much more accommodating to this very warm evening.

Ptolemy sat down while slaves appeared out of nowhere to arrange his garments in a very astute pattern around him on a couch that he had for himself. They all sat and waited for him to finish and look at them all with his permission to begin their long awaited meal.

"You may begin now." Spoke Drusilla. All of them dug into the scrumptious treats beside them all.

"Now please let me know all of your names again, I have heard much about you all from my grandmother…" Ptolemy looked at Caradawc for this.

Taking his cue, Caradawc looked at each in turn and began his introductions, "I am Caradawc, the second son and prince of Britannia, while over to your left on the couch are my brother Gweiryth, the youngest prince in the house, and next to him, you know, your cousin Alexander, who is the husband of my sister Cleopatra who is sitting over there beside my older sister Leanydd."

Ptolemy nodded at this and questioned, "Where is the eldest of your brothers, the heir to your throne in Britannia?"

Caradawc responded, "He had to stay behind to assist my father in pressing matters back home. There had been some border skirmishes that he had to suppress." Ptolemy nodded in understanding to that. "And your mother, where is she?"

Drusilla responded, "She is with her father, your grandfather and chose to stay by his side. I suggest that we make this meal a short one, since we do not know how much time that he has left and he would want to see his grandchildren."

Ptolemy loved to be the center of attention, though nodded for he loved his grandfather who had raised him since the tragic death of his parents.

In silence they ate for while until Leanydd spoke up, "Tell us about grandfather please, I have heard a lot about him from my mother, but would like to know more. How old in truth is he now?"

Drusilla looked at Ptolemy and with his permission continued, "He is eighty-four years old now." All of them nodded at this respectively for few lived to be that ancient an age.

"Is it true that he once knew Julius Caesar?"

Drusilla looked startled and then smiled at this, "Why yes, it is. For he was a very small child when he lost his parents to a battle fought against him in Numidia. It was rumored that Julius Caesar even had an affair with Juba's mother. Though no one knows the truth of that." All eyes in the room were focused for this was very interesting, even Ptolemy did not know this.

She continued, "Juba was the second of that name and had inherited the crown and rule of Numidia from his father before him. Your own line was from a great aunt of his who had married your great-great grandfather Beli, so we are related there as well as from our grandparents.

"When Juba was three his parents were killed, his mother in battle and his father, who had fell on his sword after the defeat. Juba was then taken off by Julius Caesar himself. For Julius took sympathy on our grandfather and unlike the ways of the Romans to kill the children of their enemies, he set a new precedence and spared the life of the young child that he had fallen for in his adorable innocence. Julius Caesar took him into his own household where he was raised by his daughter Julia, who had in later years died in childbirth. Julia saw to Juba's education as well as Julius Caesar. Upon his death when Octavian or Augustus inherited his wealth and was adopted by him and made heir, he inherited the care of Juba as well and saw to the rest of his education.

"When Julius Caesar met out great grandmother Cleopatra VII, the last Pharaoh of Egypt, he fell in love with her and married her in the Egyptian fashion. They had a son together by the name of Caesarion.

"After his death, Octavian made sure that there was nothing to stand in the way of his inheritance and made sure that young Caesarion was killed. I suppose out of remorse he might have then felt sorry for Juba who was now a young man and also for how it all turned out after the famous battle of Actium.

"For after the death of Julius Caesar, Cleopatra VII met and fell in love with Marcus Antonius who was part of the Triumvirate of Rome and shared leadership with Octavian. Marcus Antonius and Cleopatra had children together of which we are descended from, all in this room. He had a wife at the time in Rome who happened to be Octavian's sister Octavia. Perhaps out of pride at Marcus abandoning his sister and perhaps out of his fear of Marcus Antony taking over all of Rome, he went after Cleopatra VII and Marcus Antonii in many battles. The last of which was Actium which was a brutal defeat that had lost them all of Egypt. Marcus Antonii then fell on his own sword in disgrace and was brought to the palace of Cleopatra VII, All of them wept over his body, so strongly had they loved them and Cleopatra then went into her own mausoleum and locked herself inside with her two most faithful servants and succumbed to the bite of an asp.

"Octavian or Augustus, then took all of their children in captivity and in the precedence set by Julius Caesar, took them into his home to raise and into the care of his sister Octavia. Cleopatra Selene, Alexander Helios, Ptolemy and Arsinoe were all raised there by the matronly Octavia, who was the mother of Antonia Minor that Jubilla still writes to. For Antonia was the daughter of Marcus Antony and Octavia and was married to her the same time that he was with Cleopatra. Antonia Minor and Cleopatra Selene were a few months apart in age and eventually started a great friendship that lasted for so many years.

"Augustus then married off Juba II and Cleopatra Selene and gave them back the rule of Numidia and then Mauretania, where we all are now." Exhausted with her short rendition, she slumped gracefully against the side of her couch.

All faces were captivated with this rich history of their origins and sat there. She knew they wanted more and she fed them willingly.

"Grandfather was a wonderful man and was always there for his family, that is when he was not traveling and gathering some information for his vast compilations of geography and history. He is very well knowledgeable in botany, physics, and science in all aspects. His thirst for knowledge was unquenchable and I know that he is angry with himself for not being able to continue his search. For he would often say when people were amazed at how knowledgeable he was in so many matters, he would wave his hand and mention with all of his learning he realized how little that he actually knew. For with all of his answers he found still more questions." They all stared curiously at this revelation, though understood it well. For each face in that room had inherited his unquenchable thirst for knowledge in some form and felt the same that the more one learned, the more they felt that they really did not know at all—that so much was out there for them to grasp. Sighs of understanding at this very precise outlook into their very souls uttered by their grandfather, made them all feel closer to him in that moment.

"During your stay I will show you all of his work and his study, they are truly amazing. For there are over four hundred codices and velum manuscripts that he had authored and it looks as if he was in the process of beginning another set as well, though his ill health prevented this."

"He was a man who wanted to know how the world worked and why we are the way we are and where we all came from. He had so many quests for information it was difficult to keep up with them all. He had even discovered some islands near what the Romans call Hispania as well as some near the west coast of this continent. He had also mentioned something about some lands to the far west almost where the earth drops off where he mentioned there existed pyramids similar to the ones in Egypt, he felt they were somehow related to one another. He also found another great River way to the north of that and charted it, where he mentioned lived a people who were builders of mounds."

All heads in the room looked questionably at that last bit of information.

"Sister, why do you fill their heads with nursery tales, father had made those up for us as bedtime stories. There is no proof of that."

"You are wrong Ptolemy, for he told me that he has those treasures somewhere safe for our family should they ever need them, but only when all appears lost. Someone in this family has the information." She looked around the room and noticed that all of their faces appeared blank at the mention of this.

"Well, enough of this, now to finally meet the great man himself once again." With this she rose carefully and beckoned all of them to follow her.

They all had long finished their meal and were bursting with satiated delight at all of the foreign yet filling delicacies which entertained their palates this evening. In a long line they followed her down the large and spacious marble carved corridors with her brother right beside her.

At last they all entered the darkened chamber and saw the ancient Juba II laying on the lap of his daughter as contented as a child and peaceful. Jubilla looked up at their entrance which went almost unnoticed by her father, who only slowly moved his eyelashes and his eyes to their entrance.

"Grandfather, I have brought to you your other grandchildren, do you remember them?" Drusilla uttered patiently since she knew that he was also very forgetful and felt sad for him and his deteriorated mind.

Softly he spoke, "Yes, I do, for with you are Arsinoe and Little Juba my own son and Tonia, it has been a long while." His eyes were misty with the past and all bowed.

Drusilla hated to correct him, though knew she must for he had to know who was truly there. "No grandfather"

Jubilla interrupted and stopped her and whispered, "Drusilla, let him see them as he will for it is his day now. My children understand, for they have all seen him before when he remembered them all" She looked over at her children and they bowed to their mother's wishes.

He looked over at Cleopatra and beckoned, "Come Tonia, sit on my lap and Tatta will sing you a little song!" Jubilla placed her delicate hand on her eyes to control the rush of them at the mention of her long lost twin sister. She had wished that Tonia would have been here. She wondered if perhaps those people who were close to dying really did see those who were lost.

He looked over at Jubilla and Jubilla nodded to Cleopatra. He continued after looking at his daughter, "I will sing you a song that I know you mother will be mad at me for!" He smiled and winked at Jubilla thinking that she was his Selene.

The others gathered around closer to hear him since his voice was barely perceptible above a whisper. He sang a song which Jubilla recognized as a very tame sailors song, that he sang long ago to tease her with to annoy her mother when she was very little. She smiled as the tears began to flow at the sound of his voice singing this long forgotten song.

He sang in Phoenician which she knew her children were never taught, but he had taught her when young because he told her that all of the greatest maps were written in this language and he made sure that she knew this if she wanted to be a great traveler someday. She smiled and joined in to the astonishment of her children with the tame though slightly ribald lyrics, that were lost in meaning to those in the room. This young generation.

When the song was done, Jubilla knew that his time was drawing near the end for his breath was ragged and forced. She looked at him and continued to sing a song that her aunt had told her was his favorite lullaby sung to him by his mother when he was a baby.

It was a beautiful song in Numidian that mentioned birds coming to life and bringing the heavens down for the children to play in. Of painted rainbows that lit up the sky and of many animals that frolicked in play for the entertainment of the magical children of the forest. As she softly sung those magical and almost forgotten words she knew that her father probably thought that he was in his mothers arms once again and slowly he forced out his last breath as the song ended its verse on the lips of his daughter giving him the most precious gift that he could ask for.

VI

Jubilla helped Drusilla with the funeral arrangements and made sure that Juba II was placed in the mausoleum beside his wife and her parents. They had to travel to Alexandria in Egypt for this. All of them went. Caradawc wondered why they did not have a mausoleum here in Mauretania. Drusilla had responded that Juba had originally tried to have one built for them in Numidia in the land of his parents, but when he went down there to investigate the tomb, he had found that it was desecrated and the bodies of his parents smashed all over the floor. He was horrified by this and had the remains gathered and placed in a special containers that he had carved especially for them and ordered them to be placed beside the parents of his wife. For the tomb that Cleopatra VII had built for her and her beloved Marcus Antonii was untouched and well guarded.

Thus, all of them gathered in a caravan to make this last voyage of Juba II to be by the side of his wife for eternity. They had walked through the gates of Alexandria in which people had found out their mission and who they were. People flocked from everywhere to join them and to admire with fascination and curiosity the descendants of their last Pharaoh Cleopatra VII. Flowers were thrown in their path as they made their way slowly. The palace loomed in the foreground in the harbor. The palace they had all heard about as children. It was now occupied by a Roman general and off limits to them.

Drusilla thought how sad that Cleopatra Selene was never able to return to the land of her birth until after she had died.

They had created quite the spectacle with their large retinue carrying the mummified remains. The sarcophagus was brought over along the coast on a barge that they had all traveled on and the royal family was carried on litters and hidden from the people who were joining their funeral march in large numbers. The outer coffin was unlike the Egyptian style and painted in a vast array of bright African colors which held no boundary to the imagination. Despite this the people knew who was in this and bowed in his presence and of the children which carried the blood of their rulers.

Al last they came to the famous mausoleum. One by one they entered the long corridors that were carved deep into the cliffs beside the ancient harbor. Not a sound was heard but held back tears of those who knew and loved their King. At last they arrived in the main burial chamber that glowed in vivid Egyptian depictions painted in the most fluid colors and even in gold. The story of Isis and Osiris was revealed to all of them in gorgeous picture writing that held them all transfixed with awe.

Jubilla found her mother's final resting place along with that of her grandmother and grandfather. She bowed reverently and spoke in her mind a final prayer and blessing to them all. She had also noticed the finely carved marble sarcophagus that contained the remains of her other grandparents from her father. So much history was in this place! She was numb at the thought of actually standing beside all of them. All of those whose blood flowed deep in the veins of each person present. It is amazing how much legacy that one person can hand down. From many people we are born and many people come from us to light the way of the future. She stood transfixed in the mystery of life that flowed in her veins in this brightly lit and colorfully decorated chamber. Her past was here and her present stood silent beside her.

She whispered to her parents while the priest droned on and on with the ceremony, "Mother and Father, I thank you for this great legacy that you have left for me and yours. I thank you for your great history you have poured in our veins with love and will repay you with a vivid future and promise with my children and theirs after. Mother, I will carry on the truth for you and the future daughters and will make sure the legacy of the sun and the moon is fulfilled with Cleopatra and Helios. Your sun and moon connected. I know great deeds will come from them and their children. I will guard them for you…" She bowed her head and sang the song that her mother taught her long ago of Isis and how she protected her children and the descendants of the throne of Egypt. For she knew that the thrones of Egypt, Numidia and Mauritania and well as those from her husband may be gained back someday, such was the legacy of Cleopatra VII and the children born from her genes. All of these children who surrounded her were a new and very promising generation and she smiled at the thought of how proud they would have been had they lived to see them. Then again she believed that they all did know, such was the felling that she had.

* * * * *

"Alas, here I am the last in line of the great legacy that I have inherited. Such brave women have formatted most of what I am today. I have compiled the chronicles of the great women who are a part of me and my beginnings. I write this all down for you to see how valuable are our roots and how important that the truth be told

so that we may have a more powerful understanding of our paths before us. This volume is the very beginning of the daughters of the mighty Cleopatra VII, the last Pharaoh of Egypt. Of the daughters that she bore and their daughters. For they have traveled great distances in this known world in order to leave a better live for the next generation. I have made sure that the children born after me will never forget.

I also would like to make sure that none of which has been written is to be used as an excuse to not achieve greatness in the future generations yet unborn. Only that this knowledge should be used as a stepping stone over the turbulent waters that we had tried to avoid thus far.

We were told to avoid water in the beginning, perhaps to avoid drowning. Yet, I feel after looking over all of the history that has led to myself...I believe that we are to be weary, yet strive with all of the power born to us to conquer that water and to use it for us to grow further and to reach the skies way above us in our pursuits. For in the end no one can truly avoid water in all forms possible. For we need it to sustain life and to nourish it. Even if we were to avoid water-we would only find ourselves in a dark and desolate desert far from life and we would only die from the thirst of life left behind and avoided.

I hope that by teaching my children that though the world is not an easy place for a woman to stand alone, it is possible.

-Princess Cleopatra of the Iceni"

The End of Volume One of

The Legend of the Sun and Moon

Breinigsville, PA USA
23 November 2010
249876BV00001B/5/P